I0776936

DUPLICITY
DECEPTION and LIES
(A TRILOGY)

ALSO BY PETER EISENHUT

THE PEN PROJECT

THE BOULDER CREEK PROJECT

FINAL PROJECT

FATEFUL AFFAIRS

CONTENTS

In 1967, a young but brilliant Peter Troutman agrees to participate in a special assignment in Vietnam. He is eager to serve his country during the Vietnam War. However, he experiences more than he bargained for. The CIA involves him in espionage, assassination, and relationships that challenge his sense of morality, and affect the rest of his life.

In 1987, Peter Troutman, a senior employee of a large computer company, works undercover with the CIA and the FBI. Together, they attempt to stop the Soviets from putting an end to President Reagan's Strategic Defense Initiative. The suspense, intrigue, romance, and unexpected outcomes will not disappoint!

In 2003, a seasoned intelligence officer, Donna Wolf, strives to complete an important mission before the end of her life. Things don't go as planned. Her mission evolves into a larger covert project involving multiple intelligence operatives. Donna's daughter, an unwitting participant, struggles to discover the truth about her own involvement and about her mother's life and final actions. With the help of others, including Peter Troutman, she reveals a quagmire of deception and uncertainty, affecting their careers and their personal lives.

THE PEN

By

Peter Eisenhut

PROLOGUE

Try to imagine living in a world without small plastic water bottles, smartphones, DVRs, the Internet, or personal computers. If you were born after 1980, you might find it difficult to do. However, this was the reality of the 1960s.

In the 1960s, computers were very primitive. Organizations were just beginning to harness the power of large computers housed in custom-designed rooms. Over time, the demand for computer professionals increased. After congress passed the Civil Rights Act in 1964, organizations began to hire more women and minorities, especially for computer-related jobs.

Meanwhile, during this time, an unpopular war was taking place in Vietnam, and the United States was becoming increasingly involved. In the 1960s, the United States government required all men over the age of eighteen to register for the draft. Some volunteered to serve before they were drafted, and some went to Canada to avoid the draft. However, most of those who went to Vietnam from the United States were drafted. A lesser number were college graduates who became military officers by participating in the Reserve Officer Training Corps or by attending one of the military academies. Fewer yet were civilians, and most of them were men. Peter Troutman was one of those civilians. Most of those who went to Vietnam from the United States were told that they were there to protect our values and prevent the spread of communism. Most believed it. Peter Troutman was no exception.

He was young and socially naïve, but he was also smart. It was in the 1960s that he developed the concept of the PEN. The PEN Project was the reason he went to Vietnam. But the idea for the PEN project didn't happen all at once. There was never a "eureka" moment. It evolved over a period of years. The idea of uncertainty and probability always intrigued him. He always had an interest in how past events influenced future events. He would ask, "what if that had happened, and then what would have followed?"

The events of the early and mid-1960s influenced Peter Troutman's thoughts. His thoughts led to the development of the PEN, the Probabilistic Event Network.

1

WHAT IF

It was early on an October morning in upstate New York in the year 1961. The sun was out, but the temperature was cool, and it was breezy. The word "brisk" comes to mind. Peter Troutman and his friend, George, stood on the side of a two-lane highway with their thumbs out, holding a sign that said "Watkins Glen."

It had been more than fifteen minutes since their first ride had dropped them off about one-third of the way to their destination. Where was the traffic? Peter was beginning to feel the cold and wondered why he had let George talk him into this. What if this didn't work out? No, he realized that it was not fair to blame George. It was as much his doing as it was George's. Perhaps they had both been foolish.

Peter and George were in their sophomore year at Cornell University in Ithaca, New York. The two of them were friends. Unknown powers had paired them up in their freshman year and declared them roommates. Fortunately, it worked out. They got along. They were both in the same engineering school, they helped each other with their studies, and they had common interests. By common interest, we're not just talking about girls and booze. We're also talking about math, science, and fast cars. Although they had been out on the town together, most of the time they studied. After freshman year, George had moved into an off-campus rooming house, and Peter had moved into a fraternity house. However, they remained friends.

They were in the sixth week of their sophomore year when George called Peter to ask if he was interested in attending an automobile race the following weekend. After more than five weeks with their noses to the grindstone, they needed a break. Attending the auto race in Watkins Glen seemed like a great idea, and Peter told him so. Then George confessed that they had no way to get there. He wanted to know if one of Peter's fraternity brothers, presumably one with wheels, wanted to go. Peter told him he would ask around. Unfortunately, no one else was interested, but Peter really wanted to go. The race was only four days away when Peter called him back with the bad news. Not sure who suggested it, but they decided to hitchhike. Neither of them had access to a car, and there was no public transportation that would have gotten them there, so hitchhiking seemed to make sense. The race track was many miles away. So, they left early in the morning to ensure they would get there in time.

The big race on this day was the United States Grand Prix at Watkins Glen. It was the first time ever that this race had been held at Watkins Glen. The participants would be the top international drivers and carmakers in the world. At the time, the Watkins Glen racecourse, simply known as The Glen, was a 2.35-mile track that included hills, sharp curves, and a tricky chicane at the back end of the course furthest from the starting line. The cars were Formula 1, open cockpit, open-wheeled missiles. They looked much like those at the Indy 500.

As Peter remembered it, Honda was experimenting that year with a turbine-powered car. It would not be in the race, but it would do trial runs beforehand. News reports had described the high-pitched wail of the engine as it sped around the track. As engineering students, they couldn't wait. Although it was a three-day event, they were only going for the main event on Sunday.

They may have been having second thoughts because as they stood there on the side of the road, they began to ask a lot of "what if" questions:

"What if no one picks us up? How long do we wait? And then what?"

"What if we get there late? Could we still get into the infield?"

"What if we can't get a ride back to Cornell?"

"What if we don't get back to Cornell until late in the evening? Would we be locked out of our respective houses?"

Of course, they considered these questions before they left, but now they were getting anxious about the uncertainty of the outcome.

Despite the second thoughts, Peter and George did hitchhike the thirty miles or so to Watkins Glen; they did see the entire race from the infield; and they made it back at a reasonable time that evening. So, were they just lucky? For sure, there was a great deal of uncertainty. Outcomes could have been much different. How did they reach their decision to do this when there was so much uncertainty?

They considered the probabilities, and they considered the severity of the possible consequences. They reasoned that many people would drive to the racecourse from Cornell that morning making the likelihood (probability) of getting a ride very high.

On the other hand, what if no one stopped and gave them a ride? They reasoned that if they didn't get a ride within a certain length of time, they would simple turn around and head back. That would not have been a big downside; the time they were not able to study was time they were able to talk as friends and enjoy each other's company. What if they couldn't get a ride back? They figured the likelihood of not getting a ride back to school was even less than the likelihood of not getting a ride to The Glen. They reasoned that if the person that gave them a ride to the Glen also attended the event, they could request a return trip. However, what if they were unable to do that? Well, they figured there would be many other people going back to Cornell, and someone would eventually pick them up. If not, it would be an adventure. As it were, the person that took them did not bring them back, but he knew someone who could. Apparently, Cornell students had been going to this event for years, and many of them knew each other.

There was another "what if" experience that involved George. The previous spring, Peter had pledged to a fraternity, while George had decided to remain independent. When Spring Weekend approached, George and Peter discussed meeting women and getting dates. More "what ifs" ensued:

"How do we get dates for Spring Weekend?"

"Who do we ask?"

"What if they say no?"

"What if we can't get a date?"

As it were, George didn't think that getting a date was a top priority, and he was content to study. On the other hand, having a date for Spring Weekend was more important to Peter. Perhaps that was why Peter saw a need to join a fraternity and George didn't. As it turned out, Peter asked someone, but she turned him down, and he could not think of anyone else to ask. Was there a possible downside? Yes, he would miss some fun at his new fraternity, but he could still go and help with the beer and the drinks. It just so happened however, that his "Big Brother" was the Social Director for the fraternity. Peter debated whether to tell him his plight.

Peter didn't want him to think of him as less of a man because he was unable to get a date. However, he decided to risk it. After all, he was supposed to be his Big Brother and a worthy mentor. As it turned out, it was Peter's lucky day—well, somewhat, anyway. Big Brother knew someone who would like a date. It turns out that the someone was his sister—his blood sister, not a sorority sister. Peter knew what this meant. He had to be on his best behavior. Well, as it turned out she was only a senior in high school. Since her brother was nearby, she acted quite properly, and Peter responded accordingly. However, she was attractive and she was his date. He had no reason to be embarrassed. Other brothers looked on with envy. The upsides of that weekend outweighed the downsides, and Peter earned the respect of his new fraternity brothers.

These experiences provided valuable insights into how people make decisions. The results of actions one takes in life are uncertain. The best we can do when we make a decision, is to estimate the likelihoods or probabilities of the possible outcomes and evaluate the potential impacts these outcomes are likely to have. Sometimes we do this consciously and sometimes intuitively. Sometimes we do it well, and sometimes not so well. Nevertheless, we all do it.

****

Peter began to realize that events are not isolated but that one outcome leads to the need for another decision and to another uncertain outcome, ad infinitum.

To illustrate this point further, in 1965, Peter married Penelope, and went to work for TGW in Rochester, New York. During that time, he attended night school at The University of Rochester. What were the chains of events that enabled these things to happen?

How did he come to be married to Penelope? He would not have met her had it not been for Ben. Ben asked Peter if he wanted to go with him and two others to see some girls at a nearby all girl's college. Ben didn't have a car, so someone else provided the transportation. Apparently, Ben had been dating a girl at that school, and she had a friend who wanted a date. Yes, blind dates usually don't live up to expectations. Not a problem for Peter. He had no expectations. Besides, he was always interested and curious about things, and he looked forward to the experience. He told Ben he would be happy to go.

Ben introduced his girlfriend, Penelope, and then introduced Peter to his date, Olive. They spent the evening at a local pub, had one drink, and danced to a couple of Juke box numbers. It was not an exciting evening but it was friendly and cordial. The four of them were not party types, but were more on the reserved side.

At one point, Peter looked across the table at Ben and Penelope and wondered how they ever hooked up. They were not hitting it off any better than he was with Olive. Peter asked how they met and learned that they were both Catholic and met at an intercollegiate church event. Perhaps that was the only thing they had in common. Sometimes Penelope returned Peter's occasional glances. He sensed that inside she had a spark, energy just waiting for an opportunity to release itself. He was attracted to her.

Two weeks later, Peter found himself talking to Ben about an upcoming party at his fraternity.

"Are you thinking about asking Olive?" he wanted to know.

"No, I don't think so. Are you going to ask Penelope?"

Then surprisingly, he said, "No. I'm not going to see her anymore. Why don't you ask her?"

"Wait a minute, what happened? Are you sure?"

"I'm sure."

Since Peter really had an interest, he was very curious to know what went wrong, so he pressed. "No, really, I want to know. If I ask her out, I'd like to know what I'm getting myself into."

"She's Catholic," he said in a cynical tone.

"I thought you were as well."

"Yes, but she told me I was not worthy, and I told her she had no soul."

"I see," was all Peter could think to say. On further reflection, Peter decided that Ben was probably frustrated that she didn't want to have sex with him. So, Peter decided to ask her out.

Peter's relationship with Penelope started based on pure chance. It then developed based on conscious decisions made on both their parts and influenced by others every step of the way. Three and one-half years later, in 1965, they got married.

****

After his marriage, Peter went to work for TGW. TGW was a privately held manufacturing company with about three thousand employees, located in Rochester, New York. They made specialty machine tools mostly for the automotive industry worldwide. At the time, only rear- wheel-drive cars were on the road. TGW had a "monopoly" on the machines that made the hypoid gears that connected the drive shaft to the differential gears and the rear axle.

Peter would not have ended up at TGW if his parents had been rich. They were not. They told him before he went to college that they could only afford to finance one of his years of college. It was only his efforts and a great deal of luck that he was able to complete seven years. Some of the events were by chance; some were by design, but all were uncertain. One way he financed a portion of his education at Cornell was to apply to be part of a co-op work-study program. He was accepted into the co-op program at TGW. He received his degree in the same amount of time, but instead of working summers, he had a high-paying job working a fall semester, a summer semester, and a spring semester. That meant taking classes during two summers rather than during the regular semesters.

During his co-op work sessions in Rochester, Peter learned how to survive on his own, and although he didn't have too much of it, he was learning how to manage money. During one of his work sessions in the spring of 1964, he heard about a new company called Xerox that started up in nearby Webster. Xerox had gone public, and people were telling him how Xerox was revolutionary and how the stock price was going to "go through the roof." Peter was at the end of his work session and it was almost time to head back to Cornell. However, he was curious. He went into a stockbroker's office that he just happened to walk past. He was wearing ragged clothes and he walked in off the street with no appointment. One of the brokers greeted him. Peter told him he knew nothing about the market but had heard about Xerox. The broker told Peter that for $200, he could have a share, and he was quite certain that it would increase in value. Peter had the $200, but that was all he had, and he needed the money to eat. So, he thanked the broker but did not invest. As we now know, the stockbroker was right. Xerox stock took off and split several times after that. Well, ever since, Peter has asked "what if?"

Peter's prior co-op experience at TGW led to a nice full-time job offer when he graduated from Cornell in 1965. They hired him as a systems analyst and assigned him to the Systems Department. He reported directly to Mr. G. Mr. G was the nephew of the current president and rapidly on his way to the executive suite. He had recently joined the family business after spending time in South East Asia. Peter was not sure what he did there but thought he worked for the State Department. Rumor was that he was fluent in more than one language, including Chinese. Anyway, Mr. G's mission was to modernize the company, and he was doing just that. Only five years earlier, TGW didn't allow female employees to smoke, the office areas had no air-conditioning, and spittoons lined the manufacturing floors. Mr. G. had created a Data Processing Department and a Systems Department of which Peter now became a part. The mission of the Systems Department, was to redesign the way the company operated its business, to make it more effective at less cost.

Computers were playing an increasingly important role in business. TGW already had two. By 1966, computers were faster and more reliable than they were before 1960, when they still used vacuum tubes. The use of transistors and even solid-state circuitry not only allowed them to be faster, but also allowed them to be smaller. Smaller computers could be housed in smaller rooms, and the cost of cooling those rooms could be lower. The two computers at TGW and the tape drives that fed the programs and data into them stood on raised flooring in a room that was about thirty feet by fifty feet in size. At TGW, computer programs replaced an entire room of people whose full-time jobs had been to crunch numbers using Marchant mechanical calculators.

TGW had a large manufacturing job-shop, with each job moving through the manufacturing facility according to a predefined route. One of the assignments Peter had while in the work-study co-op program was to read the blueprint of a newly designed part for a machine tool, and determine how to route it through the manufacturing job shop. For example, go to the milling department, then drilling, and then heat treat, etc. For each step along the way, the routing sheet would also specify exactly what work to perform and the tools required to do it. These routings were handwritten and then typed onto special multipart forms. Often the routings needed modifications. The entire process was time-consuming and labor-intensive. Peter found a way to improve the process using the computer and the new Xerox technology.

Later, Peter became interested in how to minimize the overall elapsed time it took to manufacture a part. If too many jobs arrived at a workstation at the same time, they would queue up and wait their turn for service. Then the question became which job to work on next. The mathematics involved advanced queuing theory. The math was intriguing but elusive. There was no Internet in the 1960s, but Peter read technical papers, attended seminars, and consulted with experts. He learned that computer programs could simulate the process and determine the most favorable rules for routing work through a job-shop. At his recommendation, TGW began to implement these rules.

Most of Peter's projects at TGW involved changing the way things were done so that they would be done more effectively, more efficiently, or at a lower cost. Often, these changes depended upon computer applications. **Computer applications were the wave of the future!**

****

After coming to TGW full-time, Peter decided to get an MBA degree. His interest had already changed from becoming a professional engineer to becoming a systems analyst, and now he was thinking he might want to end up as a business manager with an engineering background. In short, he was still trying to figure it out. He enrolled in the University of Rochester MBA program at night. He figured that since both Penelope and he were both employed full-time, night school was affordable. However, he was especially pleased when he found out that TGW would pay for it.

The graduate MBA program at The University of Rochester was normally a full-time two-year program. However, Peter was exempted from six courses in the first year's curriculum. He did this by passing three of the courses' final exams, and by applying course credits from three other courses he took at Cornell. He was able to take two to three courses each semester and figured he would earn the MBA in less than three years at night, maybe two. Without that opportunity, the next three years of his life may have turned out differently. Once again, a sequence of events that may or may not have materialized.

Each of the events that led to his being married to Penelope, working at TGW, and eventually obtaining an MBA, happened partly by design and partly by chance. In every case, the outcomes were uncertain and could have changed direction at any step along the way. In his fifth year at Cornell, he had taken a course in stochastic processes. A stochastic process is a series of events that develop over time according to the laws of probability. He began to visualize life events like the ones in his own life as a stochastic process, but with one significant difference. In real life, the likelihood of each event occurring could be influenced by human will and human action, and as some believe, divine intervention.

****

There was another event that made Peter ask, "what if?" On November 22, 1963, President John F. Kennedy was shot and killed in Dallas, Texas. People across the nation and the world, glued themselves to their TV sets and watched in awe as the horror unfolded. Could this unfortunate event have been predicted? Peter considered the sequence of events that preceded the assassination. Were these events known or predictable in the days, weeks, and months prior to the assassination? Peter thought so.

Think about it. The President was riding in an open convertible automobile, on a route that passed three tall buildings, a bridge, and a grassy knoll, all of which would have provided a vantage point for a sniper. The parade route had been announced several days in advance. Lee Harvey Oswald, the likely assassin, worked in one of the tall buildings. The FBI and the intelligence community knew that he owned guns, was a sharpshooter, had a military background, was a communist, and had other issues with the U.S. Government. They knew that he had defected to Russia, only to be allowed back into the USA after he lied about his mother needing him home for health reasons. They also knew he was discharged from the U.S. military as "undesirable." Three weeks before the assassination, the FBI had talked with Oswald's wife, and Oswald threatened that he would blow up the local FBI office if they didn't stop talking with her. The public was also aware of his existence. He had previous arrests, which made the news, and there were photographs of him handing out pro-Cuban flyers in New Orleans.

There were credible warnings of an assassination attempt before Kennedy came to Texas. President Kennedy did several things that were admirable but he also made enemies. His handling of the Cuban missile crisis prevented Russia from having missiles near our mainland, but made enemies of Russia and Cuba. He also made enemies with the DOD and the CIA when he stopped an all-out invasion of Cuba, and settled for the failed Bay of Pigs Operation.

Kennedy also made enemies of the CIA and the DOD when he rejected their Northwoods proposal to commit acts of terrorism against the U.S. and then blame the Cuban government for those acts. He also felt betrayed by the CIA after the assassination of Ngo Dinh Diem, the tyrannical President of South Vietnam. Apparently, the CIA had orchestrated the assassination, while promising Kennedy that Diem would have safe passage from the country. The CIA didn't want that evidence to come out.

Even the Mafia had grudges against President Kennedy. The President may have shared a mistress with a Mafia leader. In addition, the Mafia may have been angry because after their money helped to elect him, Kennedy's administration actively fought Mafia corruption. There was also a possible link between the Mafia, the CIA, and the drug trade. Before coming to Texas, there was plenty of motivation for the assassination of Kennedy, and the Mafia, the CIA, or Cuban extremists could have been involved.

Peter and his fraternity brothers watched Kennedy's assassination on TV. The nation was horrified. It was almost unbelievable that this could happen. It bothered Peter greatly that more was not done to prevent Kennedy's assassination. Couldn't there have been a way to centralize and evaluate all the bits of information that led up to the assassination? Would it have been possible to calculate the probabilities (likelihoods) of the possible outcome beforehand? Peter thought so. He was convinced that if a process had existed to allow such an evaluation, an assassination could have been foreseen and prevented. Given the information available, one could have calculated the probability of an assassination three months beforehand, one month beforehand, and one day beforehand. If no countermeasures were taken, these probabilities would have increased. One day beforehand, the probability of an assassination would have been very high. Peter believed that if these probabilities had been known, countermeasures could have prevented the killing of the President.

The accused assassin was Lee Harvey Oswald. People watched their TVs in horror again two days later when Oswald was assassinated. Perhaps we could have prevented that as well.

2

THE PROJECT

No doubt, you have heard the idiom, "necessity is the mother of invention."

Sometimes horrific events must take place before the necessity is evident. Peter's reaction to the assassinations of Kennedy and Oswald motivated him to find a process that would avoid such a tragedy in the future. Toward the end of 1966, he took a course in information theory. The professor challenged the class to come up with possible applications using what they had learned about predictive analysis, conditional probabilities, etc. Peter began thinking about the stock market, but quickly realized the futility of that. There were too many unknowns and too many variables. Then he started thinking about how one piece of information would relate to other pieces of information, and how one could draw some conclusions after one had enough pieces of information. Somewhere along the line, he drew a parallel between pieces of information and events. Events related to each other. If you had enough information about related events, you could possibly reach meaningful and predictive conclusions. This was the idea upon which the PEN was based.

Peter submitted the assignment paper for the Information Theory class, but on his own time, he continued to develop the concept. In 1966, the world was ripe for new ways to use computers. Computers would be a way to do things a lot faster than in the past. For example, if you take a tour of the Arch in St. Louis, while waiting to go up in the tram, you walk past a display of handwritten mathematical equations used by the architects to design the Arch. We are talking about very advanced math, differential calculus, and hyperbolic cosine functions. You can only imagine how much easier it would have been if they were able to use a computer to do the calculations and create the blueprints.

Peter thought about the possibilities of creating a network of related events, and applying the principles of information and probability theory to be able to predict outcomes. He created what became known as the Probabilistic Event Network (PEN). It was something like a PERT chart. A PERT chart is developed at the start of a project and used to track project status. It portrays the events (activities) and the sequence in which they must occur in order to reach the project's objective. However, the PEN network differed from a PERT chart in two important ways.

First, in the PEN network, an event may or may not occur, and if it does occur, may or may not lead to any following events. It could even lead to more than one future event or objective. It was all a matter of probability. Secondly, whereas the events in a PERT chart are usually static, the events in a PEN are always changing.

****

In November of 1966, Peter talked to Professor Gavin about his probabilistic network concept. The professor was his advisor in the MBA program. (Everyone had an Advisor). As it turned out, he was very intrigued by the concept. He told Peter that if he could develop this concept, including the math that connected the events, the computer program logic, and a process for updating it, that he would count it as the project that the MBA curriculum required for graduation.

Peter had always been very good at math, but now computer programming was a new thing in which he took an interest. He involved himself in various exercises outside of his formal studies. While at Cornell, he had attempted to write a computer program to play chess. Each possible chess move could elicit various possible responses, each with a different likelihood of occurring. When he attempted it, the computers available to students were not yet up to the task, and he put the project on the shelf. Now, however, only three years later, the capabilities of computers were increasing rapidly. Peter thought that creating a computer application to apply his PEN concept would have merit, and he started thinking about real-world applications.

Professor Gavin told him that such an application might be military intelligence. Peter asked what made him think of a military application.

Gavin told him that every year the CIA was one of the employers that came to the school to interview graduates. Yes, that is right, the Central Intelligence Agency. Then he said that Mr. Armstrong who came up to the school to do the interviews was someone he knew quite well and he would arrange for Peter to meet him. But first, Peter had to prove that the concept would work.

Full-time work and night school were already tough on Peter's personal life. Sometimes he would skip supper, go right to school, take two classes, and come home extremely tired. Ironically, he could not always go to sleep right away because he would be buzzing with adrenalin. Nevertheless, he told Professor Gavin that he accepted the challenge.

With some time out for the holidays, Peter spent the next seven weeks working on the probabilistic network concept. He finally came up with a process that was able to calculate the probability or likelihood that certain predefined events would occur. Explaining it got rather technical, but Professor Gavin was eager to hear how it worked.

The process he came up with started by defining a target event that one wanted to predict. Then one would create a network of dependent events that would ultimately influence the target event. One would define appropriate rules and functions to describe the mathematical relationships between that event and the events immediately preceding it. An event that had already occurred would have a probability of 1. Then one would input apriori conditional and unconditional probabilities for each event. An apriori probability is simply one that cannot be calculated from any known data, and one that can only be estimated theoretically. Finally, a computer program would step through the network and calculate the probabilities of each event along the way until the probabilities of the target events were calculated.

In 1966, the initial input to a computer was on eighty-column punch cards. Each event in the PEN had two input cards associated with it. The first card contained a three-digit ID number, fields to define the event IDs of immediately preceding events, rules defining how those events related, and fields for apriori probabilities related to those rules. There was also a field to indicate if the event was new, deleted, or changed. The second card contained a description of the event. The plan was to read these cards into a computer and store them as two separate files on magnetic tape. The first file would be the Event Input Data File; the other would be the Event Description File. These Event Files would be updated periodically.

Peter developed mathematical functions to describe different possible relationships between events. For example, if event *"A"* occurs, one could calculate the probability that a dependent event *"B"* occurs. The probability of *"B"* would be the probability of *"A"* multiplied by the conditional probability of *"B"* given *"A."* It gets more complicated when there are several *"A"* events affecting the probability of the *"B"* event. However, in many cases, these relationships could also be defined. For example, in the case where **both** *"A1"* and *"A2"* (and nothing else), must occur before *"B"* can occur, the probability of *"B"* is the probability of *"A1"* multiplied by the probability of *"A2."* Alternatively, if **either** *"A1"* or *"A2"* (and nothing else), must occur before *"B"* can occur, then the probability that *"B"* occurs is one minus the probability that **neither** *"A1"* nor *"A2"* occurs. The probability that neither *"A1"* nor *"A2"* occurs is the probability of *"A1"* **not** occurring multiplied by the probability of *"A2"* **not** occurring. In some cases, an event *"B"* could be partially dependent upon an unknown event, an *"A3,"* for example. One could assign an apriori probability to the unknown event.

In some other situations, probabilities could functionally relate to external variables. For example, the probability of winning a gunfight could be an exponential function of the ratio of guns and people available on each side of the battle. Often, these types of probability functions could be created using historical data. Once created, these functions could then calculate probabilities based on current data. There were other possible relationships, and many of the functions were more complicated. These mathematical functions could be programmed in FORTRAN, and kept in a Rules File.

Peter also created a logical process for stepping through the network. A master computer program would integrate all the pieces of the process and work for hundreds of events and multiple weeks of data. Each week, this computer program would calculate the probabilities for each event. The results would be saved in a Calculated Event Probability File.

Each week, a report would show the current network and the calculated probabilities for each event. This report would be called the

Event Probability Report. A trend report could also be generated for any given event to show how its calculated probability changed over time.

Bottom line: Computers could use mathematical functions to calculate the probability of future events given the probability of preceding events. Analysts could periodically update and electronically save the results.

Peter completed all the design specs for the Probabilistic Event Network by Monday January 9, 1967. He also created a simple test network of five events to illustrate the concept. For the test, he could step through the process and do all the calculations manually. That evening, he presented the results to Professor Gavin. He had spent the weekend putting it together. He had a fully documented report, overhead projector transparencies, and computer printouts. After his presentation, Professor Gavin told him rather ceremoniously "Peter, congratulations! You have just satisfied the project requirements you will need to graduate."

As Peter started packing up his briefcase, Gavin added "Remember I told you about Mr. Armstrong, my colleague from the CIA. He is going to be here this Wednesday evening. I would like to show him your project report, if that would be okay. In addition, I would like you to meet him. Can you be in my office at seven p.m. on Wednesday?"

"Yes! Thank you!" Peter replied. "I look forward to it."

3

A COMPELLING OFFER

It was Wednesday, and Professor Gavin had arranged for Peter to meet with his colleague Jim Armstrong in the professor's office at 7:00 p.m. On that day, Peter had use of the car and was home by six. Penelope arrived shortly thereafter. She worked full-time for Eastman Kodak as a computer programmer. For a woman in 1967, she had a good job, and her pay was even a tad more than Peter's. However, they only had one car, and she worked on the opposite side of the city from TGW, where he worked.

Fortunately, Eastman Kodak was a large international company that employed many people. As a result, she was able to carpool with others that lived nearby. On the days when it was her turn to drive, or if she needed the car for other reasons, she would drive Peter to work and pick him up afterward. Either way, they both ended up home by six each evening. They would then have a quick supper, after which Peter would take the car and drive to the university to attend classes or to work in the library. Normally after he got home from work, and before driving to the university, he would change into clothes that were more relaxing. However, tonight he wanted to make an impression on Mr. Armstrong so he continued to wear his work attire—a sports jacket, slacks, white shirt, and tie.

Peter had told Penelope his good news about passing his project requirements the night before. She said she was happy for him. However, he neglected to say anything about the meeting he had tonight with Armstrong. He didn't think anything of it until he was about to walk out the door, and Penelope noticed his attire. "Aren't you going to change?" she wanted to know.

"Oh, I didn't tell you. The professor wanted me to meet with one of his associates who may have an interest in the project work I did. To be honest, I don't know what he has in mind. I'll tell you everything when I get home." He gave her a kiss, grabbed his briefcase, and ran out the door.

He arrived on time at 7:00 p.m., but Mr. Armstrong was already there. Armstrong and Gavin were chatting as he walked into the room. Both Gavin and Armstrong were what he would have called middle-aged. Peter learned that they had known each other for many years. He got the impression that they may have worked together before Gavin came to the university. Perhaps the professor had a secret past with the CIA?

They both stood, and Mr. Armstrong Introduced himself. "Hello Mr. Troutman. I'm John Armstrong. I'm a recruiter for the CIA. I'm pleased to meet you." They shook hands; he had a firm grip. Peter was a bit nervous at first, but made his hand as firm as he could. He hoped Armstrong didn't notice the coolness of his hand as they shook. He must have though, because then he said, "No need to be nervous, Mr. Troutman. Professor Gavin has told me all good things about you."

"I apologize for my cool hand, Mr. Armstrong. I admit that I'm a little nervous. I was not exactly sure why you wanted to meet me. Has Professor Gavin told you about my concept? I have all my presentation materials in my briefcase if you want to see them."

Mr. Armstrong seemed okay with Peter's response. "You can relax. Gavin has already done an excellent job of explaining what you created, and I have already read your report. He told me he liked the concept and believed that it could be implemented in a real-life situation." After that, Peter began to relax.

Mr. Armstrong then explained that the probabilistic network concept had an application for the military in Vietnam.

At that time, Penelope and Peter didn't subscribe to a newspaper, and they did not have a TV. Peter knew very little detail about Vietnam, or about what was happening with the war there. He couldn't help but ask, "How will the CIA use the Probabilistic Event Network in Vietnam?"

"Peter, the North Vietnamese have vowed to overtake South Vietnam and to unify the country under communist rule. The people of South Vietnam have a democratic government and they are a capitalist society. If the Communists take over, they will take away individual freedoms, just as they did in Russia, China, Korea, and East Germany. In many cases, they'll execute the dissenters. The standard of living in those countries is very low. The people are poor. We believe in the democratic form of government we have here in the USA, and we believe that capitalism is the right way to go. We are there to help South Vietnam preserve what they have. We are also there to prevent communism from spreading to other countries like neighboring Laos and Cambodia.

"In the last couple of years, the South Vietnamese and the Americans have been attacked on multiple fronts. The Vietcong, who are agents of North Vietnam, attacked restaurants, military officer living quarters, and our embassy. North Vietnam has been sending troops and military supplies from Hanoi to the border with Laos and Cambodia, ready to invade. In fact, they have come across the border in many places and have taken control of some of the border villages. If the people in those villages don't cooperate, they end up dead. The war is escalating. Many soldiers and innocent people have died.

"The military is just beginning to make effective use of computers. We have always had intelligence analysts, but a computer application like yours will allow us to analyze more events, answer more what ifs, and come to more objective conclusions than what we can do manually. Not only that, but it will allow us to do all this much faster.

"We need to be able to make sensible predictions from all the intelligence that we are gathering. I think that your Probabilistic Event Network concept will be ideal. It will help us to organize intelligence and predict where the enemy is likely to attack, and possibly when. We hope that the PEN project will help to reduce the bloodshed and save South Vietnam from communist control. I want you to help us implement it. Mr. Troutman, your support for this project will be a very important thing that you can do for your country."

Then Mr. Armstrong spoke straight and to the point. He made Peter an offer he could not refuse! "Mr. Troutman, the CIA wants to hire you. We want you to leave for Saigon in four weeks and help to implement your Probabilistic Event Network. You will work with a MACV project team to explain the logic and how to set up the events. You will also work with a programmer who will write the program code. You will report to an army Captain who will manage the implementation and use of the application."

"WOW! That is rather sudden!" Peter exclaimed. "How long would I need to be there?"

"I expect four or five weeks, but we are flexible on that," Armstrong answered. Then he added, "During the next four weeks, you will need to get a passport, attend a one-day seminar, and get a security clearance. That would mean filling out some forms. I will expedite the passport and the security clearance."

Peter had many questions. "You said that I would be working with MACV. What is MACV?"

"MACV stands for Military Assistance Command-Vietnam. The word 'assistance' is to remind us that it's not our war. We are there to 'assist' South Vietnam with their war. MACV oversees everything that applies to the U.S. military and advises South Vietnam. All branches of the U.S. military are under MACV command. MACV reports directly to General Westmoreland. It has a headquarters in Saigon, and that is where you will be working."

"Why do you need *me*? Doesn't the military have programmers that could do the job?"

"Yes, they do, but we need more than a programmer. You have developed the concept to the point where it can be implemented. We need someone who understands the math and logic that links the events to each other. You had some of those relations pre-defined, but there will be others, perhaps more complex. We also need someone who can teach the military personnel how to implement the process, and we need someone to help test the code and the process after it's implemented to ensure that it's working correctly according to your specs. We think that you're the best person for the job."

"What about compensation?"

"Not to worry. We will pay you a consulting fee of $5,000 plus all expenses."

Five thousand dollars was a lot of money back then. Peter's salary at TGW was $11,000 per year, which at the time was considered quite good, and they were also paying his tuition in graduate school. Mr. Armstrong continued: "You will also continue to get your regular pay from TGW."

"Does my employer already know about this?"

"All of that has already been taken care of with your employer." Peter looked at Mr. Armstrong quizzically as he wondered how, when Gavin chimed in.

"Mr. Armstrong and I both know Jim," referring to Mr. G, Peter's boss, and heir to the TGW Presidency. "He gave you a glowing recommendation. He mentioned your ability to work independently, to take initiative, and to figure things out without a lot of guidance."

Then Mr. Armstrong added, "There will be a written contract that you will need to sign. Officially, the contract will be with TGW, but aside from Jim, you will be the only employee named on the contract. Jim will review it with you."

"This sounds very exciting, but I need my wife to be okay with it."

Armstrong replied. "Talk to her. You can also tell her that we will have your draft status reclassified as 2-C, 'critical skills,' but you need to let me know by Friday."

After Peter left that meeting, he attended his marketing class, but found it hard to focus. His head was still buzzing. It all happened so fast. Was this really happening? How many people go to a meeting just to meet someone, and without even having a job interview, come out with an offer they cannot refuse?

Later, during his drive home, it hit him that prior to meeting Armstrong, he already had two job interviews, one with the professor, and another with Mr. G.

Not only did Mr. G initially interview him for his position at TGW, but Peter frequently met with him at work as well. He often joined several of the employees in a card game at lunch. It was a game where you took tricks, like Hearts. The game allowed an unlimited number of people to play. The employees named the game "get the leader."

Mr. G was clearly intent on building rapport and gaining the respect of those over whom he would eventually rule. Initially, he was the manager of the new Systems Department, and Peter reported directly to him. However, within a year and a half he was two levels higher and in the "executive office." As one of Peter's colleagues quipped, "I wish I could be on one of those executive training programs like Mr. G."

Near the end of the preceding summer, Mr. G had invited Peter and Penelope over to his home to dine with him and his wife, Marie. The invitation was a surprise, and Peter wondered why he and Penelope would be worthy of such attention. Of course, Peter eagerly accepted the invitation.

Jim and Marie lived in an old but fashionable home on the East side of the city. Jim and Marie escorted Peter and Penelope to a pleasant garden at the rear of the home. They offered them a drink followed by steak tartar, which they boiled in a fondue pot filled with oil, one piece at a time. The leisurely meal afforded plenty of time to talk.

Jim was soft-spoken. Marie said little, letting him take the lead. Although they were in their mid-thirties, they had no children. They learned that Jim and Marie had spent time in South East Asia, that Jim spoke Chinese, and that Marie spoke French. Although Peter was interested in hearing more about their experience abroad, they said very little. Jim seemed to be a very private person, and he directed most of the conversation toward Peter and Penelope. Jim wanted to know if they were planning to have kids, and Peter said they were holding off at least until he finished his degree. Penelope told him about her job as a programmer, and that she wanted the opportunity to work for a while before having kids.

Jim asked Peter what he wanted to do long-term. Peter didn't have a precise answer for that and said he was still trying to figure that out. However, Peter asked him what he thought the opportunities would be at TGW. Jim acknowledged that there were limited opportunities at TGW. It was a small company and not growing. The few key positions were filled with people who had to die, retire, or quit, before someone could replace them. That led to a discussion about expanding the company, and travel to other parts of the world where they had, or would have, sales offices and joint ventures. Would we consider something like that in the future? Penelope and Peter both agreed that it would be exciting.

At that time, they were flexible and ready to embrace all possible futures. They left having enjoyed the evening but still wondering why they were receiving so much attention. Thinking back on that evening, Peter wondered if Mr. G might have had more in mind than what was apparent.

****

When Peter arrived home from the University that Wednesday night after meeting with Mr. Armstrong, he talked to Penelope. It was late so they talked the next night as well. Peter wanted Penelope to have a say and point out things about which he may not have given enough thought. Although he wanted badly to go, she could have vetoed the offer, and he would have accepted that. However, she saw things the way he did. Financially, it was like winning a lottery.

"Who can turn down a chance to increase their annual salary by almost fifty percent for only four weeks of effort?" she told him. Peter also considered his responsibility to his country. He had avoided the draft with a student deferment until he started working full-time for TGW. Night school didn't qualify for a deferment, and his draft board had recently reclassified him as 1-A. If drafted, he would be gone for two years. With this opportunity, he would be reclassified as 2-C, "critical skills." Penelope said she would miss him, but only four or five weeks was much better for her than if he were gone for two years. For Peter, it would also be an exciting adventure, and he would be doing something he enjoyed. They agreed that he should say yes to the offer. Peter would leave in four weeks.

On Friday, Peter called Mr. Armstrong and accepted the offer. He talked with Mr. G and thanked him for the opportunity. He co-signed the contract with TGW. He went to the university library and learned all he could about Vietnam, and about the war. He met again with Mr. Armstrong for a "briefing." He filled out lots of forms. He packed. He even finished his course work for that semester.

Within two weeks, he received a new draft card with a "critical skills" deferment, his first-ever passport, and a Top-Secret security clearance (with "special provisions"). Spring semester at the university would begin soon. He would not be taking any more classes until the fall semester.

4

ARRIVAL

Peter left Rochester early on Friday morning February 10, 1967. It was still dark, and it was cold in Rochester, but Armstrong said it would be hot in Vietnam. He had packed accordingly. Penelope drove him to the airport and let him off at the terminal so he could check in while she parked the car. Peter had a large suitcase in one hand, a briefcase in the other, and a World War II army duffle bag slung across his back. His luggage weighed him down, and he barely managed to get himself to the check-in counter.

The duffle bag had been his father's bag during World War II. Peter had stuffed it with underwear and anything that would not need ironing. It was about three feet high and had a strap allowing him to sling it over his shoulder. He checked the suitcase and the duffle bag but would carry the briefcase onto the plane.

The briefcase was really an artist's case, a four-inch thick hard-sided case with a lock. It was large enough to transport computer printouts plus everything that he may need at his new work location. The briefcase contained all his papers having to do with his PEN concept. It also contained a small slide rule, a flowchart template, the official papers that he would need, some toiletries, a sandwich, a fresh shirt, and a change of socks and underwear. In 1967, there were no security lines, so he didn't have to open his briefcase.

Penelope returned, after parking the car, and they chatted at the gate until it was time to board. Peter removed his coat and left it with her to take back to the car. He would not need it in Vietnam. The two of them kissed and hugged each other good-bye.

"Good luck, Peter. I love you."

"I love you too," he replied, and followed the crowd across the tarmac and out to the plane.

Getting to Saigon from Rochester, New York was a three-day affair. Mr. Armstrong had pre-arranged his travel reservations and tickets. He took a United Airlines flight to JFK, and another United Airlines flight to San Francisco. Then he spent the night at a local airport hotel that had a shuttle service to and from the airport in San Francisco. Early Saturday morning, he took a commercial Pan American Airways flight to Hong Kong. This was a fourteen-hour flight. After subtracting eight hours of time zones, but then, adding twenty-four hours because of crossing the International Date Line, he arrived in Hong Kong around 1:00 p.m. the next day, which was now Sunday.

Peter found the trip exciting. He had only been out of the country once before, when he and his wife drove across the Canadian border on some back roads from New York State. As a car enthusiast he enjoyed driving fast. What he didn't realize was that the speed limit signs in Canada were in kilometers, and he had unwittingly exceeded the speed limits. Fortunately, the Canadian police didn't catch him. But now, he was traveling halfway around the world to a non-English-speaking country. He hoped he would be able to abide by the local laws and customs.

From the air, Hong Kong looked very large, like New York City. It had skyscrapers and buildings with strange shapes, modern for its time. Peter wished he could have spent some time in Hong Kong as he had heard it was a beautiful city to visit. However, an hour in the airport was all he got. His flight to Saigon left Hong Kong around 2:30 p.m. As they took off, an announcement welcomed everyone on board and gave special thanks to the military on board for their patriotism. Peter looked around. Uniformed military personnel filled the plane. He later learned that many were returning from a "rest and relaxation" leave (R&R). They were all men, except for three women who had medical emblems on their uniforms. There were probably no more than five civilians on board, including him.

Peter found himself seated next to an Air Force Lieutenant. According to the nametag on his shirt, his name was McCann. Peter introduced himself as Peter, and they began to talk.

"Are you on your way to Bangkok to join your wife?" McCann asked. He could see that Peter was married as he was wearing a wedding ring, and he could see that Peter was a civilian, so his question was reasonable.

"No, I'm only going as far as Saigon, and my wife is in New York," Peter responded.

"What brings a civilian to Saigon?" he wanted to know.

Mr. Armstrong had prepared Peter for this type of question before he left home, and he gave McCann the answer he had rehearsed. "I'm a computer analyst working under a civilian contract for MACV."

"I suppose you can't say much more than that," he responded.

"No. Sorry. If I did, I would have to kill you." Peter said jokingly, but was not sure McCann appreciated the humor, so he quickly asked, "What about yourself?"

Peter learned that McCann was returning from an R&R week in Hong Kong. He had already seen action in the air and was in his second year of service. He had been on bombing runs from Thailand but was now going to be stationed near Tan Son Nhut, the Saigon airport where they would be landing. He said that things had quieted down in the Saigon area relative to the prior two years. According to him, The U.S. had eliminated much of the Vietcong in the Iron Triangle, and the Air force was doing a great job of bombing supply lines down the Ho Chi Minh trail. Peter took what he said at face value.

As they approached Tan Son Nhut, an announcement came over the intercom. It went something like, "Those of you who are returning know the drill. Fasten your seat belts and be prepared for some serpentine, followed by a rapid descent and some sharp turns."

Peter had an aisle seat and did not have a great view out the window, but he could tell that they were now over land. He looked over at Lt. McCann, who was not perturbed by the announcement. The lieutenant smiled. In a matter of minutes, they banked sharply to the right, then sharply to the left, and then they spiraled rapidly downward. Peter could feel the blood start to drain from his head. It was like an amusement park ride. He had a new admiration for the maneuverability of the Boeing 707 aircraft. As they hit the tarmac, and decelerated, Peter looked over at McCann again. He smiled. As they departed from the plane, they wished each other the best.

As Peter came off the plane and walked across the tarmac, he was struck by how bright the sun was and how hot it was, not steamy, just hot. He had lost track of time with all the time zone changes, and his wristwatch was wrong, but he judged it was late afternoon, around 4:00 p.m. It felt like going on vacation in Arizona or Southern California. Then he noticed the many military vehicles, the military aircraft, and the armed soldiers. It was not like any place he had ever been on vacation.

He made his way through the terminal building entrance and found his way to where he could retrieve his luggage. Then he realized he would also have to go through customs. Peter showed his passport and travel papers, and they allowed him to pass without having his luggage searched. Nevertheless, he was beginning to get hot and irritable with the inconvenience.

****

Peter had been told that someone would greet him at the airport and escort him to his hotel. As he exited the baggage area, he saw a young woman holding a sign with his name on it.

"Are you looking for me?"

"I don't know. Who are you?"

"I'm Peter Troutman. My name is on your sign."

"Let me see your passport."

Peter showed it to her. "Looks like it's really you, Mr. Troutman. I'm Donna Rice; you may call me Donna. May I call you Peter?"

"Yes, of course," he replied.

"How was your trip?"

"It was long, and I'm hot and tired."

"Not the first time I've heard that," she said with a smile. "I'll help you with your bags, and then I'll drive you to the Continental Palace where you will be staying." When she spoke, her tone was firm but pleasant, and she had a cute smile. She came across as being friendly.

Donna appeared to be about twenty-five or twenty-six years old. She was about five feet eight inches tall with an athletic build; thin, but well-proportioned. She had short golden-brown hair. Her hairstyle was short, like that sported by Mia Farrow, Julie Andrews, or Lisa Minnelli. The color of her eyes matched the color of her hair. The lobes of her ears were pierced with gold studs. She was wearing tan slacks and a plain white blouse with short sleeves and an opened collar that revealed a light tan that matched her slacks. Except for the open collar, her cotton blouse was fully buttoned. She was not wearing makeup, but she had a pretty face, with nicely proportioned facial features and a clear complexion. With the pants, the absence of makeup, and the short hairstyle, her appearance was modest and not provocative, at least not in a feminine way. If anything, Peter thought her appearance leaned in the direction of "butch."

"Peter, let's get to my vehicle. You can set your bag onto this cart."

"That will be very helpful. Thank you. I also have a duffle bag."

He retrieved his duffle bag, and they loaded the luggage onto the cart. Then they made their way to her vehicle. She pulled the cart with the luggage, while he held onto his briefcase. Her vehicle turned out to be an army Jeep. It had a canvas top, but the top was down.

"It looks like that suitcase and duffle bag of yours may be heavy. Let me load it for you." Before he could respond, she lifted the duffle bag and tossed it into the back of the Jeep. Peter went for the suitcase, but she promptly took it from him and told him she had it. Donna was clearly a lot stronger than she looked. Once again, he thought that "butch" might be an apt description. He dismissed the thought and put his briefcase in the back with the suitcase. They climbed into the Jeep.

Before Donna started up the engine, she turned to him and noticed his flat-top buzz-cut hair. It was a typical hair style for young civilian men as well as military men in those days.

"I suggest you get yourself a lightweight hat before the sun burns your scalp." she said. She reached behind her and pulled out a white sailor's cap.

"Here. You can put this on. Are you thirsty?"

"Actually, I'm very thirsty . . . and hot."

"Well, you're in luck. I have something for you." She turned her body around and reached into a cooler she had behind the seats and handed him a quart-sized glass bottle. He grabbed ahold of the bottle and could see that it was seltzer water. He was a bit surprised as seltzer water was not something that he drank very often, and a whole quart of it to boot. As he opened it and took a swig, he remembered that when he was very young, he found some seltzer water in the refrigerator, and experimented with making ice cream sodas and carbonated eggnogs. As the carbonation filled his mouth and went down his throat, he remembered why he didn't drink it very often. The carbonation made him gassy and sometimes aggravated his digestive tract.

He didn't want to look a gift horse in the mouth, so he politely said, "Thank you."

Sensing his reticence, she said, "Peter, it's very hot here and very important that you stay hydrated. I heard that seltzer water is popular with the Jewish population in New York. Isn't it something you drink?"

"No, not generally. Did you think I was Jewish?"

"Aren't you Jewish?"

"No, I'm Christian. How about you?"

"I'm Christian too, Catholic. Sorry, I shouldn't make assumptions."

"It's okay. Forget it."

"In any case, safe water is hard to come by in Saigon. May I give you some advice?"

"Sure."

"When you get to your hotel, do not drink the water. Have you heard of Montezuma's revenge?"

"Of course. Do you have that problem here?"

"Yes, but here we call it Ho Chi Minh's revenge."

"So then, what am I supposed to do to stay hydrated?"

"Seltzer water is a good substitute. You can buy it at the military Commissaries. Bottled mineral water is good as well, but for me it acts as a laxative. However, if it works for you, we have imported Perrier and there is Vinh Hoa, a local brand also available in stores here. The locals that live here drink hot tea. Hot coffee, soup, or the local pho, are good too. Anything that uses boiled water is fine. The French drink wine, and many of the soldiers here drink beer. You can also find imported soda like Coke, Pepsi, and Canada Dry in the Commissary. The military imports water for the military or makes it at sea from seawater. The U.S. imports the water in the coolers where I work and where you will work. That water *is* considered safe. Since you will be here for several weeks, your body may slowly acclimate to the water at your hotel. Brush your teeth with it and rinse with seltzer water. If after a few days you still feel good, take a few sips of the tap water, increase it in bits each day, but don't overdo it."

"Thanks for the water and for the advice as well." He took another sip and put the cap back on the bottle.

She started up the engine, and they were off. She told him that the hotel was about five miles from the airport. After they came into the downtown area of Saigon, she commented on several places in the city as they drove by. They drove by the Presidential Palace, and then the new U.S. Embassy building that was under construction on Thong Nhat next to the French and British embassies. Then they traveled down what Donna said used to be called Rue Catinat. She told him that after the French left, the Vietnamese renamed Rue Catinat and many other streets. As they approached the Notre Dame Cathedral on Duy Tan, Donna began explaining what they were seeing. "The French completed the Notre Dame Cathedral in 1880. The area surrounding the entire Basilica was recently renamed JFK Square."

Jokingly, he said, "You sound like a tourist guide. Who is it you actually work for?"

"Peter, don't be cute. You can think of me any way you wish, but I think you know who I work for."

He *was* being cute, and he *did* know who she worked for. Mr. Armstrong had briefed him before he left home. He told him that his CIA contact would be Donna Rice, and that she worked for the USAID organization as a hospitality worker. Peter thought that if hospitality was a role, then Donna played that role extremely well.

Before leaving home, Peter had done some research to determine what USAID was. The university librarian was very helpful. Peter learned that President Kennedy started the U.S. Agency for International Development (USAID) in 1961, to consolidate various foreign aid programs. It was set up as an agency under the State Department. In 1966, South Vietnam received about one-fifth of the total aid provided. The concept behind this aid was that the USA needed to do more than use military force to win over Vietnam. They also needed to win the hearts and minds of the people. Aid to South Vietnam included a wide variety of support. It included providing medical care, settling refugees, building schools in rural areas, providing agricultural assistance, improving transportation, and supporting Vietnamese importers. A public Safety division provided support to the National Police.

Donna continued talking. "On November first of last year, the Vietcong landed twelve mortar shells on this square, killing five, injuring more than forty, and doing damage to the roof of the seminary. You can see a filled-in mortar shell crater over there by the statue of the Virgin Mary."

"Why would they attack a church," he wanted to know.

"We don't think the church was the target. That morning when the shells landed, a parade was in progress celebrating National Day and three years since the overthrow of President Ngo Dinh Diem. General Westmoreland and the current President were in the viewing stands, and many of the marchers were reportedly ex-Vietcong. Most of the victims were innocent Vietnamese, but one U.S. military officer that came to watch was also killed. He was a Navy Lt. Commander—someone I had met."

"Donna, I'm sorry."

"It's okay. I'm telling you this because these attacks seem to occur randomly without warning. My advice is to avoid organized events, parades, and demonstrations. We're in a war zone. You need to stay alert."

After they left JFK Square and the Cathedral, the street name changed to Tu Do and the hotel was only a short distance further. Peter commented that even though today was Sunday, there was quite a bit of traffic. He also noticed that there didn't seem to be too many traffic signals. "You should see it on a week day," she said.

As they came down Tu Do Street, they passed the Continental Palace, an exit lane, and another building set back from the street. It had concrete steps that led up to an arched entrance. As Donna turned left onto an entry lane. Peter noticed an Air France Office and the Hotel Caravelle on his right. But he was curious about the building on his left. "Donna, what is that building with the archway to our left that we are driving around?"

"We are driving around the National Assembly Building. It used to be a theater for live performances, but now the ruling body of South Vietnam meets here. They have made it one-way around the square, and the entrance to your hotel is on the other side of this square and not on Tu Do Street. By the way, the French had named it Garnier Square, but now it's known as Lam Son Square."

When they arrived at the entrance to the Continental Palace, he looked at his watch. With today's traffic, and their circuitous route, it took them about twenty minutes to travel from the airport to the hotel. Donna helped him unload his luggage.

"Peter, you can check in, but meet me in the lobby in about thirty minutes," she directed.

"Okay . . . Oh wait. What is the local time here right now?"

"It's about seventeen hundred fifteen hours. I'll meet you here at eighteen hundred hours."

****

Peter made a note of the time and reset his watch, as he muttered to himself about his need to figure out that 1715 hours meant 5:15 p.m. After he checked in, a valet took his luggage to his room. Not knowing what a fair value was, and with no local currency in his pocket, Peter tipped him one dollar in U.S. currency. The valet took a glimpse of the dollar bill and quickly stuffed it into his pocket, as if he had received a packet of heroin. The valet seemed very happy to have received it.

Peter's room was interesting, what one might expect from a historic hotel. One would say it was typical French Colonial. His room was on the first floor. The first floor was really the second floor, one floor up from the lobby, which was the ground floor. On entering the room, the bath was on his right and the main room was straight ahead.

As he walked through the main room to the windows, he immediately passed the foot of a double bed on his right. The bed was higher above the floor than he was accustomed to, and it had a dark wooden headboard and footboard. It looked old-fashioned. There was a small lamp table next to the bed. An armoire was directly across from the foot of the bed on his left. It had plenty of drawer space and a hanger bar for his clothes. The wood of the armoire matched the wood of the bed. The ceiling was high with a wooden fan in the center. The uncarpeted floors were hard and marble-like with a reddish–brown hue.

When he reached the windows, he looked out and could see that it faced the street. The windows opened like French doors and offered a view of Tu Do Street. There was a retrofitted air conditioner unit at the bottom of one window. Thank goodness for that! The drapes were open, exposing the room to the late afternoon sun. The room was very warm, so he closed the drapes and reset the air-conditioner to a lower temperature. In one corner near the window was an over-stuffed brown armchair. On the other side of the window, opposite the armchair, was a dark wooden desk with a wooden chair. The room had no TV and no phone.

Before leaving, he checked out the bath. It had a full-size tub with a splashboard and a hook to hang the shower hose. Next to the toilet was a bidet, another reminder of decades of French dominance.

Overall, his room was quite large, but the furnishings seemed sparse relative to its size, and in his mind, the room was somewhat austere. He had stayed in better hotel rooms, but this one was fine for his purposes. It even had a certain charm, *"C'est le vie,"* he thought.

After he washed up, he left, being sure to lock the door behind him.

****

Donna was already waiting for him when he arrived back in the lobby.

"Are you hungry?" she asked.

He had not eaten for at least five hours, so he was ready to eat. "Yes. I could use some food. What did you have in mind?"

"There's a café across the street called Givral. Let's go there, and we can talk some more." They walked across Tu Do Street and sat at a table at Givral.

"Peter, have you ever read The Quiet American?"

"No, why do you ask?"

"Well, an author named Graham Greene, who stayed at the Continental Palace, wrote it in 1955. He used to eat here at the Givral and joked that he spent so much time here that the Givral was like his office. The story took place while the French were still in power. The novel was about Alden Pyle, who was sent here from Washington, but his idealism got him into trouble. You should read it."

Then she changed the subject. "A popular dish here is pho. Many people here start their day with it, but I like it anytime. Are you game?"

"Sure."

"Do you prefer beef or chicken?"

"I don't know. Surprise me."

"Okay, I'll order one of each."

Donna went to the counter and, speaking in Vietnamese, ordered a *pho bo* and a *pho ga* from the Vietnamese woman on duty. Shortly thereafter, the woman brought the meal back to the table for them. Donna allowed

Peter to try a little of each type. Pho consisted of meat, green vegetables, rice noodles, and broth. Peter found Pho to be quite good, a very enjoyable meal.

He told her, "I like this pho."

"This time, it will be my treat," she said.

After they ate, Donna became very businesslike. "Peter, people you meet may ask what you do or why you're here. If someone asks you why you're here, you tell them that you're a computer analyst that works for a U.S. company that is contracted to MACV, and that is all you tell them. Earlier, you asked me what I really do. If anyone asks you what I do, you tell them that I provide guest services for USAID, and that is all you need to tell them. The job I have with USAID is a real job by the way. Our other roles are never to be mentioned in public. Please tell me you understand."

"I understand that," he said, as he looked her in the eye. "Actually Donna, I would be interested in knowing more about USAID and what you do for them, if you have enough time. What is the mission of USAID?"

"Well," she began, "the mission of USAID is to help countries such as South Vietnam become democratic and capitalistic countries. We do this primarily through economic help, education, and technical assistance. Here in South Vietnam, we share our goals with the military and other government agencies."

"How does your job fit into that mission?"

"It fits indirectly. I see a real need for what I do. Accomplishing our goals requires both military and civilian participation. The military handles the needs of military personnel. The military command regulates the travel, room, and board, of its members, and has direct control of their activities. However, the needs of civilians that come here are different, and there is no single authority to guide their activities. Civilians here don't usually take orders directly from military officers, and they are not subject to the same disciplinary process. Civilians like you are here voluntarily and for many different reasons. Some are here for a few days, some like you for a few weeks, and some, like myself, are here on temporary assignments that may be for one or two years. In addition to needing appropriate places to live, they also may have special transportation needs; some need cars, and some need drivers. They may need special security measures, like bodyguards. They may need maps of the country or the city and some assessment as to what areas or routes are safe and what ones are not. They may need to know where specific agencies, businesses, or facilities are located, and how to get there. They may need help to know who to see, or what to do about various issues they may have. If here for the first time, they need orientation to the Vietnamese culture, the economy, and the laws. They need to understand the dangers of being in a war zone, and if they have not been in the military, they need to understand the structure and social nature of military rank. My organization is here to satisfy the needs of civilians who come here as guests of the U.S. government and its various agencies.

"My USAID title is Manager of Civilian Guest Services. There are four of us right now. We work for USAID under personal service contracts. That means we are contractors, not employees of USAID. My USAID contract is for two years and my term ends at the end of this year. In addition to supporting civilian guests of MACV, such as you, we also support civilian guests of USAID, the U.S. Embassy, the USO, the Joint U.S. Public Affairs Office, and the CIA.

"In short, I escort visitors to the city, help them acclimate, and help them with any logistics or travel issues they may have. So, 'tour guide,' as you suggested earlier, is not far off the mark. I do this for three or four visitors per week. However, in your case, I'll be doing that plus a lot more. And, before you get cute, sexual favors are never part of the deal."

"I would not have thought otherwise."

"Peter, your official orientation will start tomorrow morning but I feel the need to give you some advice up-front. You're in a place that's unlike any other place you've been. Saigon is in the middle of a war zone. I'll be your primary contact. You will report to me on a regular basis while you're in Saigon. My job is to be sure you have what you need, to show you how to get around the city, and to protect you. Above all, however, my job is to ensure that you successfully complete the job you were brought here to do.

"Sunset is around eighteen hundred hours here, and the city can be dangerous after dark. You need to be careful as to who you trust and who you associate with. There are many who will try to take advantage, including gangs we call 'cowboys.' Keep your personal items close, and be sure and keep your hotel room door locked at all times. You also need to know that we have a midnight curfew in Saigon right now. I suggest that you don't leave your hotel room tonight, as you have not yet registered your presence with the embassy. I cannot tell you what to do with your personal life, but if you let things get out of hand, you will be sent back home. Do you understand me?"

Although he felt like he had just been scolded by his mother, and her lecture sounded a little over the top, he was in no position to judge. His response was, "I understand you. Don't worry."

She continued, "This is a good place to have breakfast. I would like you to be here in the morning at zero seven-thirty hours. After we eat, I'll brief you some more, and then I'll take you over to the American Embassy to register your presence. I'll introduce you to the Colonel who is in charge and the captain you will be working with. Then you'll go to the location where you will be working. For tomorrow, you won't need to bring anything with you except your passport and your wallet. As you can see, it's already dark, so allow me to escort you back to the hotel."

As they entered the hotel lobby, Peter thanked Donna again for her advice and for the delicious pho. Then she said, "Just one more thing before you go. Here is a map of the city, published by Central Command. It will help you find your way around."

Back in his room, Peter was pleased that the air conditioner was working and the room had cooled off. After he closed the drapes and sat down in the easy chair, he looked at the map. Important landmarks were indicated on the map with circled numbers. First, he located his hotel (number 57). Then he found the Cathedral they had passed earlier (number 77). It appeared to be a short walk, up Tu Do Street to the right. He could see that if he walked down Tu Do Street to the left, he would come to the river. The Majestic Hotel (number 60) was on the right, and The U.S. Embassy that he would be visiting in the morning (number 76) was only a couple of blocks more to the South.

Peter set his alarm for *zero six forty-five* and had no trouble falling asleep.

5
ORIENTATION

The next morning, Peter was up at dawn, as the noise from the traffic below began to get very loud. He showered, brushed his teeth, dressed in slacks and a white shirt, got his documents together, and made his way down the stairs to the lobby just before 7:30 a.m. He was surprised to see Donna there, as she had told him to meet her at the café.

"Peter," she called out from across the room, and waved for him to come closer. "Please go over to the café and order your breakfast . . . no need to wait for me. I have something I must do first. I'll be over there as soon as I can."

He watched her disappear into the open door of the elevator. He wondered if she was also staying at the Continental Palace. He figured he had some extra time, so he picked up a morning paper, not realizing it was not in English, and walked outside. The morning air was cool and crisp. He walked across Tu Do Street to the café and began thinking about what to order.

Inside the café, fruit and pastry were on display. It looked Interesting, but he didn't recognize the type of fruit or the pastry.

He noticed that the woman on duty was the same woman that had been on duty the night before. Speaking English, he asked what the fruit was called, what was inside the pastry, if they had coffee, and how much it cost. She didn't seem to understand his English.

"Vietnamese?" she asked.

"No," he responded, and shook his head from side to side. He didn't speak Vietnamese, but he had learned that in addition to Vietnamese language, many locals also spoke French. This woman looked to be middle-aged, so she was probably here when the French were here. As for him, *je parle un petit peu Francais*. However, he thought it was worth a try, so he said, "*parlez vous Francais?*"

She responded, "*Oui, Vous etes prets a commander?*"

"*Un moment.*" He needed more time to decide what to order.

He decided to give up on the mystery fruit and mystery pastry. Then he saw a picture on the counter offering a special breakfast *omelette*, and he noticed that one of the other customers had ordered it. It had avocado in it and looked good to him. Speaking French, he ordered. "*Oui … Je voudrais petit dejeuner … omelette au avocado, croissant, et café au lait, si vous plait.*" As for the coffee, he didn't know what to expect, but he knew he needed some wake-up caffeine, and according to Donna, it was safe to drink.

When he offered U.S. money to pay, the woman said, "No dollar . . . dong!" He held his hands out and shrugged to indicate he had no dong. The woman said, "It okay. Wait for lady." Apparently, she spoke some English after all. Then the woman asked his name. "*Quel est votre nom?*"

"*Je m'appelle Peter,*" he told her.

"*Peter, Je m'appelle Han.*" The rest of what she said was hard for him to understand. "*Prenez place je vous en prie. Je vais apporter votre repas vous.*" He thought she wanted him to sit down until she brought the food.

He found an empty table and sat down, hoping that Donna would arrive soon. He was very happy when she arrived a few minutes later. After they exchanged greetings, Donna walked to the counter, spoke to the woman in Vietnamese, and then returned to their table with a dish of that mystery fruit he was eyeing earlier. He explained to her that he had not paid.

"Not to worry. I just talked with Han, and I took care of your bill."

"Thank you for that. Han was very patient with my language difficulties. We got by with her French, which is excellent, and mine, which is poor. I tried to ask her what that fruit is that you're eating, but I don't think she understood my question and I didn't get an answer."

"Oh, this? It's called Jackfruit . . . sweet and juicy . . . very popular here . . . grown in the Mekong Delta. The fruit itself is large like a watermelon, but Han, or her assistant, has opened it up, removed the lobes of fleshy meat, and sliced it up. You're welcome to try a piece."

"Well, okay, just a taste. Hmmm . . . It's different . . . Looks like slices of artichoke or raw potato. It tastes sweet, and it's chewy like a gum-drop."

"Want more?"

"No thanks," he replied.

Donna chuckled and said, "Sounds like you're not quite sure what to make of it. Perhaps it's an acquired taste."

Then he changed the subject. "I noticed you speak Vietnamese with Han. Do you know each other?"

"Yes, I have come here off and on for about a year. Han has taught me to speak Vietnamese, and I have tried to teach her some English."

He was about to ask if Donna had taken care of the business she had to attend to earlier, but before he could, she began to talk in a very matter-of-fact manner about something else.

"Peter, before we go, I need to talk to you about currency and economics here in Saigon. I'll make it brief. In Saigon there are three currencies in use, the U.S. dollar, the military payment certificate or MPC, and the South Vietnamese Dong. Sometimes you will hear the South Vietnamese currency referred to as Piasters. Officially, one U.S. dollar equals one MPC dollar. One dollar equals one hundred eighteen dong officially, and one hundred fifty dong on the free market. Legally, the locals are only allowed to circulate the dong, and they are not allowed to possess MPCs. You will quickly see that this is not enforced. No one is authorized to use dong or dollars at the military bases or commissaries. To help you get started, I have been authorized to give you this envelope. It contains five thousand dong and one hundred MPC dollars. Any more may not fit in your wallet."

He began stuffing nine 500-Dong notes, four smaller denomination notes, and five 20-dollar MPCs into his wallet as she continued to talk. She was right; it barely fit. "You can exchange your U.S. dollars at the Saigon bank for dong, or on the street at a higher rate. You can exchange your US dollars at the military base for MPCs when you need more. When you go home, the embassy will take care of your final exchange. The money I just gave you will be deducted from your account. Another thing you need to know is that unless something is scarce, whatever it costs in the States probably costs a third of that here." Then she changed the subject. "We need to get going. I have scheduled our meeting at the Embassy for zero eight thirty hours, but the traffic may be a problem, and we need to go through a security check to get in. I want to be on time. Do you have your passport?"

He nodded yes, and pointed to his trouser pocket. "I'm ready to go whenever you are."

They walked back across Tu Do Street to a parking area behind the Assembly Building between the Continental Palace and the Caravelle Hotels. When they arrived, he looked around but saw no evidence of her Jeep. "Where is your Jeep?"

"We're taking my bike today . . . too much traffic for the Jeep."

They walked over to a red late-model Honda Motorbike (or was it a Suzuki). She unlocked the chain, pulled the bike out from the parking rack, and lowered two footrests that were toward the rear of the bike. Donna got on the front part of the seat, and motioned for him to hop on the back. He did so, as she kick-started the engine. He was still trying to find the footrests with his feet when she abruptly sped away and turned sharply to the left. He felt his body falling backward and then sideways. He instinctively reached for the nearest thing he could, her waist, and perhaps a bit more.

The bike suddenly stopped, and his body lurched forward, pushing up against her back. Donna turned her head and sternly asked, "What are you doing?"

"Donna, I have never ridden on the back of a motorcycle before. I apologize if I did something wrong, but I think I need to hold onto something."

"All right, but just watch where your hands go, or I'll let you off and you can walk."

"Yes, Ma'am!" he replied. She may have been having fun with him because he thought he saw a smile on the side of her face and maybe heard a muffled chuckle as well.

They arrived at the U.S. Embassy building, not too far from the river. Donna explained that this building was still being used until the new embassy building was completed. She said that security was the main concern. She said that the barricades they were looking at were added after the bombing in 1965. She said that the troop buildup and the additional number of employees were also reasons for new quarters. Then Donna pointed out the building she worked in next door to the Embassy. She thought she would move as well, but didn't know when.

They passed through a guardhouse; Donna showed the guard a badge, and Peter showed his passport. The guard, a marine, let them through, and they found a place to park and chain the bike. Then they entered the embassy, went up some stairs, and signed in. Peter was given a visitor's badge, and they went down a corridor to the office of Colonel Abernathy. The Colonel welcomed Peter to Saigon, and addressed him as Mr. Troutman. As they shook hands, Peter said he was pleased to be here and hoped that his process would be of help. The Colonel introduced Donna and him to Captain Weisman. Peter could not help but notice the expressions on the faces of Captain Weisman and Donna as they shook hands. He wondered if perhaps they had met before, but if they had, they didn't let on. The Colonel asked for Peter's passport and had his assistant create an appropriate ID badge for him. He explained that the embassy already had a file on him, and that his passport was all he needed for verification.

"Mr. Troutman, I'm assigning you to work with Captain Weisman until the PEN is fully implemented and tested. Hope you don't mind the abbreviation PEN for Probabilistic Event Network. The military is big on mnemonics and acronyms."

"Not a problem, sir," he replied.

The Colonel continued, "After we are done here, I need to meet with Donna Rice on another subject. Perhaps you could drive over to the computer lab with Captain Weisman. He can explain what has been done so far, introduce you to his staff, and you can get started on your mission. Are we good?"

"Yes, sir. We're good."

Just then, the Colonel's assistant returned. "Mr. Troutman, I need you to sign these forms. I see that your security clearance has special provisions. Those special provisions allow you to work at the facility, and on the project to which you were assigned, but nowhere else. And you are not allowed access to documents or materials that are above 'Top Secret', unless you are given additional clearance directly by the Colonel. The 'special provisions' also mean that you may not leave Vietnam unless you come here first and notify us. To ensure that happens, we will hold your passport until you leave Vietnam. Here is your identification document. Always keep it with you! Use it like a badge to access your work location, pass the guard here at the embassy, or gain entry to most of the military Commissaries and BOQs. You have privileges equivalent to a Second Lieutenant."

He took a quick look at his new ID. It said, *Military Assistance Command (MACV) across the top. Down further it said Civilian Non-Combatant. In a field labeled "Rank/status" it said O-1 Equiv.* The ID card had his passport picture on it as well.

Then he heard Captain Weisman say, "Let's go," He glanced over at Donna. "Don't worry Peter; I'll catch you later." So, he slipped his new ID badge into his pants pocket and followed the captain out of the building.

Captain Weisman was in his mid-thirties. He looked to be in decent shape, about one hundred and eighty pounds, five foot ten. He had a flat top of brown hair and hazel eyes. He had a pleasant rounded face. Peter followed him toward a parking area that held several Jeeps. The captain spoke as they walked. His tone was friendly and comforting, not harsh or authoritarian.

"Mr. Troutman, hope you don't mind riding in a Jeep. It's my primary mode of transportation. I'm not entitled to have a regular driver, but I enjoy driving, so it's not a problem."

"It's not a problem, Sir. In fact, this will be my second Jeep ride since arriving yesterday."

They hopped in and drove off. As they drove, Peter tried to pay attention to where they were. He could see that they were driving away from the river, but there were very few street signs. He could not help but ask, "Captain Weisman, Sir, I was wondering what is the name of this street?"

"We are on Pasteur. It was named after the famous French doctor, Louis Pasteur," he replied.

He continued. "Colonel Abernathy tends to be rather formal and adhere to official protocol. This is especially true when he is at his office in the embassy. He gives orders and needs to maintain his image of authority. He needs to be addressed as 'Sir.'

"However, I tend to be much less formal. We are analysts and technicians, not on the battlefield. I want the environment we work in to be relaxed, and I want the people in my group to talk with each other without being concerned so much about rank. Therefore, you don't need to address me as Sir. You can just call me 'Captain' if you wish, or even my first name is okay."

"What is your first name, Sir? I mean Captain."

"My first name is Betzalel."

"A very interesting name," Peter responded, "but I think I prefer to call you Captain."

The captain chuckled. "Good choice. I think my parents had a strange sense of humor when they picked it, but they died in the Holocaust when I was young, so I never really found out why they named me that."

"Perhaps it has some special meaning," Peter suggested.

"Actually, it does. According to scripture, Betzalel built the portable tabernacle that the Jews took with them while in the desert for forty years. Perhaps there is a parallel to the mission we are about to begin?"

Peter was tempted to tell the captain that he was not Jewish but decided to hold his tongue. Instead, he said, "Captain you don't need to address me as Mr. Troutman, just call me Peter."

"Okay, I'll call you Peter. Sometimes I tend to talk too much. Tell me about yourself." Peter gave the captain a quick summary of how he came to be there, but before he could say too much, they arrived at their destination at 137 Pasteur. Like so many places, it was a guarded compound with barricades and a guardhouse.

A guard checked them in at the gate. The building appeared to be an old-style apartment building, or even a long multistoried motel. It had five stories, and went back lengthwise from the street. According to the captain, Michigan State University used it until 1962, when MACV took it over. They drove through, parked the Jeep, and walked into the building through a side entrance on the first level. Peter followed him to his office on the first level, where they talked briefly.

The captain said that he wanted to introduce Peter to everyone on his project team. First on the list was Danny. Danny had a desk next to the captain's office. Peter noticed that Danny was an army Staff Sergeant. Danny appeared to be somewhat effeminate, but very congenial. The captain asked him to make Peter a basement pass. "Yes, Captain, will do."

Danny turned to Peter. "Mr. Troutman, please fill out this form and sign it." Peter did so.

"Danny, I'm pleased to meet you. You can call me Peter." Then the captain led Peter to the basement where the computer room was located.

To get to the computer room, they had to use a badge reader before going down a flight of stairs. As they descended, Peter could feel the skin on his arms cooling down. The computer, tape drives, a disk storage unit, printers, and consoles were in a separate raised floor air-conditioned room in the center of the basement. Entry required another badge read. An aisle ran along one outside wall of the raised floor room. Along the aisle were workrooms, a key-punch room, a card-reader room, and four small cubicles. A section of the wall separating the aisle from the computer room had windows that reminded Peter of a food automat he had visited in Manhattan when he was a child. He had seen this before at college, but not at TGW. The windows had locks and gave access to boxes that contained computer printouts.

The captain introduced Peter to Jim McDermott, an army Chief Warrant Officer with three bars—fully commissioned, he was told. Jim managed the computer room.

Peter asked Jim what model computers these were, but before he could answer, another fellow came up behind him and answered, "An IBM 7094-II system, an IBM 1410 system, and a communications controller are in there. My name is Bob Nunn; I'm the IBM Systems Engineer. My job is to manage and maintain the systems. I have been trying to get the captain an IBM System 360, but the red tape is slowing us down."

Aside from Peter, Bob was the only one not wearing a military uniform. His short-sleeved white shirt and necktie seemed somewhat out of place. Peter later learned that Bob was one of a handful of civilians that IBM had sent to support the war effort, and that IBM expected them to follow a certain dress code.

Bob explained the printout boxes. "That is how we do things at IBM, when there are multiple people or departments using a data center, and where security is required. In this case, there are at least seven other project teams within MACV sharing the computer room."

Then they turned their attention back to Jim. "Sorry for that. Bob can be a bit overbearing at times, but we could not get along without him.

Mr. Troutman, welcome aboard. Unfortunately, I must run to a meeting. However, if you need anything, my assistant, Chan, can help you out. If he is busy in there, just dial him on this intercom phone here by the door." Peter could see Chan through the glass in the access door to the raised floor. He was busy mounting a reel of tape onto a tape drive.

Then. the captain introduced Peter to Jeff, a Navy Warrant Officer. "Jeff will be the one you'll be directly working with to complete the implementation of the PEN. Jeff is an expert programmer. I would like the two of you to meet tomorrow morning." He looked at Jeff and said, "This afternoon, I'm going to give Peter an overview of the project and where we are with it. You guys can go into detail tomorrow."

As they left to go back upstairs, the captain told Peter that after the PEN was up and running, another individual would be part of his team and be responsible for administering what went into and out of the computer room. Her name was Lt. Nguyen. She was with the South Vietnamese Women's Armed Forces Corps or WAFC, but she needed to finish officer training school and would arrive in about six weeks after Peter completed his assignment.

"Captain, you seem to have a very diverse group of people working with you, many backgrounds."

"You're exactly right. We have purposely done it this way to maximize our intelligence as a group. Also, this is supposed to be a South Vietnamese war as much as it is ours, which is why Nguyen will be joining us."

"Captain, I'm still a bit fuzzy on the organization as to who reports to who. For example, are you responsible for more than one project? It sounded like Jim is servicing multiple projects. Does he report to you?"

"It can be a little confusing at first. John and Chan report to Jim. Jim reports to a lieutenant who manages several data centers who reports to a regional Captain, who reports to a full Colonel who is responsible for all the data centers in Vietnam. The Pen project is my only project responsibility. Bob was correct that there are multiple projects sharing the center. Most, including mine, are part of SOG. SOG used to stand for Special Operations Group, but the politicians decided that they could not put an organization with a reputation for being assassins on an organization chart. So, they added some intelligence processing functions and renamed it the Studies and Operations Group. Danny and Jeff report directly to me, as will Lieutenant Nguyen when she arrives. Meanwhile, you and an intelligence officer, who I call Sam, are also on the project as contractors. Sam has a doctorate degree as well as battlefield experience. Like you, he is contracted to us by an outside firm. In his case, I think it's the Rand Corporation. I meet with Sam at least once per week on Friday mornings, and we will create and maintain the PEN network of events. I report directly to Colonel Abernathy, who you met earlier.

Then, there is the CIA. As you know, the CIA initiated this project, and they keep tabs on what is happening through Colonel Abernathy, through Sam, and in other ways that I'm not supposed to be aware of."

"Wow!" Peter exclaimed. "This is not the regimented structure that I had expected the military to have. It sounds like a management concept I studied in school called matrix management."

"All of the projects here require this type of organization to be effective. It seems to work, and I like it. By the way, everyone on this project has a security level of at least 'Top Secret,' so that we can freely talk with each other while we work and help each other out. In your case, you have a special clearance that allows you to go above that level, but only with special authority from the Colonel. Your clearance also restricts you to matters that concern this project."

When they arrived back at the captain's office, it was lunchtime. The captain said he had a prior engagement but offered Danny to take Peter to lunch and show him the neighborhood. Peter was hoping to try his new ID badge at an officer's club, but that would have to wait for another day. Danny was very interesting. He only had enlisted men's privileges, but he knew of a reputable street vendor nearby. Peter could not say what they ate, but he was hungry and had decided to trust Danny's recommendation.

"Danny, where are you from?"

"Phoenix, Arizona."

"How long have you been working for the captain?"

"Only about three months."

"Have you been in Vietnam very long?"

"About six months."

"What did you do?"

"I was working as a supply clerk. It was boring. I'm hoping this job will be more interesting."

"What do you think of Captain Weisman so far?"

"I like him. He is not your typical military authority figure, yet he seems to have everyone's respect."

"Does the captain have any particular rules about when we come and go to the office or to lunch?"

"Well, he generally wants me to be there when he is there. He often takes me with him to meetings, but there are some meetings that he goes to on a regular basis that are above my clearance level."

As they talked, Peter found out that he had an American Indian heritage, but given the sunny weather in Saigon, his complexion was not much different from many others. He was single and about twenty-two years of age. Peter liked him.

When they returned, Danny had Peter follow him to another part of the building where they picked up his new badge to get him into the basement where he would be working. Shortly thereafter, the captain returned, and they went into his office so he could give Peter a rundown on the project.

The captain spent the next three and one-half hours going over the project plan with Peter who asked many questions. The captain seemed to enjoy answering Peter's questions and then some. The two of them mingled a lot of small talk with their project talk.

The captain said that they had already created a network of about twenty-five events. They had numbered the events by tens, from ten to one thousand, to leave room to add more events later. However, they also planned to leave room at the top end so that they could add additional dependent events later. For example, if Event 500 is a target event, and then Event 500 occurs, they may then want to add a subsequent Event 510. The captain asked Peter if he agreed with his numbering plan. Peter said that he did.

Peter asked where the intelligence came from. The captain said that he and Sam met regularly with CIA analysts who provided the intelligence needed to construct the Probabilistic Event Network (PEN). The CIA already had an intelligence database in Thailand, but in addition, information came from local sources. Intelligence sources included interrogations of captured Vietcong, newspaper articles, politicians, and the army of South Vietnam (ARVN). Some information came from aerial surveillance of troop movements, tunnel construction in the South, or traffic coming down the Ho Chi Minh Trail. Some information came from intercepted or bugged voice communications. The CIA also conveyed information it got from unknown sources. The sources and the amount of information were endless and voluminous. According to the captain, there was more information than could be processed solely by humans. That was why they needed a computerized PEN. No argument there.

The captain said that over the next three weeks, he wanted Peter to help verify the logic and the dependency rules he chose to apply. However, he made it clear to Peter that producing and testing the coded computer process was the primary reason for him being here. He said that Peter would meet with Jeff tomorrow and would be spending a lot of time with him over the next three weeks or so.

"Peter, one of the things Jeff has asked is what logic he would apply for stepping through the network. He asked where he would start. With multiple starting points and multiple endpoints in the network, he was not sure how to code it."

"I have a process all worked out. I'll go through it with him tomorrow morning when we meet."

"I would also like you to come to our project status meeting every Friday afternoon."

"I will do that, Captain."

It was about 1700 hours when the captain suggested that Peter might want to call it a day. "You're probably tired and may not have adjusted to the new time zone yet," he suggested.

"I'm okay. What are the normal work hours here anyway?"

"Zero eight hundred to seventeen hundred hours."

"I guess I'll see you in the morning then."

"How are you getting back to your hotel?" he asked.

It then dawned on him that he had never thought about that. "Guess I'll walk," he responded.

"Peter, where are you staying?"

"I'm staying at the Continental Palace Hotel."

He chuckled. "Well, you could walk, but it's a long walk on a hot afternoon. I would be happy to give you a lift. I live in the Rex, which is only two blocks away from your hotel. I can also give you a lift in the mornings if you can be ready by zero seven-thirty hours."

"Thanks Captain, I would appreciate that."

****

That night, as he lay in bed, Peter could not help but notice the sounds coming from the outside, people talking, motorbike engines, and a few distant explosions. However, after a while, the sounds began to die down. He began to fall asleep, only to be interrupted by an unusual repetitive chirping sound. It seemed to be coming from inside the room. Perhaps it was a cricket, but the sound seemed different. It began to annoy him, so he turned on the small lamp next to his bed and scanned the room in the direction of the sound. "Oh my gosh! What is that?" he said to himself. There on the wall next to the armoire, he could see what looked like a small green lizard. The sudden light caused him to stop chirping. Peter walked over to him to get a closer look. He must have spooked him because right away the creature took cover in the narrow space between the armoire and the wall. Peter didn't really know its gender, but chose to say "him" for convenience.

The next morning, Peter mentioned his discovery to the houseboy. In broken English, the houseboy told Peter that it was a gecko and that they were quite common. He also told Peter that if he were to protect it, it would bring him good luck. The gecko came out every night. Peter had to admit he was cute, but his incessant chirping was annoying and kept him awake. On three occasions, Peter attempted to remedy the situation by capturing it in a box that he planned to unload outside somewhere, but the gecko was too quick. He always managed to scurry back behind the armoire before Peter could get him. Finally, after a week of trying, Peter gave up and resigned himself to the idea that he would just have to live with it. Peter acclimated, and after a while, the chirping was hardly noticeable. In fact, it grew on him grew to the point where he decided to name him "Freddie."

6

GETTING THE JOB DONE

On Tuesday, Peter was up early, showered, dressed, remembered his two new badges, had a quick bite to eat, and met the captain in front of the hotel with briefcase in hand. "Good morning, Peter. Climb in."

"Good morning, Captain. Nice morning."

On the way to work, Peter asked the captain about the street addresses of the buildings they had passed yesterday and today. He was trying to make sense of what he had observed. "Captain, what is the logic to how the street addresses are numbered? I had noticed that the Continental Palace was number 132, but the Givral was 169, and when we drove up Pasteur yesterday, we passed number 140 long before we came to 137. However, in both cases, I noticed the numbers got larger as you went away from the river."

"Yes. It took me awhile before I figured it out, but there actually is some logic to it. If the street is heading Northwest, like Tu Do, Pasteur, or Hai Ba Trung, the numbers increase as you move further in that direction, moving away from the river. The numbers on the right side of the street are always even numbers, and those on the left are always odd numbers. As you have observed, the numbers on the right side are out of step with those on the left side. I can only speculate as to why that is. Possibly the numbers were based on the original properties and not on distances."

"Wow, do I dare ask how the cross streets are numbered?"

"The cross streets run to the Northeast. However, they are running toward the river, where it snakes down from the North. The numbers start at the Cholon boarder and decrease as you head to the Northeast. Oh, and there are some exceptions, but we can save that for another day."

"Thanks, Captain." What else could he say? Apparently, the captain had a good head for detail, as did he.

After Peter arrived in the building, he cheerily said hello to everyone. The next thing he did was to go down the stairs to the data processing area, and set up a place for himself in one of the vacant cubicles. He was eager to get started. The cubicle had no desk but the table he found would work just fine, and he also had his briefcase. He could always keep stuff locked up in that.

Although Jeff had a small office upstairs, he had also set up camp downstairs in another cubicle nearby. It made sense for him to be near the computer. Peter's meeting with Jeff went well. One could describe Jeff as a nerdy-looking guy, about five feet nine, wearing glasses. Jeff was a Warrant Officer. He sported a crew cut, but unlike the flat top that Peter had and the captain had, Jeff's was more rounded. Since they would be working together for the next three or four weeks, Peter wanted to know more about him. Jeff told him he had been in the military for about three years now. "I had no money, so I enlisted. I worked my way to Ensign, and after I reenlisted, the Navy promised that I could make a career out of the Navy and become a computer programmer. They promoted me to Warrant Officer. I never thought my assignment would be on land. Funny how things work out, but I'm doing what I always wanted to do; I'm writing computer code. What is your story, Peter? Were you in the military?"

Peter responded, "To be honest, I didn't consider myself soldier material, and my draft board was not eager to get me, so I went for education. Of course, Vietnam was not a war yet. I got a bachelor's degree in engineering and a master's degree in operations research from Cornell. Now I'm working on an MBA."

Peter wanted to tell him that he was poor as well, and paid his own way through college, but that might seem like one-upmanship, so he resisted. "I developed this probabilistic network process and when I was given a chance to come here, I jumped at it because I saw it as something I could do for my country." ("John F. Kennedy would have been pleased," he thought.)

"Where are you going to get your MBA?" he asked.

"My employer is paying for me to go to The University of Rochester at night."

"Peter, I went to RIT and got a two-year degree there."

"Are you from Rochester?" he wanted to know.

"Nearby, I grew up near Sodus Point just to the East of Rochester. I spent a lot of time sailing and fishing on Lake Ontario."

"I'm actually employed by TGW," Peter told him. "They have an apprentice program with RIT."

"Yes, I knew about that, but didn't want to be a tool and die maker. I decided that computer programing was what I wanted and here I am."

"Well, if you get back to the Rochester area, you should look me up; we can get together." Peter was glad they had something in common, other than work.

Then, they settled down to work. The technical discussions went something like this: "Peter, what is the logic for stepping through the network to calculate event probabilities? How do you decide which events to calculate first?"

"You start with the lowest numbered event that has precedents. If all the precedents have known probabilities, you calculate the probability for that event. Then, you move on to the next numbered event, etc."

"Will there always be an event that meets your starting criteria?"

"Absolutely. There must be at least one. And after you calculate that one, there must be at least one more."

"Okay, I cannot quite visualize it yet, but I'm sure you're right. I think I will program it using Assembler Language."

On Tuesday evening, Peter had supper with the captain at the Rex. They talked. Well, the captain did most of the talking. "I have lived here for about a year now," he said. "Only officers are housed here. The quarters are not bad, but it's two to a room. My roommate works in Cholon, so I don't see too much of him, except on weekends. This place has a store, the restaurant you're in now, and a bar and swimming pool on the roof." The captain spoke with enthusiasm as if he were on a vacation and describing a resort. "Do you like to swim?" he asked.

"I'm so-so on it, I easily burn, but I am interested in checking it out."

"Well, the only downside of the pool is that there are rarely any women to look at. They are allowed; there just aren't any. Of course, no women are housed here either. The Rex is a BOQ. BOQ stands for 'Bachelor Officer

Quarters.' The few women that are in Saigon either stay with nurse and Red Cross workers or they have villas or apartments."

"What about the restaurant where we are now?"

"Of course, sometimes women will come to eat here. In fact, I met Donna, your USAID hostess, here one evening several months ago. She was by herself, so she obviously has dining privileges here. The men were not very civil to her. I felt sorry for her. I went over to her table and pulled rank on a lieutenant that seemed to be harassing her. She essentially told me, 'thank you,' but that she could handle it herself—a tough cookie, I thought. I think she was embarrassed but she kept it to herself. She left shortly afterward. Don't think she finished her meal."

Changing the subject, the captain asked Peter if he had been in the military. Peter had been asked that so many times since arriving in Saigon that he thought how convenient it might be if he could just pull out a script from his pocket and hand it to anyone who asked. Perhaps he just felt a little defensive about the need to justify to military people the reason he was not in the military. However, Peter quickly dismissed those thoughts as non-productive. Besides, he really wanted to get along with everyone, especially the captain, so he told him the whole truth.

Peter enjoyed one of his favorite meals that night, baked chicken, mashed potatoes, and peas. He thought the food was prepared very well. After they ate, the captain gave him a tour of the place. Peter told him he really enjoyed the meal. The captain said they could do it again on Thursday night if he wished. Peter said that would be great. He looked forward to it.

Peter established a good rapport with the captain. Over the next four weeks, Peter had dinner with the captain at the Rex several times, and Peter went over to the Rex by himself a few times as well. His ID card gave him Lieutenant level privileges, and after a small fee, he was able to pay on a meal-to-meal basis. The price of a meal at the Rex and at other BOQ dining areas was about one-third of what it would cost at a regular restaurant. One could thank the U.S. taxpayers for that.

On Wednesdays, Peter met with the captain and answered questions about the rules used to link the events. If the captain was not sure as to what relationship rules to select from the standard set, he would ask for help. Sometimes, the captain would present Peter with a unique event relationship that would require a new rule, additional math, and additional FORTRAN coding.

Meanwhile, Jeff continued to talk to Peter almost daily about the specs and the code logic; and how he would access and use various files, especially the Rules File that contained the FORTRAN coded math. Peter also kept him informed about the FORTRAN code that he was still writing because the captain had some special situations. As the code was completed, they both participated in the testing and the checking.

That first Wednesday, the captain also talked to Peter about allowing the programs to run in a simulation, or "sandbox" mode. This seemed like a great idea. When Peter came up with the original network concept, he had not given much thought to events that were aimed at countering other events. However, as this was a military application, he began to see its relevance. The military didn't just want to know the probability of an attack by the enemy; they also wanted to know the probability of stopping it if they took various countermeasures. A simulation mode would allow the evaluation of possible changes in the inputs, including possible counter events. If countermeasures required special rules, Peter would need to design the rules and the math. However, the task of creating a job-control process for simulation would be primarily one for Jeff. It would require special database management, and it would need to be kept separate from the "official" runs each week. Peter agreed to help Jeff on this where needed, but it was quite clear that the primary objective would be to complete the job-control process for the official weekly runs before focusing on the simulation runs.

Peter was very pleased that the captain differed from the usual military officer. Whereas Peter would describe most military officers as literal black-and-white thinkers, the captain was conceptual. For security reasons, he could not tell Peter what the events really were, so they discussed situations in abstract and metaphorical terms. Peter thought they communicated quite well with each other.

****

Peter had been expecting Donna to be in touch again based on what she said on Monday. It was late when he got back to his hotel that first Wednesday night, so he didn't check his mailbox until Thursday morning.

On Thursday morning, he went to the front in the lobby and saw a note in his mailbox. It was a handwritten note from Donna.

> Peter,
> I want to meet with you on Thursday evenings at 1800 hours for status and any issues.
> Donna

The note didn't say where they should meet, and she had never left instructions on how he could reach her. He had no choice but to cancel his dinner plans with the captain, so that he could meet with Donna. He was annoyed. That evening, just before 1800 hours, he was about to go down to the lobby and look for Donna when there was a knock on his door.

It was Donna. "Peter, I apologize, for imposing, but can we meet in your room?"

He was caught off guard, but how could he say no? "Of course, come in. Feel free to make yourself comfortable in the arm chair." As she sat down, he pulled the wooden chair out from the desk, and straddled it with the chair back in front of him, facing her.

"I apologize for not getting back to you since we parted at the Embassy. Something came up that kept me busy for the past two days. I'll try not to take up too much of your time. Just give me a run-down of how you're doing. Are you fitting in with the team? What do you think of Captain Weisman? Are there any issues?"

Although she had apologized, he was still a little annoyed at her for the sudden inconvenience. He responded curtly. "We're making progress on the code and I'm getting along with everyone just fine. I think the captain is great. No issues."

She must have sensed some irritability in his voice. "Peter, I'm just doing my job. I'm supposed to maintain a good rapport with you. Apparently, I'm not doing that very well right now. I'll go now and let you be. If you need anything, you can contact me by leaving a note in mailbox number three fourteen here at the Continental Palace."

"No, Donna, wait! I am a little irritable right now. I get that way when I'm hungry. I have not had any supper yet. I didn't see your note until this morning and had to cancel my dinner plans. Next time could we either meet over supper, or meet at nineteen hundred hours rather than eighteen hundred hours? And, while we are at it, we are both civilians; can we just say we will meet at seven p.m.?"

"Well, according to protocol, it's better if we meet where no one else can overhear us. That would rule out supper." Peter kind of shrugged at that as he thought her concern for protocol was excessive. "Okay Peter, listen. Come over to the café with me. I'll ask Han to fix something for you, but you need to promise that you won't mention our involvement with the CIA or say anything about the project."

He responded quickly. "Donna, you need to trust me."

"I will try to, but I have been trained to always be wary."

They walked across the street. It was getting dark, but the street was still busy with people and mopeds. They entered the café and said hello to Han. There were several other customers, but they took a table in a corner of the room where they could hear each other talk. Donna walked over to Han and ordered something for him to eat, and she ordered a cup of tea for herself. Peter didn't know what he was eating, but he really was hungry and he felt much better afterward.

"Donna, I apologize for my crabbiness earlier, and I thank you for your consideration for my hunger. I feel much better now. How much do I owe you, by the way?"

"It's okay. It's on me. I should have been more sensitive." Then, she started a conversation. "Tell me, where have you eaten so far?"

"Aside from here, I have been to the Rex, the Brinks, and the Italian restaurant at the Continental Palace. Where do you eat?"

"I generally eat at home. I have an apartment with a small kitchen." Until he heard this, he thought she stayed in room 314 at the Continental Palace.

"Where abouts?" he asked.

"Sorry, I can't say."

"Hmmm . . . where do you go when you get tired of cooking? Do you ever eat at any of the officer messes, like the Rex?" He was testing her.

"I tried the Rex but it made me feel uncomfortable."

"How so?"

"Well, there are rarely any women there and although they are all officers, they are almost all bachelors, and sex-starved. They tend to leer and ogle at me. I won't go back there again."

Peter was pleased that she trusted him enough to be open and honest about the Rex. He didn't make mention of what the captain had said to him Tuesday night. Instead, he replied, "Of course there's no excuse for that, but you are attractive."

"Thank you, but I don't think I'm that attractive, and I don't usually wear makeup or dress provocatively." Then she changed the subject. "Peter, do you have any plans for the weekend?"

"Nothing specific, but I definitely want to explore the city and the sites while I'm here. And you?"

"Nothing really, except for church service on Sunday."

"Any chance you could give me a '*xe om*' tour on Saturday?" "Xe om" was a new term he picked up. It meant something like "taxi ride on a bike." She paused before answering. He didn't know if his pronunciation was way off, or if she was pondering the possible ramifications and implications of his request.

Finally, she responded: "Okay, can you meet me out front of the Continental Palace at nine a.m.?"

"Yes, thanks. Sounds good; see you then."

****

That Saturday, they toured Cholon. Originally, Cholon was what we would call "Chinatown" in the U.S. The Chinese first settled there in 1778. It became a separate city in 1879. As the populations of Saigon and Cholon grew, the two cities merged and became one in 1931. Cholon is known for its temples, its open-air market places, and its street food. The military also had a large post-exchange (PX) in Cholon.

They parked and chained the bike in a safe place. As they walked the streets, vendors were everywhere. Peter observed the locals preparing their food with bare hands, the same hands that also handled garbage and dirty dishes. He didn't want to appear prissy in front of Donna so he kept those observations to himself. They bought food at locations that Donna recommended, including a strange fruit that they could eat while they walked. They witnessed an elaborate wedding festival, and several colorful temples. Peter had brought his camera and he took pictures. By the time they returned to the Continental Palace later that afternoon, he had shot a full roll of film, twenty-six pictures.

After exploring Cholon, they returned to Donna's bike, and he asked her, "How did you come to have this bike? You seem very proud of it."

"I bought it. I really like it. It's practical and gets me around quickly. The bike is a 1967 Suzuki M-31, but customized. It's more powerful than your typical moped, as you have already experienced. It has a fifty-five cc two-stroke engine, rated at six horse-power, and I can go over fifty miles per hour if necessary. Of course, there is not much opportunity with all the traffic we have here. It runs well, and as you may have noticed, oil consumption is minimal—very little blue smoke. The oil and gasoline are automatically pre-mixed. The bike also has larger wheels than your typical moped, but I wish the tires had a more aggressive tread for when the roads are wet. Technically, it's not a moped because you can't pedal it. However, Suzuki calls it a moped. As you can see, the frame swoops down in front of the seat, and it has a wind deflector in front, allowing me to wear a dress if I want to do so. I even added a luggage rack on the back. I strapped a pouch to it containing a cover to protect the bike if it rains. However, if I go shopping, I still can't carry containers or bags because there is no good way to secure them to the rack. I may need to get a bin that can clamp to the rack. The trick is figuring out how to secure it. The downside is that I can still get very wet during the monsoon season when it rains a lot. That is why I also have access to a Jeep."

"I'm impressed. Not many women would have such a technical knowledge of a motorized bike."

"I doubt you will find me to be like most women."

Hoping not to get into a debate about the role of women in modern society, or possibly her sexual orientation, he simply replied, "That's a good thing, I'm sure. May I take a picture of you sitting on the bike?" She agreed and he took two, in case one didn't turn out. And then she took one of him.

"May I ask you a question?"

"What's that?"

"You seem to like your bike a lot. Have you given it a name?"

"Uh . . . what? . . . A name? Not sure what you mean."

"Like a pet. I know a guy who owns a Harley. Maxwell named his bike *Little John.* He rides with a friend named Jack, and Jack named his bike *Big Max.*"

"I see. What do you think I should name my bike?"

"Oh, I don't know. The bike is a Suzuki. How about *Little Suzie?*"

"Could I ask you something?"

"Sure."

"Are Max and Jack, by any chance, homosexual?"

"I don't know. They may be."

"I bet they are, and I bet that Max is the dominant one, and John or Jack is the submissive one."

"You may be right. Max is rather controlling."

"I also bet that there is a question you have been just dying to ask me." Peter thought he knew what she meant but didn't say anything. "It's okay," she said, "I'll save you the trouble. Despite my butch appearance, my military background, my interest in motorbikes, and my disappointing relationships with men as of late, I'm *not* a lesbian. And I don't need to get my jollies by riding a little girl named Suzie."

"Donna, I was not implying anything like that," although he had to admit to himself that he had been curious about her sexual orientation. "I obviously hit a nerve . . . didn't mean to. I'm sorry."

She looked hard at him as if trying to size him up. "You did hit a nerve. Most of the women here are afraid of me, and most of the men I meet think I'm a sex object. It's very frustrating for me. I should not have reacted that way. It's not your fault. You probably couldn't care less about which way I go anyway. You're happily married."

"Don't be frustrated. You're a unique individual with a lot going for you . . . and I do care. I find you to be a very interesting person."

Then, being genuinely curious, he asked her, "How did you become so knowledgeable about motorbikes?"

"Well, I was in the military for two years and worked in the motor pool. I went to mechanic school and learned how to maintain Jeeps and bikes. Are you surprised?"

Not knowing how to respond, he said something innocuous like "Not at all. You have a lot to be proud of." Then, he recovered and asked, "Why did you leave the military?"

"They told me I had officer potential, but the only opportunity for women officers in the army would be in the nurse's corps. Nursing and medical stuff were not for me. I also didn't like being told exactly how to do everything. The CIA gives me a great deal of autonomy to make my own day-to-day decisions and I like that. I joined the CIA a year ago. This is my first real assignment."

Peter thought she seemed very young to have the position she did. But he was also young, and he still wondered how he got into the position *he* was in. He concluded that like him, she must have a very high IQ.

"Could I ask you a personal question?" Peter asked.

"I suppose .... What?"

"How old are you?"

"How old do you think I am?"

"You look like you're about twenty-one, but that would be too young to have the military experience, a management position at USAID, and also be a trained CIA operative."

"Peter, you should have been a diplomat. I'm twenty-four. I'll be twenty-five in three and a half weeks . . . March the seventeenth. I was born on St. Patrick's Day."

"Does that mean you're Irish?"

"Of course not. Don't be silly. How old are you?"

Although he thought she probably already knew the answer, he was polite. "I'm also twenty-four, but my birthday is not until November. I was born on Veterans Day."

"So, does that mean you're a veteran?" she quipped.

He didn't respond verbally to that, but she must have noticed him rolling his eyes at her retort. "Sorry Peter, I couldn't resist. So, tell me more about *you*. Why are you not in the military?"

Here we go again he's thinking, but he was nice. He gave the same answer he had given others. However, he also told her "Like you, I am also independent-minded and like to make my own day-to-day decisions. I often think outside the box and sometimes I do things that others don't expect. I'm often viewed as non-conforming. I have the self-discipline to be a good soldier, but I don't know how happy I would be if I were one." He looked for a reaction.

She smiled and simply said, "Peter, I think you're a very interesting person also." He smiled back.

****

For the next four Thursdays, they had status meetings in his room at the Continental Palace at 7:00 p.m., and they had *xe om* bike tours on the weekends.

On the second Saturday, she allowed him to drive her bike . . . well, only after he begged. They had ridden up to the Tao Dan Park area. They had parked the bike on Truong Cong Dinh, a roadway that went between Tao Dan Park on one side and the City Gardens on the other side. They were on foot and enjoyed the exercise and the scenery. The park housed a Buddhist temple at its Southeastern end, across the street from where the bowling alley was on his map. The Gardens housed the French sports club at its northwestern end. The Cercle Sportif, as it was called, was well known. It served the French elite during the colonial times, and it was known for its swimming pool and tennis courts. Not only were the park and gardens scenic and relaxing, but they were considered a tourist attraction.

When they returned to the bike, Peter made his request. "Donna, I didn't tell you, but I also worked as a mechanic for two summers, and although I have no experience with bikes, I do have experience with racing automobiles and working on them. I have a degree in mechanical engineering and I have an appreciation for mechanical things. I would really like to drive your bike."

She was surprised that he took such an interest. "After that first Monday, I was not sure you would be into it. Now you not only enjoy riding but you want to drive. I guess we have a lot more in common than I thought. However, I have never let anyone operate my bike. Like you said, it's my pride and joy."

"Well, would you at least be willing to teach me how to operate it? You could demonstrate."

"Hmm . . . well . . . alright," she agreed.

Donna described each control. The front wheel brake and throttle were on the right handlebar. The rear brake was a pedal in front of the right footrest, and the gearshift was a pedal in front of the left footrest. She told him that normally the clutch would be on the left handlebar. However, on this model the clutch was automatically engaged when shifting gears with the left foot. Peter could not help but wonder how it got decided that on an automobile the gearshift was hand-operated and the clutch foot-operated, but on a motorbike, it was the reverse. The bike had a crank kick-start on the right. She demonstrated starting it up and shutting it down.

Then, he begged, "Please let me try it. I'll just go around the park. I'll keep it in low gear. You can ride on the back and coach me if I need it."

He thought she really was going to let him do this all along because without hesitation, she responded. "Well okay, I'll trust you." With that, they sped away, this time with Donna holding onto *his* waist.

****

On Peter's third Saturday in Saigon, he and Donna chained the bike to a post, and walked up to the rooftop bar atop the Majestic Hotel where they had a beverage and took in the view of the river. He had his camera and took pictures. It was a scenic view, but it was not long before they began talking about the war. She pointed to a place down the river where the Vietcong had set off two bombs outside the My Canh Café on the waterfront back in June of 1965. The restaurant was called the "floating restaurant" because it floated on the river like a barge. One walked a gangplank to access it. She said, "Dozens of innocent people were killed and injured. More than forty were killed. Nine were Americans, including a CIA operative and three Airforce supply officers that lived on the top floor of your hotel."

She continued, "Bombings like these tend to occur at unexpected times and places. Wouldn't it be great if we could predict these bombings?" (Of course, they both knew that was the purpose of the PEN project.) "I find it difficult to see people die, especially people I know. Perhaps I will eventually get used to it. That Tuesday and Wednesday, the first week you were here, I was called away to a place up country from here. A CIA colleague had been killed while on a mission in the field. We had a ceremony and I was asked to escort his body back to Saigon and ensure it got onto a plane home to the United States. I found that very difficult."

She paused, and he sensed she was starting to get emotional. He felt sympathetic. "Donna, I can only imagine what that must have felt like."

She regained her composure and continued, "When I was in the military, women were not allowed in combat. Technically, they still aren't, but they seem to be relaxing some of the restrictions. I didn't see action so I didn't have to deal with that kind of death until I came here, but if I pursue my career in the CIA, I know I'll see more of it. The military trained me to shoot, and I got quite good at it. I have a Sharpshooter rating. I have privileges at an army target range, and by the way, I do own a gun."

"Have you ever had to kill anyone with it?"

"No, I haven't, but who knows, I may have to someday. Peter, tell me something. Do you think you could take a life?"

"Well, I never owned a gun, and my only exposure to guns was when I was a Boy Scout. One of the leaders took us to an NRA firing range and we learned how to fire a 22-caliber rifle, and to do it safely. My father never had a gun in the house either. I was not allowed to have a BB gun like some of my friends, and my father discouraged me from even having a cap pistol. However, to answer your question, I think that if someone was about to kill me, I would not hesitate to defend myself, even if I had to kill them. Not sure if I would know how to do that though. Nevertheless, I do have a problem with some of the wholesale killing of innocent people that is occurring here in Vietnam."

"I think I have a problem with that as well," she said.

Now as he looked at Donna across the table, he noticed the shoulder bag she always seemed to have across her right shoulder and hanging on her left side.

He could not help himself from asking, "Donna, are your carrying a gun right now? Is it in your bag?"

There was no one nearby and he didn't think he said that very loudly, but she looked around to see if anyone heard before answering. "If I said yes, would you disapprove?"

"No, I have no problem with it. I believe that people who are responsible and properly trained should be allowed to own and carry guns. As for me, I have not had a need."

"Well, to answer your question, I do carry it in my shoulder bag, but I don't have it with me today. It's a Colt 45, and quite heavy, so I only take it when I'm at the shooting range, on a dangerous assignment, or outside alone at night. Otherwise, I keep it locked up in my apartment."

They did a lot more touring and took many more pictures that afternoon. When they got back to the Continental Palace, it was early evening. Donna let him off the bike and was about to say good-bye when he interjected. "Donna, do you have dinner plans or a date tonight?"

She paused, and then said, "I think we should talk."

"We can talk over supper. I'll buy. It's late and we both need to eat."

"Where do you want to go?"

"How about right here at the Continental Palace?"

****

After parking the bike, they went up three steps from the sidewalk on Lam Son and entered The Continental Shelf. The "Shelf" was an open-air restaurant and bar area, a couple of feet above the sidewalk level on the ground floor of the hotel. The Shelf was at the corner of the building. Where there would normally be walls and windows there were archways open to both Tu Do Street and Lam Son Square. A canopy extended outward from above the open archways toward both streets and ran the length and width of the building above the sidewalks. The canopy and the overhead wooden fans inside the building provided adequate cooling from the hot sun. In the late afternoon, blinds were often lowered from the street side of the canopy to block the rays of the bright setting sun. However, it was after 6:00 p.m. now and the sun was setting. The blinds had just been raised. One could relax, have a meal or a drink, and watch the bikes go by on the street. They sat down at a table away from the street, where it was quieter and more conducive to talking.

After they had ordered supper, Peter initiated the conversation. "Donna, you said we need to talk. What do we need to talk about?"

She wasted no time getting to the point. "Peter, I like you. We have enjoyed touring together, and we have shared thoughts and feelings, but I wonder if maybe we are doing too much together. I mean . . . well . . . let me put it in the form of a question. If your wife were to learn of everything we have been doing together, the day trips, sharing the bike, the meals together, not to mention being in your room every week, what do you think she would make of it?"

Her tone didn't sound threatening but he was not sure of her intent. "Donna, where are you going with this? Have I crossed a line? Have I made any unwanted advances toward you?"

"No, you've been a perfect gentleman."

"We are friends, aren't we?"

"I guess I'm afraid it may become more than that for one or both of us. Tell me, if you weren't married, would it be more than that for you?"

"If I weren't married, I would be all over you, or at least I would want to be. I think you're really great. I enjoy your company. However, I *am* married. Can't we just be business associates and friends?"

"I don't know if we can."

He took a moment to reflect upon what she had just said.

She said, "We." Did she mean the "royal we?" Did she mean herself, both of us, or just him? He never thought of himself as someone that she would take an interest in romantically. He wondered if she could possibly have those kinds of feelings for him.

"What do you suggest we do?" he asked.

"I don't know. I guess I just wanted to know what you were expecting, and let you know of my concern."

"Well, I appreciate you sharing your concern with me. The last thing I want to do is hurt you in some way."

"I don't want to hurt you either," she responded.

"I think it will be okay with us. I think we should relax and not overthink it."

****

The following week, Jeff and Peter were hard at work testing the function and the accuracy of the output of the programs. Jeff really was a whiz. They were running his code against real data in the fourth week. Before that, Peter had spent his time reviewing sample reports that they tweaked to the liking of everyone who would see them, reviewing the logic choices that the captain chose for defining the relationships between events, and answering many questions for both Jeff and the captain. In the fourth week however, the testing became much more demanding of Peter's time. He spent hours and hours manually calculating probabilities to ensure that the results were consistent with what was intended. His pen and paper and his slide rule became very useful tools. He found only a few discrepancies, a testament to Jeff's good work. However, it had to be perfect; one wrong calculation could result in all dependent calculations being in error. That meant testing every single one of them. "Zero Defects" was the order of the day. All this work had to be done at the office. For security reasons nothing went out of the building. Jeff had a file cabinet in his downstairs cubicle, so they made an extra key and Peter was able to store stuff in there overnight.

That Thursday of the fourth week, Peter had his usual status review with Donna. He had to tell her it was taking longer than they had originally anticipated but that they were making progress. She asked if he had time to tour on the weekend, and he said that as much as he would like to, he and Jeff would have to work on Saturday. During the week, they had been lucky to get two computer runs a day, but that was not enough. The computer load was less on the weekend, and they figured they could get five runs counting Friday night and Saturday night. On Friday, they told the captain the same as he had told Donna. The captain approved their extra work time.

Peter and Jeff made great progress that Friday evening and all-day Saturday. After the hard day's work, he and Jeff went over to the USO and played pool. Peter beat him in two out of three games of eight ball. Although technically Jeff was a low-level Warrant Officer, he was authorized to be in a BOQ. He also needed to be near his workplace and he often rode a bicycle to work. For that reason, he was housed at the Ambassador (BOQ), which was next to the Caravelle. After playing pool, he invited Peter to come over and have dinner with him at the Ambassador. It was not quite luxury dining that was offered at the Rex, but Peter found it to be surprisingly good.

****

Finally, in the fifth and last full week that Peter was in Saigon, the application was up and running for real, and it was getting usable and meaningful results. Peter reported all of this to Donna on Thursday. The only thing left was more documentation, a final report and instruction to the captain. Peter told Donna that he and Jeff would take care of that tomorrow and on Monday. She said she was pleased that they were almost complete with their work.

As she said this, Peter sensed a gloominess on her part.

"I just gave you good news," he said. "I got the project back on track and our mission is going to be a success. You don't seem overly joyed. Is something wrong?"

"Peter, are your mom and Dad still together?"

"Yes, they are. Why?"

"Were they always true to each other?"

"As far as I know. Why, what is going on?"

"Tomorrow is my birthday, and today I received a letter from my mom. She hardly mentioned my birthday, but she told me that she and Dad had a big fight and she said he should move out."

He walked over to the easy chair where she was sitting, put his hand on her shoulder, and said, "Sit tight. I'll be right back. I have something that may cheer you up."

He walked into the bathroom. He had not forgotten her Birthday. He had hidden a cupcake, a candle, and a large humorous birthday card in the bathroom. He stuck the candle into the cupcake, lit it, and returned to the living room with it and the card while singing "Happy Birthday." Donna's face gleamed as he set everything down on the end table next to the chair.

"Oh my God, I never expected this," she said as she jumped to her feet, came over to him, grabbed him by the neck, and planted a hard kiss on his mouth.

Then, realizing what she had just done, she backed away and sheepishly said, "Oh please forgive me, I . . . I got carried away."

"It's okay. Relax. It pleases me to know that you feel happy. Open the card."

She opened the card and read the message. She chuckled and said, "I think you're really a nice guy. Thank you so much."

Then, after a pause, she continued. "I missed you last weekend, but now that the project is almost complete, does this mean you will have some free time this weekend? It will be your last weekend in Saigon. Is there anything else you would like to see or do before you go home?"

"Yes. I will have Saturday afternoon and evening free. I cannot think of anything specifically, but I'm open to suggestions."

"I'd like to invite you to a party on Saturday night. Several of the people I work with at USAID have decided that my turning twenty-five, a quarter of a century, would be a good excuse for a party. They said I should bring a guest."

This was totally unexpected, and Peter wondered why she would pick him. "I feel honored that you would ask me, and of course I would love to be your guest, but I'm curious, why me?"

"I guess I feel safe and comfortable when I'm with you, and since it's your last weekend in Saigon, I thought you'd appreciate the opportunity to relax and unwind before you go home. To be honest, I do have an ulterior motive as well. My boss at USAID wants to meet you."

"Why does your boss want to meet me?"

"The party is at John and Linda's villa and includes a catered meal. Linda is who I report to at USAID. She has taken me under her wing so to speak and can be a mother hen at times. However, I have known her for a year now and we have become friends. She is the only one I can confide in when it comes to girl stuff. I have told her about you, all good." He looked quizzically at Donna and then she added, "I told her that you're married and that we are just friends."

"Okay, I'm game. Where is this party? Were you going to pick me up on the bike?"

"The party is way out on the North side of Saigon. It may take a while to get there. Will it be okay if I pick you up outside the hotel at seventeen hundred hours, I mean five p.m.?"

"Sounds good to me. I appreciate the invitation. I'll see you then."

****

Peter and Jeff gave their final status report to Captain Weisman that Friday, March 17. The captain had commandeered the office next to his and turned it into a "war" room of sorts. This is where he would meet with field operatives to review intelligence and update the events and probabilities in the network. In the center of the room was a large table with a complete diagram of the entire network. The captain had depicted the events by circles with an event number inside. Lines, some penciled in, connected the events. Arrowheads showed the direction of dependence. Back then, it was next to impossible to have a computer print the entire picture of a network, without resorting to "cut and paste."

Jeff was quite proud of the fact that he was able to print a separate page for each event showing the event and its connections to its precedent and dependent events. The captain had cut and taped the whole network together from the individual pages printed by the computer. The captain called it "The Big Picture." By that time, the network had more than seventy events. There was more than one target event in the network. On March 14, these target events had calculated probabilities that varied from five percent to twenty percent.

After their status meeting with the captain, Peter went down to the canteen for a coke. He was surprised to see Bob Nunn buying himself a cup of coffee. He had not seen him since that first week in the computer room. "Bob, how are you? Fancy meeting you here. Are there problems with the computer?"

"No, I was just in the neighborhood and had stopped in to see Jim and leave some instructions for John over the weekend on how to reset the console. How is your project coming?"

"Quite good. In fact, I expect to have everything wrapped up by next Tuesday. That means I'll be homeward-bound. Bob, do you have any time to talk?"

"Sure. What's up?"

"Well, the company I work for, TGW in Rochester New York, is considering upgrading their computers. Right now, they have Control Data, but IBM makes frequent calls to win them over. I'm one of the go-betweens they talk to at TGW. IBM also offers some seminars that I have contemplated attending. Anyway, I'm interested in learning more about IBM. And, to be honest, I also have a personal interest. I have been working on an MBA degree at night. Things were delayed a bit due to this assignment, but I still expect to graduate in June a year from now. What do you think of IBM as a company to work for?"

"IBM has given me the greatest opportunity of my lifetime. I'm here on a two-year assignment that I started in March of sixty-six. I'm part of a new program and contract that IBM has with MACV. There are six of us in Saigon right now, as MACV buys more computing equipment from IBM, we will need more IBMers to support that equipment. We consider it an adventure. All six of us are in our twenties like you. We are given the equivalent of officer status ranging from Lieutenant to Colonel and we all have security clearances that are at least 'Top Secret'. Mine is above that level so that I can work inside data centers that provide support to the CIA and military intelligence. IBM pays us our regular salary plus another seventy percent for living expenses. I also should tell you that all of us are unmarried, an IBM requirement. We work hard to support our military clients, but we also have free time on weekends. One of IBM's mottos has been 'respect for the individual'. That means that so long as we don't embarrass IBM, we're free to use our free time as we wish. Peter, I'm also interested in how you ended up here. You said that you have a job and go to night school. Does TGW provide technical or programming support to the government?"

"Actually, I developed the process that I'm implementing here, but I did that on my own, not under any contract. My advisor in graduate school suggested the application to the military. He had a contact in the CIA and things went from there. I also see this as an adventure, although my five weeks is nothing compared to your two years. I also see it as a way to serve my country without being in the military."

"I assume you had student deferments."

"I did for five years, but night school doesn't qualify, and with the war building up, my draft board would have classified me as 1-A. I'm married now and I hope to start a family and a career. Being drafted is not what I want. This assignment gives me a critical skills deferment. Were you in the military?"

"No, I also had a student deferment but then I went to work for IBM. I had asthma when I was young, so they made me 4-F because of that. However, like you, I also wanted to serve in some way. IBM decided that I was good at problem-solving and often thought 'outside the box,' so they made me this offer. I think that those of us that are here are thought of as 'wild-ducks.' I don't mind that label."

"That's interesting. People have always told me that I was an original thinker, and I have always considered myself a problem solver as well. Aside from being part of a minority of civilians amongst military people, perhaps you and I have something in common."

"You know, when you get your degree, you may want to consider IBM. Did you say this was your last weekend here? My roommate is spending time with his new girlfriend this weekend. I could use some company. How would you like to see parts of Saigon you have not seen yet?"

"What did you have in mind?"

"Well, this city used to be very French, and there are still some French restaurants left. My roommate is basic meat and potatoes, but I have been yearning for something more upscale. There is a place called La Cigale on the North side of the city. It also has a nightclub associated with it. If you're game, we could check it out. If that club doesn't pan out, there is another club back this way we can go to, and I know a girl that works there."

"Okay, I'm game. I assume you have transportation?"

"Oh, yes, in fact, IBM allows us to buy cars. I managed to buy a very used VW, but it does the job. It's almost 5:00 p.m. now. We could go right from here, if you like."

"Okay, but first, I need to go back to my desk, put away some papers, and lock my briefcase up for the weekend."

Bob followed Peter to his office; Peter locked everything up for the weekend, and followed Bob out to his VW. As they drove over to La Cigale, Peter commented to Bob about the heavy and chaotic traffic they were encountering. The thing about traffic in Saigon was that there was a mix of autos, motorbikes, and pedaled vehicles. When work let out at the end of each day, the streets were jammed, but what made it particularly troublesome was that no one seemed to abide by any rules. Drivers would go wherever they wanted, including opposing lanes and sidewalks if necessary. Motorbikes would dart and weave between other vehicles. The traffic scene was very chaotic.

Peter's comments about the traffic led Bob to tell a story.

"Peter, I was once in a long line of traffic heading over to Cholon. When I approached the railroad tracks, a long freight train came by and everyone had to wait for the train to pass. However, vehicles that were behind me were impatient and decided to pass on my left. So, there we were with two lanes of traffic waiting for the train to pass. When it finally did, it turned out that the vehicles on the other side of the tracks had done the same thing. So, now there were two lanes of traffic in each direction facing each other. Fortunately, most of the vehicles were bikes. Otherwise, it would have taken forever to get it sorted out."

Bob and Peter got to know each other that night. They had a great dinner, and they went to two nightclubs. Bob had a definite interest in women, but when two young ladies presented them with an opportunity for the night, Peter apologized and passed. They continued to talk to the ladies and to each other, but Peter was sure that Bob was disappointed in his lack of interest in pursuing it further. He told Peter that he had a prior acquaintance with the one lady. He explained that in Saigon prostitution was widespread and not expensive. Increasingly, young girls were forced to do this in order to make ends meet. Others were eager to form relationships with Americans because it would provide them with stability and security.

Although Bob may have figured that he would go back and see her the next night, Peter appreciated that Bob showed him respect and understanding by not dumping him and forcing him to take a taxi home.

Peter went to sleep that night feeling glad that he had gotten to know Bob. He had a newfound respect for IBM and for Bob. As he would later find out, if that chance meeting with Bob in the Canteen that Friday had not occurred, future events may have turned out much differently than they did.

7

THE PARTY

On Saturday evening, Donna picked Peter up outside of his hotel at 5:00 p.m. as agreed. As always, he was eager to ride behind her on the bike. However, that evening Donna looked sexier and more attractive than he had ever seen her. She was wearing a tight-fitting fancy white blouse and a pink skirt than barely came below mid-thigh. Her skirt was a bit more modest than a mini-skirt, but it was short enough to reveal two very shapely legs.

In early 1967 in Saigon, her short skirt was pushing the envelope of fashion and modesty. She had a narrow gold belt around her waist and tan-colored flats on her feet. Her short-sleeved blouse opened at the top, revealing her gold chain necklace. Tonight, she was wearing makeup, and it enhanced her already natural beauty. Golden earrings dangled from her ears, and her shoulder bag hung against her left hip. She certainly looked like she was ready to party. Peter could not help but notice she attracted the attention of two men standing outside the hotel as she drove up on her bike. He told her that he thought she looked gorgeous. She seemed pleased.

Peter cannot say exactly where they went that night. He thought that Linda and John's villa was in the area of Dung Dang, somewhere to the North on the outskirts of the city, but the location was beyond the borders of his map. Peter found Donna too distracting to pay close attention to the route she was taking. She was gorgeous, and he had his arms around her waist.

They arrived at the villa before 5:30. The definition of a villa may have evolved over the years. In Vietnam, the well-to-do French Colonialists had lived in villas. Villas were what we would call single-family homes in the United States.

By 1967, some of the larger villas, mansions with many bedrooms, were being used to house groups of people, like IBMers, or CIA SOG agents. However, this villa was modest and was inhabited solely by Linda and John. The war in Saigon necessitated that the property of a villa have high walls in the front and on the sides for security reasons. In this case, the eight-foot-high walls were stone. An iron gate, manned by a private security guard, provided access from the front. They rode the bike through the opened gateway, into the yard, and parked in a small area to the left of the gate set aside for that purpose. The house was two stories with what appeared to be stucco or concrete block walls. The roof was relatively flat and appeared to be tiled. The house was about forty to fifty feet across in the front with a heavy wooden door in the center. To the right and to the left of the door were two vertically long windows with wooden shutters. The second story sported three of these windows, one above the front door and another on either side. Above the second-story windows, were three small louvered windows that were probably used for ventilation.

The sides of the house went back away from the street and were about eighty to ninety feet long. A stone patio ran the entire length of the right side of the house and was accessible from the front and from the rear. Except for the small motorbike parking area, gardens surrounded the entire property. Peter could see a conveniently placed bench in the garden area to our right, and assumed there might have been more that he could not see. As they entered the front door, they found themselves in a small vestibule. Linda was there to greet them.

"Hello, Donna . . . and you must be Peter. Donna has said good things about you. John and I are glad you could come."

Linda was older than Donna and Peter, probably in her mid-thirties. She was about five foot six and a little on the heavy side, not unattractive, but what one might call, matronly.

A moment later, John appeared from the room to the left of the entrance, his office. Donna introduced him. John was about five feet eleven, had an athletic build and was quite handsome. He looked familiar to Peter, but he could not remember where he may have seen him. Peter didn't say anything. "Peter, it's a pleasure to meet you. Donna has been here a few times but why don't you let Linda show you the house while Donna and I talk about you?" He had a grin on his face. "I'm just kidding," he added.

"Okay, see you guys later," Peter responded, and left with Linda.

They walked down a main hall in the center of the house to a stairway on the left. "Let me show you the upstairs first," Linda said. At the top of the stairs, they came to an open area with a ceiling fan high above. Then, turning to their left, they walked down a main hallway in the center. There were two bedrooms on the right and a full bath on the left. At the end of the hallway was the master bedroom. It extended across the width of the house and provided a nice view of the gardens and trees beyond. Linda was quite pleased with her accommodations, and was more than eager to describe everything in detail. It was here in the master bedroom that they struck up quite a conversation.

"Linda, I hope you don't mind my asking how long you and John have been married."

"About ten years, but this is the first time we have had a house to live in together. We rent the house from the State Department and we have been here for about a year. As you can probably tell, I really like the house."

"Donna says she reports to you at USAID."

"Yes, but her department has a lot of autonomy. Donna works well independently and I don't have to give her very much direction." Linda continued, "I understand you have been working at MACV. May I ask what you do there?"

"I'm a computer systems analyst. I've pretty much completed my assignment and expect to be returning to the States next week."

"How long have you and Donna known each other?"

"About five weeks. Why?"

"Are you two getting involved with each other?"

"We're just friends, but why would that concern you?"

"Well, please excuse me, but I'll get right to the point. Although I'm Donna's boss at USAID, we have known each other for about a year, and we have become friends. I look out for my friends, and I am concerned. Donna is bright and outgoing. She is also very attractive, and when it comes to men, she has had some bad experiences. I don't want to see her taken advantage of, and I don't want her to be heartbroken when you leave next week. I know how men can behave when they are away from their wives for too long. Please, don't be that way with Donna."

"Linda, I assure you that I would never hurt her or take advantage of her. I've made no secret of the fact that I'm married, and I want to be true to my wife. I hope you don't mind my asking, but are you and John having some marital issues?"

"Why would you think that?"

"Well, based on your assessment as to how men behave, and the fact that there is only one pillow on the bed . . . I'm sorry, it's none of my business."

"Donna said you were very perceptive . . . and very outspoken. You are right. John travels a lot and he flirts, and sometimes more. I even suspected he and Donna were involved at one point before I got to know her. He and Donna see each other often. John says it's work-related, and he's not allowed to talk much about what he does. The thing is that once a man cheats on his wife, the wife will sense it whether he tells her or not and then there can be trust issues."

"Well, Donna and I are just friends."

"I hope that's true, but Donna often confides in me, and I think that she may have stronger feelings for you than she has let on."

He looked directly at Linda. "I see. Now I understand where you're coming from." After a pause, he added, "I think it best if we keep this conversation to ourselves."

"I agree," was her response.

Linda may have unintentionally revealed that John was Donna's CIA boss. Peter remembered his first day in Saigon at the U.S. Embassy. Donna had excused herself, stating that she needed to meet with her boss. Peter had looked down the hall and noticed that a man greeted her and escorted her into a nearby office. Thinking back on it, Peter now thought that man was John.

Linda and Peter walked back down stairs and to the left, down the main hallway and through the kitchen at the back of the house. Two young Vietnamese women were in the kitchen preparing food. Linda said hello as they passed and proceeded out a back door from the kitchen and into the gardens. "Peter, I wanted to show you my gardens before it gets dark. I'm quite proud of my mandevilla and hibiscus. They are not native to the area but they seem to do just fine. I also have chrysanthemums (hoa cuc) and jasmine that are often found in this area."

"Your flowers are quite beautiful, and the garden is very nicely arranged. What are those purple flowers over there?"

"Those are bougainvillea. They bloom most of the year. They were native to South America, but the French introduced them here. Then, over here, I have orchids. I want to show Donna my orchid plants. I think she might like one as a birthday present."

"Linda, I very much enjoy the beauty of a garden, and I can tell that you're quite proud of yours. The flowers all have sexy names when you pronounced them, but I must be honest with you, I can't seem to remember their names."

"Donna says you're a genius and can remember everything."

"I think Donna has given me too much credit," he said as he chuckled.

"Perhaps that goes to my earlier point?"

"Perhaps," he chuckled again.

They passed through the gardens in the back of the house to the patio on the right side. The patio was being set up for a buffet meal. They reentered the house via one of the two sets of French doors that connected the patio to the long living and dining room that extended along the entire length of the right side of the house.

"Peter, I call this the 'long room.' The dining area is toward the back of the house and at this end is the living area. John has a component stereo system set up at this end and he has removed the large scatter rug that is usually here. We thought that later after we eat, we could play some popular tunes and dance." Peter was impressed as he took it all in.

"I see you noticing the ceiling fans," she said. "The ceilings in this house are about ten feet high and ceiling fans are in almost every room." The long room was no exception; it had two.

As they passed back into the main hallway, they encountered John and Donna coming out of his office.

"Oh, so there you guys are. That was a long tour. They have a very nice house, don't they?" Donna asked.

"Yes, they certainly do," Peter replied. "The gardens are quite beautiful. Linda, thank you for the tour. You and John have a very nice place."

Then Linda asked Donna to come out to the garden with her before it got too dark. She had a birthday present for her. "John, maybe you and Peter can talk while I spend some time with Donna."

"So, that is your office," Peter said. "I see you keep it locked. You must have some rather secret information in there. You and Donna spent a long time in there. If one didn't know the true nature of your relationship with Donna, I would think they might be very suspicious that something inappropriate was going on between you." He didn't seem amused. "I'm just kidding," Peter quickly added.

"Peter, I assure you it was not inappropriate. Sometimes you just have to trust someone. The trick is to know when you can and when you can't. Let's go outside and talk."

He led Peter through the living area, telling him about his component stereo system and record collection on the way out to the patio. They stopped off at the portable bar set up on the patio area, and manned by a Vietnamese servant. John ordered a scotch and Peter ordered a glass of white wine. With drinks in hand, they proceeded to a secluded place in the garden area where they could talk privately.

"Peter, before we talk, you need to understand that this conversation must remain secret and none of it can be repeated. I mean that, literally. It can be a matter of life and death. You understand?"

"Yes, I do."

"Has Donna told you who I am?"

Donna really hadn't told him, but he lied. "She said you were her boss, and you wanted to meet me. I know that Donna works undercover for the CIA, so I assume that means **you** are CIA. Why did you want to talk with me?"

"Well, I'm her project manager, her boss, if you will. I wanted to start by thanking you for successfully completing your assignment and helping Donna with hers. I also want to give you some insight into what is going on, and I want to talk to you about some concerns I have."

"Okay," Peter replied. He still didn't understand, but he was curious enough to hear what he had to say.

"I was U.S. ARMY Special Forces, Green Berets, for several years. After that, I worked for the CIA's Special Operations Group. Now I'm in the Foreign Service and employed by the U.S. Embassy. However, the CIA does not technically employ me; I just work with them. The CIA has a rather complicated organizational structure. Have you heard of a 'matrix management' structure? Well, the CIA is more like a matrix management structure in multiple dimensions. You have the manager that holds your personnel card, you have the manager of the operation that you are part of, but then you have people who are undercover, and others that are not. I manage a project or operation that Donna is part of. The CIA also has non-employees that they call *assets*. **You** are an asset. I had to approve of your assignment here, as did the Saigon Chief of Station. As an employee of the CIA, Donna reports up to someone in Langley via the Saigon Chief of Station." John had just answered another one of Peter's questions. He and the station chief were **not** the same person.

John continued, "Donna reports to me with respect to the project. You probably realize that you're only a small part of what she does for me, and Donna is only a small part of my project. However, the job necessitates that Donna and I meet and talk frequently."

Before he could continue, Peter interjected. "I understand, and I find this interesting, but why are you telling me all this?"

"Well, I'm concerned about your relationship with Donna. I feel the need to give you some advice that will be beneficial to you as well as to Donna. Your situation with Donna is something I can identify with from my own firsthand experience."

"What situation are we talking about?"

John ignored his question and kept talking.

"When Donna first came here, Linda was suspicious. She thought I could be having an affair with her. Of course, Linda has always known that I was involved in intelligence work, but I had to take her into my confidence and trust her more than normal in order to convince her that nothing inappropriate was happening with Donna. Since then, the two of them have become friends. Linda truly cares about Donna's welfare. She has expressed concern that maybe you and Donna were becoming too involved with each other. She doesn't want her friend to be hurt. I think she may have expressed this to you when you took that tour of the house."

Peter began to realize that this talk was going to be more like a lecture. Although not in the military, he knew that when a colonel lectures a lieutenant, the lieutenant would be advised to listen and not talk back until asked to do so. Peter struggled to keep his silence as John continued.

"Linda may have also told you that she and I are on the outs right now. I love Linda but I tend to indulge in meaningless sexual encounters with young women when I'm away from her. I think it may be my macho background or the way I'm wired. I don't know. There is no emotional involvement with my encounters, just sex. I don't think that you are like me in that regard, but that was Linda's fear. Now that she has met you, she may think otherwise about you." Hearing this made Peter wonder if this conversation wasn't also for John's benefit. After all, who else did he have to confide in about such matters?

John continued. "Like Linda, I'm also concerned about Donna, but my reasons differ from hers. I generally take the position that the people I manage have a right to make their own personal decisions. I don't like to get involved. However, as a manager, I want the people that report to me to perform well. If they are upset, or heartbroken, they may not." Having had some management training in business school, Peter understood where he was coming from.

"Peter, for me to do the job I had with Special Forces and Special Ops, I had to learn something called *emotional intelligence*. To perform well, I needed to recognize my emotions and those of others, and I needed to manage them in a constructive manner. That means you don't suppress or deny your emotions; it means you deal with them. Over the years as a Green Beret and as a manager within the SOG, I saw many terrible things that made me very emotional. What I learned was that you could not just suppress those feelings and emotions. People that denied their emotions became automatons, cyborgs; they became dead inside. People that felt their emotions but didn't know how to handle them often became depressed, committed acts of violence, or made poor decisions that got them killed or got others killed. A CIA agent's ability or inability to handle emotions intelligently can be the difference between life and death. Donna is still learning. Her ability in the area of 'emotional intelligence' is not fully tested, and yours is a total unknown to me. That concerns me."

Peter wasn't sure if he should respond to that. He felt as if he knew how to handle his emotions. He was the one with the marital problems, not me, Peter thought. Nevertheless, Peter decided to play it safe and keep his mouth shut, as John continued with his lecture.

"You're newly married. I have been married for ten years. I have learned a few things that could be useful to you. For one thing, I know that if you were to sleep with Donna, it will affect your marriage. Don't think it won't. That is true regardless of whether you have feelings for Donna or not. Your wife will know something happened and she will lose trust in you. Don't think you can hide it from her. You would be better off just telling her everything upfront.

"You say that you and Donna are just friends. However, according to what I've heard from Donna and from Linda, Donna has a crush on you. Donna did not dress the way she did tonight for my benefit. Sometimes the emotions we feel are based on assumptions we have made rather than objectivity. For example, men and women might think they are in love when it's only the hormones talking. Even if your intentions are good, the two of you could end up hurting yourselves as well as my mission. You need to be careful."

The bottom line was DO NOT SLEEP WITH DONNA. Most guys would consider his lecture to be bullshit and psychobabble, but his advice made sense. Objectively, Peter had no argument. On the other hand, he never liked being told what to do. That was especially when it came to managing what he thought should be his personal choices. Being told what to do often made him want to do just the opposite. Until this evening, he had no intention of sleeping with Donna, and he had no idea she had any desire to sleep with him. He was right. He needed to be careful. Peter nodded that he got the message.

"Here is another little tidbit of advice for you, Peter. Don't burn your bridges. It's possible that you will see Donna again after you leave here next week. I'm only thirty-eight, and I often run into people that I thought I would never see again. In your case, maybe you get a job offer from the CIA, or maybe you move to Virginia and run into Donna in the grocery store. Maybe we will be so impressed with your work that we will invite you back for another project. You never know."

Peter thought that he might not mind burning this bridge, but again he remained silent.

"Anyway, you have been very patient putting up with my lecture. Anything you want to say?"

Finally, Peter was given the invitation to speak.

"John, I thank you for the talk. Your advice about emotional intelligence is well-taken. I will remember it. Deciding on the best way to handle emotions is not always easy. I do my best, but I realize that I'm still learning. I also hope that Donna lives up to your expectations. She's become a friend and I want her to succeed. Just one more thing—"

"What?"

"Something I have learned is that a woman may say they never want to see you again and at the same time love you. They are simply putting the ball back into your court. I think you should tell Linda how you really feel about her."

"That's probably good advice," he said as he stood up and glanced over to the patio. "Well, I see that food is being put out on the patio, and I imagine that Donna may want to introduce you to her colleagues. So let us head back."

When they got back to the food buffet on the patio, the food was not quite ready. Several couples had gathered on the patio, talking with drinks in hand. Peter joined Donna, who was talking with two of her colleagues. "Peter, I would like you to meet Thuy. Thuy works for me at USAID, and this is Thuy's friend Allan."

"Pleased to meet you both. Allan, do you work in USAID also?"

"Yes, but in another department. What do you do, Peter?"

"I'm a contractor here on a temporary assignment with MACV SOG, over on Pasteur." After he said this, there was dead silence until Donna interjected.

"Peter is a computer system analyst. He is not here to kill anyone." We all laughed.

As they waited for the remainder of the food to be laid out, Donna continued to introduce Peter to the other eight people who were her colleagues and guests.

The buffet was excellent. Donna suggested that Peter focus on the Vietnamese food rather than on the American food that one could get back in the States. A good suggestion Peter thought. He tried to sample everything but was careful not to take too much in total.

Wow, what a spread! He had a small cup of Pho, and followed that with Cha Gio made with pork, crabmeat, egg, and onions, all very tightly wrapped and deep-fried in rice paper. A special fish sauce was provided for dipping. He finished his selection with ginger chicken, rice, and stir-fried vegetables. He and Donna sat at a table for four with Sally and Bruce. Donna introduced Sally as someone who worked for her at USAID. Sally introduced them to her friend Bruce. Bruce was more than six feet tall, and had to be well over two hundred pounds. Bruce was an airman first class. He had on his summer Khaki uniform with short sleeves. His biceps bulged at the hem of his sleeves. He was drinking beer and already had more than one. Peter wondered how and Sally hooked up.

"Bruce, I'm curious as to how you and Sally met," he asked.

"Well, I load and unload cargo out at Tan Son Nhut. Sally came out there looking for a missing shipment, and I helped her to find it. She was grateful and asked me to come party with her, so I said yes. Kind of hard to turn down an offer like that, isn't it?"

Peter realized that he didn't bring a drink back to the table, and thought a white wine would complement his meal, so he asked if he could get anyone a drink. Sally declined, and Bruce already had a beer in front of him. Donna said she would like a glass of white wine, so Peter excused himself and headed for the portable bar. After several minutes, he came back to the table with two glasses of sauvignon blanc. As he set a glass of wine in front of Donna, Bruce was engaging her in conversation, some of it rather suggestive he thought. But Peter kept his emotions in check.

Meanwhile, Sally was left out, so Peter began talking with her. She was not particularly attractive physically, but she had a nice smile and a sweet personality. Peter enjoyed talking with her.

After supper, Linda called everyone into the dining area of the long room. In the middle of the dining room table was a large layer cake about fourteen inches in diameter; it was a white cake with chocolate icing. Centered on top of the cake were a medium-size white candle and the numeral "25" in white icing. Everyone sang Happy Birthday to Donna.

Donna cut the cake and she and Linda served. Donna brought Peter a slice and as she handed it to him, he thanked her and wished her a happy birthday.

Linda and her girlfriends all wished her a happy birthday. Then, to Peter's surprise, Bruce came over and said, "Babe, where I come from birthday girls get a big hug." Sporting a beer in one hand, he gave Donna a bear hug that could have squeezed the life out of her—not to mention spilling beer on her. Sally quickly spoke up admonishing him. "Bruce, please be careful; don't hurt her." If Donna was bothered, she didn't show it.

After some more conversation, mingling, cake-eating, and drinking, John began playing dance music. The wood floor of the living room area of the long room became the dance floor. John's 400-watt amplifier and giant speakers filled the room with quality sound. He had 45 and 33 RPM records that he was playing on two different changers, so he could quickly switch between them, allowing for almost continuous play.

The dancing started out with lively music popular at the time, music that lent itself to non-contact dancing like Cubby Checker's "Lets Twist Again Like We Did Last Summer," and like James Brown's "Papas Got a Brand New Bag." Then there was more Rock and Roll style dancing, such as "Devil with the Blue Dress On." Everyone was changing dance partners. Peter danced with Donna but also with the other women.

As the evening wore on, the music slowed down with popular hits like "The Sound of Silence," "You Don't Have to Say You Love Me," "Cherish," "You Lost That Lovin Feelin," and others. Peter was dancing with Linda when the first slow piece, "In the Still of the Night," started playing. He looked for Donna but she was already dancing with Bruce, and Linda wanted to dance with him again. However, he could not keep his eyes off Donna as he realized that Bruce was making unwanted advances, even attempting to grope. Donna seemed to be handling it, but he didn't like to see it. He also noticed that Sally was watching. She didn't look too happy either. Peter revealed his observations to Linda. "Linda, I don't like what I'm seeing. I think we should do something."

"Peter, please don't lose your cool."

"Not to worry; I have a plan. Please come with me."

"What are you going to do?"

"Please trust me," Peter responded.

He took Linda by the arm and they walked over to where Bruce and Donna were dancing.

"Excuse me, Bruce. May I cut in?" He seemed to ignore the question and kept dancing, so Peter spoke louder, "Bruce, may I please cut in? I would like to dance with Donna."

"Donna and me need to finish this number." He slurred his words as he spoke.

Donna piped in, "Bruce, it's okay, we can dance later. You should go ask Sally to dance."

"She won't dance with me," he said and continued to hold onto Donna.

Seeing their stalemate predicament, Linda said, "Hey Bruce, I want to dance with you; how about it?"

Meanwhile, Peter thought how dumb it was that he did not have a "plan B." But fortunately, Bruce accepted Linda's offer. As Bruce and Linda stepped aside and began to dance, Peter overheard Linda tell Bruce that if he got fresh with her, he should remember that her husband was a Green Beret.

Peter turned to Donna. "Donna, I would very much like to slow dance with you." She didn't respond so he took her hand and asked, "Are you alright?"

"Yes, just a little embarrassed. I could have handled it you know."

"I know, but I didn't enjoy seeing it, and Sally was not happy either. My instinct said I needed to do something. I hope you didn't mind."

"Perhaps we should talk to Sally."

Peter glanced over to where Sally was and saw that Thuy and Allan were consoling her. "Sally's okay. She is talking with Thuy and Allan. It's all okay now. You can relax."

Peter took Donna's right hand in his left hand, and put his right arm around her back. He looked into her eyes, and gave her a smile. She smiled back and they began to dance. "Peter, you're really a nice guy," she said.

The lights were dimming and people were beginning to gravitate to the person that they came with. Donna and Peter both had had a few drinks through the course of the evening. They were sober, but relaxed. Peter told her how much he was enjoying the evening and she told him that she enjoyed dancing with him. Each time they danced, they positioned themselves closer to each other. They were playing "When a Man Loves a Woman" when Donna put her head on his shoulder and they brought their bodies closer. She wrapped her left arm around his neck and he held his right arm low on her back. They pulled closer and they could feel the warmth of their bodies as they rubbed up against each other.

They didn't say much to each other; they just enjoyed the music, and the comfort of each other's bodies. As they danced to "The Unchained Melody," a very dreamy piece popular in 1966, it became clear that they were becoming sexually aroused.

Peter could see that Donna's face had become flushed, and she could feel his growing firmness against her hip. Her lips were pressing against his neck when she whispered, "Peter, what are we doing? I want you to know that I really like you, but you said you wanted us to just be friends." She remained up against him as she said this.

They were starting to breathe more heavily when he whispered very softly, "Donna, let me hold you." They stopped dancing, repositioned their arms around each other, and stood there in a tight embrace. Her body trembled, followed by an audible gasp of ecstasy and an excited giggle. Peter could feel her tears on his chin. An admonishment from Linda immediately followed. "I hope you two are behaving yourselves," which elicited a short chortle from Peter. Until that moment, they had no awareness of anyone else, but apparently, Linda was nearby. Meanwhile, Donna was probably aware that Peter was unable to prevent his own release. He was glad that the room was dark and that he was wearing black pants. It could have been a very embarrassing moment for them.

Still holding onto each other, he spoke softly and suggested, "Please come with me outside. I think we need some fresh air, and I would like us to find a place where we can talk. Perhaps we can pick up some cold water on the way. We can either drink it or douse ourselves with it as we see fit." He was trying to be funny, and she forced a laugh. They left the dance floor and headed outside, stopping for water on the way. They walked out to the garden and sat on the same bench he had been to earlier with John.

Peter turned toward her as he tried to decide what to say. She avoided looking at him, but she spoke first. She must have thought he was angry. "I didn't mean for that to happen. I know you just wanted to be friends. Please don't be angry with me."

"I'm not angry with you." He put his hand on her shoulder, and she turned her head quickly toward him as if surprised. She had tears in her eyes. He repeated himself. "Donna, I'm not angry with you!"

"After what you saw with Bruce, and then what I just did with you, you probably think I'm a slut or even worse."

"Donna, stop. I would never think that of you. This was just as much my doing as it was yours. I was hoping you wouldn't be angry with **me**. I don't want you to go home and write in your diary that I'm a creep that would cheat on his wife and try to take advantage of you."

"I'm not angry with you, and I don't think you're a creep. I think you're wonderful." As she said this, she took his hand in hers and put her head on his shoulder.

"I think you're wonderful too," he said, as he draped his arm over her shoulders and drew her closer.

The night was comfortably warm. The sky was clear and many stars were visible. They sat in silence for a long spell. It seemed that everything had become evident. There was no need to talk. After a while, they agreed it was time to head back home.

They said goodnight to each of her friends, even to Bruce, who had sobered up. Linda must have given him a good scolding. He apologized to them both and was apparently back in Sally's good graces as well.

Then they looked for John and Linda. They found them dancing together. They thanked them for a wonderful party. Donna and Linda embraced in a farewell hug as Peter shook John's hand. "John, I'm very glad we met. Once again, thank you for your advice."

"I took your advice as well," he said as he turned his head toward Linda. Peter nodded and smiled. He knew exactly what John meant.

Peter said good night to Linda. "I very much enjoyed your hospitality. I think Donna is very fortunate to have you as her friend."

They hugged, and then she said, "I'm glad you could come. I understand why Donna has taken a liking to you. "Oh wait," she said. "Which one of you is riding on the back of the bike?"

"Probably me. Why?"

"Because you get to carry Donna's birthday present. The orchid plant is in a small pot. I wrapped it with Saran wrap and aluminum foil, and set it into this shopping bag with a handle." They walked over to a nearby table and she handed him the bag. "Can you manage it?"

"Yes, I think so," he said as he took hold of the handle. "However, I think Donna will need to stop at her place before she drops me off." As he intended, Donna and John had overheard him. Donna looked quickly at Peter and then back at John as if looking for permission.

Then John said, "Sounds like a reasonable plan to me. I'll walk you to the door. Donna, don't forget your shoulder bag in my office."

The ride back was slow. They had been drinking and Peter was holding onto the potted orchid plant as if it were a baby. They didn't want to have an incident. He held onto the plant with his right arm and onto Donna's waist with his left. Every now and then, her shoulder bag would move away from her body and then swing back against his hand. Her bag was heavy, and he was quite sure why. They arrived at the back door of Donna's apartment building at around 11:30 p.m., well ahead of the midnight curfew. This was the first time he knew where Donna lived. Her apartment was near the Rex and off Nguyen Hue. Nguyen Hue was a main street on the other side of the Eden building running parallel to Tu Do. Donna shut off the engine and they set the orchid plant inside the small lobby of her building. Then, they got back onto the bike and traveled the short distance to his hotel, where she dropped him off. They both knew that a sleepover would be inappropriate and out of the question, and they avoided a tempting goodnight embrace or kiss. However, they did speak briefly before she sped off.

"Donna, please know that I really enjoyed the evening, and I'm glad you invited me."

"I'm glad I was with you, Peter. I'll see you next week before you leave."

He stood there for a few moments and watched as Donna turned left onto Tu Do and right onto Le Loi toward her apartment. Her shoulder bag was across her body and snugged against her left side. He knew she would be safe.

.

8

GOING HOME

On Monday, Peter completed everything he planned to do at work. Everything was documented, and all the loose ends were tied up. When he got back to the hotel that evening, he found his detailed going-home itinerary in his mailbox. He would leave Wednesday morning, change planes in Hong Kong, be in Los Angeles (LA) Wednesday afternoon, sleep over in LA, and be home Thursday night. He was amused to see that he would leave Hong Kong, be in the air for fourteen hours, and get to LAX before he left Hong Kong. Of course, that all has to do with the magic of the international date line, which reverses everything by twenty-four hours when you cross it in the Pacific heading East.

Peter had specifically requested the overnight in LA. Two weeks ago, he had written a letter to his friend George that he was in Saigon, and would like to see him on his way home. He would arrive in LA in the afternoon, allowing them to have dinner together, which he had offered to buy. George had accepted his offer in concept. The problem was that Peter didn't know what day he would be coming home, and George didn't know how to arrange his schedule. Peter had the same issue with his wife, Penelope. What he needed to do was figure out a way to let them know on rather short notice what days and exact times he would be there.

It was now about 6:00 p.m. At this time of year, LA would be fifteen hours *earlier* than Saigon. It would be 3:00 a.m. in LA. In New York, it would be 6:00 a.m. Peter went over to the USO and used the phone. Penelope would be getting up, and he might reach her before she left for work. He would have to wait three hours to call George. This is what he did. Fortunately, the calls went through, and they were both at home when he called. There were no answering machines in 1967. AT&T still had its monopoly and nothing could be connected to its network. If no one had answered, his backup plan would have been a Western Union Telegram.

By Tuesday March 21, everyone had agreed that the job was complete and he could go home. The captain, Danny, Jeff, and even Jim came to his send-off in the conference room. They presented him with a card and an expensive pen engraved with his initials PST. The message on the card said, *"Hope your PEN fulfills a need and is very useful."* It didn't escape him that the official name of the project had become the PEN Project. He thanked them all, but especially thanked Jeff for his ability to complete quality coding in such short order.

The next morning, Donna picked him up in the Jeep and drove him to the embassy to exchange his ID for his passport, and to turn in his MPC and Dong for dollars. Then, they were off to the airport, where they said good-bye.

"I imagine that after all this time, you're very happy to be going home to your wife. I'll miss you."

He replied, "I will miss you too. I'm very glad to have known you, and I enjoyed your company. I hope that we can keep in touch. I plan to send something to the captain at the Rex. Would it be okay if I send something to your mailbox at the Continental Palace – like pictures, or maybe a Christmas card at Christmas?"

After a pause, she said, "Yes, I would like that."

Then he asked, "Would it be okay if I give you a hug good-bye?" She smiled, and they hugged briefly but tightly. As he began to turn away, he thought he saw some mistiness in her eyes.

The trip home was pretty much the same as the trip there, but in reverse, and this time they got to subtract a day as they crossed the Pacific. The fourteen-hour flight from Hong Kong to LA gave him lots of time to think and reflect on his entire stay. He was happy with the work that he and Jeff had accomplished. He reflected on all the sights he had seen in Saigon. He reflected on the lives of people who worked and lived in Saigon. He wondered what it would have been like if he had been in the military there, or if he was an IBMer like Bob. Then he started thinking about the life of a CIA agent. That led him to think about Donna and feelings that he never expected. He recalled John's words about emotional intelligence.

Somehow, the whole six-week experience seemed like a distant dream. Was any of it real? It was now ten hours into this flight, 11:00 p.m. Saigon time. He was very tired and fell asleep. Three and one-half hours later, he was awakened by the announcement that they were beginning their descent into LAX.

This time, his overnight in Los Angeles was more pleasant and more relaxed than on the trip over. The anxiety of the unknown was not there, and he looked forward to having dinner with his friend George. He retrieved his luggage, went through customs, and caught the shuttle to his hotel. He arrived at the hotel around 2:30 p.m. George arrived around 5:30 p.m. George had taken off early from work, and it took him almost an hour to get there from work. He already had a good place in mind for dinner and that is where they went. They had a drink at the bar and then a hostess seated them at a table. They drank, ate, and talked for four hours. It was a great visit.

After leaving Cornell, Peter and George had kept in touch. They were room-mates freshman year, and later shared a rooming house off campus in their fifth year. George was down to Earth, overly modest, and a hard worker. Peter admired him for that, and they continued to be friends. George now worked for an aerospace company. He was not married yet but would be shortly thereafter. Of course, Peter told him why he was there in general terms, but mostly they talked about life and family, and reminisced about college. Peter asked about his mom and he asked about Penelope. That reminded Peter of his friend Ben at Cornell, who had introduced him to Penelope.

"George, do you remember Ben? Whatever happened to him?"

"Ben never graduated but dropped out of school in Junior year. I'm not sure, but the rumor was he tried to take his own life."

"Wow, I'm sorry to hear that. Why?"

"Well, I'm not sure, but if you remember, he was very bitter about how he had been treated growing up as a Catholic. I think he had a very low self-esteem."

"Now that you mention it, he once told me that he decided to no longer be a Catholic. When I asked him why, he told me that the nuns, the priests, and even his parents made him feel unworthy. I remember him telling me how he thought the church made suicide a serious mortal sin to stop all the unworthy Catholics from wanting to take their own lives. He was a cynic, wasn't he?"

"Didn't he introduce you to Penelope?"

"Yes, he did, but after I started dating her, I never heard from him again. George, how about you? You meet anyone yet?"

"I have, but not sure where it's headed."

"Well, I wish you the best with that."

They talked for much of the evening before George politely excused himself. He had to work the next day and reminded Peter that he had an early flight. Peter enjoyed their visit, and was pleased to be able to break up the monotony of the long trip home. That night, he fell asleep feeling grateful that he had long-term friends like George.

Peter finally arrived in Rochester, late Thursday night, March 23. Penelope was at the airport to greet him. They embraced and got his stuff into the car. She wanted to know everything, and although he was dead tired, they talked most of the night. Of course, he was careful not to say anything about who he reported to. He felt good about the work he had done, but now he was glad to be home and resume his normal routine.

****

The next week, Armstrong required Peter to meet with him for what he called a standard debriefing. Peter summarized the success he had implementing the PEN project, while avoiding details about things he didn't need to hear.

The people at TGW were all interested in his trip. He was able to tell them things that he saw in Saigon that were of general interest. He showed them some of the photos he had taken while there, such as the Notre Dame cathedral, and the traffic jam of motorbikes and taxicabs. He also had a picture of his USAID guide, Donna, sitting on her motorbike, and a picture of him with his briefcase in front of the Continental Palace. Later in April or May, he mailed copies of these last two pictures to Donna in Saigon, c/o room 314 at the Continental Palace.

They resumed their normal routines of work, socializing, and going out on "dates" with each other. They seemed happy. A few weeks after returning home, Penelope told him she was pregnant. That was unexpected but good news—although he had to wonder about the timing since he had been away. They both celebrated and called everyone with the good news. The next day they began to look for a larger apartment. They also agreed that she would not tell her employer until she had to do so. Employers expected pregnant women to stop working soon after they were pregnant. These were happy and adventuresome times for them as a couple, and they looked forward to their developing life together.

****

It was in the middle of June when the unthinkable happened. Peter and Penelope had just celebrated their second wedding anniversary. Saigon was about the furthest thing from Peter's mind when he got a call from Armstrong. He was surprised when Armstrong told him they wanted him to go back to Saigon. "Why," Peter asked. "I thought my work in Saigon was done. Did I screw something up?"

"I'm not sure," Armstrong said. "What they told me is that the probabilities calculated by the program are different than what they calculate by hand. It could be a program error."

This puzzled Peter because he knew that he and Jeff had thoroughly tested the code. "What about Jeff? Shouldn't he be able to figure out what's wrong?"

"Apparently, Jeff is no longer there. He got himself reassigned to a ship somewhere in the Pacific. I don't think they even know where he is. They want **you**. They think that you're the best one for the job."

Peter was not convinced but decided not to argue. "How much time before I must leave?"

"Two weeks if you can do it."

"I don't know. I may need three. I need to set my wife up in a new apartment, and we need to move first. What about the pay?" he was bargaining.

"If you can leave within two weeks, we are prepared to pay a bonus of $7,500. That would be in addition to what we already paid you."

"Have you talked to TGW?"

"Yes, they are good with this. There will be an amendment to your prior contract."

Peter didn't tell him that they had already selected a new apartment and were already packing. Nor did he tell him that if he was responsible for a problem, either in the code or in the logic, he wanted to go anyway. Nor did Mr. Armstrong tell him that his original contract had a clause in it that said they could bring him back at will until he had completed the job to their satisfaction. Yet, Peter could not help but wonder how his employer could benefit from him being away from the job so much. Perhaps TGW had a contract with a customer in which the Government had an interest. Peter could only speculate.

"Let me talk to Penelope and get back to you."

"Please call me tomorrow," he said.

Peter broke the news to Penelope, and they talked about it at length. He explained his need to go back and exonerate himself, and how much additional money they would have. He convinced her that it would only be for a few weeks and he would be back long before the baby was due. He also promised her that they would complete the move to their new two-bedroom apartment before he left. It was enough; she agreed that he should go. As promised, he didn't leave her in the lurch. They moved into their new place two days before he left.

9

GOING BACK

After the same grueling trip back by air, Peter landed at Tan Son Nhut the afternoon of July 9. As he descended the stairs down to the tarmac, he felt like he was suddenly being smothered. The air was heavy; it was hot; and, it was very humid. It even had a bad smell to it. The sky was overcast, not sunny. It was very different from when he had arrived in February. As he walked into the terminal, he had the feeling that the airport was busier than he had seen it before. One reason for that became evident as he went through customs. Apparently, agents were searching the bags of all civilians, except for those that flashed special badges. He assumed those individuals were either state department employees or black-ops agents. In any case, it must have been more than thirty minutes after coming off the plane before he walked out of customs with his suitcases and briefcase.

Once again, Donna was there to greet me. He noticed that she had let her hair grow a bit; it was just above her shoulders now.

"Hello Peter. Welcome back. How are you?"

"I'm doing great, Donna. It was a long trip though." He got his luggage, and they walked toward her parked Jeep as they talked. "We won't make this a regular commute, will we? You must really need me here."

"What did Armstrong tell you about why you were called back?" she responded.

A curious question. He thought that Donna would know exactly why they brought him back. The implication was that there might be some pretense as to why they did. "Not too much. What can you tell me?"

"I'm going to leave it up to Captain Weisman to explain it," she said. Peter had hoped for a different angle from her than what Armstrong told him but did not get it.

They loaded his luggage into theJeep and took off. He noticed that the canvas top was up. "Are you expecting rain?"

"At this time of year, it tends to rain almost every day, and it takes forever to get the top up."

Before they left the area around the airport, Donna drove by the site where the new MACV headquarters compound was under construction. "Peter, I thought you might be interested. MACV expects people to move into the new headquarters within the next two months. It will have Bachelor barracks for both enlisted and officers. It will have two mess halls, a chapel, tennis courts, a gym, a motor pool, central air conditioning in each building, and modern computer data processing rooms. It will be like a self-contained village."

"Will the PEN project relocate?"

"We don't know yet."

As they got onto Cach Mang, the main road into the city, she asked about his home life. "Was your wife glad to have you back home?"

"Yes, very much so. We had some good times while I was home. We even had a chance to drive to Montreal for a day and see the International Expo."

"How did she feel about you being called back?"

"Penelope and I had mixed feelings about it. While at home, I found out that she's pregnant and we got ourselves a larger apartment. However, she's not due until late September so we agreed that it would work out if I were only here for a few weeks."

Then, very politely, Donna said, "Congratulations, I hope it all works out for you." Peter began to get cool vibes after that, and the conversation for the remainder of the trip into town remained on more of a business-like level.

Donna dropped him off at the Continental Palace Hotel and said she would like him to come across the street to the café and meet with her after he checked in. He checked in, and a new houseboy named Hung carried his luggage up to his room. This time his room was on the second floor. The room was nicer than the one he had in February. It had a sofa where the armchair had been. In front of the sofa was a small coffee table. The desk and chair were still there. Even more important to him, however, was that it was an inside room away from the sounds of the street. It overlooked the rear of the inner courtyard, and it had a balcony. It was not much of a view, but it was quiet. He wondered if the room would come with a pet gecko this time.

He went across the street to the Givral Café and was pleased that Han remembered him. He sat down, and Donna gave him her introductory briefing. Then, she told him, "I'll have a colleague of mine pick you up in the morning at eight o'clock sharp to get you registered at the Embassy. After that, he will take you to work."

"I was hoping you would do that, Donna."

"Sorry, I have a meeting I must go to, but unless you have a problem with it, I'll see you Wednesday at seven p.m. in your room, just like we did before."

"No problem," Peter replied, "but as I recall, we used to meet on Thursdays."

"I have meetings with my boss on Thursday evenings," she said. Then she gave him money. "It will be deducted from your account," she said. Her next comment seemed out of place. "Peter, I suggest you keep in touch with home; send your wife a letter each week. I think she would appreciate it."

****

The next morning, a fellow named Don picked Peter up, and he repeated the process of only a few months prior. He went to the U.S. Embassy and gave up his passport in exchange for an appropriate ID. He looked at his ID. On the line for rank, he was amused that he had received an imaginary promotion from O-1 to O-2, Second Lieutenant to First Lieutenant. He wondered what differences in privilege that could possibly afford him. Afterwards, Don dropped him off at 137 Pasteur Street, where he had worked before. Peter thanked him and headed for the guard shack. The Sergeant on duty allowed him to pass after he thoroughly searched his briefcase and made a phone call to Captain Weisman. The captain met Peter at the door and escorted him in.

That afternoon the captain took Peter to an office down the hall from his. He introduced him to Lieutenant Nguyen, who had joined the team just after he had left in March. "Peter, I want you to get to know the lieutenant here. She finished her officer training and is a lieutenant with the WAFC, the South Vietnamese Woman's Armed Forces Corps."

The lieutenant was larger than most of the local women, and her eyes were more slanted than most, a Chinese influence, he thought. She appeared to be in her late twenties. She had black hair and was reasonably attractive, but she seemed to have a hardened look about her as well.

"Welcome Mr. Troutman. I look forward to work with you." Her English was not perfect but not bad either.

"I'm pleased to meet you as well," he responded. "Did you replace Jeff?"

The captain interrupted and said, "No Peter, the lieutenant is the Systems Administrator for my project. She handles all input and output to the computer, the access authorizations, and all technical aspects of my job that are not above her security grade. It frees me up to modify the event network each week and provide the appropriate inputs."

"Oh, I see."

At this point, the captain excused himself to let them have time to get to know each other.

"Peter, you not wear uniform. Are you military?"

"No, Lieutenant. I'm a civilian contractor."

"I am contractor too."

"How so? I thought you were military. You wear a uniform."

"Yes, I am WAFC. We not paid by Republic of South Vietnam. WAFC all volunteer. U.S. military pay me as contract."

"Oh, I see, but why did you join the WAFC if they don't pay you?"

"I join two years ago. My husband he captain in ARVN. He support me. Then he get killed. Now I need money . . . no clean villa . . . no whore. I get education . . . learn English . . . learn computers. I go for advanced officer training at Fort McClelland in Alabama. Now I'm Lieutenant."

"That's quite an accomplishment. How did you like the USA?"

"You have expression: 'Good place to visit but don't want to live there'. I like it here."

"Peter, you stay at the Continental Palace?"

"Yes. It's about a mile from here. With the heat and the rain, I may need to bum rides each morning. How about you? Where do you live? Do you have far to go?"

"I live in Cholon. It take twenty minutes in morning. A neighbor, he drive. He manage construction at the new MACV headquarter near airport. This on his way. You see it?"

"Yes, it was pointed out to me yesterday on the way from the airport to the hotel. Do you think this computer center will relocate?"

"No, I think we stay here."

"What do you think of this PEN project?" he asked her.

"Not sure. You create the PEN?"

"Yes, I designed it and helped to implement it."

"Why you design it? You not military."

"I designed it for business, but the military said they wanted it. They said it would help to save lives. Do you think that PEN will save lives?"

She didn't answer at first, and then said, "I do not know what it supposed to do. Whose lives will it save?" Peter thought that was a curious answer.

Then, after a pause, she said frankly, "I do not know if it can work. It has program bug. Did you come back to find bug?"

"I will try to determine what the problem is."

"It must be program bug," she snapped back. "You see. I help."

10

THE INVESTIGATION

In 1945, Computers were more primitive than in the 1960s, and consisted of a multitude of vacuum tubes and electromechanical relays. Admiral Grace Hopper, who at the time was a Navy Lieutenant and a scientist, was working in a computer lab at Harvard University. According to the story, the computer stopped working. Admiral Hopper and her coworkers investigated the cause and found a moth lodged in one of the relays preventing it from closing. She removed the moth, taped it into her logbook, and pronounced, "We just debugged the computer." Like most stories, its veracity is questionable, but the terminology survived.

Peter knew that finding the bug in the PEN program would require an investigation. Like any investigation, the process could be tedious and time-consuming. The resolution would require logical and deductive reasoning, but like most investigations, it could also require some out-of-the-box inductive thinking, and maybe even some luck.

****

First Week Back

Tuesday, July 11, was Peter's first full day of work after being called back. The first thing he did on Tuesday morning was to sit down with Captain Weisman and have him explain the problem that he had discovered.

"Captain, what was it that made you think that there was a problem?"

"Peter, I manually calculated the probabilities of two events, and they differed from the calculated probabilities on the PEN Event Probability Report.

At Peter's request, the captain stepped him through the latest version of the network.

"Based on the intelligence that Sam and I were feeding the PEN system, we thought that Event 305 should have a higher probability than the fifteen percent calculated. At the end of May, we had added a new event to the network, Event 295. Event 295 had no precedent events, and it fed directly into Event 305. As Event 295 had no precedent events, we had to estimate its probability of occurring. We gave it a low probability of only ten percent that first week because we didn't have all the intelligence yet. However, the next week the intelligence showed that the event was very likely to have already occurred. Therefore, we changed our estimated probability for Event 295 from ten percent to ninety percent. Sam and I thought that the impact upon Event 305 of such a big change would be more significant than what the Event Probability Report was showing. We expected a much higher probability for Event 305, so I manually calculated the probability for Event 305. To do the calculation, I used the latest input data, like conditional probabilities, as well as the calculated probabilities for the precedent events. It took a while to do. I manually calculated that the probability of Event 305 in the second week of June should have been thirty-five percent. The PEN program calculated only fifteen percent."

At Peter's request, the captain took him through the manual calculations he did for Event 305. It appeared to Peter that the captain had discovered a problem.

"Was the second week in June when you first noticed this problem?" Peter asked.

"Yes, that is when I first noticed it. I then went back in time to see when it started. I found that the problem existed for Event 305 the first week in June, but the difference was not as significant. I didn't find an issue in the last week of May. However, it is possible that events other than Event 305 could be wrong as well."

"You said that you manually calculated probabilities for two events. What was the other one?"

"I did it for Event 300, one of the other events that fed into Event 305. However, I found no problem. I got the same answer as the computer did."

"Other than adding a new event, did anything else happen in the first week of June or the last week in May?"

"Like what?"

"Like a change in the staff, or using a dependency rule for the first time, or maybe a lost badge to the computer room."

"Hmm," he responded. "Jeff left us at the end of May."

"Anything else?"

"Not that I remember."

After Peter left the captain's office, he went back to his cubicle in the basement. As he studied the network, he could see that Event 360 seemed to be a very important and pivotal event. If one viewed the network as going from left to right, Event 360 would be very near the right-hand side. Unfortunately for Peter, his security clearance did not allow him to know what the event was, but it was easy to discern that if Event 360 were to occur, many of the so-called target events that followed it were also more likely to occur. The latest report, generated the preceding Thursday, a month after the captain first noticed a problem, showed that the calculated probability of Event 360 occurring was only fifteen percent. If Event 305 was really at thirty-five percent or more, fifteen percent was likely an understatement of the true probability for Event 360.

Peter spent the remainder of that day and Wednesday re-doing the calculations the captain had done for Event 305. He got the same results the captain did. He also did calculations on some of the other events and for some other weeks. He did the calculations manually with pencil and paper, and some help from a slide rule. It was a daunting and time-consuming task. In early 1967, there were no hand-held calculators, only desktop calculators. Wang had not yet mass-marketed its system. Friden electronic calculators and Marchant mechanical calculators ruled the day. However, none of those were anywhere in the building where he worked. Perhaps the reasoning was that if they had computers, they would not want calculators. To requisition one would have taken more time than it was worth, so the pencil, paper, and slide rule prevailed.

The captain had only looked at two events. After hours of labor, Peter also found discrepancies with two other events in other weeks. How could he be certain of the week that the problem started?

He knew he would be reviewing code, so on Tuesday afternoon, he went to Lieutenant Nguyen's office and requested a listing of all the current coding for the PEN project. She said he would have it on Thursday.

On Wednesday afternoon, he had an idea. He wondered what change to the input data would result in the calculated probability reported by the computer program. Suppose there was a decimal point error, either in the calculation program or in the report program. In other words, could a probability of forty percent have been mistakenly represented as four percent or even as point four percent? He redid the manual calculations for Event 305 using the altered input, and sure enough, that was exactly the case. One of the input numbers, a conditional probability, was off by a factor of ten. It was quite possible that a programming error caused it, and if so, very likely it was in the FORTRAN code that he and Jeff had written.

That Wednesday evening, before he left work, he made his first entries into his daily journal, something he continued to do each evening. Then, each evening, before he left the office, he would lock the journal up in his file cabinet for the night. Oh yes, the captain had made sure that he had been given a file cabinet with a lock this time.

Later, on Wednesday evening, he reported to Donna. They met in his room at 7:00 p.m. as planned. Donna entered the room and commented on how nice the room was before perching herself on the edge of the sofa. He sat across from her on the wooden desk chair.

Donna asked if he was settled in, and he told her he was.

Then she asked if he had sent a letter back home yet. He remembered that on Sunday, she had suggested he do that. He didn't understand why she would care, but he answered, "Yes, I have. I even got some picture cards yesterday and included one in the envelope."

"I'm sure your wife would like to hear from you on a regular basis, especially now that she is expecting." Then, Donna asked, "Have you met the new person on Captain Weisman's staff, Lieutenant Nguyen?"

"Yes, I have. She's an interesting person. Was there anything about her you needed to know?"

"No. Just wondering what you may have thought of her."

"Well," he said, "too early to make any judgments, but she seems friendly enough." If Donna's question was more than just idle chitchat, he could not tell.

He reported that he had verified the problem as the captain had described it. He told her that his next effort would be to analyze the computer code to see if it had been altered.

"Sounds like a plan. Let me know when you find something."

"Of course."

"Donna, before you go, I was wondering what you were doing over the weekend. I miss those bike ride tours we used to take."

"The weather is not so good this time of year, so not as many opportunities for that."

As she arose from her seat on the sofa, she told him gleefully, "I have a date on Saturday."

"That's great. May I ask where you're going?"

"I don't know."

"I hope you have a good time," he told her.

"Thanks," she said, as she left.

****

On Thursday, Peter began to investigate the code. There were two possibilities. The code could be wrong if it was changed after he and Jeff had tested it, or the code could be wrong if he and Jeff had overlooked an error.

First, he investigated the possibility that Jeff, or someone else, had changed the code after they had tested it. This was relatively easy to do because Jeff had filed a copy of his code in Mid-March after he said the coding was done. Peter found that printout, and compared it to the printout of the latest code. They were identical! He also compared the math code that he had provided to see if it had changed. There was no change!

He began looking at the FORTRAN code he had written for the module that applied to Event 305. He could find nothing wrong. He looked to see if the code could have incorrectly changed the location of a decimal point. There didn't seem to be any way the code could have done that.

So now what, he wondered?

It was well after dark by the time he left the office Thursday evening. He remembered the lectures he had received from Donna about the dangers of walking alone at night. Rather than risk walking, he called for a cab to pick him up and take him back to the hotel.

****

Friday morning, Peter continued proving that none of the computer programs were at fault. Thinking he may not have been objective about his own code, he had Jim do him a favor and independently look at the FORTRAN code module he had written that applied to Event 305. He also looked at the calculations for Event 50, which used the same code module as Event 305. If the code was at fault, both sets of results would have been affected. However, Event 50 was not affected. The code was not the problem! If the computer program was not at fault, there was a good chance that the data used by the computer program to do the calculations had been altered by a human.

On Friday afternoon, he had his first status meeting with the captain. "Peter, tell me what you have found so far."

"Captain, I have not found any issues with the program code. However, I did find out that a specific piece of data input for Event 305 was off by exactly a factor of ten, and that accounted for the entire discrepancy in the calculated result. I believe that the problem is with the data! The implication is that the data being used by the calculation program is not the same as the data you see on the printouts of the Input Data Files. Selecting the wrong rule from the Rule File is not likely to be the problem either, because that would result in an error and the calculations would not run. Also, if the Event File accessed had unapproved events in it, that would show up on the output reports. If we look at your output reports, your calculated probabilities should belong to legitimate events. Can I assume you have already checked that?"

"Yes, but I don't mind checking it again just to be sure," he replied.

"I can do that for you, Captain. However, I think the most likely issue is that the conditional and apriori probabilities used by the calculation program are different from the correct ones that you see on your input data printouts. That would mean either the program runs against a permanently altered Input Data File, or the file is temporarily altered during the calculation run."

"Don't understand. How could that happen?"

"I don't know yet, but I would like to check the control card listings on the reports you received. That will indicate the file IDs that were accessed. We can compare the file ID on your data file printout to the file ID used in the calculation run."

"Okay, let's do it," the captain agreed.

One initiated a computer run by submitting punch cards. The cards on the top of the deck were called job-control cards. The information they contained included the authorization code of the person initiating the run, the ID of the program being run, the ID of the files being accessed, (unless embedded in the program), and the routing of the printouts. When a report was generated, the first pages of the report would have all that job-control information (JCL information). The actual report would follow. Peter wanted to see what file ID was accessed by the calculation program, and if it differed from the file ID that had the correct event data.

The captain went to his cabinet, and retrieved a report of a recent data update he made to the Event File, and the report of yesterday's calculation run. They checked the reports, and sure enough, there was a difference! The Event Data File ID used for the data update report was one digit off from the Event Data File ID used in the calculation run.

"Captain, if I give you the cards, could you submit a calculation run? It would run against the correct database. Let us use the most recent week. We will compare our result to the report you got yesterday."

"Okay, let's try it."

He gave the captain the control cards he needed to generate a calculation report that accessed the correct Event Data File ID. They looked forward to seeing the results on Monday.

****

Second Week Back

On Monday morning, Peter and the captain started talking about getting the report that they requested on Friday using the revised control card. They were in the midst of a discussion when Lt. Nguyen came in and handed the captain a report. "Captain, this is the report you requested on Friday."

As they began perusing the report, they could see that it was showing the same incorrect result that the captain had on his original Thursday report. Peter could also see that the pages that would contain the control card and JCL information were missing.

"Lieutenant," he asked, "where are the control pages?"

"Oh," she said. I do not think you need, so I remove them and throw away."

Peter began to realize that this was going to be more difficult than he thought. He tried to be tactful with his next question.

"Lieutenant, how does the captain know what control cards to use when he submits a run?"

"Peter, you not understand procedure," the lieutenant snapped back.

The captain held up his hand and then explained. "Peter, the lieutenant handles all my input and output. I fill out key punch forms, and she has them punched. She submits the cards into the reader, and she retrieves the output from my printout box."

That afternoon, Peter talked to the captain again. "Captain, unless you object, I am going to submit these cards on your behalf. If you allow it, I will use your authorization code, the same data file ID, but this time we can re-calculate the probabilities for that second week in June. That was the week for which they had done the manual calculations."

****

Tuesday morning, Peter was in the captain's office when the lieutenant delivered his report, before he could get to the box himself. The first page of the report had the message "**ACCESS NOT AUTHORIZED**" in bold letters. The lieutenant asked, "What were you trying to do, Captain?"

"We wanted to make another run using data for a week back in June. What did we do wrong? Why does it say that I am not authorized? It did **not** say that the last time?"

The lieutenant looked at the control card and then calmly explained, "No one allowed to run calculation against original data files. When I submit run on Friday, I fix that for you. Every week Chan makes copies of file. Calculations run against copy."

"Why?" We both asked in unison.

"It's for security reason," she replied. "Not a problem, Captain. I'll rerun these against the correct file. Which week was that?" Of course, the run came back the next morning with the same incorrect results they had before. Obviously, determining how the data used in the calculations was altered and covered up was not going to be easy.

On Tuesday afternoon, Peter decided to try something else. Suppose the captain were to request a calculation run against the copied data file that included temporary data change cards. The data change cards would ensure that the data was correct. The captain agreed and they did this for the first week in June with data change cards for Event 305. The only change needed would be to move the decimal point over for one of the input probabilities.

Peter also decided to run the same report using his own authorization code, but he didn't tell the captain.

****

The reports came back Wednesday morning. He asked the captain what the results were and the captain told him that once again the report showed the same incorrect results. Peter looked at the report. He noticed that the JCL indicated that the change program did run before the calculations were done, but the listing of the change cards themselves were missing from the report. There was no way to verify which changes ran. The captain called in the lieutenant, and asked for an explanation.

"Captain, data in file not wrong. Data in file same as change card. Change card run and make no change. That prove problem is code error, not data." They didn't want to argue, so they let it go.

Peter left the captain's office, went to his own printout box, and retrieved the report that he had submitted on his own. The first page of the report had the message "**ACCESS NOT AUTHORIZED**" in bold letters. He went to see the lieutenant.

"Lieutenant, why am I not authorized?"

"Peter, you not authorized to change data."

"Lieutenant, who handles the access authorizations?"

"I do," she said firmly.

"Lieutenant, can you give me authorization?"

"Maybe. I talk to Captain. We see."

On Wednesday afternoon, Peter had a task to finish for the captain. He had promised the captain I would verify that every event on the output files were the same as every event on the input files. The captain had given him several weeks of reports and on Tuesday and Wednesday, he laboriously made the comparisons. He noticed that there were additional events added since March, and some had probabilities of one hundred percent, indicating that they had already occurred. As he expected, however, everything checked out. The events on the input files were the same events that were on the output reports. No one had altered the events!

****

On Wednesday evening, he met with Donna. "How was your date?" he asked.

"It's not your concern," she said bluntly.

"Donna, I didn't mean to offend you." He paused and then added, "I was just asking as a friend you know."

"I know," she replied. "If you really want to know, my date didn't go too well. I guess I'm not into the dating thing." Her tone was disparaging.

"I am sorry to hear that, really."

"If you don't mind, I would like us to focus on business, okay? What can you tell me about the job?"

He told her what he could at that point. "I didn't find any problems or changes in the computer code. I am convinced that the data reported was different from the data used to do the calculations. The why and how of it remains a mystery." She didn't seem too surprised at that. "I'm going to ask the captain to give me a sandbox or isolated test environment. That will help me determine where all the differences are and what the true event probabilities are. After that, I can work on the why and the how."

"Peter, this is your field of expertise. I'm going to rely on you to know what is the right thing to do. Just keep me informed."

Then, before she got up, she looked at him for a long moment and then said, "Peter, could I ask you what you plan to do over the weekend?"

"I have no plans. I found last weekend rather boring. I'm not much of a reader, but I have started reading a novel on the weekends."

"What are you reading?"

"The Quiet American. You had told me about it, remember? But you never told me if you had read it."

"I did read it, but I'm not sure how I felt about all of the opium, prostitution, and casual sex."

"Well, I don't favor opium and prostitution either, he responded, but so far, I have found it to be interesting. Why were you asking about my weekend?"

"Well," she began, "there is a USO show this Saturday night, and I thought that perhaps you would be interested."

"You're not asking me out on a date, are you, Donna?"

"Peter, despite what happened between us back in March, I was hoping we could go as friends. Besides, there will be other people there."

"Okay then, count me in. Details in the mailbox?"

"Okay."

****

On Thursday morning, Peter went to the captain. "Captain, to do further testing, I would like a 'sandbox.' I want my own test environment. I want to be able to read files, print them, copy files, change them, and have reports delivered to my own printout box." He reminded the captain that the original design of this process called for a simulation mode, so they could answer 'what if' questions. and that was what he needed.

"Okay, I'll ask the lieutenant to set that up for you. You and the lieutenant should talk more. I think she could be very helpful to you."

At that point, he called her into his office. "Lieutenant, I would like you to work with Peter and give him what he needs to determine the issues with the PEN.

"Yes, sir. It is program bug, no?"

"We don't know yet," Peter interjected, "but I would like your help in setting up a simulation mode for me, so that I can work independently of the real operation. Do you have time for us to meet this afternoon, so that I can explain what I'm looking for?"

"No Peter, sorry, but Friday morning, okay?"

"Yes, that would be fine thank you. See you at nine in the morning?"

"Yes, nine hundred hours," she responded.

****

On Friday morning, Peter met with Lt. Nguyen. He told her that he wanted his own test environment. He told her he wanted to be able to read files, print them, copy files, change them, and have reports delivered to his own printout box.

"Peter, I do best I can. What files you need?"

He told her he would need the following:

- Copies of the weekly Event Input Data files starting in May;

- A copy of every PEN program;
- His own authorization code with authority to run any PEN program he wanted against his files;
- Authority to run file-management programs against his files;
- And, he wanted all output to go directly into his own printout box.

"Mr. Peter. That not easy. It take time. Is okay if I only give you some of the weeks now and more later?"

"Yes, that would be okay. Can you give me the last week in May, the last week in June, and the second week in July?"

"I do my best but do not know how long."

"Your best is all I would expect, Lieutenant. Thanks."

****

On Friday afternoon, Peter told the captain he had met with the lieutenant, but she didn't seem to think she could give him everything he was asking for right away, and she didn't know when. The captain explained that the lieutenant had told him she was not sure what she could do, but that he told her it was important, and she said she would try to have something ready by early next week.

Meanwhile, the captain asked if he would like to go to a USO show on Saturday evening. He said he was getting a group together, and it should be fun.

"Sure, thank you. Who is going?"

"So far, Danny, Jim, and Dee. Chan said he would come separately and meet us there. I expect he will come with his girlfriend."

"Who is Dee?"

"Oh, sorry. Lieutenant Nguyen's given name is Chi, pronounced *Dee*. In Vietnamese, you would verbally address her as Lieutenant Chi. However, the U.S. military requires us to address her using her family name, Nguyen." This was the first time he had heard the captain refer to the lieutenant by a first name.

"Perhaps you may want to ask Donna?" he suggested.

"Actually, she already asked *me*."

Peter left a note in Donna's mailbox that evening. He said that the captain was getting a group together for the USO show and asked if they could join him at his table. Peter suggested that he meet her at her place at 7:30 p.m., and they could walk together from there, depending on the weather. Or he could have a cab pick her up at her place. The USO, Donna's apartment, and his hotel were equidistance from each other and only a short distance from one another. Peter was hoping they would walk together.

****

Finally, Saturday came. Around mid-day, Peter found a note in his mailbox from Donna saying that she had something to attend to, and that she would meet him at the entrance to the USO at 7:45 p.m. The weather was nice and Peter enjoyed walking the four blocks to the USO. They arrived at about the same time. Donna was wearing a dark brown skirt and a gold-colored blouse. She looked nice, but not seductive. Peter told her she looked nice, and she returned the compliment. They walked in together and found the captain's table. It had been a rough week, and Peter looked forward to some relaxation.

This was not the first time he had been to the USO. They had pocket pool and table tennis. Both games were ones that he enjoyed. He had come to the USO for pick-up games a few times earlier in the year and a couple of times after returning to Saigon. The USO was also a place where he sometimes went after dinner before returning to his room at the hotel. Tonight, and any time they had a show, they removed the ping-pong table from the stage and put it away for the evening.

Jim and John came together; the captain and Dee came together; and Chan and Kim came together. Danny never showed up. He later asked the captain why, but didn't get an answer. Jim introduced Peter to John, who worked for Jim and was the computer room attendant at night. John explained that he had the evening off, but would make up for it Saturday morning. The room was set up with round tables intended to seat six, but the captain's group of eight managed to fit themselves at one table. Donna and Peter sat together, with John on her left and Kim on his right. The captain and Dee sat across from them. Everyone introduced themselves by first names. Well, except for the captain. He said, "Just call me Captain."

Peter was meeting John for the first time. John was Jim's roommate at the Brinks BOQ. Jim had said that John was the computer operator during the off-shift, so during the intermission Peter could not help but ask, "John, it's a pleasure to finally meet you, but who is minding the computer room?"

Jim interjected, "Peter, I have another employee now. His name is Jerry. Usage of the computers grew rapidly after you left in March, so I added more help. Jerry joined us in May."

There was plenty of time for conversation before the show started and again at intermission. As she was sitting to Peter's right, he struck up a conversation with Kim, Chan's girlfriend.

"Peter, do you work where Chan works?" Her English was very good.

"Yes, but I'm only there for a short time."

"How do you know Donna?"

"Donna works for USAID. Her job is to help transients like me get settled, and find their way around the city. We were staying at the same hotel and kept running into each other so we began talking and became friends." Donna was listening in and seemed to approve of his white lie. Donna added that she had given him a tour of Cholon and introduced him to pho, after which the two of them started talking about recipes for pho.

The show started with a comedian and then a musical revue. It was not bad, and it served its purpose. Besides, it was a chance to maintain a good rapport with everyone, and although it was not a date, Peter did enjoy Donna's company.

Later during intermission, Donna excused herself and went to the lady's room, and Chan excused himself and went to the bar to get a ginger ale for Kim. Peter began talking with Kim again. "Kim, how did you and Chan meet?"

"I met Chan in Cholon about a year ago when he came into the store where my mother works. I work there as well. Chan was trying to find a woodcarving of an elephant. They bring good luck you know. He spoke to me in Vietnamese, and that impressed me. I asked how he learned Vietnamese and he told me that his father grew up in Vietnam."

"What does your father do?"

"He works for the government in land management. We are fortunate. We are well off financially. My father says the government appreciates what he does."

Peter asked Kim if her parents approved of her dating an American soldier. "My father did not approve at first, but two months ago, he and

Chan came to agreement, and now it's okay. We even have secret place where we go to be alone together." She seemed sweet and innocent. Her openness reinforced that.

Donna had not returned yet when Peter noticed she was over near the bar talking with Chan. It seemed to be more than a passing conversation. When she eventually came back, she had two drinks with her. Peter had not requested it, but she handed him a brandy, and apparently had a ginger ale for herself. "Thank you," was about all he had a chance to say before the show started up again.

They all had a few drinks. Everyone seemed to be enjoying themselves. Dee and the captain seemed to be comfortable with each other, perhaps too much so. She seemed to be fawning over him. She had her arm on his shoulder a lot. Donna also noticed. Peter sensed that Donna had some prior knowledge of Nguyen, the way she looked at her.

After the show, Peter heard "Dee" invite the captain over to her place. He assumed he took her up on that. Then, Jim asked Peter if he and Donna wanted to join them for drinks back at the Brinks. Peter looked at Donna. She shook her head. He walked over to Jim. "No thanks," he said softly. "I want to see that Donna gets back, and then I'm just going to turn in. But Jim, could I hitch a ride to work with you on Monday morning?" Peter didn't think it would be an imposition because the Brinks BOQ was only a hundred yards or so away from the Continental, and Jim had to go right by his door anyway. Besides, Jim had given him rides to work before.

"Sure. Would seven-thirty hours be okay?"

"That's fine. See you out front. Thanks."

Then, when he and Donna approached the exit, they noticed that it was starting to rain.

"Peter, if you want to join them, it's alright."

"Actually, I feel like I should have spent more time with you tonight. I got involved talking with Kim."

"That's alright, I enjoyed the evening, and I got a chance to talk with the people in your group."

"Not a problem," he told her. "I'm more than pleased to escort you home."

It was raining rather hard now, so Peter suggested they take a cab. Several cabs were lined up out front. She agreed. When they got into the cab, he was about to direct the driver to Donna's apartment. He figured he would drop her off and then the driver would take him the rest of the way to the Continental Palace. However, before he could say anything, Donna told the driver to take them to the Continental Palace. When they arrived, he said, "I'm glad you enjoyed the evening. Would you like to come up?"

She put her hand on his shoulder, "It's okay. I really did enjoy the evening, and I'm glad we went together, but I'm a bit tired. Besides, this was not a date, remember? I'll just have the cab take me to my place. I'll see you next week."

"Okay, here. Please take this.... cab fare...the least I can do," he said, as he inserted the appropriate wad of bills into her hand.

After he got out, he watched the cab drive across Tu Do and turn right onto Le Loi before he lost sight of it. He went up to his room, and had no trouble falling asleep.

****

Third Week Back

That Monday morning, Peter got a ride to work with Jim. Jim and John not only shared a room, but they also shared a Jeep. Since they worked on different shifts, sharing the Jeep worked out for them.

Peter had intended to talk to Jim about the security of the computer room, but decided to take a different tact. "Jim, have you heard from Bob Nunn lately? He took me out on the town before I left in March, and I wanted to connect with him again."

"Bob is due to pay us a visit soon. I was waiting to hear from him."

"Sounds like you have not had any issues requiring his presence. Does he have a regular schedule?"

"I only call him to come if we have an issue that is critical. Otherwise, I just keep a list of things I want him to check out when he does come. As far as a regular schedule, that is not Bob. Unless we have a critical issue, he pretty much comes when he pleases."

"Yes," Peter chuckled, "that sounds like Bob."

"I'll get his phone number for you when we get to the office."

"Thanks, Jim. I would appreciate that."

"Peter, other than going out on the town with Bob, what do you do with your free time?"

"Well, there has been eating, drinking, touring, bowling, ping pong, pool, shows, reading, and shopping. I get restless if I don't do something."

"Did you say you play pool? Jim asked."

"Yes, in college, the fraternity had a table. However, the USO is the only place I know that has tables here. They are quite busy, so I have only played a few times here in Saigon."

"If you're interested, I can reserve a table at the USO. I have been thinking of getting John and Chan together to play, but we could use a fourth."

"Yes, I would be interested. Thanks for the invite. When were you thinking of doing this?"

"Haven't decided yet. I'll let you know."

After they entered the office, they exchanged pleasantries with Danny, who was already at his station. After a few moments, Jim excused himself. "I'll leave the phone number on your desk," he said as he left and walked toward the stairs leading to the basement.

After Jim left, Peter continued talking with Danny. He couldn't help but ask him, "Why didn't you join us at the show Saturday night? You missed a really good show."

"Well, you're not in the military so you may not understand this, but it's not generally acceptable for low-level NCOs like me to associate socially with officers like the lieutenant or the captain. My friends would ostracize me if they knew. You are okay because you're a civilian, and everything at work is okay, but socially that is something else."

"Gosh, Danny. I had no idea. I guess I just don't think that way. For what it's worth, I don't think the captain does either. I think he respects you and tries to include you."

"He does, and I have a great deal of admiration for the captain. It's not him, but I live in NCO quarters, and we hang with our own. Most lieutenants and captains treat us like servants. My best friend Bruce feels the same way about it, and he talked me out of going."

Peter was about to head downstairs when he noticed that the captain had his door open and was reading the Monday newspaper. "Danny, would you please excuse me? I would like to say hello to the captain before I head downstairs."

The captain had what Bob Nunn said IBM called an "open door policy." If his office door was open, you were free to poke your head in and speak. The captain welcomed it as a way to stay in touch with "the troops" and maintain morale. They had both arrived early to work, so Peter had no hesitation about entering the Captain's office and striking up a conversation.

"Hey, Captain. How are you this morning?"

"Great, did you enjoy the show Saturday evening?" he asked as he motioned for him to come in and have a seat.

"I did, and I appreciated your inviting me and Donna to join the group. You and Dee seemed to be hitting it off pretty well."

"Yes, she can be friendly," he replied.

"From what I overheard her say, I assume you went home with her," Peter ventured in what he thought was a non-judgmental way.

The captain smiled. "You know, when you have been here in a war zone for an extended period with very few women, it can be hard to resist. Just between you and me, I knew Dee before she joined the project. Many of the officers I know have Vietnamese women on the side. Technically, it's against the rules, and an officer can be charged with 'behavior unbecoming of an officer,' but it is common practice nonetheless. I have always admired Dee. I hope I can trust you to keep my secret."

"Of course, Captain. However, my guess is that the people on your team may already suspect what is going on. Maybe you need to be more discreet."

"I guess I'm not very good at discretion," he said emphatically, but then he turned the tables. "I thought maybe you and Donna had something going."

"Why would you think that?"

"Before you came back to Saigon, Donna and I had coffee. We talked about you. She seemed very fond of you. She showed me a picture of the two of you with her bike. And then you said that she had asked you to Saturday's show."

"Well, I think we are friends. We're not sleeping together if that's what you're implying. I'm married, and she's Catholic. Actually, I thought *you* and she could be interested in each other."

"You know, I actually thought about inviting her over to the pool at the Rex, but I think she would have declined."

"Perhaps she would have been embarrassed again," Peter ventured, remembering the prior experience he had told him about. "You told me that women rarely go over to that pool."

"Perhaps you're right, but to be honest, I'm a little bit afraid of her, being CIA and all, and besides, as you pointed out, she is Catholic, and I'm Jewish."

This was the first time Peter was aware that the captain knew Donna's real job. "Captain, why do you think she is CIA?"

"When I discovered the inconsistencies in the PEN calculations, I went to see Colonel Abernathy. He had Donna and Donna's boss join us in a follow-on meeting. That was when I learned of her real job. Abernathy and Donna's boss asked me to work with Donna. They told me that the CIA initiated the PEN Project and had a vested interest in its success." As the captain said this, Peter was thinking that *he* had initiated the PEN project, but he let it pass and didn't quibble.

The captain continued. "When Donna and I had coffee, she wanted to know how we could determine the cause of the problem. I was bumping my head up against the proverbial wall, and Jeff had already gone. Donna wanted to know more about the people on the project, including Jeff, and especially about Dee. I suggested we bring you back. Donna was unsure. I got the impression that something had happened between you two. However, we both agreed that you were the best person for the job, so Donna agreed to talk to her boss about bringing you back."

"Captain, I appreciate you telling me this, but I need you to also be discreet about Donna's true role, and about my CIA connection to her. Can I count on you for that?"

"Donna doesn't know about my relationship with Dee. I will keep your secret if you keep mine." Peter didn't say anything, but he thought that based solely on his behavior Saturday night, his relationship with Dee would have been quite clear to Donna.

"Captain, I had best get downstairs to my cubicle. I'll talk with you later."

"Okay, Peter."

Late Monday afternoon, the lieutenant poked her head into Peter's cubicle and told him that his test environment was all set up, and she hoped it was enough to get him started. "Peter, Captain say this important. I work all weekend. Hope this what you need. Here is list of all your file IDs. I also do the control cards so you get reports."

"Lieutenant, thank you. I appreciate the effort you put into it"

Peter was eager to get started. So, before he left that night, he verified that the control cards she gave him made sense. He submitted cards to print several reports, including Event Input Data Reports using his new test environment and the three weeks of data that Nguyen gave him. These reports were delivered to his printout box on Tuesday morning.

On Tuesday, he compared the results to comparable reports that the captain had. The last week of May was the same, and as expected, the other two weeks he printed were different. It took time to find these differences. To do so he had to compare all the input data for each event, but eventually he determined where the differences were. Three of the seventy-five events were different, and the differences involved shifts in the decimal point of an input conditional probability. Peter knew he had the same bad Event Data Input files the captain had. He now had proof that it was the data and not the program that was in error. He also knew that the problem clearly started in the first week of June. That afternoon, after finishing his analysis of the Event Input Data Files, he submitted cards to run the calculation program against his input files. The Event Probability Reports for these three weeks would be delivered to him on Wednesday morning.

****

Tuesday evening, back in his hotel room, he lay in bed but could not sleep. He began mulling over the results of his analysis so far. He was becoming more convinced that someone was intentionally altering the input data that the probability calculations were based upon. *Who could that person be?* he asked himself.

He lay in bed thinking about the possibility that someone on the PEN team could be a traitor. Whoever it was, they needed to have the opportunity and the means. If the problem did not start until the first week in June, it would rule out Jeff, as he was already gone.

Those that worked inside the raised floor area had special unrestrictive security clearances. They all had access to the computer files and computer runs. That included Jim, Chan, John, and now Jerry, who worked the off shifts when Chan was not on duty. It didn't escape Peter that Jerry started working in the computer room about the same time that the problem started to occur. Peter judged that whoever was doing this needed to be doing it on a regular basis, so he ruled out Bob Nunn. He was not there very much. He only showed up when there was a problem or a new software or hardware install. He had many other accounts to service in addition to ours. *Was it possible that the captain himself was involved?* He had an unrestricted security clearance. He also had direct knowledge of what the events were and how the events related to each other. He certainly had means and opportunity. However, as he was the one that discovered and reported the problem, it seemed illogical that he was the one.

Lt. Nguyen, or Dee as the captain called her, didn't have an unrestricted security clearance, as did those working on the raised floor area. She was not authorized to see event descriptions or to be on the raised floor. Unless she was in some way using the captain, it was questionable that she had the means.

Means and opportunity were not enough. There needed to be a motive as well. Everyone on the team was there voluntarily and had signed up for extra military terms. *What would motivate them?* Peter wondered. The antiwar movement was growing in the United States after the bombing to the North, and the defoliation in the South. Mostly, objections to the war were for ethical or moral reasons. No one he had talked with on the team had expressed any direct criticism of the war. Could it be money? Except for Danny and Chan, most of the team members were well-paid based on their rank.

Danny, who was a sensitive soul, could have been motivated by an anti-war sentiment. In addition, Danny had expressed some feelings of not belonging. He said it was because of his low rank, but it could have been for other reasons. He said he had a close friend named Bruce who didn't want him to socialize with us on Saturday night. Perhaps Bruce was more than just a friend. Perhaps Danny was homosexual. That was never discussed of course, but Peter tried to consider all possibilities. If in fact Danny was homosexual, he could have been blackmailed. That would have been a powerful motivator. On the other hand, Danny did not have access to the computer room, or did he?

Then, there was Chan. Chan's father was Vietnamese, and he had family members still in the country. Chan had a Vietnamese girlfriend, Kim. Kim's father had a job that could give him direct connections to the Viet Cong. Kim said that a couple of months ago, Chan and her father came to an agreement that allowed them to be together. The problem with the PEN started two months ago. *Could Kim's father have allowed Chan to have access to his daughter's affections in exchange for acts of espionage?* Sex could be a powerful motivator.

Peter thought about the captain again. He was a loose and free talker, and he seemed to have an intimate relationship with Dee. *Could she have persuaded him to manipulate data, or to leak classified information? Could he have been so concerned about protecting his career that he could have been blackmailed for a mistake?* Peter didn't think that was likely. He thought it more likely that if the captain was involved having unwittingly revealed information that he should not have revealed.

That last thought brought up more thoughts. *Wouldn't the perpetrator need to be working with a contact on the outside? In addition to preventing or delaying MACV's ability to see the true probabilities, wouldn't they also want to know the actual event descriptions and the actual probabilities? Were they also stealing copies of the real results and the real event descriptions?* These reports and the information they contained would certainly be valuable to the enemy. Perhaps the motivator was not money, but ideology.

"What should I do next?" Peter asked himself.

His head was spinning with thoughts. He could not go to sleep. He kept an opened bottle of brandy and plastic cups on the shelf inside the armoire. He poured a little and began to sip. Then, he laid back down on the bed and finally fell asleep.

****

Wednesday morning, Peter reviewed the Event Probability Reports that were in his printout box. For all three weeks, his test environment results were the same as the official results the captain had gotten. The probability for Event 360 in the last week of May was ten percent, the only week in which both sets of data were presumed correct. He thought about what he was going to do next. Clearly, the input data was being altered, and he needed to find out who was doing it.

On Wednesday afternoon he made a decision. He didn't consult with anyone. It was his belief that someone related to the PEN project was also a spy, and he needed to find out who it was without alerting any of the possible suspects. He had a plan. Bob Nunn had the highest level of security possible. Bob would know exactly how to go into the computer files and obtain the information he needed.

Peter called Bob on his business phone. He was not there, so Peter left a message for him to call him back at MACV. Bob called him back at about 3:30 in the afternoon.

"Bob, thanks for calling me back. How are you?"

"I'm doing great, Peter. It has been a while. I thought you went back to the States. What have you been up to?"

"I did go home, but now I'm back at MACV. Long story, but they have a problem here with the PEN application and they called me back to Saigon to fix it. I need your help, badly."

"You sound almost desperate. What's the problem?"

"Before I tell you, I need you to swear to secrecy about this conversation. Can you do that?"

"Well, within the limits of the law of course."

"Okay Bob. I want to ask you to do something for me and for your country. You may say yes or you may say no, but either way, I need you to pledge secrecy."

"You have my word."

"The PEN programs were not producing the expected results, and Captain Weisman said that they suspected a programming error. They called me back to fix it. However, I have found strong evidence that the problem is due to espionage. Unfortunately, all the people here are suspects, including the captain. I need someone who can obtain the information I am looking for without alerting the others that they are suspects."

"Jeeze, are you asking me to be a spy? I could get into big trouble."

"Bob, I'm already putting **my** life at risk. The risk to you will be minimal. You have the technical skill to do this, and you have a security clearance that allows you access. You can do this legally. Besides, you said you came here for the adventure. Well, this is it! Please hear me out."

"What is it you want me to do?"

Peter read from a list he had already created. He was looking for the following:

- Printouts of the access logs or parts thereof that show who accessed the Event Description File (#32386) and when;
- Printouts that show who and what programs accessed the Event Input Data File each week to copy or make changes to it (file numbers 32390-1 and -2.);
- Identification of who accessed and made changes to the PEN access authorization file and when (file #30000.) Don't ask how I know the number;
- Identification of who generated a PEN calculation report and when (Report #PEN 10).

"How far back in time?" Bob asked.

"At least two full weeks, a month if possible."

"Peter, I took notes as you were talking, but I want to be sure and get it right. I have a locked message box next to the computer room. I would appreciate it if you could write down what you just said, put it into a sealed envelope, and slip it into the slot for my box. One more thing. I hope you don't expect me to get this information out of the building."

"Nope, you don't even need to get it out of the raised floor area. Just put it into a Top-Secret envelope and put it into my print box. I'll retrieve it early Monday morning. Can you provide the captain and John with a good cover as to why you need to be there over the weekend?"

"That's not a problem. There is always a backlog of updates to install."

"Bob, if all of this plays out the way I think it will, you'll be proud of the results."

"And if it doesn't?"

"You may never see me again. Either way, thanks."

****

That Wednesday evening, Peter met with Donna at their usual time and place. He had not talked to her since Saturday night, so the first thing he said was, "I'm very glad that we could take time to see the show over the weekend. I enjoyed your company. I trust you got home okay."

"I did . . . and thanks for the cab fare. You didn't need to do that. I enjoyed the show and your company as well. I was glad to have a break."

"I needed a break as well," he told her. "To be honest, I have been getting bored with the same routine each evening. I could use some new ideas for places to eat and things to do. I was wondering if you had been out to any interesting places to eat lately."

"You know I have an apartment. I make something for myself, so I don't eat out very much. Where did *you* go for dinner tonight?"

"On Wednesdays, I usually eat across the street at the café. There is not enough time to do much else. Han asks if I'm expecting you, but I say no. She said that she thought you lived nearby and did not understand why she didn't see more of you."

"I never told Han where I live. It would be a security risk. I hope you didn't tell her."

"I did not. I will keep your secret. I promise."

Then they talked business. "Peter, please tell me what is happening at MACV."

"Very well, the captain has provided me with the "sandbox" test environment I had requested for further investigation. The test environment has allowed me to prove that the data used in the calculations was not the correct data. I expect the test environment will also allow me to determine what the correct results should be. I strongly believe that someone on the project or in the data center is responsible. But, I don't know who yet. Most have the means, and some have a motive as well"

"Tell me what you think of Lieutenant Nguyen."

"Well, I'm suspicious of her. I sense that she has been putting obstacles in my way. I also wonder if she and the captain have something going on based on the way they were acting on Saturday. And I'm afraid that the captain could unwittingly give her information she should not have."

"Hmm . . . I have had my suspicions as well. I didn't want to alert Captain Weisman of my suspicions, so last Saturday at the USO event, I had a brief conversation with Chan. I asked him if he thought there was something going on between the captain and the lieutenant, but I couldn't get much from him. However, I think the captain is an honorable man who would never betray his country. On the other hand, you should be wary of Nguyen and keep an eye on her."

"Donna, have you been holding something back from me?"

"You must realize that we are looking at a broader picture than what you're involved in, or even what I am involved in."

"Yes, I kind of thought as much. So, what's the broader picture?"

"I can't tell you too much."

"Tell me what you can then."

"We have been losing information. There seems to be a leak. We suspect that there could be multiple people involved. We are trying to link some suspects to other people."

"We have also had our suspicions that the lieutenant could be linked, but we have no hard evidence."

"What made you suspicious?"

"We got suspicious when we linked her to someone else that was suspicious."

"Interesting. I thought you guys did thorough background checks. How could the lieutenant pass all those background checks and still be working for the enemy?"

"We did do background checks, and we have no idea how she could have passed them and be working for the enemy. We can only speculate."

I began to show a little impatience and asked, "Why are you just telling me this now?"

"Stay calm. It was a judgement call on the part of the CIA. I didn't tell you this because we wanted you to remain objective and do an independent investigation. I had some hesitation about bringing you back, because I was afraid it may put you at risk and the job may require skills that you may not have. On the other hand, no one else could do it better. We needed you to help nail it all down. How was it done, who is involved, and what is the evidence? I would like you to keep an eye on Lieutenant Nguyen. Are you okay with that?"

Peter looked directly at her and gave her a resounding "Yes. Please stop trying to protect me. The more I know the better. I can handle it."

"Peter, I'm sorry." She sounded sincere.

Then, he told Donna about his idea and what he had asked Bob to do. "I think I have a way to determine who is responsible," he told her. "I made a decision this morning and took some action you need to know about. It can still be reversed, but I hope you will agree to go forward with it. I have asked Bob Nunn, the IBM Customer Engineer, to retrieve some critical data for me. I have asked him to provide copies of the access logs that show who has accessed what programs and data. Bob will do his thing over the coming weekend, and I'll get the results early on Monday. We should know for sure on Monday who the culprit is, whether it's Nguyen or someone else. I didn't want to alert the captain or anyone ahead of time because we don't know for sure who is involved, nor would we want anyone to alert someone else as to my plan."

"Does your security level allow you to see this?"

"Possibly not, but Bob's may. And, the information can stay in the building until we need it."

"I'm not sure; it sounds risky."

"Not so much," Peter responded. "What is the worst that can happen? We really need this information, and I know of no better way to get it."

"Peter, you're turning out to be more of a risk-taker than I thought, but if there is a spy on the team, we need to know who it is. You are the expert in this case. If you think this is the best way to get what we need, I must go with your decision. Just don't get caught."

****

On Thursday morning, Peter had copies of the incorrect data files that Nguyen had provided for his sandbox, and he also had the correct data reports from the captain. He had found where the differences were. He could now correct his data files and run the calculation program against the corrected files. He did this for the three weeks of data that he had. Rather than permanently correcting his data files, however, he submitted change cards with the calculation run that temporarily changed the data that was wrong while the calculations were running.

His first output, for the last week in May, arrived and appeared to be okay. As he expected, this report was identical to the calculation report that the captain had received. The second report, for the last week in June, didn't arrive, and he resubmitted it. It finally came and he retrieved it immediately. This good report was clearly different from the bad report that the captain had received. The good calculation report would also list all the temporary data changes that he ran to make it correct.

While reviewing this corrected calculation report, he noticed that it was possible to remove the pages from the report that listed the data changes without any indication that they had been removed. Those pages preceded the actual report and didn't have page numbers. Unless the receiver of the report was looking for those pages, they would not know those pages were missing. In other words, someone could make changes that affected the calculations, and by removing the control card pages from the printout, no one would know. Just one more thing to consider, he thought.

For some reason, the calculation run he submitted for the second week in July didn't show up in his printout box. He asked Chan if someone else had picked up the report. He thought that Nguyen might have. He resubmitted it. This time he went to the print box before anyone else could. The report was there, and it showed a probability of thirty-five percent for Event 360—the correct value.

So far, he had only generated two weeks of good new results, the last week of June and the second week of July. He needed to add more weeks. He requested the copied input data files for the last two weeks in July from Nguyen, but she only gave him the third week. He still expected to receive the fourth week. During the next three workdays, he was able to generate a corrected calculation report for the third week of July. That meant he now had three weeks of corrected but unofficial results. As soon as he received the fourth week of input data from Nguyen, he would also be able to run a calculation report for that week as well.

Computer runs were time-consuming. They were run in batch mode, not in real-time. Comparing the Event Input Data file that he had against the correct one took time. Verifying that he was submitting all the necessary control cards and necessary data changes also took time. After he ran the calculations for the third week in July, he went to the print box before anyone else could. It was there and showed a probability of thirty-seven percent for Event 360. At the Friday meeting with the captain, Peter told him of his findings for the last week of June and the second and third weeks of July using his test environment. Peter told him he had identified the input data discrepancies for those weeks, and he had generated corrected output reports for those weeks. He also told the captain that he verified that the discrepancies started in the first week in June, as they had thought, and that he had copies of those reports.

"Captain, the third week in July shows a true probability of thirty-seven percent that Event 360 will occur. I expect the fourth week to be even higher."

"Peter, I was hoping you would have that report to show me as well."

"I also had planned to have that report for you today so that we could compare the results to the official report you received yesterday. However, that is dependent upon my receiving a copy of the Event Input Data file for that week from Nguyen. I requested it but have not received it yet."

Later that afternoon, Lt. Nguyen came by Peter's cubicle. "Captain Weisman say I not give you what you need. You have problem you see me." Her tone was angry.

"Lieutenant, I only told him that I was waiting for you to provide another week of data for my test environment. I didn't express dissatisfaction."

"Well, you have it on Monday," she snapped back.

"Thank you," he said. "Enjoy your weekend. I'll see you Monday."

****

Fourth Week Back

It was Monday, July 30th. Peter was eager to see what Bob had left for him, so he arrived at work very early, before anyone else. The first thing he did was head toward his printout box. He retrieved the package that Bob had left for him and was on his way back to his cubicle when he encountered Lt. Nguyen on her way down the stairs. "Good morning, Lieutenant. You're here early."

"I like to get early start on Mondays," she responded as she made her way to the printout boxes. He guessed that she was there to retrieve the latest Event Input Data Report for the captain.

Back in his cubicle, Peter began to read the logs that Bob had provided. He had taken special care to highlight the lines that were most relevant. The logs showed that Nguyen had made several changes to the access authorization file that explained the "NOT AUTHORIZED" messages that he had received as delaying tactics.

Most importantly, the logs showed that Nguyen had used her authorization code to make an extra copy of the *correct* input data reports. Each week, it was standard procedure for Chan to make a copy of the input data file. The log showed that Nguyen initiated a calculation run against the copied file on Mondays to be delivered to herself on Wednesdays. Those calculation results would therefore be correct. She then initiated changes to the *copied* file on Tuesday mornings. That was not standard procedure. The access authorization files showed that only Nguyen had the authority to change or print the *copied* input file, and that the calculation program did not run against the *copied* file. The calculation program only ran against the original *correct* input data file. Nguyen was the only one that accessed the access authorization file. This explained how Nguyen obtained the correct calculations for herself, and then, why after that, all file copies differed from the originals, and why the calculated results that the captain saw were always wrong. The logs showed that the *correct* input data reports were delivered to the printout boxes on Monday mornings, and calculation results *(not correct)* were delivered to the captain's regular printout box on Thursday mornings.

In addition, the logs showed that the captain's latest Event Description Reports were printed on Monday mornings and delivered to a special restricted access printout box. This was a second printout box that the captain used for highly classified information like the Event Description Reports. The logs from Bob also showed that the only authorization code accessing the event descriptions (updating the file, initiating a report, or accessing the box) belonged to the captain. This was as it should be. Peter wondered if someone other than the captain could have had access to that report.

Peter looked at his watch and noticed that it was getting close to lunchtime. He was about to leave his cubicle for lunch when he spotted the lieutenant entering the computer room, a place he didn't think she had the authority to be. He watched as she went to the captain's special high-security printout box and removed a thin report. Only the captain knew the access code, so the only way she could get to it would have been from *inside* the computer room. Peter was quite sure that it was an Event Description Report. He figured that like the Event Input Data Report, it also would only be five pages in length at most. He watched her place the report into a large plain envelope. These descriptions could be very valuable to the enemy. Not only would the enemy learn what we thought they were doing, but the enemy would also learn what countermeasure events we were planning. He watched her leave the computer room carrying the envelope and start up the stairs. He followed and paused to look in through the door to the computer room as he passed. No one else was in the room. Chan was on his lunch break. Peter went up the stairs and as he came to Danny's station, the lieutenant was no longer in sight.

"Danny, did you, by any chance, see the lieutenant?"

"Yes, she just went by. I think she went into her office."

"Thanks Danny."

Peter walked down the hall to the Lieutenant's office. Her door was closed, so he went back to Danny.

"Danny, could you do me a favor?"

"I suppose; what do you need?"

"Remember back when Jeff left. Did he ever return his badge to the computer room?"

"I don't remember. Let me check."

Danny pulled out a log he kept and flipped the pages. "No, actually, he didn't. The badge went missing."

Peter assumed that when he encountered Lt. Nguyen early in the morning, she was on her way to retrieve the correct Event Input Data Report, and now she had the latest Event Description Report as well. He wondered what she would do with those reports. Did she just pick off some information she was interested in seeing and then throw the report into the trash? More likely, he thought, was that she would try to smuggle the reports out of the building and deliver them to her superiors, whoever they might be. Many who worked there would go out to lunch. It would be logical to think that Lt. Nguyen would want to get something like unauthorized reports out of the building as soon as possible and in the least conspicuous way possible.

As Peter was contemplating what would happen next, the lieutenant reappeared. As she passed by Peter and Danny, she said she was going out to lunch. They both replied together, "See you later."

The lieutenant was not carrying an envelope as she went by, but Peter thought the back of her blouse had some sharp edges. She could have used the time in her office to remove the title pages and the tractor edges from the pages. She could easily have secured up to ten report pages under her blouse, behind her back.

Then he told Danny, "I'll talk to you later. I need to get some fresh air before I go down to the canteen." He went out the front door in time to see the lieutenant get into the front seat of a black VW Beetle. She obviously knew the driver. It was far away, but he was quite sure that the driver was Vietnamese.

****

On Tuesday, Peter met with the captain as planned. "Captain, I have an idea. I know we did something like this two weeks ago, but I now have much more information. If you remember, I was not able to make temporary changes to the official Event Input Data files. The lieutenant had told me I was not authorized. I asked her if I could be, and she said she would talk to you. I assume she hasn't done so, because I still don't have that authorization."

"No, she has not talked to me about that. Would you like me to ask her about that?"

"Well, at this point, I think there is a quicker way. If you're okay with it, we can just use your authorization."

"What would you like me to do?"

"What I would like you to do is to ask the lieutenant to re-submit an event probability calculation run for the fourth week in July using temporary data change cards that I would provide. You could tell her you need to see the effect of a change you're considering or whatever. As in my test mode, these cards would temporarily correct the Event Input Data File while the calculations were performed. If successful, this would provide correct results.

"I'm also making appropriate comparisons for the same week using my test environment. This morning, the lieutenant did give me the copied Event Input Data File for that week, so I can do that now. And, I have one more request. I would also like you to allow me to use your authorization code so that I can also submit a run independently of the lieutenant."

The captain looked directly at Peter with a questioning look and asked, "Peter, tell me straight, do you think that the lieutenant may be involved somehow in changing the data?"

Peter looked him straight in the eye and said, "I think it's a possibility, Captain."

"Well, I suppose we will find out. Okay, let's do it," he agreed.

Peter expected that the output reports for all three runs would be in their printout boxes the next morning.

As agreed, the captain gave the lieutenant the cards he had provided and asked her to submit them on his behalf. Peter didn't know the reason he gave her. Also, as agreed, the captain notified him as soon as the lieutenant went down the stairs to submit the run through the card reader.

Donna had said he should keep an eye on "Dee," and he had already observed suspicious activity on the lieutenant's part, so he had no problem spying on her from afar. He secretly watched her remove the change cards from the deck that the captain had given her. He watched as she tore them in half and tossed them into a trashcan. He later retrieved them from the trashcan, and put the "evidence" into his locked cabinet.

****

Early Wednesday morning, Peter went to the printout boxes. From his box, he retrieved the Event Probability Report that he had generated in his test environment using the same change cards he had given the captain. The report would show the correct event probabilities. He peered through the glass to see what was in the lieutenant's and in the captain's printout boxes. The report on the lieutenant's box and the two reports in the captain's box all appeared to be Event Probability Reports.

After that, he hid in a nearby empty cubicle that offered him a clear view of the printout boxes. From his vantage point, he watched the lieutenant go to her printout box and remove her Event Probability Report. This report would have the correct probabilities and would be the one she would secretly keep for herself. Then, he watched the lieutenant go to the captain's printout box and remove two reports. The one report would have been the report she submitted after tearing up the data change cards. She would deliver that one to the captain. The other report would have been the one that he submitted using the captain's authorization code. It would have been correct, but now the lieutenant had it. She clearly didn't want the captain to see it. She didn't need to keep it because she already had a correct Event Probability Report that she had generated for herself. He watched as she tore the report into several pieces and tossed them into the classified waste bin. In 1967, office paper shredders were not prevalent. The procedure at MACV was that someone would make the rounds later that day, collect all the classified waste paper, and take it to a central location for destruction. Fortunately, there was plenty of time before that would happen. Peter waited until the lieutenant headed back up the stairs to her office, and he retrieved the torn pieces of the report from the classified waste bin. he added them to the other evidence that he had locked up in his cabinet.

Back in his cubicle, Peter reviewed the Event Probability Report he had generated using the corrected data in his test environment. His report showed that for the last week in July, Event 360 had a correct probability of forty percent. The captain's official report that he received on Thursday was not correct and had a much lower value.

Peter was beginning to build a case against the lieutenant. However, he was careful not to say too much to the captain for fear it would get back to her. Although the captain may not be a spy, he may have been guilty of running a loose ship or being too trusting. Regardless, Peter would report everything to Donna. Apparently, he was getting close to the whole truth.

****

The evening of Wednesday, August 2, was a regular meeting night with Donna. She came to Peter's room at 7:00 p.m. after they both had supper separately. He tried to anticipate her questions. He knew she would need more hard evidence. Right now, He had some, but he needed to report his observations and get some guidance on how to proceed.

She took a seat on the sofa, and he sat across from her on the desk chair. "Peter, what can you tell me? Did you get anything back from Bob yet?"

"Yes, I did." He gave her a summary of what he knew. He told her that he felt he was close to solving the puzzle. He told her he had a good idea as to how the data had been doctored and manipulated without detection. He told her he had reproduced the method used to alter the results; and he told her he had the corrected results for several of the past weeks. He told her that his test bed run for the prior week showed a corrected event probability for Event 360 at that point in time to be forty percent. These results were significantly higher than those on the official reports. He also said that he believed that the lieutenant was the perpetrator, a spy, and the information from Bob totally supported this. He told her he had not reported this to the captain yet.

"I was afraid this could be the case."

"What was? That I did not report it to the captain?"

"No! Stop it. You know what I mean. I was afraid it would be the lieutenant."

"Why do I think the picture is broader than what you have already told me?" Peter asked.

"Well, you asked the key question yourself. You asked how we could have done a thorough background check without seeing this coming."

"Yes, I remember. What's the answer?"

"The answer is that her identity was manufactured."

"When?"

"Before the captain knew her; before she applied for the MACV position; and before she went to the USA for officer training."

"If her identity was manufactured and was good enough to pass your background checks, doesn't that imply that some high-level people were involved?"

"It does. Now you know why I said I was afraid."

"Yes. In the past, you have been protective of *me*. Now I wish I could protect *you*."

"It's nice to know you care, but I can handle it."

"Fair enough. Any guidance as to what I should do next?"

"I would like you to keep providing corrected PEN information to the captain. Don't tell him what you have on the lieutenant. Let me know if anything changes."

"Yes, Ma'am," he replied.

****

The captain received the official Event Probability Reports on Thursday mornings. The reports included a summary diagram of the network. Each node would have an event number and the probability of occurrence. The summary fit on about five pages of printer-size paper. Of course, the probabilities on the captain's official report would not have been correct, whereas the version delivered to Nguyen on Wednesday would have been correct. However, now the captain would review a corrected Event Probability Report using correct data from Peter's test environment.

Then, as before, the captain would meet with his intelligence operatives on Thursday. They would then make changes that they would input on Friday morning, and the cycle would repeat.

Peter anticipated that Nguyen would want those five pages from both the correct version and the incorrect version of the calculation summary report, and that she would use lunchtimes on Thursdays to remove them both from the building. Once again, Peter remembered that Donna had suggested that he keep an eye on the lieutenant. Before lunch, he took himself up to the second floor of the building, went to the end of a hallway, and waited by the window. The window at the end of the hallway provided an excellent view of the guard gate and the street beyond. Sure enough, at almost precisely noon, he saw Lt. Nguyen leave the premise and get into the same black VW that he had seen on Monday. However, he could see no indication that she had a report with her. The guard would have searched her bag. If the guard had seen it with her, and if she didn't have the required security pass, she would have been detained. If she had the reports with her, she must have hidden them in a secret compartment of her purse, or somewhere on her person under her clothing, as he suspected on Monday. The only other alternative that he could think of was that the reports were still in her office. He didn't think that very likely, but just in case, he walked down the stairs and by her office. Her office door was locked. Probably just as well because just after he tried the door, the captain came around the corner. He would have caught him.

****

On Friday morning at the end of his fourth week, he received a very scary warning. It was tucked between pages one and two of a printout in his print box. It was handwritten in big block letters using a marker.

PEN WILL NOT SAVE LIVES
BUT YOU CAN STILL SAVE YOURS.

Peter's meeting that afternoon with the captain was difficult. He showed him the corrected predicted probability reports from his test environment. "Captain, Event 360 is now showing a probability of forty percent, and the target events that followed are almost as high. I'm able to do all of this in my test environment, but I wish I could get the official reports to run correctly in your official environment."

"Peter, I asked the lieutenant why the test we did with the change cards on Wednesday didn't show a higher probability."

"What did she say?"

"She told me that the data was already correct and, therefore, the change cards had no effect. She said that proves there is a program code error."

"Do you believe her?"

"No, I don't."

Peter didn't tell him about the evidence he had against her, nor did he mention the threatening note.

****

As soon as Peter returned to his hotel on Friday evening, the fourth, he put an envelope into Donna's mailbox. It contained the threat he had received and a note from him explaining where he found it.

He went for supper, and when he returned, Donna was waiting for him in the lobby. "Let's go to your room," she said. Once inside, she spoke emphatically. "Peter, I'm thinking about pulling you off this project!"

His response was a loud "WHAT?"

"I'm concerned for your safety. I don't want to see you get killed."

"Slow down," he demanded. "I'll be fine! We are very close to solving this case, and you need me to finish it. Lieutenant Nguyen is a spy, and you need me to provide the proof. You also want to know who is pulling her strings, and I can help with that. At this point, I know what she is doing and how she does it. If she wasn't a Vietnamese citizen, you could take her into custody now, but I know that you need hard evidence first. We are almost there. Just let me complete what I have started."

"Okay, maybe. First, I want you to tell me what you know in detail." Peter gave her the following detail and he laid it on heavy:

"Lieutenant Nguyen maintains the access authorizations. The authorizations are a combination of the person and the program that tries to access the file. She has made it so that no one other than herself can run the calculation program against the data file containing the correct data. She set up the access authorizations so that no one could ever run the calculation program against the original correct data files. She also has made it so that only she, the captain, and later myself can run the calculation program. For generating data file reports, only the file with the correct input data can be accessed to generate a data report.

"Early each Monday she retrieves a copy of the newly updated data report, and later at lunch when no one is in the raised floor area, she steals the updated Event Description Report from the captain's special printout box. She smuggles these reports out of the building at lunchtime on Mondays.

"Each weekend, the good input data files are copied according to procedure. Both sets are kept. On Monday, Nguyen initiates a calculation run against the correct Event Input Data File. She receives this calculation report on Wednesday in her own printout box. She stores this report in her office until lunchtime on Thursday. On Tuesday morning, Nguyen summits unauthorized change cards that she keeps in her office and permanently changes the copied version of the Event Input Data File. This ensures that any future calculation runs will be incorrect. The captain gets his bad calculation report on Thursday. These calculations are inconsistent with the good Event Input Data File Report that is the only version of the file one can officially see.

"On Thursday morning, Nguyen gets a copy of the same incorrect calculation report that the captain receives. At lunchtime, she smuggles the summary pages of this report and the summary pages of the correct version she received on Wednesday out of the building. She smuggles these reports out of the building by hiding them on her person, probably inside her blouse.

"The lieutenant is not authorized to access the Event Description File because that is above her security level, and she cannot control access to that file. Therefore, at some prior point in time she made a copy of the captain's control card, which contains his special access code for that security level. She uses the copy of his card to run the Event Description Report. The program has the captain's special security authorization code, and for that reason, the report ends up in the captain's special security print box, to which only he has authorized access. Therefore, the lieutenant must steal the report out of the captain's print box before he sees it. She purposely does this on Mondays at lunch when no one else is in the raised floor area. The lieutenant uses Jeff's unreturned access badge to enter the computer room when Chan is out to lunch. The captain would normally print more than one copy of his reports. If one more copy, or one less copy were to end up in the captain's special print box, that would not be too hard to explain.

"On the days the lieutenant smuggles the reports out, she gets picked up by a Vietnamese man driving a black VW Beetle.

"The lieutenant left the threatening note. I know this because when I first met her, I asked if she thought that PEN would save lives. She just gave me her answer.

"We already have the logs that Bob provided. They clearly show that the lieutenant accessed files and ran programs over the past month that she had no business accessing or running. In addition, we know that she frequently changed the access codes that she controlled to suit her needs."

As he finished, Donna stared at him wide-eyed. "Okay, okay already. I don't think I need to hear any more right now. It's a lot to remember. It sounds like you have nailed down every detail."

"Yes, I *have* nailed it all down, but you don't need to memorize it. I'll document it for you."

"Peter, what have you told Captain Weisman?"

"I have *not* told him that I think the lieutenant is a spy. Until now, I wasn't sure I could trust him not to tip her off. Now, however, the threatening note would suggest that she already knows that I'm onto her. However, I don't know how the captain will react when he learns. As you know, he's sweet on Dee. Another thing that I can do is get the license plate of the car and a better description of the man who will pick up the lieutenant on Monday. He may—"

Donna interrupted and excitedly said, "No, Peter, no need. That should be my job. I'll have a colleague stake out the building and I'll drive you to work and pick you up. You should be safe inside the building."

"Donna, please," he said as calmly as he could. "You don't need to drive me to work. I'll be fine. I will plan to ride to work with Jim."

"I'm sorry. I just don't want anything bad to happen to you."

"I know, and I appreciate your concern. However, I do need your help on something. I need a favor. I'm accumulating incriminating documents in my locked cabinet at work. To get them out of the building, I'll need special authorization from the MACV HQ Colonel in charge of security. I understand that he will need something from your boss before he will give it to me, and it must be for a specific day."

"What day were you thinking?"

"How about next Wednesday?"

"Okay, let me handle that."

Then Donna changed the subject. "Peter, may I talk to you as a friend?"

"Of course. What's bothering you?"

"Well... you have a family and a child on the way. It's something very important to you. It's a life I may never have. It's difficult for me to form close relationships with the job I have, but many of the people I have been close to have either left or died. That includes my younger brother, who died in a car accident when he was only sixteen, and several people I have known in Saigon who were blown to bits. There are colleagues that I can talk business with, but no one I can really confide in about personal things. I probably need a girlfriend, but there are not too many women here. There is Han, but she doesn't speak English very well. When I go back home to the States, I can't say too much about what I do, and my mom is not a very understanding person anyway."

"What about Linda? I thought you were able to confide in her."

"Oh, I guess I never told you. Since you were here in March, John and Linda have separated. Linda is back in the States."

"I'm sorry to hear that."

After a brief pause to recollect her thoughts, Donna continued. "What I am trying to say is that you should cherish what you have. This project is not worth dying for."

"Well, I appreciate your concern, but I suppose it is my choice to make, isn't it? Why are you so concerned about *me*?"

"Because I like you, and I care about you!" she replied emphatically and with feeling.

"Donna, I would like it if we could just be friends."

"Isn't that what we are, Peter? Aren't friends supposed to care about each other?" she said softly.

Her display of feelings had been more than he expected, but she was right; we were friends. "Yes, of course," he said, and smiled.

When their meeting was over, Donna started to get up from the sofa, but before it was too late, he blurted out, "Donna, before you go, I would like to ask you something. I would like to invite you to have dinner with me after we meet next Wednesday."

She paused, got an inquisitive expression, and then asked, "Are you asking me out on a date?"

"No. Uh . . . of course not. It's just that if all goes well, we will be wrapping up my mission here. I'll probably be heading home the week after next. Before I go, I wanted to show you my appreciation for all you have done for me. You have given me guidance, looked out for my interests, and I have really enjoyed working with you, not to mention the party and the USO, those bike tours, and even allowing me to drive your bike that time."

She smiled, and asked, "Are you asking anyone *else* to go with us?"

"Uh, no," he responded.

"So, if it's not a date, what would you call it?"

"A non-date?" is what he managed to get out, but he was beginning to feel like he had stepped into quicksand.

She could see that he was struggling and possibly embarrassed, so in a serious tone, she said, "Peter, I'm just toying with you. I would love to have dinner with you. Do you have anything planned for this weekend?"

"Oh, Jim and his guys are taking me somewhere tomorrow evening to play pool, and during the day, I need to tend to laundry and letter writing, and some shopping. My mother-in-law collects elephant figurines. I was thinking about going over to the shop that Kim works in for that. Also, I'm still reading 'The Quiet American'."

"Sounds like you're busy," she said, sounding somewhat disappointed. . . Peter, you said you were going to go to the shop where Chan's girlfriend works. How were you planning to get there?"

"I was going to take a cab. Why?"

"Please let me take you." She noticed his quizzical expression, so she added, "I need to do an errand over there anyway. It would not be a problem."

"The weather will be rainy tomorrow . . . not conducive to riding your bike."

"I'll bring the Jeep," she responded.

11

CHASING THE EVIDENCE— CHOLON

It was Saturday morning. Peter had something to eat downstairs and met Donna out front at 9:00 a.m. as agreed. It was drizzling rain so he was glad that she had the covered Jeep. They sped off toward Cholon and were about a quarter mile from the store where Kim worked, when Donna pulled off the street and shut off the engine.

"Uh . . . Donna what are we doing? Why did you pull over?"

"We need to talk."

"Why? Are we breaking up?"

"Peter, this is no joke. It has to do with business. I just found out that Chan has not been to work since Wednesday. Why did you not tell me?"

"Why would you need to know that?" Peter asked.

"Remember, I told you that we were looking at a people chain of possible VC supporters?"

"Yes. Do you think that Chan is involved?"

"Yes, he is involved but not how you think. We think that Kim's father, Pham Mung, is a VC supporter. We think he is using his government position to import arms for the VC."

"So is Mung using his daughter to lure Chan into revealing classified information?"

"No. Chan has been working for us. He has been using his relationship with Kim to help us determine what is going on."

"Wow! Poor Kim."

"Chan did not take advantage of Kim. He was involved with Kim before he started helping us. He didn't want to get involved with us, but because of his relations with Kim, he had a few infractions of the military rules regarding where he was supposed to be and when. We told him these would remain secret if he helped us."

"Wow! Poor Chan."

"Stop being a wise ass. I need your help! Why didn't you tell me Chan was missing?" Donna was clearly upset, but Peter didn't think it was with him.

"Sorry. I wish you had told me that Chan was important to you. I asked Jim of his whereabouts on Thursday when Jim asked me to join him and the guys for a night out tonight. Jim told me that Chan had told him on Wednesday that he may be coming in late on Thursday. When he didn't show up, Jim thought he could be sick. On Friday, I asked the captain. The captain said he was AWOL for unknown reasons. I thought that it was Jim's issue and the captain's issue, not mine."

He thought for a moment, looked at Donna, and asked, "How did *you* know he was missing? The captain said Jim had not reported it yet."

"Because he missed his meeting with me Thursday night." She sounded irritated. This left Peter wondering why she was upset with him when in fact she already knew on Thursday evening that something was wrong. Peter also reflected on John lecturing him about "emotional intelligence" back in March. He refrained from over reacting, but he was not going to let it go.

"Donna, you sound like you're upset with me."

"No, I'm not. I'm upset with myself. I feel responsible. Sorry."

"Do you think that Chan could have gone off with Kim, eloped or something? Do you think Kim would know where he is?"

"Maybe."

"From what you're telling me now, it sounds like he may be in trouble. Is that what you think?"

"I do."

"How can I help?"

"I want you to go into the shop like you had planned. I want you to buy your mother-in-law that elephant figurine, and you should buy your wife something too." Peter didn't like her telling him that he should buy his wife something, but he restrained himself, and she continued. "The sales person will likely either be Kim or Kim's Mama. Engage them in pleasant conversation. See if they have heard from Chan. If so, when? You know . . . that sort of thing."

"Perhaps you should join me."

"Kim knows you from the USO event. She knows that you work with Chan. She and her mama shouldn't be suspicious of you asking polite questions, but don't challenge or argue with their answers. Okay?"

"Got it, you need to trust me."

"I also want for you to observe the scene, like who is in the store, and is anything going on in the back room, **but don't get caught snooping.**"

"Okay. It may take me about half an hour. Will you pick me up out front of the store?"

"I'll drop you off a little closer now and spare you the rain. Then I'll drive around a bit. I'll give you half an hour and keep a look out. It won't be precise. If Kim asks how you got there, tell her by cab."

Peter entered the shop and set off a chime as he did so. He looked around and saw that Kim was helping a customer, or so he thought. When she was done, her customer went into the back room behind a heavy curtain, at which point she noticed him.

"Oh hello, didn't we meet a couple of weeks ago at the USO show?"

"Yes, Kim, we did. You remembered. I told you my mother in-law collected elephant figurines and that I would stop by. Well, here I am. How have you been?"

"I'm okay thank you. Uh, Mister Peter, right?"

"Yes."

"Well, Mister Peter, let me show you what I have." So far so good, he's thinking as she led him to a cabinet with some very interesting china figurines and the like.

As he began to admire the collection, Kim got a serious expression and asked, "Mister Peter, have you seen Chan? How is he?"

That was his opening. "Kim, I thought he came to see you on the weekends. Isn't he here?"

"No, he is not. I don't think he wants to see me anymore."

"Why would you say that? I thought he really cared about you. What happened?"

"I don't know. We had a small argument last weekend, but then, this weekend, he just didn't show up. There was no word, nothing. I left a message for him at the Brinks this morning, but have not heard anything. Peter, have you seen him recently? Did he say anything to you?"

Peter was really beginning to feel sorry for her so he said, "Kim, I must tell you something. I don't want to alarm you but I think you deserve to know this. I have not seen him since Wednesday. He was not at work on Thursday and Friday, and I'm also concerned. I was hoping that you could give *me* some information."

"Oh, do you think that something bad may have happened to him?"

"I don't think we should jump to conclusions. You said you had an argument. May I ask what it was about?"

"It was nothing. I caught Chan snooping in my father's office. He denied it and said he was just curious about the clock on the wall. However, two days later my father came out of his office and seemed very irritated about something. I asked him what was wrong, and he said that something was missing from his office. Then, he asked if Chan had been in his office. I had to admit that he was. Do you think this has anything to do with why Chan does not want to see me anymore?"

"I don't know, but Kim I do know that he really does love you." Peter noticed another customer entering the store. "You need to attend to another customer so let me pick out an elephant and we can talk again in a few moments."

Peter didn't know much about collector elephants so he picked out one that was clearly worth a few dollars but that was not too big for him to transport in his suitcase. On the way back to the counter and Kim, he passed a rack of silk scarves. What the heck, Penelope would like one, he thought. As he approached the counter, he noticed that the other customer was also going into the back room behind the heavy curtain. He remembered that back in Rochester, he had observed a similar occurrence at his local barbershop. In that case, there was a regular and illegal card game going on. He wondered what was going on in this case.

"Did you decide Mr. Peter? Oh, yes, very nice choice. This figurine is made of fine china with perfectly hand-crafted detail. I think she like it. I make sure it is well-wrapped and packaged. Did you want to ship it?"

He thought for a moment. Probably an unfounded suspicion, but something in his gut said not to let them know where he and his wife lived. Furthermore, if things went sour with Kim's father, he wondered if he would ever see the elephant again. "Kim, do you think it would be safe if I carried it home in my suitcase?"

"Yes. I think so. I package it for you. Oh . . . and what else do you have?"

"I thought my wife would like a silk scarf."

"That is very thoughtful of you. If you buy two scarves the second one is half price."

"You sold me. I'll take another as well."

She rang him up. Not cheap, but he thought it was worth it, and besides she had given him a great deal of information. She said she would be willing to accept dollars if he so chose. He had not been to the bank, so he gave her forty American dollars. It was a win-win.

As they were conducting the transaction, he noticed a movement and a shadow on the other side of the heavy curtain. Was it his paranoia, or could someone be listening to their conversation? Nevertheless, he continued. "Kim, if you learn anything more as to Chan's whereabouts, please let me know. You can reach me at the Continental Palace Hotel. Ask for Peter Troutman." He wrote his name and room number onto a scrap of paper, and placed it in her hand. "If I learn anything, I will let you know as well."

"Mr. Peter, how you getting back? I could call you a cab."

"No that's okay. I thought that while I was here, I should check out a few other shops and cafés . . . but thanks. Take care."

As he exited the shop, he caught a glimpse of a woman popping out from behind the curtain and walking over to Kim. Perhaps it was Kim's mama. He began walking down the sidewalk. It was getting very warm. The drizzle had stopped but the sky was overcast, and no sun. After he had walked about a block, Donna came by in the Jeep and he hopped in.

They drove until they came to a place where they could park and talk.

"Well? Did you buy what you came for?" she asked as she turned in her seat so she could face him.

"Yes, I did. Would you like to see?" He didn't wait for a reply and began opening the box containing the elephant. He was rather excited about his purchase and wanted to share it. He had barely opened the box when Donna stopped him.

"Peter, it's okay. I'm not a connoisseur of fine china or elephants, but I am sure your mother-in-law will appreciate it. Looks like you have something else there as well."

"I bought a silk scarf for Penelope."

"It's very nice," she said. She sounded disheartened without much enthusiasm, and she had pretty much sucked away the joy he had contemplated sharing with her. "You seem to have two of them."

"Yes, I do. Would you like to have one?" Without waiting for an answer, he said, "I would like you to have one. I bought the second one for you."

She seemed to be getting emotional but before she could say anything, he said, "Please, I want you to try it on. It will look really good on you."

At this point, she was clearly upset and she let him have it. "You need to keep them both for your wife! Please tell me about Kim and Chan!"

He took a moment to recover from her bitchiness before he proceeded. "Of course." He told her everything he saw and said while he was in the shop, including a description of the customers that disappeared into the back room, and his conversations with Kim. "I don't think Kim knows what happened to Chan or why he didn't show up Friday night as planned. I also think she is genuinely concerned for his welfare. We agreed to be in touch if either of us learns more about what happened to Chan. It may have been a mistake, but I gave her my room number at the hotel. She did reveal something that may have a bearing on this. She said that she caught Chan snooping in her father's office, and that her father forced her to reveal that to him on Monday after her father noticed something was missing. I think you already knew this from Chan, am I right?"

"Why do you think I already knew?"

"Because you told me not to get caught snooping. Do you remember? It's also something that Chan should have told you."

"Hmm"

"So, I was right. What do you want to do next?"

"You told me that you had planned a night out with Jim and a couple of other guys tonight. Is that still on?"

"Yes."

"I want you to enlist Jim's help. Chan reports to him, and they both live at the Brinks BOQ. Chan would keep evidence that he collected in his room, in his underwear draw, according to him. It's possible that there is still evidence in his room that I never saw, including what he took from Pham's office last weekend. I think that if you can appeal to Jim's patriotism and desire to find out what happened to Chan, he would be willing to search Chan's room. Jim would need to convince Chan's roommate. We need to do this before Chan is officially reported AWOL or missing. Once that happens, we lose control."

"What is it specifically that we would be looking for in Chan's room?"

"We are looking for a miniature camera, an envelope with documents, and undeveloped rolls of film from a larger camera that may also be there. It would be a Nikon and probably have a telescopic lens. If that camera is there, we only need the film that is inside, not the camera itself." Peter could sense irritation in her voice as she spoke.

"Okay. I know that you're upset by all of this, but you need to know that I'm on your side and I'm going to do everything I can to help."

"I told you I feel responsible. Chan may be dead!"

"Donna, you didn't do anything wrong. I'll try to talk to Jim before we go out tonight, and I'll let you know what we find in Chan's room."

"Peter, it's up to you, but it may be better if only Jim searched the room, but whatever he finds, I want him to give it to you, and I want you to give it to me. I'll come to your room Monday night as we already planned. Jim is probably already aware that you're doing a project for the CIA, but you need to keep me out of it. I need to maintain my USAID cover. Do you understand?" Peter knew she was upset, but it was hard not to react negatively to her tone.

"I understand. Please relax. It will be okay. We'll do the best we can. That's all anyone can expect of themselves."

"I know, but I may have lost Chan. I'm afraid I could lose you too!"

"You're not going to lose me. I promise."

Then, she changed the subject. "You said you were running out of dong. Tell me what you need. I'll give you an advance on Monday."

"Okay, maybe another five thousand dong. Thanks, Donna. Please let me off at my hotel. I'll be in touch."

****

Peter went up to his room and put his parcels away. Then, he went downstairs for a quick bite of lunch, and then he walked over to the lobby of the Brinks. He walked up to the Sergeant at the desk, showed him his MACV ID, and told him that Warrant Office Jim McDermott was expecting him. The Sergeant looked a little surprised. He probably didn't see too many "non-combatant first Lieutenants." However, there was no issue. He gave him Jim's room number and let him go up.

Peter knocked on Jim's door, and was fortunate to find that he was there. "Jim, I need to talk to you in private. It's about Chan." Jim opened the door and invited him in. It was even more fortunate when Jim told him that his roommate was not there.

"Peter, what have you heard?"

"I need your help to find out what happened to Chan. I also need to share some things with you that are highly classified and I need your word that it will remain between us."

He could sense Jim starting to groan so he quickly added, "Jim this is for your country and for Chan. Please . . ."

"Okay Peter, hit me."

"Well, you already know that I'm doing what I do at the bequest of the CIA. What you may not know is that Chan was also working undercover for the CIA." Jim winced. "Not to worry. What Chan was working on had nothing to do with you, or your department, or any project at MACV. Chan was investigating Kim's family. He found some very incriminating evidence. We believe that some of that evidence may be in his room. We would like your help in retrieving it. Will you do that?"

"What exactly am I supposed to retrieve?"

Peter repeated to Jim, exactly word for word what Donna had told him she needed.

"What will I say to his roommate as to why I need to search his room?"

"You don't need to lie. I assume the roommate will know that you are Chan's superior officer. You can say he went missing and ask when the roommate last saw him. The roommate may know something that would be helpful. Then, you could say that there was something Chan has that he was supposed to give you on Thursday that you need for a project or a meeting or something."

"When do you want me to do this?"

"How about right now? Let's get it out of the way."

"Would you like to come with me?"

"That would be up to you. As a civilian, I may appear to the roommate as out of place, but if you feel more comfortable with me there, I'm okay with that. You can say I work with you as a computer analyst and we need the documents Chan has for an installation. As far as the film is concerned, you could explain that it might identify where he was, and when, before he disappeared. It's your call."

"I want you to come with me."

"Okay, let's go."

They went to Chan's room. His roommate, Don, let them into the room. Jim introduced him. Don was very cooperative. He also wanted to find out what happened to Chan. He said he thought that Chan had been out all-night Wednesday but snuck back in after six hundred hours. He understood that Chan was going to clean up and go to work. He said that he simply thought that Chan had an all-nighter with his girlfriend, but knew not to ask too many questions. Jim said that Chan told him on Wednesday that he might be late coming to work on Thursday, so that was consistent. They searched Chan's side of the room and found a ten-inch by fourteen-inch brown envelope full of documents and two rolls of undeveloped film. It was in Chan's underwear drawer, just as Donna had said. They also found a very expensive Nikon with a telephoto lens attached on the shelf above where Chan's uniforms hung. Jim said that the uniform Chan would wear to work was not there, implying that he may have left for work on Thursday morning as Don had suggested. Peter wound the film in the Nikon and removed the partially exposed film cartridge. Meanwhile, Jim searched for the miniature Minolta, which he eventually found inside Chan's shirt drawer. Then, Jim asked Don if he wanted to join him later for pocket billiards. Peter was pleased to hear him decline as he was sure that Don would eventually become suspicious and start asking more questions.

We went back to Jim's room where Peter took sole possession of everything they found. He thanked Jim for his help and told him he would see him later. Back in his room, Peter hid the folder, the two rolls of film and the Minolta, in *his* underwear drawer with the intention of reviewing it on Sunday.

That evening, Pete and Jim joined two others. They drank, played pool, cracked jokes, and told stories. They had a good time and got their minds off the perils of war and missing comrades.

12

CHASING THE EVIDENCE— MACV

The next week was Peter's fifth week back. He spent the beginning of the week gathering the hard evidence against the lieutenant. Per Donna's request, they met again the evening of Monday August 7. He gave her everything regarding Chan that he had collected. He pointed out to her that Chan's documents had established a connection between Lieutenant Nguyen and the Pham family. Donna reminded him that he was not supposed to see that. Chan's documents indicated that the Viet Cong had their hooks into every aspect of the South Vietnamese economy and government. Peter wondered how this war could ever be won. He could only imagine the incriminating evidence that Chan had on the film. He wanted to believe that Chan had done his job very well. However, Donna was right. He didn't have a need to know, and he said no more.

"Peter, I want to apologize for my bitchiness on Saturday. I can't blame it on PMS; that was almost two weeks ago. I thought about what you said —that we do our best, and that is all we can expect of ourselves."

"No need to apologize," he replied and smiled. He was pleased that Donna seemed to have come to grips with the Chan situation and was more at peace with herself about it. They both knew that the likelihood of ever seeing Chan again was zero and there was no need to talk further about it.

They then talked about how to get the documented evidence that Peter had on the lieutenant out of the MACV building on Wednesday. Donna told him she would arrange for him to see Colonel Boehner on Wednesday at 1600 hours (4:00 p.m.). Colonel Boehner was responsible for the security of the entire building and SOG located there. He would have an authorization pass that would allow him to take anything he wanted out of the building regardless of its classification level. She told him that she would pick him up at 5:00 p.m. outside the guard gate.

He could not help but ask, "What if Boehner doesn't have such a security pass ready for me at 4:00 p.m.? Should I try to get the documents out of the building anyway?"

"Not unless you want to be caught and charged with espionage."

"Then what? Is there a backup plan?"

"I'm working on it. There will be one if it's needed. I'll let you know if it comes to that. You need to trust me."

"Okay, Donna. You know I trust you."

He figured their business conversation was over, and he was about to remind her of their non-date, when she asked, "Where were you planning to go for dinner afterwards?"

"Is La Paix okay?"

"Perfect!"

****

It was Wednesday August 9. There had been no further communication with Donna, so as instructed, Peter went to Colonel Boehner's office at 4:00 p.m. He hoped to pick up an envelope that contained the appropriate security pass.

Colonel Boehner's office was at the other end of the building. Peter arrived at 4:05 p.m. His gatekeeper was a Sergeant Daley according to his nameplate. "May I help you?" he asked as Peter approached his desk.

"Yes, I'm here to pick up a security pass from Colonel Boehner."

"Please show me your ID," he politely requested.

Peter showed him his MACV ID. Sergeant Daley took a long hard look at it. "Please take a seat Mr. Troutman. I will need your ID for a few minutes but will return it when I come back." As the minutes ticked by, Peter began to feel uneasy. What was taking so long, he wondered.

It was 4:20 p.m. when he finally returned. "Mr. Troutman, Colonel Boehner says that he needs to talk with you." Peter wondered why this would be. His uneasiness increased. Would he require a "Plan B"?

The Sergeant led him into the Colonel's office. Peter could tell from his uniform that he was a Lieutenant Colonel, not a full Colonel. He appeared to be middle aged, but looked lean and tough, leathery skin, the whole thing. The Colonel asked him to take a seat, another indication that this might take a while.

"Is there a problem Colonel?" Peter asked as calmly as he could.

The Colonel spoke in a loud intimidating voice.

"You bet there is son. You don't report to me, and I don't know who you are. I've been asked by the CIA to grant you an unconditional security pass. I got no knowledge as to why I should grant you this, or what information you're trying to take out of here. Your ID indicates you're the equivalent of a Lieutenant, but I see a young scrawny looking civilian with no military experience. Yes, I have a problem!"

Peter was rattled, but did his best not to show it.

"It sounds like you were not thoroughly briefed, sir," Peter said as calmly as he could.

"That being the case, why should I cooperate?" he gruffly responded.

"Colonel, perhaps the 'higher-ups' limited your knowledge in order to protect you. Perhaps it would have been better if the meeting we are having didn't even occur. I think there is a term called 'plausible deniability'."

"Mr. Troutman, I'm responsible for security here. I need you to tell me about the documents you want to remove from these premises," he demanded.

"Colonel, the fact is I'm only a courier," he lied. "I don't know what the documents are, or why the CIA needs them."

"Mr. Troutman, I think you know more than you're saying."

"Colonel, I'll tell you what. Why don't I just bring you the documents? You can see them for yourself. However, I'm expected out of here by seventeen hundred hours, and you really should think about 'plausible deniability'."

"Mr. Troutman, I'm expected to be out of here **before** seventeen hundred hours. You have less than thirty minutes. Bring me the documents!"

"Okay, sir. I'll be back."

Peter didn't know how this would play out, but he had no problem showing him the documents. Whether he would understand what they were, he didn't know, but if it got him the security pass, he didn't care. If he did not get the security pass, he would need to rely on Donna's "Plan B" whatever that was.

All the evidence he had accumulated was in the locked file cabinet in his cubicle. It took him about three minutes to get to his cubical, and another five minutes to transfer the documents into his briefcase, and re-secure his cubicle. It was now 4:45 p.m. He had to get back to Colonel Boehner's office before he left for the day. The plan was that Donna would meet him outside the security gate at 5:00 p.m. sharp. His understanding was that they would drive to the Continental Palace where they would review the evidence, come up with a plan to recommend to her boss, and then go out to dinner. He had less than fifteen minutes to get that security pass, get by the guard, and make it to the street. Time was running out and he was getting nervous.

He took his briefcase with the evidence and ran back to Colonel Boehner's office. He went up to Sergeant Daley and told him that the Colonel wanted to see him again. He hoped for the best.

"Please show me your ID."

"Sergeant, I was just here."

"Protocol, sir."

"Okay here it is. May I see the colonel now?"

"Thank you, Mr. Troutman, but the colonel has left for the day."

Oh crap, Peter's thinking. He didn't make it back in time; now what? He was on the verge of panic. However, the Sergeant kept talking. "The Colonel told me that if you came back, I should give you this envelope." Peter opened the envelope and it contained the needed security pass. He had no idea what happened. Perhaps the colonel thought about "plausible deniability," perhaps he had another call from a higher up, or perhaps he just didn't want to deal with him anymore. It didn't matter. He got what I wanted.

Peter left the building a couple of minutes after five. Lt. Nguyen was still there and noticed his departure. It was starting to rain as he exited the building, a typical storm for that time of year. When he got to the guardhouse, he noticed that the guard on duty was an ARVN, and not the usual marine. He showed the security pass that allowed him to take anything out of the building. Since the pass was all-inclusive, he was surprised when the guard still wanted him to open his briefcase to let him see what was inside. The guard was well armed and Peter was not about to argue. He opened his briefcase. Peter could feel his heart rate increase as the guard rifled through his stuff. The guard noticed he had several computer printouts and documents labeled "Top Secret" but he let Peter pass without further comment. However, right afterward, the guard picked up his phone and made a call.

As Peter approached the street, he looked for Donna. As it was raining, he expected her to drive up in her Jeep. He looked up and down the street but there was no Jeep in sight. His watch said it was now 5:08 p.m. Was he too late? He was starting to consider his options when he heard his name called from across the street. "Mister Peter . . . Mister Peter . . . You Mister Peter?" He noticed a taxicab with a Vietnamese driver calling him from the opened driver's window. Most cabs were either Renaults or VW Beetles. This one was a Renault. The rear windows had privacy curtains and he couldn't see into the cab. His heart began to beat a little faster as he considered the possibility of being kidnapped with highly classified documents in his possession. He walked slowly toward the cab; half expecting thugs with guns to suddenly appear and force him in. Fortunately, that did not happen. He opened the rear door. Donna was on the far side of the seat. He breathed a sigh of relief, climbed in, slid over, and sat alongside of her. She was wearing her business attire. In this case, that meant slacks and a white blouse. She was also wearing glasses and had a briefcase with her. She looked very business-like. They made small talk and he began to relax.

"How was your day?" she asked.

"I had a good day, thank you, but I'm looking forward to our dinner."

"Yes, I am also. I think the going home dinner for Charlie tonight at La Dolce Vita will be just grand."

Peter figured that this chitchat was clearly a diversion for the sake of the cab driver, so he played along. "What do you think of this present I got for Charlie," he asked. "I hope he likes it." As he said this, he opened his briefcase.

"Yes, very nice. I think that he will. Sally has not seen it yet. I can take it to her." Donna opened her briefcase and he transferred the documents from his into hers.

Then Donna said, "I have a card for him," and took a greeting card from her case and handed it to Peter. "Here. Take a look." On the front, it said, "Farewell from the gang." He opened it. Inside he read the following handwritten message:

> Although your move upstairs will leave us at six, your work will prove very valuable to us in unit 314. We wish you farewell Charlie. Thank you.

"Tell me if you think it's appropriate. Do you like it?"

"Yes, I do. I think it's very appropriate." He carefully took notice of the implied message. Of course, Charlie was a name often used to refer to the enemy, and the message was telling him that they should meet in room 314 at six o'clock. Peter thought the subterfuge to be a bit over the top and not necessary, but it amused him. However, he sensed that Donna was also amusing herself with the charade they were playing, including his efforts to play along.

Absent-mindedly, he was about to put the card into his briefcase when Donna reached out and said, "Let me have it back. I'll keep it with the present, and show it to Sally when I see her. Sally and I have a quick errand to do and then we will meet you at six. John has invited us to have cocktails in his suite at six before we go to dinner. Are you okay with that?"

Peter understood her redundant message and responded, "Yes, I'll see you there." Although Donna had never explained to him what was in room 314, he had been curious enough to walk up there one day, and realized that it was more than a dummy mailbox. He had thought it could be a second room for Donna, but her mention of her boss, John, made it clear that it was a room used by the CIA.

Peter didn't think the driver was the wiser about what they were actually doing or saying, because he asked in broken English, "How long you in Saigon? You married?" Donna responded to the driver in Vietnamese.

"What did you tell him?" Peter asked.

"I told him that we were married and had been here with the U.S. Embassy for about a year, and that we were having a going away dinner for one of my co-workers who was promoted and leaving the country."

Then she said something else to the driver in Vietnamese. Again, Peter asked her what she said and why she was speaking in Vietnamese and not

English. She said he was not that fluent in English and may not understand her English.

"I told him to let you out in front of the Continental Palace Hotel, but that I needed him to let me out somewhere else because I needed to meet my friend Sally before the dinner."

The driver drove up to the entrance to the Continental Palace. Peter got out and watched the cab drive off and disappear toward Le Loi. He assumed Donna was going to her apartment. It was still raining. He walked quickly into the Continental Palace. As he walked through the lobby, he noticed a middle-aged Vietnamese man reading a newspaper. He didn't think too much of it at first, but the man seemed to take notice as he walked to the elevator. The man arose and followed him into the elevator along with two other people. He carried a small cigar in his left hand. Two of them, including the Vietnamese man, got out on Peter's floor. As Peter unlocked the door to his room, the Vietnamese man walked slowly past him, on down the hallway and around the corner. The other person entered a room just down the hall. When Peter got into his room, he put his briefcase on the desk and opened it. His briefcase still contained his tools, some blank paper, pencils, and this morning's paper. He removed the paper and tossed it into the trash bin. About the only thing in the paper was the crossword, but he didn't have time for that now.

Then he put the briefcase into the corner where he usually kept it. His room was too warm so he clicked on the window air-conditioner. It was hot and muggy outside and although it had only been about twenty-five minutes since he left work, he was hot and uncomfortable. He remembered the message from Donna. There was not a lot of time. He headed into the bathroom. He needed to freshen up.

****

All prior status meetings with Donna had been in his room. Meeting somewhere else was a first. When he first came to Saigon and she told him her mailbox was number 314, he assumed she stayed at the hotel. After that, he thought she stayed at the Caravelle, but then she told him she had an apartment. Later, after her birthday party, he learned where that was. Then he wondered if she also stayed in room 314. One evening when he had nothing better to do, he had wandered up the stairs and could see that there really was a room 314. Being curious, he had knocked on the door, half expecting Donna would answer. No one had answered.

Now he was about to discover how the room was really used. At five minutes before six, he left his room, locked the door, and walked slowly toward the stairs. Hung, the houseboy for his floor met him along the way and asked, "Where you go for dinner tonight, Mister Peter?" He was a friendly type and they often exchanged pleasantries. Hung assumed he was on his way out to dinner, as that would have been Peter's usual evening behavior at this time. Peter told him he had a date and was going somewhere special tonight. "You have good time, Mister Peter."

Peter knocked on the door of room 314 at precisely 6:00 p.m. Donna opened the door. He immediately noticed her appearance. She was no longer the conservative businesswoman he had talked with in the taxicab. She had changed into a summery flowered dress. The bottom of the dress came just above the knee. The top of the dress was sleeveless and bared her arms, shoulders, and a vee shaped area that dipped down the front of her chest to a point between her breasts. She had a cross on a chain centered near the bottom of the vee. She had applied makeup, she no longer looked like a business executive, and she smelled nice. To Peter she looked very alluring and sexy.

"Donna, you look very nice," he told her.

"Thank you" she replied with a smile.

He entered the room and looked around. He didn't see John. It was clear to him that hotel guests did not stay in this room. The room had no bed, only a large table, and some chairs. The walls appeared to be covered with soundproof material. He noticed that the door through which he entered had an extra lockset. There was a bathroom to his left, but he saw another door far to his right. It also had a special lock on it. So, this is a two-room suite, he concluded. He wondered how this place was used. Was it used as a "safe house?" Did "interrogations" take place here? Was this a CIA sub-station? He could only guess as to what was in the other room. Donna noticed his apprehension.

"Trust me," she said. "We are safe here and so are the documents you gave me. No one can hear us."

"What about John, is he coming?"

"No, he's not. He said he could trust me to handle it."

The two of them sat down at the large table. Donna pulled the documents out of a large shopping bag and set them on top of the table. She had transferred them from her briefcase before bringing them to the hotel. An interesting deception, he thought. She had left the cab looking like a business executive carrying a briefcase, and she came to the hotel looking like an embassy employee's wife that had gone shopping.

They met for about forty-five minutes. He gave her the promised documented rundown that he had recited to her at their meeting on Friday. Then he stepped through the list of supporting evidence that they had, including a chronology of observations that he had made over the past two weeks. His hard evidence included the following:

- The access logs provided to him by Bob Nunn, tracing Nguyen's activity over the past month.
- The database of access authorizations set up by Lt. Nguyen.
- Data change cards that Lt. Nguyen tore up and threw into the trash.
- A computer printout of control and change cards from Lt. Nguyen's trash showing that she had run a program to alter the data before the probability calculations were done.
- Printouts of the correct data files for several weeks.
- Printouts of the incorrect data files for the same weeks.
- A correct set of probability calculations that he had run in his test environment. For the most recent week, it showed that Event 360 had a probability of fifty-five percent.
- An incorrect set of probability calculations for the same weeks that the captain ran against the altered data files.
- Peter's journal showing what he did and what he observed by day.

In addition, Donna provided the following:

- The CIA lab technicians had determined that the fingerprints on the threatening note belonged to Lt. Nguyen.
- The CIA identified the owner of the VW that picked up the lieutenant from work, and determined where he lived. Unfortunately, unless they searched his home and car, they could not prove him to be a co-conspirator.

Finally, if they apprehended the lieutenant on Thursday (tomorrow), it might be possible to catch her with stolen documents taped to her back. If they searched her office and her home, they expected to find other evidence, such as the badge she used to enter the computer room, the data change cards she used to alter the database, and the captain's access codes.

After reviewing the evidence and rehashing prior evidence, Peter and Donna agreed that Lieutenant Nguyen should be arrested and held for questioning. They could also assume that the lieutenant was onto them and might be a threat if she was allowed into the building where she worked. Once the lieutenant was away from the computer room, she would no longer be a threat, either to them or to the computer room. Donna thought that her boss would agree, and that there was enough evidence to convince the National Police to make an arrest, or at least let the CIA detain and question her. According to Donna, the CIA's objective was not only to stop the lieutenant from doing more damage, but also to determine for whom she worked.

Donna said that she would be in contact with her boss regarding tomorrow, and then they would meet with Colonel Abernathy (at the Embassy) Friday morning, and decide what to do next. Peter made a point of saying that he still needed to run reports from prior weeks to show a trend, and that he would need to instruct the captain on how to correctly run reports himself in the future. Peter told Donna that he thought the captain was clean. He chose to remain silent about what the captain had told him regarding his prior intimacy with the lieutenant. Donna instructed Peter to stay home tomorrow, and wait to hear back from her as to when he could meet with the captain. Peter reluctantly agreed.

Peter pulled back the drape covering the window and looked out. It was about 6:45 and already getting dark outside, but the rain had stopped.

"Donna, how do you feel about us riding your bike to dinner?" We were planning to go to a French restaurant called La Pais that was about a mile away to the North. They could have taken a taxi, but Donna enjoyed her bike and Peter enjoyed riding on the back of it.

She walked over to the window beside him. "I think that is a great idea. I was hoping we could take the bike, and in anticipation, I parked it behind the assembly building next door. However, I think we should take our rain ponchos just in case the rain starts up again. Before we go, I need to put these documents into the other room and call my boss on the single side band (SSB) radio to tell him everything is go. It will be a few minutes."

"Okay, no problem. I'll use the bathroom while I'm waiting."

A few moments later, they walked out of room 314 together and went to the stairs. Peter said that he would need to stop in his room on the way down to pick up his poncho. As they entered his room, he noticed that his briefcase was no longer in the corner where he thought he had left it. Nothing else seemed disturbed. The briefcase had vanished! Donna watched him as he looked all over. Peter's confusion was apparent.

"Okay, what's the problem?" she asked.

"My briefcase is gone. The only one that had a room key other than myself was Hung. I think we should find Hung, and ask him who was in the room and who ended up with my briefcase."

"Yes, I agree," she said, "but try to be a bit more diplomatic and less accusatory about it. There may be other possibilities."

They went to his station; he was not there but Peter caught a glimpse of him moving down the hallway. They caught up and intercepted his progress. "Oh Mr. Peter, you back so soon. You have dinner?"

"No, we were delayed, but my lady friend and I need your help with something. Please come to my room to see."

The three of them went into his room and Donna shut the door behind them. Hung was clearly nervous. Since Hung was his houseboy, Donna let Peter take the lead. Peter pretty much ignored what Donna said about being diplomatic and got right to the point.

"Hung, here is my problem. My briefcase is gone and we know that you are the only one besides me that has a key to my room. My key is right here." Peter pulled his key from his pocket and waved it in front of his face. "I want to know who has my briefcase!"

"Mr. Peter I no tell."

"Hung, I will give you two choices. You can tell me everything you know, and if you do, I will give you three thousand dong and we would still be friends. Your other choice is to remain silent. If you do that, I will report you, accuse you of theft, and you will lose your job and all the tips that go with it."

As Peter said this, he could see Donna cringing, but Peter knew that what motivated Hung was money, friendship, and authority—probably in that order. Fortunately, Hung made the right choice.

"Okay Mr. Peter, I tell you. A man come to my station and said he wants to borrow key for ten minutes. I stay at my station and not see what he did. I not know he take your briefcase."

"Hung, how much money did he pay you for that?"

"No money."

"Hung, if he paid you no money then why did you give him the key?"

"I sorry Mr. Peter. He say he police. The man show me badge."

After that, Hung gave Peter a description of the man. It sounded to Peter like the man that followed him up the elevator and past his room a little over an hour ago. Peter remembered that the man he saw smoked, so he asked, "Hung, did this man smoke?"

"Yes" he smoke big cigarette." Peter thanked Hung for his help, gave him the promised currency, and let him go back to his station. Then he and Donna discussed the implications of this new development.

First, Peter started, "Does this mean that there may be a link between Nguyen and the police? Could they be working together?"

He guessed he was stating the obvious, because Donna all but ignored that question, and then asked, "Was the briefcase locked?"

"Yes."

"What was in the briefcase that could be useful to the thief?"

He thought for a moment before he remembered. "Unfortunately, I left an entry badge in there—the one that allows access to the basement where the computers are." Then, he remembered something else. "When we left MACV the guard took extra notice of the contents of my briefcase, and then appeared to make a phone call as I entered the taxi. The guard could be in on it." They both looked at each other and simultaneously realized the possibility of someone being able to enter the building and the computer area, and then setting off a bomb. "No, wait," Peter said. "Isn't it more likely they were going after the documents, and may not even be aware of the badge until after they open the case? And besides, won't Nguyen be interrogated before they would have enough time to plan an attack using someone other than Nguyen?"

"Maybe," Donna responded, "but what happens when they open the case and find no documents? Will they come back here to look for them, and try to get you to tell what you did with them?"

"I hope not, and I don't think so. I think they'll realize that the CIA already has them. And I think they'll realize that Lieutenant Nguyen is about to be arrested. Perhaps they'll try to prevent that."

"Maybe, but one thing is for sure; I must report this to my boss. I need to go back upstairs and use the secure SSB radio phone again."

"Okay, I'll wait for you in the lobby."

She was about to leave the room, when she turned toward him with an inquisitive look. "You just gave Hung three thousand dong. Do you still have enough for dinner?"

"Oh, damn! I guess I wasn't thinking, was I."

Donna suppressed a giggle, as she continued to look at him. It was humorous, and they both laughed.

"You can relax, I have it covered. Uncle Sam should pay for this. I have access to piastre (money) upstairs in our safe. It's intended for times like this. I'll meet you in the lobby."

Peter grabbed his poncho and they left.

13

A NON-DATE

Peter waited in the lobby while Donna went upstairs to talk with her boss about the implications of his stolen briefcase. She returned ten minutes later. His watch said it was already 7:20 and their dinner reservation was for 7:30. They would be late.

Donna had parked her bike next to the National Assembly building, not far from the hotel entrance.

"How did it go with your boss?" he asked as they walked.

"He thanked me for the update, told me not to worry, and said I should enjoy my evening."

Before they got onto her bike, Donna turned to Peter and handed him a fat envelope. "Here, put this into your pocket." He did so without opening it. He assumed it was reimbursement for the money he had given Hung.

Then she added, "I want to apologize for putting you at risk." She seemed genuinely concerned.

"Not a problem."

"I also want you to know I thought you did a masterful job of handling the situation with Hung. It was not as diplomatic as it could have been, but it was effective."

"Forget it. If okay with you, I would like us to put it aside for now and enjoy a nice dinner and each other's company—no more business talk for the remainder of the evening. Besides, I'm getting hungry."

"Not a problem, just don't get grouchy."

They unchained her bike, removed the rain cover, and secured it to the luggage rack. La Paix was in the Da Kao section of the city. They sped off on her bike up Hai Ba Trung and then North on Bai Lo Thong Nhat toward La Paix on Dinh Tien Hoang. The streets got darker as they left the downtown area, and it was starting to drizzle again, not what he had hoped for. Fortunately, the restaurant was no more than a mile away, so they didn't get very wet. Peter had never been to this restaurant, but knew of it from the time that Bob had taken him out on the town to a restaurant and nightclub just down the road.

The French name for the restaurant was La Paix. To the Vietnamese, it was Hoa Binh. Either way it meant "peace." Their reservation was for 7:30 and they arrived about fifteen minutes late, but the maître de was very nice about it. After exchanging *bonjours,* they were shown to their table and seated. The dining room was small with only a few patrons. That was good because they could talk, without shouting at each other. The tables were covered with white linen tablecloths. The walls had prints of Monets, or were they Manets? Peter never knew, but they made for a pleasant atmosphere.

As they sat down, Peter ordered them each a glass of Beaujolais. They toasted to what they thought would be the completion of a successful mission and started to relax. The menu was in French and Vietnamese. They each knew some French and Donna knew some Vietnamese, but they ended up keeping it simple. They shared the *hors de oeuvre de jour.* It consisted of breads, cheeses, pates, and something else. It went well with the wine.

For the main course, Donna ordered *coc au vin.* According to the menu, it came with *pomme de terre sautéed avec buerre, et petis pois.* Peter thought that meant chicken cooked in wine with boiled potatoes sautéed in butter and small peas. For himself, he ordered the boeuf bourguignon, or beef burgundy. The beef burgundy included mushrooms, onions, bacon, and carrots. It was served in the center of a large plate and surrounded by boiled potatoes. Parsley was sprinkled on top. They say presentation is everything, but this was the most delicious meal he had the entire time he was in Saigon. The portions for their meals were more than generous. Of course, they each had a second glass of wine with the main dish. They shared an éclair for dessert. The sharing was almost a necessity because after the meal they were "stuffed."

****

Their dinner conversation at La Paix was not only about the food and the view out the window (raining again), but they also talked about John and Linda, Donna's experience with men and dating, about trust, religion, her family, his family, etc.

"Donna, last week you told me that Linda and John had split, and she had gone back to the States. What happened?"

"Well, it seems that John had an eye for other women. One day, she found him in his office with the house cleaner. He denied anything was going on, but she says she knew otherwise. Although he told her the encounter was meaningless, and that he loved her, she just could not handle it anymore."

"At your birthday party, John told me the same thing he told Linda and I believed him. I believe he still loves her. However, if he was doing it right under her nose that was too much, I think. I don't blame her for leaving. Do you think they'll get back together?"

"I don't know. I try to keep in touch, but John is still my project boss. The truth is, I really can't blame him all that much either. I would never get involved with him for various reasons, but I can understand his situation somewhat, and I have not lost respect for him."

Peter asked Donna about her family growing up. "My father was born in Italy, came here in the nineteen twenties, and became a naturalized citizen. He enlisted in the Army Corps of Engineers and was a veteran of World War II. He was hard working and operated a construction company." Peter didn't say anything, but he was quite sure after Donna spoke of her father, that Donna's last name was not Rice. She continued, "My mother worked at the medical facility in Bethesda Maryland. That's where they met and were married before he joined the war effort."

"Did you go to high school in Bethesda?"

"Yes, but it was a Catholic high school. My mother and father were both very Catholic."

"Did you date when you were in high school?" He wanted to know.

"My father was leery of boys, and when I finally had a steady boyfriend, my mother was always afraid that I might be sinning. She made me go to confession once per month. Meanwhile my parents gave unlimited freedom to my younger brother Brian. Unfortunately, Brian died in a car crash seven years ago, his senior year in *public* high school."

"That sounds terrible, Donna. I'm sorry."

"I still think of him, and sometimes I wonder if I had been given the same freedoms, could it have been me. After that, my mom was not the same, and I don't think my mom and dad were intimate any more. I think that maybe my mom blamed him. I think my dad may have a girlfriend on the side, but if true, he keeps it quiet. I cannot blame him; I think he deserves more from mom."

Then she quickly looked up at Peter and put on her cheery face. "You probably don't want to hear all of this. Tell me about *your* family."

"Sure. I grew up in Hyattsville Maryland, not very far from Bethesda. In fact, my father worked in Bethesda for a while. He was an office manager for a trade association. When I was fifteen my family moved to Massachusetts, but left me behind living with a friend, so I could finish the school year. My two brothers and I were always given a lot of freedom, but this was the most I had ever had. That was when I started dating and had a regular girlfriend. To be honest, I had no idea what I was doing, sexually or otherwise. The otherwise included a night drinking beer with friends of my friend, and riding around in a souped-up car doing mischief. The good news is that I survived, stayed out of jail, and learned a lot."

"Have you done anything wild while in Saigon?"

"Nothing I would call wild," he told her, "But I did spend some time with the captain and with Bob, the IBM rep. Neither was particularly wild though. The captain took me bowling one weekend, apparently to the only bowling alley in Saigon. It was up near the Tao Dan Park where we went. He said he missed doing that. You know about the USO show that we attended, and the captain and I often had lunch and sometimes dinner together. A couple of times he invited me over to the Rex to listen to bands that played there. Rather normal activities I would say.

"Now Bob on the other hand is something else. Bob lives the stereotypical bachelor life. The Friday night before your birthday party, Bob and I went to La Cigale, just down the road from here, and then to another club in town. We met two local Vietnamese women. I think he knew the one, but she had brought a friend. They offered to spend the night with us and make us very happy. Apparently, the friend would have spent the night with me for less than what it would cost to buy an umbrella on a rainy day in Saigon. That was about two thousand dong, expensive for an umbrella, but cheap for a prostitute."

"And did you?" She wanted to know.

"Absolutely not! I was not interested. I know Bob would have though, if he had not been with me. However, I did hear him tell his friend that he would see her the next night. Bob is somewhat of a womanizer, but I give him credit for understanding my wishes. He did not abandon me."

"Peter, after you got the information from Chan's room this past Saturday, didn't you go out with the guys? You never told me about what you did."

"Oh, yes, that's right. We went over to the USO and played pool and ping-pong. Of course, there were only three of us and not four as originally planned so we had to take turns at ping-pong, and we played a lot of eight ball. Jim is a very good pool player. He went through an entire rack before I even got my turn. By the way, the two of you have something in common."

"What's that?"

"You're both left-handed."

Peter looked across the table at her. He noticed she seemed far away. "Donna, you okay?"

"I'm sorry. I was thinking of Chan."

"You know, if you want to talk about it, I'm willing to listen."

"Well, I did talk to John. He told me it was not my fault and gave me an analogy to an officer in charge of troops in battle. He said that the officer is required to make a judgement and give battle orders that the men are required to carry out. Invariably some of those men will lose their lives. The officer is doing his job; he can't blame himself. In my case, Chan did what he did at his own discretion. However, it still saddens me. Peter, I do appreciate your offer, but I'm dealing with it. I'll be fine."

"Well, the offer still stands if you should change your mind. Okay?"

"Okay."

"So, I just told you about my wild date with Bob. What about you? Have you had any wild dates lately?"

"No. I really don't go out much."

"Why not?"

"I think my jobs have a lot to do with it. Both of my jobs have kept me very busy, and I'm not really into the club scene. Aside from the fiasco I told you about two weeks ago, I have had only two dates in the past year, both of which were disappointing to me. I think I already told you about my bad experience at the REX. Most of the military men here seem to be looking for only one thing. They buy you dinner and they expect sex in return. Peter, I hope you're not going to be like that tonight."

"Don't worry Donna. I don't expect anything, and besides," he jokingly reminded her, "You're Catholic, and I'm married."

"Do you think that's enough of an excuse?" she quipped. Perhaps Donna was hinting that she wished things were different. Peter began to wonder if he secretly wished the same.

He had tried very hard to keep his relationship with Donna much the same as his relationship with the captain. Both had some authority over him, but both allowed him to speak freely and actually listened to what he had to say. He had gotten to know both the captain and Donna as colleagues and they certainly enjoyed working together.

With respect to Donna, however, he also enjoyed the "xe om" tours of Saigon that she had given him on her bike. After that first ride, they sometimes joked about his holding on while riding on the back of her bike, but that relationship was more like a tour guide and tourist. It was no different than if she had been a six-foot-tall man. (Well, almost no difference). They had become friends and, except for that situation at John and Linda's dinner party in March, there had never been anything sexual going on between them, or at least it was not apparent. However, tonight, he felt that he and Donna were getting to know each other on a more personal level than they had in the past. Perhaps it was the wine, or the romantic setting but he secretly wondered if this would be a turning point in their relationship.

He paid the bill; it was less than four thousand dong, including a tip, or between thirty and forty U.S. dollars, depending on which rate of exchange you assumed. They waited for the rain to stop and left La Paix at about 9:45 p.m. As they stepped outside, they realized that it was still drizzling but the temperature had cooled down significantly. They put on their ponchos and set off to retrace their route back to the National Assembly Building.

The roads were wet, and pools of water remained in some places. They were probably moving at about twenty-five miles per hour along Thong Nhat. Before they got back to Hai Ba Trung, they came to a cross street.

As they approached the intersection, a car passed them and then made a sharp right turn passing in front of them and cutting them off. Donna reacted quickly but instinctively by putting on the brakes and veering to her right. The rear of the car just missed clipping them as it sped off down the road to the right. Unfortunately, Donna's reaction combined with the wet roadway set the bike into a slide. The bike went sideways and horizontal to the ground all at once with the rear of the bike shooting out faster than the front. Peter reacted by pushing his hands down on the seat and extracting his right leg from under the bike before it hit the pavement. He then went into a slide on the pavement much like sliding into home plate. He could feel a burn on his leg as he slid and finally came to a sitting position on the pavement.

He sat dazed for a moment, but then looked over to Donna. She was also separated from the bike, but she was on her right side with her arm underneath of her. He was able to stumble over to Donna without feeling too much pain. He put his right hand on her left shoulder. "Donna, are you okay? Say something."

"I think I hurt my wrist."

"Can you sit up?"

He helped her to sit up and looked at the expression on her face. She was clearly in pain. "Can you tell me if you're hurting anywhere else?" She put her head on his shoulder as she said, "I don't think so."

"Let me see your wrist." The night was dark, but he wanted to get an idea how bad it was. She put her right hand across her lap and he gently put his hand around her wrist. "Try to move your hand."

She tried. "It hurts," she whimpered.

"I don't feel that your bone is out of place. I hope that it's only a bad sprain, but we need more light. Give yourself a moment and then see if you can get to your feet." She held on to him and pulled herself up. As she did so, she commented that she might have banged up her right leg too.

"Can you walk?"

"Yes, I think my leg is just scraped."

Meanwhile, another biker had stopped. His rider jumped off, and was up-righting Donna's bike. He asked if they were hurt. Donna spoke first and with conviction. "Thank you but I think we will be fine."

Peter limped over to check out the bike. It didn't seem to be too badly damaged. The light was dim, but he could see that the air deflector shroud was cracked, and the right side of the seat was abraded and torn. By this time, Donna had made it over to the bike as well. They were both suspicious of the "good Samaritans." Were they "cowboys" intent on taking advantage of the situation? "We are good. Thanks for stopping," Peter said as strongly as he could muster. Our demeanor and towering presence may have been enough. Our "Samaritans" returned to their bike.

"Peter, I don't think I can operate the throttle with this wrist."

"Not a problem, it's my turn to drive, if you can hold on with your left hand."

He got onto the bike and kicked the starter. Fortunately, it started right up. As he tried to place his right foot onto the footrest, he realized that the footrest had broken. Donna got on behind him, while the other two bikers watched. Then seeing that their help was not needed, they sped off up the street to the right.

Peter went very slowly, but got them another four blocks with no issues. As they approached the rear of the National Assembly Building, Peter felt a tug on his left side. "Peter, please take us to my place. You remember where it is, don't you?"

"Yes of course," he said, disappointed that she didn't want to go to his place.

So, he continued past his hotel, went up Le Loi, turned right onto Nguyen Hue, and entered a small parking area near the door of her building. Then he heard, "Ride the bike right up to the door. We can bring it inside."

He shut down the engine and they dismounted right outside the door. In the dim light from an overhead lamp, he noticed that in addition to her wrist, she had really messed up her dress and possibly her leg. He saw blood drops on her right shoe. He felt concerned and wanted to be sure that she would be okay. "Please let me see you to your apartment. We can take a better look at your wrist and get some ice for it."

"Okay, I would like that."

At Donna's request, he brought the bike inside the door and secured it in a vestibule area inside the doorway apparently intended for that purpose. Two other bikes were already there. "Is there an elevator?"

"It's down the hall but not working."

They had no choice. They slowly walked (limped might be a better description) up two flights of stairs and entered the living room of her apartment. The apartment was small, but it had a kitchen, a living room, a bedroom, and a bathroom. He went to get some ice from her refrigerator's freezer as she made it to the bathroom. As he made his way through the living room toward the kitchen, he could not help but notice an exercise mat and dumb-bells in one corner of the room. She obviously kept herself fit. When he returned to the bathroom with the ice, he found her sitting on the edge of the tub with her right leg in the tub and her left leg out. She had pulled her muddied dress up above her knee and she was struggling to clean the blood and debris from her right leg with her left arm. Her injured right wrist was across her lap. He set the ice tray in the sink and tried to help with her leg. As he used the washcloth and the water sprayer, she rested her left hand on his shoulder. He touched her leg just above the knee while observing her muddied dress. As he did so, she winced.

"I'm sorry about your dress. You really looked pretty tonight."

"Peter, you're not going to get fresh with me, are you?"

"I'm trying my best not to." She chuckled a little. "But you may want to look at your thigh if you have not already done so. Please let me have a look at your wrist." He could see it was swelling and beginning to turn bluish. He dampened a washcloth with cold water and wrapped it around her wrist. He then put some ice in a hand towel and suggested she hold it against the washcloth, which she did willingly.

"Donna, I would like to suggest that you visit a medical center in the morning."

"I hate hospitals," she replied.

"Well, I'm with you on that, but they can verify that your wrist is not fractured. They can demobilize the wrist so that you won't injure it further every time you move, and they can do something about the pain. Please, do that," he insisted.

"Alright, I will. I really made a mess of our evening, didn't I?"

"It's okay; not your fault."

At this point, she started to cry. He gently put his hand on the side of her face and looked into her eyes. "Your wrist hurts, doesn't it?"

"Yes."

"Is that why you're crying?"

"No."

"Why are you crying?"

She put her head on his shoulder and pulled closer before answering. "Because I like you. I wish you weren't married."

Peter should have known that this could be coming but somehow it surprised him. He was not sure what to say, but responded, "I like you too," which he suddenly began to realize was true, in more ways than he had originally thought.

"Donna, I need to go, but I want you to promise me that I will hear from you before tomorrow night. I want to know how you are, but I also need to know what is expected of me on Friday. In the meantime, I'll be around if you need me or want to talk." As she started to pull away, he pulled her back and kissed her on the forehead. He then stood up and let himself out.

Peter limped over to the Continental Palace and made it back to his room by 11:30 p.m. He later learned that curfew was now 11:00 p.m. and not midnight as he had thought. Fortunately, no one stopped him.

He used the bathroom, cleaned up, took two aspirins, and undressed for bed. As he removed his pants from his burning leg, he could see that the entire upper part of his thigh was reddened and bruised. He could not help but wonder what Donna's upper thigh looked like. Images of the accident scene raced through his head. He realized how lucky they were that the roads were wet and they were wearing their plastic ponchos as they slid. Their injuries could have been much worse otherwise. With those thoughts in mind, he fell into a sound sleep.

14

ASSASSINATION

When Peter woke up the next morning, his first thought was that he had overslept and would be late for work. Then he remembered that Donna had advised him to stay home. He slipped out of bed, and as he got to his feet, he could feel the pain in his right leg, another reminder of what had transpired the night before. He looked at the clock; it was 8:00 a.m. He showered, brushed his teeth, and began to think about what he would do all day. He wondered what Donna would be doing and what the captain would be thinking when he didn't show up at work. What the hell, he told himself, he should just relax.

He went downstairs, got some fruit, and decided to take a short walk. The sun was out and the temperature was still below 80 degrees F. He remembered that he was running low on dong. Donna had reimbursed him for the money he gave to Hung, but he had spent it on dinner. So, he went to the nearby bank and replenished his stash. Although he knew he might be leaving the country in a week, he was not concerned about being stuck with dong. The embassy had assured him that they would give him the opportunity to change everything back to dollars before leaving the country. His leg was bruised, but it felt less stiff after he walked. He returned to his room and hid the excess dong that would not fit into his wallet.

Later, he went over to the Givral for a late lunch. As he arrived and seated himself, he noticed that Han was catering to two men at another table. When Han noticed him, she came over and said hello to him in English. Her English had improved considerably since he first met her.

They engaged in conversation. "Han, I notice that your English has improved considerably"

"Yes," she said. "Donna has been helping me to learn. By the way, do you know where Donna is today? She promised she would stop by but I have not seen her."

He considered answering her directly. He wanted to tell Han about their misfortune the night before, and explain why Donna had not kept her promise to stop by. However, he took another look at the two men she was talking with at the other table. He sensed that they were glancing over at them and showing some unexplained interest. One of them fit the description of the man with the cigar that he saw in the Hotel yesterday evening. He was middle-aged, Vietnamese, and smoking a small cigar. Was he the same person that asked Hung for the key? The man seemed to show a particular interest. After looking in his direction, he had turned to the other man and said something. Then the other man had turned to have a gander and reported back to him. Peter wondered if they had asked Han to get information from him.

"Han, I have not heard from Donna today, and I have no idea where she is." Then he asked her a question. "Han, I am curious, who are those two men at the other table? They look familiar to me."

"Pham Xuân Ãn is a reporter for Time," she responded. "You have probably seen him at your hotel because Time has an office over there." *[After the war was over, Peter learned that he was a top spy for North Vietnam.]* "The other gentleman is a National Police Inspector. The two of them come here often."

"Han, do you know the Inspector's name?"

What Peter heard was, "Yes, he is Inspector Dran."

This information raised alarms in Peter's mind, but he didn't know what to do about it. Although he was suspicious, he could not be sure that the police inspector at the other table was the same man that took his briefcase. Peter decided that at least he could get a warning to Donna as to the possibilities about what he saw. He thought about walking to Donna's apartment, but decided the better of it. The inspector had noticed him. Suppose he was the one that took his briefcase and followed him to see who his contact was. Instead, Peter decided to write a note. After finishing lunch, he wrote a note, and had it put into Donna's mail slot at the Continental Palace.

Donna – I had lunch at Givral…Saw a middle-aged Vietnamese Police Inspector having lunch with a Time Magazine reporter. The police Inspector smoked a cigar, and seemed to fit the description of the man I saw in the corridor yesterday before I came to the third floor. He may be the same man that stole my briefcase. Han pronounced his name as Dran. (??) –Peter

He knew it was weak, but it was all he had. Unfortunately, other than the cigar, he could not think of any particularly distinguishing features that the man exhibited. However, Han pronounced his name as *Dran*. Perhaps the name could be traced.

Then, Peter returned to his room. He finished reading "The Quiet American," and fell asleep. Around 6:00 p.m., he started getting hungry again and went down to the lobby. He was not sure where he was going to eat. As he passed the desk, he heard his name. "Mr. Troutman, there is a message here for you." The attendant removed an envelope from his mail slot and handed it to him. It was a note from Donna.

Peter, Nguyen is out of the way … OK to talk with the captain … Possible stress fracture … Bad sprain … Wearing a light cast to limit motion … Bike in the shop. P.S. Got your note.

With that, Peter decided to walk over to the Rex for supper. Perhaps he would see the captain. He waited in the buffet line, got his meal, and started looking for a table. As he did so, he spotted the captain sitting alone on the far side of the room. The captain noticed him and motioned for him to come over. "Captain, may I join you?"

"Have a seat. You're limping. What happened to you?"

"Donna and I had a spill on her bike last night. I have a bruised and scraped-up leg . . . nothing serious. Donna got scraped-up, but also has a badly sprained wrist."

"Sorry to hear that. Glad it was not worse."

Changing the subject, Peter asked him, "How did things go at work today?"

"Lieutenant Nguyen was not at work this afternoon. She went out at lunch, but never made it back. I got a call from Donna around thirteen-thirty hours asking if I knew where she might be. I thought that was strange. Do you know anything about that?" Peter's face revealed surprise. "Peter, you seem surprised."

"Yes, I am. The plan was for someone to follow Nguyen after she left work at lunch and then have her arrested by The National Police. After she was in custody, they were supposed to notify the CIA. The CIA wanted to interrogate her to discover who she was working with. Donna knew the plan, so I don't know why she would have called you to find out where Nguyen was, unless something went awry."

"I'm in the dark here. I knew you were suspicious of Nguyen, but I didn't know they were about to arrest her. What did she do?"

"Captain, Donna gave me the green light to give you a briefing tomorrow at our status meeting. I'm prepared to detail everything I discovered and passed on to her."

"Peter, I have a meeting with Colonel Abernathy first thing in the morning. I don't know what to expect. I would like some input now if you can provide it."

"Well, let me try to summarize then. I can give you more detail tomorrow. Every week, Nguyen stole your reports that described the PEN network and the events contained in that network. I'm talking about the Event Description Files that she was not authorized to have. She got those reports out of your special printout box by entering the raised floor area and taking them from inside. As you know, these events included actions planned by the National Liberation Front (NLF) and the North Vietnamese Army (NVA). They also included counteractions planned by the Army of the Republic of Vietnam (ARVN) and the United States (US). She also stole the reports that portrayed the *true* likelihood of those events occurring, reports that she kept hidden from you. She passed these documents on to the NLF leadership.

"Nguyen then manipulated the data and reran the calculations to make it look like the NLF/NVA actions had a lower likelihood of occurring. The manipulated results were on the reports that you received. That lowered the perceived need for you and your associates to plan counter-actions by the ARVN/US."

"Peter, what if Nguyen reveals her relationship with me or even directly tries to implicate me? If she were to implicate me, even falsely, it could really screw up my career. Once again, I swear I had no knowledge that she was an agent for the NLF. I also have no recollection of how she may have used me. I never gave her information that she was not supposed to have."

"Captain, I do need to ask you this. Although it would have been unintentional on your part, is it possible that you may have revealed to Nguyen that Donna worked for the CIA?" (Peter was still pondering the question that the captain asked as to why Donna had called him earlier.)

"Jeez, I don't know when or how. I'm beginning to feel foolish like I've been played, but I cannot for the life of me explain what Nguyen may have gotten from me."

"Well, Nguyen may have initiated a relationship with you to keep you from being suspicious of her. Try not to beat yourself up over this"

"You said you would not say anything to Donna about me and Dee."

"I kept my word. I cannot speak for the CIA, but if you were under suspicion, I don't think Donna would have allowed me to talk with you."

"I hope you're right. You and I should talk more after I return from my meeting with the Colonel."

****

The next morning, Peter was up early. On the way to the café across the street, he picked up a newspaper. He could not believe what he read.

VIETNAMESE WAFC LIEUTENANT NGUYEN CHI SHOT IN THE HEAD

There was a picture of a body. It was Lieutenant Nguyen. The article went on to suggest that the CIA had done this. Peter's blood ran cold. Donna's note had said, "Nguyen is out of the way." Could Donna have done this? After all, she was a certified sharpshooter. No way, she would never have done that, he thought! Could the captain have done this? He had a lot to lose if he was a co-conspirator. However. Donna had said it was okay to talk with him. No! No! He did not believe either of them could have done this.

He no longer felt hungry and he decided to skip breakfast. He walked to work that morning. Fortunately, he still had his credentials to get into the building—in his wallet. Once inside, he went directly to Danny's desk. "Danny, I need to see the captain as soon as he gets into work. He is expecting me to meet with him. In the meantime, I'll be in my cubicle. Would you mind calling me to let me know when he arrives?"

"Yes of course, not a problem."

Peter started to head for his cubicle when he remembered that his badge to the downstairs had been stolen. He went back to Danny's desk. "Danny, I just realized I have forgotten my badge this morning. Can you give me a temporary one to use?"

"Okay, but I need for you to sign something first."

Peter signed the appropriate form, headed for his cubicle, and waited for Danny to call him when the captain arrived. Danny called him around 10:00 a.m. He climbed the stairs, thanked Danny, went into the captain's office, and shut the door. The captain was sitting at his desk sipping on a cup of coffee. "Did you see the morning paper?" Peter asked.

"Yes," he responded. "Do you think the CIA did this?"

"I hope not. They wanted to interrogate her. It would not have made sense for them to do it. I was instructed to give you the details of the evidence that I found against Nguyen, and then to instruct you on how to run correct reports yourself in the future. I'll be here today and the early part of next week. I'll ask Jim to re-copy all the data files with the correct data, and then I'll run PEN reports for all weeks with the corrected data, including probability trend reports for the target events."

Peter then gave the captain a documented and detailed version of the case against Nguyen, so that he would understand exactly what she had done and how she did it. However, he didn't tell him about the evidence he had illegally obtained from Bob. He did tell him about the stolen briefcase and why he needed a temporary badge to the basement.

"Captain, I'm sorry it worked out this way; I know you and Dee were close. Are we good?"

"We are, Peter. You did what you had to do and you did it well. I appreciate your protecting me and my team."

****

That evening, Peter treated himself to a dinner at La Dolce Vita, below the Continental Palace. It was excellent. He took a short walk afterwards and was back in his room by nine. He had finished writing postcards to various family members and was preparing for bed. He had changed into a tee shirt and black pajama bottoms, and had just brushed his teeth, when he heard a knock at his door. It was late; his watch said 9:45 p.m. He wasn't expecting anyone. So, he walked to the door and before he opened it, he asked, "Who is it?"

"Peter . . . it's Donna . . . may I come in? I need someone to talk to."

Her voice was unsteady and she seemed upset. Before opening the door, Peter quickly checked himself and decided that he was adequately clothed. Standing in the dimly lit hallway, she looked gorgeous, but something seemed off. She was wearing a flowing knee length dress with a halter-top, which bared her arms and shoulders. She seemed to have on makeup. She was carrying a shoulder bag. As usual, the strap was on her right shoulder and the bag hung along her left side. However, the bag was much larger than normal. The lower part of her right arm was in a brace. The image was incongruous and she seemed agitated. He invited her in. She entered the room and he closed and locked the door behind her.

"Here, let me take your bag. It looks heavy."

He helped her remove the bag from around her neck and set it against the wall next to the armoire. Then, he turned toward her and put his hands on her shoulders as they stood near the door. He could see that her mascara had run, a sign that she had been crying. "Donna, you're upset. What's wrong?" He could not help but wonder if she had had another disappointing date.

She looked directly at him. "I killed someone," she said in a very matter of fact way. "I'm having trouble dealing with it."

Her words rattled him, but he regained his composure and spoke. "Uh . . . Please, come sit over here on the sofa."

He slowly escorted her to the sofa. She perched herself on the front edge of the cushion with her body bent forward. He knelt on the floor in front of her and brushed his hands lightly across the sides of her face.

"Donna, tell me what happened. Did you kill Lieutenant Nguyen?"

She looked at him with some surprise. "No!" she said emphatically.

"Then who did you kill?" he asked.

"I killed Inspector Trang of the National Police!"

For a moment, he was speechless. All he could muster was "Wow!" He needed time for it to sink in. "Donna, let me pour us a brandy. It will help you relax." He didn't say it, but he thought he needed a brandy as much as she did. He got up and went over to the armoire and pulled down a pint-sized bottle of brandy and two plastic cups from the top shelf. He poured two brandies, and set the cups on the coffee table in front of the sofa. Then he planted himself on the floor in front of Donna with his back resting against the side of the table.

"Please, tell me what happened."

Donna then began to recount the details of the events that ended with her killing Inspector Trang of the National Police.

"My boss had a close working relationship with a commissioner at the National Police headquarters in Saigon and they had arranged to tail Nguyen when she left the Pasteur building at noon yesterday. They were supposed to call us after the arrest was made. However, they never called us, so I called the captain to find out what I could, and my boss called his contact at the National Police. The captain said that Nguyen went out for lunch but had not returned. The Commissioner told my boss he had not received any feedback yet, but would let us know when he did." Donna paused to sip her brandy.

"A short time later, the Commissioner called my boss back and told him that there had been a problem. He gave us an address in Cholon with instructions to go there. When my boss and I arrived, there were police vehicles and police officers everywhere. The police were asking questions and interviewing people. My boss showed credentials and we were admitted into the home. I saw the body. Nguyen had a bullet to the forehead. She was definitely executed." Donna paused and took another sip of brandy.

"The police on the scene said that they had followed a black VW to the location, and that both the driver and Nguyen had entered the home. When the police went in, they found Nguyen dead, and the driver had disappeared. The police impounded the VW, the same VW you had described, but we weren't able to determine the owner. I spent the rest of the day with my boss talking with people and doing our own investigation. No one saw anything."

"Then what?" Peter asked.

"Then this morning I got a call from my boss saying that an Inspector Trang had a lead. We both went to the police headquarters and talked to him. Trang was a plain-clothes police inspector. According to Trang, they thought they had discovered who the driver of the VW was. He was either a suspect or a witness but had yet to be located. Later in the day, I got a call from Trang. He said he discovered where the suspect lived and I could tag along with him when he went to question him. He said that my boss had agreed. According to Trang, the person of interest would not be home until 6:00 p.m., so he would pick me up around 5:30 in front of the square."

Another pause as she seemed to be searching her memory. This time Peter had a sip of brandy.

"So, did Trang pick you up?" Peter asked.

"Trang picked me up as planned and we then drove to a home in Cholon. Trang smoked a small cigar in the car on the way, something I found annoying. When we arrived, he squashed the butt into the ashtray in front of me and we got out. We walked up a flight of stairs and knocked. No answer, but we could hear someone inside. Trang broke open the door and we entered. As we entered, a young Vietnamese man aimed a gun at us and shouted something in Vietnamese. He got off a shot that missed us. Before he could fire a second shot, Trang fired back, hitting him in the stomach. The man fell backward into a sitting position and looked like he was going to fire again, but Trang shot him again, this time in the head. He fell back dead onto his back. His gun hit the floor and dislodged from his right hand. Trang walked over to him, holstering his own gun as he did so. Trang reached the body, and was about to bend over and retrieve the man's revolver when everything suddenly clicked in my head." Donna had another sip of her brandy before she continued.

"I don't know if these were conscious thoughts or just instincts, but they all weighed on my judgement. Picking up a gun and disturbing a crime scene was not proper protocol. I originally thought that what I heard the man shout 'I want to kill you' in Vietnamese. I now realized that what he really said was 'you want to kill me'. . . The scent of the small cigar was like the faint scent I detected in your room on Wednesday evening; Hung had said the police officer he saw smoked a 'big cigarette'. . . I remembered your note. 'Trang' could be heard as 'Darn'. . . It was unlike my boss to have agreed to my going with him without notifying me. . . I thought it unusual that a national police inspector would not have another police officer with him. . . And how did Trang know where to pick me up?"

They sipped more brandy.

"I had my small shoulder bag with me, not the large one over there. I quickly and quietly removed my Colt 45 and took off the safety. Yes, Peter, I told you I sometimes carry a gun. Before leaving, I debated whether to bring it but I'm glad I did. I had preloaded it before I left home, and the hammer was already back and ready to fire. I don't think Trang knew I had it, and he probably didn't think I could fire a gun anyway given his earlier comment about my wrist. I'm glad I'm left-handed. . ."

After another sip of Brandy, she continued. "Meanwhile, Trang picked up the revolver from the floor. Then he quickly turned toward me and pointed the gun right at me. We both fired almost at the same time, but mine was a split-second sooner. His shot missed, but not by much. My shot hit him in the head. He fell back. The gun fell from his hand as his head landed on top of the unidentified man already on the floor. I went over to him and watched him die. His eyes had a look of surprise."

Then loudly and with agitation in her voice, she says, **"Peter, I can't get that image out of my head!"**

Peter reached for her again and looked into her eyes. He spoke as calmly as he could. "Donna, easy, it's going to be okay. Talking about it is the best thing you can do."

"Peter, I have never killed anyone before. I know it was self-defense, but still . . . I took a human life, and it makes me feel bad. And the other two . . . why did they have to die?" She took the final sip of her brandy.

"I don't have the answers," Peter said. "I've never even come close to what you must be feeling right now, but what I do know is that these feelings are very normal. In your line of work, this could happen again. If you become so jaded that you stop feeling, then you may as well be dead yourself. I think you *must* feel, but be able to manage it."

He then asked, "Why do you think Trang wanted you dead? It sounds like he set you up."

"I think so too, and I walked right into it. I think he wanted to blame Nguyen's death and the witness's death on the CIA. I was just the sacrificial lamb."

"Donna, can you tell me what happened next?"

"I left. I went out the back door. I don't think anyone saw me. I went home. I wasn't sure what to do so I showered and changed my clothes. I had some water, but couldn't eat. I realized I would need to report this to my boss. I also knew that if the National Police or the NLF were looking for me. I knew that I should not stay too long in my apartment, so I packed a suitcase. Then I called my boss. I very calmly summarized what happened; I left out some of the details, and I didn't tell him how I was feeling. He asked if I was okay. I lied and said that I was. He asked if any one saw me. I told him I didn't think so. He advised that I play it safe and keep a low profile until I heard back from him. He suggested that I stay away from my apartment. He said he would have Joe, a colleague, shadow me, in case someone came looking. He said I could stay in room three-fourteen, if I had no other place to go. It has a blow-up mattress and each member of our team keeps 'GO' bags there, with toiletries and changes of clothes, documents etc. So, that's where I went, but after about a half hour in that room, everything started to hit me, and I started feeling bad about the three deaths and the images. I couldn't sleep. I felt alone. Then I thought about Wednesday night. You told me how much you liked my dress and the way I looked. I thought about how much I enjoyed your company and how comforting you were to me after the spill. I really wanted to talk to someone I could trust."

Before she could say more, Peter told her she could spend the night if she wished. She looked at him with a question mark. "You can have the bed; I'll take the sofa," he said. "It's not a problem."

15

AN AFFAIR TO REMEMBER

Donna had risked telling Peter details that her boss would probably reprimand her for revealing. Peter was sure that her boss—was it John?—would not think he had a "need to know." However, she needed to confide in someone, and he had listened. She seemed to feel better. He judged that she was okay with his offer to spend the night.

He took the empty brandy cup from her hand and set it on the coffee table next to his. Then he moved up onto the sofa. Donna moved slightly to her left and back on the cushion making room for him to sit next to her on her right. "How is your wrist doing?" he asked.

She lifted her arm so that he could see. He placed his left hand under her arm as she explained the brace. "It keeps me from moving my wrist. However, it's removable, so I can wash when I want to. It's easy to remove and put back on. Watch." She quickly removed the brace to demonstrate. Peter noticed the discoloration on her wrist and forearm.

"Does it still hurt?"

"Yes, but only when the brace is not on. They gave me some pain pills at the field hospital that I could take if I needed to, but I have not taken any since yesterday."

"What about your leg? How is that doing?"

Without hesitation, she pulled the hem of her skirt up to mid -thigh, and bent her leg up to show him the scrape and bruising on the outside of her right leg. As she did so, the hem of her dress moved further up her leg. The bruises were still there but slightly more yellow than before and what had been bloody scrapes were now scabbed over. He commented that they were looking better, but as he spoke, he could not resist moving his hand lightly along the exposed injury on the side of her leg, and then slowly toward the top of her thigh under the hem of her dress. He looked up at the expression on her face, but removed his hand just as he heard her say "Peter . . ." Her tone was more like a question than it was an objection.

He stood up so that he was in front of her. His right leg had ended up against the inside of her left leg and when she brought her right leg back down it ended up on the outside of his left leg. It was not planned that way; it just happened. With his shins braced against the front of the sofa, he leaned over and slid his hands under her hair that flowed down the sides of her head. He began to massage her temples.

She looked at him questioningly and asked, "Peter, what are *we* doing?"

Peter was not sure, but thought they were both looking for a declaration of intent. His response was, "Donna, I want you to let yourself relax. Is what I'm doing okay?" He heard a soft but unsure "yes."

"Put your head back on the cushion," he said. She did, and he continued the massage, including the back of her neck.

She closed her eyes and then she said, "What you're doing really feels good."

After an unknown amount of time, Peter began to feel her legs against his. Her face had become flush, and her breathing had quickened. He was feeling it too. She opened her eyes and looked dreamily at him. He felt the urge to kiss her but was still hesitant.

Then she said, "Peter, I'm getting hot." He hadn't heard that term in a while and was not sure what she meant.

She saw his possible lack of understanding and then said, "Peter, I'm becoming sexually aroused."

Peter thought she knew he was aroused as well, but he asked her, "Do you want me to stop?"

She put her left hand on the back of his head, looked him in the eyes, and said, "No. Please don't stop."

He kissed her tenderly on the mouth and started to pull away, but she said, "Peter, I want you to love me," and pulled him back.

"And I want you to feel loved," he whispered back.

She pulled him toward her and at the same time drew her legs up so that her feet rested on top of the cushion of the sofa. Things went very fast after that. He told her she deserved all the love he could give her. He reached behind her neck and untied the strap of her halter-top. He kissed her neck and moved his way down to her nipples. Then, he moved his hand down between her legs. Her panties were wet and he removed them. She sat upright and attempted to undo the rope tie around the waist of his pajama bottoms. The task required two hands so he helped her, and then he slipped them off. As he slipped off his top, she put her good hand on his erection and the coolness increased his pleasure. For a moment, he thought she was going to take him in her mouth, but instead she looked up at him, put her arm around his neck, and said, "Peter, I want you to make love to me." Peter put his hands on both sides of her head and kissed her on the mouth. As he did this, they fell lengthwise onto the sofa. Peter was inside of her and kissing her all at once. They held each other tightly and they both started laughing and crying at the same time from the intense pleasure. Orgasms came easily for them both.

Afterwards, they fell asleep next to each other. As he came to, he slid off the edge of the sofa. Donna was sound asleep, so he picked their clothes up off the floor, got his pajama bottoms and tee shirt, and made his way to the bathroom. He used the toilet and washed up. When he came back into the main room, Donna had awakened and was sitting up on the sofa. She seemed totally out of it. He sat next to her.

"You were asleep. I tried not to wake you. Sorry. Are you okay?" She nodded in the affirmative. "There are fresh towels and a wash cloth on the shelf next to the sink. I set your bag over there. Let me know if you need anything. You okay?"

"I have to go," was her response as she quickly grabbed her bag and darted into the bathroom.

She returned ten minutes later, wearing a long pull over top. She sat down next to Peter on the bed where he had waited for her. "Which side of the bed do you prefer?" he asked.

"Peter, I feel a bit awkward. You may find this hard to believe, but I've never slept in bed with a man before."

"Well," he said sincerely, "If you feel more comfortable, you can have the entire bed and I'll take the sofa."

"No, I didn't mean it that way. I want you next to me." With that, they got under the covers, hugged, and quickly fell asleep.

****

The next morning, when Peter awoke, Donna was already up and in the shower. She was "bright-eyed and bushy-tailed" as they say. She came out of the bathroom fully dressed and greeted him. "Good morning. I'm hungry. If you would like, I can get us something and bring it back while you're getting washed and dressed"

"Thanks, but I won't be long in the shower. Please wait for me and we can go together."

"Okay, I should have told you the whole truth. I need to go upstairs and check in."

"Oh, It's okay Donna. Come back here when you're done and we can go out then."

He noticed she left her large shoulder bag with the rest of her clothes and who knows what else. Out of curiosity, he was tempted to rummage through it. Did she have her gun? What was her real name? Of course, he refrained from doing so.

They had a great day together. She told him not to react if he noticed someone following them. Earlier when she went upstairs, she had verified arrangements that she had made to have a protection detail shadow them. After they had a late morning breakfast-brunch, they went to a commissary and she bought some additional clothes, etc. He bought some condoms and another bottle of seltzer water. That day they talked about everything, everything except what had happened the night before.

That evening, they had a brandy and a light supper on the top floor of the Caravelle next door, and they enjoyed the 10th floor's beautiful view of the city. When they arrived, the weather outside was clear and the sun had not yet set. From the bar, they could watch the sun set, and as night fell, they watched the lights come on across the city. It was romantic to be sure. But Donna had her small shoulder bag in which he assumed she carried her gun, and Peter noticed a man sitting at the end of the bar that he assumed was their shadow. It felt good to know that they were "protected."

When they returned to their room, Peter told her he wanted to make love to her again. She was not shy at all. She let him totally explore her body and she totally enjoyed it. They made love, and this time he made sure that he used a condom. They went to sleep at around eleven. He thought he heard her whisper that she loved him as he fell asleep, but perhaps he only imagined it.

For some reason he awoke in the middle of the night. It was dark. He moved his arm to Donna's side of the bed. She was not there. He clicked on the lamp next to the bed. The clock on the night stand said two in the morning. He looked around. Donna was not in the room. Perhaps she was in the bathroom. The door was shut. He knocked, but there was no answer. He knocked again and called her name. "Donna are you in there?"

He heard a feeble "yes."

"Are you okay?"

He heard a feeble "no."

"May I come in?"

"I suppose," she said with resignation.

He entered the bathroom. Except for the night light plugged into the socket, she was sitting in the dark on the closed lid of the toilet. She had been crying. He stooped down beside her and asked softly, "Donna, what is going on?"

She raised her head, looked directly at him, and began to speak excitedly and loudly.

"You want to know what's going on? What is going on is that I'm in love with a married man who loves his wife and who has a child on the way. That is not the way things are supposed to be, and I don't know what to do about it. After Friday night I felt guilty that maybe I took advantage of your emotions. I was needy, and asked you not to stop, and maybe you kept going when you would have preferred to stop. But then . . . the way you were tonight. I'm a good Catholic girl, and you had condoms I didn't even know about. It made me wonder if I was wrong about you. Maybe all you cared about was the sex, and now I feel guilty about allowing you that privilege. When I was young, my mother made me go to confession every Saturday evening. Peter, is what we are doing a sin?"

Then, she looked away and started crying again.

"I guess we should talk about our relationship," he suggested.

"I guess so," was her response between sobs.

Peter started. "Well, I think that what happened between us on Friday night would never have happened if we didn't have strong feelings for each other. Is what we are doing wrong? Is it not supposed to happen? I suppose only God knows that. But I know it feels right to me. Maybe God has a plan for this to happen. I can't say that what we have is not supposed to happen. I don't feel guilty or regret what we did, and I don't want you to feel guilty or have regrets either."

He continued. "I know that my feelings for you are a lot more than sexual. If my behavior earlier tonight offended you, I apologize, but I honestly thought you were enjoying it. Yes, it is true that I still love my wife, but I also care deeply for you."

She interrupted. "How can you say that, and still love your wife?"

"I think it's possible to love more than one person. This may be a poor analogy, but if you love someone, and that loved one dies, you don't stop loving them. Even if you remarry and love your new spouse, you still have the memory and love for the first one. Perhaps it's hard to understand, but that's what I believe and how I feel."

"You're right. It's a poor analogy. Your wife is not dead!"

"Okay, I said it was a poor analogy. The point is I care about both of you."

He continued, "Donna, I think we need to be realistic about our relationship. I'll be leaving in another three days, but I will always remember you and the way we felt about each other. Rather than longing for a life that we cannot have together, I think we should be grateful for what we do have. I think we should enjoy the opportunity we have with each other now. I know you would like to be married and have kids. Perhaps you're envious of my life, I don't know, but I'm convinced that someday you will meet someone who you will also love, and that the life you want will happen for you. I would like to think that you would still remember us even then. However, there is no reason why you can't love and be happy in the meantime. That is all I have ever wanted for you . . . to be happy. Please, come back to bed."

She remained seated on the toilet seat lid, and then spoke. "Would it be okay if I go to church tomorrow? I don't mean confession, just church; it has been a while."

"Of course. You don't need my permission, you know."

"I know, but I would like you to come with me. Will you?"

"Absolutely, it has been a while for me as well."

Then she pulled him toward her, kissed the side of his face, and spoke softly into his ear. "Peter, I did enjoy the sex. And I promise I will always remember you too." With that, they returned to bed and they both went back to sleep.

****

On Sunday morning, they had breakfast downstairs, and had a cab pick them up in front of the hotel. Donna told the driver to take them to the Tan Dinh Church, not Notre Dame as Peter had expected. The church was on Hai Ba Trung in the direction of the airport. When they arrived, Donna requested that the cab return in an hour and one-half.

As soon as they stepped out of the cab, Peter was struck by the image of the church before them. The entire structure was pink. He observed a tall bell tower before them with a steeple on top, perhaps reaching eighty feet in height. Smaller towers with steeples flanked the sides of the building. Before entering the nave of the church, they passed under an arch and into an open vestibule that was underneath the main tower. It was at this point that a priest who recognized Donna greeted them. "Glad to see you come back to us Miss Rice."

As they entered the nave, Donna crossed herself as was customary. He took her lead and did the same. They walked about a third of the way down the center aisle to a place where they could kneel and sit. The pews were very basic. They were hard wooden benches with a single two by ten-centimeter size board to lean back against. The pews were not intended for comfort. As he looked down the main aisle of the nave, Peter was impressed by the marble alter up front, and the crucifixion replication high above. The arched top of the nave may have been fifty feet above the floor. Support columns lined both sides of the nave. Arched entryways spanned the columns, and led to additional seating and access aisles to the right and left of the nave. He judged the ceilings in the side areas to be about twenty-five feet above the floor. At the head of these side areas, closer to where they entered, were chapels that popped out from the sides of the building. At the altar end of the nave, archways on each side provided access to a one-story horseshoe-shaped structure that wrapped around the backside of the altar. They didn't go down there, but later Donna told him they used those rooms for classes, meetings, conferences, and the like. The columns and the walls of the inside of the nave were pink complimented by cream-colored trim. The pink color and the images of Christ combined with outdoor light coming in from above the columns, to create an ethereal aura. He had the feeling of being in a fairy tale or perhaps heaven itself.

The church was only half-full. Most of the attendees were Vietnamese. A different priest than their greeter conducted the basic service, after which those who wished to take communion were asked to stay. Peter looked over at Donna who said they should leave. He knew that in the eyes of the Church neither of them were worthy of communion.

The priest who had originally greeted them spoke to them again as they exited. He appeared to be Vietnamese, but he spoke perfect English. "Miss Rice, what did you do to your wrist?" he asked politely.

"I took a spill off my bike Friday evening."

"I am surprised you didn't stay for communion."

"I may not be worthy Father."

"Then you must come to confession."

"Perhaps I will, next Friday," she replied.

Then he turned to Peter. "I am Father Jo. I have not seen you here before. I notice that you did not opt for communion either. I hear confessions on Friday evenings."

"I'm Peter Troutman. This is the first time I have been here. However, I *am* worthy! I'm just not Catholic. I don't believe in the confessional." A look on Donna's face indicated she was not happy with his tone.

"I welcome you to our church anyway, and I hope to see both of you again next Sunday." Then he turned to speak to the next person exiting.

Peter looked at his watch. They had a forty-five minute wait before the cab would return. They discussed the possibility of walking but it was a long way, the weather was warm, and rain was possible. It would not have been a nice thing to do to the cab driver either. They thought better of it and found a sheltered place outside in the garden area where they could sit and talk.

"Peter, I didn't realize you were not Catholic. Perhaps you didn't know that in the Catholic Church you're not supposed to take communion unless you are 'worthy,' which means you are Catholic and you have confessed your sins. Only the priest can decide if you have sinned, and if so, absolve you. I didn't like the quip you made to Father Jo about your worthiness."

Peter felt bad. He had come to church with her because he wanted to support her, and now he let her down, by saying something stupid.

"I owe you an apology. I know you needed my support this morning and the last thing I wanted to do was to embarrass you. I should not have said it. I'm sorry. Please forgive me."

"Why did you say it?"

"It was your exchange with Father Jo that set me off. I was annoyed by the implication that we were not worthy. I think that we are both worthy, and I don't think we have sinned." He was thinking of how the Catholic Church made his friend Ben feel so unworthy he tried to kill himself.

"Although you're not Catholic, I get the impression that you have been to a Catholic church before. Do you practice a religion?"

"Actually, I have deep spiritual beliefs. I told you once that I think differently than most people. My religious beliefs are different as well."

"Tell me what you believe."

"Okay. I believe in a spiritual God. I believe that all of us have a good spirit within us, some more, some less, and that spirit is my concept of God. My wife is Catholic, or I should say *was* Catholic. Before I married her, I needed to know how accepting I would be of her, and how accepting she would be of me. I read about Catholicism and about other religions as well. I was convinced that all organized religions have something good about them. However, I didn't find even one that was right for me, so I formed my own beliefs and religious concepts. I try to respect other peoples' rights to believe and practice their own religious, political, and economic ideologies, just so I'm free to practice my own."

He continued, "I agreed to be married in a Catholic Church. She agreed that she would not try to convert me, and we found a liberal priest who was okay with that. We also agreed that we would share our beliefs and attend both Catholic and Protestant churches. We agreed that if we had children, we would expose them to all religions and allow them to make an educated choice rather than force them to practice a certain religion. Regarding Catholicism, I don't want my children to go around feeling guilty and unworthy all the time."

Donna put her hand over his and said, "I agree with you. I often felt that way about myself, you know, guilty and unworthy. I like your idea of exposing your kids to multiple religions. You're fortunate that your wife agrees."

At this point, their cab arrived and they returned to the hotel. As they walked through the lobby, Donna noticed a note in the mailbox for room 314 and had the desk clerk hand it to her. "What is it?" Peter asked.

"It's from Joe." Peter assumed Joe was the person who was following them everywhere they went. "He's delivered a suitcase for me. Will you come up with me?" This was good news for both of them. Donna needed fresh clothes, and Peter never liked it when women commandeered a bathroom by washing things in the sink, and hanging them over the shower curtain rod. They retrieved the suitcase and then returned to their room.

They were hungry, so Peter offered to get some food from the café across the street, and bring it back to the room. As he entered the café, Han greeted him. He told Han he was leaving next week and that he was pleased to have met her and enjoyed her special pho.

"Donna will miss you," she said. "Tell her I say hello." Peter thought she figured out that he was bringing the food to Donna. When he returned to his room, he mentioned this to Donna.

Nothing of significance happened the rest of that afternoon. They were both tired. They ate, shared a newspaper, and talked.

Later that evening, they prepared for bed and were about to turn off the lamp when Donna said, "Peter, could I ask you something?"

"Sure, what's on your mind?"

"Promise you will be honest with me when you answer."

"Of course. I promise."

"Well, do you think we are compatible? I mean like if we were to be together as a couple."

He looked at her and contemplated why she would ask that. Was she looking for self-validation, or further justification for their affair?

"Yes, I do think we are compatible. We're able to talk to each other, like right now. I think we have the capacity and ability to resolve issues that may exist between us. I have appreciated how tolerant you have been of my idiosyncrasies, such as my tendency to overreact. Although I may not do as good of a job of being as tolerant as you, I do try."

Then she asked, "If you were not already married, do you think you could be married to someone like me?"

"Yes, of course I could. In fact, if I was not already married, I would ask you to marry me right now. If I did, would you say yes?"

"Would you expect me to quit my job and move to Rochester?"

"No, if you were to continue doing what you're doing, I would support that. As far as moving to Rochester, I'm not sure it would matter where your home base was if you were always in the field. However, I would like to finish the five courses I have left and get my MBA. After that, I could live and work anywhere. I have thought about IBM. They have locations everywhere. Their Federal Systems division is in the DC area, which is close to CIA headquarters in Langley. I think that we would be able to resolve issues like that. Tell me about kids. Do you want kids?"

"Yes, I have always dreamed of that. However, I think it would be difficult if I were still doing what I do now."

Peter could see that she was struggling with life choice issues. "Donna, I think that choices between career and family are always difficult, but many women are able to have both. I know you're good at your job. I also think that when you're ready, you will be an excellent wife and mother. All marriages require some compromises and some sacrifices. You and your husband would need to decide how to balance work versus raising children. Perhaps you work for a while, then have children, and then go back to work when they are older. Perhaps you hire a nanny. Perhaps when the kids are old enough, you enroll them in a nursery school. Your husband may need to play a more active role in sharing the duties of raising a child. When you're married, you have faith in your spouse. If you and your husband are compatible, you can agree on how to handle issues as the issues develop."

Peter looked at her wondering if she would answer his hypothetical marriage proposal. She seemed to be confused as to what to say next. Then she got misty-eyed, came over to his side of the bed, put her arm over his neck, pulled him toward her, and kissed him hard on the mouth.

"Peter, I love you, but I'm very tired tonight, and we will have a busy day tomorrow. Would it be okay if we just hold each other tonight?" They fell asleep in each other's arms

16

MOVING ON

On Monday, Peter finished correcting data files, generating reports, and instructing the captain on how to proceed after he left. The final PEN report on Monday morning showed the probability of Event 360 to be sixty percent. The target events that surrounded Event 360 all had high probabilities above forty percent. A trend analysis showed that all the target events crossed the ninety percent threshold near the end of January 1968. around the time of the Tet holiday. Peter did not know what the actual events were, but he did not think any of the events in the PEN network that could be countermeasures had significant probabilities. He concluded that a momentous event would occur around the time of Tet.

Before leaving the captain's office that afternoon, Peter engaged him in a conversation about how the results of PEN would be used. Peter really wanted to know that some good would come out of all the work he had done. "Captain, I know that you review these results with the Colonel, but who sees the results after that? More importantly, who decides what actions to take?"

"Peter, you ask an excellent question. The Colonel, Sam, and I review it first. Then we make recommendations, which the Colonel takes to his superior and to the CIA station chief. Usually that would be enough to decide on actions. The decisions would be passed back down the military chain to the appropriate field commanders. However, if critical enough, the recommendations and intelligence would go up the line all the way to General Westmoreland, the Secretary of Defense, and in some cases, the President himself. If it means getting ARVN involved, there is a parallel chain of command. Sometimes it can get very political, and in my opinion, politicians don't think the way we do. Whereas you and I try to maximize the probability of successfully solving a problem, a politician seems to be concerned about minimizing the possibility of being removed from office.

"For example, suppose our intelligence showed that North Vietnam had an army of troops on the Cambodian border and was planning an invasion that would capture villages on this side of the border. You and I would probably recommend sending troops into Cambodia to destroy them before they could act. A politician on the other hand, might decide that doing so would make it look like we were the aggressors and that we were invading another sovereign country. The politician might decide to wait for them to attack, so that we can say we were defending ourselves. If our defense were to fall short, the politician would blame the CIA for bad intelligence, or blame ARVN for not doing its part.

"You didn't hear this from me, but there have been rumors, all denied by officialdom, but supported by PEN, that the North Vietnamese army and the Vietcong might be planning a coordinated Tet Offensive. It's still months away, so there is time to act. I hope that perhaps officialdom will take notice and appropriate counter events will prevail."

"Captain, I hope we take appropriate action also. I have confidence that you will make good arguments in support of the intelligence."

****

Late on Monday afternoon, Peter thought about Bob and the significant contribution he made to the cause. He needed to thank him before he went back to the States. He called him on a secure phone. Bob answered.

"Bob, this is Peter Troutman. I want to thank you for the significant contribution you made." His response caught him totally off guard.

"Mr. Troutman, thank me? I should not even talk with you. What have you gotten me involved in?" He was speaking loudly; he was livid.

"Bob, what do you mean?" Peter asked.

"I met Nguyen. I talked with her. You never told me I would be responsible for helping the CIA to put a bullet through her head. She was an honored ARVN female lieutenant."

"Bob please calm down. The news article you read on Friday was wrong. She was a spy, an agent for the Viet Cong. The CIA did **not** take her out! The CIA wanted her alive so that they could interrogate her and find out who she was working for. Unfortunately, the CIA never got the chance. She was killed by someone that wanted to keep her from talking. You did not help the CIA to kill her." Bob was silent so Peter continued.

"On the other hand, what you **are** responsible for is helping to expose an enemy agent, and allowing the PEN project, and possibly other projects, to continue operating. There is no trace of your involvement, and I thought what you gave me was very professionally done. I cannot tell you what the PEN project is, but I am hoping that in the long-run it will save lives. If you still feel I have deceived you, I apologize. It was not my intent to deceive you. I wanted to show my appreciation. I have something for you, but I'll be leaving day after tomorrow. Is there any chance we could connect up before then?"

After a pause, Bob calmly replied. "Peter, I don't always adjust to things right away. Perhaps I overreacted. Where are you?"

"I'm at work."

"I know you don't have transportation; I'll pick you up at five p.m. You can buy me a drink." Then he hung up.

It had been Peter's intent to give Bob a fifth of Johnny Walker, a whiskey Peter knew he liked. The only problem was that he had not bought it yet. He also had another problem. He had forgotten that for the first time since coming to Saigon, he had a houseguest that would wonder where he was. It was 4:00 p.m. He had one hour to figure this out.

He called Bob right back and asked, "Bob, could you drive over to the Continental Palace instead? I would like to ask my friend Donna to join us for drinks and for dinner afterwards. Are you okay with Italian food?"

"Peter, I sure have underestimated you! You dog you. Italian is fine. I'll see you both at five."

Peter then found a cab and had the driver take him to the nearest Commissary. He had the driver wait while he bought a fifth of Johnny Walker, and then he had the driver take him to the Continental Palace. Donna was not there, so he began writing a note, but at five minutes before the hour, she came in.

"Peter, you must have left work early," she said, showing her surprise. "I didn't expect you to be here."

"Yes," he said and gave her a hello kiss. "Something came up and I need to ask a favor of you. I would like it if you could join Bob Nunn and me for a drink and I should buy him dinner as well. I want to thank him for what he did for us. I apologize for the short notice, but he didn't respond to my phone call until an hour ago." It was a white lie. He should have discussed it with her on Sunday, and he should not have waited until late afternoon to call Bob. "Are you okay with that? I would understand it you can't do it."

"When?"

He looked at his watch as he sheepishly replied, "right now?"

"Okay, but you need to hold him off long enough for me to freshen up. Where are we going to eat?"

"I thought we could have drinks at the bar here at the Continental Palace and then dinner at La Dolce Vita. He likes Italian."

"Okay . . . suggestion . . . go on downstairs and make a seven o'clock reservation for dinner. Hold Bob off. I'll meet you at the hotel entrance as soon as I can get there." Then she pecked him on the cheek and headed for the bathroom.

By the time Peter got down the stairs, Bob was already waiting in his vehicle. Peter looked around and saw a place where Bob could park. Peter had the Johnny Walker with him in a brown paper bag. "Bob this is for you. Why don't you put this into your car? You can park your car over there," he said and pointed to the spot he had in mind. "Then meet me back here. I'll treat you to a drink and dinner at La Dolce Vita, but I need to reserve a table while you're parking."

Peter walked several yards down the sidewalk and entered La Dolce Vita. He made a reservation for three at 7:00 p.m. and then walked back to the entrance to the Continental Palace. Bob was already waiting. "Peter, I thank you for the Whiskey. All of this is really not necessary you know." He looked around, and then said, "Didn't you say that you were going to have your friend join us?"

"I did. Here she comes now."

After Peter made introductions, the three of them headed up to the bar on the ground floor of the Continental Palace. The fact that someone was following them didn't bother him. He knew who it was and Bob didn't notice. The three of them had drinks, and talked while Donna's protector watched from the far corner of the bar.

The conversation was mostly chitchat. They could not talk business because Bob didn't know who Donna really was. After their first round of drinks, Bob asked if curfew tonight was at 2300 hours and when should they head over to La Dolce Vita. Donna promptly said she thought curfew was at 2300 and suggested they head over to the restaurant at 1850, to be there before their reservation at 1900 hours. That prompted Bob to tell a joke. "Hey you guys, that reminds me of a joke. I think the two of you can relate to it. It goes something like this." Peter held his breath hoping it would not be too off-color, as Bob began without a pause.

"A rooky male reporter was sent to Saigon to do a human-interest story about an unmarried female army Sergeant. In Saigon, the number of men outnumbered the women by at least twenty to one. The idea was to portray the life of such a woman living in a man's world. The reporter found an appropriate female Sergeant on a Saturday evening, quietly sitting alone at a bar sipping a drink. He approached her and tried to engage her in conversation. He said, 'Excuse me, Sergeant, but you seem to be a very serious woman. Is something bothering you?'

'Negative brother,' the Sergeant said, 'Just serious by nature.'

The young reporter looked at the Sergeant's awards and decorations and said, 'It looks like you have seen a lot of action.'

The Sergeant's short reply was, 'Yes, brother, a lot of action.'

The young reporter, tiring of trying to start up a conversation, said, 'You know, you should lighten up a little. Relax and enjoy yourself.'

The Sergeant just stared at him in her serious manner.

Finally, the young reporter said, 'You know, I hope you don't take this the wrong way, but when is the last time you had sex?'

The Sergeant looked at him and replied, '1958.'

'Well, there you are,' he said. 'You really need to chill out and quit taking everything so seriously! I mean no sex since 1958! Isn't that a little extreme?'

The Sergeant, glancing at her watch, said in a matter-of-fact voice, 'You think so? It's only 2132 now.'"

They all laughed and Bob continued with, "Peter, don't we love that military time!"

Then Bob wanted to know where Donna and Peter met. Peter said in the lobby of the hotel as she was staying there as well. Peter was quite certain that Bob assumed they were sharing a room. Bob wanted to know what Donna did, and why she was in Saigon. Donna told him she was a provider of host services for USAID.

"Oh," Bob said. "USAID is one of IBM's accounts. In fact, I sometimes teach a class over there. Perhaps I'll run into you there." Then he started chatting with her. Finally, in full character for Bob, he said, "Donna, I understand Peter is leaving Saigon in a couple of days. You know this guy is married, don't you? Unlike Peter, I'm not. Would it be all right if I call you? Maybe we could get together."

Peter looked over to Donna and wondered how she would respond, or if she expected him to respond. Donna responded quickly, and Peter was surprised by what she said. "Bob, I appreciate your offer, but it won't be possible. I just found out that I will be transferred back to the States. I leave on Wednesday, same time as Peter." Then she turned to Peter and said, "Peter, I found out earlier today but I didn't have a chance to tell you."

Donna reminded them that it was time for dinner. Peter paid the bill and they got up to leave. Their protector followed them out. They exited the hotel and entered La Dolce Vita from the street. Of course, Donna's protector didn't follow them into the restaurant, but probably kept an eye on the door. Anna Faby greeted them as they entered. She was the owner's wife, and often greeted people as they came in. Peter had eaten there a couple of times before and she acted as if she remembered him. One could describe the decor inside the restaurant as somewhat basic, austere, or rustic. There was a pronounced look of wood: simple wooden tables, wooden chairs, wooden railings, and large wooden support posts. The archways that led to the outside were fitted with heavy wooden French-style doors. What looked like a metal wagon wheel was mounted on one of the walls. However, Peter thought that what really set the room apart was the floor. The floor was a terrazzo-type material with a reddish pattern. This was not unusual. Terrazzo floors were often found in hotels and public buildings in Saigon. Table clothes with a red and white checkered pattern covered the restaurant's tables. The table clothes complemented the floor color quite nicely. The red terrazzo floor and the red and white checkered table clothes combined to give the decor a needed bit of class.

Peter liked Italian food, and there were not too many places in Saigon where one could have Italian food. The food here was not the best, but it was good and the service was friendly. He and Donna stuck to basics— spaghetti and meatballs for him, lasagna for Donna. On the other hand, Bob ordered a more sophisticated and more expensive dish. He ordered the most extravagant item on the menu. He ordered a beef tenderloin served with a green vegetable and risotto. Bob had a glass of an expensive Chianti Reserve as well. Perhaps he was reacting to his disappointment that Donna was not going to be around to date him. Peter was okay about it though. As far as Peter was concerned, for what Bob did for him, he deserved anything he wanted—well food-wise that is. They talked a bit more as they ate, mostly chitchat. After dinner, Peter paid the bill and Bob thanked him profusely for the drinks and dinner. The three of them walked down to Bob's vehicle where they exchanged best wishes and said goodnight. Peter and Donna watched Bob drive off. Bob had plenty of time before curfew.

He and Donna returned to his room. They sat on the sofa and talked. She asked Peter if he was getting jealous when Bob started coming on to her. "Maybe a little," he admitted. "I also thought it was insensitive of him to ask you for a date in front of me." Then he asked her, "If you were still in Saigon, would you have dated him?"

"Peter, you told me he was a womanizer and slept with prostitutes. What do you think?"

"I think not," Peter responded. "I guess I'm feeling a bit vulnerable right now. It was wrong of me to ask."

Then, he changed the subject. "Donna, I was surprised when you said you were also leaving on Wednesday. What's going on?"

"Peter, I found out earlier today. My boss gave me the news over the phone but didn't say too much more. He told me that I'm to leave on Wednesday, but that the details will come. He also said that he wants me to meet with him and the Chief of Station tomorrow to go over details about the situation. I have this fear that I may be in trouble."

"I don't think you should be concerned. I think they should give you a medal. They are probably just trying to protect you."

"But, if my boss and the station chief were to talk with the National Police Commissioner and explain that their inspector was a traitor, they might call off any hunt for his killer. After all, they would not want the bad publicity of having a traitor working for them."

"That may be true, but what about retaliation from the Vietcong? Your boss may think that to be a possibility. In any case, it is possible that your cover has been blown and they know who you are. If true, that would limit what else you could do here. Besides, you completed your assignment. Doesn't it make sense that you should leave? I don't think you are in any trouble with your bosses. I think they are protecting you. Worrying won't help. You need to relax," Peter said, as he put his arm around her and pulled her close.

"I hope you're right. Peter, there's one more thing I need to tell you."

"What's that?"

"My local boss, John, wants to meet with you tomorrow as well. He will send a car to MACV tomorrow at 3:00 p.m.to pick you up."

"Why?"

"He needs to debrief you. I'm concerned that he may be testing me. I may have let you know things that I was not supposed to let you know."

"I see. But unless he tortures me, I promise I will not sell you out."

"I need you to take this seriously."

"Trust me. I am taking it seriously."

"Let's go to bed," she said, as she gave him a peck on the cheek and rose from the sofa.

****

They were both up early on Tuesday. Donna had her meeting with her station chief in the morning. She also had to finish cleaning out her apartment and make travel arrangements. Peter had to wrap things up with everyone at MACV, and then meet with Donna's boss, John.

He started the morning at his workplace, making sure that all his things were cleared out, and that all documents were secure or returned to the persons that owned them. Then he said good-bye to each person individually. After he saw the computer room guys downstairs, he walked upstairs and turned in his two building badges to Danny. He saved the captain for last, and they had lunch in the building café. The captain asked about Donna, but he told him he could not say too much. They agreed to keep in touch. Peter gave him his address in Rochester New York, and the captain gave Peter his APO address.

That afternoon, everyone gathered in a conference room and they presented him with a going-away cake and a bottle of brandy. Everyone was nice and polite but somewhat downbeat, he thought. Perhaps they could not believe that Nguyen was a spy. Perhaps they could not get over the death of a co-worker. Perhaps they felt the future of the team and their assignments were uncertain. Perhaps they were just learning that he was a spy of sorts. Whatever it was, they kept it to themselves. Peter expressed his regrets about the unplanned loss of their co-worker, and he thanked them for their cooperation in preventing the further loss of classified information to the enemy.

John's driver arrived at precisely 3:00 p.m. and took Peter to the embassy. Peter went to the receptionist and told her he had an appointment with John—and it dawned on him, he didn't remember John's last name. He tried to remember the party at his house back in March. Did he give his last name, or was it just John? Fortunately, John's representative came over to greet him and escort him to John's office. When they arrived, Peter noticed the name and title on his door was Jon Wilson, Inter-agency Liaison. Turns out, Peter didn't even have his first name right. He always thought it was *John,* not *Jon.* Peter thought to himself, "N*ext time you have an interview Peter, do your homework first."*

The representative escorted Peter into the office, and Jon greeted him. They shook hands.

"Good afternoon, Peter. It has been a few months since I last saw you."

"Good afternoon to you. Nice office."

"Peter, can I have my secretary bring you a cup of coffee?"

"No, Jon. Thanks, but I'm fine. What is it that you need to talk about?"

"I want to start by thanking you for a job well done. I know you got a little more than you bargained for, but you stepped up to the challenge. You proved to be a good analyst and a good detective. I could not have expected more. Thank you. And Peter, if you're interested, I would gladly recommend you for future assignments." Then he told Peter what he would do in terms of references, thank you letters, and future contacts the CIA might have with him.

"I appreciate your confidence in me. I was glad I could do something for my country. I enjoyed the work." Then without thinking, he added "But I had never expected it would result in people being killed."

"Lieutenant Nguyen was a spy working for the enemy. Lest you think otherwise, the CIA had nothing to do with her death. The news report was wrong. However, you mentioned *people*. That implies that you know more than you should. How did you know there was more than one person? Tell me what you know, and how you know it. What did Donna tell you?"

Whoops, he's thinking, he had better not betray Donna.

"Jon, with all due respect, your reaction just gave it away." As he said this, Jon began smiling, but he continued. "I can assure you that Donna didn't tell me anything that I didn't have a need to know. I can also assure you that whatever I know about this will remain with me."

"Peter, that's what I needed to hear. As part of this debriefing, I'm also obligated to remind you that your non-disclosure agreement requires that everything about your work here must remain secret for as long as it remains classified. I'm also required to tell you that nothing we have discussed is to leave this room. Are we good?"

"We're good." Then after a pause, Peter said, "I'd like to ask you something, off the record so to speak. I know that Donna met with you earlier today. Is she in trouble?"

"No, but I'm taking precautions regarding her safety and regarding her state of mind. I have decided to give her a well-deserved break. She can tell you all about it tonight when you see her."

"Jon, I need to know something. Is there any chance that the National Police may try to stop her at the airport as she tries to leave?"

"She also asked that and I told her not to worry. I have taken steps to preclude that from happening."

As they shook hands to say good-bye, Jon said, "Peter, I know that you and Donna have had something going between you. I sincerely hope you don't mess up your marriage the way I did with Linda. It's all about 'emotional intelligence.' I hope you're better at it than I was."

That evening, Donna asked how his debriefing went. "It went very well," he told her. "I didn't have to tell him what I knew, and he didn't try to find out if you broke any rules with me. He just wanted to be sure that I would never talk about anything that I did know. He also told me I did a great job and he thought that I should interview with the CIA in the spring when they come to Rochester. He said I could use him as a reference if I wanted. He said he would see to it that an appropriate thank you letter went to my employer."

"Peter, I'm glad for you."

Then, he asked Donna how her meeting went.

"You were right, I'm not in trouble," she replied, "but I don't think I'm getting a medal either. I have a new assignment back in the States. Please understand, I can't tell you about it."

"I understand," he replied.

"Donna, when I talked with Jon, I told him I was concerned about the possibility of the National Police detaining you at the airport. He told me he had made arrangements to ensure your safe passage."

"Yes, I met with both him and the station chief. They told me they had a meeting with the Commissioner and told him the CIA had evidence that his Inspector Trang was a traitor. They said the Commissioner promised not to interfere with my leaving. Afterwards, I met separately with Jon. He reassured me that he was looking out for my best interests. Jon also provided me with a special exit visa, approved by the Commissioner, and he provided me with details of my new assignment."

Then Donna told Peter the details about their orders to leave. Early tomorrow morning, Wednesday, August 16., a colleague would drive them to the embassy and the airport. They would fly on the same flight to Hong Kong, but she would be debriefed, have a medical exam, meet with a psychoanalyst, and then get some R and R before flying the rest of the way home. "All standard procedure," she assured him.

He asked if she needed any help getting her things ready to travel. She told him that her apartment was declared safe. She had been able to go over there during the day and retrieve everything she needed to take with her. She also told him that someone was assigned to pack everything else from the apartment into a crate that would be shipped home to her mom. "And Peter, do you remember the orchid that Linda gave me for my birthday? I had it on a windowsill. It did very well. I was able to leave it with Han. My colleague had interviewed her and decided there was no risk if she knew I was leaving the country."

Peter asked about her bike. She told him that one of her colleagues gave her a fair price, but she was sorry to have to part with it. However, she gleefully added, "I saved the pictures you took."

They talked about the possibility of staying in touch. He told her he knew she had a secret she had been keeping from him.

"What secret?" she asked.

"I know that your real name is not Donna Rice." She looked surprised.

"It's okay, I understand, he said, but to stay in touch I need to know how to reach you."

"After two weeks, I'll be living with my mom. I'll write down her name and address and phone number, but Peter, please understand that giving you this is against the rules, and if anyone knows my true identity, it could endanger lives, including yours. I will give it to you when we reach Hong Kong. As far as staying in touch, I want that, and I want us to remember each other, but please be discreet. I don't want you to risk your marriage over something that we cannot have together."

Tuesday night they finished packing, and made love for the last time. She told him she would always remember him, and he promised the same.

****

The next morning someone who introduced himself as Joe picked them up in front of the hotel. Right away, Peter recognized him as Donna's "protector." Peter said, "Hello, a pleasure to finally be introduced." Joe remained expressionless and didn't respond. They went to the embassy, turned in their IDs, and retrieved their passports. Peter converted his remaining local currency and MPCs into dollars, and received his travel documents. Once again, he would fly Pan Am to Los Angeles. He was disappointed that there could be no overnight in Hong Kong for him, only for Donna. His flight to Los Angeles would depart Hong Kong Wednesday afternoon, same as in March. Joe drove them to the Tan Son Nhut Airport. They checked their luggage. Peter's would go all the way through to Los Angeles.

For Peter, waiting in line to board the plane felt like awaiting an execution. Donna may have felt the same thing. It did not help to notice two Vietnamese men watching the line. Were they undercover police? The two of them knew the end for them was in sight, and it was difficult to know what to say to each other. They boarded the plane, and discovered that their assigned seats were not near each other. Her seat was up near the front and his midway back.

After they landed, Donna looked back at him before leaving the plane. It seemed to take forever to deplane, but when he did, she was there waiting. She ran toward him, gave him a long hard kiss, and shoved something into his pocket. Then she looked up at him with tears in her eyes, and as she noticed his tears, she quickly turned and headed for the baggage area. Peter stared for a moment, wishing he could chase after her, but knew he could not. Then he turned and went the other way toward his connecting flight. As he waited, he pulled the note from his pocket:

Mrs. Paul Cinelli (my Mom)
9906 Rosedale Ave
Bethesda, Maryland
Tel: 301-555-1212
I trust you, Donna

17

LIFE GOES ON

Peter arrived home late Thursday night, August 17. He was exhausted and felt like he had been through an emotional ringer. He remembered Jon's advice about "emotional intelligence." He sucked it up and made a point of focusing on his wife. He wanted to get back to a normal life. However, this was not to be, at least not yet. Penelope's water broke on Saturday evening. Their daughter was born in the back seat of their car, in the middle of the city, at two in the morning, on the way to the hospital. Managing his emotions was very difficult.

He and the Captain made good on their agreement to exchange greeting cards at the end of 1967. It was common practice to exchange holiday cards and notes with family and friends, especially if they were any distance away. Peter sent him a Hanukah card. He told him he was glad to be home, that he had a new daughter and he was back in graduate school. He also said, "A part of me misses you and the team. I hope our efforts make a difference, and that things are going in the right direction."

The captain responded with a religious Christmas card in which he congratulated Peter on his new daughter and wished him and his family the best. Then he added, "The team is doing well and they also wish you well. Things are looking up as we approach the holidays. I talked to Jon the other day. He said *he was making plans for the holidays in Nam, and looking forward to celebrating the coming of our savior from on high.*"

Peter understood the message. The captain knew that Peter's security clearance was no longer active. The message was clearly in code, but discreet enough to avoid any suspicion by Penelope or anyone else who may read it. It pleased Peter that his work was still useful to them. It did not please him that the likelihood of a TET offensive was trending upward. However, he was pleased that they thought the higher-ups would take appropriate action.

Unfortunately, that was the last time Peter ever heard from the captain. Peter sent another card the following year, but the captain's APO address was no longer active and the captain never received it. Years later, Peter visited the Vietnam war memorial in Washington D.C. He found the captains name on the wall.

As for the rest of the captain's team, Peter never heard from them again either. Peter had hoped that Jeff would call him if he made it back to Rochester, but Jeff never did. He never heard from Bob Nunn again either, but years later, he was able to find out what happened to him through people at IBM. It was not a happy ending for Bob. Apparently, he died in an automobile accident somewhere in Europe.

And then there was Donna. Before they left Saigon, Donna had given Peter her home address and they had agreed to stay in touch. They exchanged Christmas cards and notes in December of 1967. He told her about the birth of his daughter and wished she and her family a wonderful Christmas. She replied with a polite note saying she was enjoying being home again and wished him and his family the best.

A year later, Peter sent another Christmas wish to her. He had enclosed a note asking how she was doing, and telling her his latest news. In 1968, He had received his MBA degree, turned down a permanent job offer from the CIA, and by September, had left TGW and had started a job with IBM in East Fishkill, New York. He was disappointed when she didn't reply. He called the telephone number she had given him. Her mother answered and told him she was not home. He left a message, but she never called back.

After their experience in Saigon, he wanted to remain friends, and thought the feeling to be mutual. It bothered him that he didn't hear back. He didn't understand why. But at least her mother's response had told him that she was still alive. Perhaps he was being too idealistic or naive and expected too much. However, he knew that if he was to have a successful marriage, he needed to put thoughts of Donna to the back of his mind. He needed to focus on his wife, his new daughter, and his new career at IBM. And that is what he did.

EPILOGUE

The Tet Offensive occurred just as the PEN predicted it would. The attack on Saigon began January 30, 1968, on the eve of Tet, the lunar New Year celebrated by Vietnamese. It was an all-out assault on multiple cities by the North Vietnamese and Viet Cong. To the best of Peter's knowledge, North Vietnam began planning for the Tet Offensive in mid-1967. A change in leadership in Hanoi was moving their tactics away from guerilla style warfare and toward a more conventional war with massive deployments of troops. Intelligence gathered by the U.S. intelligence community in the South was aware of this change and its possible consequences. Most likely, the CIA Chief of Station in Saigon informed Washington of a possible Tet Offensive. But the politicians in Washington, including CIA headquarters, didn't want to hear it.

The Tet Offensive was reportedly a surprise, but the intelligence was there; it should not have been a surprise. To remain politically in favor, the military leaders and the Johnson administration had deceived the American public into thinking that we were winning the war. Our government could not publicly acknowledge the threat of a Tet Offensive. The strength of the enemy was consistently under reported and enemy losses over reported. Prior to the Tet Offensive, the U.S. forbid sending troops into Laos, Cambodia, or North Vietnam, places where the North Vietnamese army would stage for the Tet invasions. High level government officials made decisions that were based on politics.

Clearly, the PEN project didn't prevent the Tet Offensive. However, the advanced intelligence may have helped prepare our troops to defend the cities under attack. The U.S. and ARVN troops won the battles militarily, but the TET Offensive cost us politically, and five years later in 1973, the U.S. officially pulled out its troops, leaving the ARVN and unofficial special forces to defend the South.

Peter Troutman and many others question if American involvement in Vietnam had any positive effect. In 1956, the U.S. did not allow a vote to unite the communist North Vietnam with South Vietnam. A war ensued. The North Vietnamese took over the country in 1975. As many as

3.5 million people died supporting the war effort between 1956 and 1976. The United States and South Vietnam fought the war to stop the spread of communism. And yet, after twenty years of fighting, Vietnam became a united and communist country. One might ask, "What if . . .?"

CODE NAME BOULDER CREEK

By

Peter Eisenhut

1

TEDDY

The weather in mid-April 1987 was typical for Colorado Springs. One day could be warm and sunny, the next day cool and rainy. Today would be warm and sunny. The temperatures would reach into the seventies by mid-day.

Jim Hoffman hoped the nice weather would boost his spirits. So far, 1987 had not been a good year for Jim. His wife was ill from a long bout with Parkinson's disease. Her condition was slowly deteriorating and he could no longer provide the support that she required. He had arranged for a caretaker to come in during the day while he was at work, but he could see that at some point she would need to be in a long-term care facility. His wife's illness had overloaded him with medical and caretaker bills. He needed money badly. Medical plans at most small private companies were inadequate or non-existent. Jim's company was no exception. He had asked his boss for help. His boss told him he wished he could help, but he just could not do it.

Jim reasoned that selling his house would help resolve his financial difficulties, but he was not having much luck. Several deals had fallen through. He was no longer under contract with anyone, and he had arranged to meet with yet another real estate agent. She had called him unexpectedly. On the phone, she sounded promising. She said she was an independent broker and could offer a lower commission. She also said she had several buyers that had already expressed an interest. Jim thought this might be another false lead, but he had nothing to lose except his time. No need to dress up for this. After all, it was Saturday morning, and he had yard work to do later. So, he donned a work-shirt and jeans and set off to meet this woman at a coffee shop not far from his house.

Jim arrived at the coffee shop and surveyed the scene. The shop had an outdoor patio, and the weather was perfect for sitting outdoors. Each table had an umbrella to provide shade from the sun. Most of the tables were already occupied, and as he had never met this lady before, he wondered how he would know who she was, or if she was even there. He stood at the edge of the patio and slowly scanned one table after another until he spotted a woman seated alone. Their eyes met, and she motioned for him to come to her table. Now he wondered how she knew who *he* was.

Jim walked over to her and she rose from her seat. As they shook hands and introduced themselves, he could not help but notice how attractive she was. She wore a knee-length tan skirt with a matching jacket and a silky white top. Her long brown hair and light-colored skin complemented her outfit. She seemed like the typical agent—very professional. He had met enough of them to know. And yet, unlike other real estate ladies he had met, he sensed an uncertain allure about her. Her dark sunglasses added to the mystique.

"Mister Hoffman, my name is Ursula Behr." She spoke with an air of authority and confidence. "My last name is German, like yours, I assume."

"Pleased to meet you, ma'am," he said as he extended his hand. He was raised on a Colorado ranch, and he was ex-military. That was how he addressed a woman he just met.

"Mr. Hoffman, here is my business card. As you can imagine, I acquired the nickname, Teddy. Please call me Teddy. May I call you Jim?"

"Yes, ma'am . . . I mean, of course . . . Teddy," he said as he took a quick look at her card and tucked it into his wallet for safekeeping.

"Jim, tell me how you like your coffee."

"Uh, black," he replied.

"Please have a seat. When I return with the coffee, we can talk about your needs."

When she returned, she had two cups of coffee and two crullers.

"Oh, what do I owe you for this?" he asked.

"Jim, this is on me. I believe I can help you. Please tell me a little more about your situation."

"Yes, okay, I need to sell my house to bring in some money to help pay my wife's medical bills."

"I see. May I ask what she suffers from? Is it cancer?"

"No. It's Parkinson's."

"I see . . . but don't you have insurance with your employer?"

"Very little, and at some point, I'll need to move her to a long-term care facility. There is no insurance for that."

"I'm very sorry, Jim. May I ask what you do for work?"

Teddy had already done her homework and already knew the answers to all her questions, but she did not let on. Jim had a great job as a contractor to the U.S. Air Force's newly reorganized Space Command. His company played a major role in redesigning the network that would transmit satellite reconnaissance data from the ground stations to the Cheyenne Mountain complex. The work was highly classified. Jim was a Junior Partner in the business, and on the surface, the business was doing well.

"I work for a company that has a contract with the government," he told her. "I design data networks."

"I see. It sounds very technical."

They continued to chat and get to know each other better as they finished their coffee and crullers. Then Jim said, "Teddy, I haven't had much luck with previous agents. What can you do that they couldn't?"

Teddy responded without hesitation. "Three things Jim . . . First, I'll represent you, not the buyer. Second, I will not be exclusive. Technically, you, the owner, are selling the house. I'll advise you and bring in potential buyers. My fee will be half the standard fee—three percent, not six. Third, I already have interested parties lined up. Jim, you were asking $150,000 for your house. I think I can get you that price, especially now. The time of year and the economic environment are both favorable. You have no downside with me. I was showing a couple around the area last weekend and they saw the sign in your yard. They expressed an interest. I can bring them over to look at your house. I will call first of course. We can meet here again next Saturday to review our progress. Are you okay with that?"

"Yes, I am. Thank you," he responded. What else could he say? Teddy was very convincing.

****

Next Saturday morning, they met again. This time the weather was cool and rainy so they sat inside. The conversation got more personal than the previous Saturday. Teddy asked Jim about his wife and then pressed him for more details about his financial needs.

"Jim, I think the market value of your house is around $150,000. How much will that leave you after selling expenses?"

"I have $70,000 left on my mortgage from ten years ago."

"So, you would net about $75,000 after expenses."

"No, unfortunately, I also have a second mortgage for $25,000, so I'd only net about $50,000."

"But still, do you need more than that for your wife?"

"I already owe more than that, and I will need even more."

"How much more?"

"Another $100,000."

"Have you no other sources? You have a high-paying job, don't you?"

"Yes, but our contract will end soon. Much of what I'm paid is based on the contract revenue we receive. I have already spent my share, and we don't have another contract going forward."

"But surely you can find another way to get the money you need."

"I thought I had found one. But I made the mistake of trying to make money by betting on basketball games. I thought I knew what I was doing, but I didn't. I got in over my head and ended up owing $20,000 to a loan shark. I don't know how I can pay it off, and I'm starting to get threats. To be honest, I'm scared. I need another way."

"I see," she said in a sympathetic tone. "Will your company's design be the one that the government implements?"

"Yes. Why do you ask?"

"Jim, I have an idea that may help you if you are willing to do something that is not quite legal. Do you want to hear about it?"

It got his attention. "Of course, as long as I don't end up in jail."

"I have a connection to an organization that helps people who are in situations like yours. They are like a charity, and they could give you a $100,000 to help your wife."

"What is illegal about that?"

"They will want something in return," she said and then paused.

"Are you going to tell me what?"

"I will, but you will need to tell me *yes* or *no* before we leave here."

"What happens if I say no?"

She took a sip of her coffee, looked him in the eye, and said, "If you say *no*, we will never see each other again."

"Before I answer, tell me the status of the two couples that saw my house last week?"

"The one said they could not go above $140,000. The other is on the fence. If I talk to them more, I think they will offer the full $150,000."

Jim paused while he weighed the choices in his mind. If he declined to hear what she offered, he had a chance to sell his house and net $50,000; if he listened to her proposal and said *no*, he would get nothing; if he listened to her proposal and said *yes*, he would net $150,000, and he would have the money he needed for his wife.

"Okay, Teddy, please let me know your proposal."

"This organization will deposit $150,000 into your bank account with a letter stating the charitable reason for the gift. They will do this as soon as you have completed what they want—"

"And that is what?" he interrupted.

"They want you to provide documents describing your network design and the associated protocols that are used."

"Ooh . . . Teddy. That's a tall order. You are asking me to steal classified documents."

"Well, not quite Jim. You should be able to make copies of the documents. So, nothing will go missing. If the copies were in your briefcase, and you accidentally misplaced your briefcase, it would be excusable if anyone found out. But if you do it right, no one will know."

"I don't know. I need time to think."

"Think about your wife. The risk is much less than the risk you took by gambling on sports, and you want your wife to get the treatment she needs . . . don't you?"

"What are you going to do with these documents?"

"Jim, you know I can't tell you *that*—and it's best for you if you don't know."

After a long pause, he finally gave in. "Okay, I'll do it. When do you need this?"

"One week."

"Teddy, can we make it two weeks? Here's why. We're scheduled to make copies for the Air Force the week after next. It would be easier to do this unnoticed at that time."

"Okay Jim, two weeks it is."

"Where and how do I deliver it?"

"When you have the documents ready, you leave a message on the number on the card I gave you. I'll give you details then."

****

Almost two weeks later, on a Friday at lunchtime, they met again. According to Teddy's instruction, Jim brought with him a very thick attaché case loaded with documents. He arrived as instructed at precisely noon, the busiest time, especially on a workday. They sat at a small table for two. Jim set his attaché case on the floor under the table and gently slid it toward her side. They ordered sandwiches and ice tea, after which Jim excused himself for a few moments to use the restroom and wash up. When he returned, the food and tea were already on the table. Jim and Teddy chatted while enjoying the lunch—all very friendly. Teddy told Jim that she had an offer for him on the house and handed him an envelope. Jim opened it and was pleased to find a written offer and a binder check for $2,000, a sign of good faith.

Then Teddy asked, "Jim, did you bring the documents?"

"Yes, just as you instructed. Everything is there as you asked. When will the hundred-grand be in my bank account?"

"If all the documents are there, the money will be in your account within the next two hours. Jim, it was a pleasure doing business with you. I wish your wife the best."

With that, Jim said, "Thank you," got up, excused himself, and walked to his car, leaving the attaché case behind. Teddy had a smile on her face as she watched him leave and thought about what would happen next.

Jim went directly home after lunch and gave his wife the good news about the offer on the house. Then he called the bank and checked the balance in his bank account. Sure enough, a deposit of $100,000 was there waiting to be cleared. Teddy had kept her word. Now, he and his wife could sell the house and move into a less expensive garden apartment. Later when needed, she could go into a long-term care facility. Jim was pleased that his wife would have the resources she needed, and he felt the relief he had needed for so long.

Unfortunately, Jim's jubilation was short-lived. An hour later, he began to feel the burning in his gut and in his chest. Perhaps it was something he had eaten for lunch, he thought. His wife called an ambulance, but it was too late. Jim died that afternoon of an apparent heart attack on the way to the emergency room.

2

MORNING ROUTINE

Jon Wilson was in the hallway of a large office building. Alarms were sounding and people were flooding the hallways. "What is going on?" he asked aloud. "An incoming missile attack," he heard. He looked up as if it would be possible to hear or see something above him.

The next thing he knew, he was awake, staring at the fan hanging from his bedroom ceiling. *Just a bad dream*, he surmised. He immediately rolled over to his left and shut off the alarm. Then, he rolled back to his right. Mary Lou, his girlfriend, was just beginning to stir. He got up slowly, hoping she might enjoy a few more minutes of peace, and made his way to the bathroom, to relieve himself, brush, shower, and shave.

When he returned to the bedroom, Mary Lou had fallen back to sleep. He had already laid out his clothes for today, so he quietly picked up the pile and went off to his den to dress. He had a very important meeting today and he needed to look very professional. Today he would be wearing his gray suit, a white shirt, and a dark blue power tie that Mary Lou had given him for Christmas.

Jon and Mary Lou had been living together for almost a year. They got along well. Each had been married once before. Neither had kids, and except for Mary Lou's mother, neither had a family. Jon's marriage ended twenty-one years ago while stationed in Saigon. Back then, he had a supportive wife whom he adored, but the stresses of his work and his attraction to other women got in the way. At that time, Jon was officially an employee of the Department of State, and he had an office at the U.S. Embassy. However, his real job was working covert operations for the CIA. He was also an ex-special forces officer. He was six feet tall, weighed about

190 pounds, and was handsome. His charming personality was icing on the cake. Women could not resist him. Of course, this had been upsetting to his wife. To make matters worse, she wanted to have kids and live the American dream in a stable environment. He could not give that to her. Saigon was a war zone. As one might expect, his marriage did not end well. Over the years that followed, Jon became accustomed to the notion that the traditional American dream was never going to be his. You know, a wife, kids, a house in the suburbs with a white picket fence and a dog, etc. At fifty-four years old, Jon was more mature now. He cared for Mary Lou and had learned to remain loyal. However, he was not sure about getting married again.

Mary Lou McGuinness was twenty years his junior, and she was attractive. She was about five feet eight inches tall, trim, and very fit. Mary Lou had light-colored skin and light-colored hair. Her light hair belied her name, but McGuinness was not her maiden name. She and Jon had met two years ago while jogging along a path overlooking the Potomac River. He fell in love with her short wavy light brown hair, her cute seductive smile, and her obvious intelligence. They dated and decided to live together in Jon's condominium almost a year ago, when her lease expired. Mary Lou understood Jon. She told him that it was okay with her if they did not marry. She told Jon she felt secure in their relationship, and she was happy.

Jon had told her about his prior marriage, and she told him about her own misfortune with marriage. She told him that she had grown up in a rural town in North Carolina, received a degree from Duke University, and then married her high school sweetheart. She said that she and her husband lived in relative poverty in the same rural town where she grew up until they divorced due to her husband's drinking. Meanwhile, her father died, and her mother moved to the west coast. After her divorce, Mary Lou went to live with her mother in Oakland, California. While there, she worked at a travel agency by day, and earned a master's degree in management at night.

According to Mary Lou, however, living with her mother was difficult. Her mother was a devout Catholic and did not approve of her dating unless she got an annulment, and they did not agree on many other things as well. Mary Lou needed her independence, so after only four years, she came to D.C. to look for work, and make a new start in life. She was able to land another job working for a travel agency, but since she had experience and a master's degree, she quickly became the manager of the Travel Star Agency in nearby McLean, Virginia.

Jon worked at the CIA's headquarters in Langley, Virginia, about a mile from where Mary Lou worked. When they moved in together, they decided they only needed one car. Jon had just bought himself a fancy dark blue BMW, so Mary Lou sold her old clunker, and they shared his car. Normally they would drive to work together, but today would be different. Today, she would take the car to McLean herself, and Jon would take the Metro. Jon was a high-ranking officer at the CIA in charge of special projects. He had set up a meeting for today with his intelligence counterpart at the Pentagon. Other high-ranking officials from other agencies would also attend. This was a very important meeting concerning new intelligence he received affecting the nation's security. He would walk to the nearby Grosvenor Metro station and take the Metro all the way to the Pentagon.

Jon fetched the daily paper from the front door of his condominium apartment and took it to the kitchen. As he began preparing the coffee, he could hear Mary Lou stirring in the other room. She found the aroma of freshly brewed coffee very inviting and it would not be long before she would join him in the kitchen. Meanwhile, he poured himself some orange juice, swallowed his blood pressure pill, prepared a bowl of cereal and milk, and opened the newspaper.

Today was Thursday March 17, 1988. "Iran-Contra Indictments Returned" was the headline! The Iran–Contra affair was a complicated arrangement between Israel, the United States, and the rebels in Nicaragua. Using Israel as an intermediary, the U.S. had sold arms to Iran. The U.S. hoped to improve relations with Iran and get their help to free hostages held by Hezbollah in Lebanon. Meanwhile, Ollie North had arranged to divert some of the proceeds from the arms sale to aid the Contras in Nicaragua who were fighting the communist-backed Sandinista government. The entire operation was illegal.

Jon was only halfway through the article when Mary Lou entered the kitchen. "Good morning sweetheart," he told her and gave her a good morning kiss on the mouth. "Sorry I woke you up earlier than normal. I have—"

"It's okay Jon," she interrupted, "you told me you had an important meeting this morning—thanks for making the coffee. Did you remember to take your blood pressure pill?"

"Yes, I did. . . No need to remind me," he added.

"I'm just looking out for you. . . Do you know what time you will be home tonight?"

"I think so. I plan to work out of my temporary office at the Pentagon after the meeting. However, I will probably leave earlier than normal and catch the Metro around five. Be home by six thirty."

"I was thinking that maybe I could pick you up at the Metro station. You could call my work number before you leave the Pentagon. I don't like the idea of you walking from the station in the dark and in the cold. What does the paper say about today's weather?"

Jon went back to page one.

"It says lows this morning below freezing, but highs in the low forties—forty-five percent humidity—cloudy—no rain. Not so bad."

"I worry about you."

"It's okay Babe. You don't need to worry, but I'll call you before I leave work and we can take it from there. Okay?"

"Okay, but today is Saint Patty's Day, and I saw where Kelsey's is having a special corned beef and cabbage dinner. I was thinking that maybe we could go. I could pick you up at the 'Kiss and Ride' and we could drive right from there. What do think?"

"It's a date," he said, as he gave her a peck on the neck.

Then Jon went back to his den, picked up his attaché case, made his way to the front closet, put on his winter topcoat and hat, and said, "Bye" to Mary Lou. As he walked out into the hallway, he heard "Don't forget to call me." Rather than wait for the elevator, to make it all the way up to the nineteenth floor, he took the stairs down the first six flights and then took the elevator from there. He felt good as he walked out the main entrance of his condominium onto the street. Jon's only medical issue was high blood pressure and he took pills for that. Otherwise, at fifty-four years of age, he was still in great physical shape and he welcomed every opportunity to stay that way. It was cold out, and it was breezy, but he did not mind. He enjoyed walking. The Grosvenor Metro station was only a half mile away, and the fresh air felt good to him.

****

It was around 7:30 a.m. when Jon arrived at the station, the start of peak rush hour. The station was busy. He inserted his fare-card into the turnstyle reader, took it back when it popped up on the other side, and walked down to the platform. Jon was beginning to feel the cold, so he made his way to a covered waiting area. Several others were already huddled inside. The train would be there in about seven more minutes.

When the train arrived at Grosvenor, no one got off. Jon squeezed his way onto the train and was lucky enough to find a seat. After settling down, he began to think about the meeting he had set up for 9:00 a.m. Yesterday, he had received information from an operative named Chan. Chan worked in the U.S. embassy in Beijing as a communication data processing specialist. However, his real job was spying for the CIA. After reviewing the information and verifying its veracity with his key staff, Jon made the decision to request this morning's meeting. The information was critical to national security, and action was required.

As the train moved through the tunnel below ground, the constant whirring from wheels and air movement lulled Jon into a dreamy state. The early hour and the walk in the cold probably added to his semi-conscious state. He began to mentally reminisce about Chan. Officially Chan was dead. Figuratively, Jon had killed him, but technically, he had saved his life, for which Chan would be forever grateful. Chan had worked under-cover for Jon in 1967 in Saigon. The mission was to root out a network of enemy agents, Viet Cong, and North Vietnamese sympathizers. Chan had a serious girlfriend named Kim who lived in Cholon, the Chinese district of Saigon. Chan suspected Kim's father of being an enemy ringleader. During a visit to the family's home, Chan was successful in photographing a document containing the names of enemy agents in the Saigon area. Unfortunately, the father became suspicious and used a ruse to summon Chan for a "family meeting" at the end of the next workday. However, Chan had a meeting that evening with his CIA contact, Donna Rice, to turn over the roll of film containing evidence. Chan was suspicious of the reason given for the family meeting. The father had claimed that his daughter thought she was pregnant, and the matter required a family discussion. Although Chan and his girlfriend had frequent sex, he did not think it possible that she was pregnant. However, he and Kim were truly in love, and he was not about to abandon her. He felt the need to go, and although he sensed some risk, thought he could talk his way through it. He tried to contact Donna, but unable to do so, he called Jon and explained the situation. The father was to have a driver pick him up at his bachelor officer quarters (BOQ). Jon asked where the camera was and learned it was in Chan's room at the BOQ. Jon told Chan to keep the appointment with Kim's father and that he would notify Donna on his behalf. Of course, none of this is what really happened.

Jon had not told Donna or Chan anything more. He did not want Chan to have his family meeting. Surely, that would mean interrogation followed by death. Instead, Jon arranged to pick up Chan as he left work and before he could return to his BOQ. Chan resisted at first, but the two agents that Jon sent to intercept him were convincing. They took Chan's wallet and ID and whisked him off to an undisclosed location. Chan found himself on a CIA flight to Hong Cong before the night was over. Meanwhile Jon arranged for a mutilated body from a morgue to show up in the future with Chan's identification. Chan's death had to be believable and he could not risk sharing the truth with anyone. Jon often had mixed feelings about what he did.

Although Chan had no family, there were people who would miss him. He felt bad for Kim who lost a lover. Kim would initially think that Chan ran out on her and may later think her father had killed him. Jon also felt bad for Chan but did not see an alternative to what he did. In addition, he felt bad for Donna, who he considered a friend as well as an agent. For a while, Donna thought she was in some way responsible. No one could know the truth, and Jon carried this around with him.

Something caused Jon to stir and regain his senses. The man sitting next to him had gotten off and left his newspaper on Jon's lap. It was the Washington Post, the same as Jon was reading at home. Jon began reading the rest of the paper he had started earlier. He read an opinion piece predicting that the Cold War with the Soviet Union could soon be over and that the U.S. could be the victor. The opinion was based upon several factors. These included President Reagan's Strategic Defense Initiative (SDI), the new Intermediate Nuclear Forces Treaty (INF), the economic downturn in the Soviet Union, and the initiation by Chairman Gorbachev of a more capitalistic and democratic government. The writer went on to say that the hardline Communists in the Soviet Union would try to prevent this from happening.

The next stop was Metro Center where he could change to the Blue Line. Most people would get off at Metro Center. The station would be crowded, and he hated crowds. He took a deep breath, got off the train and fought his way through the crowds to the lower level of the station, and waited for the next Blue Line Train.

3

INTELLIGENCE

The Blue Line train headed away from downtown and across the river into Virginia. Only a few riders got off at the Pentagon Station. Jon left the train, walked the length of the station, and entered a special entrance to the Pentagon. Screening was fast; he had an attaché case but no weapon—nothing marked classified in his case. One of Jon's agents would bring all the information he needed for the meeting. Up on the second floor, he said hello to a receptionist who offered him coffee, which he declined. Then he went to the temporary office assigned to him for the day and hung up his coat and hat. No sooner had he done so than he heard a voice behind him.

"Good morning, Jon."

Jon turned to face the General standing in the doorway. "Good morning, Ken." General Ken Morehouse was Jon's counterpart at the Defense Intelligence Agency (DIA). As a Deputy Director, he had one star on his shoulder. Jon knew the General as Ken, but in public, he would address him as *General*. Jon and Ken had graduated from West Point in the same year, more than thirty years ago. Ken and his wife Kathy knew Jon and Mary Lou socially. They were friends and they respected each other.

"Jon, did you hear the news?"

"No. What news?"

"Just happened early this morning. Iran is accusing Iraq of using poison gas."

"My gosh! It's one thing after another. I'll be sure and get the full report from Jim later today," Jon said, referring to Jim Miller, his administrative assistant. Jon didn't say it, but he already knew what was going on. President Reagan did not want Iran to succeed against Iraq. As a result, the CIA was feeding intelligence to Iraq and looking the other way whenever they used mustard gas, cyanide gas, or Sarin gas.

Together they made their way down three floors to the conference room where the meeting would take place. The two exchanged pleasantries along the way but said nothing of the issue they were here to discuss. They showed their IDs to the soldier guarding the door of the room and he allowed them to enter. Others had not yet arrived.

The conference room was below ground level; it was impenetrable and safe. The room was set up with an oval table surrounded by ten cushioned chairs. An overhead projector was set up at one end of the oval table and pointed to a wall with a screen that pulled down from the ceiling. An easel stand with flip charts were nearby. The room was spy-proof. The only communication was a hard-wired red phone located in a far corner of the room. The electromagnetic shielding and soundproof construction allowed no other communication in or out. The thick reinforced walls were considered bombproof, and no one was allowed in or out without proper credentials.

The General was first to speak. "Jon, what is this meeting about? It sounded urgent."

"Yes, it is, but I would rather wait until everyone is here. My assistant should be along soon with the documents I will present."

Just then, the others started to arrive. The meeting started at precisely 9:00 a.m. or 0900 hours to the General. Jon had brought the matter to the attention of the President's Deputy National Security Advisor on Tuesday, and he had agreed to call the meeting and allow Jon to present his information. He had invited the appropriate members of the National Security Planning Group (NSPG). The President set up the NSPG to plan actions regarding the country's national security and interests in the Strategic Defense Initiative (SDI). The NSPG was a subset of the larger National Security Council (NSC). Ronald Reagan had made the SDI initiative public in March of 1983. Since then, the U.S. had spent billions to create the nuclear defense shield that the President envisioned. The Soviet Union and the USA had been stockpiling nuclear weapons for years. Both countries now had the capability to launch Intercontinental Ballistic Missiles carrying nuclear warheads. Doomsday was a real fear. President

Reagan was committed to the concept of either eliminating all nuclear weapons or building a defense mechanism that rendered them useless. Only five people were invited to today's meeting. The Deputy National Security Advisor represented the President. Jon represented the CIA. The General represented the Department of Defense, Intelligence. An Assistant Deputy Director represented the FBI. Finally, an Under Secretary responsible for International Security represented the Department of State. Each of the invitees had also brought their top assistant. Jon had met with these individuals before, and they had some familiarity with the subject that Jon was about to present.

The President's Security Advisor began the meeting. "I want to thank all of you for coming today on short notice. Jon Wilson approached me on Monday with information that I thought you should hear ASAP."

Then Jon spoke. "I also want to thank you all for coming this morning. The good news is that I'm not going to talk about Iran or Nicaragua." Jon could see the relief on the faces before him, especially the two from the Department of State. Jon had always thought that the State Department knew a lot more than they revealed. Congress may have thought so as well. Only last month they had rejected a funding request to support the Contras.

"Before I begin, I want you to know that anything we say in this room must stay here. Nothing can be revealed to the public or to Congress except as authorized by the President. We can't afford to have any leaks," he said as he looked at the Undersecretary of State. "This information is highly classified and our national security is at stake. My boss, the CIA Director of Intelligence, has reviewed and fully authorized this presentation. What I'm going to tell you is that we are facing a serious security threat to our ballistic missile defenses and to the implementation of the President's Strategic Defense Initiative or SDI."

Jon could see that he had everyone's attention and continued with his presentation. "I believe that most of your NSPG meetings have dealt with broad issues concerning types and numbers of anti-missile weaponry, and of topics to negotiate with the Soviets. You also know that although the Pentagon and Congress approved the broad architecture for the SDI, funding to do more development work is a problem. In the meantime, programs that are already in place need to continue and must evolve. If this does not happen, we won't maintain our advantage over the Soviets.

"One of these programs is the Satellite Defense Support Program under the Air Force Space Command. Currently, we have multiple satellites in space that serve as an early warning system for a possible nuclear attack. These satellites continuously send information from infrared sensors, digital photographs, and signal intelligence down to ground stations here on Earth. The ground stations forward the information to appropriate computers and personnel, such as those in NORAD, for analysis and action. This program continues to grow and evolve, as we improve technology and add satellites.

"I have just received intelligence from a source in Beijing, China that the Soviets are involved in slowing this evolution. According to our source, the Soviets are working with the Chinese to introduce viral Trojan sleeper code into our Satellite Defense Support management and communications software. This would not only cause immediate havoc, but also potentially delay the development of the full SDI program. We expect that on or about the middle of May, the Chinese will deliver this code to the United States via their embassy. We believe the intention is to imbed this code into a software release planned by the IBM Corporation. Precisely how they would do this, we do not know, but—"

"Jon before you proceed, I'd like to request something." It was the Deputy National Security Advisor. "You referred to *viral Trojan sleeper code*. This is a new concept for some of us. Would you mind giving us a short tutorial on what that is?"

"Okay . . . sure. What we are talking about here is computer code secretly installed onto a computer with the intention of doing harm. The term *Trojan* refers to the fact that the bad code poses as legitimate code. Information from our source indicates that the code may be *viral*, which means that it can replicate itself and spread to other computers—kind of like a chain letter. The term *sleeper* means that it will not do harm until some external event triggers it, such as a date."

"Thanks Jon. I'm sorry for interrupting, but I thought that information was very helpful."

"Do any of you have any other questions before I proceed," Jon asked as he reclaimed the floor. . . "If not, I have asked my assistant, Jim, to show you several documents on the overhead projector. There will be more time for questions after that."

Jim took documents out of his locked briefcase and prepared to put them onto the overhead projector as Jon explained what they would see.

"The first three documents are intercepted messages between an agent identified as Teddy and the Soviet Consulate in San Francisco."

Jon turned toward Jim. "Jim, please show them the first one. This document makes the connection between IBM and Soviet involvement."

Date: March 5, 1987
To: Ivan Boskovitch, Deputy Consul
Subject: Project Westlake
Transcribed phone message to the Soviet Consulate in San Francisco
This is Teddy. Westlake relocation completed. Assets now in place and new communication channels established. Operation Westlake resuming.

"Westlake was an IBM location that relocated to Boulder Colorado," Jon said. "Then there was this message:"

Date: May 19, 1987
To: Ivan Boskovitch, Deputy Consul
Subject: Project Westlake
Transcribed phone message to the Soviet Consulate in San Francisco.
This is Teddy. I have received the requested documents.

"Jon, a question?" It was the President's Security Advisor again.

"Yes, of course."

"These intercepts occurred quite a while ago. Was some action taken at that time?"

"Yes, it was. Being new on the scene, you may not have been briefed. I'll let the FBI fill you in."

"The FBI did investigate this. In July, we uncovered a plot to destroy satellite ground stations on government property in the Denver area. We arrested two individuals who were students at the University of Colorado and who were members of a pro-communist, anti-government group. Those two individuals pointed us toward another individual, who may have been the ringleader. However, he disappeared before we could talk to him. We found his remains a week later in Boulder Creek. In addition to a cache of explosives, we recovered documents that gave them access to the ground station. We thought these documents were the ones that Teddy referred to in her message. We kept the details quiet. Although we continued to hunt for Teddy, we thought we had nipped the imminent threat in the bud. We are only just now learning otherwise."

Jon reclaimed the floor. "Thank you."

He once again turned to Jim. "Jim, please show them the next document. This document clearly shows that there is an attempt to interfere with an IBM software upgrade in Boulder. *Panda* is a new name. We don't know who that is. We assume Boskovitch relayed this message to the Soviet embassy in Beijing, China."

> *Date: February 20, 1988*
> *To: Ivan Boskovitch, Deputy Consul in San Francisco*
> *Subject: Project Westlake*
> *Fax message received by the Soviet Consulate in San Francisco*
> *IBM S/W upgrade planned for mid-May. Panda needs computer code in Boulder before this. Please ensure. Teddy.*

"The next set of documents is a thread of electronic messages that we intercepted between the Soviet and Chinese Embassies in Beijing. As you can see, we took the liberty of translating from Chinese into English."

Jon read each of the following three documents aloud:

> *Date: February 25, 1988*
> *To: Tin Lee, Ministry of Foreign Affairs in Beijing*
> *Re: Project Westlake*
> *After you received the network specs & communication protocols last August, you estimated the project would take six months. Please advise as to the current status.*
> *Igor Malinsky*

> \-

> *Date: March 10, 1988*
> *To: Igor Malinsky, Soviet Embassy in Beijing*
> *Re; Project Westlake*

Please be advised that code will be available for shipment on or about May 1st of this year. Please let us know shipping requirements. Upon your final payment to COSTA VI, we will ship as requested.
Tin Lee

Date: March 15, 1988
To: Tin Lee, Ministry of Foreign Affairs in Beijing
Re: Response to your advisement
Send code to Soviet Consulate in S.F. via your Consulate and then private courier. Transmit two IBM 3480 tape cartridges in shielded diplomatic pouches. Payment will arrive with Costa VI immediately upon verification of shipment.
Igor Malinsky

"Okay, the implications are that a theft of classified information occurred sometime before August of last year, and that the Chinese Costa VI is using the information to create malicious computer code that will be sent back to the states for use in May of this year."

Jon continued. "Adding to this is the slow progress made over the past year and one-half to upgrade existing computer code and data tables. The IBM Corporation is heavily involved in the effort to expand our existing process to accommodate new data types and more satellites. They support multiple computers used by the Air Force Space Command to manage satellites. The original IBM group was in Westlake Village, California. Early last year, they relocated to Boulder Colorado and the size of the operation was increased. The work they are doing is highly classified and both IBM employees and government personnel have access to information and secure communications networks. The Air Force has reported multiple issues with coding errors found during attempted upgrades. Each time, IBM swore that the code was thoroughly tested, and that the errors were not present before delivery. In addition, from time to time, glitches appear to occur in the processing of data. One day, everything went dark for no apparent reason. If the Soviets had planned an attack that day, we would have been vulnerable."

Not a moment went by when, "Mr. Wilson, I must register my protest regarding the apparent wiretapping and eves-dropping that your organization has apparently conducted." It was the Undersecretary of State. "As you know, it is against State Department policy to do this kind of thing and it endangers our abilities to work with our diplomatic counterparts. In fact, if this came out in the open it could be the cause of the nuclear war that we are here to avoid."

"Well then, I guess we best keep this under wraps," Jon retorted. He had a genuine dislike for the State Department, ever since the fall of Saigon in January 1975. He blamed their indecision and excessive desire to be diplomatic for the abandonments and deaths of thousands of Americans and American sympathizers. However, Jon realized he had to keep his emotions in check and quickly followed up. "Please allow me to continue. There will be more time for discussion later."

Jon continued. "In light of these developments, I have the following recommendations:

First—I recommend that the Inspector General do an audit of the security procedures followed by the personnel associated with the U.S. Air Force's Defense Support Program. I would look to the General Morehouse to initiate this request;

Second—I recommend that the FBI investigate the possibility of non-military actions that would adversely affect the Defense Support Program. This investigation would focus on the processing of data from reconnaissance satellites, and on updates to software and databases. It would determine if a foreign agent is interfering with the process;

Third—I recommend that the FBI request that IBM do an internal audit of security procedures at the Boulder facility focused on their contract with the Air Force. I know someone who is currently part of the audit staff at IBM, someone I worked with in Vietnam. I would highly recommend that we reactivate his security clearance and have him work with us for the duration of the audit. I have every confidence that if there is an issue at IBM, he will find it;

Fourth—I recommend that all the interagency activities be coordinated by General Morehouse of the DIA under the code-name, *Boulder Creek*;

Finally—I recommend that the President be informed of the situation at the President's next security briefing."

Jon paused to let his recommendations sink in. "You've been very polite," he told them. "Any more questions?"

"I have a question." It was the Undersecretary of State again.

"Yes. Please go ahead." Jon replied as politely as he could.

"When President Reagan met with Chairman Gorbachev in Iceland, they seemed to agree that reducing the chance of nuclear war was a good thing. Reportedly, Reagan even offered to share the defensive technology with the Soviets. So, why would the Soviet Union want to sabotage our efforts in this area?"

"Well, not everyone in the Soviet Union agrees with Gorbachev. The Soviets have a powerful hard-core contingent led by the KGB that would like to keep the status quo. They fear that if the U.S. were to continue developing its missile defense shield, the Soviet Union would be at a disadvantage. They are especially concerned that President Reagan may put nuclear weapons in space. The Soviets no longer have the resources to keep up and they fear a long-term loss of world-wide power to the United States. They are also against Gorbachev's concept of Perestroika, which gives more power to the people of the Soviet Union. The hard-core Communists fear a loss of centralized control over the members of the Union that would further erode their world-wide influence."

"Okay, thank you. May I ask another question?"

"Sure."

"What happens if we do nothing?"

Once again, Jon reminded himself that he needed to keep his emotions in check. After all, how could the State Department not understand the significance of what he had said? "Sir, if we do nothing, there is a good chance that the Soviets will inject malicious code into our process that will take our anti-ballistic early warning systems down. If this happens, it will offer the Soviets an opportunity to launch a missile attack—"

Before there could be a retort, the General spoke. "I endorse Jon's recommendations. If these are acts of espionage, I can envision situations where the Soviets could attack us without warning, or even create an accidental attack to demonstrate our inability to protect our country. However, even if the Soviets did not launch missiles, taking down our early warning system would be a serious problem for us. It would delay the implementation of our SDI programs. It would make the United States look weak. It would give the Soviets more international prestige, and lower ours. I'll contact the Inspector General later today."

There were no more questions. The President's Security Advisor adjourned the meeting.

****

Jon spent the rest of his day at his Pentagon office. He sent a secure message to his boss summarizing the results of the meeting, and then spent the rest of the day dealing with other issues. At the end of the day, he called Mary Lou as agreed, and began his journey home on the Metro. On the way home, he thought about his presentation earlier in the day. It went well, he thought. He had every confidence that Ken would ensure the implementation of his recommendations. He arrived at the Grosvenor Metro Station at 6:20 p.m. Mary Lou was at the Kiss & Ride.

Jon opened the passenger door, tossed his attaché case onto the back seat, and climbed into the passenger seat. He pulled her to him and gave her a kiss. "It's nippy out. I appreciate your picking me up."

"How was your day?" she asked.

"I did the best I could for America," he responded.

"I'd love to hear about it. You ready for corned beef and cabbage?"

"You bet."

4

THE ASSIGNMENT

Peter Troutman was a member of IBM's Internal Corporate Audit staff. It was early April, and he was in the fifth week of a six-week audit of the management practices at an IBM location in Endicott, New York. He sat at a temporary desk, writing notes to himself about irregularities he had observed earlier in the day. The ringing of the phone disturbed his concentration. It was Greg, his manager back at the home office in Bethesda, Maryland.

"Peter, I want you to return to Bethesda and meet with me on Monday. I have an exciting new project that I want you to be involved with."

"Sure, but what about the project I'm doing now? Will I come back here after we meet? Michael is depending on me to finish up something for his meeting with management."

"Yes, I understand. I'll talk with Michael. I think you will have some time during the next two weeks to finish up."

Peter returned to his apartment in Rockville, Maryland on Friday evening. He had been away from home for almost two weeks, and welcomed the opportunity to catch up on personal matters—such as grocery shopping, doing his laundry, reading tons of mail, and paying bills. He lived alone, but he loved his living arrangements. He had a very nice large luxury one-bedroom apartment. It had a kitchen, a dining room, a living room, and a walk-out patio. Except for the kitchen and the bathroom, it was fully carpeted. The bedroom had a large walk-in closet. He even had a washer and dryer in the apartment.

Peter was now in his mid-forties, had two daughters in college, and lived separately from his wife whom he intended to divorce. When

243

he separated from his wife almost two years ago, he had arranged for a *temporary assignment*. That simply meant transfer from one audit team to another, but without moving his official residence, which was still in New York State. A temporary assignment also meant an additional income of about twenty percent in the form of a living allowance. He could spend it in whatever manner he chose, without filling out an expense report. He had it made.

On Monday morning, he drove the short distance from his apartment in Rockville, Maryland to his office in North Bethesda. Several other companies had offices in the same office park, including the Marriot Corporation and Martin Marietta. IBM itself owned a building in the park referred to as "The Rusty Bucket"—another interesting story.

When built in the 1960s, the builders used an experimental steel alloy imported from Japan to create the facade. Over the years, the surface oxidized and became the color of rust. By 1988, the building looked like a rusty bucket. The building made national news in 1982 when an ex-employee drove his car through the glass doors and shot up the place. During a seven-hour siege, he murdered three people and injured nine. However, IBM also rented office space in several other buildings in the office park.

The audit office was in rented space above a coffee shop. Peter parked in the underground garage and made his way up the elevator to the third floor, where he would meet with his manager, Gregory Stevens. As Peter walked down the hall toward Greg's corner office, he could detect the faint aroma of coffee. He said hello to Susan as he passed by her desk. Susan was the department's secretary. "Good morning, Peter," she replied. "Welcome back." Greg was already in his office, sipping his morning brew, and puffing on a cigarette. "Good morning. I had Susan get us coffee," he said and motioned for Peter to have a seat.

"Oh, thanks," Peter replied as he took a seat and removed the lid on the cup of coffee that Susan had left for him.

Both Peter and Greg were in their mid-forties. After several promotions, each had obtained the level of *Senior*. At IBM, that was akin to what *Colonel* was in the military. Both had management experience at IBM, but Peter excelled at detective work, and Greg excelled at management. Peter's title was *Senior Auditor*, and Greg's title was *Senior Audit Manager*. Greg's department was part of IBM's Corporate Internal Audit Group. Their department was responsible for auditing the operation of organizations that were in IBM's Federal Systems Division. Peter and Greg made a good team, and they respected each other. The two of them sipped coffee as they talked.

"Peter, on Friday, I received a call from the FBI field office in Denver, Colorado. They want us to do a security audit of the Boulder facility. They want *you* to lead it."

"Okay, when will the audit start?"

"I have a meeting scheduled with the Denver office Thursday morning. They asked that you be there with me. I assume they will tell us what they are looking for then."

"Sounds serious. If the FBI is involved, does that mean that this is part of some sort of criminal investigation?"

"I don't have any details. Hopefully we'll get what we need on Wednesday."

"Greg, may I ask you something?"

"Sure . . . What?"

"Isn't Boulder involved in doing work for the Air Force?"

"Yes."

"If we are going to do a security audit, won't we need security clearances?"

"I asked that question, and they told me they will take care of the paperwork and explain everything on Thursday."

"One more question please. Why do they want *me* to lead the audit?"

"I should be asking you that question. They specifically asked for you. I was afraid to ask why."

Peter chuckled. "I guess we'll find out on Thursday."

Susan would make the travel arrangements for Peter and Greg to fly out to Denver on Wednesday. Until then, Peter would learn about the operation of the Boulder site and brush up on how to conduct a security audit. He would also spend time talking on the phone with Michael and the auditors in Endicott and filling out expense reports. Tuesday evening, he repacked his suitcase while listening to the evening news. The big news item was that Arab hijackers had killed their second hostage in Kuwait. Of greater interest to Peter was the news that Russia had signed a pact with

Afghanistan to stop the fighting there and remove their troops. The pact had the support of the United States.

****

The five-hour flight from Dulles Airport was uneventful. They landed at Stapleton, rented a full-size sedan from Hertz, had a late lunch, and went directly to a Marriott's Inn, where they would stay for the night. After seven hours of travel, they would rest up for the early morning meeting with the FBI in Denver, and an afternoon meeting with the IBM management in Boulder.

The next morning, Greg and Peter met in the hotel lobby. Both were wearing business suits with white shirts and neckties, appropriate IBM attire. Greg was wearing a black suit and a red power tie; Peter a gray suit and a dark blue tie with a floral design. They enjoyed breakfast at the Marriott before leaving for their nine o'clock meeting at the FBI Denver Field Office. Greg drove. As it turned out, the FBI office was not very far away. If they did not need the car after the meeting, they could have walked. They arrived for their meeting ten minutes early and parked in the open parking lot across the street from the main entrance to the building. The white stucco-faced building spanned the entire block on 19th Street between Stout Street and California Street. From the parking lot, they could see five floors. A lower floor seemed to be a half story below ground, and the main floor appeared to be a half story above ground. The main floor had tall windows two stories in height that surrounded the building. A rim ran above the tall windows and separated the next three floors of windows. A wide concrete stairway led from 19th Street to the main entrance. The building looked like it could have been an old main post office building. Greg and Peter walked across the street, up the stairway, and into a lobby on the main floor. They observed a sign telling people where to go. A corridor to the right was for *fingerprinting services*. A corridor to the left was for *official use only*. Greg and Peter proceeded straight ahead to a manned security checkpoint between the entrance and the lobby that seemed to have been added as an afterthought.

The guard spoke to Peter first. He was matter-of-fact in his demeanor.

"Do you have a bag or briefcase?"

"No." The guard could see he did not.

"Are you carrying firearms?"

"No."

"Please open your jacket."

"What is the nature of your business here?"

Greg had not told him the name of the person they were to meet with. "My manager set up the meeting—"

"We are here to see Special Agent in Charge, Roger Colby," Greg said from behind.

"Please wait your turn, sir. I was asking him, not you. I will do you next."

"Yes, we are here to see Special Agent Colby," Peter replied.

"Now, please step through the scanner. Then, proceed into the lobby area and to the reception desk on the right. The receptionist will contact the person you are here to see, and someone will come down to escort you to your meeting."

"Now you, sir," he said pointing to Greg.

A young woman greeted them at the reception desk. "Welcome to FBI Denver. Please sign in."

She waited for them to finish and verified they had signed. Then she politely asked in perfectly correct English, "Gentlemen, whom are you here to see this morning?"

"We have a nine o'clock appointment with Special Agent in Charge Roger Colby," Greg replied.

Then the polite young woman asked them to please take a seat, and someone would be there shortly to escort them to a conference room where Special Agent Colby would join them.

Five minutes later another polite young woman greeted them.

"Hello, gentlemen. I'm Agent McCarthy. Please clip on these visitor badges and follow me."

They followed her into an elevator, up to the third floor, and down a long corridor. They passed several conference rooms enclosed by glass walls. People who met in those rooms were exposed to the world—like being in a fish bowl, Peter thought.

"May I ask where we are going?" Peter asked in a whimsical way.

She chuckled. "Just a little bit further. Agent Colby has asked that his meeting with you be in his private conference room outside of his office."

She led the way into a small conference room with a mahogany table surrounded by several red cushioned swivel chairs. The room had no windows and no glass walls.

"Please be seated. Agent Colby will be here shortly. Would you like coffee?"

Peter and Greg shook their heads in the negative. Greg replied for the two of them. "No thanks. We're all set. Thank you."

Within a few minutes, Agent Colby arrived and stood in the doorway. "Hello gentlemen. I'm Special Agent in Charge Roger Colby." His presence was commanding. He was a white male in his early forties. He had an athletic build, weighed about 180 pounds, and stood six feet tall. He had a full head of dark black hair. He sported a black business suit, a white shirt, and a red power tie. Colby and Greg were dressed alike. This observation prompted Peter to have an idle thought—that he kept to himself. They were both wearing their power suits, but if the two of them had a power struggle, Greg would not have a chance.

Peter and Greg arose from their seats and introduced themselves.

"Did my assistant offer you coffee?"

Greg answered. "Yes, she did. Thank you. We're all set."

"Then please be seated and let's get started."

Colby gave them a moment to settle in their seats and then began. "I talked to Mr. Stevens on the phone on Monday and gave him a summary of what this is all about, but I want to repeat it for your benefit Mr. Troutman. Initially, the Department of Defense requested this audit. As you know, IBM in Boulder is engaged in providing software to the Air Force under a long-term contract. The Department of Defense is concerned that a security weakness could compromise the computer code or prevent its delivery altogether. I understand you have a template that your audit team follows when it does security audits. Is that correct?"

Greg answered, "Yes, sir. We have guidelines that we follow."

"Can you tell me more? What are some of the things you look at and what types of questions do you ask when you do an audit?"

"Yes, sir," Greg continued. "You may think of our audits as operational or process audits. We verify that the process that IBM management is following is according to IBM's documented policies and procedures. We also observe situations that may require new or revised policies and procedures. We then report our findings and recommendations to the IBM managers responsible for the operation."

"I see. How many people do you normally have on an audit?"

Again, Greg answered as Peter patiently listened and occasionally nodded in agreement. "Usually six, but it can vary depending upon need."

"I see. Well, for this audit, your normal process is fine, but in addition, we will want more focus on the code creation and distribution process itself. Do you have the right mix of skills?"

Peter and Greg looked at each other, and then Peter spoke. "Mr. Colby, we have three on our team with those specific skills right now, but there is someone on the Santa Teresa team that I would recommend adding to our team for this assignment," he said as he looked at Greg.

Greg nodded. "Yes, I assume you mean Noah Bosch?"

Peter met Noah in Santa Teresa when he helped them with an audit at that facility. Socially, Noah was a nerdy type. However, when it came to computers and programming, he was a genius. Unlike some geniuses, he was not arrogant, and he was likable. He saved the day on the Santa Teresa audit. He figured out how a disgruntled employee was able to hack into an IBM database and manipulate files. Peter was very impressed by this and wanted him on the Boulder audit.

"Exactly," Peter acknowledged. Do you think we can get him?"

"I'll try," Greg responded. "That would free up people to finish the audit we are still doing up in Endicott." Then he looked at Colby. "Mr. Colby, do you think that four people on this audit would be sufficient?" What is the time frame you are looking at?"

Colby responded. "The time frame I'm looking at is four weeks."

Peter and Greg looked at each other, almost in shock. Greg spoke up. "We really want to accommodate you, but normally our audits take six or seven weeks. What is happening in four weeks?"

"Unfortunately, I can't tell you right now, for security reasons. Okay, I'm looking for results, but the final report does not need to be complete at that time. By the way, your audit report may need a security classification. We need to talk more about security clearances. You two and your team will need security clearances, one reason why your team should not be too large. However, obtaining clearances for the two of you won't take long."

Peter and Greg looked surprised but remained silent.

Recognizing their puzzlement, Colby continued. "In case you were wondering, I can get you two approved quickly because each of you is already in our system, and your status is *current*. You have already had background checks. All we would need would be updates to your information. Then we will have you sign non-disclosure agreements, and your status will become *active*."

Peter and Greg eyed each other, not having known of each other's intelligence background.

"Agent McCarthy will have you sign non-disclosure statements and paperwork that will apply solely for the duration of this audit. These clearances will be at a level sufficient for you to do your jobs. However, I need to know the particulars of your team members. Please select your team as soon as possible. They may need to fill out the entire SF 86 forms, and background checks may be necessary. It may take a while to get them the appropriate clearances. However, I can expedite and obtain *interim* clearances. That should save some time. I'll give you forms that you can give to them. Mr. Stevens, you will also sign a form indicating your responsibility for the team's actions. Are we good?"

"Yes, sir," Peter and Greg said almost in unison.

Colby then picked up the phone on the wall of the conference room and called Agent McCarthy. "Agent McCarthy will escort you to another room where she will have you sign papers. In the meantime, I'd like to borrow Mr. Troutman for a few minutes. He will catch up." Both Peter and Greg looked at Colby with surprise and then each other as they wondered why.

Colby could see some angst on Peter's face, and after Greg left the room he said, "Please relax. Jon Wilson wanted me to say hello. He had specifically asked that you lead this audit. He thought he might be here today but could not make it. He wanted to meet with you and suggested that perhaps you could meet with him this coming Saturday at the Pentagon. Is it doable for you? If it is, I'll let him know." Although, this caught Peter by surprise, he tried not to show it.

Jon Wilson was CIA. Peter had known him in Saigon in 1967. On a couple of occasions after that, Jon had made use of Peter's expertise in process analysis and probability estimation. But this was different. Peter wondered why the CIA and the FBI would want him to lead an audit internal to IBM.

"Did Jon say why he wanted to meet?" Peter calmly asked.

"Yes, it has to do with this audit, but I was advised to allow him to give you the details when you see him."

"Please tell him yes. I will be there. What time?"

"Ten in the morning. That okay?"

"Sure."

"Well . . . Stevens is probably wondering what I'm doing to you. Mr. Troutman it was a pleasure and I look forward to the next several weeks."

With that, the two of them shook hands, and Colby motioned to a room a few cubicles away where he would find Greg.

****

Peter and Greg returned to their car. They were in the process of removing their jackets and carefully setting them on the back seat when Greg asked, "Peter, would you mind driving this time?"

"I don't mind. Why?"

"I haven't had a cigarette since this morning. I hope you don't mind if I smoke while you drive."

"I suppose. Perhaps you could crack the window. We probably don't need the air-conditioning anyway. It's only about sixty degrees out."

"Thanks. I really need it."

Peter found his way to Route 36 and began the drive to Boulder where they would meet with John Armstrong, the Manager of the Boulder IBM site. They had scheduled the meeting for two o'clock that afternoon. The Boulder site was about an hour's drive, and it was only eleven o'clock now. They would have time to stop for lunch on the way. They had not gone far before Greg asked the question that was eating at him. He could not hold back any longer.

"Peter, aren't you going to tell me what you and Colby talked about?"

Peter chuckled. "I was wondering how long it would take you to ask. Do you remember on Monday, you told me that they specifically asked me to lead the audit and to be at this meeting?"

"Yes."

"And you asked why?"

"Yes."

"Well, Colby didn't tell me why, but he told me who made the request."

After a few moments of silence that seemed forever, Greg asked, "And the answer is?"

"Have you heard the expression *if I tell you, I will have to kill you?*"

"Come on now, stop toying with me."

"Okay, someone else was supposed to be at the meeting today. He couldn't make it. It's someone that I have known for a long time. I will meet with him on Saturday in D.C., and he will tell me more at that time." Then turning to face Greg, he added, "After that, if there's anything more I can tell you, I will." Without responding, Greg lit up another cigarette.

"I thought you were trying to quit."

"I was. I made it several hours, but the urge got too great. Maybe I don't have the willpower. You ever smoke?"

"I did . . . a long time ago."

"How did you quit?"

"Well, you're right. It's not easy. I quit three times before it stuck, but the trick is not just willpower."

"What then?"

"After I quit, I volunteered as a facilitator for the American Cancer Society, and I ran clinics to help others quit. It will take a while, but if you are really interested, I may be able to help you."

"Can you just give me the crash course?"

"Okay. What I learned was that smoking is partly a nicotine addiction, and partly a psychological addition. To break the habit, you need to understand the reasons and the triggers that prompt you to light up. Usually, the triggers are emotions or feelings. You need to figure out for yourself what they are. Then you need to reprogram the way you react to those feelings. That's kind of it in a nutshell."

"Well, I guess that explains why I haven't been able to quit."

They didn't say much after that. They stopped for lunch in Boulder, and then continued to the IBM site north of the city.

****

The IBM site was only a few minutes' drive from downtown Boulder, but the surroundings were like night and day. Downtown Boulder was an assembly of buildings and concrete, and it was busy with cars and people. IBM was in the country surrounded by fields and rolling greenery as far as one could see. As Peter drove up IBM Drive from the Diagonal Highway, he was surprised that there was no guard gate. He drove directly to a public parking area to the left side of a large IBM office building. The building was three stories high with a central entrance. Greg and Peter parked the car, grabbed their suit coats from the back seat, and made their way down a concrete walkway leading to the entrance. Although still early in the season, they could smell the scent of freshly cut grass. The landscaping on either side of the walkway was green with grass and shrubbery, well maintained. A tree on the right of the walkway was in full bloom. Was it a cherry tree? Before they entered the building, they looked at each other. Peter motioned to Greg to tighten his necktie and smiled at Greg's slightly annoyed expression at being reminded.

They checked in at a reception desk in the lobby and received visitor badges. The young woman at the reception desk promised that an administrative assistant would arrive shortly to escort them to their meeting with John Armstrong. As they waited, Peter wondered how easy it might be to slip past the reception desk unnoticed.

An Administrative Assistant named Virginia led them to a large corner office on the third floor. The windows offered an excellent view of the scenery outside. One could see the mountains off in the far distance. As soon as they entered the office, John Armstrong got up from behind his desk, introduced himself, and shook hands with Greg and Peter. He immediately motioned for them to take seats around a table to the right of the entranceway, and dispensed with further formalities.

"I'm known around here as Big John. We use first names here so you can call me John." He seemed more than six feet in height, big-boned and stocky, yet not intimidating. His fifty years could not hide the fact that he had developed a slight paunch and was a little overweight. More importantly, he was friendly and made you feel welcomed. Big John reminded Peter of a Captain Weisman that Peter worked for in Saigon many years ago. Just by the tone of his voice and his demeanor, Peter felt relaxed and knew they would get along.

"Peter, I like your tie," he commented. Coincidently, he wore a gray suit, just like Peter.

The three of them discussed the arrangements for the audit and the objectives of the audit. Big John said he had talked with Roger Colby and was very much in favor of this audit, as they had some unexplained coding issues over the past several months. They repeated the discussions they had with Colby and agreed that all four of them were on the same page. Several questions were answered as well.

"When will the audit start?" John wanted to know.

"The full team will be here on Monday, the twenty-fifth of April," Greg replied.

"Where will the team sit?" Peter asked.

"The site is suffering growing pains so space is at a premium. We have provided temporary office space—modular units—off to the right rear of the building," Big John explained. He promised that before the start of the audit, the space would have furniture and a door with a badge lock."

Then Big John asked, "How long will the audit take?"

"Our plan is six to seven weeks," Greg responded.

"Do you normally have a kickoff meeting?" Big John asked.

"Yes, we do," Greg answered. "We usually have that on Day One."

"Who are your key employees, and what responsibilities do they have?" Peter asked.

Big John said he would provide a list and introduce the audit team to some of them at the kickoff meeting.

"Will these people be able to talk to us freely?" Greg asked.

"Yes, if you don't ask them something classified above your level. My key managers and technical people will be at the kickoff meeting, and I will ask for their full cooperation."

"What badge access would we be entitled to have?"

"You will have access to the building and to your office area which will have restricted access."

"I will also need access to the raised floor," Peter said, referring to the computer room.

Big John's answer was, "I'll work on that. There may be security restrictions."

"Before you leave here," Big John offered, "let me give you a personal tour of the building. While we are on the tour, I'll have Virginia get you a layout of the building, an organization chart, and some documentation on Boulder's mission."

Peter found the tour to be quite useful as it gave him a general feel for the overall layout. The third floor was where the administrative offices were. That included Human Resources, Accounting, Finance, and John Armstrong's office and conference room. Programmers and systems analysts were on the second floor. Those on the project to provide the Air Force Operating System (AFOS) were on the left side of the building and the others on the right side. The computer rooms were on the first floor, separated by the lobby. A stairwell in the left rear of the building allowed easy access to the AFOS computer room and offices directly above. An entry door from the outside near the stairwell allowed AFOS employees to enter the building without going through the lobby. Big John also pointed out the cafeteria in the rear of the building behind the elevators. "Excellent food," he claimed. Finally, Big John took Peter and Greg down a long corridor that ran the width of the building and down a stairwell on the right side of the building to the modular units where the audit team would sit. Big John apologized for the distance from the AFOS project.

After the meeting and the tour with Big John, Peter and Greg continued to prepare for the audit. Peter reviewed the information that Big John had given him. The layout of the building had more meaning after seeing it first-hand. Then Peter arranged for six-week stays at the Boulder Residence Inn for four individuals. Greg initiated action to get Noah onto the audit and decide whom the other auditors would be.

Next week, after they were back in Bethesda, they would review the audit guidelines, and begin preparing for the kickoff meeting. Peter would also use next week to finish what he was doing for Endicott. Greg would review the status of the Endicott audit and talk to the individuals that would join the Boulder audit. He would have them complete the SF-86 security clearance forms. Peter hoped that would include Noah.

****

Peter Troutman and Greg Stevens arrived back at Dulles Airport on Friday afternoon. They retrieved Peter's car from long-term parking and drove back to Bethesda. Peter dropped Greg off at the office parking lot, and then went to his own apartment-

The time was about five thirty when Peter walked into the vestibule of his apartment building. He opened his letterbox and retrieved his mail. There was an envelope from Jon Wilson. He opened it right away.

Peter,

Rather than make the trip all the way to the Pentagon on Saturday, I thought it might be easier if we met locally. Turns out, we only live about three miles from each other.

Please come to my place (10 a.m. is still good). I have an office in my condominium. My address is 10101 Grosvenor Place, Apt 1901, Rockville MD 20852. Go South on Old Georgetown, East on Tuckerman Lane, and South on Grosvenor Pl. You can get to it from Rt. 355 as well, just south of the Metro station. Please have the guard at the desk notify me when you arrive.

I also left you a phone message. My phone number is 301-555-5300. Please call me right away to confirm.

Respectfully,

Jon

Hmm, Peter thought. This is different. Peter thought it odd that he would want to meet at his home on a Saturday. Although they had a lot of respect for each other, it was not as if they were close friends. "Well, I guess I will see what this is all about in the morning," he thought. He called the number on the note. A recorded voice requested that he leave a message. He did.

5

THE BIG PICTURE

Peter was up early on Saturday morning. Although he did not understand the purpose of a home visit, he was eager to see Jon again. Peter had worked with the CIA in Saigon in 1967. He was an asset to an operation that weeded out an enemy agent working for the North Vietnamese. Peter remembered the final debriefing with Jon, the praise he received for a job well done, and the offer to work for the agency after finishing his graduate studies. Although Peter decided to work for IBM, Jon continued to be a supporter of his career, including initiating temporary work assignments with the agency. Peter had worked for the Agency on four assignments after Vietnam. However, he had not seen Jon since the first of the four assignments, and he looked forward to their meeting again.

Although he had never been to Grosvenor Park before, he had no issue finding it. A small visitor parking area in front of the building was full, so he drove around to the rear of the building. He parked the car on the open top level of a two-level garage. Residents could enter the rear of the building through a door just off the parking level. However, a sign directed visitors to follow a walkway to the lobby in the front of the building. As he walked the short distance to the main entrance in front, he marveled at the building's architecture. The building looked as if two buildings, placed at slight angles to each other, had been hinged together by a central column that contained the main elevators and stairways. The red brick high-rise had a modern appearance. Peter counted twenty stories. The units had balconies that were integral to the building facade except at the ends of the building where the covered balconies curved outward like discs. The

257

facility looked almost new. The landscaped open areas surrounding the building were still being developed, but they looked promising.

Peter walked into the main entrance and up to the guard behind a large reception desk. The guard looked up as he approached.

"Good morning. I'm here to see Jon Wilson," Peter told him.

"Do you know his unit number?"

"No, but I have his phone number if that helps."

"That won't be necessary. Please sign the guest register," he said as he motioned to the register to Peter's right.

After Peter signed, the guard pulled the clipboard back toward him and read the entry. "You are Peter Troutman. Is that correct?"

"Yes."

"May I see identification, please?"

"Ooh . . . kay," Peter responded as he pulled out his driver's license, and then commented on how tight security was.

The guard looked at the license and returned it. "Sorry for the inconvenience, sir, but the people that live here pay to have a secure facility. I'll call Mr. Wilson on the intercom and let him know you're here."

After calling Jon to let him know he had a visitor, the guard allowed Peter to proceed. Peter entered the elevator and pushed the number 19. Jon lived on the nineteenth floor in unit 1901.

Jon answered the door.

"Peter, come on in," Jon said as his left hand rested behind Peter's right shoulder, and his right hand offered a warm handshake. "It's good to see you again. How long has it been? Damn, I wish I could stay young like you. You haven't changed a bit. You're still thin and not a single gray hair. How are you?"

"I'm doing great, Jon. It's good to see you again too. And, as far as looking great, you are looking pretty good yourself."

"Come. . . I want to introduce you to my significant other."

They walked down a hallway, and Mary Lou met them as they entered the living room.

"Peter, this is Mary Lou. Mary Lou, this is Peter."

"Very nice to meet you, Peter," she said as she gave him a pleasant smile.

Then she turned to Jon. "Jon, I'm going up to the market and do some other errands. There's a fresh pot of coffee on the stove. I'll leave you two to yourselves.

She looked at Peter. "See you later," she said and disappeared down the hall and out the door.

"Peter, how about some coffee?"

"Sounds good . . . This looks like a really nice place you have Jon. I bet the view is spectacular as well. Have you and Mary Lou been here long?"

"This place was completed two years ago. I'm the first owner. Mary Lou moved in afterwards. Tell you what . . . let me give you a tour. We can have our coffee after. Mary Lou would be upset with me if we were to spill any on the carpet."

The condominium had a large master bedroom, a second smaller bedroom they did not see, a large living room, a dining area, a kitchen, one large bath, a laundry room, and a balcony. The views from the master bedroom and from the living room were impressive.

After the tour, they went back to the kitchen for coffee.

"We can take the coffee into my den. I use the second bedroom as a den and as a home office."

They entered Jon's office. Peter was amazed to see that Jon's home office—the second bedroom—was almost as large as the master bedroom. The office was ten feet by fourteen feet but with no windows to the outside. The entry door from the hallway was on the left side of the room. The first thing Peter saw as he entered the room was a reclining chair in the corner against the back wall.

The office had everything Jon needed. A large wooden desk was at the center of the far wall to the right after you entered the room. The desktop supported a fourteen-inch CRT monitor and a keyboard on the left, and a telephone and writing surface on the right. On the same wall to the left of the desk, Jon had a powerful UNIX-based computer with a state-of-the-art 9600-Baud modem and a matrix printer. He could send and receive messages and view certain documents from the CIA library, and he could make encrypted phone calls, over a secure phone line. A five-foot-high bookcase stood to the right of the desk along the wall to the right of the door as you entered. Several items were on display atop the bookcase. One of these items specifically caught Peter's eye. It was a sixteen-inch-high white *snowman.* Attached to the top of the lid it had a Styrofoam ball for a head with two small brown felt eyes, a red smiling mouth and a carrot nose. A candy-caned scarf encircled the bottom of the head. On top of the head was a black felt hat with a red band above the brim. Two arms extended from under the lid and black-mitted hands held a sign that read, *"Let it Snow."*

"That is a very interesting *snowman* you have on the top of the bookshelf," Peter commented.

"The *snowman* was actually a novelty container for a quart-sized bottle of Old Grand Dad, my favorite bourbon. Mary Lou gave the snowman to me as a Christmas present. We drank the bourbon, but the container was so decorative that I decided to set it on top of the bookcase. It gives me pleasure to look at it and to remember sharing Christmas with her . . .

"Peter, please have a seat over there in my *think chair*. I call it my *think chair*, but sometimes I'll sit there in the dark and fall asleep, so Mary Lou calls it my *sleep chair*. I'll sit over here at my desk."

Peter took the seat offered him and carefully set his coffee down on a small table next to the chair. Jon set his coffee on the desk, sat in the desk chair, and spun so that the two of them were now facing each other. Jon began to talk.

"Peter, tell me what is happening with you. You are here without your family. Are you still married?"

"I'm here on a temporary two-year assignment. I'm legally separated from my wife and intend to get a divorce."

"I see. Now is that the same wife you had when we were in Saigon?"

"Yes."

"Well, it lasted much longer than my marriage, and I am surprised you stayed together that long, considering what happened between you and Donna." As soon as he said this, he realized he might have said too much.

"Jon, I always thought you probably knew about my involvement with Donna. I remember the party at your house in Saigon twenty-years ago. You lectured me on *emotional intelligence* and advised me not to become involved with her. Donna said she got a similar lecture from your wife, Linda. I'm sure Linda also told you how hot things got with Donna on the dance floor that night, but after that, nothing more happened. We listened to your advice, and I returned to the States a few days later. We never expected to see each other again, but then you called me back to Saigon a few months later.

For the next several weeks, my relationship with Donna remained professional, but then too many things happened—Chan gone missing, my stolen briefcase, the bike accident, the assassination, the attempt on Donna's life, and her need to defend herself. Our relationship changed. One night she showed up at my door. She was very upset and said she needed to talk. She told me she killed a police detective, and that you suggested she stay in the CIA safe-room at the hotel. She couldn't handle it. She needed to talk about her feelings, and she needed to be with someone. Things went from there. We fell in love. She didn't want you to know we were together—didn't think you would approve. I'm sure you knew though. You provided us with a protection detail and arranged for us both to leave the country eleven days later—probably saved our lives. We knew our relationship could not last, but we promised to cherish what we had and to stay in touch. She even broke protocol and gave me her personal contact information so that could happen. However, I have not seen her since."

"So, I guess your wife never knew?"

"No, she never knew." Then, Peter could not help but ask, "Do you ever hear from Donna?"

"Only occasionally. You know she's married now and has two kids?"

"I do," Peter responded. "I tried to contact her after I moved down here. I was able to talk briefly with her mother. She gave me Donna's P.O. box in Langley. So, I sent her a short letter updating her on my status. I just suggested meeting for coffee and catching up on old times. More than a month later I got a polite response. She apologized for the delay in getting back to me and said her travel schedule made it very difficult. She said she remembered me, but was happily married with two kids in college. She said she didn't think it would be possible or wise to meet. She said she was sorry to hear I was getting divorced, but pleased to hear that I had a successful career, as she always thought I would. John, I'm not trying to start anything up with her, but I get the feeling she's putting me off. I just don't understand why."

"Maybe she just needs to put the past behind her," Jon responded. It was lame, but it was all he could think to say.

"Well, I just hope she is doing well. If you see her, please let her know that I wish her the best. . . Jon, what about your ex-wife Linda? Do you keep in touch with her?"

"No. Life with me wasn't what she needed. We have both moved on. I don't even hear from her at Christmas anymore."

"Sorry."

Jon seemed eager to change the subject.

"Peter, let's talk business!"

He had Peter's attention.

"Please understand that this discussion that we are about to have is privileged, and you cannot reveal it to anyone. Do you agree?"

"Yes, sir."

"Okay then, as you may already know, I'm the one who recommended you be the leader of the audit at IBM Boulder. As you may have surmised, there is more to this than what you've been told. The audit is part of a much bigger investigation, involving national security."

Jon paused to take a sip of his coffee; Peter did likewise. Then Jon continued.

"Peter, I need someone on the inside. I need someone who can determine what I need to know without arousing too much suspicion. I believe they told you that the audit was to determine vulnerabilities in the software distribution process. Is that correct?"

"Yes, it is."

"There is a specific vulnerability that I'm concerned about. It relates to an event that we expect to happen in about four weeks. I believe that for you to be effective in exposing this vulnerability, you need to know what it is that we are looking for. That's why I'm reading you in."

Jon paused to take another sip of coffee.

Peter took the opportunity to ask, "Jon, does my security clearance allow you to tell me the bigger picture?"

"I was coming to that. Your Top-Secret clearance is good, but in addition, this assignment will be compartmentalized and include a code name."

"Okay."

"I have the authority to do this. All the paperwork is here."

Jon unlocked the top drawer of his desk and pulled out a multi-page document.

"I know that Colby already had you sign a standard non-disclosure form that the FBI uses. Colby had your manager sign the same form, and he did not want to arouse any suspicions by treating you differently. This form is different. You can read through it, but essentially, it's a more specific non-disclosure agreement. It includes the specific terms of our agreement, and a section indicating that I read you in on the project. Also, notice that this is an inter-agency project. It includes the Department of Defense, the CIA, and the FBI. The project code name is *Boulder Creek*."

Looking at Peter's expression, Jon sensed another question.

"Peter, do you have a question?"

"Is Colby fully aware of my status?"

"Yes, Colby is, and you may talk freely with him. However, Greg won't have this special clearance. In fact, no one else at IBM will . . . only you."

"Okay."

Jon continued. "Now, here is the bigger picture. IBM plans to distribute software to the Air Force sometime in the middle of May. The software is a major upgrade to the operating systems installed in more than a dozen computers that monitor and track reconnaissance satellites. These satellites are the basis for our early warning system about a potential nuclear attack by the Soviet Union. Various data transmission circuits and microwave links transmit information from these satellites to computers on the ground. These computers then transmit information to NORAD, located in the Cheyenne Mountain Complex near Colorado Springs. Computers at NORAD process the information. NORAD notifies the Strategic Air Command if military action is warranted. We have actionable intelligence that a person or persons acting on behalf of the Soviet Union will attempt to insert a computer virus into the IBM software. If the Soviet plan is successful, the computers in Cheyenne Mountain, and any other computers that they communicate with, might also become infected. This would include computers that process early warning information from radar stations as well. We believe that the virus will be hidden on a tape cartridge, and arrive onto the IBM premises just before the distribution date. An individual or individuals at IBM will then imbed the virus into the IBM software. If we allow this virus to infect the IBM software, the corrupted software could take out our entire ICBM defense system. If the Soviets were to take advantage of that, it could potentially be Armageddon for the United States."

"Wow!"

"Exactly," he responded. "I want you to find out how they will do this within IBM. We must stop it before it's too late."

"Okay. I would imagine that there must be others outside of IBM who may be part of this conspiracy as well?"

"Yes, we believe so. We have investigators from the FBI, the CIA, and from the Defense Department trying to determine who is involved. We do suspect someone by the name of *Ursula Behr*, aka *Teddy*. Also, the name *Panda* has popped up. If you come across those names, please let me know. Peter, whatever you find out, you can only report it to me, or to Colby. You can't reveal any of this to others on the audit team, or to IBM management. If in doubt, check with Colby.

And Peter, I'd like you to give me a status-report every weekend. Call me here on my private line—you already have the number. If I'm not here, you may leave a voice message. My voice mail is password protected, and no one else knows the password. It's secure."

"*Hmm*," Peter thought to himself.

"Oh, and one more thing, I know you are not doing this because you need the money, but you will receive some compensation for your efforts and for the possible risk involved. I'll see to it that you receive a deposit of $5,000 in your bank account by the end of next week."

Peter never asked where the money came from. Jon had told him once that he had a special CIA account set up to compensate assets who worked with him. It was legal but very secretive. Peter signed the forms. Jon locked them in his desk and promised to file them on Monday.

The two shook hands and said good-bye until the next time.

6

KICKOFF

Michael Cuccia and Deborah Smith flew from Dulles Airport in Virginia with Peter and Greg on Sunday, April 24. When they left, six hours earlier, the weather in Virginia was rainy. They arrived at Denver's Stapleton airport Sunday evening, around 5:00 p.m. The weather in Denver was cool, but clear. After collecting their luggage, Peter went to secure the rental car while the others waited for Noah Bosch to arrive from San José a half hour later. The plan was to save a few dollars by sharing one car—After all, they were auditors.

Peter returned with the car about forty minutes later. When he arrived at the terminal, he was amused at what he saw. Greg, Michael, and Deborah, who liked the nickname Debbie, were waiting at the curb dressed in casual business attire. Debbie and Michael each had two large suitcases. They would be staying awhile. Then there was Noah. He stood between them wearing jeans, athletic shoes, and an open sports jacket that displayed a Star Wars T-shirt underneath. He only had one suitcase, and it was not that large. He did not look like the stereotypical IBM professional, and he looked as if he was only planning to stay for a couple of days.

Peter hoped that the other team members would accept Noah. He was different and appeared to be a little off to some when they first met him. Peter had worked with him before, and they had become friends. Peter had learned that Noah was mildly autistic, and lacking in social skills, but he had also learned that Noah was highly intelligent and very reliable.

Peter got out of the car and walked over to the curb. "I assume the four of you have already introduced yourselves," he said. "Let me help you load the car."

IBM always rented a full-size Ford from Hertz. However, with the five of them plus luggage, it was a tight squeeze, and it took a while to load the car. They fit four large suitcases and two briefcases in the trunk. Greg sat in the passenger seat and held his overnight bag on his lap, while Debbie and Noah sat in the back with their shoulder bags. No one complained though, and Debbie did not seem to mind being flanked by two male companions.

After finding their way out of the airport—a challenge, by the way—the first order of business was to eat. One thing about travel is that it always throws you off your usual routine. The two-hour time difference meant that back East, it was now around 8:30 in the evening. Meanwhile, on the West Coast, it was only 5:30 in the afternoon. That meant that Noah was ready to eat, and the rest of the team was either starving or too tired to eat. Peter spied a diner in Westminster. He pulled in and parked in the back.

"This is good . . . enough variety that we can each have what suits us," Greg proffered.

"I'm ready for a chicken dinner," Noah said.

Then Debbie piped in, "I'm just going to have a salad."

"Watching your figure, Debbie?" Michael quipped.

"You should talk," she shot back in a jesting manner.

Neither of them looked as if they were over-weight. However, they were both single, in their thirties, and starting to add pounds. Debbie made no secret of the fact that she was trying to maintain her figure, and Michael worked out every chance he got; he was just trying to stay in healthy shape. Debbie had no family. Raised in upstate New York, her foster parents had recently passed away. Michael came from a large Italian family and grew up in an Italian Neighborhood in New York City. His parents now lived in St. James out on Long Island. He had brothers and sisters and knew how to get along in a family environment. Debbie and Michael had been with the team for over a year now, and they worked well together. Although they were both single, they got along more like a brother and sister, than as a potential love interest.

Then Noah entered the conversation. "Did you know that a chef's salad has just as many calories as a chicken dinner?"

"No, I don't think so," Debbie said.

"It's true," Noah snapped back.

Noah was probably correct, but Debbie didn't want to hear it. "If you want to keep the weight down, it's not so much what you eat as it is how much you—"

"Welcome to our family Noah," Greg interrupted. Noah was about five years younger than Debbie and Michael. His title was *Staff*, one level lower than Debbie and Michael's level of *Advisory*, but he was a rising star. Peter had told everyone about Noah, but this was their first time meeting him. Noah was nerdy, and Greg wanted to be sure that Noah would fit in with the team. "Peter said you did some good things for Santa Teresa. Tell us more about yourself."

"Yes, I worked with Peter on the software development audit at Santa Teresa. We found that someone was hacking into a data base and altering data and—"

"It was Noah that discovered all this," Peter said. "He figured out who was doing it, and how he did it. He saved the day for us."

"No really . . . it was . . . I was just doing my job."

"So, Noah, what do you do when you are not saving the day," Debbie asked.

"I ran a ten-kilometer last weekend . . . and I play chess . . . and video games."

"Very interesting," Debbie said politely. "I see you are wearing a Star Wars shirt. You must like Star Wars."

"Yes. I have collected all their memorabilia too. . . What do you like to do, Debbie?" he asked.

"I just finished reading a good book—'*The Bonfire of the Vanities*' by Tom Wolfe. Have you heard of it?"

"No, I have not heard of it," Noah replied.

"I've heard of it." Greg intruded. "But I haven't read it. What is it about?"

"Well, it takes place in New York City. It's a satire about the interaction between three characters. They have very different viewpoints concerning race, social class, politics, and wealth. One is a WASP who works on Wall Street. Another is a Jew who is a lawyer, and the third is a journalist who came from Great Britain—"

"That reminds me of a joke," Greg responded. "Three men go into a bar. One is a . . ."

The chitchat continued as they ate.

After the meal, Greg asked Peter if he would take care of the bill. Peter knew Greg's reason for asking. Anyway, it really didn't matter who took care of the bill; it all went onto a travel expense form—*Dinner for five audit team members*. Greg would sign it. IBM had provided both him and Peter with travel debit cards. Reimbursements went directly into a bank account set up for the purpose. Peter paid the bill and walked outside toward the car.

He found Greg leaning on the front fender finishing the last drags on his cigarette. Michael and Debbie were walking around the building, and Noah was off by himself admiring a classic 1967 Ford mustang. As Michael and Debbie came around the building and passed Noah, Michael also noticed the Mustang.

"Wow!" Michael called out. "That is quite a beauty, Noah. Looks like a GT-350. That was the muscle car to have back then . . . 1967, I think."

I was in elementary school then," Noah replied.

"Would you consider trading your bike for it?" Debbie taunted.

"I like my bike," Noah replied matter of factually.

As they continued toward the rental car with Noah following, Peter saw Michael say something privately to Debbie.

After they all returned to the rental car, Debbie leaned forward from the back seat and asked, "Greg, how long will you be in Boulder?"

"I'll leave Tuesday morning."

"Does that mean we need to drive you to the airport?"

It sounded like a challenge. Greg remembered her annoyance once before when he asked her to do that. Nevertheless, he let it pass—after all, she was a good auditor—and he chuckled.

"You won't have to do that, Debbie. I've arranged for an airport shuttle."

As Peter pulled the car out of the parking lot, Debbie asked Greg, "Do we have a dress code for this audit?"

"The same as always, Debbie—Business attire. That means jackets and ties for the men and full coverage for the women. However, you may remove your jackets when you are at your desks and don't have visitors. When Peter and I were here two weeks ago, we noticed that the management here, including the women, all had suits. The men wore neckties. We did notice some employees dressed more casually, and Peter asked John Armstrong about their dress code. John said that the programmers and computer technicians were allowed to dress more casually."

"In San José and in Santa Teresa, people who work in the computer rooms are told *not* to wear neckties for safety reasons," Noah added.

Debbie looked at Noah. "Noah, did you bring a suit?"

"Only the jacket I am wearing, and slacks," he answered.

"Do you have a necktie for when you are not in the computer room?" she asked.

"Yes," he said . . . and then added, "I brought my Star Wars tie."

Peter may have been the only one in the car that knew Noah was being sarcastic and only said that to get a rise out of Debbie.

"Noah, you can't wear a Star Wars tie at our kickoff meeting tomorrow," she protested.

Not wanting the children to fight, Greg interrupted. "Noah, let me know if you need a tie for tomorrow. I have an extra one you can borrow."

"Thank you, Greg," he responded.

"Peter, how about some music on the radio?" Debbie asked.

Peter looked over at Greg in the passenger seat. "Greg, would you mind? I haven't figured it out yet—don't want to fiddle with it while I'm driving."

"Sure—Debbie, is Pop music good?"

"Yes, thanks."

Greg tuned in a station playing the top releases. Next up was Whitney Houston singing "*Where Do Broken Hearts Go.*"

Debbie started singing along.

"*I know it's been some time. But there's something on my mind. You see, I haven't been the same . . .*"

It was a little annoying, but no one said anything.

About a half hour later, around 9:00 p.m., they arrived at the Residence Inn. The IBM audit team used Residence Inns most of the time. It provided reasonably priced long-term stay accommodations. Each weekday evening, they provided a cocktail hour serving complimentary food and wine. This facility even had a pool. Each member of the team would have his or her own unit. Each unit had a queen-sized bed, a kitchenette, a refrigerator, a safe, and a fireplace—wax logs only, of course. After checking in, everyone said goodnight and went to their place to unpack and retire. They would be up early for the continental breakfast and for the short drive to the IBM site, where they would get oriented and be ready for the kickoff meeting at 9:00 a.m.

****

The team arrived at IBM bright and early the next morning. The kickoff meeting with Armstrong and his staff took place in a large conference room on the main floor near the lobby. It went very well. John Armstrong started the meeting. He told his staff that Corporate Audit had come to do a security audit of the AFOS project. AFOS stands for Air Force Operating System, he told them. He welcomed the five auditors from Corporate. He told Debbie, Michael, and Noah—the three that he had not yet met—that he was John Armstrong, the Site Manager—sometimes referred to as Big John.

Then, Armstrong introduced his key staff to the auditors. First, he introduced Virginia Simpson, his Administrative Assistant. She was available to help the auditors with any administrative issues. Then, he introduced Robert Stanley, Manager of site physical security; He was responsible for access badges and keys. Then Armstrong introduced John Engels—sometimes referred to as *Little John*. Little John was only five feet nine and thin. He reported directly to Big John who was six feet and weighed at least two hundred pounds. Little John managed the AFOS project. Big John told the auditors that the AFOS software was installed on IBM model 4381 computers that the Air Force used to manage reconnaissance satellites. The initial systems had been running for almost a year. The current activity was to provide a major code update that would enhance productivity and utilization of memory.

Big John introduced Little John's key staff person, Brian Goodman. Brian would be the primary AFOS technical interface to the audit team. Then, Big John introduced Georgy Belinsky. Georgy was Supervisor of the computer room where AFOS code was stored, tested, compiled, and finally distributed to the Air Force. He reported to Little John.

Finally, Armstrong introduced Greg Stevens as the Manager of the Corporate Audit team serving the Federal Division of IBM. Greg summarized what the audit intended to accomplish. The audit would evaluate the security associated with the AFOS project. The focus would be on determining security vulnerabilities in the coding and distribution process. The plan was that the audit would take approximately six weeks with an interim report halfway through. Greg then introduced Peter Troutman as the lead auditor, and the rest of the audit team.

At the conclusion of the meeting, Armstrong made it clear to his people that they were to cooperate with the auditors. They were to provide the auditors with whatever information they requested, as long as it was not above their security clearance. He also told the audit team that if there were any issues, he wanted to know about them. Armstrong characterized the audit as routine. He said that IBM and the DOD required audits on a periodic basis. He made no mention of the FBI's involvement.

Immediately after the kickoff meeting, Big John told the team he had provided them with a private office area, not shared by anyone else. It had been set up in the modular units recently appended to the backside of the building. He also provided the team with electronic access badges. The badges would allow them to enter the building using the employee entrances. The badges would also allow them to access their private office quarters. The access badges had been pre-programmed by computer to only access specific authorized locations in the building. Peter hoped his badge would allow additional access. He would worry about that later.

In addition, Big John asked the team to continue to wear their corporate badges, which had their photos. Virginia escorted the team to their new offices. The auditors' office area had four desks, a worktable, and a cabinet. The desks and cabinet were new. They still had the keys taped to them. More than sufficient, Peter thought.

After that, the team had lunch together in the cafeteria. During lunch, Michael and Greg began discussing the Endicott audit. They had a preliminary review with Endicott management last week, and each auditor, including Michael and Peter, had written a draft of what they wanted to say. However, the final report was delayed because Peter and Michael were pulled off the audit to come to Boulder. Michael had worked hard on that audit and wanted to be sure that his findings were accurately reported.

"When are we going to see the final audit report," Michael asked Greg.

"Later this week, Michael," Greg answered. "Over the weekend, I reviewed the draft that you and Peter put together, but the final report is not yet completed. If possible, I'd like to review some items with you this afternoon. I want to make sure your input is properly represented."

"I assume that Peter and I don't need to be at the presentation meeting in Endicott."

"No, Michael, I think that any issues with Endicott management were resolved when we met with them last week."

"Now that they are done, will the Endicott auditors join us here on this audit?" Noah asked.

"No," Greg responded. "They will begin a new audit in Oswego."

"How will you have enough auditors?" Debbie asked.

"I'll bring a newbie onto the team. He works in Endicott . . . says he is interested in becoming an auditor. We'll see how it works out. I'm also borrowing an auditor from Poughkeepsie. We will have six."

"Greg, when are you planning to fly out of here?" Debbie asked.

"Tomorrow morning. Why?"

"Greg, I know what I said yesterday, but if you need a ride—"

"No, I'm all set. Thanks, but I've already reserved the shuttle service."

****

On the first night of a new audit, everyone wants to go out for dinner. This is especially true if the audit is at a location no one has been to before. That Monday night everyone was ready to explore the territory and check out the town. The whole team piled into the car and with Peter driving, they went looking for an eating-place called *Casa de Mama*. The place was Greg's idea. As the name would suggest, it was a Mexican restaurant. After driving around for a while, and finding themselves on the outskirts of town, they wondered if they had bad directions. However, they finally found it. To be honest, it did not look like much from the outside. It looked like it may have once been Mom's house—literally. The place was on the outskirts of town and surrounded by a field with animals. A fenced-in yard with chickens was immediately out back. It was a far cry from what the team was used to in Baltimore, Washington DC, or in Noah's case, San José California. After a few glances at each other, and at Greg, they decided to stay. It did not matter. They were hungry.

The hostess sat them promptly and she was courteous—was she *Mama*? After Margaritas, tortilla chips and a choice of guacamole or queso dip, the team enjoyed a wonderful meal of . . . everything. There was *mucho* to choose from—burritos, chimichangas, enchiladas, quesadillas, fajitas, chili, Spanish rice, fried pinto beans, and more. No one could decide, so they just ordered everything and put it in the center of the table. The meat fillings consisted of various forms of beef and chicken. People could take whatever they felt like—a true family meal with sharing. Greg saw it as a good team builder. Peter particularly enjoyed the chicken—without regard to its possible origin.

The auditors only went out to dinner as a team for two more nights that week. One can only eat out so many times before the effects on one's digestive tract become an issue. Michael and Debbie were also trying to stay trim. They were the first to decline a group dinner. Each weeknight, The Residence Inn provided substantial five o'clock hors d'oeuvres in the common area. In addition, each of the resident units had a kitchenette with a cooking facility.

One night, Michael invited the team to his unit for a veal dinner that he made. However, that was an exception enjoyed by everyone. Usually, each member of the team preferred to eat alone, and not so much. Perhaps they welcomed the solitude and the break from each other.

7

AUDIT

After meeting with Robert Stanley, Manager of Site Security, the audit team knew the types of controls that secured the Boulder facility. Computer-controlled badge access provided physical security to the building and to rooms. Physical locks and keys protected the contents of closets, cabinets, and desks. Computer-controlled passwords protected magnetically stored files. The audit team found that these access controls were consistent with the requirements of IBM and the department of defense (DOD). Of course, the vulnerability was that badges, passwords, and keys could be lost, stolen, or lent. Security also depended upon having trusted employees.

To ensure that employees would be trustworthy, IBM investigated the backgrounds of potential employees before hiring them. The background checks required by the DOD were even more stringent. Most of the employees had *Secret* level security clearances. *Secret* level required background checks every ten years—*Top Secret* level every five years. While these controls were consistent with IBM and the DOD, the vulnerability was that people change over time. Peter often read about trusted employees who, after twenty years with their company, were guilty of embezzlement.

Peter observed that there was no screening of what people brought into the IBM facility or took out of the facility—unlike the FBI facility in Denver. During the meeting with Robert Stanley, Peter asked a pointed question. "If someone were to walk out of here with an IBM asset, how would you know it?"

Robert mentioned two things. First, they had several security cameras strategically placed. They kept Video *tape* recordings for a minimum of one month. Second, they periodically did inventories of what they had in the building, including documents. Peter considered his response.

"What you are doing is good. However, no amount of security can prevent all possible breaches, and when a breach does occur, a good security system will have a way to detect the breach—the sooner the better. The auditors will look for both prevention and detection."

As instructed before any audit, Peter told the audit team to focus on the lack of controls and be able to explain the possible significance if controls were lacking. Peter told them *not* to be looking to prove an actual crime. If they suspected one, they were to inform him and then the proper authorities. However, on this audit, Peter's personal mission went well beyond this. He was looking for evidence of an actual crime that the CIA believed to be in progress. No one could know this.

****

Peter and Noah worked together to audit the code development and distribution process used by AFOS. Peter assigned Michael and Debbie to do everything else. Everything else included managing personnel and facility security. During the first week, Peter and Noah began to understand the process and establish rapport with the people involved. Two people were key to the AFOS process. Peter and Noah sat down with each of them to understand their role in the process.

First, they sat down with Brian Goodman. He was the lead systems analyst on the project and reported directly to John Engels or Little John. His office was on the second floor, just above the AFOS computing center, as were most of the AFOS programmers. Brian invited them to have a seat at his work-table. Brian was a *Senior Systems Analyst*. His level was equivalent to that of a third-line manager—one having two levels of management reporting to him. Although, he did not have employees reporting directly to him, he had a great deal of influence and power. He was very knowledgeable, personable, and respected by his colleagues. He was the same level as Peter. His office was spacious and he had a window.

They exchanged pleasantries, and then Brian summarized the AFOS program and his responsibilities. For a large program, such as this, multiple programmers wrote the code in modules. The programmers did not enter the computer room. They created source code from terminals and personal computers that resided in their offices. These connected to the computers on the raised floor in the computer room downstairs. The products of their endeavors were stored on random access devices or tapes inside the computer room. They also received printouts on printers that were near the offices from which they worked. Brian was responsible for the functional design and integration of all the parts. He was also directly involved in compiling and functional testing the entire code package on the 4381 computers at IBM and at customer sites.

"Brian, we appreciate your time. I hope you won't mind if we ask you a lot of questions."

"No, of course not. That's why you're here . . . right?"

"Who has access to the programmer's source code files?" Peter asked.

"I do, and each programmer has access to their own code."

"Don't people in the computer room have access? I mean . . . how do they compile the object code if they don't?"

"Oh, I'm sorry. I misunderstood your question. The computer room has read and copy access, but they can't change the code. Only the programmers that created the code can change it. My access allows me to link files together and create volume headers, but I can't change the code without the programmer knowing it."

Peter gave Brian's answer some thought. If Brian could link files together, he could link to a file containing viral code, but it was too early in the process to press this point or to sound accusatory. Peter decided to change the subject.

"Brian, could you explain the process for creating a tape cartridge for delivery."

"Of course," he began. "It's my responsibility to determine what individual program modules to combine, and in what order. I don't need to enter the computer room to do this. The source-coded program files are on a direct-access storage device. Each program module contains a header label created by the programmer. Using a job-control language (JCL), I instruct the computer operator to mount an empty tape cartridge onto the tape drive and create the volume header label for the entire tape. The JCL instructs the computer as to which files to access, compile, and load onto the output tape cartridge. The computer uses an event logger to record the transactions as they occur and provide an auditable record."

"What is the output media that gets delivered to the customer?"

"The output tape cartridge is an IBM 3480 design holding two-hundred megabytes of data. IBM uses a standard labeling format. Each cartridge has a volume header label magnetically stored on the tape. If more than one cartridge is required, the volume header label will indicate that. In addition to the volume label, each file or program module on the tape has its own header information defined by the programmer that created it. The AFOS tapes use a fixed record length variable block size format. That allows each program module to have its own block and its own header. Data is encoded onto the tape using a standard EBCDIC format. In addition to a magnetically stored volume header, each tape cartridge has a paper label affixed to the casing. The blank labels come in a big roll, like postage stamps. For AFOS, the computer room operator can tear the labels off the roll as needed, fill in the required information by hand, and affix them to the tape cartridges. The information put onto the labels complies with guidelines established by the Boulder site."

"Brian, how do the tapes actually get distributed to the customer, the Air Force in this case?"

"Ngai Wu is responsible for recording the information about each tape that goes to a customer. He currently stores this information on a personal computer and a floppy disk."

"How do the tapes get shipped to the customer? Do you mail them . . . use a shipping company . . . what?"

"No, we contact the customer and they come and take possession. Keep in mind that the product is classified. When the Air Force comes to take possession, we photograph them and their IDs before they leave."

"Impressive!" Peter responded. "What about backup? Does IBM keep a master copy?" Peter already knew the requirement to do so, but wanted to hear it from Brian.

"Oh, yes. We keep two master copies of everything that we deliver to a customer. That applies to the commercial products as well."

"Where do you keep them?"

"There's a room on the basement level below the computer room. We call it *the vault*. It's protected from fire. Everything in the room is *government-classified or IBM-restricted*. Access is limited."

Peter turned to Noah. "Noah, is there anything you would like to ask?" Noah had listened intently. JCL, tape design, and computer room operations were Noah's areas of expertise. Peter was very glad he had Noah on the audit.

"Uh . . . not right now," Noah responded. "But, I may want to talk with you again later . . . if that would be okay."

Brian picked up on Noah's shyness. "My door is always open Noah. You guys come by anytime. I'll be glad to help any way I can."

****

After talking with Brian, Peter and Noah met with Georgy Belinsky. He was the manager of the AFOS computer room. Georgy's office was located on the first floor, just outside the computer room. Georgy had attended the kickoff meeting, but this was the first time they had a chance to talk one-on-one. Peter and Noah found his office and introduced themselves. Then Georgy introduced himself.

"Just call me *Georgy*, like in Georgy Porgy the nursery rhyme."

"Is your name Russian?" Peter asked.

"Yes, it's a Russian version of George. In Russia, it's pronounced more like '*e-your-gee*' with the accent on the middle syllable and a hard gee. My parents were born in Russia, but I was born in the States in 1954 after they arrived. So, my friends always called me *Georgy*."

"Very well, *Georgy* it is. We look forward to working with you. As you already know, Noah and I are here to . . . ."

Peter rehashed the official purpose of the audit in more detail than was done at the kickoff meeting. Then Georgy summarized his job. The exchange was all very cordial and business like. The next order of business was for Georgy to give Noah and Peter a tour of the computer room.

Access to the computer room required a badge with the appropriate coding. Very few people had it. When they arrived at the door to the computer room, Peter inserted his badge into the slot. It did not work! It was very important for Peter and Noah to have access, especially with the added investigation that Peter would do. Peter had brought up the subject again after the kickoff meeting. After a long discussion, Peter—with Greg's support—convinced Big John to allow it for both he and Noah. The argument for Noah was that Peter would need his technical support. Noah was the computer expert; he even had operator experience. Big John said they would receive new access badges very soon. However, Brian had mentioned the *vault*. They would need access to that as well. Peter would remember to take care of it—first thing in the morning.

Georgy chuckled. "You need special access," he said. Then he used his badge to open the door. Noah and Peter followed. The AFOS computer room covered half the floor of the building. According to Georgy, the room included an IBM 3090 computer, two IBM 4381 computers, a bank of 3480 tape cartridge drives, two random access disk storage devices, a printer, and some related equipment like communication controllers. Georgy pointed out each piece of equipment like a proud collector would show off his stable of antique automobiles. This was his domain!

According to Georgy, security for the room was provided in two ways. First, the room itself was physically separate from the computer room used for commercial purposes. To access the AFOS computer room, a person had to have a badge that authorized them to enter. Authorization was only given to those with an appropriate security clearance that also had a need to be there. Most programmers did not have authorized access to the computer room. Secondly, once they entered the room, a person could only access that equipment and those files that they had authority to access. This was controlled by using passwords. Georgy said that he and his second in command had administrative access, but they could not make changes to program files.

Then Georgy introduced us to two of his employees, Ngai Wu and Bob Jones. They helped with things like tape loading, labeling, and record keeping. All three were proficient at operating the equipment and everything else that needed doing inside that room. However, Georgy Belinsky was in charge. If the computer room were a ship, Georgy Belinsky was the captain, and the other two were his mates.

Between Brian and Georgy, Georgy was the one Peter was most interested in. Jon Wilson told Peter that the virus would be in the form of object code delivered on a 3480 cartridge. Brian worked with source code and did not operate the 3090 computer or the tape drives. Nor did he create the final package delivered to the customer. No, Peter believed that if anyone was to add viral object code to the shipped product, Georgy was in the best position to do it.

There is an old saying: *keep your friends close, and keep your enemies even closer*—or something like that. Peter had learned this concept from his association with Jon Wilson. Peter thought another old saying would apply here as well. *You catch more flies with honey than you do with vinegar.* Peter intended to apply both concepts to Georgy Belinsky.

Over the next few weeks, Peter made a point of initiating friendly conversation with Georgy every chance he had. It seems the two had a few things in common. Both were going through a divorce; both had kids not living with them; and both had recently transferred from another IBM location. In addition, both had separated from their wives more than a year ago. It was natural that another common interest was women. Having these things in common, fostered conversation, and even enabled some degree of bonding.

Peter learned a lot about Georgy over the next three weeks. He learned that Georgy was supporting a wife, two kids, and the house they lived in when he lived in California. He learned that he had a mother who was in an assisted living home because she had Parkinson's disease. He learned that Georgy liked to bet on sporting events. Though he did not admit to a gambling addiction, Georgy was able to tell Peter where to go to place a bet. Then to top it off, Georgy said he had a sister who was not allowed to leave the Soviet Union. The financial implications were more than enough to make Georgy a prime target for anyone who wanted to coerce him into doing something he would not otherwise want to do.

****

The team had completed three weeks of auditing. At eight o'clock Saturday morning, Peter made his regular status call to Jon Wilson. Although he had not yet found evidence of a viral tape cartridge, he was quite certain he knew who the insider was at IBM. He was eager to tell Jon what he knew. Jon would still be in his home office. There was a two-hour time difference so it was ten o'clock where Jon was. He would probably be having a second cup of coffee.

He dialed the number and Jon answered on the third ring. "Hi, Jon . . . this is Peter Troutman. How are you?"

"I'm good. I'm just having another cup of coffee. How are *you* doing?"

"I am enjoying *Boulder Creek.*" Jon had told him that by saying the code word, he could be certain it was really him. Rather silly, Peter thought, but he played along.

"What have you got for me?" Jon asked.

"Jon, I think I know who the IBM insider is. His name is Georgy Belinsky. He's the computer room manager for the AFOS project. I assume you want to know why I think it's him, so here it is in a nutshell. After three weeks of studying the process here, I believe that he's the only one that has the *means*. Furthermore, he has *motive*. I'm on friendly talking terms with him. He confided in me that he's divorced with three kids—He pays child support—His Mom and Dad were born in Russia—His Dad and a sister are still in Russia—His Mom is in a nursing home in Loveland—He uses party drugs—and he likes to bet on sports. Sounds like more than he can afford."

"Sounds like *means and motive*," Jon replied. "Have you found any evidence of *opportunity* . . . a viral cartridge or a means to acquire it?"

"No, I haven't Jon, and that is beginning to bother me because IBM plans to deliver the AFOS code update next week."

"Peter, I just received new intelligence that may give you something to go on. It's an intercepted message sent to the Russian Consulate in San Francisco. Let me read it to you: *'Cartridge has been received by Panda. IBM operative notified. AFOS release planned for next Wednesday.'* We've heard the name *Panda* before, but we still don't know who Panda is."

Peter thought for a moment. Then he said, "I may be able to help with that. Georgy told me that he often goes for Pizza on Saturday nights before he goes partying. Panda Pizza is where he goes to get pizza. He recommended it to me. I think I know where I'll go for supper tonight."

"Thanks Peter. Let me hear from you early next week."

"Okay, Jon. I'll talk to you then. Bye."

That evening, Peter and Michael—the only other auditor in town that weekend—enjoyed pizza and beer at the Panda Pizza Palace. They even ran into Georgy Belinsky who picked up an order from the take-out window. They exchanged pleasantries as Georgy passed their table on his way out. He held two calzone boxes in his hands.

8

SECURITY SWEEP

Monday began the fourth week of the audit. The first thing Peter did once everyone arrived at breakfast was to call an impromptu meeting of the team. They met right there at the Residence Inn in a small room next to the breakfast room.

"Thank you for indulging me. As you know, we are scheduled to do a security sweep tomorrow night. **I have decided to do it tonight instead.**" He could hear the silent *why* as he said this.

"Excuse me," Michael said. "Didn't we need to clear this with Robert Stanley? Can we just change the date like this?"

"There is nothing that says we must have special clearance or give advanced notice. By not telling them ahead of time, the audit will be more representative of what really goes on. In addition, if we don't forewarn the Security Department, we will test their response as well," Peter replied excitedly. Things he had recently seen disturbed him—things he could not reveal to his team. The team noticed his agitation, but said nothing.

Then Noah asked, "What do we do if a security person or another employee sees us snooping and questions us?"

"If that happens, it's a good thing. Other employees and especially the security force *should* ask what you are doing. Do not confront them. Let them know who you are and what you are doing. Document the encounter on the Issue Form and make note of the person that questions you. I'll provide copies of that form later."

"Peter, I've never participated in a security sweep before," Debbie asked. "What do I need to do?"

"Glad you asked that Debbie."

"It will be fun. I made copies of the *Check List*," he said as he gave a copy to each of them. "Each of you will take a route and go room to room. Each place you go, you will look for any of the issues on the *Check List*. For each issue you find, you will fill out an *Issue Form*."

SECURITY SWEEP CHECK LIST
- Look for unlocked desks, cabinets, and closets.
- Look for computer terminals that are powered on. See if you can access files.
- Look for classified material that is not where it belongs.
- Look for hallways with NO lighting.
- Look for building exits that are blocked.
- Look for unauthorized ways to enter the building or restricted areas.
- Look for documents left in fax or printer hoppers.
- Look for electronic media that is not where it belongs.
- Look for anything else that looks like a security risk.

"Here is a summary of what is on the *Issue Form*," Peter said as he passed out a sheet to each of them. "The information on the form will provide input to the audit report. A stack of the forms will be printed up for us later today. As you can see, it's quite simple." The team read the following information on the sheet Peter handed them:

ISSUE FORM CONTENT
- The time and date that you discovered the situation
- The exact location of the situation
- A description of what the issue is
- A statement of the significance or the finding
- Your initials

The team left the IBM site early that evening and had supper at the diner on 28th Street. They returned to the IBM site at 7:00 p.m. Most of the AFOS employees had gone home by then, but a few remained—not a problem. Michael got Debbie started checking the programmer's offices on the second floor. Then Michael went upstairs to Armstrong's suite. He also checked all the entrances and exits of the building. Noah and Peter both went to the computer room. After finishing their review there, Peter went to the offices surrounding the computer room, an area that included Belinsky's office. Meanwhile, Noah took the nearby stairs down to the vault. He glanced at his watch. It was already after 8:00 p.m.

****

When Noah exited the stairwell at the bottom of the stairs, he found himself in a dimly lit corridor that ran the length of the building. The temperature felt much warmer than upstairs in the computer room. This was Noah's first trip to the basement, so he took a few moments to explore the length of the corridor. He saw no offices, just storage rooms and utility rooms that housed generators, HVAC, telecommunications, network hubs, and the like. Except for the distant muffled hum of motors, the basement was quiet. After a few moments, he spotted a short aisle that led to the vault.

Noah's job was to see that the records in the vault were appropriately secure, and to take an inventory of the AFOS tapes that were in the vault. Two master copies of every tape released to the customer or to the field for testing, were required to be there. The vault was a large room the size of two management offices, twenty-one feet wide and twenty-eight feet deep. It had three main aisles that ran the length of the room. Along each aisle were racks of files that went from floor to ceiling. The vault was fireproof. The materials that made it fireproof also made it soundproof.

Noah approached the solid heavy metal door of the vault and inserted his badge. As he pushed the door open, he heard a woman's voice yelling **stop**. He peered down the center aisle, and at the far end of the aisle on the back wall, he could see the back of a man bent over a tabletop. The man had his arms under the raised knees of a woman who lay on her back atop the table. As Noah began to walk down the aisle toward them, the man straightened up and turned toward him. The woman yelled, "Get off me" and used the opportunity to push herself free.

"What are you doing to her?" Noah called out. "Miss, are you okay? Did he—"

It was too late. She had already fled down the aisle to the left and out the door behind him.

The man adjusted his trousers and belt as he faced Noah. Noah read the name on his badge . . . *Don Reston.*

"Please don't report this," Don begged. "It was a misunderstanding. She was embarrassed when you barged in. That's why she ran off. No big deal—who are you anyway? I've never seen you before."

"I'm one of the corporate auditors. Whose badge was used to get in here?"

"What? . . . Mine."

"She wasn't authorized to be in here, was she?"

"No, but—"

"No . . . but, you let her in."

"She insisted."

"Well, I must report what I saw," Noah said. It looked to me like your advances were not welcomed."

"Please, I didn't hurt her. Things were going fine until you showed up. Damn you! I'm going back to my office," he said angrily and stomped out.

Noah made an entry on his Issue Form, described what he saw, and noted the time 8:20 p.m. He then completed the job he went there to do.

****

Meanwhile, Debbie was checking offices on the second floor. So far, she had only found one office with an unlocked cabinet, an office with the light left on, and another with tape cartridges from an unknown vendor. She was nearing the end of her rounds when she spied an office at the end of the hallway, also lit. She entered the office. There were two desks—a shared office. The one desk was neat, tidy, and locked. The other was unlocked with papers on the desk. No one was there. Debbie took a long look up and down the hallway. There was no one in sight. Debbie began assessing the situation and was about to write up an incident report when a young woman appeared at the door.

"What are you doing in my office?" She asked sternly.

"Oh hello, I didn't know anyone was still here. Is this your office? Are you Barbara Brown, or Jennifer White?" These were the two names on the nameplate affixed to the door jam.

"I'm Barbara Brown. Who are you?" She seemed very agitated.

"I'm Deborah Smith. I'm with Corporate Audit. You really shouldn't leave your office unattended like this."

"My office mate was still here when I left, but I was gone longer than I expected. I guess she went home," Barbara said in her own defense.

"Well still, you need to plan ahead. These papers are classified and there is classified material in your desk."

"I'm sorry," she said as she walked to her desk, sat in her chair, rested her head in both hands, and started crying.

"Really it's not that big of a problem," Debbie said, thinking she may have been too harsh in her tone. "Are you alright?"

"No, I just had a bad experience with someone I know—at least I thought I did. I'm upset."

"Do you want to talk about it?" Debbie asked with compassion.

"No! I can't talk about it. Write me up if you want," she angrily said as she stood up suddenly. She threw everything into her desk, slammed the drawer shut, and locked it. "I don't care. I'm going home." She went quickly out the doorway almost knocking Debbie over in the process.

Debbie had no choice but to write up the incident. On her Issue Form, she put a time of 8:35 p.m. She evaluated the last few rooms on her list and then headed downstairs toward the lobby and the car.

****

The team had agreed to meet back at the car at 9:00 p.m. As soon as everyone was back, Peter asked, "Anyone find anything of great interest?"

Michael was first to answer. "I had an interesting experience. I was investigating Armstrong's suite. He had left his door unlocked—a no-no—so I walked into his office and looked around. Apparently, I tripped a motion detector, and an armed security guard greeted me at the door. With his hand on his holster, he asked me who I was and why I was there. I explained, but he told me he had not been briefed, and ordered me to leave immediately. I was not about to argue so I left."

"Did you put all of this on the Issues Form?" Peter asked.

"I did."

"A job well-done, Michael. Thanks!"

"I had an interesting experience too," Noah said. "When I went to the vault, two people were already inside. I am quite certain that they were about to have sex." Everyone's ears perked up when they heard this. Peter had already started the engine and was pulling out of the parking lot.

"Did you write it up?" Michael asked.

"I did, but I wasn't sure what rule they broke. Is there a rule that says you can't have sex on IBM property?"

"Damn good question," Peter said. "I assume they had authorized access to the room."

"When I came in, I interrupted them. The girl was angry. I am not sure that she wanted to have sex. She left before I could talk to her. I don't think she had authorization."

"Interesting . . . did you talk to the guy?" Michael asked.

"I did. I got his name. The guy asked me not to report it. He said she was embarrassed and that was why she ran out, but I am not sure."

"Noah, did you get the girl's name?" Debbie asked.

"I only got a quick glimpse of her badge, but her first name may have been Barbara."

"Can you describe her?"

"Black hair, black skirt, and a white blouse," Noah replied.

"Peter, turn the car around," Debbie demanded. "We need to go back and report this to Security. I think she was *raped*!" That pronouncement got everyone's attention.

"Why do you think that?" Peter asked.

"I found an office with the lights on, the desk unlocked, and papers left loose. While I was in there, a girl named Barbara Brown appeared—said it was her office. She was wearing a black skirt and white blouse, and she had black hair. She was very upset . . . started crying . . . didn't want to talk about it . . . told me she was going home . . . and left in a huff."

The team went back to the main Lobby and met with the Security Manager on duty. Noah and Debbie answered questions while the Security Manager filled out the appropriate forms. "Thank you for reporting this," he told them and turned to resume his nightly routine.

"Wait. Shouldn't we report this to the Boulder Police?" Debbie asked.

"I know you don't want to hear this," the Security Manager said, "but there's nothing the police can do unless there's more evidence of a crime. You both said that Miss Brown did not appear to be physically injured, and you said that she didn't want to talk about it. It would really be up to her to report this as an assault or as a rape—"

"But I heard her shout, *Stop*!" Noah said.

"I hear you," the Security Manager responded. "But, let me say this, if I was making love to my wife and a stranger barged in on us, I'm sure she would yell *stop* as well. I'll keep this report on file, but the names will remain confidential. If someone reports a future incident involving Mister Reston, or if the young lady comes forward, we'll pursue it then. In the meantime, let me mention that Security has requested more cameras. We should probably have one in front of the vault. Perhaps you guys could help us out with that."

"Perhaps . . . thank you for your help," Peter said. He then turned to his team. "Guys, we need to get going. It's late."

As they started to leave, Debbie turned to Peter. "Peter, maybe I should talk with her and get her to report it."

"Debbie, I think your feelings may be getting in the way of objectivity," Peter cautioned. "Our job is to report the facts to IBM as we know them. In this case, we don't have all the facts. Perhaps it was consensual or even a misunderstanding with her boyfriend. Perhaps she ran off because she was embarrassed. If we make this public, and there was no attempted rape, it could ruin both their reputations. On the other hand, if she wasn't authorized to be in the vault, perhaps she was afraid of being charged with a security violation. I think we should let Miss Brown and IBM decide what actions to take."

Debbie persisted. "Peter, I don't agree. I—"

"Debbie," Michael interrupted. "Why don't we sleep on it? Barbara has already left the building—nothing more you can do about it tonight."

Debbie shook her head in resignation.

The four of them exited the building. On the way out to the car, Michael asked, "Peter, we haven't heard what *you* found tonight."

"Nothing as exciting as what you guys found," he lied.

It was after ten o'clock before they were back at the Inn.

9

THE BOMB

It was 7:30 Tuesday morning and the audit team was eager to start their day at IBM. This morning they were to make their first major report to Big John and his staff. They left the breakfast room and walked as a group out the lobby door of the Residence Inn and toward the rental car. Peter led the way. As they walked into the morning sun, Debbie put on her shades, and Peter put on his driving glasses. They were about fifty feet from the car when Peter caught a glimpse of something. As he got closer, he noticed what looked like a small black rectangular box sitting on top of the rear tire. It was almost unnoticeable in the shade of the wheel well.

Strange, he thought. He ventured closer and crouched down to get a better look. *Oh my God!* He felt a rush of adrenaline, and his heart beat faster. He quickly stood upright and turned to face the others.

"GET BACK . . . AWAY FROM THE CAR!" he yelled and moved towards the others with his arms outstretched.

"Peter, what is going on?" Michael shouted.

"Is there something wrong with the car?" Noah wanted to know.

Peter gathered the three into a huddle and spoke softly. "Listen, I think someone has planted a bomb under our car."

There was a sudden silence.

"We need to return to the lobby. I'll speak to the manager and he and I will call the police. Not a word to anyone. We don't want panic. Okay?" he said as he looked each of them in the eye. "Let's go."

They all returned to the lobby, and Peter asked the desk clerk to summon the manager. She seemed reluctant at first, and Peter had to tell her it was extremely important and could not wait. The manager came out seeming a bit annoyed. He was even more annoyed after Peter explained the problem. After all, this kind of bad publicity was the last thing he needed. "Let me go have a look at it," he said. Obviously, there was a trust issue here.

"Sir, you need to believe me. This is serious and dangerous. The sooner we get the authorities out here to investigate, the better. I understand you don't want the bad publicity and you don't want to start a panic either. If that thing goes off, matters will be a lot worse. Please!" The manager made the call.

Both Peter and the manager talked to the authorities on the phone. Once Peter knew that help was on the way, he asked the manager for another favor. "I will of course stay here to talk to the authorities when they arrive, but my three colleagues need to get to work at IBM. Any chance you could arrange transportation for them?"

"Of course, we have a van."

"Thanks."

So far, no one else in the lobby was aware of the situation. Peter went back to his colleagues to explain what was happening. Debbie seemed scared. He tried to reassure her. "Debbie, it's going to be okay. I'll need to stay and talk to the authorities when they arrive, but the manager here is arranging transportation for you guys to get to IBM. I'll get another rental car and catch up to you later. Michael, please tell Big John that we need to reschedule our meeting."

Debbie still seemed distraught. Peter put his hand on her shoulder. "Debbie you will be fine. The safest place you can be right now is inside the IBM building. Try to relax here in the lobby until the van is ready."

The Boulder Police, and the County Sheriff, were just now arriving. Fortunately, they had sense enough not to use their sirens, Peter thought. They went to the front desk, spoke to the manager—who had taken over the front desk—and then turned and began walking toward Peter. "Are you Peter Troutman?"

"Yes, I am."

"I'm Detective David Redman. We have called the County bomb squad. They need to come from Longmont so it will be a few minutes. In the meantime, we are roping off the area where your car is. Things are starting to get busy here. Would you mind if we go sit in my car and talk?"

By the time the bomb squad arrived, people were already beginning to gather and gawk. Three patrol cars and a truck with the words *bomb squad* written on the side could not help but attract attention. Peter watched from Detective Redman's car window as two officers controlled the growing crowd and kept them a safe distance from the rental car. At the same time, he saw one individual begin dismantling the bomb while another supervised.

Detective Redman asked questions, and Peter did most of the talking.

"Mister Troutman. Start at the beginning and tell me everything that happened."

Peter described in detail what he observed.

"Mister Troutman, tell me why you are here."

"I'm employed by IBM and I'm here with three others on company business," he answered without additional detail.

"Mister Troutman, do you have any enemies?"

These were all standard questions, and Peter answered them as truthfully as he could without revealing the true nature of his mission. Although Peter had some thoughts about the answer to the last question, he did not share those thoughts with Detective Redman. "No, sir. I have no idea who would want to do this."

Detective Redman said that was all for now and asked Peter for contact information. Peter gave it to him.

"Detective, before you go, I have a question. Will I be getting my car back?"

"No, we will need to impound it . . . check for fingerprints and the like."

"We may have some stuff in it, like the rental agreement, a hat . . . don't know what else."

"I'll make sure you get that back. Mr. Troutman, here's my card. If you think of anything else, please call me."

They shook hands and parted company.

Peter made a dart for the safe-haven of his residential unit. Before he shut his door, he saw the local news van drive into the parking lot. Once inside, the first thing he did was to call Special Agent Roger Colby. Unfortunately, Colby was not available and Agent McCarthy forwarded his call to Colby's voice mail. Peter left the following voice mail message:

Last night I found a tape cartridge that may contain a virus. I marked the cartridge and put it back where I found it, so as not to arouse suspicion. However, I would suggest holding up shipment of the AFOS release to allow investigation. In addition, police and bomb squad are here at Residence Inn this morning. I must postpone this morning's meeting.

Peter also placed a call to Jon Wilson and left a similar message on his recorder. Then he called Greg. Once again, no one answered, and he left the following message for Greg:

Letting you know that this morning someone attempted to blow up our rental car. Everyone is okay, at least physically. It was quite a scare. I arranged transportation for the team to go to IBM while I stayed behind to deal with the authorities and get a new rental car. I asked Michael to reschedule the status meeting with Armstrong. I will try to call you later.

After that, he called Hertz and secured a replacement rental car. It took a while trying to explain to the rental agent why he needed one.

****

Peter arrived at the IBM site shortly after lunch. He had a brief meeting with Big John to make sure he was up to speed on the audit and the bomb scare. Apparently, Big John was already on board. Colby must have called him. Big John said that Colby wanted the AFOS code prepared for shipment tomorrow as planned, but that he would delay the actual shipment to the customer. The FBI would use the time to determine if a virus was on the tapes. As far as the bomb scare was concerned, it seemed like everyone in Boulder was already talking about it.

Big John asked Peter if he still wanted to do the security sweep planned for that evening. Peter told him there was no longer a need; he had found what he set out to find. He told him that his team did the security sweep last night instead of tonight, and he told him he discovered a tape cartridge in Georgy Belinsky's office that may contain viral code. Big John expressed his displeasure with Peter for changing the plan without consulting him first, but he knew the auditors had a right to do so. He let the matter drop.

"Peter, I don't understand something. If you found the viral tape cartridge, where is it?"

"I left it where I found it."

"What I don't understand is why you didn't take it so that it couldn't be used."

"Possessing it is not much of a crime. Using it is. I think the FBI wants leverage to go after the big fish that are behind all of this."

"I see."

"While the shipment is on hold, I would like to have Noah review the computer event logs. He would need Ngai Wu to print them. He is looking for an irregularity in the tape preparation process. You okay with that?"

"Of course, but you don't really need my permission."

"I know, but I may need your help with the cooperation aspect."

"You have it," Big John responded.

After leaving Armstrong's office, Peter went to the auditor's office and met with his team. They were anxious and wanted to know what was really going on. Debbie was still scared. Michael spoke for the group.

"We've had the feeling all along that there is more to this audit than you have told us. We want to support you and stand with you, but we need to know what's going on . . . and, now that our lives seem to be in danger, I think you owe us an explanation. We're scared for our safety."

"Hey guys," Peter spoke in a sympathetic tone. "I really do understand how you feel, but I need you to stick with me. I really do. You're right; there is more to this audit than you were told. Unfortunately, for security reasons, I'm not allowed to tell you everything . . . but as you said, I owe you an explanation. I will tell you this. The FBI requested this audit. This is not abnormal. We have done other audits requested by the FBI as well. For example, the FBI requested the audit we did in Manassas last year. Usually, when the FBI requests an audit, it's because either a crime has been committed or the FBI thinks that one is about to be committed. In either case, our objective is to determine the vulnerabilities that would allow a crime to occur, to prevent one from happening in the future. In this case, the work we are doing on this audit is *extremely* important to our national security."

"Peter, does that mean that you have a higher security clearance than the rest of us?" Noah wanted to know.

"Sorry, I can't answer that."

"Peter, who do you actually report to?" Michael asked.

"Sorry, I can't answer that."

"What about our *safety*?" Debbie asked.

"You should not be concerned. We don't even know who the target of the bomb was. Was it the audit team . . . was it me . . . or was it put on our car by mistake? In fact, we don't even know if the bomb could have exploded or if was just meant to scare someone. I have already notified the FBI of what has happened and I'm confident that the FBI will take measures to protect us now that this has happened. Please, work with me," he pleaded. "Michael has rescheduled our status meeting with Big John to give us more time. Our focus now should be preparing for that meeting. What was the time, Michael?"

Michael answered, "Tomorrow afternoon . . . time is not firm yet."

Peter knew that they were not satisfied, but he did not know what else to offer them. There was so much more he needed to know himself.

The team spent the rest of Tuesday afternoon attempting to prepare the details of the status report for the meeting the next day. As you can imagine, however, they found it difficult to focus. They left work earlier than normal. As they were about to get into the new rental car, Debbie began to act strangely. She did not want to get in. Michael convinced her that everything would be all right and he helped her into the front seat.

****

That evening, the team stayed in. Peter and two others enjoyed the sloppy Joes and wine provided by the Inn in the common area. Debbie stayed in her unit. All four were in their units for the night at an early hour. It was around 8:00 p.m. when Peter answered a knock on his door.

"Mister Troutman, I'm Agent Sanders with the FBI. Sorry to bother you but we need to talk."

"What about?"

"*Boulder Creek.*"

"Are you alone?" he asked as he opened the door looked outside.

"Yes."

"Okay, come in. . . . Have a seat."

She took a seat on the edge of the sofa.

"Mister Troutman, I talked with Roger Colby this afternoon. He filled me in on what happened here this morning. He wanted me to talk with you. I've been fully read into the project so we can discuss freely, but our discussions need to be secret, hence the venue—nice place. IBM treats you well. I should see if Colby will allow me to stay in a nice place like this."

"Where are you staying?"

"Tonight, I'm staying at the Dumpy Motel on Route 36—28th Street according to the locals. All I could do on short notice." Peter wondered if she was referring to the Dunphy Motel, but without waiting for his response, she got back to business. "Colby said you left a message for him today, indicating you may have found the computer virus. You were supposed to give him a full report this afternoon."

"Yes, I left him a phone message that I was unable to make it to Denver due to the recent developments."

"He understands that, but it's because of the recent developments, that he's asked me to work with you. You tell me what you know, and I'll tell you what I know."

"Maybe you should go first," Peter suggested.

"Very well . . . I've been working on this project for about a year, before it became *Boulder Creek*. I'm a forensic accountant by training. A year ago, a one hundred grand payment was made to someone named Jim Hoffman. He was a network designer that worked for a contractor in Colorado Springs. Within hours after the wire transfer to Hoffman's bank, Hoffman died. The coroner ruled his death suspicious. That's how I first got involved. I eventually determined that the payments came from an offshore affiliate of a company by the name of Panda International. However, we did not see a connection to what is happening with IBM until recently. It turns out that the Air Force plans to install tomorrow's code release on the computers that make up the network designed by Hoffman. I recently determined that Panda International has links to Panda Pizza, the place where you had supper Saturday night. DEA has put surveillance on them because they think Panda Pizza may be dealing drugs."

Peter tried, but could not remember seeing her there on Saturday. Did she learn of his presence from DEA?

"Okay," she continued. "You were supposed to give Colby a highly classified report this morning. Your team was to give Armstrong and staff a less classified report this afternoon. Whoever did the bombing, probably wanted to prevent that from happening."

"Any information as to *who* that might be?" Peter asked.

"I was hoping you could tell *me*," she said.

"No idea."

"Mister Troutman! What was it that your team was about to do that was worth blowing you to bits? I need to know."

"Agent Sanders, we're on the same side remember. Relax. I'll tell you everything I know."

"Yes . . .?"

"Last week, Noah—he's one of my auditors—and I looked for tape cartridges that were not ones that IBM would have purchased. If we had found any, it would have signaled a security problem. We also reviewed computer logs to verify that all cartridges were clean and formatted before being loaded with code. Aside from Big John, only two people could have had any awareness of what we were doing. They were Georgy Belinsky, the computer room manager and Ngai Wu, his employee that packaged products for shipping."

"Did you find something?"

"Only two instances over the past year where cartridges may not have been used or labeled correctly. By chance, we also found one cartridge that had made its way out of the data center. As a test, we took a cartridge that we labeled as *Secret* off site to our car and brought it back the next morning. What we proved was that it could happen, and there were no controls to prevent it. Last Thursday, I went to Big John—"

"Who?"

"Oh, I'm sorry . . . John Armstrong, the IBM General Manager. He verified that the AFOS code release was scheduled for Thursday morning of this week. Colby had already briefed Armstrong that there may be a plot to imbed viral code into that release by using a cartridge from the outside. I told Armstrong we planned to do a security sweep tonight as part of our normal audit routine. The sweep would include a full search of the computer room and AFOS offices. If there was a viral tape, I hoped the sweep would find it. I asked him if he could give us a master key that would allow us to open desks and cabinets. He did not agree, citing IBM's philosophy of *Respect for the Individual*. No one was to have known of our plans except Big John, Colby, and possibly Robert Stanley, Manager of Site Security. I don't think any of them would have intentionally told Belinsky or his employees about our plan, but it may have been leaked. If Belinsky, or someone he worked for, knew of our plan, they could have been fearful that we would have found the viral tape. Perhaps that was motivation for the bomb."

Peter paused and seemed to be thinking. "But back to the question of who was behind the bomb. I don't know, but I would suspect that Panda Pizza may have had some involvement."

"You think Panda Pizza could be involved in the bomb? What did you see Saturday night when you were at Panda Pizza?"

"I saw Georgy Belinsky come in. I saw him go down the hallway toward the men's room and office. He reappeared about ten minutes later and went to the take-out window where he picked up two calzone boxes. He paid in cash, and then walked by my table as he left."

"Did you speak?"

"We exchanged pleasantries."

"What do you think he had in those boxes?"

"I think that one of those boxes contained an IBM tape cartridge. I think the other box contained a calzone and possibly some drugs."

"Basis?"

"During the audit, I have had several friendly chats with him. He told me he was divorced and that his mother was in a nursing home. He told me that on Saturday nights, he likes to go to Panda Pizza and then he goes clubbing. Anyway, it seemed to me he might need money and be easy to influence. He recommended Panda Pizza to me when I told him we would be around on weekends and were looking for places to eat and things to do. That's the reason we were there." Peter did not mention the other reason—his conversation with Jon Wilson.

"My audit team and Belinsky use the same side door to enter the IBM building each morning. Yesterday morning, I followed Belinsky into the building. I saw Belinsky bring a calzone box into his office. I assumed he put it into his desk. After seeing this, I decided to do the security sweep last night instead of tonight. During the sweep, I went into Belinsky's office and searched for the calzone box. I found the empty box in the trash bin.

I retrieved it. I found no residue of food. That supported my theory that it contained the tape cartridge. I found the cartridge inside his desk."

"Wasn't his desk locked? . . . Never mind, I don't want to know."

"What did you do with the cartridge?"

"I assumed it contained the computer virus that we are looking for, and debated whether or not to take it, to prevent it from being used. I decided to leave it in the desk. However, I did put a subtle mark on it using a permanent marker."

"Good choice!" she said. It may be risky, but if we allow Belinsky to imbed the virus into the software release, I think we will have a stronger case against him when we find it . . . as long as we find it before it gets installed on the network computers."

"Well maybe. You are assuming that we can prove that the tapes readied for shipment contain a virus."

"When will the software be ready for shipment?" she asked.

"Tomorrow, the software will be compiled and copied onto tape cartridges and readied for delivery. The Air Force expects to take ownership on Thursday according to Armstrong. When I told Armstrong of my observations, he said that Ngai Wu would hold up delivery long enough for Noah to review the computer logs, and shipping documents. Noah can do that tomorrow evening. The computer log may give hint as to how the virus was loaded or copied onto the cartridges before delivery. I also expect that Noah will find the cartridge that was in Belinsky's desk. Once the compiles are completed and the tapes readied for delivery, Belinsky would not have any further use for it. He probably wiped it clean but it may have other trace evidence on it. If we find it, I'm witness to the fact that it came from Belinsky's desk. On the other hand, if Belinsky was aware that we would look for it, he may have used it and then disposed of it. If that is the case, the computer logs may still tell us something. Can the FBI put an official hold on shipments to the installation sites? The FBI lab could then use that time to prove that the cartridges contain a virus. They could compare a cartridge ready for shipment to a cartridge that we know does *not* have the virus. Then they could go after Belinsky. They could get him to talk!"

"Yes, I think that is what the FBI should do, but we need to prove there is a virus before we question Belinsky. That goes for you too, you know."

"Of course, . . . one more thing." Agent Sanders looked up, but before she could ask *what*, Peter said, "My team is concerned about their safety."

"I can't blame them." Her expression became reflective. "You were all very lucky. If you had not spotted the mercury tilt switch on top of the wheel, you would all be gone. We found two blocks of C4. That was enough to destroy everything within a hundred feet—Peter, how are *you* doing?" she asked with a great deal of compassion.

"I'm good, but I'm concerned about my team. Is there anything you can do?"

"I'll see if I can get your team a protection detail."

"Okay, thanks," he replied, without being sure how realistic that would be, "But, I was thinking of something else. Would you consider talking with them in the morning before we leave for work?"

"What would I tell them?"

"I think you could let them know that the FBI is watching over them. You could say that the target of the bomb may be random or perhaps they got the wrong car and they were not the intended target. Let them know that you are investigating the bomb. Let them know you are analyzing the bomb components and hope to determine who bought those components, etc. You could also let everyone know that it's unlikely that whoever did this, would try again now that this is in the news. I don't know. I'm thinking out-loud here. I just need them to feel safe. Perhaps you could help."

"I can talk to them at eight in the morning under one condition."

"What's that?"

"You buy me breakfast?"

"Okay. It's a deal. Thanks. I really appreciate this."

"Mister Troutman, this was a very productive meeting. I'll be here at eight and then I'll talk with Colby and bring him up to speed on everything we discussed, and I'll see if I can reschedule your meeting with him for Thursday morning. Do you still plan to meet with Armstrong tomorrow?"

"Yes, unless I'm told otherwise. By the way, you can call me Peter."

"Peter, thanks," she said with a smile. "I'm Carol. Until tomorrow."

10

AFTERMATH

On Wednesday, the morning after the bomb scare, Peter was up early. He went over to the lobby and picked up a local newspaper. The bombing attempt made the front page.

ATTEMPTED CAR BOMBING

by Lois Lane

Boulder Daily News

Tuesday morning, someone planted a car bomb under a car parked at the Residence Inn in Boulder. The bomb was discovered before it exploded. Boulder County deputies arrived on the scene and brought in the bomb squad from Loveland. The bomb squad dismantled the bomb and removed the components from the scene. The car was impounded. The perpetrator and their motives are unknown. The FBI and the Boulder County Sheriff's department are investigating. Authorities said that if the bomb had exploded, it would have destroyed everything within one hundred feet. Authorities did not identify the intended victims.

Incidents like this bring back memories of the May 1974 car bombings that took the lives of six. The reasons for those explosions were never fully determined.

Peter breathed a sigh of relief. The article did not reveal names and did not mention IBM. He made his way to the complimentary breakfast bar and was the first of the audit team to arrive. He helped himself to juice, scrambled eggs, and one sausage link, and then found a large empty table. It was after eight as each of the team members and Agent Sanders

"

filtered in one at a time. As they helped themselves to breakfast and looked around for a place to sit, Peter stood up and motioned for them to join him. Everyone was there except Debbie. Peter asked Michael if he would call her room to see if she was okay, and mention that we had someone with us we wanted her to meet. Michael came back to the table and said she would be right down.

Peter introduced everyone to Agent Sanders. Debbie apologized for being late and mentioned that she had not slept well. Carol introduced herself to the group and said it was okay to address her as Carol. She said that Peter asked her to speak to them and address the concerns they had about their safety. It went well. She was friendly and seemed especially understanding. She listened to their concerns and assured them that that the FBI had their back. Debbie asked, "Carol, have you ever had a near death experience?"

"No, not personally, but I have known several agents that have. . . Why?"

"I was going to ask what you did to get through it."

"It's not uncommon for an agent to see someone get killed, or even kill someone themselves. The best advice is to talk about it and let feelings come to the surface. Sometimes that means talking with a professional like a psychologist, but Debbie in this case, no one died. Are you having trouble dealing with this?"

"I know I am reacting to this more than the rest of you. I need to tell you something. When I was just out of college, I toured Europe. I met a boy in Ireland and we shared his car. One day we were checking out of a hostel and I offered to go get the car and bring it to the front so that we could load some things. He stopped me and said no. He told me to finish packing while he got the car." Debbie's voice became shaky as she said, "I saw him get into the car and I saw the explosion. . . I never saw him again. **It could have been me!**"

"Debbie, I'm so very sorry," Carol said with a great deal of feeling.

"Debbie, I had no idea," Peter said. "If you need time, it's not a problem. Maybe take off a few days if you need to."

"I may do that, Peter. I'll let you know. Look, I don't want you guys feeling sorry for me. I went through this before and I had plenty of help as to how to handle it. I will work it out. It just takes time."

"Well, just know you have our support," Peter said sincerely.

"Debbie, do you have someone that you can talk to about this?" Carol asked.

"I do back home."

"Debbie if you need to talk to somebody here, please feel free to call me . . . okay? And if any of you feel threatened, or want to talk further, please call me." She gave each member of the team her business card.

Peter thanked Carol for speaking to them and said that they should leave for work soon. When they got to the new rental car, a sheriff's deputy greeted them. He had checked out the car. They were good to go. Apparently, the FBI really did have their backs.

****

On Wednesday afternoon, as rescheduled, the team gave a status report to Big John. Greg did not attend, but Peter had summarized the report over the phone with him on Tuesday, and Greg was okay with it. Peter told Big John that so far, they had not found any serious issues, or violations of either DOD or IBM policy and procedures. However, there was more work to do. The meeting included discussion about difficulties that the auditors were having getting information they needed from the organization. For example, Michael was trying to compare the badge access listing to a current listing from Human Resources that said who was still working at the facility. He did not think that the Human Resource Department was cooperating. Noah felt he was getting resistance from Belinsky, the manager of the computer room when he asked to review the administrator's computer logs. These types of issues were common for every audit—nothing new. Big John promised to talk with the managers involved to resolve these issues. No one mentioned the bomb scare, or the belief that a virus was about to be imbedded into the AFOS software. At the end of the meeting, Armstrong thanked Peter for an informative presentation. Peter gave kudos to Debbie for putting the written report together in an organized way.

Meanwhile Georgy Belinsky was doing his job. That day, he created twelve tape cartridges for delivery to the Air Force. He also created two additional cartridges that IBM would keep as a backup. These two would go into the vault. He finished the work by three in the afternoon and took the rest of the afternoon off.

After the status meeting, Noah talked with Ngai Wu, Georgy's technician who helped him resume his analysis of the computer logs. His objective was to determine if there could have been unwanted code introduced into the process. He found several things that did not seem right, but he did not find everything he needed in order to know exactly what occurred. He was concerned that the paper labels on the cartridges did not relate to the magnetic information stored on the tape. He told Peter he needed more time.

The team stayed later than usual Wednesday evening, making up for time lost on Tuesday. Belinsky had left for the evening and Noah took Peter into the computer room to show him a cartridge he found. Peter had alerted him to the fact that he was looking for specific cartridge that he had marked on Monday. Noah asked why he was looking for it. Peter could not tell him the reason. What he did tell him was, "I'm sorry, I can't tell you, but it's very important that we find it. You need to trust me on this." The team had been hearing that a lot lately, but they knew that more was going on than they were authorized to know, and they were willing to play along. That evening, after normal working hours, Noah found the cartridge that had the subtle mark on the case—the one Peter had put there using a permanent marking pen. Peter was convinced that on Monday when he saw it in Georgy's desk, it contained the virus. This evening, it was in a stack of cartridges to be disposed, and the label said, *error-prone and unreliable*. The label number was not on the shipping list. Peter took the cartridge with him. He then called Big John and left a message that he had a cartridge that he would turn over to the FBI in the morning.

Carol called Peter that evening and told him that Colby wanted to meet with them first thing in the morning. She could drive and bring him back. She was still staying at the Dunphy Motel, so it would be no problem. She would be there to pick him up at 7:00 a.m.

****

By 7:15 Thursday morning, Carol and Peter were on their way to Denver to meet with Colby. Carol was driving. Peter had given Michael the keys to his car the night before and left him in charge of the audit. The hour it took to get to the FBI office gave Carol and Peter the opportunity to talk and learn more about each other.

Carol told Peter that she had an advanced college degree in accounting. Peter told Carol he had an advanced degree in business administration. Carol told Peter that she had a daughter and a son that were in college. Peter told Carol that he had two kids in college as well—two daughters. Carol said that after having kids, she had gone to work for the FBI where she worked as a forensic accountant. Peter learned that she separated from her husband three years ago and they divorced two years ago. Carol learned that Peter had been with IBM since getting his MBA, but had worked for another company prior. His main expertise was planning and process analysis. He had legally separated from his wife. Both ex-spouses got the houses they had lived in. They found that they had a lot in common. Then they asked each other the traditional question: "how did you ended up doing what you are doing?"

"Carol, what made you want to work for the FBI?"

"It's kind of personal, but the short of it is that my father was swindled out of a lot of money, and they never figured out who was responsible. I saw how it hurt him—he got depressed. I guess a part of me is still trying to solve his case. . . That's probably more than you wanted to know." Her mood had turned somber as she said this. Then, almost like turning a switch, she perked up and asked, "Peter, what about you? How did you get involved with a project like this?"

"Oh gosh, I'm sorry, but it's not something that I'm allowed to discuss," Peter replied. Well, that was not totally true, but he did not feel comfortable telling her about his connection to the CIA until he knew her better. He resorted to his favorite cliché. "Perhaps you have heard the cliché, *I could tell you, but then I would have to kill you.* It's kind of like that."

"Tall, dark, handsome and now mysterious," Carol thought, but did not say it.

Instead, she said, "I've heard that expression before. Where does it come from?"

"No idea."

Then Peter changed the subject. "Carol, I wonder if you could help me out with something? When I was here six weeks ago, Greg and I had to go through security before we got to the visitor's desk. I was wondering if you must do that since you have a badge and everything."

"Yes, but I go through a separate line. Why do you ask?"

"I'm concerned about my briefcase. I don't want it to go through an x-ray scanner. I didn't have it last time so wasn't sure of the procedure."

"Maybe you should tell me what's in your briefcase."

"I have a magnetic tape cartridge and two rolls of film."

"Sounds like I should put the cuffs on you for stealing classified information."

"Ha-ha. The cartridge was not marked classified, and I doubt there is any classified information on it anymore. It was in the disposal bin. However, the cartridge *did* contain the virus and it *was* in Belinsky's desk on Monday. It may have trace evidence on it. Armstrong said it was okay to give it to the FBI," Peter said, knowing that it was not quite true. "As to the film, it belongs to me."

"I'll tell them you're with me, but they may still want to manually search your briefcase and my bag . . . shouldn't be a problem."

****

Peter and Carol had no issue with the security screening. They met with Colby for about an hour in his conference room. No one else was present. Peter gave them a copy of the general report he had presented to Armstrong and his staff yesterday. Colby looked at it quickly and then set it aside. Carol put hers into a shoulder case she carried. The real purpose of the meeting was to discuss the possible virus delivered to the Air Force yesterday.

"Peter, you called and left a message for me late Tuesday morning after the bombing," Colby began. "You said you found the virus. After that, I talked with Armstrong. We decided to let the Air Force take possession, but they have agreed to delay the installations until the FBI lab can verify that the cartridges are okay. However, the computer lab called me just before you arrived to tell me that they looked at the contents of the tape and did not see any unexpected files. They think the tapes are okay."

"With all due respect sir, I am quite certain they are not okay, **and I don't think releasing them is a risk you would want—**" The tone of Peter's voice was presumptive and didactic. Noticing Colby's reaction, Carol interrupted.

"Sir, I think what Mr. Troutman is trying to say is that he has more evidence for you to consider before making a final decision."

"Sorry, sir," Peter said calmly. "I did not mean to sound confrontational. In fact, I do have something to give you."

Peter lifted his brief case off the floor, set it on Colby's desk, opened it, and handed Colby the cartridge. "This is the cartridge that I found in Belinsky's desk Monday night. I believe he received it from Panda Pizza, and I believe it contained the virus we were looking for. However, yesterday afternoon I found it in a disposal bin. A physical label was on the casing indicating that it was no good. It had no label when I saw it Monday night."

Colby picked up the cartridge and studied it. "How do you know this cartridge is the same one you saw Monday night? Don't they all look alike?"

"Turn it over. Notice the small red dot on the lower left of the case."

"Oh yeah."

"You may not want to handle it too much. If we are lucky your lab may find fingerprints on it that belong to someone at Panda Pizza. However, what is still on the magnetic tape is unknown. The virus may still be on there, but I doubt it. One of my auditors—Noah Bosch—is analyzing the computer logs and hopes to explain the role that the suspect cartridge played in the AFOS distribution process. However, it would be helpful to know what exactly is still on the tape. He specifically wanted to know what volume and file labels were still detectable, if any."

"All right, I'll have the lab analyze it. Anything else?"

"Well, yes . . . I know that the FBI lab is the best in the world, but Noah asked me *how* you would detect the viral code on the AFOS tapes . . . assuming there is viral code of course."

"What are you getting at?"

"The virus portion of the tape would be very small. It may be a separate file, or it may be part of a legitimate file. Noah was afraid that it might not be on a separate file with its own header. Apparently, your lab already discovered this. The AFOS cartridges only contain *object code*. Humans can't read object code—only computers can. If the virus is imbedded in a legitimate file, Noah wondered how you could distinguish the good code from the bad code."

"Mister Troutman, I must admit that this is not my area of expertise, but you are welcome to talk with Special Agent Don Matthews. He is the supervisor of the FBI computer lab here in Denver. He may be able to answer your technical questions. I'll give you his phone number and let him know to expect your call."

"Thanks. I appreciate that, but would it be possible to talk with him now?"

"Mister Troutman, he knows how to do this stuff. Are you suggesting otherwise?"

"No sir. Noah Bosch is analyzing the computer logs created when the tapes were created. Based on this analysis, he believes that the virus is embedded in a legitimate file. I'm sure your lab would want to pursue this possibility. His information may be useful to your lab and may expedite your process. Noah also proposed a way to determine if the virus is embedded in a legitimate file. I would like to discuss the proposal with Agent Matthews."

Colby gave Peter a hard look as he contemplated his decision. "I'll tell you what . . . Let me see if Special Agent Matthews is available. If he is, I'll invite him to join us."

Fortunately, Agent Matthews was available. After introductions, Peter informed him of the type of evil code they were looking to find and the fact that it would be functionally dormant until triggered by an unknown future event. Then Peter asked, "Have you had a chance to examine the AFOS tape yet?"

"Yes. We didn't see a file on the tape that wasn't supposed to be there, but if there was one, it wouldn't be a problem."

"What do you mean," Peter asked.

"The installation process looks for specific file headers. If a file doesn't have a header, or if the header isn't on the list of expected headers, the installation is aborted."

"I see. But, if the virus was attached to a legitimate file, and didn't have its own header, would you know that?"

"Do you think that could be the case?" he asked.

"Yes, my auditor, Noah, thinks that may be the case. What would you do then?"

"Not sure . . . Never had a situation like this. We would probably send the tape to our lab in Quantico. They could attempt a reverse compilation of the code. It would be time consuming and costly. Is it worth doing?"

"It most certainly is!" Peter said emphatically. However, Noah has a proposal that would save time and effort."

"What is it?"

"He suggested comparing the code on the AFOS cartridge to the code on a cartridge that did not have the virus—one you knew did not. He suggested that if the FBI had the *source code*—the code readable in English before being complied into *object code*—the FBI could do its own compile and create a cartridge that they knew did not have the virus. IBM does not normally provide source code but may make an exception in this case due to the serious nature of the issue. If not, IBM may authorize creating a new AFOS cartridge under FBI supervision. Then we would know it was created without introducing the virus. Is that something that you could arrange with John Armstrong?"

Agents Matthews and Colby looked at each other, seeming to give this thoughtful consideration, and then agreed.

"Yes, I think we could talk to him about it."

Peter hoped they would coordinate with Armstrong and work out a way to create another cartridge that would be virus free.

Most of the meeting had been devoted to the viral tape cartridge. Carol had said little, but now it was her turn. Colby spoke, "Sanders, what is happening with respect to tracking the source of the virus, and the people involved. Do you have anything new to report?"

"Yes, sir. Peter has reported observing a connection between Georgy Belinsky at IBM and the Panda Pizza Palace. If a virus was embedded into the AFOS tapes at IBM, Belinsky is the one most likely to have done it. As a result, I have started an investigation into the possible motivation of Belinsky and any money flow to him. As Peter has indicated, Panda Pizza may have delivered the viral cartridge to Belinsky in a calzone box. There is the possibility that the Manager of Panda Pizza is involved in more than dealing drugs. I have requested more information from DEA to see if Belinsky showed up on their radar. Unfortunately, many pieces to the puzzle have yet to fit together. I hope to have something more informative by next Wednesday."

"Thank you both," Colby said. "I look forward to meeting with you next week. I hope we know much more by then."

"Before we leave, sir, I'd like to ask you a question. My audit team is very concerned about the attempt on their lives. What can I tell them? Has any progress been made on identifying who did this?"

"I can't give you details yet," Colby responded, "and I don't want anything I say to be leaked to the press. However, I'll tell you in confidence that we have a suspect that we plan to take into custody once we have enough evidence to hold him. We hope he will talk and tell us the brains behind the operation. As of now, we have no proof that the bombing is connected to the work your audit team is doing."

"Do you think that there could be a link to Panda Pizza?"

"There may be, but I don't want to speculate." Tell your audit team that the FBI is investigating. Tell them that we don't expect another attempt, and that our agents will protect them."

"Okay, thanks, sir."

"And Agent Sanders, I have made an office and computer resources here in Denver available to you as you need them. If you need anything more, please let me know."

****

Peter and Carol left Denver around 11:00 a.m. After about twenty minutes, Carol was the first to speak.

"Peter, you're being rather quiet . . . everything okay?"

"Yup, he replied," curtly.

"Are you upset with me for speaking up for you when you seemed to question Colby's judgment?"

"What? . . . No, I'm not. Thank you for doing that."

"So, what's bothering you?"

"I'm not sure that the FBI bureaucracy is going to prevent the virus from being installed. It sounded like if they can't prove the AFOS cartridges have a virus, they just might go ahead and release them. If that happened, it could be the end of life, as we know it. That's why I used the tone I did."

"Do you really think it would come to that?"

"Even if the chance of that was only ten percent, would you risk it?" he asked.

"I think you should give Colby more credit. I also think you need to be more positive in your thinking."

The warning caught him by surprise, but he knew her criticism was valid.

"You're probably right. I'm sorry. It's not every day that someone tries to kill me and my team. It's been a tough week."

"May I make a suggestion?"

"Of course."

"Sometimes when bad things happen to you, it helps to take a break. Take your team out for supper or a sports event. Maybe get away from it all together. Go home this weekend. Come back refreshed."

"Thanks Carol, those are good ideas. Changing the subject, what are you doing for the rest of the week?" he asked.

"What I told Colby—tracking the money flow. I'll be going up to the Loveland Office this afternoon. You told me that Belinsky's mother is in an assisted living home up there. I plan to check it out and try to find out who pays for it. However, I plan to go home for the weekend and then work from Maryland on Monday. Why do you ask?"

"Just curious."

She dropped him off at the IBM site and wished him well.

****

Immediately upon returning, Peter called Big John's office and asked for a meeting. He talked to Virginia. "Come by at two o'clock," she told him. Then Peter went back to the audit office and talked to the team. They knew he had gone to Denver with an FBI agent in the morning and they wanted to know what he learned about the bombing attempt. He projected a positive face when he told them exactly what Colby instructed him to say. No one had the slightest inkling about an actual computer virus that could destroy the Air Force satellite monitoring system. Peter figured that Noah may soon figure it out, but he had not said anything so far.

Then Peter brought up the idea of a break. Peter thought Carol's suggestion about taking a break would be a great idea for everyone, including himself. He suggested to the team that they all go to dinner tonight, and then to a place that had miniature golf and batting cages.

Michael reinforced the idea of a well-deserved break and helped to bring the idea to a consensus.

****

Peter was in Big John's office at two that same afternoon. "Peter, come in and have a seat," John said. "I assume you want to talk about testing the software that we just released to the Air Force. Am I right?"

"Yes, you are."

"Colby called me and told me you are convinced that the software contains a virus. He asked if I could release the source code so that the FBI could compile a version of the code that they knew did not contain the virus. My answer was no. He wanted to know if there was another way that we could create a cartridge known to be virus free. He indicated that you might have another idea. I wanted to talk with you before I got back to him. What are your thoughts?"

"Well, I understand the IBM policy to not release the source code, but I thought that perhaps you could make an exception in this case, due to its significance."

"You should know that to make an exception I would need to get approval from Corporate. Not only would that take time but it would also start a controversy that could end up in the news. Colby also mentioned FBI supervision. I don't want the FBI here overseeing anything we do! Talk about getting people upset and a possible news leak. Even if an IBM employee turned out to be guilty, I could lose my job over it. Why are you so sure that there is in fact a virus? Are you sure that you aren't just basing your opinion on your gut feel?"

"Someone tried to bomb us."

"Yes, but it may not be connected."

"John, we had credible intelligence that a virus would be planted in this software release. There are multiple agencies involved in this investigation. They include the FBI, the DEA, the CIA, and the DIA. Although neither of us knows the entire story, I am convinced that there is more than a ninety percent chance that the software you just released contains a virus. However, suppose there was only a ten percent chance. Would you want to take the risk that there was a ten percent chance that our National Defense Early Warning System could become useless? I recommend that we find out one way or the other."

Armstrong smiled. "How do we find out?"

"Brian Goodman told me that the Air Force approved a beta test of this software two weeks ago. Were any code changes made between then and yesterday?"

"Not that I know of, but we can verify that with Brian."

"I understand that IBM keeps two master copies of the beta test software. If there were no changes to that code, then my thought is that we could send them one of the two master beta test cartridges. They could make the comparison and return the cartridge when they finish. What do you think?"

"Hmmm . . . maybe. Let me call Brian right now and see what he says about code changes. I'll put him on speaker."

"Hi Brian, this is Big John. I'm here with Peter Troutman, the auditor. He needs to know if any code changes were made after the beta test cartridge was released. In other words, should the code on this week's release be the same as the code on the beta release?"

"Yes, absolutely no changes—anything else?"

Big John turned to Peter. "Peter, anything else?"

"No that is all we needed for now," Peter responded.

"Thanks Brian," Big John said as he pushed the button on the phone and disconnected the call. "Now Peter, just to be clear . . . the beta test tape will go to the FBI lab, and they will compare it to the AFOS tapes already released. If the two tapes have identical code, it proves that there is no virus. Is that the plan?"

"Yes, it is. John, I would like to request one more thing. I'd like us to deliver one of the original beta test cartridges, not a copy. That way we can be absolutely sure that it hasn't been altered."

"Sounds reasonable but—"

"But . . . something is bothering you?"

"If one of those tapes leaves the vault and the computer room, it must be signed out and the computer room personnel will know it. Wouldn't that arouse suspicion?"

"Maybe you could ask Brian to sign it out," Peter suggested.

"Perhaps, he could use the pretense that the Air Force wants to field-test it on a different computer configuration so that they can measure the performance change. Wouldn't that be believable?"

"When do we need this?" Big John wanted to know.

"I'm thinking tomorrow, so they can work on it over the weekend. If you want, I could arrange with the FBI lab to have someone stop by tomorrow afternoon to pick it up."

"Tell them to keep it low key. I don't want them flashing their badges," John quipped.

"They could simply have a courier come to the lobby and ask for you," Peter suggested. "You could have Virginia take the cartridge down to them in the lobby."

"Okay, go ahead and arrange that with the FBI Lab. In the meantime, I'll figure out a way to get the cartridge to Virginia by tomorrow morning."

"Great, thanks . . . uh . . ."

"Did you want to say something else?"

"Yes, on another, but related subject. I want Noah to have access to the computer event logs. He tells me he has encountered some resistance from Georgy. The computer logs can help to detect if any of the released cartridges were altered. He is not asking for admin access—although he would love having that—but only to have someone print the logs for him as needed and on a timely basis. Could you perhaps stress the need for more cooperation in this regard?"

"I'll see what I can do."

"Thanks John."

Later, Peter found Noah and talked to him about accessing the computer logs and told him that Big John said he would address the issue.

****

That evening, the team left work early—early for them anyway. After a short stop at the Residence Inn to change into comfortable clothes, like jeans and tennis shoes, they were on their way to a fun night out. It would have been natural for them to go out for pizza. Under normal circumstances, a place like the Panda Pizza Palace would be perfect for the occasion. However, Peter nixed the idea of going there after considering the possibility that Panda Pizza may have tried to kill him. Instead, he took the team to the local Pizza Hut. It was nearby on Route 36—Boulder's 28th Street. Although the Pizza Hut was only five minutes away, they ordered ahead to save time. They ordered two large pizzas. That was more than enough for four people. One pizza had pepperoni and onions on one-half with sausage and peppers on the other half. The other pizza had hamburger and mushrooms on one-half, and three vegetables on the other half. The idea was to share. Peter ordered a pitcher of Pepsi for the table.

After the supper, they went up the road to a place called Putt and Bat. The idea was to play miniature golf, but the batting cages caught Michael's eye. He said he needed some exercise before the golf and it would not take too much time. He got himself the required helmet, selected a bat, and walked into the fastball cage. Turns out Michael played ball in college. Almost every one of his swings connected. Debbie watched from the walkway. She was enamored with Michael—not in a girlfriend-boyfriend way, but in a sister-brother way. You could hear the twang of the metal bat as he lined them into the far net. He was good!

Meanwhile, Peter decided to hit a few balls himself. What better way to unwind, he thought? He swung hard at every pitch, trying to take the leather off. Much of the time, he swung at air or fouled the ball off, but when he did connect, it felt good. A good leader is not supposed to show frustration, anger, or fear. Peter had all those feelings pent up inside. Who would not be frustrated if they could not prevent Doom's Day? Who would not be angry if someone tried to kill them? What leader would not be fearful if his troops were about to lose confidence in his ability to protect them? Every swing of the bat was therapy!

After the batting cages, they went back inside, returned the equipment, and collected Noah who was racking up a high score on an electronic pinball machine. "Hey guys," Peter called out. "What do you say we play miniature golf?" The course was a country western motif. Each hole had its own unique scene. One was *Bone Hill*. If the ball went into the center of the open grave at the top of hill, it would propel directly to the hole on the other side. The 18th hole was interesting. It was a representation of Cheyenne Mountain near Colorado Springs. If you hit it directly into the tunnel, you had a hole in one. It was fun. Each of them was able to laugh at their misadventures—the ball that went into the pond, the ball that knocked another's ball into the hole, the ball that got stuck inside the snake's mouth, etc. When they finished, Debbie had the low score. Peter bought her a soft ice-cream cone to celebrate. She seemed happy. She would fly home in the morning. Perhaps after the weekend she would feel better and decide to return. Peter hoped so; the team needed her.

Before retiring for the evening, Peter pulled Michael aside. "Michael, may I talk with you for a few minutes?"

"Sure. What's up?"

"I want to talk about Debbie. I've talked with her and tried to allay her fears. Tonight, she seemed happy, but I'm still concerned that she may not stay with us after this weekend."

"Considering what she told us on Wednesday, that's understandable."

"Yes, of course it is, and I feel for her, but I was wondering if you have any more insight as to where she is on this right now. Greg is putting some pressure on me and we have no one to take her place. I know that you are like a big brother to her and I was looking for your input."

"Peter, I have talked to her and I have tried to understand her, and I have tried to convince her to stay. Right now, I'd say it's fifty-fifty. I think she needs the weekend to get away from it and reflect. Maybe she needs to see her therapist."

"Okay Michael thanks. I'll talk to Greg in the morning and tell him what you told me—I won't mention the therapist."

"Peter, could I change the subject and ask you a question?"

"Sure."

"Are you planning to go home this weekend?"

"No, why do ask?"

"I'm planning to stick around. I was going to ask about using the car."

"Oh . . . what were you planning to do? Are you thinking of anything in particular?"

"I have no idea . . . any suggestions?"

"How would you like to go white-water rafting?"

"Really?" he said with a look of disbelief.

"Yeah. Why not?"

"What do you know about it?"

"They have openings on Saturday afternoon. The meeting place is in Fort Collins. They have a locker room and you put on wet suits. River temperatures are in the low fifties and you will get wet. Then a bus takes you to the Poudre River, where you receive helmets and listen to a lecture on safety. Either six or eight people will be in each raft—including one or two guides—who know what they are doing. The trip lasts about an hour on the river and the rapids this time of year are generally class four."

"Uh . . . don't know. It sounds dangerous. Have you done this before?"

"Only once . . . not here though. I called the company last weekend to get information and they described it all to me. I also have a brochure from a local tourist office here in Boulder. It sounded like it would be a fun adventure. What do you say?"

"What will it cost?"

"I think they said twenty-five dollars apiece. This is still early in the season and the pricing is quite favorable at this time of the season."

"What about the car? Do we have to pay for our use of the car on weekends? It's not business use."

"The car is like the hotel and food. Like the hotel, we rent the car at a monthly rate regardless of how much we use it. Like the food, we pay for the gas we use over the weekend."

Michael stared at his feet for a moment, raised his head, looked directly at Peter, smiled, and said, "Well I guess we only live once. Count me in."

"We will have a good time, Michael. I guarantee it. Let's plan to meet for breakfast Saturday morning before we go, okay?"

"You got it."

****

On Friday morning, Noah met Georgy in the computer room. Georgy seemed a bit irritated. Obviously, Armstrong had already given him instructions, and he was not very comfortable about what was happening. By Friday afternoon, Noah had finished his analysis of the computer logs from Tuesday and Wednesday. It was apparent to him that when creating the released AFOS software, Belinsky did not follow the required protocols. Noah concluded that if someone wanted to modify the code before shipment, he or she could have done so. He also concluded that some of the controls needed improvement. He had specific recommendations. However, while he could say that it was possible to bypass the controls and modify the code, he could not say if it really happened.

Later in the day, Peter entered the vault and observed that only one beta test cartridge remained. He contacted Don Matthews at the FBI and confirmed that they had a beta test cartridge in their possession. Everything seemed to be happening as planned.

11

PROOF

Monday May 23 began the fifth week of the audit. It would be another week of perfect weather—Sunny, no rain, and temperatures in the sixties and seventies. The very good news was that Debbie would be back. She arrived Monday night. On Tuesday morning everyone told her how pleased they were that she returned. The audit was already a week behind plan, due to the unforeseen events resulting from the bombing. The team very much needed her help.

Early Wednesday morning, Peter received a call from Carol.

"Hi Peter, I'm back."

"Are you back in Boulder, or in Denver?"

"Right now, I'm in Loveland. Tonight, and tomorrow night, I'll be in Boulder."

"The dumpy motel on Route 36?"

"That's the one. Anyway, Colby would like to meet with us tomorrow afternoon at four thirty. Can you do it?"

"Sure. What's on the agenda?"

"Project status."

"Four thirty? . . . I'll need to check with Michael about using the car."

"I could pick you up at IBM at three thirty, and we could ride together."

"Oh . . . Okay, sure . . . thanks. See you then."

****

Later Wednesday morning, Peter received a phone call from Agent Matthews at the FBI Lab.

"Mr. Troutman, this is Agent Matthews. I need to give you a heads-up. We compared the beta test cartridge that we received last Friday with the production cartridge. I know you don't want to hear this, but we found no difference."

"Uh . . . You are right. I did not want to hear it."

"I need to release the production cartridges to the Air Force."

"Agent Matthews, I'm sure you did everything correctly, and I have no basis to challenge your findings. However, I have a meeting scheduled for tomorrow afternoon with you and Colby. Could you please hold off until then? Just give me a chance to see if I can explain it."

"Well, you realize you have already had another chance, but okay until tomorrow's meeting . . . better safe than sorry, I suppose."

"Thanks, I appreciate your patience. See you tomorrow."

Almost immediately after hanging up the phone, Peter began to wonder if Matthews had a copy and not the original beta test cartridge as requested. True, on Monday, only one cartridge remained in the vault. However, if Georgy had knowledge of why Brian Goodman requested the tape, he certainly had enough time to make a copy that included the virus. The next step would be to recheck the vault, and then to talk with Georgy.

Peter walked into the vault and shut the door behind him. He went to the shelf that held the beta test cartridges and the production cartridges. As expected, one beta test cartridge was still missing. Both production cartridges were there. As he left the vault, he could see Ngai Wu, Georgy's assistant. He was the keeper of the sign-out logs. The beta test cartridge should have been signed out to someone.

"Ngai, how are you this morning? Could I have a moment?"

"Sure, what's up?"

"I was wondering if I could see the cartridge sign-out logs."

"Sure, they are over in my work area. Were you looking for something in particular?"

"Yes. I want to see who the beta test cartridge was signed out to on Friday," Peter said as he followed Ngai to his work area.

"Here it is," Ngai said as he pointed out the entry on the page. "Looks like Brian Goodman borrowed it."

Peter noticed the time stamp was Friday, 10 a.m. "Thanks Ngai. That's all I needed."

As Peter walked out of the computer room, he passed Georgy's office. The door was open, and Georgy was sitting at his desk. Peter knocked politely on the doorjamb. "Hey Georgy . . . got a minute?"

"Sure, come in," he said politely.

"Georgy, I was in the vault, and I noticed that one of the beta test cartridges seemed to be missing. I was wondering if you knew why."

"Well, last Friday I think it was Brian who came to me and asked me to let him have it."

Peter continued to play dumb. "Did he say why he wanted it?"

"All he said was that the customer was concerned about a possible difference between the beta test version and the production version."

"I see, and did you give him the original?"

"I did. Normally I'd make a copy, but he insisted on the original."

"Okay, thanks. That's all I needed."

Peter's next stop would be Brian. However, he was not there, so Peter left a message for him to call and went back to the auditors' office. Lunchtime came and went. Peter was about to call Brian when his phone rang.

"Hello, this is Peter."

"Hi Peter. This is Brian Goodman returning your call."

"Thanks for calling back. I have two simple questions."

"I see that you signed out an AFOS beta test cartridge last week." My first question is when did you request it from Georgy?"

"Peter, I'm not sure I should be answering this. Why are you asking?"

"Okay, look. I know that Big John asked you for it. Brian, I'm going to trust you to keep this between you, Big John, and me. I'm the one that requested this from Big John. He probably told you to keep it quiet, and if any one asked about it, he probably told you to say that the customer needed it again—perhaps to test it on a new computer configuration or something. Please just tell me when you requested it from Georgy."

"I asked Georgy for it late Thursday afternoon. Do you need a precise time?"

"No, but I do have another question. When did you receive it?"

"Friday morning."

"And did you receive it directly from Georgy, or did you get it from the closet yourself?"

"I got it from Georgy."

"And what did you do with it after you received it?"

"I gave it to Big John."

"Big John?" Peter said with skepticism.

"No. You're right. I left it with Virginia."

"What time was that?"

"Hey you're really given me the third degree here. Did the cartridge get lost or something?"

"Something like that. Brian, I don't mean to be coming down on you, but I really need to trace what happened to it."

"About eleven . . . I gave it to Virginia around eleven."

"Thanks Brian. That's all I need. And please don't mention this conversation to anyone other than Big John."

"You aren't going to tell me anything more?"

"Brian, I can't. Big John may want to tell you more, but it would be up to him."

One more stop—Virginia would know when she received the cartridge and when the FBI picked it up. Peter decided to walk up there, rather than call. He needed the exercise and he could have a coffee while he was there. Besides, he enjoyed talking with Virginia.

"Hi Virginia. How is life treating you?"

She offered Peter a cup of coffee as she always did and they chatted for a few moments. Then Peter asked her about the package. "Virginia, last Friday, someone called you from the lobby and asked about a package that Big John had. Do you remember what time that was?"

"I do remember. It was late in the day. John wasn't here, and I kept the caller on the phone while I looked for the package. Turns out it was buried on my desk, but I didn't know it. John hadn't said anything to me, but there was a note on it from Brian Goodman. Anyway, I took it down to the lobby. The man said he was from the FBI and he showed me his ID. I gave him the package." She paused for a moment. "My Gosh, I hope I didn't do something wrong."

"No . . . No, you did fine. I just wanted to verify. Oh . . . Do you happen to remember what time that may have been?"

"I'm not sure. . . I think it was after three."

"Virginia, you're a sweetheart. I owe you."

After gathering all this information, Peter realized that he was losing his argument that the production cartridges contained a virus. All the facts so far indicated that the FBI received an original beta test cartridge last Friday. However, he was not ready to give up. He wanted 100% certainty before he would agree to the release of those cartridges. In his opinion, the consequences of being wrong were too high. He knew it was only remotely possible, but what if Georgy made a copy of the AFOS production release cartridge—containing the virus—and labelled it as the beta test cartridge. Georgy had all night to do this. He also had plenty of time to substitute this copy for the actual beta test cartridge, either before he gave it to Brian or later while it was on Virginia's desk. If Georgy still had the actual beta test cartridge, he probably hid it in his desk—probably with the intention of returning it to the vault when Brian returned the one that he borrowed.

It was mid-afternoon when Peter met with Noah.

"Noah, I need your help with something very important."

"What?"

"I need you to review the computer event logs for the period between four o'clock last Thursday and four o'clock Friday afternoon. I'm looking for an entry indicating the creation of a tape with a volume header labeling it a beta test release. The tape would have been created using a source tape with an AFOS volume header dated last week."

"When do you need it?"

"Tomorrow by three o'clock."

There was a pause. "Peter, you know that I don't have admin access to the computer. How do I produce the logs?"

"Any way you're able to get access! Perhaps you could hack into the computer?" He noticed the expression on Noah's face. "I'm kidding," he quickly added lest Noah take him seriously. "I don't think that Georgy will do this for you, but perhaps you could convince Ngai or the other assistant—was his name Bob? He should be there on second shift. Ask him to print the log for you. Tell him that Big John wants you to see it. I don't know. Please come up with something. **I really need this!**"

****

It was late in the day when Michael drove the team back to the Inn. He and Peter had been sharing the driving. After they got back, Peter told Michael he needed to use the car after supper.

"Do I dare ask why?" Michael said as he handed over the keys.

"Best you don't," Peter responded.

Peter had a quick meal at the Residence Inn—sloppy Joe, carrot sticks and broccoli stalks. He washed it down with a glass of red wine for courage, and then he set off to do what he had to do. He drove to the IBM site. He still wore his suit and tie from earlier in the day—important to maintain the look of authority, he thought.

He parked the car in the area on the side of the building where they parked every day and headed for the door they normally used to enter. He inserted his badge—nothing happened. He tried again. Nothing happened! Then it dawned on him. He remembered the orientation meeting the team had with Robert Stanley, the Manager of Site Security. His exact words were, "After seven thirty in the evening, everyone must enter through the main lobby entrance." Peter looked at his watch. It was already 7:45. After a quick glance back at the car he decided to walk to the main entrance. He entered the lobby and flashed his badge as he started to pass by the guard at the lobby desk—

"**Whoa! . . . Sir!** It's after seven thirty. You need to sign in," the guard stated in a commanding voice.

Uh oh . . . Peter did not expect this. It was the first time he had entered the building after 7:30 p.m. As he made his way over to the desk, he thought about forging someone else's signature. The thought fleeted quickly as he realized he had a legitimate reason for being there—another security check. He signed in, recording his name, his badge number, and his reason for being there. Then he made his way down the hallway and proceeded directly toward Georgy's office.

The lights in Georgy's corridor were dimmed for the night. That was a good thing. He walked past Georgy's office to the computer room at the end of the corridor. He peeked inside. He could barely make out the light on a tape drive blinking. Someone was working—probably Bob Jones. Peter returned to Georgy's office, entered the office, and turned on the light. If someone came by and saw him in there with the lights off, it would look suspicious. If someone came by and the lights were on, he could appear to be leaving a note on Georgy's desk. He pushed the chair aside, knelt in front of Georgy's desk, and went to work. He retrieved a small black case from his inside jacket pocket and removed two small tools from the case. He inserted the *wrench* and then the *rake* into the key slot. It only took him thirty seconds this time, a whole thirty seconds faster than when he did this a week and a half ago. He opened the drawer where he had found the original viral tape cartridge. Aside from some junk, it was empty! No tape cartridge in the other drawers either.

"Now what?" he murmured to himself. He was running out of options.

Just then, a guard—not the one at the lobby desk—came down the corridor and noticed the light.

"Hello, sir. I am doing a security check . . . just routine. I need to know who you are and why you are in Mister B e l i n s k y's office." He pronounced the name slowly as he read the nameplate on the wall next to the office door.

Peter quickly tucked the tools back into his pocket, rose from the floor, and faced the guard.

"I see you are wearing a Boulder IBM visitor badge, and a second IBM badge," the guard said. "Mister Troutman . . . are you an IBM employee from another location?"

"Yes, sir. That's correct. I'm a member of the Corporate Audit staff. I signed in, so you can verify my access rights at the lobby desk."

"May I ask why you are here now?"

"Actually, we are doing a security audit, and I'm pleased to see that both you and the gentleman at the lobby desk are doing everything right."

"With all due respect, sir, you didn't really answer my question. Why are you in this office, and why were you kneeling on the floor?"

Peter could feel his heart thumping, but he remained cool.

"I need to meet with Georgy . . . Mister Belinsky . . . in the morning. I was about to leave him a long note, but I dropped my pen on the floor. After this, I plan to head to my desk in the auditors' office on the other side of the building."

After writing down Peter's name and badge number on his clipboard, the guard remained in the doorway and used his two-way to radio the lobby. This forced Peter to play out his role and begin writing a long innocuous note to Georgy.

After what seemed like an eternity, the guard spoke to him again. "The lobby says you are legit. Sorry to have disturbed you, sir. You have a pleasant evening. Please turn out the light when you are done here."

Peter watched as the guard disappeared down the hall. He took a breath, relocked the desk, and went back to doing what he came there to do. Where else could Georgy have hidden the cartridge? The file cabinet in the corner was a likely place. Using the same process as before, he unlocked the file cabinet in about ninety seconds. The cabinet had four drawers. He started at the bottom and worked up. He found the cartridge in the second drawer from the bottom. He pulled it out and looked at it. Sure enough, it had the small mark he had placed on it when he did an inventory two weeks ago. Peter removed the cartridge from the drawer and relocked the cabinet. Now, all he needed to do was smuggle it out of the building. He tucked the cartridge under his jacket, turned off the light, and headed back down the hall, but he did not go to the lobby. He went to the audit office instead. He opened his own desk and placed the cartridge into his bottom right drawer. He mused at the idea that building security was so much tighter at night than during the regular workday. The more he thought about it, the less sense it seemed to make.

****

Thursday afternoon, Peter told his team he had a meeting in Denver. They all knew what that meant. Peter gave Michael the keys to the car. They watched as Peter removed something from the bottom drawer of his desk and placed it into his briefcase. Then Noah gave him a folder and said, "I hope this helps."

As Peter walked out the door of the office, he heard Debbie say, "Please come back with some good news about the bombing." They all knew that there was more going on.

It was 3:25 p.m. and Carol was already waiting for him as he exited the building.

"Good afternoon," he said. "I appreciate your picking me up. How was Loveland," he asked as they walked to Carol's car.

"Actually, I just got back to Boulder about an hour ago. The information you gave me about Belinsky paid off. Turns out a foreign company has been paying for his mom's care."

"Panda International?"

"It looks that way. I'll give a report to Colby at today's meeting."

Peter tossed his jacket and his briefcase onto the backseat. He kept the folder from Noah with him as he got in the passenger seat and fastened his seat belt. As they drove off, he began to read the computer event log.

"What are you reading?" Carol wanted to know.

"It's evidence that—"

Just then, the steering wheel started shaking in Carol's hands. "Oh my God," she exclaimed. "What is happening?"

Peter glanced over to her. "Hang on to it. It's probably a flat tire."

"Oh jeeze! That's all we need. We're going to be late." She sounded pissed.

She slowed and pulled onto to the shoulder.

"Carol . . . it's going to be okay. Relax. Shut off the engine and let me check it out."

"Peter, please be careful. This is not the best place to stop."

Peter got out, walked around the front of the car, got to the driver-side front wheel, and then returned to the passenger door the way he came. He looked around. They were on the outskirts of town, surrounded by fields on both sides of the road. He could see two oil pumps in the distance to the right of the car. They were in the country—and on their own.

"What do you see?" she asked as he returned.

"Carol, we have a flat on the driver's side front tire. Please pull the emergency brake up as hard as you can. Here let me help," he said as he gave it an extra tug. "Now if you would be so kind as to pop the trunk, I'll see what I can do."

Peter then tucked his tie inside his shirt, rolled up his shirtsleeves, and made his way to the back of the car. They were in luck. The car came with a full-size spare, a jack, and a lug wrench. He removed all three and set them on the ground. Only one more challenge. Where under the car should he place the jack? He walked around to the front and looked underneath the passenger side for a logical place on the frame. Ah, that must be it on the side behind the wheel. It would be the same on the driver's side. He would be standing in the roadway and would need to be careful. He made his way to the passenger door and spoke to Carol again. "Please turn on the flashers. Also, you may want to get out from the passenger side and stand behind the car while I do this."

They met each other behind the car.

"Peter, I want to help. Tell me what to do."

"Well, I think I'll be all right, but you can watch out for traffic and warn me if someone looks out of control." He knew it would not help much, but she needed to feel involved. He then picked up the jack and the lug wrench and returned to the front of the car.

He jacked the car up part way and loosened the lug nuts. One was on so tight he needed to kick the lug wrench with his foot to break it loose. Meanwhile, every car that passed by gave an unnerving loud swoosh behind him. Finally, the nuts were loose. He jacked the car up to bring the wheel up off the ground, and removed the nuts and the wheel, all the while trying very hard not to soil his clothes. He rolled the wheel to the trunk. Carol looked on with a sorrowful expression on her face. She also seemed antsy. "How are you doing?" she asked with concern.

"Making progress. It'll be okay. We'll be back on the road in no time."

As he started back to the front of the car with the spare, he saw Carol try to lift the wheel with the flat. "Carol no!" he yelled back.

"I'm just trying to *help*."

He temporarily set the spare aside the car and walked back to her. "I know you are, and I appreciate that, but the wheel may be too heavy for you to get into the trunk, and there no need for more than one of us to get dirty. Carol it's okay. I'm sorry I yelled at you."

Peter was about to begin tightening the lug nuts onto the new wheel, when he heard the short burst of a siren to his rear. He looked up and saw the flashing lights of the police cruiser. The cruiser had pulled onto the shoulder and stopped about a hundred feet behind. He decided to let Carol handle it while he continued to tighten the lug nuts. As he returned to the trunk with the jack and lug wrench, a patrol officer greeted him.

"Hello, I'm Officer Doolittle. I'm with the Boulder County Sheriff's Department. This is a very dangerous place to change a flat. I thought it might help if I had my car back there with the flashers on. I was chatting with your partner. She says you're FBI. You may know we are working with the FBI on the bombing two weeks ago. You involved with that?"

"It was assigned to someone else," Peter quickly responded.

"Well, we just took someone into custody yesterday. The FBI was supposed to interrogate him today . . . thought that might be *you* guys. I hope they can get him to talk and tell who is behind it. We haven't had a car bombing in these parts since 1974 when a group of Chicano activists blew themselves up. . . You seemed to be just about finished with the flat. Is there anything I can do to help? . . . Here, let me lift that wheel back into the trunk for you."

"Thank you. Any chance you have a paper towel to wipe our hands with?" Peter asked.

"Sure do, I'll be right back." He returned with a roll of toweling.

"Ah, perfect," Peter said.

Then Carol asked, "Officer, we are late for a meeting at FBI headquarters. Do you have a way to contact FBI headquarters to let them know we'll be late?"

"Yes ma'am," he relied. "I can call dispatch and they can do that for you. Who should they call?"

"Roger Colby," she said.

"Roger Colby? Isn't he the top guy?"

"He is," Peter added, "but you would reach his Administrative Assistant." Peter carefully reached into his pocket—despite the towel, his hands were still dirty— and pulled out a card. "Here is his card with the information on it."

"I'm glad to help any way I can," Officer Doolittle said as he took the card. "You guys have a nice day."

****

Peter and Carol arrived at the FBI building only twenty minutes late. They made their way through security and got a visitor badge for Peter. Peter still had his tie tucked into his shirt. His jacket was over his right arm, and his briefcase dangled from his left arm.

"Carol, would you mind waiting for me. I need to use the restroom and my hands are still dirty as well. I won't be long."

"Not a problem."

Peter came out of the men's room looking much more presentable and he felt better as well. Carol pushed the elevator button. The door opened and Peter followed Carol in. She pushed the button for floor *three* and stepped back. As the door closed, she turned and looked at Peter.

"Peter, hold still," she said

"What's wrong," he asked, as she came toward him and reached for his necktie. As she gently tugged at his tie, their eyes met briefly. She backed away quickly.

"Your tie wasn't straight," she said sheepishly as she realized her over-exuberance.

They arrived on the third floor and walked down the long corridor to Colby's office complex. Agent McCarthy greeted them.

"Good afternoon," she said. "I got a call from the Department telling me you had a flat tire on the way here. Is everything alright?"

"Yes, we're fine. I'm glad to know you got the message," Carol responded. "I was worried that you may not have—"

"As it turns out, Colby's four o'clock has run over. Coincidently, it's with the Sheriff of Boulder County . . . and I see he's just finishing up with his meeting now."

After the sheriff left, Colby came out, said hello, and told McCarthy to show everyone into the conference room. He needed five minutes. Don Matthews arrived shortly thereafter and joined them.

****

Colby began the meeting by giving the standard speech about the classified nature of the meeting and warned against leaking anything to the public. Then he said he had some positive news regarding the bombing.

"You will be pleased to know that we have the person who planted the bomb in custody. He has identified the person that put him up to it, and we hope to take him into custody next week."

"May I ask who that is?" Peter wanted to know.

"Sorry . . . protocol."

"Then can you tell us if the bombing is related to the Boulder Creek project? Was the audit team the target?"

"Yes, to both questions. They wanted to stop the auditors from discovering their plan to plant a virus. However, if they think their plan succeeded, they would have no reason to try again to kill you."

"Okay, that's good to know. Thanks."

Carol was next on the agenda. Colby asked her to describe what she found with respect to the flow of funds, and how the pieces of the financial puzzle fit together.

"Good morning gentlemen," she began. "Last week you asked how I was coming along with my financial analysis, and I told you that many of the pieces were not yet together. In the past week, much of it has gelled. Here is what I have:

"A holding company named Panda International operates here in the United States. The main office in the States is in Oakland California. According to a source in the CIA—Peter's eyes widened as he heard this—Panda International is owned by a company in Poland, which in turn is owned by the Soviet Union. Money between the Polish company and Panda International flows through a financial company in the Cayman Islands named PFC Limited. I assume PFC may stand for Panda Financial Company, but it does not really matter.

"Panda International operates as a franchiser. They control Star Travel, and they control Panda Pizza. There are three Star Travel locations. One is in Fairfax Virginia, one is in San Francisco, and one is near here in Westminster. There are four Panda Pizza locations. The one here in Boulder reports the most business—an anomaly that could be explained by drug traffic. The owner of the Boulder Panda Pizza franchise is Anthony Rizzuto. He has no felony convictions, but his brother John does. His brother owns a construction business, Demo Construction. They specialize in demolition. Money has transferred between the two businesses and between the brothers' personal accounts. Their personal bank accounts seem to have more money than can be explained by their business incomes. In addition, they seem to be living a life of luxury—nice homes, golf club memberships, expensive cars, and various investments.

"This past week I visited an assisted living home in Loveland. Georgy Belinsky's mom resides there. I determined that to pay for her care, the home draws money from a special bank account set up for that purpose. The money that goes into that account comes from PFC. If you recall, last year we found that money from PFC had gone into a bank account belonging to Jim Hoffman. We believe he stole copies of the design for the satellite-management network . . . Questions?"

Colby spoke, "Agent Sanders, I think you have done a very thorough job—Excellent work! Your input will be very helpful when we apply for warrants. Is your report documented?"

"Yes, sir. It is. I'll be sure you get a copy," she said.

"Now Mr. Troutman, Agent Matthews is here to tell us his finding at the computer lab. He had someone analyze the cartridges you provided to us last week. As you suggested, he found nothing on the tape you gave us last Thursday morning."

Agent Matthews joined in. "Our lab did find fingerprints on the casing. A comparison to our criminal database showed that two prints belonged to the manager of the Panda Pizza restaurant. On the other hand, we have not found the virus. John Armstrong at IBM refused to lend us the source-code, and he would not allow an FBI agent to go to the IBM site and supervise the compilation of a new tape from the source code. However, Armstrong did agree to give us a copy of a beta test tape that was known to be virus free. He asked us to disregard the volume header and compare the compiled code, one file at a time. Armstrong assured me that the new tape would not have the virus. We picked up that tape Friday afternoon and brought it back to our lab. We compared that tape to the ones we put on hold last week. They were identical. Therefore, our conclusion is that none of the tapes contain a virus."

"Then how do you explain the fingerprints on the original cartridge I gave you?" Peter asked.

"How could there be a virus if these two tapes are the same?" Don Matthews shot back.

Peter smiled. "Touché," he responded. "After you called yesterday to alert me of your finding, I did some investigating. The tape you picked up Friday afternoon was **not** the beta test tape. What you received was a copy of the production tape with the virus, but with an altered volume label and a phony paper label."

"That is quite an imaginative story," Agent Matthews said. "How can you prove it?"

"Here is the proof," Peter said as he opened his briefcase, removed a cartridge, and handed it to Colby. "This is one of the two master beta test cartridges. When I received your call yesterday, I knew something was wrong. Armstrong notified Belinsky Thursday afternoon that the Air Force wanted to test the beta code for use on a new computer model—it was a pretense. He directed Belinsky to provide one of the two master beta test tapes. Belinsky had time to plan what he would do. He knew that if he gave you a tape without the virus, you would discover his bad deed. His mission would be a failure. Two weeks ago, I inventoried the two master beta test tapes that IBM had in its vault. I marked them. The cartridge you have does not have the mark. This one does. I found it in Belinsky's office. Belinsky was directed to provide the original, not a copy. He said he provided the original. He lied."

Matthews asked to see the cartridge Peter had just handed Colby. Colby put it on the table in front of him. "Could you please show me the mark?" he asked as he looked at Peter.

"Here it is, on the short edge below the label," Peter said, as he reached across the table and pointed to the mark.

"And you say the one I have does not have the mark?"

"Correct. Do you have it?"

"I left both tapes in my office. I'll take your word for it for now. But, how do you know that he didn't make a copy of this beta test tape?"

"If that were the case, why would he lie about it, and why hide it in his office rather than return it to the vault? . . . There's more."

"More?"

"I asked Noah to look at the computer event logs for last Thursday evening. Let me show you what he found." Peter handed him a page from the computer log. Noah had highlighted the period from 7:00 p.m. to 7:30 p.m. "The log shows that Belinsky was the operator and that for the period highlighted, the operator turned off the logging. That was just enough time to create a phony beta test tape. Furthermore, a witness identified Belinsky as the computer operator during this period. The same witness also saw him make trips to the vault before and after this period."

Peter pointed to the cartridge in front of Agent Matthews.

"Please take this cartridge back to the lab. Check it out. Compare it to a tape that has the virus. That's your proof!"

For a few moments, everything went silent. No one said a word until Matthews broke the silence. "We will analyze it," he said. Then he turned to Colby and back to Troutman as he added, "However, we won't have results until next week due to the holiday coming up."

12

HOLIDAY WEEKEND

It was about 6:30 in the evening when Peter and Carol left Colby's office. It made sense to stop for dinner on the way back to Boulder. Peter suggested the diner in Westminster—the same one that he and his team had stopped at more than four weeks ago.

They both removed their jackets and left them in the car. Peter also ditched his tie. They were shown a booth, sat down, and opened the menus that the hostess set before them. Carol took a deep breath and let it out slowly. "It's been a busy day, time to relax," she said.

"I'm with you on that."

"What were you thinking of having for dinner," she asked.

"Well, it's more like lunch, but I am in the mood for a Reuben sandwich and a side of potato salad. I don't see it that often on menus, and I really like Reuben sandwiches, especially with potato salad."

She smiled. "You know what? That sounds good. I think I'll have that as well."

They waited for their dinner to arrive. The ensuing conversation started innocently enough.

"Peter, the Memorial Day weekend is coming up. Are you heading back home?"

"Not planning to. Are you?"

"No. I'm not either. Is there anything to do around here?"

"Well, when I go on an IBM audit, I try to take advantage of the area we visit. It's my chance to be a tourist at no extra travel cost."

"That's an interesting concept. What are you planning?"

"I was thinking about driving up into the hills to check out the scenery and maybe explore a couple of trails. I was also thinking of driving down to Colorado Springs. They have something going on called Territory Days, which is an annual street event in the old city . . . street performers, vendors, artwork, and so on. It may also be possible to do the Pikes Peak cog railway. Then maybe in the evening, I'd check out a country western bar and dance club. I'm still rather flexible, but I am looking to relax a bit. It's been a tough two weeks."

"Sounds like a lot to do in one day. How far is Colorado Springs?"

"I think it's about an hour and a half away."

"Are you doing any of this with other members of your team?"

"No. They are all leaving town for the weekend . . . just me."

"Why would you want to do it by yourself? I would think it would be more fun if you went with someone. Oh, I know, you plan to pick up a cute chick along the way and talk her into spending the night with you . . . right?"

"Ha-ha," Peter chuckled. "Only in my dreams, Carol."

"Still, someone to share it with . . ."

"Carol, would you like to come with me?"

She smiled. "I thought you would never ask."

****

Carol had talked her boss into paying for her to stay at the Residence Inn in Boulder for the weekend instead of a flight home and back. Early Saturday morning, Peter knocked on Carol's door.

"Come on in. I'm almost ready."

She looked the part. She was wearing jeans, a long-sleeved western shirt and walking shoes. She sported a white cap. Her brown hair was in a ponytail and exited the rear of her cap above the strap. She wore a pair of orange-tinted sunglasses.

"Carol, I have good news," he said with excitement. "We're on a standby list for the cog railway to go up to Pikes Peak. When I called, they recommended that we bring a sweater and a jacket as it may be rather cold up on the top."

"Okay. Give me a moment."

"Do you have a camera?"

"Sure do! Do you?"

"Yup."

Once Carol had her things together, they made their way to the car, and shut the doors.

"Peter, before we start out, I would like us to have an understanding about something." She sounded serious. "It's very important to me that you allow me to pay for my share of the expenses."

"Sure . . . not a problem," he said, but wondered why this was so important to her. Perhaps she did not want him thinking of this as a date. "Do you want to do this as we go, or wait and tally up at the end of the day?"

"As we go . . . Speaking of which, where do we go first?"

"Here is a map you can look at," he said, and handed it to her. "You can navigate. As you already reminded me, there are only so many hours in the day. We can't do everything. Originally, I thought we could take an excursion up the road from Boulder and back down again. Route 119 follows Boulder Creek for quite a way. It would give us a scenic view of the mountain above Boulder." Recalling a picture of the map in his mind, he continued. "Then we could join up to Route 86 . . . get over to Route 25 . . . that will take us right to Colorado Springs. However, we scheduled our appointment for the railway in Manitou for twelve-thirty. If we do that, we may not have any time for the Territory Days. I think we'll need to select one or the other. What would be your choice?"

"How much time does the railway take?"

"Two hours to Colorado Springs, Fifteen minutes to Old Colorado City for Territory Days. Then fifteen minutes to the cog railway depot. Then perhaps half hour to park and pick up tickets, and three hours round trip to Pikes Peak."

"I see," she responded. "You said we are on standby. What do we do if they don't accept us?"

"We have options. We could drive up, or we could hike in the area, or we could check out The Cave of the Winds, or Cliff Dwellings, or Manitou Gardens."

"Somehow I'm not sure that gardens would be your first choice."

"It would be okay. This is for your enjoyment too . . . not just mine. So, do you have a preference . . . hills or Territory Days?"

"Peter, I'm okay with whatever you decide."

"Okay then. Here is my thought." He spoke rapidly. "The hills will be here tomorrow and they're nearby. The Pikes Peak opportunity is today and Territory Days is in the vicinity. Why don't we head directly to Colorado Springs, check out Territory Days, and then proceed to Manitou Springs to get the cog railway? When we get back to Colorado Springs, we can check out the Territory Days some more. Then we can head back to Boulder and have supper somewhere. I'd like to check out a country western place that I heard about. It's supposed to have good steaks. Tomorrow, if you're interested, we can do the drive along Boulder Creek." He was speaking too fast.

"Peter, slow down. You really do need to relax." Let's play it by ear, okay?"

"I agree. Nothing's cast in stone. I'm flexible," he said as he started up the engine.

****

They arrived at Old Colorado City just before ten o'clock. A sign directed to a parking area about six blocks away that ran a shuttle service to one end of the festival. Peter picked up an event guide that contained a map of the layout and a schedule of the events. The festival was on both sides of Colorado Avenue, the main street through town, and went for more than three blocks. As they walked down the avenue, Carol decided to buy a T-shirt, and Peter bought a stylish wide-brimmed western hat with a cord to keep it on his head in case of wind. He liked the fact that it was crushable. It would fit in his suitcase. Carol looked for a hat for herself but could not find one to her liking. The festival had something for everyone. As they continued down the avenue, they passed a fortuneteller, a raffle for a pick-up truck, paintings by local artists, and other things. The festival had many activities for kids like face painting, pony rides, train rides, a Muppet show, and an ongoing mock cowboy gunfight. According to the event guide, a country western band would play at eleven o'clock. It was in a park area a couple of blocks down from where they came into the festival.

"Carol, are you interested in this live band?" he asked as he showed her the promo in the guide.

"Sure, let's do it. If we have time, I could use a cup of coffee first. How about you?"

"Great idea. According to the map, there should be a place over there somewhere. . . Oh yeah, I see it now."

The coffee place also had muffins. "Peter, would you be interested in sharing a muffin with me?" Carol asked cheerily.

"I would. Thank you."

They made their way to the stage in the park while drinking coffee and munching on a blueberry muffin. The concert lasted about forty minutes. They both enjoyed the music.

Unfortunately, although they had only traversed about half of the festival, it was now twenty minutes before twelve.

"Peter, did you enjoy the band?"

"I did. I really enjoy country western music. Did you?"

"I did as well. There is a radio station back in Baltimore that I listen to all the time."

"WPOC?" he asked.

"Yes . . . you too?" she said as if just making an important discovery. I think we have something in common—"

Peter started to comment but looked at his watch. "Carol, I wish we had a little more time here, but if we are to keep our appointment, we need to head back to the car. We have less than forty minutes to get to the railway depot. Are you okay with that?"

"I agree," she said.

****

Peter and Carol parked their car in a lot across from the Pikes Peak Cog Line Depot. Peter had reserved a parking ticket along with the railway tickets. He had made the reservation over the phone, but now they needed to pick up the actual tickets and pay. Peter went to the window. The lady at the window said that since they were on standby, they would need to wait until their number was called. However, she thought their chances looked good.

"You can pay for the parking ticket now," she said. "There's no need to go back to the car with it now. Just have it when leaving."

While they waited, Carol noticed a sign that advised bringing plenty of water, a warm jacket, and *oxygen*. Peter and Carol knew about the need for water. While in Colorado Springs, they had bought a quart of water each. Carol had her shoulder bag with her. She had stuffed their jackets in her bag. They already had on their sweaters. It was fifty-five degrees at the Depot, but a sign said the temperature at the summit was only in the high twenties.

"What about oxygen?" Carol asked. "Do you think we'll need it?"

"I don't know," Peter said, "but we can buy a can of it for about ten dollars just in case."

They did not wait very long. After a couple of no-shows, they were in. Peter went back to the window and picked up the actual tickets. Carol gave him cash to cover her share. Then, they got into another line to board according to their seat ID.

One thing that tourists do is to talk with other tourists. Asking others where they are from, or something about their situation, is common. Sharing an enjoyable experience with other people—even strangers—is rewarding. On this day, Peter and Carol were tourists. Peter took note of the fact that despite her conservative occupation, Carol had no issue initiating conversation with people they met on that day. They both enjoyed the company of other tourists as well as each other.

While waiting in line to get onto the rail car, Carol started a typical conversation.

"I really like your western hat," she said to the woman standing next to her. "I should probably get one to take back home."

"Oh, do you like it? I got it back in Colorado Springs at Territory Days."

"Peter and I were just there, but we ran out of time. We wanted to do this. We were lucky to get tickets."

"Do you remember the location of the shop?" Peter asked.

"About halfway between 25th and 24th Streets near the beer garden," the man with her replied.

"We may have some time after this on the way back," Peter said to Carol. "Perhaps we can get you a hat then."

"Where are you two from," the man asked.

"Maryland. You?"

"We are from Tennessee," he replied.

"We are celebrating our fortieth wedding anniversary," the woman added. "I'm Sally and this is my husband, Bud."

"Oh my! That's quite an accomplishment," Carol exclaimed.

"Are you on vacation?" Bud asked.

"Actually, I'm out here on business, and Carol was able to join me for the weekend."

"How nice," Sally said.

The line moved a bit, stopped, then moved, until finally they boarded the rail car. They found themselves in the second car of a twosome. Carol and Peter sat facing downhill with their backs toward the uphill direction. The seats alternated between rearward facing and forward facing. Two other people sat facing them. The train started to move and began a steep ascent towards its objective. The wooden seats were hard and slippery. Occasionally, when the grade became steep, Peter found himself sliding forward toward the people facing him. The cog rail cars traveled no faster than ten miles per hour and the ride to the top lasted more than an hour. However, the scenery and the humorous commentary from the conductor were more than enough to offset the discomfort of the seats. Along the way up they saw some wild life—critters according to the commentary.

Peter and Carol saw several marmots—super squirrels. Carol said she spotted the brown bear announced by the conductor at the five o'clock position. They both saw Bighorn sheep on one hillside down below them. Every point of interest announced by the conductor was a photo opportunity. The windows were open at first, but as the train ascended and the temperature got cooler, people began to shut the windows. As far as pictures were concerned, it did not matter; the windows were quite clean.

When they arrived at the summit, they got off the train and looked around. Snow covered the ground, and it was cold. There was also a stiff breeze, and Peter was glad he had his new hat with a draw cord under his neck. They would have at least half an hour to take pictures and enjoy the scenery, and perhaps have a donut or a hot chocolate at the Summit House as well. Peter and Carol took a few swallows of water and proceeded to the sign that marked the summit—*14,110 feet,* it said. It was almost like a ritual to take a picture of oneself by the summit sign. It proved that you had been there. Everyone did it. While they waited for a group in front of them to take their turn at the sign, they took in the scenery around them. Except for the sound of an occasional vehicle driving up to the peak, it was remarkable how quiet it was. At fourteen thousand feet, the sounds of civilization were left far below. Looking downward, snow still covered the tops of the mountains around them. Farther down, one could see blue pools where the ice covering mountain tarns had already melted. Looking horizontally beyond the edge of the peak one saw fluffy clouds that one would normally see by looking up. It was like being in heaven and looking down upon Earth.

The group in front of them finished. Now it was Peter and Carol's turn to take a picture of the sign. Carol took one of Peter next to the sign, and then Peter took one of Carol next to the sign. As Peter finished, he felt a hand on his shoulder. It was Bud. "Let me take a picture of both of you together. It will be a chance to use my instant Polaroid camera—no multi-day wait for the film to be developed."

"Ah sure," Peter said as he motioned for Carol to go back to the sign.

Bud snapped the picture and walked toward the sign. "While we wait a few minutes for it to develop, would you mind taking a picture of Sally and me? You can use Sally's camera."

"Not a problem," Peter said as Sally handed him her camera.

Peter took two pictures just to be sure. When he finished, he handed Sally her camera. Meanwhile, Bud was in the process of checking on the Polaroid print when suddenly he seemed to faint. Peter, Carol, and Bud's wife all rushed to keep him from hitting the ground.

"Oh my God! Are you okay?" Peter asked as he guided him into a sitting position, and then knelt beside him.

"I don't know, I got very dizzy, and my arm is tingling," he said.

"Perhaps it's a lack of oxygen," Peter suggested.

"Today is only our second day here. The altitude is new to us and Bud has a heart condition," his wife said.

"Carol . . ." Peter was about to ask her for the can of oxygen, but she already had it out of her bag.

"Here, she said."

Peter placed the nozzle over Bud's mouth and nose, and pulled the trigger. "Try to relax and breathe."

After a few minutes, Bud said, "I'm feeling much better now. Thanks."

"What about the tingling in your arm?"

"It's gone. I'm okay."

"Good. Get up slowly," Peter advised, and held on to him just to be sure.

Then Peter handed the can of oxygen to Sally. "Please take this in case he needs it again." He watched as Bud and Sally walked into the Summit House.

Carol came over to Peter and put her arm around his shoulder. "Peter, that was really nice what you just did. Are *you* all right? You're shivering."

"I think I need to get warm," he said, and they walked into the Summit House with their arms around each other. Inside, they once again encountered Bud and Sally who were sipping hot chocolate.

"**Oh Peter**," Sally called out. "I'm so grateful to you and your wife for helping Bud. What can I do to repay you?" The look on Sally's face indicated how grateful she was.

"Nothing. I'm just glad he's okay. Make sure he drinks plenty of liquid. It will help."

"Peter and Carol, we almost forgot the Polaroid. It just came out"—apparently, not that *instant*. She handed Peter the image. He held it for both to see. "It's a very nice picture of us," Carol commented. "We thank you."

"I'll get us some cocoa," Peter said as he tucked the picture into his shirt pocket.

****

Peter and Carol stopped at Territory Days on the way back and Peter helped Carol find the Western hat she wanted. Then on the way out, Carol took interest in a plant display. "Are you a plant lover?" Peter asked.

"I wish I had more time for growing plants. My daughter was suggesting I buy some plants to spruce up the decor of my apartment and I was just getting some ideas."

"What is your apartment like?"

"It's a two-bedroom garden apartment complex. I have a small balcony that gets lots of sun and if I keep the curtains open, it lets lots of sun into the room. I think plants and flowers would do well there."

They enjoyed talking and they were in no hurry. Before they left to head back to Boulder, they stopped for gas. Carol paid with a credit card. "Let me pay for the gas," she said. "You can buy us dinner." It was close to 7:30 p.m. when they re-entered the Boulder city limits.

"Peter, are you getting hungry? What do you want to do for supper?"

"Well, someone at IBM told me about this place called the Blue Columbine Corral. They said it has food and live country western music. Would that be all right with you?"

"Sounds good to me. Let's do it."

The two took a seat at a dimly lit booth. They had a good view of both the dance floor and the bar, which were well-lit. The place was busy but not crowded, as many of the college crowd had left for the weekend. Carol ordered ribs and Peter ordered a rib-eye steak. Both dishes came with the establishment's special potatoes.

A country western band started playing around 9:00 p.m. Peter ordered a couple of drinks. Then they watched as people started to circle around the perimeter of the dance floor doing Texas two-steps, Texas polkas, cowboy cha-chas, shuffles, and other steps too complicated to describe.

"Carol, do you do any of these dances back home?"

"I've tried line-dancing but that is about it. Have you done this?"

"Never, but I think I would like to try it. I've been watching the two-steps. Looks rather simple—Step-step, quick-quick," he said as he demonstrated with his hands on the table.

"I don't know, I might embarrass you," she said tactfully.

"Don't care. No one knows us here. C'mon. Please, let's try."

It took a few practice steps on the side of the dance floor, but they got the hang of it. Then the band started playing a country waltz.

"It's just a basic waltz step Carol, we can do it."

After that, they decided they were not ready for the polka or the Cowboy Cha-Cha that followed, so they returned to their table.

Peter was thinking of another drink, and turned his head toward the bar where he noticed Belinsky.

"Carol, that is Georgy Belinsky from IBM. We should say hello."

"Really? He's a prime suspect who will be taken into custody on Tuesday."

"Oh . . . you didn't tell me. Do they have enough evidence?"

"Thanks to you, they have enough to hold him. They will make him think they have more than they do. They want him to talk and reveal who is pulling his strings."

"I see . . . Carol, what are you looking at?"

"Looks like some chick is cozying up to him at the bar. Do you think she's a prostitute?"

"Maybe," Peter replied after turning to look, "but he comes here a lot. He may know her—They're heading for the dance floor." As he watched them dance, Peter began to think he may have seen Belinsky's dance partner somewhere before, and he was curious to know more.

"Carol, I'd like to talk to Belinsky. It's okay. I see him every day. He still speaks to me, and he's the one who told me about this place. However, I'm interested in the woman he's with. I may have seen her before."

"What? Have you been playing around on weekends?" she teased.

"Carol, stop it. Please do me a favor. Play along. I won't blow your cover. I promise. Let's go back out on the dance floor. Trust me."

They made it to the dance floor and began dancing to a country waltz. Meanwhile, they watched Belinsky and his partner retreat to a small table in the bar area.

"Are they avoiding us?" Carol commented. "Belinsky's dance partner is looking very hard at us."

"I noticed that. I think she may recognize me. Let's go say hello. Please do me a favor, check out her hair and her eyelashes."

Carol looked puzzled. "Ooh . . . kay," she responded.

Peter led Carol over to the table by the bar, and Peter started the conversation.

"Georgy, how are you tonight? You had recommended this place so I thought I would check it out. I'd like to introduce you to my friend *Jean,*" he said intentionally not using her real name. "She's here for the weekend . . . and your friend?"

"Oh . . . well we just met."

"I'm Angie," his friend said as she leaned forward. "I didn't get your name."

"Peter."

"How do you and Georgy know each other?" she asked.

"We both work for IBM," Peter replied.

"What do you do for IBM?" she asked.

"Peter is with Corporate Audit," Georgy interjected.

"Interesting . . . does that mean you pore over the accounting numbers?" she asked.

"No. Not at all. We go from location to location and make sure that the management at each location is complying with IBM policies and procedures. What is it that you do?"

"I'm into pharmaceutical sales," she said.

"Do you come here often?" Carol asked"

"No. Actually, this is the first time. Georgy is showing me how to dance. I was watching you two out there. You seemed to know what you are doing."

"Thank you, but we are kind of new at it ourselves," Carol answered.

"Where are you and Jean from?"

"Maryland . . . and you?"

"Oakland . . . I came here on business but needed a break. Have you two found anything of interest for tourist around here?"

"We have," Peter said with some exuberance. "We went to Pikes Peak this afternoon—very scenic. I even have a picture of the two of us at the top—more than fourteen thousand feet up. Here, have a look," he said, as he removed the Polaroid from his pocket and handed it to Angie.

She looked, smiled, and handed it to Georgy.

"Have you ever been up there Georgy," Peter asked.

"No, but I once went to the nearby Cave of the Winds and the Manitou Cliff Dwellings. That whole area is impressive," he said as he handed the picture back to Peter. "Peter, why don't you and Jean join us? We already have a third chair and I see one over there you can grab."

"Okay, thank you," Peter said and pulled up the extra chair. He and Carol sat down and the waitress brought them drinks.

The chitchat continued for a few minutes until Georgy and Angie excused themselves and headed back onto the dance floor, leaving Carol and Peter time to talk privately.

"So, I'm *Jean* now?"

"I didn't see any point to letting them know your real name."

"Okay Peter, please explain what that was all about. Do you know her?"

"You know, women can look a lot different when they have makeup, fake eyelashes, and possibly a wig. Do you think her hair was real?"

"I think it was a wig," she said. "There was a moment when the light reflected on it. It seemed too shiny for real hair. You mentioned eyelashes. I also think those were fake. Why is this important?"

"Did you pick up on how she pronounced Georgy's name? It was more like '*e-**your**-gee*' with the accent on the second syllable. I think she may be Teddy."

"Teddy?"

"Ursula Behr, the person of interest that was involved in the network design theft that you investigated. She seems to match the description we were given."

Carol looked for her out to the dance floor. "I suppose," she said as she spotted her, "but you know something more, don't you?"

"I can't be sure, but I may have met her."

"**What**?" she said loudly.

Peter could tell Carol was getting impatient, but he asked one more question. "Did you notice a scar on her neck below her left ear?"

She looked Peter straight in the face sternly. "It was barely visible, but yes, she has the scar. Now, please explain how you know her."

"She may not be who I think she is. If she is, I met her only briefly. The woman I met had short brown hair, and she wasn't wearing makeup. I'm only remembering a possible scar now that I'm thinking back on it. I'm still trying to get a good picture of her in my head. The woman with Belinsky has black hair and eye makeup, so I can't be one hundred percent sure. It seemed that she did not want me to know who she was. However, if she is the woman I once met, she may be a Soviet agent, and probably recognized *me*."

"I hope she didn't. I don't want to see another attempt on your life."

"Before we sat down at their table, I noticed a gentleman sitting at the bar. He seemed a bit overdressed for the venue. He was wearing slacks with creases, and a white shirt. Perhaps he was there after work and simply removed his tie and jacket. Except, today is Saturday and it's a holiday weekend. He seemed to be looking at us. Carol, have a look. Do you see the man at the end of the bar? Is he one of yours?"

"One of mine?"

"You know, a Fed."

"Why do you think he's a Fed?"

"Check out his clothes and his shoes. His shoes are just like Colby's— black, heavy-duty, but dressy with laces."

"Well, I've never seen him before."

As they sat and talked, they watched Belinsky and Angie do a Texas Two Step, and then they watched Georgy try to show Angie how to do a Cowboy Cha-Cha.

"Peter, look at them. Georgy and Angie seem to be really hitting it off. She's all over him."

Finally, there was a break in the music, and Georgy and Angie turned to make their way off the dance floor and back to the table. They were about twenty feet away when Peter suddenly pulled out his pocket camera, aimed it at Angie, and snapped the shutter.

Carol was surprised. Georgy and Angie also noticed. Georgy smiled, but Angie's face showed instant horror, immediately followed by a look of anger.

"Peter, why did you do that?" she yelled with irritation in her voice, as she approached the table. Peter thought he detected a slight accent.

"I'm sorry. I really didn't think you would mind," Peter said, as sincerely as he could make it sound.

"Why did you want a picture of *me* and *Georgy*," she asked, trying to make sense of it. "How many more have you been taking?" she asked with a tone of disapproval. The expressions on both Georgy's face and Carol's face indicated their puzzlement at such a reaction.

"Well okay, Peter responded calmly. It happens to be the last picture on my roll, and for me, a picture of dancing at the Blue Columbine would be a good memory to top off a day of fun."

Realizing she had lost her cool, Angie regained her composure and apologized. "Peter, I should not have reacted that way. Please accept my apology."

"Apology accepted."

"Jean, one more dance?" The band was playing a slow country waltz.

"Of course, . . . love to."

Peter held Carol close to him. They felt the warmth of each other's body. The drinks only enhanced their mood. They were relaxed and happy.

After the dance, they kept their arms around each other. Carol looked up and asked, "Would it be all right if we head back to the Residence Inn?"

"Sure."

The two of them walked out to the car arm in arm. The cool night air breathed new life into them. The Residence Inn was only ten minutes away. They talked and laughed the whole way. They were both feeling good. Peter pulled up in front of Carol's unit and parked. His own unit was across the parking lot, but very close. He could walk. He shut off the engine.

"Peter, I had a very good time today."

"I'm glad you enjoyed it. I really enjoyed it also, and I especially enjoyed being with you."

Carol opened the passenger door. As she started to get out, Peter said, "Let me fetch your hat from the back seat."

Peter got out, opened the rear door on his side of the car, ducked his head, and reached inside. As he backed out with her hat and turned around, Carol was right there at the car door to greet him.

"Carol did I tell you how cute you look when you wear this hat," he said as he moved toward her and placed the hat on her head with both hands.

She giggled and stood there with a smile on her face.

"Of course, you look cute when you're not wearing the hat too," he said softly as he moved his head toward hers, removed her hat, held it behind her with both hands, and kissed her very tenderly on the lips. She looked him directly in the eye, put her arms around his neck, and kissed him back.

"Peter, would you like to come in," she asked.

"Yes, I would like that," he said without hesitation.

****

Peter woke up before 7:00 a.m. For a Sunday morning, it was early. As he gained consciousness, he began to realize where he was. He turned and saw Carol fast asleep bedside him. He smiled and remembered the pleasure they had shared only a few hours before. He tried to go back to sleep, but now he found himself rethinking the observations they made at the Blue Columbine. He quietly got up and made his way to the sofa. Was that woman Teddy? Was she Mary Lou? Did he need to do anything?

He was deep on thought when he felt a warm body snuggle up to him on the sofa. "Peter, are you all right?"

"Sure. I tried not to wake you."

"You didn't, but why did you get up? You seem troubled. Are you having second thoughts about what we did?"

"No. . . . No, Carol, it was perfect! When I first woke up, and I saw you next to me, I felt happy. I remembered the good time we had yesterday and how much I enjoyed dancing with you last night. I also remembered the pleasure of making love to you, and how much you seemed to enjoy it too. But you were sleeping and seemed so peaceful, so I came in here and started thinking about the case."

"You're sweet," she said and kissed him.

"Maybe I'm making too much of it," he said, "but I think that on Tuesday we should tell Colby everything we saw. I'm just not sure what to make of it."

"Okay, but you're still not telling me everything, are you? How did you meet Teddy? Whatever is troubling you, maybe I can help resolve it."

"The woman I met is associated with the CIA. The person that brought me onto this project is a high-level CIA officer. He introduced me to the woman. If the woman we met last night is the same person, she could be under deep cover, or she could be a traitor. Then there is the matter of Teddy. Are Angie and Teddy the same person? And what about the man at the bar, was he FBI, or DEA? Was he tailing Belinsky or Angie? On the other hand, perhaps what we saw was all one big coincidence. I'm trying to decide if I should call my CIA contact and let him know what I may have seen. If Angie is the person who I think she is, and if she thinks I recognized her, she would not want the CIA to know it."

"Wouldn't your CIA contact expect you to tell him what you know and suspect?"

"Of course, . . ."

"If you didn't tell him, you wouldn't be doing your job, and if she's an enemy agent she would do more damage."

"True."

"If she is not an enemy agent, the only downside I see is possible embarrassment."

"Yes, but I'm concerned that if she is an enemy agent, she may think that I recognized her."

"Oh . . . now I understand. You could be a target."

"Yes, and my CIA contact could also be compromised."

"How so? . . . Am I missing something?"

"What I did not tell you was that the two of them live together. She could be intercepting all his messages."

"Oh my God!"

"Also, if I tell him, he will be devastated by the news, assuming he even believes me."

"I think you should forget about his feelings; he's trained to deal with that."

"There is something else I didn't tell you."

"What?"

"The name of my CIA contact is Jon Wilson. I have known Jon for more than twenty years. I respect him and consider him a friend. He confided in me how much he cares for his girlfriend, Mary Lou, and how happy he is. Maybe I'm just a romanticist, but I don't want to see him hurt."

"Peter, may I suggest a course of action?"

"I'm listening."

"I think you should call your CIA contact and tell him everything you know or suspect. The more information he has the better it is for both of you.

"I want you to call him from my phone here in my unit. I'm going to shower and dress while you do that."

"I need to shower and dress also. Why don't I go to my place to make the call?"

"**Because she could be in your unit right now waiting for you, that's why! . . . And you saw how she reacted when you took her picture.**" Carol had raised her voice. "Peter, I 'm sorry I didn't mean to be impatient with you, but if she is what you think she is, she may decide not to take any chances. She knows who you are, and Belinsky could have told her where you are staying."

"You could be right."

"After I return from the shower, we can go over to your place together. I have a way to find out if it's safe. I have had some training in this type of thing. Please trust me."

"Okay."

Peter made the call, but Jon did not answer. Peter left a detailed message on his voice recorder. Then he put his clothes on from the night before and waited for Carol to come out of the bathroom. He watched as she slipped on a pair of jeans, a plain shirt, sox, and walking shoes. Then she went to the room safe, retrieved a holstered snub-nosed 38-caliber revolver, and attached it to her belt. The gun rested on her left hip with the handle pointing forward. Then she slipped on a denim jacket for cover and put her FBI ID folder into the left pocket of the jacket.

"Holy Cow, are we going to war?" Peter said loudly.

"I hope not. Peter, the likely-hood of you being a target is rather small. Ursula Behr—or whatever her name is—would need to believe that you recognized her, **and** she would need to believe you had a reason to tell your CIA contact, **and** she would need to believe that taking you out would make a difference to her mission. However, it's better to be safe than sorry. You ready to go?"

They walked out the door but did not head toward his unit, as Peter expected.

"Where are we going?" he asked

"To the lobby. When we get there, I want you to ask the desk if anyone has come asking for you, left you a message, or asked for a spare key. While you are doing that, I'm going to check out your unit—I need your key. If all is safe, you'll see me standing outside your door. You can come over and join me then, . . . okay?"

"Yes," he replied, with a slight tone of resignation.

He followed her directions. Much of the staff knew him, so he had no problem asking questions. Betty was on duty this morning.

"Morning, Betty. I was wondering if anyone had asked for me yesterday."

"Let me check," she said as she reached under the counter. "Yes, there is a note here for you." She handed him a sealed envelope with his name and unit number written on it. "There should also be a message on your phone. Did you see it?"

"Thank you, Betty—no, I haven't been in my room. I was away yesterday."

"Doesn't most of your group go home on the weekends? I'm surprised to see you here at all this weekend."

"Most of my crew did go home this weekend, but I decided to be a tourist this weekend and take in some of the sights."

"Where did you go?"

"Pikes Peak—"

"Mr. Troutman, please excuse me for a moment I need to help this person out."

While Betty turned away to help someone else, Peter opened the envelope. The message inside was very cryptic:

YOU HAVE SOMETHING I WANT.
WHERE ARE YOU?

The message did not say who left it. As soon as Betty finished talking with the other person, Peter asked her, "Betty did the person who left this message for me give their name?"

"I don't know, but the message came in over-night. We time-stamped the envelope. Jennifer was on duty last night. Perhaps she would know more. It's only eight thirty now. I may still be able to get ahold of her. Would you like me to try?"

"Would you please?"

Peter was in luck. Jennifer was available and Betty put Peter on the phone with her.

"I remember a woman came in around two thirty and wanted to know what unit you were in," Jennifer said.

"Did you tell her?"

"No, but she said it was important. She said that she was just with you, that you mistakenly had her camera, and she needed it back before she left for the airport. I called your number on the phone for her. No one answered, so she said she wanted to leave you a note. She wrote something and I put it into an envelope. I wrote your unit number on the envelope and put the envelope into our message slot behind the desk. . . Oh my . . . I just remembered. She said she needed to add something to the note, so I pulled it back out. She could have seen the unit number."

"I see. Thank you, Jennifer." Peter thanked Betty as well, walked outside, and began walking towards his unit.

****

While Peter was at the lobby desk, Carol had gone looking for maid service. She found a woman named Carmen—according to her nametag. Carmen was in the doorway of the maid's storage closet loading clean linen, towels, soaps, and shampoo onto her cart. "Excuse me miss," Carol asked politely.

"*Un momento, por favor*," she answered as she put another item onto her cart before turning toward Carol.

"Uh. . . Do you speak English?" Carol asked.

"A little," she answered.

"Carmen," she said pointing to the nametag. "My name is Carol. May I ask a favor of you?"

"Si."

"I would like you to go to unit number one-o-seven."

"*Cuando?*" she asked.

"Ahora—Now," Carol replied.

"Oh . . . I do hundred one . . . hundred three . . . hundred five, and then—"

Carol stopped her. "It's okay. I'll give you five dollars."

Carol had thought about flashing her FBI badge, but officially using civilians in that way could be against the department rules—especially bad if anything went astray. Instead, Carol pulled a five-dollar bill from her pocket and waived it in front of her.

"Please," Carol pleaded. "This is very important!"

"*Gracias*," Carmen said as she reached for the five-dollar bill.

"No, not yet. Here is what I want you to do," Carol said as she put the bill back into her pocket. "I want you to take your cart to unit one hundred seven and knock on the door. If no one is in the unit, I want you to come back here and tell me. Don't go in! If someone is in the unit, tell them you are the maid and will come back later. Then come here and tell me. Do you understand?"

"That's all? And you give me five dollars?"

"Yes, that's it. You understand—do not go in—come back here."

As Carmen started to walk toward her cart, Carol could hear her mutter, "*No . . . no comprendo . . . por que'?*" Then she turned, faced Carol, and asked the logical question, "Miss Carol, why not *you* do this?"

"If there is someone in the room, I don't want them to see me through the window. Meet me right here when you are done."

Five minutes later Carmen returned with the verdict. No one was in the room. Carol gave her the five dollars and made her promise not to tell anyone.

Immediately, Carol went to Peter's unit to check out the room as she told him she would do. Carol put one hand on the doorknob and inserted the key with the other. The doorknob turned before the key turned. THE DOOR WAS NOT LOCKED!

Just to be safe, Carol un-holstered her revolver and entered the room cautiously, gun in hand. She pushed the door all the way open before she crossed the threshold. No one was behind the door. She swept the room with her eyes. Everything looked normal. The bed covers were undisturbed from the previous day. She entered the bathroom—No one! She re-holstered her gun, went back to the front door, and waited for Peter.

He arrived a few minutes later. "Peter, what did you find out at the desk?" she asked with eager anticipation.

"I talked on the phone with Jennifer. She was on duty overnight. She told me that a woman came and asked for me around two thirty . . . made up a story about me having her camera and tried to get my unit number. They called my room and got no answer. The woman left after leaving me a note but may have discovered my unit number in the process. My unit number was on the envelope."

"Oh dear! You might want to check your things to be sure nothing is missing—or planted. When I entered the unit, the door was not locked."

Peter looked around the room, checked something on the desk, and then turned to Carol and proclaimed, "I see no evidence that anyone other than the maid was here. Would you mind standing guard while I shower and dress?"

About fifteen minutes later, Peter came back into the living area. Carol was on the couch. He walked slowly over to her and kissed her. Then he looked hard at her and smiled.

"What?" she said with some trepidation.

"I told you I liked the way you looked in your western hat. I was just imagining you wearing it now with your revolver on your hip."

"Peter . . . Stop!" she said with feigned indignation.

"I'm sorry. It's just that I was hoping today would be more romantic than it has been so far."

She smiled. "Peter, the day has just started. Why don't we find someplace nice to eat? It's already ten o'clock . . . maybe brunch?"

"Good idea. There is a diner on 28th Street."

****

After they went back to Carol's unit and she returned her revolver to the safe, they went to the diner on 28th Street. The diner displayed two American flags, one on each side of the entrance—very appropriate for Memorial Day. A hostess seated them in a non-smoking section without waiting too long—only two couples in front of them. They enjoyed a leisurely and enjoyable brunch. Peter ordered his favorite breakfast, orange juice and poached eggs over corned beef hash. Carol ordered hers, a fruit bowl and French toast. They both had coffee and they talked. Though neither of them admitted it, they both knew they had jumped into the relationship rather quickly. Neither wanted it to be a one-night stand, but neither knew where it was headed either. Carol needed to know more about what she was getting into. They began to talk. They ended up really getting to know each other that day. Religion was one of the first things they discussed.

"Carol, today is Sunday. Do you need to go to church?"

"No, I was brought up Protestant, and I do go to a Unitarian church back home, but I don't *need* to go. Did *you* want to go to church?"

"No," he answered. I have attended different churches over the years, and I believe in a spiritual God, but I'm not very religious in the traditional sense."

"Do you see your kids much?" she asked, changing the subject.

"I see my older daughter. She just finished her senior year at the University of Maryland. She has an apartment in College Park. She applied to several graduate schools—hasn't made a decision yet."

"What about you?"

"My ex-husband has the house in Columbia, and that is where my son David is for the summer—I see him when I'm home. My daughter has a summer job near San Francisco. Karen just graduated from Stanford University and she just found out that she has been accepted in Stanford's medical school—I don't see her so much."

"Wow! She must be smart like her mom."

"I think she's a lot smarter than me," Carol replied.

They continued to talk about family during the rest of their meal.

After brunch, they took a Sunday drive up into the mountains along Boulder Creek. It would be relaxing, and they could continue to talk and get to know each other better. Yes, there really was a Boulder Creek. It ran from Barker Reservoir in the mountains down through the city of Boulder and then northeast toward Loveland. It did not go very close to the IBM site or anything else that related to the project. Peter wondered why they named the project what they did. They drove to the western side of town, and up Canyon Road (Route 119). On the way up, they passed bikers. They would pedal two miles up on a twenty-degree slope.

"Totally impressive, but not for me," Peter said. They followed the route as it turned southward and went all the way to Barker Reservoir. At Barker Reservoir, they got out, walked around, and took a few pictures. Then they headed south on Route 72. All along, the scenery was beautiful. At times, it was like another world and one could not even see civilization. Then they got daring—at least Peter did. He was driving. They turned left onto Gross Dam Road—an unpaved road—and went toward Gross Reservoir. This made Carol nervous.

They were a few miles down the road when Carol said, "Peter, are you sure you know where we are?"

"Well, it's on the map," he replied, but he could see a worried expression on her face. "Are you all right?"

"Peter, I'm sorry, but we are driving a family sedan on a rutted unpaved road with no one in sight—not even farm animals. I'm just a little nervous. What if we have a flat tire, like we did the other day? Or, what if we slide off the road?"

Peter brought the car to a full stop.

"Peter, are you going to yell at me?" she said with trepidation.

He turned toward her and surprised her by pulling her toward him and kissing her hard on the mouth. "I wanted this to be a relaxing drive. I'll find a place to turn around, and we can head back to the main road," he said sympathetically.

Of course, finding a safe place to turn around was not easy. There were no shoulders and no turnoffs. The road barely had room in case another vehicle came the other way. Doing a three-point turn with a full-sized four-door sedan risked backing off the edge into a gully or even down the side of a mountain. After one failed attempt, Carol understood the situation, and she finally said, "Peter, it's okay to keep going."

At Gross Reservoir, they stopped and each took another picture. Then they took Flagstaff Road back into Boulder. Flagstaff Road was quite winding, including a few almost hairpin turns, but at least it had wide paved lanes. As they came back into town, they came to the famous Chautauqua Park. Peter parked on a nearby street and they walked into the park. They held hands as they toured the facility and walked down a trail that led to an overlook, but Peter sensed that something was not right.

When they returned to the Residence Inn, they went to the lobby. Lisa was on duty today. Peter asked if there were any messages. "Yes," she said. "Someone called and asked for you by name. I rang your room and you were not there so I connected them to your voice mail. They may have left a message. In addition, the management wanted you to have this." She handed him an envelope.

"Okay, thanks, Lisa."

Carol and Peter then proceeded to *his* unit.

"As he opened the door with his key, Carol said, "Peter, I still have some concern that someone may try to get to you."

"They looked around and everything seemed to be in order."

"Carol, you have been very jumpy since brunch—unlike the brave warrior I saw this morning when you wore your revolver and checked out my room."

"I know—what did the management have to say?" she said changing the subject.

Peter opened the envelope and read the letter. "It's an apology for the incident last night. They also say that Security is keeping special watch over my unit, but if I wish to change rooms they would arrange it—"

Just then, Carol said, "Peter, excuse me, but I'm just noticing that the red light on your phone is blinking. You have a message."

Peter picked up the receiver and dialed 411. He put the phone on *speaker* so that Carol could also hear the message.

Peter this is Jon Wilson. I listened to your phone message. Your message disturbed me. Mary Lou told me she was in Oakland visiting her mom. However, your thoughts may be correct. I have also picked up on several other indicators that Mary Lou may not be who I thought. I appreciate you letting me know. On the other hand, Mary Lou just called me collect—eight o'clock my time—and said she was in Oakland. But, she still could have been in Boulder last night. I expect Mary Lou to be back home late tomorrow afternoon. I'm trying to keep my emotions in check. I expect to share info with the FBI on Tuesday.

"Carol, I really appreciate you being concerned about me. I also know you may consider it your job to look after me, but the letter and the phone message from Jon should put your mind at ease, at least in that regard."

"Yes, in that regard, it does," she answered.

"But?"

"Peter . . . I need to be honest with you. I care about you—not just because it's my job to protect you. I didn't have sex with you last night without having real feelings for you, and this afternoon you were very patient with me when I started freaking out about the road. I like you a lot, *but . . .* I'm scared."

"Why?"

"Peter, you told me you were legally separated. A lot of men say that, and then they go back to their wives."

"Carol, I have not been with my wife for almost two years. I really am separated, and we really are getting divorced."

"I want to believe you. My husband cheated on me—just like Jon said in his message—and it caught me totally off guard. Perhaps it was partly my fault. I was travelling a lot and not there when he needed me. Then after I left him, I was with someone else. Bruce swept me off my feet and told me he loved me. I believed him until I found out that he lied. After sleeping with me, he would go back to his wife and sleep with her, sometimes on the same night. I was hurt when my husband did this. I was hurt even more when my lover did this. Bruce got me pregnant—I never told him. I had an abortion and had my tubes tied. I guess you could say I have trust issues. Now I find myself having feelings for you. It scares me."

Peter paused to collect his thoughts before responding. "Carol, I want to be honest with you too. I really like you a lot, and I would like our relationship to continue. In the short time that I have known you, you have given me something that I have not had in a very long time. I'm not just talking about sex. I'm talking about your willingness to share ideas, experiences, and most importantly to me . . . feelings."

"Peter, why are you getting divorced? Was it infidelity?"

"No, that was not the reason."

"Please tell me why."

"My wife regretted having kids instead of pursuing a career. She blamed me for that. I did what I could to support her ambitions after the kids were older, but I guess it was too late. She also viewed her father as a chauvinist and my father as a Nazi. She made her views known in public and to the kids. I made a decision to divorce her, and then arranged my temporary assignment with IBM to facilitate that. I have not been with anyone else since I left home—"

"I need you to be honest. Have you been with other women?"

"There was a time after I decided to divorce and before I left home when I had two brief affairs. In both cases, they knew I was married, and I would like to think that those affairs ended with a degree of mutual respect."

"What did those affairs give you? Why did you need them? Was it sex?"

"No. It helped to restore my sense of self-worth. Perhaps they needed that as well."

After a long pause she asked, "After all that I told you, do you still want to be with me?"

"Yes, I do. Do you still want to be with me?"

"Very much," she said as she stood up, walked over to him, and put her arms around him. "I need you."

That night, they held each other closely and made love.

****

They agreed to part on Monday morning. Peter's team would be arriving Monday evening—no need for them to know what was going on between him and Carol. Besides, they both had personal matters to attend to—like laundry.

Monday morning, they shared a late breakfast together, and then went to a Laundromat. Carol packed her suitcase and then checked out of her unit. Peter returned to his unit to sort his laundry. Carol came over to Peter's unit to say good-bye around noon. Colby had already made a reservation for her Monday night at the hotel near the FBI office in Denver. She told Peter she had an early morning meeting with Colby early Tuesday morning.

"Carol, when did Colby set up this meeting?"

"Late Friday . . . Why?"

"May I ask what the subject is?"

"According to Colby, he has information regarding Ursula Behr."

"Do you think I should have been invited to the meeting?"

"I asked him that on Friday. His answer was that you were not involved in that part of the Boulder Creek Project."

"I see. Carol, I want you to tell him everything we saw on Saturday and everything we heard from Jon Wilson regarding the possibility that Ursula Behr, Teddy, and Jon's girlfriend could be the same person. Please, I think he should know."

"Okay, I will," she said.

"I would also like you to give him this," he said as he handed her a sealed envelope.

"What is it?"

"It's the picture of us on top of Pikes Peak, and the note left for me in the lobby."

"I don't . . . Oh yes . . . I see," she said as soon as she understood.

When it was time to say good-bye, they said how much they liked each other. She told Peter she did not know where she would be after tomorrow. She hoped he would stay in touch—apparently, she still had her doubts. He tore a page off the pad of paper provided by the Inn, wrote down his contact information, and gave it to her. She did likewise.

Her parting words were, "I'll call you tonight."

****

Later, after a quick supper, Peter took a glass of wine out to the pool and slumped down in one of the lounge chairs. He was tired—very tired. He fell asleep.

A repeated jostling of his shoulder awakened him. It was Michael—grinning ear to ear.

"What are you doing out here?" Michael asked.

"I most have dozed off."

"How was your weekend?" Peter asked.

"Great! Just got back. I went to New York. We had a family get together—a cook out—the whole works. How was yours? Did you stay here?"

"I did stay here but I had a good weekend. We went to Pikes Peak."

"*We?*" Michael exclaimed.

Peter looked around; it was dark. Then he remembered he expected a phone call. "Uh . . . what time is it?"

Michael looked at his watch. "In Maryland it's a quarter after eleven."

"Damn . . . Michael, I need to excuse myself. I'm expecting a phone call. I'll see you tomorrow at breakfast. We can talk then, okay?"

As he got up to make a hasty retreat, Michael was still grinning.

Back in his room, Peter checked the message light. It was not blinking. He waited with anticipation but the phone never rang. His spirits dimmed. She did say she would call . . . right? His mind raced through the events of the weekend. The whole weekend was beginning to seem like a distant dream. With his emotions already drained, it took him a while to go back to sleep.

13

NIGHTMARE

Meanwhile, back in Maryland, Jon Wilson was having a difficult Memorial Day weekend of his own. On Friday, he had met with the CIA Director—his boss—who was pressuring him to locate Teddy and to ensure that no computer virus would end up in the satellite monitoring system. Earlier in the week, Jon learned that the Air Force had the AFOS tapes and was ready to install them, but that the FBI still did not know for sure if they contained a virus. Jon found the slow progress frustrating. Then on Friday, he got a coded message from the Chinese embassy that Chan had been missing for two days. This was not good news.

Later, on Friday, Jon received notification from an FBI source that an Ursula Behr had a plane reservation to fly from San Francisco to Boulder that evening. The FBI would trace her activity and let him know on Tuesday what they found. This was good news! He called Ken Morehouse and gave the General an update on what he knew. He hoped that Ken would have some new information for him in return, but that was not the case. However, as head of the Boulder Creek Project, Ken agreed that it was time for a status meeting with the principal players involved. He would schedule a meeting with the FBI Washington Director of Security, Donald Gavin, and with the FBI Denver Special Agent in Charge, Roger Colby. They would review the status of the Boulder Creek Project and the latest information about Ursula Behr. They would bring Roger Colby into the meeting via a telephone conference call. Ken called Jon back just before leaving for the weekend and told him the meeting was set for 1400 hours EST at the Pentagon on Tuesday.

After Jon got back to his condominium that Friday evening, he received a call from Peter Troutman. Peter explained that he would not be reachable on Saturday so he was checking in on Friday instead. He told Jon, "I personally gave Colby a version, known to be virus-free. The lab will compare it to the tape sent to the Air Force. They said they hope to know results next week."

Then, Jon used the opportunity to give Peter a heads up regarding the status of Ursula Behr. "I have intelligence that says Ursula Behr is on her way to Boulder. FBI may be tracking her. I don't know why she is going there. I'm just giving you a heads-up. Let me know if you hear anything."

Meanwhile, Mary Lou had left early Friday morning to visit her mother in Oakland. She planned to return late Monday afternoon. Although he could never talk with Mary Lou about his work, she was able to read his moods rather well, and they often helped each other unwind at the end of a trying workweek. However, this Friday, he had come home to an empty apartment. He was on his own—no one to unwind with. He had no idea how stressful his weekend would become.

****

On Saturday morning, Jon took an early morning jog and then retreated to his home office where he tried to make sense out of everything. The home office not only served Jon as a place to get work done but also as a place where he could escape from the pressures of the real world, at least temporarily. As he sat in his easy chair, he kept thinking about Mary Lou. He had tried to call her in Oakland Friday night and again that morning, but each time the call went to voice mail. She did not return the call. As he thought about this, he realized that he did not recall anyone ever answering the phone when he called in the past. It always went to voice mail. Jon found this to be annoying, frustrating, and puzzling. Therefore, later Saturday morning, he called Linda, one of his employees who was at work that morning and asked her to identify the owner and location of the phone number. Within an hour, she called back and told him the number was an unlisted number with a San Francisco exchange. That was curious because Mary Lou's mother lived in Oakland, not San Francisco. Perhaps there was probably a logical explanation, he thought. He asked Linda how that could be possible, and she explained about the possibility of a foreign exchange line between Oakland and San Francisco. With a foreign exchange line, calls to San Francisco billed as local calls rather than expensive toll calls.

"Jon, I can't legally access the Pac Bell customer service records without a warrant. Should I proceed?"

"No, it's okay. Thanks, Linda."

****

The forecast for Sunday was warm and humid, so Jon decided to wear something summery. This led to a decision to rearrange the clothes closet that he shared with Mary Lou. He used the left side of the closet and she the right. It was large enough, but his summer clothes were not where he could easily get to them. He would re-hang the winter shirts and suits at the far end and the summer and warm weather clothes would be more accessible near the center. As he did this, he could not help but notice that on the shelf above Mary Lou's section, several things were missing that were normally there. For example, a wig, a makeup box, and a very small jewelry container were not there. He wondered why would she need to take those things with her to visit her mother.

It was a holiday weekend and he intended to unwind. He went down to the exercise room for a workout, something he normally did on Sunday mornings. When he returned, he went to his office and took the Sunday paper with him. He had just settled into his easy chair when he noticed the red message light on his message recorder blinking. He walked across the room to his desk, pushed *Play,* and listened to a message from Peter Troutman.

Hi Jon. This is Peter. I wanted to report to you that I happened to be talking with someone last night who may have fit the description of Ursula Behr. It was at a Country Western dance club and she cozied up to Georgy Belinsky who is the IBM computer room manager, and most likely to be the IBM inside man. I talked with them both. She said her name was Angie. I got the impression that she recognized me, and as she spoke, I thought her voice and mannerisms were familiar. I did not think much of it at the time, but afterwards I thought she reminded me of Mary Lou. I still don't know what to make of it. Perhaps it's my imagination gone wild . . . just thought you should know. By the way, this woman had a small scar on her neck below her left ear. Talk to you later. You have my number at the Residence Inn.

After listening to Peter's message, Jon felt a rush of adrenalin. Mary Lou had a small scar on her neck. He was confused. How could she remind him of Mary Lou? Mary Lou was in Oakland . . . wasn't she? He began to feel very uneasy.

Before returning to his easy chair, he decided to tune in some classical music on the FM receiver that was in the corner between his desk and the bookcase. While doing this however, he noticed the need to do some dusting, especially on the top of the bookcase. Although he had a cleaning service come in weekly, the office was off limits for security reasons. Jon was responsible for cleaning his office, and it had been at least two weeks since he had done so. He needed to relax, but could not. The paper could wait— all bad news anyway. He went and got some dusting spray and a cloth. He began removing things from atop the shelf one by one and set them onto his desk. When he got to the snowman, he barely noticed a round spot next to the snowman with almost no dust. As he set the snowman onto his desk, he thought he felt a faint vibration in the palm of his hand. Then he realized that there was something loose inside the snowman. Naturally curious, he removed the tight-fitting lid and peered inside. A faint green light allowed him to see that there was a miniature cassette recorder and an attached mic. He could see the reels on the cassette turning. Obviously, the sound of the classical music had set it off. He stood there for a moment in disbelief. Who did this, he wondered? Could it be the cleaning service? Could Mary Lou have done this? She did go into his office from time to time. How long has this been here? His phone calls and messages would have been recorded. Oh my God, he thought, how much intelligence was compromised? He was upset, and anxious about how he could talk about it with Mary Lou when she got home tomorrow afternoon. Yet he knew he needed to keep his cool. Perhaps there were logical explanations—was the cleaning service involved?

Later in the day, Jon returned Troutman's call. Perhaps Peter could shed more light on his observations. No one answered, so he left a voice message and said he shared his concern.

****

On Monday morning, Jon tried again to call Mary Lou before she left for the Oakland airport. With the three-hour difference in time, it would still be a while before she would leave for the airport. He would offer to meet her at the airport here, or at least pick her up at the Metro. Once again, he was not able to reach her. He missed her but was annoyed that he kept getting voice mail and she did not call back.

He had not slept well Sunday night, musing over the situation. Why did she not return his calls? Why was her phone number not an Oakland phone number? Why did Mary Lou take a wig with her? Who planted the tape recorder and how much information did it compromise? Worst of all, was Peter's implication correct? Was Mary Lou an enemy agent? These things bothered him immensely.

He needed to talk to the FBI or to Ken. He had no choice. He had to tell what he knew. An investigation was required, and he had valuable information. Everyone was on holiday—No one to report to until Tuesday.

It was late Monday afternoon when Mary Lou walked in the door of the condominium. She had just returned from her weekend trip to visit her mother in Oakland. She had taken the Metro from the airport to the nearby Grosvenor station, and decided to walk the short distance back to the condominium. She entered the foyer and set her purse and bag down in the foyer.

"Jon I'm home," she announced as she quickly made her way to the bathroom.

"How was your trip?" Jon asked as he moved from the living room toward the bathroom door.

"Tiring, but it is good to be back." she replied from the other side of the door.

"How is your mother?"

"She is fine. Mother is thinking about moving again."

"Where to?"

"She wasn't sure—how was *your* weekend?" she said changing the subject.

"Not bad," he replied. He could not tell her the truth. In fact, he was very concerned about the Boulder Creek project, and about some of the suspicions that he had about Mary Lou.

"I'll be out in a minute, and I'll tell you about my weekend."

Mary Lou came out of the bathroom and came into the living room where she gave Jon a big hug and kiss.

"Sorry, I really had to go."

"Not a problem. I was thinking about preparing some supper for us, like cheese burgers and potato salad. Perhaps we could start with a couple of beers. What do you think?"

"I think that would be fine," she said, "but I have been sitting all day, and I'd really like to slip into some other clothes and take a jog first. Did you want to come?"

"No, it's okay. In the meantime, I'm going to finish some work I need to do for a meeting tomorrow. We can relax with a beer on the balcony when you get back and we can talk."

After she left, Jon noticed that her purse and suitcase were still in the foyer, so he carted it off to the bedroom. He set the purse on the bed and stared at it for a moment. He had to know more. He went to the purse, opened it, and started removing the contents. What he found shocked him! There was an entire billfold containing some money, and more importantly, a driver's license. He memorized the information before replacing it. The owner of the license was Angeline Ursula Behr, residing at an address in Oakland, California. The photo looked very much like Mary Lou would look if she had long black hair and wore glasses. Was it Mary Lou? He cared about Mary Lou. He loved her. How could this be her? He thought Mary Lou loved him. He did not want to believe that she could be a spy. He felt sick in the pit of his stomach. He was very upset—emotionally wounded—depressed. Mary Lou would return home from her jog very soon. What would he say to her? There was no way he could hide his feelings from her. She would know something was wrong. Is it still possible that there could be a plausible explanation?

Should he confront her with this latest discovery? Would she tell him that Angeline was her sister who shared the visit with their mother? Perhaps the three of them went to a comedy club and for some reason Angeline asked Mary Lou to hold her billfold. Then after Mary Lou was at the airport, she realized she still had her sister's billfold, but it was too late to return it. Would that be plausible?

If he said nothing to Mary Lou about why he was feeling so down, maybe it could ride until morning. Then again, she may figure it out anyway. He could not be sure he put everything back into the purse in its proper order. She would probably notice. In any case, he knew he would need to report all of this to the FBI when he met with them in the morning. Jon had a few minutes before Mary Lou would return from her jog. He used it to call Ken on his home number. Ken did not pick up, so he left a message. He could not take a chance that Ken's wife, Kathy, would hear the message, so all he could say was, *"Ken, I have new information. The Meeting with you and the FBI in the morning is urgent."* He was about to leave a more informative message on Ken's work number when Mary Lou returned from her jog.

****

On Tuesday morning, Jon was in his temporary office at the Pentagon waiting for his meeting with Ken. He was still clearing his head from a rough night—too many unanswered questions. Why hasn't the FBI found the computer virus? Was there another Soviet operation using the second viral cartridge? Could he trust Mary Lou? Last night, he had asked her questions about her trip. Her answers were vague and almost defensive. He would discuss all of this with Ken. Ken would understand, and the two of them would decide on what to do. It was a plan and he began to feel at peace with himself knowing that he was doing something. As he sat at his desk, he relaxed and felt his angst melt away, almost as if a sedative coursed through his veins.

It was time for his meeting. He began walking down the corridor towards Ken's office. Suddenly, the EMERGENCY ALARMS SOUNDED! He asked someone what was happening. "We are under attack by incoming missiles," he was told. The scenario seemed familiar to him. He remembered a dream he had not too long ago. All he would need to do would be to roll over to his left and shut off the alarm at the side of his bed, and all would be okay again. He turned and reached for the clock with his left arm, but as he did, all he felt was the corridor wall. Then he turned the other way hoping to feel the comfort of Mary Lou beside him. As he turned, he found himself face-to-face with the General.

"Ken, what should we do?" he asked.

"I'm sorry Jon. We are under attack. I let you down. We did our best, but we never found the computer virus."

"It's not your fault. I wanted to meet with you. I had new information about the identity of Teddy. I should have told you sooner. I guess it's too late now. I'm so sorry."

"Forget it! We need to get downstairs underground. Hurry!"

Just then, there was a loud thud immediately followed by a tremendous shaking. People were screaming. Both Jon and the General lost their balance and crashed against the wall. Jon could feel pain in his head and in his arm. Then something hit him right in the chest. He sensed a loud ringing in his ears. He cried out but to no avail. As he tried to move, he felt extreme heat engulf his body, and then there was total blackness. Doomsday had arrived!

14

BAD NEWS

The Memorial Day weekend was over. Early Tuesday morning, Carol walked the three blocks from her hotel to the FBI building in Denver. Agent McCarthy showed her into Colby's meeting room at 8:00 a.m. sharp. When she entered the room, she encountered a man, already seated. He immediately rose from his seat. There was instant recognition. She and Peter saw the same man at the Blue Columbine Saturday night.

"Hello, I'm Special Agent Richard Tracey. I believe we spotted each other Saturday night."

"I'm Agent Sanders. Another mystery solved."

"I believe we both have observations to report," he said.

Then another agent appeared. "Agent Sanders, this is my boss Special Agent Larry Hopkins."

"Pleased to meet you," she responded.

Roger Colby entered the meeting room with his second in charge, Special Agent Bernard Smith. They were fifteen minutes late. Colby had been in his office since 7:30 a.m. monitoring the arrest of Georgy Belinsky. It did not go as planned. Then as if that was not enough, he got a call from General Ken Morehouse, Deputy Director of Defense Intelligence, who informed him of a situation in the D.C. area. He would keep these matters to himself for now. Once they entered the room, the meeting started. Colby introduced Agent Sanders. "I believe we have already met, sir," was Agent Tracey's response.

"Yes, I'm sorry for the delay. I got caught up on another matter," Colby responded, and then continued. "Agent Sanders did an initial investigation last year in Colorado Springs that implicated an Ursula Behr using a code name Teddy, so I want Agent Sanders to hear this. I asked our surveillance division to track Ms. Behr. Her name popped up again recently, and Agents Hopkins and Tracey are here to report their findings."

"Okay, thank you, sir," Agent Tracey responded. "I was alerted Friday afternoon by my counterpart in San Francisco that a person named Ursula Behr was about to board a flight from San Francisco to Denver. He said she had gone off the grid more than a year ago and remained off the grid until recently. After she boarded, he called me again and gave me a detailed description of her. I picked up her trail when she got off a flight at Denver's Stapleton Airport Friday evening. Ms. Behr rented a car at the desk in the airport terminal and boarded a van to the rental car lot. I almost lost her, but was able to pick her up driving out the gate in a compact Dodge Dart. I followed her to the Dunphy Motel in Boulder. She paid cash in advance for a two-night stay under the name Angie Smith. An important detail may be that she wore glasses. Saturday morning, I followed her to the Panda Pizza Palace in Boulder, where she met with someone in a back room for about an hour. Afterwards she had something to eat, and then left. She made a couple of stops in the area, including a travel service, and then returned to her motel. She left the motel again at six in the evening and went to the Panda Pizza again. This time, she was not wearing glasses. She remained at Panda Pizza until a gentleman—I later learned was Georgy Belinsky— left with a calzone to go. Ms. Behr left immediately after him and followed him to his apartment—apartment number one sixty-five in the Boulder Garden Apartment Complex. Ms. Behr watched his apartment from her car in the parking lot.

"Shortly after nine, Belinsky left his apartment, and Ms. Behr followed. He went into the Blue Columbine Corral and she went in ten minutes later. I followed, and took a seat at the bar. From my seat at the bar, I watched Ms. Behr dance and make moves on Georgy Belinsky. I also watched Belinsky and Ms. Behr converse with your Agent Sanders and another gentleman who I later identified as Peter Troutman." This got Colby's attention, but he said nothing. "I saw Sanders and Troutman leave the Blue Columbine around eleven. At twelve fifteen in the morning, I watched Belinsky and Ms. Behr leave the Blue Columbine together. Belinsky and Behr then left the parking lot in separate cars. It appeared that she was following him by prior agreement. I continued to follow Ms. Behr, and I followed her to Mr.

Belinsky's apartment. He was waiting for her to arrive and the two entered his apartment together. I sat in my car, unseen by them, until she left at ten past two.

"I followed Ms. Behr to the Residence Inn in Boulder. I watched her enter the lobby and then—five minutes later—proceed to unit one-o-seven. The time was two thirty. I saw her ring the doorbell, knock on the door, and then when no one answered, I saw her—in my opinion—pick the lock and gain entry. She remained inside the unit for about twenty minutes and then left. She returned to her car. I followed Ms. Behr to the Dunphy Motel, where she stayed the night. She remained there until she checked out Sunday morning around ten.

"After leaving the Dunphy Motel, Ms. Behr made a stop at the Panda Pizza Palace and then drove to Stapleton Airport where she boarded a two o'clock flight back to San Francisco. I notified my counterpart in San Francisco. He saw her get off the plane, followed her out to the street, and saw her get into a taxicab. The cab company said they dropped her off at the Soviet Consulate in San Francisco.

"Meanwhile, I went to the car rental agency, where she had returned the car. They showed me a copy of her rental contract. The name on her California driver's license was Angelina Ursula Behr. The license number and name matched, but the Oakland address was phony. The contact phone number she left went to voice mail. We later determined that the phone number belonged to the Soviet Consulate.

"I have documented all the details of my observations in this report. I am leaving you with an official copy."

"Thank you very much. You did a fine job," Colby told him. "I'm going to talk with Agent Sanders now. You are welcome to leave."

Special Agent Hopkins spoke up. "If she's going to comment on Ursula Behr, we would like to stay. We feel it would be pertinent to our mission."

Colby tried to be tactful. "Agent Hopkins, your surveillance is part of a larger project that is highly classified. However, we will get back to you if we have further questions or need further assistance. Thank you."

Agents Hopkins and Tracey left the room. As soon as the two of them left, Agent McCarthy stuck her head into the room. "Sir," she said to Colby, "Agent Matthews is in your office . . . says it's important."

Colby turned to Agent Smith. "I think Matthews has a report from the lab regarding the AFOS software. Would you mind handling that while I converse with Sanders? . . . Thanks."

Then he turned to Sanders. "Sanders, you have some explaining to do. Perhaps you would like to speak of your observations now."

"Yes, I would. Thank you, sir."

Colby asked, "Agent Sanders, perhaps you could tell me why you were at the Blue Columbine."

"It was purely incidental, sir."

"Did you know that Belinsky or Behr was going to be there?"

"No, sir."

"What about Mr. Troutman? Did he know?"

"Peter . . . I mean Mr. Troutman may have known. He knew that Georgy often went there, and he also had intelligence from his CIA contact that may have given him some information that I wasn't privy to."

"Why did you talk to Belinsky and Ursula? Who initiated the conversation?"

"I believe it was Mr. Troutman's idea. He said that he and Belinsky were on speaking terms and that Belinsky was the one that told him about the Blue Columbine."

"What did you talk about?"

"Sir . . . am I being interrogated?"

"No, I'm sorry. Some things have happened. I'll tell you about them in a few minutes. Please bear with me."

"Please tell me everything you can remember about your conversation."

"Hmmm . . . Belinsky introduced her as Angie. He said they had just met that evening. They had danced a couple of times and she had said that she was new at country western dancing—"

"What did you and Troutman say to them?"

"Peter introduced me as Jean, and said I was just visiting for the weekend. We told them we had been to Pikes Peak."

"You don't think she or Belinsky knew you were FBI?"

"No, I don't." Colby's expression indicated relief.

"Sir, there is more information that Mr. Troutman wanted you to have. He said I could talk freely about this with you."

"What?"

"When we were at the Blue Columbine, he thought he recognized Angie or Ursula. He thought she could be the girl-friend of his CIA contact. He believed that the woman at the Blue Columbine was in disguise, but he noticed a telling scar on her neck. He was also sure that the woman recognized him."

"Did he give names?"

"No, but his contact did." Colby looked puzzled. "Troutman made a phone call to Jon Wilson early Sunday morning to report his suspicions. He reported details to him in a voice message. Wilson returned the call later in the day and left a message for Troutman. I listened to the message. Wilson seemed to agree with Troutman's suspicion. He said the girl-friend's name was Mary Lou. Peter wanted me to give you this envelope."

"What is it?" Colby asked.

"Open it."

"It's a picture of you and Troutman at the top of Pikes Peak. There is a message from someone, and there is a note from Troutman." Colby read the note from Troutman aloud.

Please find fingerprints of Ursula Behr on the message and on the photo. Compare to fingerprints of Mary Lou McGuinness, girlfriend of Jon Wilson.

"Can you explain this?" Colby asked.

"Troutman and I had been to Pikes Peak earlier in the day. We showed the photo to Georgy and Angie when we talked to them at the Blue Columbine."

"What about the message?"

"Troutman went to the lobby of the Residence Inn Sunday morning and was given the message by the person on duty at the desk. Apparently, someone left it for him during the night shift—probably Ursula Behr. Agent Tracey said she went to the lobby around two thirty."

"I see. So, tell me again what happened after you left the Blue Columbine."

"We went back to the Residence Inn."

"Something I'm curious about Sanders. Tracey said that at two thirty, Troutman was not in his room. Where was he?"

"He was . . . with me, sir," she said with hesitation. If the person at the Blue Columbine was Ursula, his life was at risk. I asked him to stay at my place." That revelation solicited a look of curiosity from Colby, but he did not say anything.

"Were either of you aware that she tried to get into Troutman's unit?"

"Not until we heard from Agent Tracey this morning. However, I had suspicions Sunday morning. While Peter was in the lobby, I checked out his room and found it to be clear. However, I noticed that the unit was unlocked when I entered. Later, on Sunday, Troutman and I both listened to that message from Jon Wilson. The message also said that Mary Lou called him 'collect' from Oakland. If she was the same person as Ursula, we knew she was no longer a threat to us."

"Are you sure she called from Oakland, not San Francisco?"

"I'm sure that is what Mr. Wilson said."

"All right, thanks."

"Sir, you asked that I bear with you. You said some things were happening that you would tell me about."

"Okay . . . and I will. I may need your help with something. Would you mind giving me about fifteen minutes and then coming to my office? I want to be by my phone."

Fifteen minutes later Sanders returned and Agent McCarthy showed her into Colby's office. Colby was on the phone. He motioned for her to take a seat.

When he was off the phone, he began talking. "Agent Sanders, let me tell you the good news first. Matthews has reported that the computer lab worked over the weekend and found the virus in the AFOS tape. Troutman was correct. You can tell him when you see him. The bad news is that Georgy Belinsky is dead. My agents went to his apartment this morning to take him into custody and found him slumped over his kitchen table. Initial indication was that he committed suicide or overdosed on drugs. We will analyze two packaged pills found on his kitchen table as well as a suicide note. Sanders, when you talked with him at the Blue Columbine how did he seem?"

"He seemed fine . . . in good spirits."

"The agent at the apartment says he thinks the scene may have been staged. It appears that death occurred more than twenty-four hours prior to this morning. Tracey's report had Ms. Behr at his place early Sunday morning. She may be the last person to have seen him alive. The autopsy will determine the time of death more precisely. We don't think it was suicide. However, until we prove otherwise, it is officially an apparent suicide—understood?"

"Understood," she repeated.

"I must ask about Troutman's whereabouts and your whereabouts that night. Could Troutman have left your unit during the night? Okay look, I'm not trying to judge your personal relationship—although we could have a separate discussion about that. I just need to rule out the possibility that Troutman is involved in the death or the staging of the scene."

Sanders shook her head. "He was not involved—what was it you wanted me to do for you?"

"I scheduled a meeting with John Armstrong at IBM for twelve thirty today. The purpose would be to notify him of Belinsky's death, to tell him we found the virus, to arrange to receive new tapes, and to return the beta test tape that he lent us. We kept a copy, so we can test the new tapes when we receive them. Mr. Armstrong said he was very busy today. I wanted to have the meeting before the rumor mill started, and I didn't want to tell him the bad news over the phone. I told him it was very important and he agreed to squeeze me in. However, I may not be able to go. My calendar says that I have a conference call scheduled for noon to discuss the status of the Boulder Creek project with the principals involved. I can't be on the call and still make it to the Boulder meeting. I would like you to go up to IBM in my place."

She was surprised he would ask her to do this. Colby was showing a great deal of confidence in her ability and people skills, she thought. The additional responsibility could be a great opportunity for her. On the other hand, she was still trying to sort out the intense emotions she still felt from the weekend. She wondered if her emotional involvement with Peter would interfere with her ability to do her job effectively. She wanted to ask Colby many questions—like why me? But she simply said, "Yes, sir," and nothing else.

"Sanders, there's more bad news. Jon Wilson was also found dead this morning."

"Oh God! No! . . . How?"

"On the surface, it looks like he died in his sleep of a heart attack. His girlfriend—Mary Lou—said she couldn't awaken him this morning. She called 911. They came quickly but could not revive him. Then she called General Ken Morehouse who is a good friend of Jon. Morehouse is also a Deputy Director at the Defense Intelligence Agency and in charge of the Boulder Creek Project."

"Does Peter know this yet?"

"No, you will need to tell him."

Agent Carol Sanders returned to her temporary office down the hall from Colby. She spent the rest of the morning trying to sort things out in her head. How would she present all of this to Armstrong and to Peter? It would be difficult telling Armstrong they found a virus in the product his employee delivered, and that his employee committed suicide. It would be even more difficult telling Peter his friend died. He would be upset. At ten minutes before noon, Carol was about to leave her office for Boulder when Colby called her on her desk phone and told her to come to his office.

"Come in," he said. "There has been a change in plan. My conference call on the Boulder Creek project has been postponed until tomorrow morning at ten-thirty our time."

"So, does that mean you don't want me to go to Boulder?" she asked.

"No, it means I'm coming with you. You're driving," he responded. Carol felt as if a heavy weight had just been lifted off her.

****

Meanwhile, back in Boulder, the team was having a normal workday. Around mid-morning, Michael asked Peter if he wanted to walk down to the cafeteria for coffee. He reminded Peter that he promised to tell him about his weekend. Peter obliged and told him about the very enjoyable weekend he had with a female companion. Of course, Michael had thought it was someone from back home and was surprised when Peter told him who it was. "Carol and I had a great time and I really like her," Peter told him. "She even lives near us in Maryland, but I don't know where this is headed. She went back to Denver last night to be ready for an early morning meeting today. She was supposed to call me last night but never did. So, I don't know. We'll see."

No sooner did they get back to their office than John Armstrong called Peter Troutman to an unexpected meeting. "I need you to be in my office this afternoon at twelve thirty," he said. "It's very important!"

When Peter arrived, Virginia greeted him and escorted him into John's office. He was surprised to see FBI agents Colby and Sanders as well as John Engels the AFOS Program Manager. Armstrong introduced Engels to Agent Colby and to Carol. "John, this is Special Agent Roger Colby and his assistant, Agent Carol Sanders. Agent Colby is the head of the FBI office in Denver. He asked for this meeting earlier today and said it was very important. I will let him tell us what this is about."

Colby stood as he spoke. "Good afternoon. I'll get right to the point. The Air Force requested our involvement. We found that the AFOS update tapes recently released to the Air Force contained a computer virus that, if executed, could knock out the entire satellite management network. That is why we are here. There is a chance that the master tapes held at IBM are also contaminated. The Air Force needs IBM to recreate new master tapes from scratch, and then re-release the updated copies. Peter Troutman, your lead auditor, has been instrumental in bringing this to light, and he can explain the technical details of what needs to be done."

"I can have Georgy do that," John Engels volunteered. "How many cartridges were there? Was it twelve?"

"Unfortunately, your employee Georgy Belinsky was found dead this morning. We believe the cause of death was a drug overdose. It may have been suicide."

"Holy Shit!" Engels exclaimed. He was stunned. It took a moment for this to sink in. "Why would he do that?" he asked.

"We believe that Belinsky was directly involved in embedding the virus onto the tapes. We went to his apartment this morning to take him into custody and question him. I'm sorry to have to tell you this," Colby said.

No one knew what else to say until Armstrong directed Engels to handle the job of recreating the tapes from the source code. He also instructed Engels to make an announcement to the AFOS employees that Belinsky died this morning in his apartment from an apparent drug overdose. "You don't need to mention anything more," Armstrong instructed.

"Yes, sir. I'll take care of it," Engels replied as he left the room.

"Mr. Troutman," Colby added, "it's okay with the FBI if you want to inform your audit team and your manager as well."

"Mr. Armstrong, before Agent Sanders and I head back to Denver, I'd like to meet with Mr. Troutman for a few minutes. Is there a private room that we could use?"

"Of course, you may use my private conference room. It's free for the next half an hour."

****

Peter and Carol followed Colby to the conference room. They were about to enter when Colby turned to Carol, and asked her to wait for him in the other room. He wanted to talk with Peter alone. Carol began to wonder why he had brought her along. Perhaps he just wanted a chauffeur or someone to talk with in the car, she thought.

Peter and Colby entered the room and Colby shut the door. Once seated, Colby got right to the point. "Peter, I have more bad news. I am very sorry to have to tell you this, but Jon Wilson died this morning of an apparent heart attack."

When Peter heard this, his mouth dropped open. **"No way!"** he responded. He stood up and started to pace the room, clearly agitated by the news.

"Are you alright? Please . . . sit down and tell me why you say that."

Peter sat back down with his head between his hands. He was upset. He remembered what Jon had taught him about managing his emotions. He got a grip on himself, lifted his head, and began to talk

"As you know I met with Jon only four weeks ago. The man was in great physical shape. I think he was murdered."

"Why do you think he was murdered?"

"When I met with him, he read me into the Boulder Creek project. He told me about Ursula Behr. He thought she could be the person managing the plot to put the virus into AFOS. I think he figured out the whereabouts and identity of Ursula Behr. I think that is why he was murdered. Jon asked that I inform him of any leads regarding her whereabouts, as I'm sure he asked you to do the same. This past Saturday night, Carol and I just happened to be at the Columbine Corral when we saw Georgy and a woman who I thought was Ursula Behr—Did you talk to Carol about this?"

"Yes, but I wanted to talk with you separately," Colby said. "You may recall details that she didn't. What did you see at the Blue Columbine Corral?"

"Over the next hour or so, we saw a woman who resembled the description we had of Ursula. We watched as she made moves on Georgy—"

"What do you mean by *moves*?"

"It looked to me that she was trying to seduce him. She was acting very friendly towards him. At first, I thought she was a prostitute, but they danced, talked, and shared a table near the bar. They seemed to enjoy each other's company. Perhaps he already knew her. Carol and I decided to walk over to the table and say hello. I knew that Belinsky was about to be arrested but I was still on speaking terms with him and he had no idea. I was curious about the woman. I needed a closer look. She introduced herself as Angie from Oakland California. She seemed to match the description of Ursula, but what got me most interested was that I got the feeling she recognized *me*."

"*Feeling?* Something she said?"

"No. It was nothing overt. More the way she looked at me. In fact, Carol thought she had spotted me from across the room before we introduced ourselves."

"Okay. Please continue."

"The four of us engaged in friendly conversation. When she talked, her voice and mannerisms seemed familiar to me. I couldn't figure out why she seemed familiar at first, but later I decided she reminded me of Mary Lou McGuinness, Jon Wilson's live-in girlfriend. I wasn't sure, and I did not let on that I recognized her. I did notice a faint scar under her left ear, but I couldn't remember if Mary Lou had such a scar—I only met Mary Lou once and it was very briefly.

"Meanwhile Carol and I both observed a man sitting at the bar. He seemed to be watching Belinsky and Angie. I guessed that he was either a DEA agent tracking Belinsky, or an FBI agent tracking Ursula. Was he an FBI agent? Was he tracking Ursula?"

"Yes, he was. The woman came from San Francisco on Friday using the name Ursula Behr. She had a roundtrip ticket. My agent kept tabs on her until Sunday morning. Tell me what happened next."

"I don't know. Carol and I left. Angie was all over Belinsky, and the man at the bar was still there when we left."

"What time did you leave?"

"Shortly after eleven."

"Where did you and Carol go after you left?'

"We went back to the Residence Inn where we are staying."

"Did either of you see or have contact with Belinsky or Ursula after you left the Blue Columbine?"

"No."

"Can you vouch for Carol?"

"Where are you going with this?"

"Relax. I'm not concerned about your personal relationship with Carol—although under normal circumstances, I might be."

"Yes. I can vouch for Carol."

"Carol said you were with her the entire night. Did either of you ever leave?"

"Not until after the sun was up the next morning."

"Did you know that your unit was broken into?"

"No, but the next morning both Carol and I suspected that it may have been. The Residence Inn told me that someone might have learned my unit number during the night. They left me a cryptic note. Carol checked out my unit and said that the door wasn't locked when she entered. However, I found nothing out of place or missing." Then, changing the subject, Peter asked, "Did you receive the envelope that I asked Carol to give you?"

"Yes, I did."

"Do you think that Ursula and Mary Lou could be the same person?"

"We don't have enough to prove that connection yet. We will check the fingerprints on the surface of the photo as you suggested. Peter, I have another question. Were you ever inside Belinsky's apartment?"

"No! What are you concerned about?"

"The suicide could have been staged. But if it is murder, trace evidence could implicate innocent people."

"Do you think that Ursula murdered Belinsky?" Peter asked.

"It's possible, but right now we don't know. My agent followed Belinsky and Ursula to his apartment. She was there for two hours and left around two ten in the morning. We don't know what went on inside the apartment or what happened after she left. And, as of now, we still don't have an exact time of death. Another question, how did you know that Belinsky was going to be arrested this morning?"

"Uh . . . I think that Carol mentioned it. Should she not have told me?"

"When did she tell you?"

"I believe it was Saturday night at the Blue Columbine. Yes, she was surprised when I suggested saying hello to Belinsky, saying he was about to be arrested."

"Did anyone else know? . . . Did you tell anyone? . . . Did you tell Wilson?"

I told no one. I didn't even know you had enough evidence."

"Peter, please let me know if you remember anything else that may help. . . Oh, one more thing, did you call Jon Wilson to warn him of your suspicions about his girlfriend?"

"I called him Sunday morning, He didn't answer, so I left a message. I called on his private line. The message machine is in his home office. He told me he keeps it locked when not there. I thought it was secure. I got a return message around dinnertime later that day. He seemed to agree with my suspicions and indicated he also had indications that Mary Lou wasn't who she claimed to be. . . Agent Colby, I gave you all the information I can recall. Can you answer a question for me now?"

"What is it?"

"I thought a great deal of Jon Wilson. He was a mentor to me. If you get any information regarding his funeral or memorial service, I would very much appreciate being informed?"

"I'll be sure and send it to you."

"Thanks."

When the two of them exited the conference room, they encountered Carol. She had been waiting in the lounge area surrounding Virginia's desk. Colby turned to Carol as she arose from her seat. "Agent Sanders, why don't you talk with Peter for a few minutes? I need to go to the men's room and drink some water . . . Be back soon."

Carol came over to where Peter was standing. She seemed concerned. "Peter, we just found out about Jon a couple of hours ago. I'm so very sorry. Are you alright?"

Was it the way she said it, or was it a delayed reaction to the bad news? Either way, Peter's emotions came to the surface and his eyes began to swell with tears. Carol put her arms around him and hugged him. Virginia pretended not to notice.

"I'll be okay. I appreciate your caring."

"I *do* care, Peter."

"I was hoping you would call last night."

"I know. I want to apologize for not calling you. I didn't sleep well—too many things racing through my head all at once. But, I do care."

"I really hope we stay in touch," he whispered.

"I would like to—"

Before she could finish, the sound of Colby's voice interrupted her. "Sanders, we need to go."

"Peter, I'm sorry. He has me on a short leash. We can talk later."

"Mr. Troutman, take care of yourself. I'll call you with the details you asked for," Colby said as the two of them left.

Peter went back to his office. He told his auditors about the discovery of a computer virus and about Belinsky's *suicide*. Then he called Greg and repeated the bad news.

****

The next morning, the local paper had a terse article on Belinsky's death. Peter thought that the reporter probably knew more than the paper allowed her to print.

IBM MANGER FOUND DEAD

by Lois Lane

Boulder Daily News

Georgy Belinsky, a computer room manager for IBM Boulder, was found dead in his apartment Tuesday morning. According to the authorities, he died of an apparent drug overdose. They could not say if the overdose was accidental or intentional. The County Medical Examiner will conduct an autopsy. He is expected to report his findings within a few days. Authorities on the scene would not reveal any other details.

****

Two days later, Peter got a call from Colby giving him details on Jon's memorial service. It would take place the following Monday evening at a funeral home in Vienna Virginia. Peter intended to go.

15

TRIBUTE

Jon Wilson had passed away in his sleep the previous Monday. Kathy Morehouse was the first person that Mary Lou called early Tuesday morning. Mary Lou seemed shocked, and angry all at the same time. She was upset, almost hysterical. Kathy had calmed her down and assured her that Ken would handle everything. Ken called the paramedics. He also notified the FBI. Mary Lou spent all day Tuesday dealing with medical people and investigators. She told Kathy she was unable to cope; much less stay in the condominium they had shared. Ken and Kathy had invited her to stay at their place in Vienna Virginia until she was able to get herself back together. She gladly accepted their offer.

Ken and Kathy Morehouse lived in a three-story colonial-style house not far from the center of town on a quiet street. It sat on a scenic landscaped third of an acre of land, slightly raised above street level. Ken and Kathy had no children at home, and with three bedrooms, three bathrooms, and a den with a sleeper couch, they had plenty of room for a guest. Three bedrooms were upstairs on the top level including a very large master bedroom with a private bath that Kathy loved. It had a large window with a view to the rear. The other two bedrooms shared a bath and faced the street. Kathy had eagerly prepared one of the bedrooms facing the street for Mary Lou and eagerly awaited her arrival.

On Wednesday morning, Mary Lou drove Jon's BMW from her condominium in Rockville to Vienna—about an hour away. She and Jon had been there several times before, and she knew the way. When she arrived, she drove halfway up the paved driveway and stopped before reaching the two-car garage. She got out and followed the paved walkway from the driveway to the main entrance centered in front of the house. She walked up the wide stairway, under a pillared canopy, and rang the doorbell. Kathy opened the double-glass doors and showed her in.

She entered the main level of the house. A large living room with a fireplace was on the right. Behind the living room were a dining area and a kitchen. The dining area opened to a large raised deck behind the house. On the lower level, a recreation room had a full-sized pool table, and Kathy had a laundry room. A door on the lower level led to a ground-level patio out back. Wooden stairs connected the patio and the upper deck. The house was ideal for parties and receptions, especially on warm summer evenings, something that Ken would often have as part of his official—and unofficial—duties.

Later that Wednesday, Ken returned from his day at the Pentagon. He drove past Mary Lou's BMW and into the garage where he could enter the lower level of the house from inside the garage. Jon had no family and before he met Mary Lou, he had named Ken his executor and trustee. Ken would make all the funeral arrangements. Ken had prepared an announcement for employees at the CIA and at the DIS. Ken wanted it released the next morning, but he wanted to be sure that Mary Lou saw it before releasing it. After supper, Mary Lou sat on the sofa in the living room and the three of them talked. Mary Lou's eyes filled with tears as she read the death announcement that Ken handed her.

> *We are saddened to report that Jon Wilson, a twenty-year veteran of the CIA and a former military officer, passed away unexpectedly at his home Monday night, May 30, 1988.*
>
> *Jon served as a military officer for Special Forces in Vietnam. Later, in the employ of the State Department and the CIA, he proved to be a talented operations officer, and an inspiring project leader. He cared deeply for the people he worked with. The classes he taught at the National War College about emotional intelligence are noteworthy. On behalf of the men and women of the CIA and the DIS, I offer our sincere and heartfelt condolences to Jon's loving partner, Mary Lou, and to his close friends and associates.*
>
> *There will be a special memorial service on Monday, June 6, 1988 at 5:00 p.m. It will be at the M&K Funeral Home, located at*

999 Maple Avenue, Vienna, VA. A reception for family, friends, and associates will follow at a location to be announced. Burial will be on a date to be determined at Arlington National Cemetery.

"Mary Lou, are you okay with this announcement?" Kathy asked.

"Yes, but where is he? Why can't I see him?" She was angry.

Ken interjected. "You may see him after the autopsy."

"Autopsy? Why is there an autopsy?" she screamed.

"Mary Lou, we talked about this. Because of Jon's work, and the untimeliness of his death, his body was taken to an FBI lab for a forensic autopsy. After the autopsy, you may be able to see him if you wish. I assure you this is routine in these situations."

"What do they expect to find?"

"They need to verify that he did not have any chemicals in his body and that he died of natural causes."

"I don't understand. He had a heart attack! How could they think otherwise?" She sounded agitated and excited. "Do they think *I* had something to do with it?"

"Mary Lou, we don't think that. Ken is just telling you what the standard procedure is."

"Sorry. I find this very upsetting. Don't I have any say in the matter?"

"Because you two were not married, you have no legal status in the matter. What is it that you are concerned about?"

"I don't like the idea of him being cut up," she said in a matter-of-fact manner. I don't think I want to see him again after that. I saw him before they took him away. He looked like he was sleeping. He would not be the same after that. Ken, I wanted his body cremated. When will they complete that autopsy?"

"I don't really know, but I'm hoping that it will be this week. I'm making all the arrangements. I'll let you know as soon as the autopsy is completed. After that, he can be cremated, and if all goes according to plan, you will have an urn with his ashes in time for the memorial service."

"Okay, thanks," she said despairingly.

****

Early Sunday evening, Mary Lou helped Kathy prepare dinner—veal cutlet scaloppini. The addition of red bell peppers, suggested by Mary Lou, made it more interesting. She and Kathy seemed to be getting along just fine. After Ken finished his yard work and washed up, the three of them sat down at the dining-room table and began to enjoy their meal.

"Kathy, this is delicious," Ken said.

"Mary Lou helped. It was a joint effort," Kathy replied.

"Then I thank you as well, Mary Lou."

"Ken, I need to ask you something," Mary Lou began. "Tomorrow is the memorial service, but Jon still has not been cremated. Ken, please tell me what is going on. Can we still have the service?"

"Yes. I am sorry for the delay, but we can still have the service. If all goes well, he will be cremated in the morning."

"I don't understand. Is the autopsy done?"

"Yes, but I'm still waiting for the report."

"What's holding it up?"

"They're just overloaded with work, and these things take time."

"What is it that they are looking for? You would tell me if they found something, wouldn't you?"

"Certainly . . . I'm sure there is nothing to worry about." Ken was lying to her. He knew that they had ruled the death suspicious, but before the FBI lab released the remains, they wanted to verify the exact manner and cause of death, and they had just received a key lab report late Friday.

"You have both been very nice to me this past week and I thank you. However, I'm starting to feel more normal again, and I need to move on. I've decided to spend time with my mother in Oakland."

"That sounds like a good idea," Kathy said after suppressing her initial surprise. "Did you tell your mother of Jon's passing?"

"No, I can't. She never knew about Jon. She is a very devout Catholic, and she would never accept my living with someone unless we were married. In her mind, I'm still married to my first husband. I never got a church annulment."

"Oh, I'm sorry. I didn't know," Kathy replied with sympathy.

"When are you planning to leave?" Ken asked.

"Wednesday morning, but I'll need to go back to the condo before I leave to pack some things. I hope you don't mind."

"No, why would we?" Kathy asked.

"Kathy, may I help you with preparations for the reception?"

"Yes, of course, I would appreciate some help tomorrow. You can come with me to pick up food."

"Since the reception is at our house," Ken added, "Kathy and I would like you to stay overnight afterwards. Then, Tuesday morning you can drive over to the condo. We'll help in any way we can. I wish I could do more to help during the day tomorrow but I must go to work—oh, and Kathy, I'll need the car. I have a very early meeting at the Pentagon. I'll get to the funeral home on time however. Several people from work may ride with me. Mary Lou, can Kathy share *your* car?"

"Not a problem," she replied.

"Oh, and that reminds me," Ken continued, "The funeral home has asked for a payment before the service. Mary Lou, can you have a check for them tomorrow as well?"

"I suppose, but do they need it tomorrow? How much do they need?"

"Twenty-five hundred, Ken replied. Didn't I give you the invoice?"

"Yes . . . yes you did . . . not sure if I have enough in the account to cover it though. The bank has not given me access to Jon's money, only mine. I'll need to stop at Travel Star and the bank tomorrow to deposit my last paycheck—I'll need to put gas in the car too. Kathy, if you tell me what you need from the store, I can pick that up for you. It may save you time."

"Thanks Mary Lou. There are some last-minute things that I need. I'll give you a list."

16

WARRANTS

On Monday, Ken was up early—before 6:00 a.m. He tried not to awaken Kathy or Mary Lou as he showered, put on his uniform, went downstairs, and helped himself to juice and cold cereal. He would have time for coffee later. He left the house by seven. It was important that he be on time for his 8:00 a.m. with the FBI. In theory, he would be at the Pentagon within one-half hour, but traffic was often unpredictable. He and Kathy only had one car. Often—when Kathy needed the car—Kathy would drop him off at the Metro station, about a mile away. However, today he needed the car, and he was leaving the house earlier than normal. Mary Lou had agreed to help Kathy with preparations for the memorial service in the evening. Mary Lou had said she would share her car with Kathy if necessary.

As he was the only one in the car, Ken could not take the fastest route—Interstate 66 only allowed High Occupancy Vehicles to the East of the Beltway. Rather than head south toward Interstate 66, he went the other way through town, took the Beltway going north to The George Washington Memorial Parkway, and then South to the exits for the Pentagon. Coming back that evening, it would be different. He would have passengers, and they would go directly from the Pentagon to the funeral home in Vienna.

Ken parked in his usual parking space. As a VIP, he had a reserved space, not far from the door closest to his office. Today however, he would go directly to his meeting. He entered the complex, made his way across the courtyard to the opposite side, and then took an elevator down to the underground level where the meeting would take place. The room was the same fortified and secure conference room where in March Jon had requested him to launch the Boulder Creek Project.

This morning's meeting was very important. The FBI would present the results of months of investigation relevant to the Boulder Creek Project. The attendees at the meeting included several top-level figures. The President's National Security Advisor sent a deputy to represent the President. Assistant FBI Director, Donald Gavin, who was in overall charge of the FBI portion of the investigation, represented the FBI. His primary responsibility was national security investigation and he operated out of the Washington D.C. office. He brought with him an assistant, Special Agent Gary Bloom. The Special Agent in Charge of the Denver Field Office, Roger Colby, also attended. Brian Matheson of the CIA was there in place of Jon Wilson. General Ken Morehouse, and his assistant, Colonel Robert Smythe, represented the Department of Defense. General Morehouse, who was the overall coordinator of the Boulder Creek Project, had called the meeting. He introduced everyone, gave the standard security lecture, and explained that he had asked the FBI to present the results of their investigation in support of the Boulder Creek Project. Then he yielded the floor to Director Gavin.

Director Gavin began by saying, "The primary purpose of the Boulder Creek Project—as I understand it—was to stop an attempt by a foreign government to sabotage the Air Force Space Command's Satellite Management Network. I believe we have been successful in doing that. The Boulder Creek Project resulted in several investigations going on simultaneously. I have prepared foils summarizing the results of each sub-investigation." With some help from Agent Bloom, he then proceeded to show and explain the following foils:

Death of Jim Hoffman

- Hoffman's death occurred May 8, 1987.
- The Coroner ruled his death suspicious.
- Hoffman's company was responsible for the design of the Air Force satellite management system.
- Although no theft was reported, Hoffman is known to have been archiving copies of the Air Force computer network the night before he died.

- Evidence indicated that on the day he died he had met with an Ursula Behr, who also referred to herself as Teddy.
- On the same day he died, $100,000 was wired into his bank account. This money was traced to Panda International.

Attempt to put a virus into the AFOS software

- The FBI determined that the AFOS delivery to the air force contained a harmful virus.
- the software was not installed in the air force computers.
- IBM provided replacements that are virus free.
- Installation will occur over the next three weeks.
- No additional viral software was found at IBM or elsewhere.
- The FBI determined that Georgy Belinsky planted the virus in the AFOS tape cartridges delivered to the air force.
- Evidence indicated that Belinsky obtained the viral code from Panda Pizza Palace in Boulder.

Bombing attempt of IBM auditors in Boulder

- An attempt was made to assassinate a team of four IBM auditors that were attempting to determine how a virus could be put into the AFOS shipment.
- The bomb maker was found and arrested and will stand trial.
- John Rizzuto, the person who hired the bomb maker, was also arrested and will stand trial. He is the brother of the owner of Panda Pizza Palace, Anthony Rizzuto.

Death of Georgy Belinsky

- Mr. Belinsky was found dead on Tuesday May 31 when the FBI went to his home to arrest him.
- The coroner ruled his death a homicide.
- Evidence links his death to Angeline Ursula Behr
- She was seen at the scene around the time of death
- We found her fingerprint on an opened drug package next to the body.
- We found **no** fingerprints on the suicide note.
- Evidence links the cause of death—potassium cyanide—to pills disguised as ecstasy obtained from Panda Pizza Palace in Boulder.

Illegal activities of Panda International

- The FBI determined that Panda International was an internationally based company that owned Panda Pizza Palace, Star Travel Agencies, and Panda Finance Corporation.
- Panda International was engaged in illegal activities. These activities included:
  ◇ Financing drug trafficking
  ◇ Money laundering
  ◇ Financing espionage activities for the Soviet Union
  ◇ Paying for murder for hire
- The owner of Panda Pizza, Anthony Rizzuto was arrested and charged with conspiracy to commit murder, drug dealing, extortion, loan sharking, money laundering.
- The Justice Department has frozen the assets of Panda Finance—an offshore division of panda international—and is building a case to stop all operations of Panda International in this country.
- The operations of Star Travel Agencies and the panda pizza chain remain under investigation.

Identity of Ursula Behr-aka Teddy

- After the death of Jim Hoffman, the FBI was looking for Ursula Behr. We interviewed and ruled out many people before we traced an Angeline Ursula Behr from San Francisco to Boulder on May 27. We established her connection to Panda Pizza and to Georgy Belinsky.
- A person who has met both Ursula Behr and Mary Lou McGuinness believes that the two Are the same person. His brief encounter with each, and the likelihood that Ursula Behr was in disguise, raises doubts about his observation. We do not yet have fingerprints known to belong to Mary Lou McGuinness. Until we obtain fingerprints from Mary Lou McGuinness, we cannot prove that they are the same person.
- The FBI compared fingerprints known to belong to Angeline Ursula Behr —taken from various sources —to all known databases. They found no matches.

- General Morehouse has had contact with her this past week. We have requested that he provide us with an article that she handled. This morning he provided us with a copy of the memorial service announcement that he gave to Mary Lou on Wednesday. It will take time for the lab to analyze it and lift her prints.

Death of Jon Wilson

- Jon Wilson did not die of natural causes.
- As of this past Friday, Jon Wilson's death was ruled a homicide. The medical Examiner found sedatives as well as unknown poisonous substances in his system. They found an injection site on his arm.
- Mary Lou McGuinness was the only one with Mr. Wilson at the time of death.
- After he died, Mary Lou had time to remove all evidence before the medics, police, or FBI arrived.

"Gentleman, the FBI believes that Mary Lou McGuinness, aka Angeline Ursula Behr, aka Teddy, may very well be the Soviet Agent that we are looking for. We believe she is directly responsible for at least three murders. Right now, she is a person of interest, but until we obtain her fingerprints, a murder weapon, or incriminating documents, we may not have enough proof to make an arrest. However, we do believe we have enough evidence to hold her for questioning. We would like to meet with her in her condominium and have her take us through last Monday night step by step. In addition, her condominium is now a crime scene. That gives us enough for a search warrant. We met with a judge late Friday and the warrant is already in process. We included the lifting of fingerprints in the requested warrant. We also believe she may flee. She has publicly stated that she plans to leave town on Wednesday. We want to move on this today. Does everyone agree?"

Everyone agreed in unison, except for Ken Morehouse.

"When?" Ken asked.

"This afternoon and certainly by tomorrow," Gavin responded.

Ken spoke, "This afternoon and early evening, we will have a memorial service and reception for Jon. Some of you, who knew Jon, may want to honor him with your presence. The reception afterwards will be at my house in Vienna. We have a large patio and deck out back. You are all invited. However, I would like to ask a favor. Out of respect, for Jon and those who want to honor him, I would appreciate it if you could hold off the arrest until tomorrow morning. As you may know, Mary Lou is staying with my wife Kathy and me. We will keep tabs on her, and I'm sure you guys at the FBI will as well. I should also mention that Kathy and Mary Lou have been friends. Kathy knows nothing of Mary Lou's misdeeds, or about *Boulder Creek*. I'd like to keep it that way. We expect that Mary Lou will return to her condo in the morning to pack. You can take her into custody tomorrow at the condo. She told us that she has tickets to fly out of here Wednesday morning to be with her mother. I did check, and she does have tickets to Oakland."

"We will handle it Ken," Director Gavin curtly replied.

17

THE SERVICE

Kathy left the house with Mary Lou around 4:15 p.m. about fifteen minutes later than they had planned. Mary Lou had driven to her bank in Maryland, and probably stopped at her condominium and did a few other errands as well. Kathy told her she was worried about how long she was gone. Mary Lou dismissed her concern. "I had more errands than I thought—things to buy for travel on Wednesday—the bank—gas. And I did bring you everything you had on your shopping list," she said in her own defense.

"Yes, and I thank you for that," Kathy replied. "I also appreciate your help making the salad. I was worried about getting all of that done before we left, but we made it. The food is all ready, and the house is clean. I feel much more relaxed now."

As they talked, Kathy noticed that Mary Lou seemed nervous. "Mary Lou, are you okay?" Kathy asked, with sympathy. Kathy remembered how nervous she had felt when she attended her sister's funeral not long ago.

"I'm fine, Kathy," she replied unconvincingly.

They were the first to arrive at the funeral home. The funeral home was a large two-story brick-faced building on the South West side of town. It was at a major intersection that was very accessible with plenty of parking. A cedar tree stood on either side of the main entrance. A host greeted them at the door as they entered.

"Are you here for the Wilson service?" he asked.

"Yes," Mary Lou replied, "but the Director has asked for a payment, and I have a check for him."

"Let me show you the way to his office."

Mary Lou gave the Director his check, and then she asked about the cremation. "I was hoping that Jon's remains would be here tonight for the service. Was that possible?"

"Yes," he replied, "General Morehouse was very persistent. The cremation occurred on Saturday at our affiliate to the South of here. I am pleased to inform you that his remains are here with us tonight. Everything has been set up in the Chapel. Let me show you the way."

The Director escorted the two of them down a hallway to a lounge adjacent to the chapel where the service would take place. They signed a guest book on a small stand near the entrance to the lounge. They entered a red-carpeted anteroom set up like a large living room, a lounge with easy chairs, and a sofa. Attendees would wait here for others until 4:45 p.m. The room had a pleasant scent of fresh flowers— roses perhaps? The red carpet and the red curtains concealing the room's only window gave the room a general hue of the color red. Once everyone arrived, attendees would enter the adjoining chapel where the service would take place.

While they waited for the others, Kathy and Mary Lou entered the chapel. Kathy wanted to check out the set up. She and Ken had spent a great deal of time on the arrangements. Ken had been there, but this was the first time she had been here. She wanted to ensure that everything would be perfect. Upon entering the chapel, she was struck by the general hue of baby blue and white. Coming from the anteroom, one could imagine the transition from hell to heaven. Kathy was pleased with what she saw. The chapel was much longer than it was wide. It had two aisles, one on either side of the room. In between the two aisles were rows of cushioned pews. There would be more than enough seats, she thought. A lectern from which people could speak was at the front of the chapel. It stood on a slightly raised altar just above the floor level; it had a microphone. A table was set up on the floor just below, between the altar and the seats to the right. On top of the table was a beautifully crafted wooden box containing Jon's ashes. A picture of Jon sat on a tripod next to the box. Kathy put her hand atop Mary Lou's shoulder and spoke. "Mary Lou, Ken said he would do what he could to have Jon's remains here for you. It looks like he succeeded. You should thank him."

"I will," she said politely.

Shortly thereafter, a non-denominational pastor arrived, and then Ken, who drove directly from work, arrived. He brought a couple of uniformed people with him. People introduced themselves and mingled until everyone arrived just before 5:00 p.m. There were perhaps fifty attendees in total. The anteroom was crowded. Attendees included several CIA employees and a few FBI employees. Most were there to pay their respects. A few were there on official business.

Peter Troutman also came to pay his respects. The audit team had flown home for the weekend and planned to return to Boulder on Tuesday. Earlier that day, they had been in the office at IBM in Bethesda. They were working with the boss, Greg Stevens, on the final report for the AFOS audit. They planned to present to Big John and to Roger Colby later in the week. Peter explained to Greg that a good friend had died and he needed to attend the memorial service. Peter could not tell Greg who Jon was, but Greg did not ask—perhaps he already knew. Peter left work early at 3:00 p.m. so he could be there in time. Jon had been good to Peter over the past twenty-one years. Peter owed him this.

As Peter entered the anteroom—lounge area—others were already going into the Chapel. He went to the guest book and noticed a familiar name, *Donna Wolf,* higher up on the list. He had not seen Donna since Saigon, more than twenty years ago. He thought about the wonderful relationship they enjoyed while working for the CIA. Her real name was Donna Cinelli back then. He had tried unsuccessfully to get in touch with her several times since then, but to no avail. Last year, he had contacted Donna's mother who told him that she was married and was now Donna Wolf. The relationship with Donna had been an open issue in Peter's life. He wanted closure. Peter entered the chapel and took a seat near the rear. He looked for Donna and despite the years, he recognized her right away. She was sitting near the front of the chapel and to him, as beautiful as ever.

The service itself was nice, but short. The pastor was the first to speak. He stepped up onto the altar and positioned himself behind the lectern.

"Hello everyone . . . I'm Pastor Norman Greene. Kathy and Ken Morehouse asked me to say a few words. Jon was not a particularly religious person, but he was a good man. He believed in doing the right thing. He had integrity and he was compassionate. Throughout his career, he worked with others from various cultures and various religions. He respected others and he was tolerant and respectful of other's ideas and beliefs. I have no doubt that God will find a place in heaven for Jon. Although Jon's life was short in terms of years, it was long in terms of deeds." Pastor Greene then read a passage from the Book of Wisdom 4:7-15 in the Revised Standard Version of the Bible. After his reading, he invited Kathy Morehouse to say a few words."

Kathy took her position behind the lectern and introduced herself to those who did not already know her. "Jon had no surviving family members," she said. "Ken and I may have been the closest thing to family that he had, and we agreed to arrange his funeral. Ken and I were good friends with Jon for many years. Ken will tell you more about that in a few minutes. Many of you here tonight worked with Jon. You may know him as a colleague or perhaps as a boss, but Jon was much more than that. He also enjoyed being with people and having fun. He enjoyed music; he enjoyed dancing; and he enjoyed a good party. Over the years, we did lots of that. We'll miss him. More recently, we came to know Jon's *significant other*, Mary Lou. Mary Lou has been staying with Ken and me this past week. I know this is hard for you, Mary Lou, but please say a few words."

"Good evening, I'm Mary Lou. I want to thank Ken and Kathy for their support. I was with Jon for the past two years. Kathy mentioned other interests that Jon had. Jon was a jogger and we first met jogging along the river near the Pentagon. I know that some of you may not approve of the fact that we were not married, but we talked about it. It was not something that mattered to Jon. He said that so long as we loved each other that was all that was important. As you can imagine it was a shock when I tried to wake him last week." Mary Lou got tears in her eyes as she tried to continue. "I'm sorry, I'm still upset. Please forgive me," she said as she headed back to her seat next to Kathy. Kathy put her arm around her to comfort her as Ken went up to the lectern.

"I want to thank all of you for coming. Jon would be happy to know how much he was appreciated. I'm Ken Morehouse. I'm still on active duty so some call me *General*. Jon just called me *Ken*. We graduated in the same class at West Point many years ago. We have been friends ever since. While I stayed with the military, Jon chose the CIA. We both saw a lot of bad things happen to people during our careers, but Jon found a way to help those who needed it. He taught courses and counseled individuals on how to deal with emotions and emotional trauma. He liked to help people. Like the pastor said, *he was a good man.*

"I want you all to know that Kathy and I will have a reception, some of you may call it a repast—a new word I just learned—at our house immediately after this service. There will be a light supper and wine. . . Oh, Kathy just corrected me to say that we will not leave for the house immediately, but we will be here in the anteroom for about fifteen minutes before we leave here. Our house is less than a mile away. Directions are on the pedestal outside the anteroom by the door. Also, by the door is information on Jon's interment at Arlington National Cemetery. The date is set for the seventh of September."

After the service, people began to file back into the anteroom. Peter waited in the rear of the Chapel near where he had been sitting. He hoped to speak with Donna. He thought he might catch her on her way out of the chapel, but the opportunity faded quickly. He saw her near Jon's remains up front and she was talking to the General. Peter started toward the aisle on the right, opposing the flow of traffic. He did not get very far when he heard someone behind him and felt a hand on his shoulder.

"Mr. Troutman . . . Mr. Troutman, may I have a moment?" As Peter turned, he found a hand extended.

"I'm Brian Matheson," he said.

Peter automatically took his hand and they shook.

"Please to meet you," Peter said. "Have we met?"

"No, but I have heard good things. I need to talk with you."

"What about?" Peter asked.

"Mr. Troutman, I reported to Jon Wilson, and I'm taking over his project load. I need to talk with you about Boulder Creek."

"I see," Peter responded, unsure if this person was on the level.

"I've been going through Jon's notes. He wasn't much for keeping records, and I talked with Roger Colby this morning. I'd like to get a better understanding of what you did. I understand that you may be entitled to additional compensation, and we can talk about where the project goes from here. I was hoping we could meet within the next few days to make sure we're on the same page."

"Sure. I'm in Boulder for the remainder of the week," Peter replied. Any chance we could meet on Saturday?"

"Can you be at Langley on Saturday at ten?"

"Okay. I'll see you then."

Peter then turned back toward Jon's remains. It was too late! Donna was no longer in sight. She must have left with the General out a door near the front of the chapel. Peter assumed that the door must have led back to the hallway. He was disappointed, but he had more of an obligation, he thought, to talk with Mary Lou. Since he had met her at Jon's apartment, protocol required him to express his condolences. He also needed to verify that he had indeed seen her at the club in Boulder. Mary Lou was on the left side of the Chapel talking with Kathy. He approached them.

"Hello, I'm Peter Troutman. I thought you and the General have done a wonderful job." As he said this, he noticed that Mary Lou seemed eager to leave, so he immediately turned his attention to her.

"Mary Lou, we met briefly at your apartment almost two months ago. I'm very sorry for your loss. I hope you're managing okay."

"Thank you," she said. "Kathy is helping me through this." As she talked, he noticed the scar at the top of her neck just below her left ear. He had not imagined the scar; it was there.

Then Kathy asked, "Mr. Troutman, did you work with Jon?" It was a safe question to ask; He could answer it without divulging any secrets.

"Yes, I did. It was more than twenty years ago, but we have stayed in touch." Probably their presence in Vietnam, and what they did there, was still classified, so Peter did not mention it. "I have always had a lot of respect for Jon and I feel very badly about his death."

Peter tried to converse with Mary Lou but found it difficult. Something did not click. She seemed on edge. Did Mary Lou think he recognized her in Boulder?

Then, he spied the General again. He had re-entered the side door in the front of the Chapel. This time, Peter watched as another man engaged him in what seemed like a heated debate. Then the man left and walked out the door. Peter wanted to meet the General, so he excused himself and went in that direction. He introduced himself to the General. Although they had never met, Peter already knew he was the head of Defense Intelligence.

"Hello, General. I wanted to introduce myself. I'm Peter Troutman. I thought you arranged a very nice tribute to Jon. I thought a great deal of Jon and he has helped me throughout my career."

"I know who you are. I want to thank you for your help with Boulder Creek. Jon had good things to say about you. You are welcome to come over to our house for the reception." Peter never knew all the players on Boulder Creek, but this revelation did not surprise him.

"Do you know if Donna will be there?" This caught Ken a bit off guard.

"How do you know Donna?" he asked.

"I worked with her many years ago. I was just hoping to say hello."

"Well, unfortunately, I was just talking with her, and she apologized that she was unable to make it to the reception . . . Sorry, but *you* are still welcomed."

"I thank you, but I have an early flight in the morning. I'll have to decline . . . General, you may already know this," Peter said softly, "but Mary Lou and Teddy are the same." The General looked surprised that Peter would know this. "I hope justice will be served."

"Peter, walk down the hall with me." The General draped his arm over Peter's shoulder and escorted him out the door and down the hallway to a place where no one would overhear their conversation.

"Peter, I just learned this, but you must keep this to yourself. It's classified, and my wife can never know this." As he continued, his tone seemed to get testy. "In case you didn't notice, not everyone in the chapel tonight was here to pay their respects. An arrest is imminent, but out of respect for Jon, I have asked that it be in the morning, and not tonight."

"General, thanks for telling me. We're on the same side," Peter said as he extended his hand.

"Peter, I'm sorry if I got testy."

They shook hands and parted company.

Peter walked down the hallway to the men's room before the long drive home. When he came out of the room, he noticed the same man as before talking with the General. They seemed to be having another heated debate. Then, the man left, and shortly thereafter, everyone else left. Peter did not give it another thought.

****

Whereas about fifty people had attended the memorial service, less than twenty-five came to the reception at Ken and Kathy's house. Considering the hour, and the distances involved, this was not surprising. Nevertheless, one couple that lived in Jon's apartment building managed to be there. Several of Jon's employees attended, including Brian Matheson and his wife, as well as his administrative assistant Jim Miller and his wife. Others included three people who worked in Mary Lou's travel agency. Also present were several members of the FBI, including Special Agent Gary Bloom. Agent Bloom was there on business.

As the guests arrived, Ken and Kathy made a point of introducing everyone to everyone else. Many of the guests did not know each other, and Ken and Kathy thought it important to encourage friendly conversations between them. Ken knew many of them formally from his work, and he wanted them to feel comfortable being at his house. He also hoped that the few who knew the true circumstances of Mary Lou and Jon's death would be careful not to say the wrong thing. Earlier in the evening, Ken had a conversation with Donald Gavin, and Gavin promised that his agents would not make an arrest until morning. Yet . . . despite the assurance, Ken was not sure he could trust the FBI. It would be a disaster if Mary Lou was tipped off by something that was said. In Ken's mind, it would be an even bigger disaster if Kathy suspected something. If Kathy got suspicious, she would go right to Mary Lou and start asking questions. Mary Lou would be forewarned, and Kathy could be hurt—emotionally if not physically.

As it were, most of the conversation between guests was at a friendly but superficial level—small talk. Almost everyone there had a security-clearance of some type. So, a question like *"Where do you work and what do you do?"* was understood to be a non-starter. Ken gave several people a quick tour of the house. Some people marveled at how nice a house it was, or what a nice deck they had. Some people made favorable comments to Kathy and Ken about the funeral and reception, others about the food.

During the evening, several guests re-expressed their condolences to Mary Lou. They said things like: *We're so very sorry. —How are you holding up? —What are your plans? —This must have been a real shock for you. —He seemed so healthy. —I did not realize he had a heart condition. —Did he take medication for his high blood pressure?* Mary Lou did a masterful job of responding to everyone without revealing anything close to the truth.

The guests mingled between the living room, the kitchen, and the outdoor deck. The kitchen had large sliding doors that opened onto the deck in the back of the house. The weather was nice and Kathy was pleased to be able to use the deck. It was a large deck and the ideal place to set up the hors d'oeuvres and the wine bar. Guests could help themselves to canapés, nuts, or cheese and crackers while enjoying a choice of red or white wine. Then they could prepare themselves a dinner plate from the buffet set up in the dining room. Kathy had borrowed a large crock-pot from her neighbor and made a hearty beef stew with tender chunks of beef, potatoes, carrots, and onions. She also made a delicious Thai chicken dish consisting of a bed of white rice topped with boneless chicken breasts and covered with a curry sauce. Slices of green olives in the sauce gave it a special flavor. It was delicious. In addition, Mary Lou had made a tossed salad containing lettuce, tomatoes, shredded carrots, black olives, and shredded green and red peppers. For dessert, Kathy had made a fruit and gelatin mold. There was more than enough food and beverage.

The sun set around 8:30 and the reception ended around 9:30. Mary Lou helped with the cleanup and then she thanked Kathy for helping her through her ordeal and for a lovely service.

"You are welcome, Mary Lou, but you should thank Ken as well. He went out of his way to give Jon the memorial that he deserved. The two of them were very close, you know."

"I know. The two of you have been wonderful, but I have imposed on you way too much. I was thinking I should drive back to the condo tonight." Ken's ears perked up when he overheard this, but Kathy saved the day.

"No! No!" she said. "You need to stay here tonight. It's late. You must be tired, and it's a long drive. Please spend the night. You can start fresh in the morning."

"Well . . . okay, but I should be out early . . . like by seven thirty say."

"Not a problem." Kathy gave her a hug.

Mary Lou thanked Ken, said, "Good night," and then went upstairs to the guest room. As she approached the window to lower the blinds, she noticed a black sedan parked on the other side of the street.

18

HOMEWARD BOUND

After enjoying a quick breakfast with Ken and Kathy, Mary Lou was ready to go. She told them she wanted to get an early start. She kept looking at her watch. It was now 7:30 a.m. Ken helped load her suitcase into the back seat of her car, as she thanked them profusely for being so supportive in her time of need. She hugged them both, slid into the driver's seat, and started the engine. As she drove off, she could see the black Ford sedan in her rearview mirror. It was following her.

The Ford followed her onto the D.C. Beltway and across the state line into Maryland. *Must be a Fed*, she thought. There was no way she could shake him. It made her nervous, but she made a point of not exceeding the speed limit. Being stopped and delayed was the last thing she needed. She drove directly to her condominium and onto the top level of the parking garage behind the building. She removed a small bag from the rear seat, and a larger bag from the trunk. She then made her way into the rear entrance of the building.

The Fed parked his car on the shoulder of the main road above. He had no need to follow her into the parking area. From his vantage point, he could see everything. He could see that the garage had two levels. The top level was uncovered. He watched Miss McGuinness enter the building. He could still see her car. He also observed that the garage had a lower level. The lower level had a separate entrance and exit. There was no indication of a ramp connecting the two levels. However, all cars that entered or exited either level of the garage had to pass in front of him before returning to the main road.

"Command, this is Tec-One," the Fed said as he spoke into his radio. Do you read me?"

"Loud and clear. What is the status?"

"Suspect parked on the top level and just entered the building."

Special Agent Gary Bloom oversaw this operation. "Roger that," he replied.

"Command to team . . . Suspect is in the building – lobby level."

The rest of Bloom's team had arrived earlier and were already in position and waiting. They wore business suits and had radio-phones with ear buds. Agents Johnson and Cummings were executing a search warrant in Jon and Mary Lou's unit on the nineteenth floor. Agents James and Smith were waiting in the lobby.

The plan was that Agent James and Agent Smith would arrest Mary Lou when she came in from the garage and went to use the elevator.

"Agent James to Command . . . I've had my eyes trained down the hallway past the elevators expecting her to come through the door from the garage. She never did. The elevators and stairs go down to the lower level. The mailboxes are down there. She could be down there. Over."

"James, go down to the lower level and find out what is going on!"

"Wilco," Agent James responded.

"Command to Johnson . . . Any sign of her on the nineteenth floor?"

"Negative," Johnson replied.

Bloom continued. "Watch the elevators and stairs on the nineteenth floor in case Mary Lou ends up there."

"Roger."

The time was now 8:42 a.m. Seven minutes had gone by since Mary Lou entered the building. That was more than enough time to stop at the mailbox, get the elevator, and make it up to her unit. Where did she go?

"Command to James . . . No sign of suspect upstairs. What are you seeing down below?"

"Nothing, sir. No sign of her on the lower level. However, there is another set of stairs connecting the two levels of the garage before one enters the corridor leading to the lobby and the elevators. It's possible that she took those stairs from the top level to the lower level of the garage, and got into another car. Over."

Special Agent Bloom felt a sudden sickness in the pit of his stomach.

"Command to Tec-One . . . Our suspect is a no-show. What are you seeing?"

"Her car is still there, and she did not come back out of the building."

"How many cars left the lot from the lower level?"

"Only three."

"Describe the cars that left."

"First, there was a dark blue BMW driven by a man wearing a suit . . . no passengers. Then a black Mercedes sedan driven by a man came out. I couldn't see any passengers . . . windows were tinted. Then, there was a Volvo driven by a middle-aged woman. One more car is leaving right now. It's a black Lincoln sedan driven by a man. Windows are tinted."

"Can you see the license plate?"

"Uh . . . Maryland plates, nothing special."

"What about the Mercedes?"

"What about it, sir?"

"The plates!"

"Uh . . . I'm trying to remember. I think they were diplomat plates."

"Do you recall any letters on the plate?"

"The Mercedes came out from the lower level and the angle was not good, but I recall the letter *D*, then an *F* . . . and I think the next letter was either a C or an O."

"Any numbers after that?"

"Three . . . but I couldn't make them out. . . Sorry, sir."

"Did you see that car go into the lot before it came out?"

"No, sir. No cars have entered the lot since I have been here. You don't think *she* was in the Mercedes . . . do you sir?"

Special Agent Bloom considered the possibility but refrained from saying anything. She could have taken the stairs down to the lower level of the garage and gotten into a car that was already there waiting for her. There were many black Mercedes sedans with diplomat plates in the D.C. area. If these plates had the letters *D* followed by *FC* that would be a car registered to the Soviet Embassy. Could be that at least one of those diplomats lived here. On the other hand, it would be a perfect escape. Without a full plate number, it would be difficult to find. In addition, even if they did find it, the FBI was not allowed to stop and search a car with diplomat plates unless there was an immediate threat to public safety.

"Stay there and keep watching. Block the entrance if you need to but check every car that leaves. Let me know if our suspect could be in any of them."

"Wilco."

"Command to team . . ."

****

The team received instructions on what to do next. They searched the building—she was not there. They interviewed people—no one saw her. Perhaps the driver of the BMW saw her—he was gone. They reviewed the list of registered plates that paid for garage parking. Two cars had diplomatic plates. One was black. Neither car was there now. They searched the cars in the parking garage; she was not there. Was there a security camera? Yes, but no tape. Special Agent Bloom put out an alert for the black Mercedes with the diplomatic plates and a possible female passenger. The FBI would also watch the airports. Perhaps they would get lucky and be able to arrest her when she left the car. What else could they do? Apparently, Mary Lou had escaped.

The FBI searched her condominium for all the evidence they could find and added to their collection of fingerprints. Meanwhile, they got a special court order and went to Mary Lou's bank. The bank reported that Mary Lou McGuinness had cleaned out her account *yesterday*. She must have cleaned out her safety deposit box as well; it was empty.

Special Agent Bloom was distraught as to what he would report to the Assistant Director. He muttered to himself, *"Damn, why did we listen to the General? We should have taken her into custody last night"*

****

Mary Lou McGuinness could feel the vibrations penetrate her body, as she lay curled up on the floorboard between the seats of a black Mercedes.

A minor inconvenience, she thought.

Her escape plan had been in place for some time. After she had parked her car on the top level of the garage, she used her badge to enter an enclosed stairwell connected to the main building. She did not walk through the entrance to the lobby and the elevators. Instead, she went directly down to the lower level of the garage. She walked out the door and set her luggage down on the pavement.

Her driver from the Soviet Embassy was waiting for her in a black Mercedes sedan. He had driven up to the door and popped the trunk. "Good morning, madam," he had said in perfect Russian. He did not look like your typical chauffeur. He was wearing a gray business suit and tie—no hat—no badge. His car could have passed as a private luxury car. He had picked up Mary Lou's luggage and loaded it into the trunk. Then he held the rear door of the car open, helped her onto the floor between the seats, and covered her with a black cloth. Her escape plan was working.

****

That evening, the FBI interviewed the owner of a black Mercedes. He lived on the third floor and denied knowing Mary Lou McGuinness or Jon Wilson. The FBI also verified that he drove straight to the Soviet Embassy that morning, but they could not verify the exact time he left the garage. There was no way the FBI could verify that Mary Lou was in that car. She may have been, or she may have been in another similar car. Regardless of what car she was in, it was not even clear where they went. If someone drove Mary Lou to the Soviet Embassy that morning, she may have left the embassy in another vehicle. Perhaps she would remain at the embassy overnight—not likely, according to Agent Bloom. Possibly, they drove directly to an airport or a train station.

The FBI followed up on all possibilities. No one matching Mary Lou's description, or Teddy's description, boarded a plane at any of the three airports in the D.C. area. No one showed up to use the ticket that Mary Lou had for Wednesday morning to fly from National Airport to Oakland, California. Spotters at the train and bus stations in both D.C. and Baltimore came up with nothing. She had vanished.

It was Wednesday afternoon before the FBI finally figured it out. Apparently, The Department of State allowed Soviet diplomats to travel between Washington D.C. and New York City after receiving prior permission. The Soviet Embassy in the District of Columbia had received prior permission to transfer a diplomat from D.C. to the consulate in New York City. The diplomat from D.C. would replace a diplomat at the Soviet Consulate in New York City who would return to Moscow. Late Tuesday morning, a car bearing Soviet diplomatic plates was on its way to New York City. It arrived at the Soviet Consulate in late afternoon. Later, a car with

Soviet consulate plates drove a diplomat and his administrative assistant to JFK Airport on Long Island. On Tuesday evening, June 7, 1988, Boris Askov and Inga Sarnoff boarded a Pan American 747. It was a direct flight from JFK to Moscow. They had Soviet diplomatic passports and credentials. Airport security cameras, reviewed the next day, showed that Inga resembled Mary Lou McGuinness. The FBI compared fingerprints on the check-in paperwork to those of Mary Lou McGuinness. They were the same! Two weeks later, the Department of State declared her *Persona Non Grata*. Her whereabouts were unknown.

19

FINAL REPORT

On Tuesday, the morning after Jon's memorial service, Peter and Greg returned to Boulder along with the rest of the team. They spent Tuesday afternoon reviewing and fine-tuning the audit report. The next day, Peter and Greg presented the report to FBI Special Agent in Charge Roger Colby. They met with him in his Denver office late morning. Agent Don Matthews also attended. Agent Sanders did not. After discussing the report in detail—and to Greg's surprise—Colby approved presenting it to IBM management without any changes. The detailed written report was marked Secret for the DOD and the FBI and Registered IBM Confidential for IBM. Peter had made sure that nothing in the report was above that security level. He considered that he might need to have a second version of the report at a higher security level, but that was unnecessary. It would be up to the higher-ups in the FBI or the DOD to write reports on the Boulder Creek Project, not him.

After reviewing and approving the report, Colby revealed that John Rizzuto was under arrest, and charged with various counts associated with the car bombing. The person that made the bomb and placed it on the car had turned on him. At this meeting, Greg also learned that the FBI lab had located a virus in the tapes that were delivered to the Air Force and that IBM had redone all the tapes, and re-released them to the Air Force—something Peter had already known. The Air Force rescheduled the tapes for installation—only a month later than originally planned.

"Mister Stevens," Colby told him, "You and your team did an excellent job. Troutman here was instrumental in revealing the vulnerability that allowed a virus to show end up in the AFOS software. He was very persistent at the right times. I just want to say thank you."

"I appreciate the compliment," Peter replied. Peter was especially pleased that Colby was willing to give him praise in front of his manager.

Peter and Greg were rising from their seats to leave when Colby said, "I would like to meet with Troutman privately before the two of you leave. I hope you don't mind. We won't be too long."

"Ah . . . sure," Greg said, sounding slightly annoyed. "Peter, I'll be out at the car having a smoke. See you in a bit."

Then Colby had a second meeting with Peter regarding the Boulder Creek Project. Colby asked a few questions but had no issues. Then, Colby once again expressed his sorrow over the loss of Jon Wilson, and asked Peter about the service.

"Did you attend the service? How was it?"

"Yes, it was a very nice service. General Morehouse and his wife Kathy did a wonderful job. I went to the service but was unable to attend the reception at their house afterwards because I had an early flight back here on Tuesday. I apologized to the General."

"Unfortunately, I could not make any of it," Colby said. "I was in D.C. on Monday, but something came up and I had to get back here Monday night. Have you talked with Brian Matheson?"

"Matheson? . . . Why?"

"He is Jon Wilson's second in command at the CIA, and now that Wilson is gone, he is trying to get up to speed on all of Wilson's projects. He was at our Boulder Creek Project status meeting this past Monday morning, and afterwards I brought him up to speed on many of the details. During our conversation, I told him about your contributions. Sometimes the CIA will use people and after they no longer need them, they ignore them and treat them as if they never existed. I wanted to be sure that didn't happen to you. I told him how instrumental you were to finding the viral software and exposing the people behind it. I told him that you deserved compensation for your contributions. He seemed to agree and said he would contact you."

"I see. I appreciate your speaking on my behalf and saying that you appreciated my efforts. I have worked on projects for Jon in the past, but the only praise I ever got was from Jon—usually too much secrecy involved for me to expect anything else. Anyway, to answer your question, Matheson introduced himself later that Monday at the memorial service. We agreed to meet this Saturday at Langley to talk about my involvement, compensation, and future possibilities."

"That's good. Just be careful about what you get yourself into," Colby warned and then changed the subject. "Before you leave, I think you deserve to be brought up to speed on some of the things you were involved with."

"I appreciate that. Were you able to prove that Mary Lou McGuinness, aka Teddy, killed Jon?" Peter asked.

"Yes, we were, and the fingerprints that you obtained were very helpful. We found a real good one on the photo of Pikes Peak. Then, yesterday when the FBI went to Jon's apartment, they were able to obtain several prints of McGuinness, and the prints matched. That was good work—risky, but good."

"What about Belinsky?"

"He was definitely murdered, and we had enough evidence to convict her for both murders. Unfortunately, when we went to arrest her yesterday, she managed to escape. Her embassy helped her to flee the country and return to Moscow. That means no further evidence is required and you won't need to testify in court."

"Well, I guess that's a plus," Peter said with some sarcasm.

"This meeting is probably your last meeting with me on the Boulder Creek project. The FBI considers your assignment completed. You do know, though, that the project remains classified and you still can't talk about it."

"Of course, but I was wondering about Panda International. Will they be shut down?"

"As you know, Agent Sanders—or should I say Carol— is still working on that. It will be a few weeks yet before that is complete but we expect to shut down all their operations in the United States. We will wrap up the Anthony Rizzuto investigation along with it."

Colby also revealed that the investigation of John Rizzuto's brother Anthony—who managed Panda Pizza—was still underway at that time. Selling drugs, money laundering, conspiracy to commit murder, and treason were on the table.

"I haven't heard from Carol in more than a week. How is she?" Peter wanted to know.

"So here is your dilemma," Colby responded. "I know you two were involved in some way. None of my business of course, except—now that you are no longer on the project—she can't talk to you about her on-going work."

"I understand. Perhaps you could just let her know I asked about her."

"I will. You have a good day now."

****

Peter walked out of the FBI building and across the street to the parking lot. He found Greg leaning against the car smoking a cigarette, possibly his second one. "Sorry to keep you waiting, Greg."

"Not a problem," Greg replied curtly, and took another drag on his cigarette.

"I see you found something to bide the time," Peter said as he pointed to the cigarette in Greg's hand.

"Please don't start in on me," Greg responded as he defiantly took another drag on his smoke. He showed no inclination to snuff his cigarette so they could be on their way, so Peter turned his back to the car and positioned himself next to Greg.

After surveying the scenery—mostly cars and traffic—and taking in a breath of fresh air, Peter commented, "Sure is nice weather today, isn't it?"

"If you say so," Greg responded despondently.

"I'm sorry, Greg. You seem annoyed. What is bothering you? Does it have anything to do with Colby wanting to speak to me in private? You seemed annoyed then as well."

"I was. He made me feel like a kid being told to leave the room so the adults could talk . . . but it wasn't just that. I forgot to call my wife yesterday after I got here, and when I called today, she said she was too busy to talk to me."

"Well, I'm sorry about that," Peter said in a sympathetic tone. "Did you apologize?"

"I tried but she hung up before I got a chance."

"Greg, you told me you wanted to stop smoking but didn't know how. I just observed something that may help, if you're willing to hear me."

"All right, go ahead," he said begrudgingly. "You're probably going to say it anyway."

"What I noticed is that you tend to smoke when you are feeling hurt in some way. Your feelings trigger your desire to smoke. Smoking helps you relieve the tension and cope with the feelings."

"Hmmm . . . maybe. What do I do about it?"

"You have two choices. First, you can put your feelings into a different perspective and perhaps the intensity of your feelings will lessen. Your wife will forgive you—Colby was very pleased with our report. Focus on that. The other thing you can do is find a different way to help yourself feel better. For example, you could just take a walk. Instead of a smoke, you could have a hard candy, or a stick of gum . . . even a cup of coffee or a soda might work. I wouldn't recommend alcohol or putting your fist through a wall though."

"May I ask what you and Colby *did* talk about, or is that above my security level?" Greg asked in a slightly sarcastic tone.

"Well, some of it was personal, but since you were just open with me, I'll share it with you. Colby was concerned about my relationship with one of his female agents."

"Oh my God Peter, I hope we're not talking about sexual harassment in the workplace."

"What? No, of course not," Peter responded, surprised that Greg would think that. "I don't think you met her, but I told you that after the bomb scare, one of Colby's agents met with us. She did a wonderful job of helping us get through it—especially Debbie. Her name is Carol Sanders. Colby assigned her to work with me. We met the evening of the bomb scare and rode together to three meetings in Denver after that. We got to know each other well. Anyway, we spent the Memorial Day weekend together. I have hopes of seeing her again. However, Carol is working on matters that are highly classified and Colby is concerned that if we see each other, she may divulge information that she shouldn't."

"Aren't you still working with her?"

"No."

"Colby?"

"No. My work is done. Tell you what, let's head back to Boulder, and get some lunch. I'll tell you a cigarette joke while we drive."

As they headed back to Boulder on Route 36, Peter told Greg the following riddle:

"A man is sitting in a rowboat and he's fishing. Not getting much action, he decides he needs a smoke. So, he takes a cigarette out of the pack he has in his pocket and puts it in his mouth. Only then does he realize he has no matches—no way to light up. What should he do?"

"I don't know . . . Quit smoking?" Greg ventured.

"Great idea, but unfortunately he just could not get himself to do that."

"So, what does he do then?"

"He removes another cigarette from the pack and throws it overboard."

"Huh?"

"He just got a cigarette lighter."

****

On Thursday morning, John Armstrong, the entire AFOS management team and key staff, the Manager of Site Security and his key staff, and the Manager of Human Resources, gathered in Armstrong's conference room to hear the final audit presentation. Peter and Greg had the other three members of their audit team there to participate and to answer any questions that might arise. John Armstrong called the meeting to order and introduced Greg Stevens.

"Let me start by expressing my condolences on the loss of one of your employees," Greg began. "From what my auditors tell me, he had a likeable personality and will be missed."

"Now, regarding the audit . . . I have distributed copies of the report with a *secret classification* to each of you. I will summarize what is in the report. You will find more detail in the report. The audit team is here to answer any questions.

"In general, the Boulder site complied with the rules, policies, and procedures required by IBM and by the DOD. The auditors were favorably impressed by the physical security and the attitude of the security staff. The auditors were here after hours on two occasions. For the most part, they found that cabinets and doors were locked, and that files and documents were protected. The auditors also reported that the security staff demonstrated an appropriate level of attention to monitoring the facility and responding to situations that occurred. However, the auditors did find that it was possible to corrupt the AFOS computer files with unwanted program code, and that this intrusion could go undetected. The intrusion of unwanted computer code onto computers is becoming an increasingly serious problem internationally. Such unwanted code is often called a virus. In the past two years, viruses with names like 'Vienna', 'Lehigh', 'Suriv-3', 'Jerusalem,' and 'Cascade' have infected IBM platform computers and computer networks. Viruses can reproduce themselves and spread from computer to computer over the existing networking links. While some viruses are created as pranks, many are designed to inflict damage by destroying files and programs, including operating systems. Our audit found that the AFOS process was vulnerable to the intrusion of unwanted code. We have several recommendations that will help to minimize the vulnerability and improve the ability to detect a virus before shipping the product to the customer. I am going to let Peter speak to the specific recommendations."

Peter put each of the following recommendations—one at a time—onto the overhead projector: He and his audit team discussed each one and answered questions. Noah answered most of the technical questions.

RECOMMENDATION #1:
Independently approve the use of all tapes prior to their first time use.

RECOMMENDATION #2
As soon as a tape is approved for use, label it with a unique serial number.

RECOMMENDATION #3
Record the tape's serial number onto the volume header when you record data on a tape for the first time.

RECOMMENDATION #4
Introduce operator controls to prevent data from being recorded on tapes unless the serial number on the volume-header matches the serial number on the cartridge casing.

RECOMMENDATION #5

Before you mount a tape, verify the serial number against a list of preapproved serial numbers. If not on the list, do not read it or record on it.

RECOMMENDATION #6

In the future, use tape drives the read the bar code serial numbers.

RECOMMENDATION #7

Modify the file management software to prevent manually altering the tape volume headers without re-initializing the tape.

RECOMMENDATION #8

Consider using automated tests and procedures to verify that object code is free of unwanted code. do this before delivering it to the customer.

RECOMMENDATION #9

Improve the timeliness of communications between Human Resources (HR) and the security department.

RECOMMENDATION #10

Perform background checks more frequently on employees working on sensitive projects.

RECOMMENDATION #11

Install a security camera outside the door of the vault and an emergency phone inside the vault.

After the audit team finished its presentation, Greg and Peter answered additional questions from John Engels.

"Mr. Stevens, you said that we were vulnerable to a virus infecting our AFOS product. Did you find one?" This was an interesting question, because Engels already knew the answer, but others in the room did not.

Greg answered, "Yes we did. However, as you already know, the Air Force delayed the installation until IBM could provide replacement tapes that were clean."

Everyone at the meeting already knew that the Air Force put a hold on the AFOS installation, and that IBM recreated the tapes. What they just verified was that the discovery of an actual virus was the cause.

Unlike most audit presentations, no one argued over words or the degree of severity implied by the auditors. Being vulnerable to the intrusion of unwanted code already had measurable consequences. Everyone knew of Belinsky's death and they knew that he was directly involved in creating the tapes that were shipped. The official cause of his death had not been made public. However, the newspapers reported his death as suspicious and there were leaks to the media that the FBI was involved. One could only imagine the severity if the issue had the bad code not been discovered before installation at the customer site.

Then Engels asked the million-dollar question. "Peter, I would like to know the actual mechanism by which the computer virus made its way onto the AFOS tapes. How do you know that your recommendations will prevent it from happening in the future?"

Peter was ready for this. Colby had told him what he could say—and what he could not say. "That's a very good question John. I can't tell you precisely. What I can tell you is a hypothetical scenario. Someone could have placed viral object code onto a tape or a floppy and brought it into the computer room from the outside. Once inside, the virus could have been merged onto the distribution tapes. If we had not done this audit, that might have gone undetected. Our recommendations will lessen the likely-hood of this happening in the future."

"Who do you think did this?" Engels asked, knowing he would not get an answer.

"That would be a question for the FBI."

"I understand. Thank you, Peter."

At the close of the meeting, John Armstrong thanked the auditors for doing an excellent job. He thanked the audit team for identifying security weaknesses in the code distribution process; and he specifically thanked Peter and Noah for preventing the installation of bad code on the customer's computers.

****

After the meeting on Thursday, the team headed home. Noah shared a ride to the airport. Having two cars, they were not as cramped as they were when they first arrived. After returning the two rental cars, the five of them waited for the shuttle to take them back to the airport. Noah's flight to San José would leave from a different gate than the others, so

Peter and Greg used the opportunity to thank Noah for his participation on the audit. Peter made a special point of thanking Noah for providing the timely evidence that prevented the virus from being shipped. They shook hands.

After saying good-bye to Noah, the other four took a flight to Dulles where they would retrieve their cars from long-term parking and return to Maryland. As it happened, Peter's seat on the plane was next to Debbie. The seats were three across. Debbie had the middle seat and Peter had the aisle seat. Having long legs, he needed the legroom, and he always asked for an aisle seat. Every now and then however, his leg would find its way into the aisle—only to have his foot run over by the service cart.

The plane was ready to take off and was about to start down the runway. Debbie said that take-offs made her nervous. She reached for Peter's hand as they took off and he obliged. They were no sooner up in the air when she turned toward him and asked, "Why did they do it?"

"Why did they—"

"Why did they try to bomb us, and who were they?" she repeated.

He paused before he answered. He looked around to make sure that they would not be overheard before he answered. Only the young kid siting by the window next to Debbie was within earshot, and he was engrossed in peering out the window.

"Debbie, the FBI released the names of two individuals arrested by the Sheriff's department. One was the bomb maker. He had a record. The other was the manager of a construction company that the C4 explosive came from. They will be convicted and spend time in jail."

"Peter, that's not what I mean. There must have been someone else behind this. Who were they . . . and why?"

"Isn't that the same question that Little John asked us at the meeting?"

"Not exactly. Little John was asking about the *virus*. I'm asking about the *bombing*. Are the two related?" She asked in a not so soft voice.

Peter noticed that the teenager looked up when he heard the words *virus* and *bombing*. Peter moved his head closer to Debbie and spoke softly.

"Debbie, you know I can't answer that directly, so let me say this. A good auditor can observe many events and pieces of information over a span of time and make realistic conclusions. In other words, connect the dots. **Debbie, you have that ability . . . more than you think**. In this audit, you knew several key pieces of information:

"The fact that I can't tell you everything should tell you something as well, but given the information you have, you should be able to draw valid explanations for what happened and why. One logical explanation from that information is that someone did not want us to complete the audit. A logical reason is that there was something they did not want us to find."

The look on Debbie's face indicated that she was still not satisfied. "Debbie, you don't seem satisfied with what I just said."

"I don't suppose you can tell me anything more, like who was really behind all of this?"

"I can't reveal who they are, but I will say that the people behind all this have failed and are being brought to justice. I am satisfied that today the world is a much safer place than it was before we started. Let me say one more thing. A trait you have that makes you a good auditor is that you are persistent. You pursue the evidence until you have all the facts and are certain of what occurred. That is generally good. However, sometimes you must accept that you may never know all the answers, and sometimes it may not be worth pursuing—"

"Peter, do you know what our next assignment will be?" she asked, changing the subject.

"No, I don't, but I expect it will be another two weeks before the other part of the team finishes the audit in Oswego. . . . Why?"

"Peter, I am aware that sometimes my emotions get in the way of objectivity, and I'm thinking of leaving the team. I already talked to Greg, but I haven't decided yet."

"Well Debbie, for what it's worth, I would like you to stay. We all must deal with our emotions. Emotions can be good you know. Perhaps your emotions give you the drive and motivation you need to pursue things. Could I tell you something?"

"Sure."

"This past Monday I was not at work. I attended a funeral service in Virginia of a friend who died unexpectedly."

"Yes, Greg told us you were at a funeral."

"Well, this friend once taught me a lesson on emotions. The bottom line is you can't suppress them. You must let yourself feel them. The trick is to manage them . . . Anyway, I think you are a good auditor. I enjoy working with you, and I hope you will stay."

"Thank you," she said and squeezed his arm.

Peter glanced over to the window seat and noticed the teenager. He had his eyes shut with his head cocked slightly towards them. Had he been trying to listen? So what, he thought. It would make his day more interesting.

After this conversation with Debbie, Peter closed his eyes and put the seat back—making sure to keep his foot out of the aisle in case he fell asleep. He began to think about Carol. He had not seen her for more than a week. He did not want to talk business with her. He did not see a dilemma as suggested by Colby. He missed her. He decided he would call her that evening after he got home. It had been a long day. He was tired and it was not long before he fell asleep.

20

A NEW BEGINNING

The evening after returning home from Boulder, Peter dialed Carol's number, but she did not answer. Perhaps she was still away on assignment, he thought. A week later, he called again and repeated this a few days after that. He left messages on her voice recorder. He wondered if she would ever return his calls. Perhaps that one weekend together went too fast. Perhaps she would just like to put it all behind her. As much as he liked her, he could accept that. It was the uncertainty that was driving him nuts. Then he remembered his words to Debbie: *"Sometimes you have to accept that you may never know all the answers, and sometimes it may not be worth pursuing."* Damn, he decided. This is worth pursuing!

He was very pleased when she called back several days later. "Peter, I just got your message. I have been on the road, on assignment. I just got back home and I plan to be in Columbia for the Fourth of July weekend. I'm very pleased that you called. To be honest, I wasn't sure I would hear from you again. Would you like to come to Columbia for lunch on Saturday?"

He did not say it, but he was not sure he would hear from her again either. He was very glad he did.

"I would definitely like to come for lunch. Did you have a place in mind?"

"My apartment . . . Do you like Reuben sandwiches?" She already knew he did.

"I love Reuben sandwiches—potato salad too. Can I bring something?"   "No, just yourself. After lunch, there is activity going on down at the Columbia Lakefront and . . . if you want . . . you can spend the night. There is a Volksmarch hike on Sunday. I mean . . . unless you already have other plans. I know I haven't given you much warning."

"Carol, I would love to do this. No, I have not made any other plans. Uh . . . you need to give me directions to your place."

"Okay. Do you have a pencil handy?"

"Hang on. . . Okay shoot."

Peter wrote down her directions on a scrap of paper. Carol lived in an apartment complex in Columbia, about twenty-five miles to the North.

"Would noon be okay?" she asked.

"Perfect! I'm looking forward to it. See you at noon on Saturday."

Peter was very happy she returned his call. It sounded like maybe there was hope for a long-term relationship after all. He needed to bring a gift—something romantic—something in which she had shown and interest. Yes! He knew exactly what he would bring!

****

Peter arrived at her door at five minutes before noon. He set his gift down on the deck by her door and rang the bell. She opened the door and they immediately grabbed a hold of each other in a tight bear hug followed by a long kiss on the lips. When she invited him in, he almost forgot the gift. "Oh wait, I have something for you," he said as he picked up the potted plant, handed it to her, and then made his way inside.

"Oh wow," she exclaimed, "I'm going to take it into the kitchen. Follow me. What is it?"

Peter followed her to the other side of the partition wall on his left, through the dining room, and into the kitchen. "It's a potted Mandevilla," he answered. "Actually, it's a special version called a Rio Dipladenia with deep red flowers. I remembered you looking at one in Colorado Springs and telling me that your daughter had suggested something to spruce up your decor and your balcony. The lady at the nursery tells me that you should keep it indoors in the winter, water when the soil is dry, and set it outside when the temperature reaches above sixty degrees. I hope I haven't over stepped my bounds on this."

She set the plant on the kitchen counter and removed the colored tissue paper that Peter had used to disguise the plant's identity and make it look festive. "Peter, it's perfect!" she said gleefully. Then she turned around, ran towards Peter, put her arms around his neck, and kissed him on the lips. I love you," she said impulsively. Did she mean to say I love *it?* Peter wondered. "I'm so glad you came. Let me show you around."

Carol gave Peter the "Cook's tour" of her apartment. They walked from the kitchen, back through the dining room, and across an open area to the living room. At the far end of the living room was a balcony. "I can put the plant out there on the balcony," she said. On the other side of the sliding glass doors Peter noticed two chairs and a small table. "For now, it can go onto the table. We can do that later after we have lunch. Or, perhaps I can set it on top of a small stand in the corner of the balcony. Yes, then when the weather cools in the autumn, I could bring the stand inside. It could go over there." She pointed to the corner inside the living room next to the sliding doors. Peter smiled at her enthusiasm. "Let me show you the other end of the apartment." They walked back to the open area and down a hallway. "This is the guest bedroom," she said as they passed a bedroom on the right. I wanted a two-bedroom apartment so that my daughter and son can visit. Here is the master bedroom down here on the right and the bath, down here on the left. The bath is very large, has a separate anteroom with a sink, and has an entrance from both the hallway and the master bedroom. However, I only have one bath and if everyone visits at once it can get crowded."

The door of her bedroom was open and as Peter peaked in, he noticed she only had a single bed. "How long have you been here?" he asked.

"A little more than a year now. As you can see, I'm in need of some new furniture." She noticed Peter's look of curiosity. "We'll work it out" she chuckled. Peter smiled.

"You have a very nice place," Peter commented.

"Thank you. How about we go back to the kitchen and prepare lunch?"

"Great idea. Tell me what I can do to help."

Back in the kitchen, Carol explained that it would only take a few minutes to have lunch ready. The table was already set. She had pre-made the sandwiches; they only needed grilling. "Perhaps you wouldn't mind fetching the potato salad from the fridge. A serving spoon is in the drawer over there. Would you like beer? It's in the crisper at the bottom of the fridge. The glasses are already on the table."

Peter did what she asked. He poured himself a beer. "Would *you* like a beer?" he asked.

"Yes, but I'm not sure I want a whole one," she answered.

"Not a problem, I'll share mine."

Carol had made her Reuben sandwiches with corned beef, Swiss cheese, Russian dressing, sauerkraut, and pumpernickel bread. She had bought the potato salad at the local deli. A kosher dill pickle completed the plate. It only took a few bites before Peter told her, "Carol, this lunch is delicious. You did a great job."

As they ate, they talked. "So, Carol, what have you been doing over the past month? I missed you."

"I know. I should have been more responsive to your phone calls. I have been very busy and I have been on the road a lot with work."

"Will you succeed in closing down Panda International?"

"Peter, I think there are some things we shouldn't talk about."

"Okay . . ."

"Colby told me that you met with him about two and a half weeks ago. He said you asked about me, and then he gave me a short lecture. He said that if we were to continue seeing each other, he did not want me talking to you about my investigations. He said you would understand."

"Hmmm . . . He gave me a similar lecture. I do understand. I don't expect you to tell me anything that Colby does not want you to tell me. However, when I asked you that question just now—and perhaps I should have chosen my words more carefully—I just wanted to know how you were doing. I know you have been working hard and I want you to succeed and feel good about what you're doing. If that isn't the case, I would hope you would tell me."

"I'm doing well. I feel like what I'm doing is important, and I'm optimistic that I'll succeed."

"I'm pleased to hear that. When you complete this assignment, I think you will deserve a salary increase—"

"Yes, but I'm not going to be home that much, and I may not have a lot of time for a relationship. But I want to be honest with you. My job was not the only reason I didn't respond to your calls. Our weekend together was intense. It brought out emotions I had not felt for a long time. I felt overwhelmed and scared. I had told you then how I felt and you seemed to understand. I needed time to sort things out in my head. I needed to be sure that what I felt was real, and not just a passing fantasy. And I needed to be sure that you would still be interested in me."

"And . . .?" Peter hoped that this was not going to be the *let's just be friend's* speech.

"And I want to go ahead with this if you still do."

Peter walked over to her and put his arms around her. "Nothing in life is easy, but I feel confident we'll make this work. Here, let me help with the dishes and then we can relocate the plant."

****

Later that afternoon, Carol drove Peter around Columbia. She was eager to show off her town, and her enthusiasm was apparent.

"How long have you lived here," he asked.

"Almost twenty years. Columbia was founded in 1967. I moved here with my husband shortly after that."

"I have heard that Columbia is a planned community. What does that mean? It sounds socialistic."

"The town was developed by James Rouse to be a place that would foster the integration of people of all races, creeds, and economic levels. It was in the planning stages for at least five years. The regulations are quite tolerable and make a lot of sense once you think about it. You would not want your neighbor to paint his or her house purple or put a neon sign in the front yard, would you? Peter, Columbia has everything," she continued. "We have parks, lakes, pathways for walking and biking, a community college, a hospital, several restaurants, venues for concerts, senior centers, and a great shopping mall."

"I get the feeling that you enjoy living here," he said.

"I do she answered—very much. I think you would enjoy living here too." Was she hinting at something? Peter let it pass.

One of the places they drove by was the Wilde Lake High School. "My daughter Karen graduated from this school," she said. "As you can see, the building is round, and inside it has no walls dividing the classrooms. Students can advance at their own pace. It is an interesting modern-day experiment—mixed results. Karen did well though."

Peter said he recalled seeing something on the evening news about Wilde Lake High School a couple of weeks ago. "What was that?"

"Yes, I think you may be referring to the U.S.-Soviet peace march. About two-hundred people walked from Takoma Park to the high school. Similar marches took place throughout the U.S. and the Soviet Union. The marches started right after President Reagan returned from the summit with General Secretary Gorbachev to nail down the terms of the nuclear arms reduction treaty and to agree on other matters of common interest."

"Yes," he said. "I think that is what I was listening to."

"Kind of ironic, don't you think? I mean here we are trying to save our country from impending nuclear destruction at the hands of the Soviets, while at the same time our leaders are pretending that the Cold War is over."

"Yes, I agree with you, Carol. I think we see too much duplicity in our line of work. Sometimes it bothers me."

"Amen to that!"

After driving around and seeing many of the sights that Carol had mentioned, they ended up at Lake Kittamaqundi. This was where the outdoor festivities were taking place. Carol and Peter bought sodas, sat on the lawn, and listened to one of the performing bands. Then they began to visit the many booths. Aside from admiring some of the artwork, Carol could see that arts and crafts were not really Peter's thing. "Peter, there is a visitors' museum up the stairs over here. They show a short movie about the formation of Columbia. If you are interested, we could go see it."

"Okay, sounds good. Let's do it," Peter said.

After about three hours at the Columbia lakefront, Carol and Peter headed back to her place. They debated whether they felt like beer, cocktails, or coffee. Although late in the afternoon, coffee won out. Carol brewed a pot of fresh coffee. They took the coffee and a few plain cookies with them and went out on the balcony. They placed the coffee and cookies on the small table, pulled the two chairs near each other, and sat down. The deep red flowers of the Dipladenia plant looked good in the corner. The balcony faced east and as the sun moved west over the southern end of the building, the balcony was no longer in direct sunlight. For a warm summer evening, that was good — for them and for the plant.

Carol and Peter talked. As they did so, they began to realize how much more they needed to learn about each other. Their relationship had been like lighting a fire with newspapers and kindling. It started with a blaze, but now they needed to add a few small logs before it went out. They told each other more about their careers and more about their families.

Carol told Peter how difficult it had been for her to have two kids and become an FBI agent. After she graduated from college, she went to work. Over the next four years, she worked as an accountant, passed her CPA exams and had two kids, first Karen her daughter, and then David her son. Then after that, she decided she wanted to be an FBI agent. To become an FBI agent, she had to get herself into top physical condition, pass a battery of written and physical tests, and then be away from home for six months to attend the FBI training facility in Quantico Virginia. She made it. Over the next nineteen years, she traveled fifty percent of the time and worked an average of fifty hours a week.

"Peter," she said with a great deal of emotion, "most FBI special agents are men. Over the years, I have had to struggle for comparable pay and I have had to deal with sexual harassment—and no, before you ask, I have never been raped. Only now that I have almost twenty years in the agency, can I say that my pay is on par with the average man who has the same experience and years of service. And although the pay hasn't been great, I stayed around because I love doing accounting detective work."

Peter told Carol how much he enjoyed his work as well. "Audit is not what most people think. It's also a form of detective work. But at IBM I also have had experience as a business analyst and as a manager."

He did not mention his experience in Vietnam, but he did tell Carol more about his parents, his siblings, and his two girls. Ann, his oldest, had just graduated from the University of Maryland. She had decided to attend graduate school at Michigan State University in Lansing. "Carol, I would like you to meet Ann before she goes off to graduate school. Perhaps you could make it down to my place in Rockville."

"Yes, I'd like that. If I did my math right, Karen and Ann are the same age. I'd like you to meet Karen. She will be here tomorrow and sleep here tomorrow night. She is why I did not invite you to stay here tomorrow night, but it would be nice if you could stay through dinner tomorrow."

"I would love to meet her and your son as well. You mentioned fireworks. When do they do that?"

"I may have misled you on that. The fireworks are not until Monday night. Peter, I . . . I'm a little bit apprehensive about Karen. Don't get me wrong. I want you to meet her, but I don't know how she will react. She was very upset after my divorce, and then she was upset with me after I broke it off with Bruce. When I mentioned you on the phone, she did not seem overly enthused and—"

"Carol, I'm sure it will be fine."

"I hope so," she said, and put her hand over his wrist.

"Hey, you know what? I would like to buy you dinner tonight . . . at a restaurant of your choice. Do you have a favorite place?"

"I do," she said excitedly. "It's a place called The Coho Grill at Hobbit's Glen. They have a bar, decent food, and they may have live music."

"That sounds perfect. Do we need a reservation?"

"Peter, I hope you don't mind, but I anticipated that we would go out to dinner tonight, and we already have a reservation at seven o'clock."

Peter smiled. "It's fine, but I want the dinner to be my treat, okay?"

"Okay," she said.

Later, the two of them went to the Hobbit's Glen. It was only ten minutes away. Carol wanted to drive but Peter said that since it was his treat, he would drive. Carol gave in. They had a very enjoyable meal, Peter paid the dinner bill, they had drinks, and they danced until around eleven. Carol suggested that if they were going to hike in the morning, they might not want to stay out too late.

****

They were back at the apartment by 11:30. Peter fetched his overnight bag from the back seat, and they made their way up to her apartment with Carol clinging to his other arm.

"Where do I take my bag?" he asked as soon as they were inside.

"Follow me," she said and led him into the living room. "I didn't tell you but the sofa opens up and becomes a queen-sized bed. I thought we could sleep out here."

"Sounds good . . . where do we put the coffee table?" he asked.

"Over there against the far wall." They each took an end.

When they opened the sofa, Peter was surprised that it already had sheets on it. "It already has sheets?"

"I planned ahead. The sheets are fresh."

Then they took turns in the bathroom. Peter went first, changed into pajamas, and waited on the edge of the sofa bed for Carol to return. When she returned, he almost could not believe how beautiful and sensuous she looked. She was wearing a very sexy negligee that came down to mid-thigh. It was not totally opaque either. He could see her nipples and he could see that she was not wearing panties underneath. Peter's face lit up as she approached him. Then she clasped her hands aside his head, pushed him back on the bed, and planted a hard kiss on his mouth.

"What's gotten into you?" he said as she landed on top of him.

"I want you," she said.

Her knees straddled his waist as she broke the kiss and pushed herself upright. She was about to mount him when he decided to have some say as to how this event would go down. He quickly performed a maneuver and reversed their positions. Now he was on top.

"And I want you too," he said and put his mouth back over hers. She shrieked, but she did not resist as he lifted her legs. She put her arms tightly around his back as he entered her and ejaculated. Her body shook and she seemed to be wailing and crying all at once. When they finished, they rolled over on their sides. Peter could feel tears on her cheek and he looked at her face. She opened her eyes and smiled. He was relieved to see that she looked happy—not sad—not angry, but happy.

As they lay exhausted side by side, Peter thought about what just happened. He had not seen this aggressive side of Carol before, and while he was aware of her ability to take charge, she seemed more controlling today than in the past.

In the past? he asked himself. What *past*? For God's sake, he had only known her for seven weeks, and this was only the third time they had had sex. Perhaps they should talk about this, he thought. He would try to be tactful.

"Carol, are you okay?" he asked.

"Yes, I'm more than okay," she said softly as she moved her hand across his face. "Are you? I'm sensing that something is bothering you."

"It's just that our love-making tonight was very different than a month ago. Your aggressiveness surprised me. I didn't know what to make of it."

"Sometimes I get over-enthusiastic about expressing my feelings, but with you, I don't feel that I need to hold back. I feel comfortable with you. I don't ever want you to feel threatened by my aggressiveness. I hope that wasn't the case tonight. I have no desire to dominate you, and I was pleased when you regained control. I trust you, and I feel comfortable letting you have control. I really liked what we did."

"To be honest, I liked it too. You really turned me on. If we trust each other and share control, I think we'll be fine . . ."

"Peter, about tomorrow, I know I planned everything for the weekend without you having much of a say, but we can change the plan. We don't need to do the Volksmarch tomorrow if you aren't interested."

"The Volksmarch is good. I've never done one of these before and I think it will be interesting. Besides, the fresh air and exercise will be good for us . . . right? And you said Karen was coming in the afternoon. I really want to meet her . . . that is if you still want me to."

"Of course, I still want you to," she replied.

****

Carol's alarm went off at six thirty. The two of them were up, took showers, and put on old clothes for hiking. They both wore the same thing: short sleeve t-shirt, jeans, white sport socks, athletic shoes, and a baseball cap. As in Boulder, Carol had put her hair up in a ponytail that poked out the back of the cap. After a breakfast of juice and cereal, they were on their way to Savage Mills Park.

The Volksmarch was interesting—something new for Peter. The Volksmarch was a six-mile walk through the woods with check points— rest stops along the way. They registered at the start, paid a fee, picked up a card and a trail map, and began following the trail. They stopped at each manned checkpoint along the way to have their card stamped and enjoy water and a snack. They could proceed at a pace of their own choosing— very enjoyable. Peter and Carol got plenty of exercise hiking that Sunday, but the day was hot, even in the morning.

When they got back to Columbia, they were ready for another shower.

"Peter," she said. "I'm heading into the shower. You are welcome to join me if you wish."

"Sounds like a good idea. Okay if I soap you up?"

After a pause, he heard, "Ah, sure that sounds like fun . . . just so you remember that Karen will be here at two."

It was around three o'clock when Karen's father dropped her off. Carol introduced Peter to Karen, but most of the conversation that afternoon was between Karen and her mom. Aside from polite exchanges, the rapport between Peter and Karen was getting off to a slow start. That evening, Carol took the three of them out to dinner at a local restaurant. Carol hoped that it would help break the ice. During dinner, Peter initiated a conversation with Karen.

"Karen, I understand you want to be a doctor."

"I think so."

"Where will you be going?"

"Stanford," she replied.

"I understand that is a great school—hard to get into— expensive too."

"My Dad is helping with the bill."

"Do you have a summer job?"

"Yes."

"May I ask what?"

"I'm working in a hospital near San Francisco. That way I'll get a taste of what being a doctor might be like before I start graduate school."

After the meal, Karen began to ask some direct and pointed questions.

"Peter, who do you work for?"

"I work for IBM in North Bethesda. I'm on IBM's Internal Audit staff"—she would have asked that next.

"Peter, tell me . . . how did you and my mother meet?"

This, of course, is a very common question, but, in this case, he could only reveal a small portion of the answer. "We met in Boulder, Colorado. A case that your mother was working on overlapped with a project I was working on at IBM, and she was assigned to work with me." As he answered, he could see that Carol was paying close attention to the conversation.

"I don't quite understand," Karen continued. "Was the FBI investigating IBM? Why would you be teaming up?"

This time, Carol interrupted. "Karen knows that I'm not at liberty to discuss the nature of the cases I'm working on."

"Then what about *you*, Peter?" Karen asked. "Can you discuss the projects *you* are working on?"

"Not in this case. The project was classified."

"So, you worked together, then what? How did it become more than that?" she asked in a somewhat demanding tone.

At this point, it was apparent that Carol was beginning to feel uneasy with Karen's questions, but she gave a quick answer. "By happenstance, we were both in Boulder over the Memorial Day Weekend, and we needed something to do. Peter asked me to go with him to a festival in Colorado Springs and a cog railway ride up Pikes Peak, and I accepted."

"Sounds like a fun date," Karen said.

"Well, it wasn't even supposed to be a date, Karen—just two colleagues touring together," Peter added.

"But it was fun, and one thing led to another," Carol said.

"So, does that mean you two are seeing each other now?"

Peter looked at Carol. "Carol, are we seeing each other?"

"Yeah, I think that's what they call it these days," Carol replied.

Karen saved her big questions to the end. "Mom, are you and Peter sleeping together?"

Carol was clearly annoyed that Karen would ask that in front of Peter. "Karen, you don't—"

"It's okay. Karen, I care a lot about your mom, and yes, we are sleeping together."

"Are you married? You better not be!" she said.

With that, Carol got up and said she was going to the rest room. She was clearly annoyed.

After a few minutes of silence, Peter reinitiated the conversation with Karen. "What has your mom told you about me?"

"Not too much."

"Okay, listen. I know that you have your mom's best interests at heart. I know that you don't want to see her get hurt again. Your mom may not have told you everything because she does not want to worry you, but I'm going to be straight with you. Yes, I'm married. However, I physically separated from my wife, and obtained a legal separation one year ago.

Here in Maryland one year is enough, but New York requires two years before the divorce papers can go to the court. So, I'm in limbo."

"You are right. I don't want her to get hurt again. The last man she was involved with lied to her and she was hurt badly. I don't want that to happen again. Do you love her?" she asked.

"I *do* love her," he replied, not noticing Carol come up behind him as he said this. Did she hear?

Carol did not sit back down. She stood there and glared at Karen. "Are you done interrogating Peter?" she asked sarcastically.

Karen looked at her. "Mom, I want you to be happy, and I don't want you to get hurt again."

"I know," Carol replied, but her disappointment with Karen's behavior was apparent in her tone. Carol picked up her credit card and receipt from the table and secured it in her purse. "I think we should go back home now," she said. With that, the three of them rode home in silence.

****

Peter understood the significance of meeting a girlfriend's family. He hoped he would pass the test. After they went back to Carol's apartment, Peter got his things together and was ready to go when Karen approached him. "Peter, I think mom is upset with me. I was hard on you. I'm sorry. I don't want you to leave because of me."

"You don't need to be sorry. It probably was best to have gotten this out in the open as we did. I understand where you are coming from, and I don't blame you for anything you said. As far as my leaving, I wasn't planning to spend tonight here anyway. Besides, I think it's important to your mom that you spend time together. Where is your mom by the way? I need to say good night to her."

"I think she's in her room."

Peter walked down the hallway and found her sitting on the edge of her bed. She had been crying. "Peter, I'm sorry. I didn't think she would be that rude to you. I was embarrassed."

"It'll be okay. Of course, she was wrong to embarrass you, and I told her that, but I think she feels badly that she upset you. She wasn't very tactful, but she apologized to me. I told her I didn't blame her for how she felt. She was expressing her feelings—legitimate feelings. She cares about you and wants to protect you. That's a good thing, isn't it? Maybe in the long-term it's best that it all came out in the open. Carol, I think things will turn out all right between her and me . . . I really do. Please make good use of the time you spend with her tomorrow. It's going to work out."

Carol rose from the bed and put her arms around him. "Did you mean it when you told Karen that you loved me?"

"I did."

She kissed him on the mouth. "I love you too," she said.

"May I call you tomorrow night?" he asked.

"Yes."

Peter returned to his apartment in Rockville. He slept well that night.

****

Apparently, the Fourth of July weekend was enough to keep the fires burning. New logs had been added to the fire. Carol and Peter were both very pleased that their relationship was more than just a weekend fling. Eventually, Karen accepted her mother's relationship with Peter. Peter and Carol began dating on a regular basis—more or less. They were in love. However, with their travel schedules, time together was limited.

During the next two months, Special Agent Carol Sanders helped the FBI to build a strong case against Panda International and shut down its illegal operations in the United States. Shortly after Carol returned to the D.C. area, the FBI promoted her to the next GS grade, and reassigned her to the Baltimore satellite office. The reassignment reduced her travel time.

Meanwhile, Peter did a lot of thinking about his future. After two years of it, he was tired of audit assignments and he was tired of travel. With the loss of Jon, there may not be any more CIA assignments either. Perhaps he should transfer from Corporate Audit to another organization within IBM, one with less travel. He was also tired of bachelorhood. He had a strong desire to share his life with someone. Carol and Peter discussed the possibility of renting a townhouse together. She wanted it to be in Columbia. She would commute to Baltimore and he would commute to Rockville or Gaithersburg. Then there was Donna. He just could not seem to forget her. Jon's funeral was scheduled for September the seventh. Should he go? Would Donna be there? Too many things were still up in the air. He needed closure.

21

CLOSURE

Today was Wednesday, September 7, the day that Jon Wilson's ashes would be buried at Arlington National Cemetery. Peter had learned that the parking at the cemetery was an issue and visitors could not leave their cars at the administration building where they were to gather. The driving part was not fun either, so Peter decided to take the Metro. Grosvenor was the closest station to his apartment—near where Jon had lived—just a short drive. He could take the Metro right to the station for Arlington Cemetery. It would be a short walk from there. As he walked out of his apartment, he looked up at the overcast sky. It had rained the night before and the grass was still wet. He hoped it would clear up. He took a small umbrella with him in case it rained, but he also hoped that the day would not be too hot or humid. There was nothing worse than dressing up in a suit and tie and perspiring heavily.

Peter parked his car and walked into the Grosvenor station. He had an old fare card from several months prior. It still had a couple of dollars on it. It would get him onto the train, but not enough money to let him leave the station in Arlington. He mused that unlike that fabled man in Boston, no one in Washington will ride forever beneath the streets of the city. Every station has machines that let you add fare when exiting the train. He inserted his card into the turnstile. It read the card and popped back up almost instantly. It worked! The platform and the train were crowded—still rush hour. He was lucky to find a seat near the door. Then at the next stop—the Medical Center—he voluntarily gave up his seat to an elderly gentleman with a cane. He held on to the post beside him as his eyes alternated between strange faces to an occasional glimpse of the tunnel walls moving past the window on the other side of the car. It did not take long before his mind began to wander. He recalled a conversation he had with Carol over the recent Labor Day weekend.

"Carol, I'm thinking about going to Jon's funeral at Arlington on Wednesday morning, but I'm still undecided. Now that he is gone, I will probably not do any more intelligence assignments. A part of me is okay with putting all that behind me, but another part of me says I want to remember Jon always. I feel like I owe him something."

"Peter, it sounds like the two of you bonded in some way that went beyond the assignments you had. Why do you feel you owe him?"

"He was a mentor to me, took an interest in my career, and always encouraged me."

"But there is more than that, isn't there? She asked . . . like shared experiences?"

"Yes, but those experiences were highly classified; I can't talk about them."

"You look perplexed," she said, trying to appear understanding.

"I keep asking myself if there was more I could have done or said to preclude his murder."

*"Peter, you know there was nothing you could have done differently. You warned him, and he acknowledged that even **he** suspected her. The ball was in his court."*

"I guess I just need closure. I want to say good-bye and I wish he could hear me say it."

"Peter, I think you should go on Wednesday. I think you'll get that closure."

Peter had struggled with his decision to attend. A part of him just wanted it to all go away. Donna, CIA, Jon, and secrecy were things he wanted to put in his past. Another part of him said he should go. Carol helped him make the final decision. She convinced him that the best way to have closure was to go. She was right, but Peter had never mentioned the full extent to which he wanted closure. He never mentioned anything to Carol about his relationship with Donna in Vietnam. He had missed

Donna at the memorial service and hoped she might attend the funeral. Yet, he was apprehensive about how things would play out.

****

Peter changed to the Blue Line at Metro Center. This time he found a seat near the door and kept it. Arlington National Cemetery was the first stop after crossing the Potomac River. They arrived quickly. He exited the train and followed the signs telling him which way to go. When he got to the street level, he was pleased to see that the skies were clearing and the sun was poking out. Perhaps it would be a nice day. He took a deep breath of fresh air. His apprehensions began to dissipate—he was ready for whatever would be.

He walked from the Metro station to the cemetery's administration building where he joined a dozen other guests. He assumed that some dressed in suits were Jon's co-workers at the agency while others wore military uniforms. He did not know any of them. To his disappointment, Donna was not there, nor was Matheson. Perhaps they chose to remain in the shadows, he thought. The guests would wait for Ken and Kathy Morehouse to arrive with Jon's urn. After what seemed like eons they arrived. Then a 'host' gave instructions as to what to do next.

Ken and Kathy Morehouse had arranged everything with the funeral home three months prior. As a captain in the Special Forces, and a holder of a Silver Star Medal, Jon was awarded a burial with full honors, and a few extras. When the appropriate time came, the guests watched four military men transfer a box containing Jon's ashes from a white hearse onto a caisson pulled by six horses. They draped the American flag over the box. The military escorts saluted, and Peter held his hand over his heart. The guests then boarded three automobiles and followed the caisson carrying the remains. The procession moved at a snail's pace as it wound its way over two hills to the gravesite. In terms of the weather, it was clearing. Nevertheless, most of the guests appreciated riding in cars, rather than walking, because the gravesite was what seemed like a mile away. However, two uniformed members of the military followed the procession on foot. Upon arrival at the gravesite, a member of the military escorted the guests to folding chairs covered with green cloth, placed a few yards from the grave. The guests stood as the military escorts removed Jon's remains from the caisson and set them above the grave. Military saluted; others held their hands over their hearts. The guests sat down while a chaplain spoke, and then stood again for the military honors. Once again, the military saluted and the non-military attendees showed their respect by holding their hands over their hearts. The sound of the seven rifles fired in unison split the still morning air. A second volley, and then the third and final volley followed. The three-volley salute symbolized Duty—Honor—Country. Guests remained standing for the playing of taps. The bugler played it perfectly with the power to bring tears. After everyone sat back down, the military folded the flag and the officer in charge presented the flag to the General. It seemed fitting. Jon Wilson had no actual kin, but General Ken Morehouse and Jon Wilson were closer than most blood brothers were.

After the ceremony, Peter said hello to Kathy Morehouse and then asked for a moment alone with Ken. Kathy was used to this type of request. She knew that she was not privy to matters that her husband discussed that were of a business nature. She walked away as Peter walked over to Ken and extended his hand.

"Peter Troutman, how have you been?"

"I'm good . . . you?"

"To be honest, I'm glad this is over."

"General, you picked a nice day. I think Jon would be very happy with everything you did for him."

"Sometimes things work out. I'm pleased you could come but now that Boulder Creek is finished, I am surprised. I know you worked with Jon in Vietnam. Did you also know Jon on a personal basis?"

"I first met Jon in Saigon. I was there as a contractor. Jon and his wife, Linda, were assigned to the Department of State at the time. I worked with him and—"

"And Donna?" Ken said, remembering their prior conversation.

"And Donna . . . but it was more than that. Jon and his wife Linda had a party at their house on the outskirts of Saigon. That's when I first met Jon and Linda. Linda had arranged a birthday party for Donna. I thought Linda was a very nice person. I liked her. Did you know Linda?"

"Sure did. My wife and I went to their wedding. I was sorry to see them split up."

"I was too. They each talked to me that evening. They revealed that they were having marital problems, but it was clear, at least to me, that they still loved each other. I got to know them. Jon was a mentor to me and he believed in me. I felt like I owed him something . . . and I miss him."

"That makes two of us. I've known Jon since West Point. He believed in me as well. I may have let him down."

"How so?"

"I did not know about Mary Lou until it was too late. Jon left a message on Monday. Jon said he had suspicions about Mary Lou. Kathy and I were away for the holiday. I didn't hear the message until the next day."

"Don't know if it would have made a difference," Peter replied.

"Why not?"

"Nothing you could have done, General. You may not know this, but I saw a woman in Boulder on the Saturday night before he died. She had disguised her identity, but I thought she could be Mary Lou. I called Jon on Sunday and left a message on his private line—the one in his office. I mentioned what I saw, including the scar on her neck. I know he got the message; he returned my call later in the day, but I wasn't there. He left me a message that he had also discovered some information that maybe she wasn't who she said she was. He said he was upset, but that he was handling it. I don't know—perhaps if we had talked more. Anyway, the point is you do the best you can with what you know at the time. I don't think that there was anything we could have done—no point second-guessing ourselves— and then, suppose we *were* able to save his life . . . what then? If he learned all the details about Mary Lou, he would have been devastated. Would he have enjoyed living after that?"

Peter's eyes seemed to tear up as he finished. "We can't be second-guessing ourselves."

Noticing Peter's display of emotion, the General put his hand on Peter's shoulder and gave a squeeze.   "You all right?" he asked.

"Sorry . . . I'm okay." Peter forced a smile and then continued. "Speaking of Mary Lou, I was disappointed to hear that she escaped. How did *that* happen?"

"What did you hear?"

"Roger Colby informed me back in June that Mary Lou escaped. He said that—but I'm having trouble getting my head around it."

"I hope you didn't come here today to lay into me about *that*. The FBI has already given me enough grief."

Ken's reaction caught him, by surprise. "No! . . . General, I didn't mean to hit a nerve. I remember you explaining the situation to me at Jon's memorial service. The FBI should have been able to handle it."

"Sorry, it's still a sore point with me," the General responded.

"Like I said, you can't be second guessing yourself. I'm sure you did what you thought was right at the time, and I'm sure it would have been difficult trying to explain the situation to Kathy if Mary Lou was arrested for espionage and murder during the memorial service. The two of them seemed to have connected. Besides, saving you that conversation with Kathy, her escape to the Soviet Union saved the government a lot of time and money."

"I suppose that's one way to look at it. . . Peter, where do you go from here?"

"That's a good question. Intelligence work is *thankless* work. I mean due to the secrecy of it, almost no one knows what you do. For example, on this project, my persistence prevented a computer virus from destroying a computer network vital to our national defense. It was my observations and a fingerprint that I provided to Colby that established the connection of Ursula Behr to Mary Lou McGuinness. Although Colby privately acknowledged my help, I'm sure that officially *he* took all the credit. More importantly, all five of the intelligence related assignments that I have done for Jon have resulted in people getting hurt—or dead. I tend to feel other people's emotions. I'll always remember when Jon personally lectured me on *emotional intelligence.* It helps me deal with my feelings, but it does not stop me from feeling. The thing is that after each of the assignments that I did for Jon, he would sit down with me. He would thank me, and he would make it all feel worthwhile. Jon is no longer here. He's gone. I've decided to close the book on this part of my life and move on. Today has helped me to do that."

"I understand what you are saying. Sometimes you need a change. Next year, the government will be under a new administration. I've been thinking of retiring myself. Kathy and I have been thinking of moving to Prescott Arizona."

"That really sounds good. I read that Prescott is one of the top ten best places to retire. General, could I ask you something? Jon told me that the CIA thought the Soviets had produced *two* cartridges containing viral software, but we only found one. What do you think happened to the other one?"

"Peter, my guess is that it was just a backup. It probably resides in a vault at the Soviet Consulate in San Francisco. We may never know"

Just then, Kathy approached. "It's time to leave Ken," she said.

"My apologies . . . I kept him longer than I intended," Peter said. "I wish you both the best."

Peter and the General shook hands.

"Peter, the best to you as well. Here keep this, just in case you need to talk." The General pulled out a business card, wrote something on the back, and handed it to him. Then everyone went to their respective cars and returned to the main gate.

Peter had wanted closure that day. He got most of what he wanted. He was very pleased to have talked with the General—who seemed to understand him. Yet one piece was still missing. Now that he found himself falling in love with Carol, he wanted closure with Donna that much more. Donna was not there. Despite that, Peter was glad he came.

As he walked back to the Metro station, he looked up at the sky. It never rained. The clouds were gone, the sun was shining brightly, and the temperatures were in the sixties. Peter felt more relaxed and more at peace than he did at the start of the day. It was a good day, he decided.

****

Final clarity came to Peter that evening in his Rockville apartment. He knew what he wanted and how he would get there. He would transfer to another position at IBM. He would rent a townhouse with Carol, move to Columbia, and they would live together. He would put the CIA, Vietnam, and Donna behind him, and move on. He would begin a new phase of his life. He had closure at last!

HER FINAL PROJECT

By

Peter Eisenhut

PROLOGUE

Jon Wilson died in his sleep of an apparent heart attack the night after Memorial Day, 1988. Wilson's death was unexpected and a total shock to his colleagues. He liked to jog and seemed to be physically fit. His personality was very congenial and compassionate. Those who knew him liked him and respected him. Early in his career, he had served in Vietnam as a special ops officer. At the time of his death, Wilson was a high-level officer in the Central Intelligence Agency. They interred his remains with honors at Arlington National Cemetery.

In March 1988, Wilson had received intelligence that the Soviet Union had launched a mission to sabotage the missile defense system of the United States. The CIA, the Department of Defense, and the FBI launched a joint investigation and revealed that Wilson's girlfriend, Mary Lou, was involved. Wilson received this news the weekend he died, and it was noteworthy that Mary Lou was the one who discovered the body and called it in. For this reason, his death was suspicious, and the FBI conducted an extensive autopsy. They ruled Wilson's death a homicide by lethal injection.

The FBI investigation proved that Mary Lou was a covert Soviet spy who played a key role in the Soviet's mission to undermine our missile defense. Her real name was Inga Sarnoff. She had used several aliases during her mission, and Jon Wilson was not the first person she had killed. Unfortunately, she managed to escape and leave the country before the FBI could arrest her. The CIA blamed the FBI for allowing that to happen and took it upon themselves to find her and bring her to justice. Then, almost fifteen years later . . .

1

SHARING INTELLIGENCE

On Wednesday evening, April 2, 2003, CIA officer Donna Wolf flew into Juan Santamaria International Airport near San José, Costa Rica (SJO). It was her first trip outside the United States since her illness, but one she had looked forward to for a long time. After meetings in the morning, she had taken a commercial flight from Baltimore's BWI with a change in Miami. There had been inclement weather, and it had delayed the plane in Miami by almost an hour. She was glad when she finally reached her destination.

At SJO, she retrieved her bag, passed through border control, and then went to the car rental area to pick up her car. Being very observant, she couldn't help but notice that all the full-sized rental cars were Toyota Camrys. She chose a white one, but then she noticed that the right rear tire was about to go flat. She resolved the matter calmly and suppressed her frustration at being delayed another forty-five minutes. They gave her another Toyota Camry and directions to her hotel.

The InterContinental Hotel in Escazu was on Route 27, just southwest of the City of San José. Following the directions, Officer Wolf headed south. She was tired, and the country roads were not well lit. She strained to keep her eyes opened and focused on the road and the road signs. After she passed two small towns already asleep for the night, and took a wrong turn, she wondered if renting a car had been such a good idea.

The official nature of her mission entitled her to have a limo from the U.S. Embassy pick her up at the airport. She also had the option of staying at the Embassy. However, she did not plan that all her time in Costa Rica would be official business, and she preferred the freedom to come and go as she pleased. She had decided to rent a car and stay at a comfortable top-rated hotel. Officer Wolf had used her official diplomatic passport to enter the country, but as a precaution, she had pre-registered at the hotel under the name Donna M. Rice. The hotel would not know her diplomatic status or who she worked for.

By the time she got to her room, it was almost eleven o'clock—one a.m. back in Baltimore. It had been a long day and she was exhausted. She collapsed on the bed and went right to sleep.

****

Early the next morning, Officer Wolf drove to the U.S. Embassy. The U.S. Embassy was in Pavas, a district to the west of the city of San José, and to the north of Escazu. As the crow flies, it was not that far from her hotel, but a mountain and a river necessitated going east toward the city and then back the other way to the west. Despite the traffic heading into the city and the bright sun in her face, she arrived in only fifteen minutes. She was expected, so after showing her credentials to several people, she could park her car and be escorted to the office of Eduardo Perez. Ed Perez was the CIA Chief of Station in Costa Rica.

Ed Perez was in his sixties. He had been stationed in San José for more than four years and was in his second year as Chief of Station. Although it had turned silver, he still had most of his hair. He was about six feet tall and had an athletic build. He had retired from the military as a Colonel and now had about twenty-three years with the CIA.

They greeted each other with a polite hug and a kiss on the cheek, as was the custom in Costa Rica. "How are you, Donna?" he asked sincerely while his hands remained at rest on her shoulders. "When I saw you in Maryland last year, you were not doing well. You're looking really good now." Ed and Donna had known each other for a very long time and had become close. Early last year, after she was diagnosed with cancer, Ed had made a special trip to Langley as an excuse to visit her.

"Yes, I'm much better now," she replied. "The cancer is in remission. As you can see, my brown hair has turned darker and has some gray in it, but it's good to have it back, and I'm keeping it short," she said as she brushed her hand across the side of her head.

"Your hair looks very nice."

"Thank you." She knew that Ed was perceptive enough to realize she was also tinting it. No need to mention that. "When you last saw me, I was wearing a wig. It was hot and itchy—"

"Yes, and glasses."

"I still have them as backup, but I'm wearing contacts now . . . I'm so glad to see you, Ed. I missed you."

"I missed you too. Please sit. How was your trip?"

"Grueling," she responded. "Got delayed in Miami, and then when I arrived, I was delayed further because the rental car they offered had a soft tire . . . a negotiation ensued—I need to brush up on my Spanish. The trip took eleven hours door to door. Didn't get in until eleven last night—one a.m. my time. I'm not fully awake yet."

"Sorry . . . where are you staying?"

"At the InterContinental in Escazu off Highway 27."

"Oh yea, I live near there you know."

"Yes, I remember," she said, remembering the night she spent at his upscale condominium a couple of years ago.

"Perhaps a second cup of coffee will help to get you going?"

"Sounds good."

"Cream, no sugar?"

"You remembered.

"Make yourself comfortable. I'll be right back."

After a few minutes, Ed returned with the coffee. He sat down, and they enjoyed several minutes talking and having coffee together. He and Donna had worked with each other many times in the past. They were colleagues and friends, but after Donna's husband died eleven years ago, they became more than just friends. The younger generation would call it friends with benefits.

Donna turned sixty-one years old last month. She had more than thirty years with the CIA, but was not ready to retire. In 1966, after college and two years in the military, she had worked as a CIA field agent in Vietnam. However, in 1967 she was forced to kill an important enemy agent, and then she allowed herself to become pregnant by someone she worked with. She left the CIA and it took six years of counseling and motherhood to get back on track. After that, she rejoined the CIA and her career took off. She loved her work and had received several promotions, but then she learned she had cancer. She considered retiring, but she had treatment and the cancer was now in remission. She felt good now, and despite her age and her illness, she was still a good-looking woman. She had an attractive face without the need for makeup and she still had a figure. She had resumed visits to her local fitness center, and was regaining her strength. One project had kept her going—one she had been working on for fifteen years and one she was determined to complete. Ed knew it was the reason she was in Costa Rica.

Their conversation turned to business.

"So, what's on tap for today?" she asked

"Well, the information you shared with me when you were here a year ago has paid off. We discovered that your spy, Inga Sarnoff, entered Costa Rica more than three years ago under an assumed identity. We know where she is and what she has been doing."

"Well, as you know, I'm here to start extradition proceedings so we can take her back to the United States for trial."

"Yes. I'm ready to help you with that, but I'm going to warn you, it may be an uphill battle. I have set up a meeting this morning with the Costa Rican *Organismo de Investigación Judicial,* or OIJ. It's the equivalent of our FBI and DOJ in the United States. We need to plead our case for extradition. I expect that the Costa Rican Dirección de Inteligencia Seguridad Nacional or DIS will also attend. The DIS is their counterpart to our CIA. By the way, we should get going. The OIJ is on the other side of the city, and traffic is usually heavy. We have a car waiting for us downstairs."

****

The chauffeur held the door open for them and showed them into the back seat of a black Lincoln Town Car. Ed sat on one side of the car, Donna on the other, allowing an appropriate amount of space between them. They moved slowly through heavy morning traffic. Looking out the window, Donna watched motorcycles weave in and out between the cars, buses, and trucks. She wondered how people could put up with this every day. She recalled what the traffic was like around the D.C. area back in the States. Commuting from Maryland to Langley was such an ordeal that she had requested an office closer to home, and she was permitted to work out of an office at the National Security Agency (NSA) nearby.

An hour later, they sat on one side of a conference table in a secure meeting room at the San José headquarters of the Costa Rican OIJ. Facing them on the other side of the table were Director Jorge Rojas of the OIJ and Director Geraldo Alverez of the DIS. Officer Perez had worked closely with both men in the past. According to protocol, they would address each other by their titles. Each Director also had an Executive Assistant with them. They would remain silent. As was the custom for an important business meeting, all attendees were dressed in business attire. The men wore suits and neckties. Officer Wolf wore a long-sleeved white blouse and a dark skirt that came down just below the knees. Officers Perez and Wolf were here to share intelligence on a matter that would be of interest to both parties with the intent of gaining their support to extradite a Russian spy back to the United States to stand trial. Protocol and decorum were important.

"Officer Perez," Director Rojas began, "I understand you have important information that you want me to know about . . . and I don't believe I have met your associate." It was apparent that Director Rojas was well-educated and spoke very proper English.

"Please," Officer Perez replied, "allow me to introduce Officer Wolf. She's an experienced CIA officer and is here on a temporary assignment. We understand that you have concerns about last year's national election, and that you have initiated an investigation into election fraud and meddling by outside parties. The result of that election was that the Socialists gained political power by establishing a new PAC party and electing fourteen members to the legislature. I want to assure you that the CIA was not in any way involved with that election, but with the help of Director Alverez of the DIS, we do have intelligence that you may be interested in. That's why Officer Wolf is here."

"I see," Director Rojas replied and looked at Officer Wolf across the table.

"Director Rojas, may I . . .?" Officer Wolf said as she returned his glance.

"Yes"

"My job is to track individuals that spy on the United States. I have tracked a certain individual for fifteen years. She's known to have orchestrated a plan to destroy our missile defense system and has murdered three people in the U.S. and at least two more in other countries. One of the people she murdered in the States was a high-level CIA officer that I worked with. She has been in your country for at least three years now as a legal expat Canadian resident using the assumed name of Maria Martin. In your country, she has tutored the children of government officials, including the daughter of Alejandro Gomez, who I understand you put in charge of the election meddling investigation—"

"Whoa, what are you suggesting?"

"*Nada*. We have no evidence that *Señor* Gomez has done anything wrong, but it's possible that Maria Martin is taking advantage of the relationship in some way. Maria Martin is not who she says she is. Her real name is Inga Sarnoff. She's a Russian spy!"

"And you have evidence of all of this, no?"

"Of course, and we will turn it all over to you."

"Uh . . . what are you asking in return?"

Now, Officer Perez got back into the conversation. "We would like you to bring Maria Martin in for questioning, perhaps even an arrest," he said with an air of authority.

"Well, I don't know if we have enough evidence to charge her with a crime in Costa Rica."

Officer Wolf looked puzzled. "Director, isn't it a crime to gain residency using a false identification?" she asked.

"That's just it! We have a very thorough residency application process in Costa Rica. I don't understand how she could have been accepted if she was not who she said she was."

Officer Wolf started to answer, but Perez spoke before she could.

"Director, I know you don't want to hear this. I'm sorry, but we have proof. All her documents were forged. She assumed the identity of a Canadian citizen who had passed away. She had help from her Russian handlers and may—we don't know for sure—have bribed someone in your immigration department. We do have proof that she lied on her application, and we can prove that her documents were forged or stolen."

"I see . . . but you are looking for something in return for this information, are you not?"

"We are!"

"What?"

"Director, we have prepared extradition papers," Officer Wolf replied. "We wish to take Inga Sarnoff back to the United States to stand trial for murder and espionage."

At this point, the DIS Director, who had not said a word until now, finally spoke up. "I thank you for the intelligence you have provided. It will help us with our investigation into possible Russian tampering with our election process—"

Director Rojas interjected. "Director Alverez, *por favor*. Why do you think the Russians are meddling in our elections? And do you think that Maria Martin is part of that?"

"Yes, Director, I do. The CIA provided us information about a secret meeting that took place in the fall of the year 2000 at the Russian Embassy in Managua, Nicaragua. The meeting was attended by the Sandinista Party of Nicaragua and the Communist Party of the Russian Federation. Our intelligence indicates that the Russians have a long-term plan to regain influence in Central America, including Costa Rica. As you know, they had supported the Sandinistas until 1992, when the Soviet Union dissolved. However, the FSLN party is still strong in Nicaragua, and there are rumors that the radical leftist Daniel Ortega may regain the Presidency at some point. At the same time, increasing numbers of Nicaraguans and Russians are coming across our border, many of them illegally. If Costa Rica becomes more socialistic and more sympathetic to Nicaragua, the Russians may increase their influence. Meanwhile, the Nicaraguans are encroaching into the Costa Rican territory of Isla Calero and have plans for a missile base there. They have already established a military base. It's only a matter of time before the Russians resume openly sending arms to Nicaragua. Knowing that we have no military, they may think we will be intimidated, and assume that we will not be successful when we take our grievances to the international courts. Our intelligence indicates that they have supported Socialist candidates in our country and that they have paid to have dirt sent to the media regarding more conservative candidates. We believe their objective is to influence relations between our country and Nicaragua to allow them more influence and control over both our countries."

"Director Alverez, do you have proof of any of this?" Director Rojas asked. "We are a country of laws. We cannot take legal action unless there is strong evidence of a crime."

"Unfortunately, not enough to stand up in court," Director Alverez replied. "We only have bits of intelligence that allow us to create a plausible picture of the future. However, we will continue to investigate."

"And what about Maria Martin? Do you have evidence that she had been working to influence our election?"

"We have some Director, but again, not enough to stand up in court. We continue to investigate."

"It seems to me," Director Rojas responded, "if we proceed with extradition proceedings for Inga Sarnoff, that will alert the people being investigated and have a negative impact on the outcome of our investigation. Furthermore, Costa Rica does not have the death penalty, and if there was an extradition, the death penalty would be off the table, and I am not sure why the USA would want to waste the time and expense to bring this to trial in the United States if the death penalty is off the table. Same with the charges of misrepresenting the residence application. Any arrest would alert the people involved in the election fraud, and by the way, if found guilty by the court of illegal entry, the only penalty would be deportation back to Russia. That's hardly a just punishment, in my opinion. Yes, Director Alverez is correct. We need to continue investigating until we get all the facts about the meddling in our election and the influence that Russia exerts over our elected officials."

Sensing where this was heading, Officer Wolf tried to speak up. "Director Rojas, with all due respect, I don't—," but Officer Perez held up his hand and stopped her before she could say it.

"So, Director, are we at a standoff on this?" Officer Perez asked, directing his question to Director Rojas.

"Perhaps, but we *will* consider your objectives, and if Inga Sarnoff should try to leave our country, we will alert you, and she is all yours to do as you wish. We would also welcome your continued help in providing evidence that the Russians have interfered with our election."

They all shook hands and the meeting ended.

****

The limo arrived out front of the OIJ at a few minutes past noon. Officers Wolf and Perez were properly shown into the rear seat. As they rode back to Perez's office, they began discussing the situation.

"You know," he said, "Directors Alverez and Rojas made a good point. It will probably take a while for them to complete their investigations and approve extradition. And once we have her, it will be a great deal of expense to convict her in the United States. And with the death penalty off the table, we no longer have a bargaining chip in exchange for useful information—not that she would give us any anyway."

"What do you think we should do, Ed?"

"It's already afternoon. Let's have lunch. You hungry?"

"I am."

"We can talk more about our game plan and have lunch at the embassy."

They had lunch and they talked, but by the time they returned to his office, nothing had been resolved.

Finally, Ed said, "Let me make some phone calls this afternoon and see if there is another approach for us to take—" He looked into her eyes. "Donna, we don't get to see each other very often. Have dinner with me tonight."

She smiled. "Are you asking me out?"

"I am."

"I'd love to, but I'm very tired. The trip here yesterday and the meeting today took a lot out of me. Could we do it tomorrow?" she asked.

"Yes, for sure. I really want to spend time with you while you're here. How about coming over to the office tomorrow morning? We can talk more when we meet. In the meantime, go back to your hotel and get some rest. Okay?"

"Okay." She got up and turned to leave.

"Oh, wait. I almost forgot!" he called out.

She turned back. "What?"

He reached into the top drawer of his desk and pulled out a mobile phone. "Here, take this. Your phone is no good here. You can use this to make local calls while you're here. Just keep in mind, it's not secure."

"Thanks, Ed. See you in the morning," she said as she tucked the phone into her purse and walked out.

2

JUDI and JOE

Meanwhile, on that same Thursday morning, Joe Garcia was at his office, sitting at his desk, and reading his emails and text messages. He and a business partner owned and operated a successful security consulting and design business located on the north side of the city of San José.

His business had four rooms in rented office space. He had a receptionist in the outer room, his partner's desk in another, and his in a third. The fourth room was a combination storage room and office for a second employee who helped with sales and the installation of security products. Officially, his clients included private individuals, local businesses, and government agencies.

He specialized in security surveillance. Although not everything he did was legal, he never had an issue with law enforcement.

It was still early in the morning when the following message popped up on his computer screen:

> *Joe,*
> *Urgent. Must meet with you at once. Please call me.*
> *Judi*

Joe knew Judi as a friend of Maria. Maria was one of Joe's clients. Unlike Maria, who was middle-aged, Judi was in her early thirties. She worked as a waitress at a nearby chain restaurant. For some reason, she put an "*i*" rather than a "*y*" at the end of her first name. She also had tattoos in subtle places. Perhaps it reflected her need to be unique. She said her last name was Smith, but she looked Spanish. Once, when asked, she

456

implied that she was from San Diego. Her slight Spanish accent supported that, so perhaps that was true. Joe had worked for Judi and Maria since 2001, and they had become friends.

Joe called Judi and asked her what could be so urgent.

"So, Judi, either the nice weather has increased your desire for male companionship, or you need my help with something. What's going on?"

"Sorry to disappoint, but I need to talk to you about Maria."

"What's going on with Maria?"

"I can't talk about it on the phone. I need to meet with you. Can you meet me this morning at La Favorita Park?"

"Don't know. Possibly. What time?"

"Ten."

Joe looked at his watch. It was already nine fifteen. "Kind of short notice, don't you think?"

"Joe, please. This is very urgent. I'll bring coffee."

"Okay," he gave in. "I'll see you there at ten."

Joe was bright and had college degrees in engineering and computer science. His father had worked for the government as a criminal investigator, and Joe wanted to follow in his father's footsteps. After college, Joe began a career at the OIJ investigating drug and sex trafficking. However, he had felt stifled every time he got the chance to do something meaningful. He also became disillusioned by the degree of corruption he was finding inside the government. Then, seven years ago, his father and stepmother died in a suspicious car accident. So, at the age of thirty, he decided to take some risks and start a new business.

Joe knew that Maria and Judi were Socialists. He also knew that the three of them were really working for Vladimir Petrov. The public knew Petrov as an influential supporter of socialist causes. Joe had worked for Maria for more than three years, and his work had been instrumental in the recent success of the new PAC political party. Maria had hired him to provide surveillance of opposing candidates and supporters. The intent was to reveal their corrupt actions, use that against them, and get reformers into office.

However, Joe was not a Socialist, and politics was not his thing. The job paid well, but the reason he agreed to have Maria as a client was because he wanted to fight government corruption and nothing else.

Joe told his secretary that he needed to go out for a meeting and would take the company car. Although he traveled to work on a motorcycle, he and his business partner leased a late-model Toyota Corolla for local travel when working.

The trip took twenty minutes. He arrived a few minutes early and parked the car on the road bordering the park. La Favorita was a small neighborhood park, nicely landscaped, with several benches. As he approached the center of the park, he saw Judi approaching from the other side, where she had chained her motorcycle.

Judi was wearing jeans and a casual tube top. The top engulfed her torso from just above her pierced navel to just above her nipples, exposing her tan arms and shoulders. A black tattoo peaked out from her tube top just above her left breast and complemented her jet-black hair.

They met at a convenient bench and sat down. She opened a small picnic bag, and poured coffee into two paper cups. Joe watched with a smile on his face.

"You really did bring coffee," Joe said gleefully. "Thank you!"

"I'm a woman of my word," she quipped.

"Judi, what's so urgent about Maria that you couldn't tell me over the phone? Is she okay?"

"Petrov contacted me in the wee hours of the morning. He thinks Maria may be in danger. He said that intelligence sources told him that a CIA officer from the United States entered the country last night. Petrov thinks she may be here to arrest or possibly assassinate Maria."

"I think you need to fill me in on some details. Why would Petrov think that's the reason for a CIA officer to be here?"

"Okay, Petrov told me that prior to coming here, Maria was a spy in the United States, and the U.S. wants her for espionage and murder."

"Oh my, I see!" he said with a display of surprise. "I didn't know this about Maria. Have you warned her?"

"Petrov said he would take care of that, but today she's on a job somewhere, and Petrov said he didn't want to alarm her until we knew more. Petrov told me this CIA officer rented a car at the airport last night. He gave me the plate number. Early this morning, I came to the U.S. Embassy and waited for her car to show up. I assume she met with the CIA Station Chief. Then, about two hours ago, a limo came and they left the premises. I followed the limo to the OIJ and watched them go inside. That's probably where she is now. In any case, her rental car was still at the embassy when I went by on the way back here."

"Where do you think I fit into this?"

"Petrov says you have the expertise to get the information we need. He wants you to find out exactly why she's here and what her intentions are. Petrov says you have sources at the OIJ, and you may be able to find out what the meeting is about. He wants you to pick up where I left off."

"Hmmm, I see. I'm kind of tied up today. I could use your help on this. Will Petrov approve?"

"I think so. How can I help?"

"Do you know what hotel she's staying at?"

"No, I asked that. He said she may be at the InterContinental, but can't be sure. Apparently, she used the name Donna Wolf to get into the country and rent a car, but may have used another name to register at a hotel."

"Judi, here's what I need you to do. Follow her back to her hotel today and find out what room she's in. As soon as you know her hotel and her room number, send it to me in a text message. If she sees you that's okay. You will need to come up with some story as to who you are and why you're at the hotel. If you talk with her, find out everything you can. She may reveal something of value. Okay so far?"

"Yes, but I'm supposed to work today."

"What time?"

"My hours are from four to ten."

"I think you should tell them you can't work today, or at least tell them you'll be a couple of hours late. What I need you to do is find a way to get into her room. I know you're good at improvising, so I'm sure you will think of something. If she has a phone or a laptop with her, you could steal it, but then she would be suspicious. Better if you could just take a photo of her contact lists or get onto her laptop and email any useful info to yourself, or perhaps you will find something else that's revealing. And once inside her room, if you can plant a bug for me, that would be perfect."

"Whoa. You're the expert. How do you expect *me* to do all of that . . . and where would I get a bug?"

"I have the devices you need in my car . . . come."

He gave her a wireless microphone/transmitter and a receiver/ recorder. Then he gave her some suggestions on how to proceed.

"This is state-of-the-art stuff," he told her. "Not very heavy and not very big. This is the transmitter, also called a bug. It has Velcro on the back and here are several Velcro strips that can be taped onto a surface. Obviously, you need to place the bug where not only she won't find it, but also where the room maid won't. Don't put it where the sound will be blocked, or near the TV, or near a fluorescent lamp. The best place might be to tape it to the back of the desk or the chest of drawers, or if possible, the back-side of the headboard of the bed. Okay so far?"

"Where do I put the recorder?"

"You don't. As soon as you tell me her room number, I'll make a reservation for you at the hotel." He noticed her expression. And knew what she was about to protest.

"No, it won't cost you," he added. "I'll prepay the reservation. Think of it as a prepaid vacation. However, you will need to show your driver's license when you check in, so I need to know the name on your license. Is it Judi Smith, or is that an alias?"

"It's really Judi Smith. I thought I told you I was married once, but I kept the last name after we split."

"Okay . . . When I make the reservation, it will be for two people, you and a husband. His first name should be Joseph if that comes up. I will text you back as soon as the reservation is made, but check-in time may be as late as four, so you need to be late for work. When you check in, make sure to get a second key for your husband. Text me your room number as soon as you check in. I want you to put the recorder into *your* room. Plug it into the wall socket—no need to run down the batteries."

"What about the batteries in the bug? Won't they run down?"

"Oh . . . hope not. The bug is voice-activated. Let me demonstrate how it works," he said and proceeded to do just that.

"Wow, impressive," she said with only mild enthusiasm.

"Meanwhile, this afternoon, while you're doing all that, I'll check my sources at the OIJ. Then tonight, I'll pay you a visit in your new quarters, and we will see where we are on this."

So, Joe, were you considering spending the night? I wouldn't mind."

"Judi, we've discussed this. You know how I feel about mixing business and pleasure."

Judi made no secret of her desire to have sex with Joe. He had allowed this once in what he considered to be a weak moment. She proved to be more sexually experienced and kinkier than he was. They were from different social classes and backgrounds, and Joe decided that she was not someone he wanted to have a long-term romantic relationship with, but it did not dissuade her from trying. He often wondered why she found him so desirable. Was it his good looks and his intellect, or was it because his inexperience with women allowed her to feel more in control?

"Well, you know what they say about all work and no play. I think you should reconsider."

He gave her a hard look.

"Okay," she said with a sincere tone of resignation. "You can't blame a girl for trying. But Joe, there is something else I need from you."

He gave her a questioning look. "What do you need from me?"

"Your car."

"What? My car? Why?"

"You want me to follow this woman back to the hotel, check in, and strike up a rapport with her. I need a cover story as to why I'm staying at an expensive hotel. It's not likely I would ride a bike. It's more likely I would be driving a rental car, especially if I'm traveling with a husband."

"Okay, but the car belongs to the business. My partner may need it."

"Take my bike. When you come to my hotel room tonight after I get off from work, bring my bike. We'll see how things go from there."

He knew she was right. They exchanged keys. He walked across the park to the bike and watched Judi get into his car and drive away. Then, he adjusted the bike to accommodate his longer legs, donned an ill-fitting helmet he found behind the seat, and took off in the opposite direction.

3

CASUAL ENCOUNTER

Donna left the embassy and retrieved her car. As she headed east on Via 104, she sensed that another car was following her. After she turned south toward Route 27, she glanced into her rearview mirror only to see that the same car was still behind her.

Could be a coincidence, she thought.

However, when she turned onto Route 27 and headed west, the same car was still behind her. Now, she began to seriously consider that she was being tailed on purpose. Sure enough, when she pulled onto the side road toward her hotel and into the parking lot, her tail did the same. Although she was a little nervous, she had played this game before and knew enough not to panic. As she walked toward the hotel entrance, she noticed a young woman exit the car and follow her. Donna entered the hotel, walked to the elevators, and pushed the up button. As she waited, the woman caught up to her.

"Hello," the woman said with a friendly smile. "I believe I may have been following you all the way from the embassy. I hope I didn't freak you out."

"Yes, I noticed," Donna replied. "I was wondering why you were following me. Did you have business there?"

"I'm sorry if I made you nervous. Yes, my husband just got transferred there, and they put us up here at the hotel until we find a place to live."

"Oh, I see."

The elevator arrived and they both got in. Without thinking, Donna pushed the button for floor six, her floor, and then she asked, "What floor?"

"Six please," the young woman responded politely.

Still unsure about this woman, Donna scolded herself—*should've asked her first. It's been too long since I was in the field, but perhaps I'm just being paranoid.*

Donna left the elevator first and the young woman followed. They arrived at Donna's door first.

"Have a nice day," the young woman said as she walked by. Donna watched her stop at another door far down the hallway.

****

Once inside her room, Donna locked the door, and set her purse on top of the desk. It was getting heavy. She was tired. Time for a nap, she decided. She removed her shoes, her skirt, and her blouse, hung them up carefully in the closet, and threw herself prone on the bed. She quickly fell asleep and woke up two hours later. When she awoke, she felt refreshed. It was only 3:30 p.m. She looked out the window—a beautiful day. She felt like she needed a swim, so she put on her swim suit, pulled a cover-up garment over her head, and took the elevator down to the outdoor pool. Although it was Thursday, most of the seats with umbrellas were occupied, but then she saw someone leave, freeing up an umbrella with two lounge chairs. She went over and plunked down on one of the chairs. No sooner had she settled down than she heard someone to her left trying to get her attention. It was the young woman who followed her from the embassy earlier. The woman waved and walked over.

"No open seats," she said.

"You're welcomed to join me under this umbrella. The other lounge chair is free," Donna said extending her arm toward the chair.

"Oh, thank you so much. I shouldn't get too much sun. This is perfect. By the way, my name is Judi Smith."

"I'm Donna."

"Donna . . .?"

"Donna Rice."

"Where are you from, Donna?"

"Maryland."

"You?"

"New York City."

Donna noticed her accent. It was not quite what one would expect of a New Yorker.

"Your accent seems—"

"More like Spanish? I know. I get that a lot. I grew up in Puerto Rico but moved to New York City, where I went to college and met my husband. I think I mentioned that my husband is in the process of transferring here."

"Have you started your house hunting yet?"

"We plan to start big time this weekend. What about you? You were at the embassy. Are you here on business?"

"No, I'm here on vacation, but I have a friend who works at the embassy and I hope to spend some time with him while I'm here. We had lunch."

"Oh, I see," she responded.

"You said your husband just started working at the embassy. What's his name?"

"Joseph Smith." After saying this, she realized that she would eventually be caught in a lie. "What is *your* friend's name?"

"Edward Gardner," Donna replied, knowing that her lie would probably go undetected or be of no consequence.

The two of them chatted for a spell, and then Donna was ready for a swim. She noticed that Judi was not wearing a swim-suit and politely asked to be excused.

"It's okay," Judi said, "go ahead."

Donna removed her cover-up, hung it on the back of her lounge chair, and jumped into the deep end of the pool. The water was cool and refreshing. Donna relaxed and swam a couple of laps before joining Judi on the pool's edge.

"I need to go and fetch my husband from work," Judi said apologetically. "I'm told that the traffic is bad at this time of day, so I need to allow plenty of time. Perhaps I'll see you again tomorrow."

Donna replied, "I look forward to it. Drive carefully," and almost immediately dove back into the pool for another swim.

She stayed in the pool for another fifteen minutes or so before coming out of the water and heading back to her lounge chair. She dried off and laid back in the chair. She closed her eyes and dozed off. When she awoke the sun was very low in the sky and she decided it was time to go back to her room. She put her cover-up back on, grabbed her towel, and made it all the way to the elevators, before she realized something was wrong. Her room key was not in her pocket. Thinking it must have dropped out near where she was sitting, she went back to the pool to look for it. Unfortunately, she couldn't find it anywhere. So, she went to the main desk in the lobby. Not having any proof with her of who she was, she had a hard time convincing the lady on duty to give her a new key.

"We pride ourselves on keeping our guests secure," the lady stated. "We can't just give out a new key to anyone that asks."

"But my identification is in my room, and I need a key to get it."

"Please wait here for a few minutes, madam. I will have a security guard escort you to your room and you can show him your identification when you get there."

The security guard was a young man who seemed very polite and understanding. He opened the door to her room and held it open for her to enter. He suggested she look around and make sure nothing was missing from the room. She noticed her laptop still atop the desk. She checked her purse. Her phone and wallet were there. No money was missing. Everything seemed to be as she left it . . . and then she noticed it.

Her key-card was on the floor on the far side of the counter that supported the TV. *Did I really forget to take it with me?* she asked herself. She showed the security guard. "Happens all the time, Madam," he said.

She handed him a five-dollar bill, USD, and thanked him for his troubles. Satisfied, he wished her a good evening and left.

Later that evening, after a light meal and an attempt to watch a TV show in Spanish, Donna got herself ready for bed. As she lay in bed, she recounted the events of the day and scolded herself. *How could I misplace my room key? It's just not like me. Perhaps tomorrow will be a better day.* Then she took a deep breath, let it out slowly, closed her eyes, and fell asleep.

4

EVENING PLANS

The next day on Friday, Donna and Ed met again at the embassy and talked.

"How did you sleep?" he asked.

"Very well, thanks. I'm fully refreshed."

"Donna, I talked with Director Rojas again earlier this morning. He said that the OIJ further considered the situation and agreed to arrest Maria Martin on the illegal entry charge early next week, and he will allow us to interview her. He said they will consider allowing us to extradite her if we can guarantee that the death penalty is off the table. He said they are also investigating her for possible espionage within Costa Rica. The OIJ wants to interrogate her, and he wants to have time for a search warrant of her house while she's in their custody. He said it may be a week or two before she could be released into our custody."

"Why the change in heart?"

"I think they realize that other than the possibility of minor charges, their investigation is going nowhere any time soon. I think they want information from her, like the names of those in the government that have been compromised. Otherwise, they probably want her out of the country as soon as possible to prevent her from doing further damage."

"But what's our bargaining chip? Why would she talk to us? And even if she does, what would she give us?"

"Well, one idea is that the OIJ uses our threat of extradition as their bargaining chip. They will tell her that if she confesses to a crime here, they will not allow her to be extradited. The penalty here is less than what we would impose, especially if she gives them names."

"You mean that after all the work we did to track her down, she will get off on a minor charge?"

"Even if she doesn't confess to anything, the OIJ may have enough to hold her long enough to get more evidence. But, if that falls through, they will just let her go—kick her out of the country. If they deport her, we could try to intercept her before she ends up in Canada or Russia. Then, if we bring her back to the United States, the death penalty would not be off the table. This would be the OIJ's bargaining chip. But let me ask you, after fifteen years, do you still have enough hard evidence to convict her of the murders she committed in the United States? And, you know, if we keep futzing around for too long, she may get wind of our intentions and flee before we can arrest her. If we don't intercept her, and if we don't convict her, won't she just reinvent herself and continue spying and murdering people elsewhere? And, as the Deputy Director of DIS asked, 'Is the expense worth it?'."

Donna gave him a hard look and slowly let out her breath.

"Ed, tell me what you suggest," she demanded.

"Donna, I know you have invested a great deal of your time and energy tracking her down, and if you were to take her out, I would look the other way."

"You don't mean that," she said sharply.

"Actually, I do. But in the meantime, I think we should play it by the book, keep our options open, and see how it plays out."

Donna shook her head slowly from side to side. "I suppose you're right," she said with resignation.

Then, after a long pause, "Ed, are we still on for tonight?"

"I don't know. Something has come up. Earlier this morning, before Rojas called, I got a call from Langley. It was your boss, Brian Matheson. I think he forgot about the two-hour time difference. But anyway, he asked how you were doing and wanted to know the status of our endeavor. I told him you were doing fine and filled him in on our stalemate with the OIJ. Then he asked—directed—that I have you do something for him later today. He wants you to meet with a contact near the city of Heredia. He said that this gentleman is a professor at the National University up there and you should meet him at five thirty this evening. He told me where. It's a coffee shop called La Copa Máxima. Every Friday and Saturday evening from five to eight, they have a classical Spanish guitarist. Many of my associates have gone there and say it's an excellent place to relax after work over a cup of coffee and a pastry. I'm sure you'll enjoy it." Then, remembering that Donna only drank coffee in the morning and tea the rest of the day, "They have tea as well," he added.

"Did he say what the purpose of the meeting was?" "Kind of. He said that the professor has a package that he needs back in Langley, and to save time, he wants you to bring it to me so that I can then send it to Langley via the embassy's secure mail service. Other than that, he said you might find the professor interesting to talk with."

"What's in the package?"

"No idea. He wouldn't tell me. You can ask the professor."

"How will the professor know who I am?"

"Matheson said that he already told the professor your pseudo name. You're still using Donna Rice, aren't you?"

"Yup. How do I get there?"

"I'll give you directions in a minute. But first, regarding dinner, I told Matheson that I was hoping to have dinner with you tonight, and we talked about where I was going to be. Originally, I was thinking of us eating at a place called Jurgens, but the location would not be convenient for me. However, we can still do Jurgens tomorrow. So, I thought that tonight we could meet at the Hotel Grano de Oro. I can be there by eight, if that's not too late for you. You could give me the package, and then we could have dinner. The hotel has a bar and a restaurant. I've been there before and the food is good. You okay with that?"

"Sure. How dressy is it? What should I wear?"

"What you are wearing now is fine," he said as he noticed her dressy white blouse and black slacks. "I really like what you're wearing now."

"Please tell me how I get to the coffee shop and then to the hotel."

"Okay. Let me sketch out a map and directions for you."

Ed turned to his desk, pulled out a sheet of paper and a pencil, and began drawing a map. After a few minutes, he turned back to Donna and showed her what he drew.

"Wow, impressive!"

"Well, thanks, but I think my drawing skills could be better."

"Good enough for me."

"Alright, so to orient you, here is your hotel down here," he said and circled the initials IC for InterContinental.

Then he repeated the process for the coffee shop, and circled the initials CM for Copa Máxima, near the top of the page. "I'll write the address here."

"And finally, here is the *Hotel Grano de Oro*," he said as he moved his hand to the lower right of the map and circled the initials GO.

"Ah," Donna uttered and pointed to the area marked as Rohrmoser. "Doesn't Maria Martin live in Rohrmoser?"

"Yes, she does. Her residence would be just about here on the map," he said and added yet another circled set of initials. "I think you already have her address," but then cautioned, "Officially, you should not contact her. If she knows we're about to arrest her, she might flee. You know that, right?"

Donna gave him a look, making it clear she did not like being talked down to.

He got the message. "Sorry, I didn't need to say that, but I do have a suggestion. The traffic going North from here on Route 39 and Route 3 can be very slow. If you leave from your hotel, I would suggest you head back to the airport on Route 147, the way you got to your hotel on Wednesday, and then take Route 111 from there. Anyway, take the map with you."

"Okay, thanks. It'll help."

"And here, take this as well," he said and handed her an envelope.

"What's this?"

"It's just more information about tonight. You can look at it later."

"Okay."

"There's really nothing more we can do on the Martin project until we hear back from the OIJ next week, so it's a chance for you to enjoy the rest of the afternoon. I'll see you tonight, and we can talk about spending time together this weekend."

"I look forward to it. See you later." She put the map and the envelope into her purse and left the office.

****

Donna went back to the hotel and used the free time to make a few phone calls. She made one to her daughter, Brandy, to see how things were at home. She made another to Matheson in Langley to get a better understanding of what he wanted her to do that evening. Then she looked up *La Copa Máxima* in the phone book and called it to verify the venue and the menu. After that, she went downstairs and had a salad and an iced tea. She explored the InterContinental hotel, noting it had a nice lounge with entertainment on Friday and Saturday nights. As she entered one of the shops, she spied Judi, who noticed and came over. They chatted for a while.

"Hi Donna. What have you been doing today?"

"Touring the city," she responded. "What about you?"

"Well, I've been hanging out around here. My husband took the car this morning . . . said he might need it, so here I am."

For a moment Judi seemed to be gazing at Donna's body and Donna picked up on this.

"What are you looking at?" Donna asked out of curiosity.

"Sorry, but I was just noticing that you seemed to be dressed up—not like a typical tourist."

"Oh, well, I haven't been here long enough to know what is expected, and anyway, I plan to go somewhere this evening."

"Do you have dinner plans?" Judi asked. Perhaps you and your friend Ed would like to join Joe and me for dinner?"

"Oh, that would be a wonderful idea, but unfortunately, Ed and I already have other plans."

"A romantic evening?"

"I hope so."

"Where is he taking you?"

"Well, he mentioned a nice restaurant in a hotel called the *Grano de Oro,* but he said he was taking off from work early, and I'm leaving around four to go meet him." She looked at her watch. It was already three. "I wanted to browse through the shops before I went."

"Are you looking for anything special?"

"I'm looking for a birthday present for my daughter."

"Well, I won't keep you. I hope you have an enjoyable evening."

As soon as they parted, Judi contacted Joe and filled him in on what she learned from Donna. Then she rode her bike to her four o'clock shift at the restaurant where she worked.

5

THE ASSASSINATION

On Friday evening, an agent using the code name DR entered La Copa Máxima, a coffee shop and eatery in Heredia, Costa Rica. The location was convenient. The National University campus was nearby. The international airport was a few miles to the southwest, and the metropolis of San José a few miles to the southeast. It was still early in the evening. A guitarist was setting up his gear on one side of the room. The aroma of freshly ground coffee beans permeated the air. The agent paid little attention, walked directly to a secluded corner of the coffee shop, and met with a distinguished-looking man dressed in business attire.

"Good evening, sir. I'm DR."

The man dressed in business attire replied, "Please be seated. May I order you a coffee?"

"I'm sure the coffee here is excellent, but I prefer tea."

It was a prearranged exchange of words for security reasons. Although the two had talked a day and a half earlier, they had never met.

"We are pleased that we can work with you, and we agree to protect your identity," the man dressed in business attire said, and motioned for the waitress.

"Likewise, we have a common interest," DR responded.

After the waitress arrived and took the order for tea, the man in business attire continued the conversation.

"I understand that you've been given some preliminary information about this operation. Is that correct?"

"Yes, that's correct."

"As compensation for your help, we have arranged to have $20,000 deposited into your overseas account. Are you okay with that?"

"Yes, I'm fine with that." DR smiled, thinking, *the money was unnecessary—the motivation to do the job was there without it.*

The two continued to talk as business associates and enjoyed coffee and tea together while the guitar music played softly in the background.

Before they parted, the man dressed in business attire said, "It's very difficult to bring a gun into Costa Rica. I assume you did not. Am I correct?"

"Yes, that's correct. Have you taken care of that?"

"My position in the government allows me to own a hand gun. I keep my hand gun and carry permit in a case under the seat of my Ford sedan. It's parked in behind the building. It's the blue one with the tinted windows. The case includes a silencer and an ammo clip. I'll assume it has been stolen. I plan to file a report in the morning, but I don't ever expect to see it again. You'll also find an empty carton on the seat. Take it with you. Your target probably has a desktop computer. It may contain valuable information. Remove the hard-drive, insert the drive into the metal sleeve and into the carton. The carton has a name and hotel address on it. Deliver it to the address written on the label before eight tonight. Oh, and one more thing. It's important that you protect your identity. Are you prepared to disguise yourself in the manner we discussed?" DR nodded in the affirmative. "Before you arrive at the target's home, you must be wearing it, and you must keep it on until you complete the total mission."

Then he handed DR an envelope and said, "This envelope contains the home address of your target and directions to get there. I assume you've already been given background information on her, so I won't repeat that. Questions?" he asked, noticing a puzzled expression on DR's face.

"Yes. Have you assessed the security at the address?"

"It has the typical wrought iron security fencing topped with razor wire, a locked pedestrian gate, and a locked garage gate. You can expect that the doors into the house itself will also be locked."

"Anything else?"

"Yes. Should I expect the target to be at home?"

"Our surveillance indicated that on Fridays she usually returns from the National University campus in Heredia after six thirty in the evening. It's only five twenty-five now so you have time," he said glancing at his watch. "However, you will probably need time to put on your disguise, and the traffic can be unpredictable. So, you had best be on your way."

With that, DR, the would-be assassin, stood up, said good-bye to the man dressed in business attire, and exited the rear of the coffee shop.

DR retrieved the empty carton and the gun-case from the Ford, walked to the front of the building, and got into a late model Toyota Camry.

DR took a few moments to apply some makeup and don the disguise. The disguise was a ladies' black loose-fitting long-sleeved top, a silky neck-scarf, a ladies' wig, a pair of stylish glasses, and dangling earrings. This complemented the black slacks, and black walking shoes already being worn. *Now I like the way I look*, DR muttered sarcastically. *I never looked better.*

Then DR opened the gun case and removed a Sig 2022 hand gun, a silencer, and a magazine containing twelve 9 mm bullets. The gun was small and light weight. It would tuck under the waist band of the pants and be concealed by the loose-fitting top. The silencer would fit into a pants pocket.

Before starting up the engine, DR opened the envelope and read the enclosed note. It had the name and address of the intended target. The address was a house in Rohrmoser, an old neighborhood on the eastern side of Pavas, a district within the Province of San José, west of the city. Rohrmoser was considered an upscale neighborhood. Many high-level government officials and ambassadors lived there, and several embassies, including the U.S. embassy, were nearby.

Following the enclosed directions, DR went southwest to Route 1, and then followed Route 1 southeast toward the city of San José. Along the way, Route 1 crossed the Rio Virilla, and at this point the river had carved a deep canyon below the bridge. The sun had not yet set, and while crossing the bridge, DR could still make out a blue ribbon of water far below. Seeing it for the first time, normal people would marvel at the scenic view, but DR was not a normal person and remained focused on the mission.

About thirty minutes after leaving the coffee shop, DR arrived at the home of the intended target, and parked the car on the street at a location close to the residence. DR got out of the car and walked toward the residence carrying a shoulder bag containing the empty carton and a small tool kit. The gun was tucked into DR's waistband under the black loose-fitting top.

The residence was a small one-story house placed endwise to the street. A short, paved driveway to the right of the house led from the street to a gated garage. As expected, eight-foot-high security fencing topped with razor wire ran along the sidewalk and then up the left side of the driveway all the way to the garage. Two-thirds of the way up the driveway, a pedestrian gate and a path led to the main entrance on the other side of the house. DR walked to the gate and pressed a button on an intercom mounted next to the gate. No one answered. DR walked to the gate protecting the garage and peered in between the bars. No car. Clearly, the target was not yet home. DR saw no easy way to get past the locked gates, to say nothing of the doors into the house which would also be locked. Looking around, there was no sign of a security camera on this house, and none were visible nearby.

The sun had set and twilight was fading. With the low humidity, the temperatures were cooling quickly. While walking back down the driveway, and following the sidewalk back to the car, DR was thankful for the warmth of the black pull-over. On the way back, a pedestrian walking a dog said, *"Buenas tardes señora"* as he passed. DR responded with a simple *hola* and nodded politely. The darkness, the disguise, and the lack of a nearby security camera should protect my identity, DR thought. Back in the car, DR patiently watched the residence. A lamp came on at the pedestrian gate, and then later, another inside the house shined through the security bars covering the two windows facing the street—probably on timers. The only other light would be from sparsely spaced street lamps.

At 6:35 p.m., a car pulled up the driveway and stopped just short of the garage gate. A middle-aged woman got out and used a key to open the two halves of the security gate. She swung them outward, got back in the car, and pulled all the way forward. As she did this, DR donned a pair of latex gloves, readied the gun and silencer, grabbed the shoulder bag, and walked quickly up the driveway to the entry of the garage. The woman reached for her purse, got out of her car, and swung the car door shut. As she turned to walk back toward the garage entrance and shut the gate, her assailant confronted her..

"Buenas noches señora."

She stopped short and looked up. A look of panic spread across her face as she saw the gun and realized it was too late to respond. While still six feet away, DR fired two bullets. The first hit her squarely in the chest, and the other hit her in the throat. Blood-spatter landed on the side of the car and on the garage wall to the left. She fell backwards and landed with a thud on the concreate floor. Her purse spilled next to her. She lay motionless. Her white blouse was slowly saturated with blood. It was a ghastly sight, but DR watched, suppressing any signs of emotion, until assured that she was dead!

DR remained calm and cool and retrieved the two bullet casings from the floor, being careful not to pick up any trace of blood, and then retrieved the woman's purse and found the keys needed to get inside. To help block any view of the body from the street, DR closed the garage gates and relocated a trash bin between the gate and the body. At the rear of the garage, there was an exit door that led toward the house. Rather than risk stumbling over the body, DR walked around the passenger side of the car to the exit door, and then walked from the garage across a covered patio to a sliding glass door that led into the house. One of the woman's keys worked and the door to the kitchen slid open.

As soon as DR entered the kitchen, an ear-splitting beeping pierced the air, loud enough to awaken the soundest of sleepers. *Oh no, a security alarm. Wasn't I told otherwise?* DR looked around, but no security alarm panel was in sight. The cluster of keys was still in DR's hand. *Two remote fobs; only one car.* DR pressed the red buttons on each. The beeping stopped! DR breathed a sigh of relief, but hoped that no one else had been alerted by the alarm.

DR passed through the kitchen and a small dining area and began looking for a bedroom or den that might have a personal computer. The house was very well-kept, with nice furniture, premium woodwork, and tile flooring. Artwork hung from the walls. According to the information that DR was given, friends and associates of the target knew her as Maria Martin. They knew her as a retired teacher and expat from Canada who was in her fifties. She taught English at the National University in Heredia. She also tutored the children of government officials. She did the tutoring in the client's homes. It paid well.

Typically, a tutor of her caliber could earn more than 500 U.S. dollars per month, about 150,000 colons in the local currency. In 2003, if you were a resident and not a tourist, that much money went a long way in Costa Rica. Maria Martin probably rented the house from a government official. However, DR considered the luxury of the neighborhood, house, and furnishings, and knew she was either living rent-free or had more income than what came from teaching and tutoring. If she did retire from a teaching job in Canada, a small pension of only $1,000 per month, would make a big difference, but DR knew the truth.

DR exited the dining area, passed through the living room, and continued down a short hallway. At the end of the hallway, facing the street, was a large master bedroom. The door was open and the light was on. DR took a quick look inside and didn't notice a computer, but did notice suitcases that were almost completely packed, and wondered why she was planning a trip. Had she been pre-warned of an impending threat? Then DR exited the bedroom and went back up the hallway. On the left side of the hallway, was a shut door. DR opened the door, flicked on the light switch, and went into a good-sized den. A newspaper lay on a side chair. It was in a foreign language—not English or Spanish—the Cyrillic letters suggested Russian. A desktop computer sat atop an old wooden desk. As instructed, DR disconnected the power cord, removed the casing of the computer, pulled out the tool kit from the bag, removed the hard-drive, and inserted it into the protective sleeve and carton that was provided.

Then, feeling the need to make a strong political statement, DR took a sheet of blank paper from the printer, pulled a magic marker from a container on the desk, created a makeshift sign, walked back into the garage, and put the sign next to the body. The sign said:

¡JUSTICIA PARA UN ESPÍA RUSO!

After collecting the tool kit, the gun, and the carton with the hard-drive, DR calmly walked out of the garage, made sure to lock all doors and gates, and went back out to the rental car. DR added the target's keys to the bag with the gun and shells and stowed the bag under the seat.

Now the hard-drive needed to be delivered. The address on the carton was for a Juan Diego, room 299, at the Hotel Grano de Oro. The hotel was two miles east of the residence on the other side of Sabana Park and on the western edge of the city of San José.

DR arrived at the hotel around 7:25 p.m. and parked the car on the street, hoping no local hoods would try to vandalize it. Still wearing the disguise, DR walked quickly into the hotel lobby and approached the manager at the lobby desk.

"Please hold this package for Señor Diego in room 299."

"I would be happy to deliver it to his room, madam."

"No need. He told me he would pick it up after returning from dinner."

"Okay, madam. I will hold it for him. Who should I say it's from?"

"DR."

"*Bueno lo har*é," the manager responded in a friendly tone.

"*Gracias.*"

DR then exited the hotel via a rear door and returned to the rental car in just enough time to dissuade two locals eyeing the car from making their move. *The police should really do more to patrol the neighborhoods.* Back in the car, DR drove to a nearby McDonald's restaurant, and parked in a space toward the rear of the restaurant that was unlikely to draw attention. A commercial dumpster was only ten yards away. The weapon and the clothing went in, even the shoes.

Now it was time for a break. DR walked into the McDonald's, used the restroom, and then returned to the car. Satisfied that the mission had been successful, DR looked forward to an enjoyable dinner later in the evening.

6

HOT POTATOES

Donna was pleased. Her duties for the evening had gone as planned. She had a smile on her face as she anticipated a relaxing dinner with Ed.

It was almost eight o'clock, but Ed was nowhere in sight. So, she asked the hostess if there was a reservation for dinner under Ed's name. There wasn't. Perhaps he had forgotten, or perhaps he used an alias. The dining room seemed busy, so just to be sure, she requested a table for two in the name of Donna Rice, and took a seat at the bar. She ordered a Sauvignon Blanc and waited for Ed to show up.

Almost immediately, some guy sat down on the bar stool next to her and they engaged in friendly conversation. He told her a joke, and they were both laughing when she felt a heavy hand on her shoulder. She turned. It was Ed.

"May I interrupt?" he said with an authoritarian tone.

At sixty-one, Donna was still attractive, but she also knew how to handle herself. Ed knew this, and she didn't think Ed had any reason to be jealous, but she began to explain anyway.

"Oh, Ed, this gentleman was telling me he comes here frequently and that he works at the U.S. Embassy."

The fellow turned to face Ed, and as soon as he did, the expression on the fellow's face suddenly changed from looking cheerful to looking fearful.

"Hello, Juan," Ed said sternly. Then Ed turned his head toward Donna. "I know this gentleman. I was supposed to meet with him ten minutes ago.

Looks like I found him. Juan and I need to talk about something in private. Donna, please stay put. I'll try not to be long."

Then, Ed looked directly at Juan. "Juan, you come with me," he commanded.

Ed and Juan proceeded toward the lobby of the hotel as Juan began to apologize profusely. "I'm sorry, Sir. I was distracted. The time got away from me."

"Are you aware of the time? It's eight o'clock. And what distracted you more Juan? Was it the drink or was it my lady friend?"

"I didn't know she—"

"**Juan** . . . I went to your room ten minutes ago and you weren't there. Where's the package?"

"It's still at the desk."

"Then you go retrieve it and take it to your room. I'll be there in five."

"Yes, sir."

A few minutes later, Juan came back to his room. Ed was waiting. They went inside.

"Here, sir. I'm sorry I was late. Time got away from me," he said and pointed to a carton that was about eight inches by six inches by three inches in size lying on the bed. Juan's name and room 299 were handwritten on the front.

Ed grabbed Juan's wrist with his left hand, placed his right hand under Juan's chin, and pressed his right forearm upward against Juan's chest, pinning him against the wall.

"Listen carefully. If you want to keep your job, you need to take your assignments more seriously. You understand?"

"Yes, Sir."

"Okay, you're still welcome to take advantage of your stay here tonight, but I don't want to see you. Understand?"

"Yes, sir."

With that, Ed released his grip, took the carton, went down the hall to a door leading to the parking lot, and went directly to his car. He hid the carton under the passenger seat, relocked the car, and went back to the restaurant bar.

"Donna, I'm sorry for that."

"Ed, you seem agitated. Is everything alright?"

"I'm fine, but I think I could use a scotch."

"Ed, he wasn't bothering me in any way."

"No, I know. That's not it."

"Tell me what's going on then."

"I can't talk about it here. Maybe tomorrow when we go touring."

"Are we going touring tomorrow?"

"Why don't we talk about what we will do tomorrow?"

"Okay, but before we do, the host has informed me that a table is now ready in the name of Donna Rice."

"Oh, damn. I screwed up, didn't I? I forgot to make a reservation."

Donna was amused and laughed. "I guess you're not perfect, but I love you anyway," she said and affectionately rubbed the back of his shoulder.

Since it was late, they had light meals, but they had plenty to talk about.

"Donna, before I forget, did you go to the coffee shop and did the professor give you a package for me?"

"Yes, everything went as planned. The professor gave me a small carton. I put it in my shoulder bag and brought it to the hotel, but it was heavy and . . .I hope you don't mind . . .I don't have it with me. Do you need it now? We can go get it."

"No, just make sure I get it before we leave. Thank you for doing this. How was the professor, by the way? Matheson said you might find him interesting."

"I think creepy might be a more apt description."

"How so?"

"I got there shortly after five, took a small table to myself, and ordered tea and what I believed was a Spanish version of a crumpet. It was very good, and the guitar in the background gave it the right ambiance. I was relaxing and enjoying my cup of tea when a slick-looking Spanish gentleman asked to join me at my table. He said his name was Professor Smythe, and he was there to meet Donna Rice, so I assumed it was the person I was to meet. He seemed to be unnecessarily covert, like he was playing a part in a bad cloak-and-dagger movie. Unlikely that his real name was Smythe either, considering his complexion. After he introduced himself, we talked about what he does. He said he teaches international politics at the nearby University of Costa Rica. And of course, he wanted to know what I did, and

I gave him the usual vague answers. But as the conversation continued, he started getting personal, told me how he enjoyed foreign women and how sexy he thought I was for an embassy courier, etc. I asked him about the package he was supposed to give me and he said he wasn't sure if I really wanted it badly enough. I think he was trying to bargain. At some point he put his hand on my leg and at that point I told him he could either give me the carton, or the people I worked for would ensure he ended up dead. Then he apologized and said he was only teasing me. Like I said, creepy."

She continued. "After he gave me the carton, I asked what was in it, and he said he was not allowed to tell me. However, I had talked with Matheson before I went, and I already knew what was supposed to be in it. Matheson told me it was a hard-drive from the office at the university where Maria Martin worked. Matheson said he would review it with me after Langley had a chance to analyze it. I was feeling uncomfortable with this guy, so I told him I had another appointment and needed to leave. If not for the creep, I would have stayed longer. It was around six when I left."

"This place is no more than forty minutes away from the coffee shop. Did you go somewhere else on the way?"

"Traffic was pretty bad, but I still had plenty of extra time, so I stopped at a pharmacy on Via 104." She paused. "Can we talk about the weekend? What have you got in mind?"

"Of course. The last time you were here, we didn't have much time for touring. I thought I would treat you like a tourist and give you a grand tour of the San José area."

"What is it that attracts tourists to Costa Rica?"

"In addition to the beautiful scenery? Well, Costa Rica is also known for its bananas, coffee, hummingbirds, volcanoes, and its *chicas*."

"*Chicas*? . . . What are *chicas*?"

"*Chicas malas* . . . prostitutes. It's legal down here, or at least it is if they don't advertise or have a pimp. It's becoming part of the tourist industry, especially for male foreigners."

"Ed," she said sternly, "I hope *you're* not sleeping with them."

"Well, *chicas* help—"

"No, never mind. I don't want to know."

He smiled. "What I was about to say is that the *chicas* are an excellent source of intelligence for us. But not to worry, we will skip that part of our tour," he said mockingly.

"Okay, but where are we going, and what should I wear?"

"Yes, of course. I thought we could start off with a drive up to the *Poás Volcano*. They say it's best to see it early in the day before any clouds roll in. The observation deck is a short walk from the visitor center. If you want to exercise, there are several hiking trails as well. The views and scenery are unbelievable. Then I think we should go see hummingbirds."

"Yes, you said that Costa Rica is known for hummingbirds. Why?"

"Yup. Costa Rica is famous for its hummingbirds. We have more varieties than anywhere else in the world. You like birds, don't you?"

"Yes, I do, but you never struck me as a hummingbird type of guy," she said with a grin on her face.

"Well, Freddo Fresas is a good place to see hummingbirds, and have lunch. Then, I thought you might be interested in touring a coffee *fincá*."

"A *fincá*? That's a farm, isn't it? My Spanish is not that good."

"It's a plantation. In this case, they grow coffee plants. I scheduled a tour for the afternoon at the *Doká Estate*. After that, we can head back to San José in plenty of time for dinner, certainly by seven. I'd like to take you to Jurgens for dinner and afterward, perhaps we could go dancing. How does that sound?"

"It sounds perfect, Ed."

7

A WEEKEND TOGETHER

Donna's room phone rang at nine the next morning. She slept later than expected and had just stepped out of the shower. She barely made it to the phone before it stopped ringing.

"I hope I'm not too early," Ed greeted her from the hotel lobby.

"Good morning, Ed. Tell me again what you've planned for today. I'm not sure what to wear. I heard hiking, and I heard Jurgens. Isn't Jurgens a rather upscale place? Will we have time to change before dinner?"

"I suggest dressing for dinner, but not quite that dressy, and bringing a pair of dress shoes with you. Wear walking shoes during the day. Also, bring a jacket to wear at Poás. Sometimes it can be chilly up there. I'm planning to wear a jacket for dinner but no necktie if that helps, and as far as shoes are concerned, I'll wear sneakers during the day . . . oh, and bring your camera."

"Okay, I'll be down in about fifteen minutes."

Twenty minutes later, she came down and walked up behind him.

"Hello stranger," she said, catching him off guard. He turned to face her and smiled. In Ed's mind, she looked like a typical tourist. A white sunhat topped her short brown hair, and a pair of Foster Grants dangled from a lanyard around her neck. She was wearing black slacks, a casual white top that showed off her still shapely figure, and white tennis shoes.

"Wow! You look really nice," he said with enthusiasm, and offered to carry her travel bag and jacket.

"Thank you, *sir*," she said mockingly.

They walked out together and, almost in unison, put on their sunshades to protect them from the morning sun. It was a beautiful day, not a cloud in the sky, and temperatures in the mid-seventies. He tossed her travel bag onto the back seat of his RAV4 and they drove off.

****

Donna watched Ed shift gears as he negotiated his way onto Route 27. She could not help but ask about the vehicle they were in. "Is it front-wheel drive? I don't remember it from when I was here before."

"I got it after you were here. Yup. It's all-wheel drive, but if I need it, I can lock it into four-wheel drive. The roads, including some we will travel on later today, leave a lot to be desired. RAV4s with four-wheel drive are very popular in Costa Rica. Expect to see quite a few on the road. Their popularity means they are less costly to maintain. And before you ask, the gas mileage is good . . . about twenty-five miles to a U.S. gallon."

The car ride gave them plenty of time to talk and catch up.

"You never told me what you did with your free time yesterday after our meeting in the morning. Anything interesting?" he asked.

"Yes. After I took a nap, I walked around the hotel. As I checked out the gift shop, I ran into a woman whom I had met the day before. Her name is Judi. She said that her husband was transferred to the embassy and they were temporarily staying at the InterContinental. She said they were from New York City, but something about her seemed off. She said her husband's name was Joseph Smith. Do you know him?"

"No, and his name was Joseph Smith? Not ringing any bells."

"I told her I was here on vacation, and that a couple of years ago, I considered bringing my daughter and grandson here on a vacation, but I got sick, and it didn't happen, so I was glad I could do it now. She asked what I planned to do and see. I told her that I planned to spend time with a friend and do some touring over the weekend. She told me about some interesting places she had heard about. She told me that the more of Costa Rica she saw, the more she loved it, and she was looking forward to living here. I told her I didn't know if I would want to live here, but it seemed like a great place to visit."

"I think you would like it if you did live here," Ed suggested.

Donna reached over and affectionately squeezed his shoulder, but didn't reply to his comment. She knew where Ed was coming from.

By the way, I noticed that the hotel has live entertainment on Friday and Saturday nights. Would you be interested in doing that?"

"If *you* are. Yes, I would."

From the hotel, Ed headed north-west. Along the way, they passed a McDonald's Restaurant. Donna commented, "I'm surprised to see so many McDonald's in the San José area."

"Like being back home, I guess. Did you know that the first McDonald's in Costa Rica opened in 1984?"

"Really?"

"Yea, it was in a two-story building in downtown San José. Now they're everywhere."

Donna glanced out the window and looked around.

"Are we headed toward the airport?" she asked.

"Yes, I thought we would go through the city of Alajuela just north of the airport. It's on the way to Poás."

They arrived in Alajuela a few minutes later.

8

THE TOUR

Alajuela was like an old rural town one would find in the U.S. Mostly old buildings, residences now turned into store fronts, nothing taller than three stories.

"Would you like coffee?"

"Oh, yes," she said. Just the thought of coffee perked her up.

"Tell you what," he said as he pulled to the curb alongside a small park, "I'll go across the street and get two coffees, and in the meantime, you can check out the park."

"Okay."

She walked into the park and observed a very large pedestal supporting a statue of a man holding a rifle in one hand and a torch in the other. The plaque said it was Juan Santamaria, a national hero.

When they were both back in the SUV, he asked. "So what do you think?"

"I don't know. Juan Santamaria is the name of the airport, isn't it? And it says he was a national hero. What did he do to deserve such esteem?"

"Well," he explained, "the story as I understand it is that in 1855 a military activist from the U.S. by the name of William Walker organized an army of revolutionaries, and they successfully took over the government of Nicaragua. The objective was to convert large areas of Nicaragua and Costa Rica into slave states like those in the Southern U.S. The next year, he unsuccessfully tried to invade Costa Rica. The Costa Rican army then went north to encounter Walker at a stronghold in Rivas, Nicaragua. After several soldiers lost their lives trying to overtake the stronghold, Juan Santamaria, a poor drummer boy in the Costa Rican army—and I should mention he was born here in Alajuela—took it upon himself to burn down the enemy stronghold under the provision that the Costa Rican government would provide for his mother for the rest of her days. He was successful, but as they never found his body—supposedly burned up in the fire—it's uncertain if he really died. However, his mother lived happily ever after."

"Interesting. I suppose every country needs a national hero," she said in a cynical tone.

"You're not impressed?" he said as he smiled and gave her a quick glance. "These stories give hope and build the morale of the common citizen."

"What happened to William Walker?" she asked with a bit more enthusiasm.

"After another major battle in Rivas in which he did not do well against an army from Honduras, he left the country and went back to the States. But then, he returned in 1860 only to be captured by the British, who turned him over to the Hondurans. The Hondurans executed him by firing squad."

Can't really respond to that, Donna thought to herself. They sipped their coffees in silence for a few minutes before Ed started up the SUV and they drove off.

They were driving along some very winding and poorly maintained roads when Ed broke the silence.

"Donna, how is your daughter Brandy doing?"

"Fine."

"I only talked to her briefly when I was up your way. We ran into each other at the hospital. I introduced myself and told her I was a long-time friend. She said she already knew who I was. We were both concerned about you then. It seems like perhaps the two of you are closer now than you had been. Is that the case?"

"I think my sickness brought us together. She took care of me the whole time, for which I was very grateful."

"Could I ask you something personal?"

She turned her head toward him as he kept his head fixed on the road. "What do you want to know?"

"You told me that you were reluctant to tell Brandy who her birth father was, and I was wondering if you ever told her."

"No. I haven't told anyone. I never told him or Brandy. Neither of them knows."

"Is that a secret that you would take to your grave?"

"Ed, I thought about what you said to me about that. And I understand your need to know who *your* birth mother was, but my situation with Brandy is different. Brandy and her birth father never knew each other whereas you and your birth mother had bonded with each other before she disappeared. You needed to understand why she wasn't there for you anymore."

Ed began to think of his mother and his need to find her. For a few moments, he became lost in his own thoughts and began to mentally reflect on his life and the emotions he had growing up.

He remembered growing up near San Diego, California, and that when he was almost three, his mother disappeared. She was no longer there to hold him, or to read to him, or to scold him when he needed it. He missed her terribly. Then, two years later, his dad remarried. He wondered if his mother had abandoned him. How could she? Hadn't she loved him?

He recalled his childhood years in California and how devastated he felt when, at the age of sixteen, his dad passed away. He remembered hoping that his birth mother would show up at the funeral. She didn't. Then, after the funeral, he remembered how his stepmom explained the situation.

"Ed, you're older now and I think you will understand what I'm going to tell you. Your birth mother had been in the United States illegally, and overstayed her visa. She was from Mexico and when she returned to attend her mother's funeral, they would not let her return to the United States. In her absence, your dad hired me to be your nanny, but during the next year, we had an affair. Your birth mother sent a letter to your dad acknowledging there was no way she could ever return to the U.S. or gain custody of you. Your dad filed and was granted a divorce."

He was happy with his stepmom. She was from Costa Rica, and he remembered how much he enjoyed the time he spent there visiting his stepmom's family or on vacation. She was a loving woman. He was happy with his dad as well. He was a good, loving father. His family had money and they were able to provide him with a good home and a good education. And yet, he always felt a void left by the absence of his birth mother.

He needed to discover the truth about her. If still alive, he wanted to see her, and he finally succeeded in finding her. He was forty-two years old then, and this was his first year with the CIA after retiring from the military. He found her in a small town in Mexico. The people there were poor, and the crime level was high. She was not well.

His birth mother told him how she was unable to convince the bureaucracy to allow her back into the States. She said she tried to re-enter illegally. They captured her, and sent her back to Mexico, but not before she was raped. When Dad told her he wanted a divorce, she fell apart mentally and physically. Drugs and prostitution became part of her life after that. She knew she may never see him again, but resigned herself that he would be well-taken care of in the States. She cried and asked for his forgiveness. Ed remembered how he hugged her and told her what she wanted to hear, and how sad he felt when she passed away a year later.

"Ed, watch where you're going!" Donna shouted.

Ed quickly returned to planet Earth and braked hard, just in time to avoid colliding with another vehicle that had suddenly pulled onto the roadway in front of them.

"I'm sorry. You okay?"

"Yeah. He pulled right out in front of us, didn't he?"

After they regained their composure, Ed resumed the conversation.

"You were saying that your situation is different. I know your situation is not the same as mine, but finding my mother and knowing that she loved me turned my life around. It was important to know that I was loved and not abandoned. I would think it would be important for Brandy as well. I think you should reconsider."

"Actually . . . after I thought I might die last year, I did reconsider. I think that Brandy should know, but not while I'm still alive. And of course, once she knows, her father will know."

"Why wait till you're gone?"

"Because I think the negative impact will be less then. The main reason I never told anyone is because I didn't want to ruin his life or anyone else's. He was married and had kids. How would he and his kids react? In addition, I always feared how I would feel towards him if we did reconnect.

After all, I was married and I cared about my husband. On more than one occasion, he tried to reconnect with me, but I could not imagine seeing him and talking with him without telling him the truth."

"You're both mature adults, and it has been a very long time. His kids are grown up, he's divorced, and your husband passed away many years ago. Why can't you tell Brandy and her father the truth now? Why do I have a feeling there is more to it than what you have said so far?"

"Ed. You and I have been very close. I'm willing to tell you but you must promise that what I say stays between us."

"Of course. You know you can trust me."

"Brandy's birth father was very instrumental in exposing Inga Sarnoff as a spy and later tracking her whereabouts to Central America. The projects he was involved in were highly classified, and yes, he's still alive."

"So, you're protecting him. You must still care about him."

"Ed. I care about a lot of people. I also care about you, probably more than you realize," she said as she placed her hand on his shoulder.

"Yea, I know. I didn't mean to sound jealous. I care about you too, you know."

"The country side is quite beautiful up here," she said, changing the subject.

****

Ed and Donna arrived at the *Poás* visitor center shortly after eleven thirty. They took time to get some information before proceeding up the path to the observation deck. Donna learned that the volcano had erupted three dozen times since 1828, when they started keeping records. She also learned that there had been no lava flows since 1952. Rather, these eruptions were explosions caused by high-pressure steam and sulfur gas that could spew ash and debris several thousand feet into the sky. There had been big explosions in the 1950s and again in the 1990s. The last significant explosion was in 1996. Many of the explosions damaged nearby property.

They put on their jackets and made their way to the observation deck, where they stood at the rail gazing into the blue water that filled the crater of the volcano. It was chilly, and he had his arm over her shoulder. She had her arm around his waist.

"This is truly an amazing view," she said. "Whenever I see something like this it makes me feel small compared to the power and the magnitude of what is before us."

"I know what you mean," he echoed. "This is one of my favorite places. It makes me realize that there must be a higher power out there, and my problems are small compared to the universe. I find it to be calming and peaceful."

"And romantic?"

"Yes, that too."

"Have you been here a lot?"

"Not a lot. This is my third time." She seemed to be fishing, so he continued. "The first time I met someone here on official business. The second time, I came alone and brought my camera. I took photographs. It's becoming a hobby for me. I hope to really get into it after I retire."

He was about to tell her she was the only woman he wanted to be romantic with, when they both heard something behind them.

They turned to find themselves facing another couple that had just walked onto the deck. The couple asked them if they would take their picture.

"Of course," Donna responded. They were young and probably on their honeymoon. After she took two pictures of the couple and handed back the camera, the couple asked if they would like their pictures taken in return. Ed was about to offer his camera when Donna spoke.

"Oh no, but thank you anyway." She knew to avoid having their picture taken together. She was here on official business, and her relationship with Ed could not be in the open. She looked at Ed. He seemed to understand.

As they began to walk back to the car hand in hand he asked, "Donna, doesn't it bother you that we can't just be a normal couple like them?"

"No, we aren't like normal people, but we learn to adapt."

****

The next stop was hummingbirds and lunch. Somehow, Ed found his way back to the main road, Route 146, and headed south. They were in the country. Aside from coffee *fincás*, they also passed acres of strawberry patches. Twenty minutes later, they drove into the parking lot at the Freddo Fresas Restaurant, a rustic log-type structure with red metal and tile roofs.

The restaurant was famous for its food and for its *fresas,* or strawberries. Ed talked to the host and was assured that he had a table for thirty minutes later, while Donna picked up a brochure about hummingbirds and began to read.

"Ed, did you know that there are fifty different species of hummingbirds in Costa Rica? Two are unique to Costa Rica; others migrated here all the way from Canada. The smallest of the birds can beat their wings up to eighty times per second and hummingbirds are the only birds that can fly backwards."

He smiled at her enthusiasm. "No, I didn't know all that," he replied.

Then they walked across the roadway to the hummingbird park, where they meandered along the red clay paths and past a fish pond. Bird feeders filled with sugar water were hanging at strategic spots from the small trees along the way. Ed watched as Donna seemed fascinated by two hummingbirds sharing the same feeder. The one would stick his beak in the food and then the other, alternating in perfect harmony. She was right. Hummingbirds were not so much his thing, but it pleased him that she was enjoying it. They continued down the red clay path to a clump of trees.

"Oh, look, an oriole," she said excitedly, pointing up to the branches. "You would think we would see orioles in Maryland, but I rarely see them—a lot of cardinals, but rarely an oriole."

After their walk and a few pictures, they headed back to the restaurant. They had a chicken dish and shared a strawberry and whipped cream dessert.

"Are you ready for the *Doká Estate*?" he asked.

"Absolutely, let's go."

****

Doká was a medium-sized coffee *fincá* in the middle of nowhere. Ed found his way back to the main road and headed south for a short spell before turning off onto an unmarked country road and then another before finally arriving at their destination.

Most of the coffee *fincás* in the area were family-owned and operated, from generation to generation. *Doká* was no exception. One of the owners, named Poncho, greeted them.

"Hello Ed, nice to see you again. I see you have brought a lady friend with you." His English was rather good.

"Good to see you as well, Poncho. This is my friend Donna. Donna, meet Poncho."

"Any friend of Ed is a friend of mine," he said and gave Donna a gentle hug. Poncho explained how they were trying to sell their coffee directly into the United States and how Ed had connected him to the right people. He said he and his brother did most of the work these days, but his dad still played a role, and they were trying to persuade his son José to work in the business full-time. He would be their guide.

The tour covered the entire process of making coffee. They joined a tour group of about twelve other people and followed Poncho to a small grove near the main building. Poncho gave everyone a welcome and a short summary of their business and what to see on the farm. In addition to coffee beans, they also grew fruit and flowers, but today they would focus on coffee. Poncho showed them what coffee plants and the "cherries" they produced looked like. He said that researchers were experimenting with different hybrids that would resist disease, and that there were more than a hundred varieties of the Arabica coffee plant. Then, they started the tour of the facility.

The group saw the seeding stations and the plantation where they grew the coffee trees. Poncho explained that they harvested the "cherries" over a period of three months, because they ripened at different times and they had to be a certain degree of ripeness when picked. Next, they saw the drying fields, the milling and husk removal, the bean grading and sorting, decaffeination, and the roasting machines.

Poncho showed them the difference between light roasted beans and dark roasted beans. He explained how the temperature and time of roasting were important as both affected the final taste. Poncho explained that for quality control purposes, they periodically tested or "cupped" the finished product to ensure that the temperature and length of roasting were optimal. Someone asked about the difference in taste and this led to some interesting facts that were surprising to some. Poncho told them that if measured by volume, the dark roast has less caffeine and less acidity than the light roast. Also, while roasting can make the coffee of a low-quality bean taste more burnt or even bitter, Poncho said that a high-quality bean like his would not suffer such degradation in taste.

Finally, they saw the packaging process and the warehouse where they stored the coffee beans before roasting. Since it was already into April, they had already completed the harvest and processed the beans. And they had already shipped most of them. However, they still had a warehouse with an ample number of bags of unroasted beans stored in special sacks, and of course, they also had plenty of bags of branded roasted beans and ground coffee in the gift shop.

Afterwards, they had the opportunity to taste all the coffee they wished to drink. One of the employees showed them how they made coffee "the old fashioned" way, using a *chorreador*. A *chorreador* is a tall wooden tripod stand with a coffee container underneath. A cotton bag is suspended from a hole in the top of the stand and is filled with ground coffee. Boiling water is poured into the bag and seeps through the ground coffee and into the container below. "Interesting," Donna commented privately to Ed. "It's the same process 'Mr. Coffee' built into a compact appliance."

Donna thanked Poncho for a job well done, and took the time to fill out a survey. She used a fictitious name and left a personal cloud-based email address she used for just such occasions. And of course, before leaving she had to buy a bag of their branded dark roast coffee to take home with her.

Back in the car, Ed asked, "So what did you think of the tour?"

"It was great, Ed. I'm glad you planned it. I found it interesting and educational. I never knew how they got the caffeine out of the coffee, and now I know." Then she reached over and gave his arm a friendly squeeze. "Thanks."

Ed took several turns onto unmarked country roads without hesitation, which led Donna to ask, "Ed, do you come up here very often?"

"No, why?"

"Because you seem to know exactly where you're going."

He chuckled. "Well, this is only the second time I've been to the *fincá*, but the first time, a colleague at work, who had been here more than once, wrote down very precise directions which I memorized. But just in case I have a senior moment, I put his directions in the glove compartment."

A few more turns, and they found themselves heading south to the city of San José via Heredia. Ed glanced over at Donna. She had her eyes closed and her mouth agape. She was asleep. He briefly wondered about her stamina and her health.

Donna didn't wake up until they approached the outskirts of San José.

"How long have I been asleep?" she asked.

"The better part of an hour. Have I tired you out?"

"No, I'll be fine," she said as she looked out the window. "Where are we?"

"We're between the city of Heredia and the city of San José."

"I'm seeing a lot of new residential developments," Donna commented.

"Costa Rica is really starting to boom. We have major manufacturing and technology companies like Bridgestone and Sprint/Nextel that are expanding their presence here. We have a stable government and a low poverty level. It has become a very attractive place to live and to retire to. Many people from the U.S. come here when they retire."

"Ed, you're close to retiring, aren't you?"

"Maybe two more years. I'm seriously considering staying here after that. I really like it here. What about you?"

"I thought about retiring when I was sick, but I wanted to complete this final project and bring Inga Sarnoff to justice."

"The project is very important to you, isn't it?"

"Yes! Matheson read me in after Inga Sarnoff escaped in 1988, and I've been tracking her down ever since. I haven't told you this, but not only did she murder Jon Wilson and at least two others, but she also tried twice to kill Brandy's father. I feel like I owed it to them to bring her to justice. Now that the project is about to end, I think I'll retire at the end of this year."

"I think you would like retiring here. We could be together."

"Perhaps."

9

A ROMANTIC EVENING

Jurgens was on the eastern side of the city, not far from the OIJ and the Russian Embassy. Ed was able to park the RAV4 in a lot, a short distance from the restaurant. Before they got out of the vehicle, they each grabbed their travel bags from the rear seat. They removed their hats and their shades; they exchanged their athletic foot-wear for dressier shoes; and they covered their tops with jackets suitable for dinner.

When they entered the restaurant, Ed and the host greeted each other in Spanish. Then the host addressed Donna.

"*Nos complace tenerte como nuestro invitado.*"

"I'm sorry, *no hablo español*," she replied and smiled.

"He said he was pleased to have you as their guest." Ed offered.

"Ed, have you been here before?" she asked as they followed the host to their table.

"Many times. They know me. I bring business associates here for lunch . . . sometimes for dinner. The Russian Embassy is nearby as well . . . and it's amazing what one can overhear," he added in a soft voice."

"I see."

"But . . . tonight is special for you."

The host seated them in cushioned chairs at a table for two with a white linen table cloth. The food or *comida* was delicious with a French flair. Donna enjoyed the tilapia with a Dijon mustard sauce and mashed cassava, and Ed enjoyed a curry shrimp dish with rice. Each plate came with carrots, a popular vegetable in Costa Rica.

They complimented their meals with a shared bottle of Sauvignon Blanc. Donna asked Ed about the cassava.

"This looks and tastes a lot like mashed potatoes, but it's not. Are you familiar with it?"

"Cassava . . . very popular here in Costa Rica. It comes from the root of a cassava tree. They shave the root down, cut it up, and fully cook it to avoid toxicity. Tapioca comes from cassava root."

"Toxicity?"

"Cyanide poisoning. Good way to do away with an enemy agent." he quipped.

"Ed, you're more cynical than I am. Let's talk about something more pleasant."

"Sorry. Too many years in the agency. Like I said, we're not normal people. Not to worry though. The chef here knows what he's doing. You're right, this is a very romantic setting and I'm a very lucky man to be sharing it with such a beautiful lady."

He refilled their glasses with wine and made a toast. "Here's to our friendship and future happiness." He wanted to add the word *together* but knew she was not ready to commit to that.

The dining room was cozy and intimate. A window view of a garden lit with colored lights added to the ambiance. The dim lighting, delicious food, excellent service, and the sweet talk between them that ensued, made it a very romantic dinner. The wine helped as well.

After dinner, they took a short walk before returning to the car. They had their arms around each other as they turned down a side street. It was dark and there was no one around. It reminded Donna of a time several years ago when they were on assignment in Mexico City.

"Ed, do you remember when we were in Mexico City, and two thugs came out of nowhere and tried to rob us?"

"It's okay. No need to worry about that here. Costa Rica is one of the safest countries in Central America—very low crime rate, especially when it comes to violent crimes. But I do remember, I was impressed with the way you handled yourself. You weren't about to give up your purse, passport, and cash. We disarmed them in less than a minute. We could have beat the crap out of them. Hell, we could have killed them. I was about to do just that when you told them they had better run if they wanted to live. I know a lot of operatives that would not have been so compassionate. I had a new admiration for you after that."

She knew it was *discretion* and not *compassion* that motivated her that night, but she did not correct him.

****

They arrived back at the InterContinental around ten that evening. The lobby lounge had a duo, a female vocalist and a male guitar player. The place was busy but they were able to get a small table without a long wait. The music was relaxing and not too loud.

"What would you like to drink madam?" the waitress asked.

"I think I'll have a brandy . . . straight up. The house brand is fine."

"Sounds good. I'll have the same," Ed told the waitress.

"Ed, I really enjoyed today, and as always, I enjoyed your company."

"Well, I tried very hard to please you and I was hoping our weekend would continue into tomorrow."

She gave him a hard look. "Ed, are you telling me that you did all that so that I would want to sleep with you tonight?" She was giving him a hard time to see how he would react.

"No. No. I didn't mean it like that!"

She smiled. "I know you didn't. I'm just playing with you. You're welcome to join me in my room tonight, but I want you to tell me something first."

"What's that?"

"I need you to tell me the truth. Are you seeing anyone else right now?"

"No."

"Been with any chicas?"

"Not lately."

"Ed, you're what some women would call a silver fox. You're handsome, in good shape, and you have money. I would think you could have sex with any cute young chick you choose. Why me?"

"I don't think of you as a cute young chick. I think of you as a mature, intelligent, and attractive woman. I trust you, and I feel comfortable being with you. You understand me and I can share my feelings with you. I think you will agree that in our line of work, we can't always do that with other people. Everything is classified, and we must always be on guard. If we say the wrong thing to the wrong person, we could put them in danger, put ourselves in danger, or be charged with violating our security agreements. I think you understand that."

"I do understand that. I had a very difficult time trying to be a mom and a wife while at the same time traveling—many times to a secret location where I would become someone else undercover. My husband John accepted that, but it also meant that we were not that involved with each other."

"Donna, think of it. We've risked our lives, and we've taken the lives of others. We've experienced things that set us apart and we think differently than others. Very few people are like us. The situation we talked about earlier after dinner is an example of that. If we were like normal people, we would have given those thugs the money they asked for. But it's likely they still would have tried to kill us so that we wouldn't report them. No, we're not normal people . . . that's why I want to be with you."

"Uh, because we're not normal?"

"No. Because we're able to share and feel comfortable with each other, Something we can't do with others." His tone showed a slight frustration at her response.

"Ed, I'm—" Just then, their brandies arrived. "Can we talk more about this later? I don't want anyone to overhear us. For now, let's just enjoy the music and the moment . . . and the brandy." They clinked glasses. "To us and what we have together," she said sincerely. To Ed, her words were reassuring.

****

They walked hand in hand to the elevator. They had the elevator to themselves, and once inside, she pulled his head towards hers and kissed him hard on the mouth. "I want you to understand that no matter what, I care about you."

When they entered Donna's hotel room, she immediately took a seat on the edge of the bed.

"Ed, please sit down next to me," she said as she patted the area on the bed next to her. "We need to talk."

"What's wrong?"

"Ed, I want to apologize if I seemed to belittle what you were saying to me earlier. I know you were being serious. I really do like you and enjoy being with you, and I can think of no one I would rather retire with than you. Whether it's in Costa Rica or elsewhere wouldn't matter. It's just that I have a problem."

"Tell me."

"I'm fearful of where this might lead."

"Donna, I've never known you to be afraid. What's going on with you?"

"If we were together, I'm not sure I would live up to your expectations."

"How so?"

"When I was sick, I went through hell, and I thought I would die. As you know, I faced death several times during my career. I thought I was invincible, or I just didn't think about it, but when I was sick, I changed, and it scared me. Although the doctors tell me that I'm cancer-free now, it could come back and if it does, it would put you through a lot more than I would want. I remember how I felt when my husband John got sick, and I know how it was a strain on Brandy when I was sick. I wouldn't want to put you through that."

"You're fortunate to have Brandy as your daughter, but if you were to get sick again, I would stand by you just as she did."

"There's more. You said we were not normal people, and that's certainly true. If we were to live together, we would need to share some of those abnormal things with each other. Some of them may turn out to be slightly immoral or illegal. I wonder if we would still love each other after that."

"But this is something I already expect and accept."

"Maybe. But there's more. I don't have the same sex drive that I had when I was last here. I guess my hormones are different now. In fact, I had surgery and don't even have all the same equipment, and I have a scar across my middle. You may not enjoy looking at it. And since my surgery, I tend to be prone to infection down there."

"But I still care about you."

"Ed, what if you need sex more than I can give you?"

"Well, I'm not going to find the nearest cute young chick if that's what you're suggesting." His tone indicated some annoyance.

"I'm sorry I didn't mean—"

"No, it's okay. I understand where you're coming from. I screwed up my marriage by sleeping with cute young chicks, but that was a long time ago. Look, my sex drive isn't what it used to be either. But more importantly, it was not meaningful sex with them. There was no sharing of the mind, no sharing of experience, no sharing of dreams. I don't want that. I want to be with you, with or without sex."

She gave him a serious look. "Ed, what I need is for you to love me and hold me close."

"I do love you," he said as they embraced, "and no matter what happens between us, you won't disappoint me. Please don't be afraid."

"Ed, I know you keep a go-bag in your car, so why don't you retrieve it while I use the bathroom."

He left, retrieved his bag, and stopped in the lobby's restroom before coming back to the room. While she waited, she washed up and put on a nightgown. After she let him back into the room, she sat up in the bed and waited for him. He undressed and joined her.

"If you make love to me, I need you to use one of these," she said and handed him a sealed condom. He laughed.

"Ed, what's so funny?"

He opened his other hand, showing her a second condom.

10

SUNDAY

Sundays in Costa Rica were a day of rest and church going. Most of the citizens (often called Ticos) were Roman Catholic. Local businesses closed, either due to religion or regulation. However, they often made exceptions for the booming tourist and business trade. Hotels still booked rooms and still provided food for their guests—although the day was dry with respect to liquor sales.

Donna woke up happy. She looked over at Ed. He was still asleep. He looked relaxed and peaceful. As she listened to the sound of his breathing, she thought about how lucky she was to have him in her life right now. She couldn't resist giving him a gentle kiss on his cheek before heading off to the bathroom. When she returned, Ed was up. He gave her a good morning hug and took his turn in the bathroom. "Are you hungry? she shouted so he would hear over the running water. "They have a nice buffet downstairs. You interested?"

"Sounds good. Let's do it," he responded.

After breakfast, Donna asked, "What now?"

"Did you bring a swim suit?"

"And if I say no?" she joked.

"Well, we're not going to swim in the nude if that's what you're suggesting."

"Ha-ha. I did bring a suit. The hotel here has a pool, and I went to the pool and swam Thursday afternoon . . . thought I told you. Anyway, you don't have a suit with **you**, do you?"

"I was thinking we could go over to my place."

"Okay. Let's go back upstairs, get our stuff, and we're off."

Donna got into her rental car and followed Ed to his place. Ed lived on the fourth floor of a condo built in 2001. Ed moved in right after it was built. Ed had explained that the U.S. Embassy was the owner of the building and that he and a few other embassy employees—and possibly CIA employees—paid rent to live there. The condo was high-end. Ed had two bedrooms—he used one for an office—a common bath, a small washer and dryer, a living room, kitchen, dining area, hardwood floors, and a bay window that afforded a view of the nearby mountains. The condo was located at the edge of the city of Escazu, not far from the hotel and very convenient to the embassy.

Donna changed into her two-piece swim suit. Despite her ordeal with cancer, she still looked good, and the scar from her recent surgery was too low on her abdomen to be visible. When she met Ed in the hallway, he smiled and told her how great she looked. She returned the compliment. Ed still looked like an athlete. They walked out to the pool together, moved two lounge chairs under an umbrella, and spent the rest of the afternoon enjoying the water and sunshine. Occasionally, a neighbor would come down and Ed would say hello and introduced Donna as a business associate. Some may have already known he was the CIA Chief of Station and that Donna was probably a CIA officer, but no one ever spoke of it. Neighbors were friendly and would engage in small-talk but knew not to ask too many questions.

After a while, they went back inside. Ed made gin and tonics and then prepared a light supper. While he was busy doing that, Donna made her way down the hallway to the bathroom. On the way she noticed photographs that Ed had framed and mounted on the walls. She did not remember seeing them the last time she was at his place. One of the pictures caught her eye and was of special interest. It was a photo of the *Poás* volcano. It was awesome, just the way she remembered it was the previous morning. And she thought the skillful matting and framing really set it off. When she returned to the kitchen, she walked up behind Ed, put her hand on his shoulder, and told him how much she liked the picture.

"I'm glad you like it. Like I said, when we were up there yesterday, it's my new hobby, and I'm trying hard to hone my photographic and art skills. I have a long way to go, but I think it is something I'll pursue after I retire."

"Well, I think you're doing a great job of it. Keep it up," she said.

He turned, smiled, and handed her a drink.

"Here's to our future," he said.

After supper, it was time to part. The weekend together came to an end, and after a hug and a kiss, Donna drove herself back to the InterContinental. She would meet with Ed in his office at nine the next morning.

Later that evening, Ed was about to put a load of dirty clothes into his washing machine when the phone rang.

11

QUANDARY

Sunday evening, CIA Station Chief Ed Perez received a call at home from Director Rojas of the OIJ. "I apologize for calling you at home, but this is something you need to know. Maria Martin was found dead this morning in her home. She was murdered. It's already on the local news."

This was quite a surprise. Ed's immediate response to the Director was, "I didn't expect this. Did the DIS do it?"

"Did you?" the Director threw right back at him.

"No, of course not."

They both laughed.

"What about Officer Wolf, your associate? Can you account for her whereabouts?"

"I don't know. When did the death occur?"

"Our investigators think it occurred on Saturday, but it's possible it could have occurred Friday night. We will know with more certainty tomorrow after the coroner is finished."

"Officer Wolf was with me all day Saturday and Saturday night."

"There is one more thing I will tell you. Our investigators discovered that Maria Martin's computer hard-drive is missing. As you can imagine, her hard-drive would have much information on it that would be valuable to your American CIA. Do you know anything about that?"

"No, I don't! I would think the hard-drive would also have information that would be valuable to people in your organization and to the DIS as well. There are probably names and information on that hard-drive that would incriminate Costa Rican officials."

"If so, I would not cover it up," Rojas responded

Perez understood that Rojas was not about to implicate the OIJ or the DIS. Rojas would need the CIA or even the Russians to take the blame, although Perez didn't think it likely that the Russians would kill their own . . . but then again.

"Look," Rojas continued, "I hope you are right about Officer Wolf's whereabouts, but right now the evidence we have points to her, and Russian intelligence may suspect her as well."

"How would Russian intelligence know why Officer Wolf was here in Costa Rica?"

"My guess is that they were notified when she entered the country. They probably have had their sights on her, know who she is and what she does for the CIA. If they think she did this, and if they think she has the information on the hard-drive, she may be a target, and the Russians may go after her."

"Why?"

"*Señora* Martin's body had a sheet of paper on her lap with the words '*justicia para un espia ruso*' written on it. Very few people knew that Maria Martin was a Russian spy, and had a motive to kill her. In addition, a neighbor claims to have seen a strange woman leave Maria Martin's house Friday night. We are still reviewing the security cams."

"Is it possible that the room we met in last week was bugged?"

"I highly doubt it, but I *will* check it out."

"What about Director Alverez? Is it possible that Alverez arranged the assassination? Even if the meeting room wasn't bugged, he could have anonymously informed the Russians of our mission and placed the blame on the CIA rather than himself. I know Alverez, and it's clear to me that he's conservative and that he doesn't want socialists to be in power. At our meeting, one of you made a point about not wasting time with court orders, and most importantly that the OIJ did not want to alert the Russians or the socialists in the government of the status of their investigation into election tampering. I think the death of Maria Martin accomplished those objectives."

"I talked with Director Alverez. He had an airtight alibi for Friday evening from eight o'clock onward, and on Saturday, he was at his kid's football game. And . . . with all due respect, Martin's death would accomplish CIA objectives as well."

"So, do you have enough evidence to arrest anyone?"

"Not yet."

"I see. Director, if possible, could you send me fingerprints and photos of the body so that I have proof that she is, in fact, Inga Sarnoff."

"I will, but there's one more thing. Director Alverez thinks that Officer Wolf's life may be in danger. There is mounting evidence that she may have done this, and he thinks that the Russians may go after her in retaliation. My advice is that she leave the country as soon as possible. I won't have her stopped, if she leaves now, but at some point, I may need to question her."

"Gracias. Director, thank you for keeping me informed and for the advice."

****

On Monday morning, officers Wolf and Perez met at the U.S. Embassy to discuss the situation.

"Did you see the newscast this morning," he asked.

"I did. Do you have any details?"

"Yes. I talked to Director Rojas last night. He thinks that the Russians will think that you did it and target you. You didn't do this, did you?"

"Surely you can't think that."

"If you did it, I don't need to know. You would have my support. However, there is something you should know. The news this morning mentioned that Maria Martin's hard-drive from her computer was taken. Friday night, I received a hard-drive from you and another from Juan. That seems to be more than a coincidence.

"Ed, what are you implying?" Her annoyance was evident.

"I'm not accusing you. Please hear me out. Juan has a room at the *Hotel Grano de Oro,* and we often have information from the field delivered to him. Normally, he then brings it to me, and I review it and have my people analyze it. I told Matheson that we transfer intelligence that way frequently. In this case, Matheson instructed me to go to the hotel, get the package from Juan, and then forward it directly to Langley via our private secure mail service. Matheson said it was for his eyes only. So, on Saturday morning, before I came to pick you up, I took the cartons I received from Juan and from you to the Embassy and arranged for their delivery to Langley. Now that I've heard the news, I think that one of those cartons contained the hard-drive stolen from Maria Martin's house. The strong implication is that the CIA in Langley orchestrated the hit."

"Ed, **I had no part in this!**" She was loud, and her tone emphatic.

"Okay, calm down. I believe you, but it's beginning to look as if we're being set up. I told Rojas you were with me on Saturday, Saturday night, and Sunday. I hope I did not dishonor you by saying that, but we needed an alibi. But then he said the murder may have occurred Friday night. You said you went to the coffee shop in Heredia and then went to a pharmacy before meeting me at Gran de Oro. Do you have receipts?"

"Uh . . . no, I don't. I've been paying cash for the small stuff because the credit card fees are exorbitant. And anyway, I don't get reimbursed for personal stuff, so I don't need receipts."

"Did you go somewhere else on the way?" As he asked this, he read her expression. "No, you didn't . . ."

"Relax. All I did was drive by. Rohrmoser was on the way to the *Hotel Grano de Oro*, and as I said, I had plenty of time. I just wanted to see where she lived. I was curious. After I passed by the house, I went to the pharmacy, as I told you, and then to the hotel where you met up with me."

He gave her a look and shook his head.

"I'm sorry. I should have mentioned this the other night."

"Tell me what type of passport you used. Was it *personal, official,* or *diplomatic*?"

"To enter the country, I used my *diplomatic* passport, but I also have my *personal* one with me, in case I need it."

"That's good. You were conducting official business, so at least you have diplomatic immunity here. They can't prosecute you, but they could still detain you and question you. However, what's worse, someone could kill you. Director Rojas suggested you leave the country as soon as possible . . . yes, I know . . . it's a stretch, but it's better to be safe."

"Who would kill me? The Russians? How would the Russians know I was here and about my interests in Inga Sarnoff? Only six of us were privy to that . . . weren't we?"

"Well, I asked that question, and the Director suggested that the Russians may have been tracking you from the time you entered the country. It wouldn't have taken much to bribe an immigration employee to keep them informed. I also suggested that the Russians could have bugged the meeting room at the OIJ. Of course, he denied that was possible. In any case, here is a newspaper article from this morning's paper. You can take it with you."

"Gracias," she replied and tucked it away to read later.

"The Director also agreed to send me proof that she was Inga Sarnoff. I'll forward it to you when I receive it." Then he looked directly at her. "There is flight out of SJO at two forty this afternoon. It goes to Charlotte, North Carolina. A connecting flight will get you to Baltimore around midnight. I already alerted my secretary. She can get you on those flights right now if you agree."

"Do you really think—"

"Please say yes."

"Okay."

"Wait right here. I'll have her print out boarding passes."

He returned within five minutes and handed her two boarding passes. "You should leave now. Come here," he said as he pulled her toward him. They hugged as he told her *"Hasta que nos encontremos de nuevo."*

****

Donna Wolf went back to her hotel, packed her things, and checked out using the TV in her room. Her account was settled—no need to go to the front desk in the lobby. She headed down to the lobby and was about to exit the hotel for the parking lot when she saw *la policia* and a tow truck about to tow her rental car. *Oh God*, she said to herself as she remembered the map with the x's. She had left it in the car. She quickly reversed direction and exited via another door. Fortunately, she was able to grab a waiting taxi and go directly to the airport. At the airport counter, she presented her official government passport and her boarding pass, but instead of returning her documents, they asked her to step aside. Her heart began to thump. Were they going to stop her? She watched as the guard who took her passport talked on the phone. It seemed like a year before he came back, returned her passport, and returned her boarding pass.

"Sorry for the delay," he said. "You are free to proceed." She breathed a sigh of relief.

Once seated on the plane, she pulled out the article that Ed Perez had given her and began to read it in Spanish. La Extra was known to be the most widely read newspaper in Costa Rica. It also had a reputation for being the seediest.

Diario Extra—Monday, April 7, 2003
By Carman Diaz, reporter

Maria Martin was found murdered in her home Sunday morning when two of her neighbors went to take her to Sunday Mass. Señora Martin was known by her neighbors to be a Canadian expat who tutored children. She was fifty-one years old.

Interviews with people on the scene revealed some interesting facts. A neighbor reported that he witnessed an unknown woman sitting in her car across the street just after sundown. Another neighbor claims to have seen a woman get into a rental car parked nearby sometime after 7 p.m. An anonymous source tells us that the hard-drive from the woman's computer was missing and that evidence found in the home included a passport in the name of Inga Sarnoff, a Russian spy wanted by the United States for murdering a high-level U.S. CIA official fifteen years ago. Another anonymous source told us that a female using an official U.S. government passport is known to have entered Costa Rica last Wednesday and met with someone at the U.S. Embassy the next day. Speculation is that this could have been an assassination orchestrated by the American CIA.

The San José police and the OIJ are investigating.

Next to the article was a picture of Inga Sarnoff lying dead on the garage floor with her blouse covered with blood and a sign on her lap that said, *'¡JUSTICIA PARA UN ESPÍA RUSO!' Oh my God,* she thought. How could they print this stuff? Was there no crime scene security? The release of this information would certainly not help a legitimate investigation. She shook her head and stuffed the article back into her pocket.

Then Donna began to muse over the events of the past several days. The outcome was not what she expected, but she had no regrets that Inga Sarnoff was dead. Sarnoff was evil. The woman had killed multiple times. In 1988, she had assassinated Jon Wilson, her friend, and a high-level CIA official. She then escaped arrest and fled to Moscow. Donna had spent the last fifteen years tracking Sarnoff down. Two years ago, she had provided

Ed Perez with intelligence that Sarnoff may be in Costa Rica. She was elated when he notified her that the information had paid off.

The demise of Inga Sarnoff was especially rewarding for Donna Wolf. When she learned she had cancer, her own future had become very uncertain, and she was glad she had a chance to avenge Jon's death before the cancer ended her own life. She had surgery and chemo—she was better now. She felt good and, for the moment at least, was cancer-free. She felt at peace and was glad to be on her way back home. She relaxed, put her head back against the head-rest, and fell asleep to the drone of the engines.

12

HOME

It was late Monday night—early Tuesday morning actually—when Donna arrived home to her townhouse in Guilford, Maryland. Tabby greeted her as soon as she stepped into the hallway and set her luggage down. Tabby was her cat—very friendly. She reached down and petted him as he rubbed against her leg and purred, happy to see her. Donna's daughter Brandy had come over every day while she was gone to feed him and clean out his litter box.

Donna felt so grateful to have Brandy as a daughter, but the relationship had been strained for many years. Donna's frequent travel away from home and her often covert operations with the CIA didn't help. The early years living with her mother, who did not look favorably upon out-of-wedlock affairs, including that of Donna's father, was not helpful either. Brandy needed a father so when Brandy was six, Donna married John, whose wife had died. He had a son a year older than Brandy. John was a good father and it was a good relationship for all four of them until Brandy got married and moved to Ellicott City. When John passed away about ten years ago due to a bad heart, Donna sold the house they were in, moved to a garden apartment complex in Jessup, and then to her current townhouse in Guilford. Although she still reported to the CIA in Langley, Donna was able to work out of an office at the National Security Agency at nearby Fort Meade.

The relationship with Brandy got better with time. Last year, when Donna was diagnosed with ovarian cancer, they became even closer. Brandy was very attentive and took care of her when she needed it. Brandy scheduled her appointments and went with her to each one. While Donna was in the hospital, Brandy took care of Tabby, her housekeeping, her mail, and so on. Donna and Brandy had become close.

From the age of four, Brandy wanted to know who her birth father was, but Donna had kept it a secret. However, circumstances had changed. Brandy was in her mid-thirties and more mature now. She was divorced and shared custody of her teenaged son, Brian. Brandy could understand now, Donna reasoned. And then there was the conversation she had with Ed. He had told her how important it was for him to learn about his birth mother. With her recent illness, Donna had come to realize that she would not be on this earth forever. After her death, there would be fewer reasons for keeping the secret about Brandy's birth father. Donna reconsidered her decision. She typed a letter to Brandy explaining the circumstances and reasons for the secret, and secured the letter in her safe deposit box at the bank. Donna also left a letter for Brandy's birth father. No one would see these letters until after she passed.

She felt good that she had completed her project to track down Inga Sarnoff. Tomorrow, she would contact her boss and talk about retiring by the end of the year. She would have more time for Brandy and her grandson Brian. Tonight, however, she was only thinking about how grateful she was to have Brandy as her daughter and how tired she was from her trip to Costa Rica. She collapsed on the bed, happy to be home, as Tabby cuddled up next to her.

****

On several occasions over the next few weeks, Donna met with Matheson at Langley, to discuss the aftermath of the Inga Sarnoff Assassination. Matheson made it clear what he wanted.

"I am disappointed about the bad publicity we are getting," he said. "The Russians have spread the word that you and the CIA are responsible for the death of Maria Martin, aka Inga Sarnoff." It looks bad for you and for the CIA. But to the Russians, it also looks bad. To lose one of their own makes them look weak. I am receiving intelligence that the Russians are planning revenge. They are now aware of who you are and what you have been doing to them for the past fifteen years. They may try to tap into your files and steal classified information. I must also warn you that your life may be in danger."

"What do you want me to do? Should I retire now?

"No. I have a plan that will turn lemons into lemonade, to use a cliché."

"What is it?"

"I can't tell you everything,"

"I'd like to know my role, Donna demanded."

"Okay. Over the next few months, I'd like you to help the technical staff set up some bogus files and documents that might attract the Russian's interest. But other than that, I would like you to continue as normal, doing everything you're already doing."

"You said my life could be in danger. Will they come after me?"

"They may, but we'll have eyes on you. We'll protect you."

"Will this operation have a name, and who else is involved?"

"No names. I can't give you any more details at this time. I need to avoid leaks and ensure plausible deniability. Look, I know you have invested years into this project. Many of the spies you have been tracking, including Sarnoff, report directly to Ivan Markov, one of Russia's top spies. We believe that Markov will be running the operation to take you down. This is our chance to take him down first. I need your support."

His answers to her questions implied that the operation may be off the books. Yet, she had worked with him for years and felt he could be trusted. She wanted very badly to see the completion of the project she started fifteen years ago, and she wanted to see it soon. Her eagerness was partly because she wanted to retire, but it was much more than that. She also had strong personal reasons that she kept to herself.

"Okay, I'm on board," she finally said.

13

GARCIA'S OFFER

Three weeks after the death of Maria Martin, Joe Garcia received a message at his security company office in San José.

25/4/03
POR FAVOR, REÚNETE CONMIGO—2 P.M. MAÑANA EN LA HABITACIÓN 305 DEL INTERCONTINENTAL—VP

It was written in Spanish, but it was a request from Vladimir Petrov to meet him in room 305 at the InterContinental Hotel tomorrow at 2:00 p.m. It was not publicly known that in addition to being a supporter of socialist causes, Petrov was also the chief intelligence officer at the Costa Rican office for the SVR-RF. The SVR was the international intelligence service for the Russian Federation. Petrov's position was the equivalent of the CIA's Chief of Station, Eduardo Perez.

Joe knew who Petrov was, but wondered why such a meeting would be required. He and Judi had already provided Petrov with reports of their surveillance activity regarding Maria Martin. On the other hand, after three weeks, the Costa Rican OIJ did not have enough evidence to arrest anyone for her murder. The Russians had reason to believe that the CIA was responsible, and were doing their own investigation. They would need to know what he knew.

****

Tomorrow came. Joe went into the office that morning and did some homework in preparation for his meeting. He needed to make sure that he had his details straight.

The seasons were changing early this year, more typical of the month of May than April, and by noon it was starting to rain. When it was time to leave for his meeting with Petrov, Joe put on his rain slicker and made his way to the garage and got into the Toyota Corolla that he shared with his business partner. Traffic was terrible, but he arrived at the InterContinental with a few minutes to spare. He made his way up to room 305 and knocked on the door.

Petrov opened the door, let him in, and glanced up and down the hallway before closing the door. As Garcia passed through the foyer and entered the main room, he was surprised to see another man rise from the sofa to greet him.

"Joseph Garcia, please meet Ivan Markov," Petrov said politely. "Markov is a comrade who is here from Moscow."

"Pleased to meet you, *Señor* Garcia. I hear good things about you," Markov said in Russian.

"Uh, pleased to meet you as well," Garcia responded, doing his best to pronounce clearly in Russian.

Markov smiled. "Russian is not your native language?" he said in broken Spanish.

"No, sir," Garcia responded, switching to English. "My native language is Spanish. I speak fluent Spanish and English, but I'm still learning Russian."

The rest of the conversation was in English.

"I am here to talk about the death of Maria Martin," Markov began. "The SVR is investigating her death, and we intend to hold her killer responsible. We believe the killer is Donna Wolf, an agent with the American CIA. We have had eyes on Wolf for some time now. We believe she's responsible for the exposure of several of our agents. Some have turned up dead, and others have had their missions compromised. We knew that she was here last year prior to the elections, and then we learned that she may be coming to Costa Rica again. I alerted Petrov. We were suspicious about the purpose of her trip. Petrov tells me that he asked you to investigate her arrival and do surveillance of her activities while she was here. He also told me that you had worked with Maria Martin. We thought you may have additional insight as to what happened. I would like to ask you some questions."

"What would you like to know?"

"When did you first learn that Maria Martin had at one time been a covert Russian agent wanted by the United States?"

"Not until two days before she was killed," Garcia replied.

"How did you find out?"

"Judi told me."

"Judi?"

"One of my agents," Petrov interjected.

"Was it you that killed Martin?" Markov asked.

"What! . . . Look—"

"Relax. I joke," Markov said with a grin.

Then Markov got serious. "*Señor*, please tell me what information you have. I need to know how she died and who did it," he said sternly.

"Well, I gave a summary to Petrov after she was killed, and I gave him my written report on the eleventh of April. I wish I had more, but I'll tell you what I know. On Thursday, more than three weeks ago, the third of April to be exact, Petrov's agent, Judi, met with me. Judi informed me that a CIA officer named Donna Wolf had entered the country Wednesday evening using a U.S. government passport. Judi told me that Petrov wanted me to track Wolf and find out why she was here. I had a listening device and an informant in the Director of the OIJ's office. I learned that CIA Officer Donna Wolf and the CIA Chief of Station, Ed Perez, had a meeting that morning with the OIJ Director. The purpose of the meeting was to discuss the extradition of Maria Martin on the grounds that she was a Soviet spy wanted by the CIA for murders fifteen years ago. I know that the Costa Rican DIS also came to the meeting. I didn't have ears inside the secure facility in which they met, but it's almost certain that someone in that meeting ordered the hit. According to the coroner, Maria was murdered the next evening, Friday evening."

"The newspapers blamed the CIA. Do you not agree?" asked Markov.

"It's entirely possible and consistent with the evidence, and it was probably Wolf that did it. I know that she was at Martin's residence that Friday evening around the time of the murder. I also know that before she was in Martin's neighborhood, she met with an unknown man at La Copa Máxima in Heredia, and I know that after she was in Martin's neighborhood, she delivered that package to someone at the *Hotel Grano de Oro*.”

“What do you think was in the package

“I don’t know for sure, but the package delivered to the hotel could have been the stolen hard-drive from Martin’s house.”

“How did you learn this?”

“I was tailing her on Friday evening.”

“Why—”

“I had asked them to track Wolf,” Petrov interjected.

“Judi and I were working together to find out what Wolf was up to. It was prudent to tail her. Judi had determined that Wolf was staying at the InterContinental Hotel. Then, Judi posed as the wife of a newly hired employee of the U.S. Embassy and struck up friendly conversations with her at the hotel. That was on Thursday afternoon and again on Friday afternoon. On Friday, they talked about things to do and places to eat. Wolf mentioned places that included *Hotel Grano de Oro*, and Jurgens. I knew from my experience working with Maria, that these places were favorite places for having business meetings and sharing intelligence. On Friday afternoon, according to Judi, Wolf mentioned that she was having dinner that night with a friend who worked at the U.S. Embassy. Wolf didn’t say what time the dinner was, but she said she was leaving the hotel around four o’clock to meet that person somewhere. It seemed too early for dinner and we surmised that something may be going down. We had planted a bug in Wolf’s hotel room, and on Friday afternoon we heard her talking on the phone with a place called *La Copa Máxima* in Heredia. Judi had another commitment that evening and I had the car, so I was the one that tailed Wolf when she left the InterContinental at around four o’clock. I followed Wolf from the InterContinental to the coffee shop.”

“What happened there?”

“Wolf arrived at *La Copa Máxima* between five and five thirty. I observed that she met with a gentleman who I did not know, and that he gave her a package. I don’t know what was in the package. It could have been money, could have been directions, or it could have been a weapon. When she left, I followed her to Rohrmoser. I was a few cars behind her when she made a left turn from Via 104 and headed into the Rohrmoser neighborhood. Unfortunately, traffic was very heavy, and a car had stalled in the intersection, and I didn't make the light. When I got into the neighborhood, her car was no longer in my sights. However, I assumed she may be heading towards Maria Martin's house. I had been there when I worked with her, so I knew the address. I passed by the house and found Wolf's car parked on the street near the house. I kept a safe distance, and waited until she returned to the car."

"Then you did not actually see her enter residence?"

"No, but I saw her exit the residence and return to her car later."

"While you waited, were you not concerned that Martin might be in danger?"

"I didn't believe that a female CIA officer would also be an assassin, but things did seem off."

"Did you intervene? What did you do?"

"I called Maria's cell phone in the hope that she may still be on the way home from work. No answer. I left a warning message. I considered walking up to the house, but Wolf returned to her car before I could do that, and my mission was to follow her, not to engage her."

"So, you sure that Officer Wolf killed her?"

"Wolf was there, and we now know that Maria is dead. But there was additional evidence as well. One of my sources in the OIJ said that a security camera showed a woman leaving Maria Martin's residence on Friday evening but the video was grainy, and while they couldn't say with certainty that it was Wolf, they couldn't rule it out either. My source also told me that a man walking his dog said he passed by a woman on the sidewalk coming from the direction of Martin's house around six fifteen that night. His description matched that of Wolf. And then what about the sign that was left on her body? Who else would have been emotional enough to leave a sign, accusing her of being a spy who was brought to justice?"

"Yes, some women can be that way," Markov stated in a matter-of-fact manner. "Did you follow her after that?"

"I did. I followed her to the *Hotel Grano de Oro*. She carried a package into the hotel and left it with the desk clerk. It may have been Maria's hard-drive. I later saw her have dinner with a man I thought was CIA. Again, my sources say that both are on security cameras in the area of the hotel." Garcia knew that his account of events was not precisely true, but it was what he needed them to believe, and it could not be disproven.

"So, it sounds like you are quite certain that the CIA is involved and that Officer Wolf is the assassin. Is that correct?"

"Yes, sir. That's correct! I informed Petrov of everything I saw later that evening and gave him a written report on April eleven."

Then, changing the subject, Garcia continued. "May I ask a question? Earlier, you said that over the years, Wolf has caused you great harm. Are you planning to take her out?"

"We're considering it. She has exposed many of our operatives and it needs to stop."

"If you want to go after Maria's killer, I want to help you do that. You probably know I was a friend of Maria. We worked together for three years. We exposed the corruption in the Costa Rican government and helped to form the new Citizens Action Party. I liked her. She even gave me private lessons to help me learn Russian. If anyone wants to retaliate, it would be me."

"How would you help?"

"Agent Markov, I have special skills—security, computer hacking, reconnaissance, and communications. While Wolf was here, I learned some things about her. I learned that she's a cancer survivor. I also learned that she's divorced and has a daughter—"

"How did you learn these things?" Petrov interjected.

"On Thursday, Judi was able to lift Wolf's room-key and entered her room while she was at the swimming pool. This allowed her to transfer information from Wolf's personal mobile phone and to bug the room with a listening device that I provided. Then when Wolf talked with Judi on Friday, Wolf had said that she planned to go sightseeing the next day with her friend. The next morning, Judi saw Wolf in the lobby of the InterContinental with her friend. I believe he was the same man I saw at the hotel the night before. That night, she and her friend slept together—spent the entire night. I later learned that her friend was Ed Perez, the CIA Chief of Station here in Costa Rica. They never said anything incriminating and never mentioned Maria Martin, but they did talk about personal stuff."

"They were well trained," Markov commented.

Garcia continued. "After Wolf left the country, I did additional research using the Internet. I discovered that Officer Wolf lives alone in the Washington D.C. area. The daughter's name is Brandy. She's divorced and living alone as well. Addresses and phone numbers are available. I could set up the kill scene for you."

"Don't know if we need more help. You have already helped by providing this information. The SVR also has special training, you know."

"Sir, may I suggest something that you may want to consider?"

"Okay, feel free."

"Wolf has access to highly classified information that may be of interest to you. Rather than taking her out right away, you may want to access her files. I have the skills needed to hijack her IDs, security keys, and passwords. I could set it up so that the CIA computers think it is her every time you access a file. This could go on for a long period of time before it's detected. In the meantime, you would learn things like what the CIA has learned from Maria's computer, except that now we're talking about a bigger picture with information on more tactics, contacts, and agents. Once you have all the information you want, or they change the access codes, or Wolf leaves the CIA, then you can take her out if you still desire, but you may not want to do it publicly."

"How do you mean when you say not publicly?"

"Maria's murder was publicized in Costa Rica. The idea that she was a Soviet spy was leaked to the media. I don't know if you want to kill Officer Wolf in retaliation and make it publicly known that your SVR did it. It may be viewed as an escalation of tensions between the United States and Russia. Perhaps you want to make it look like Wolf dies from an accident or natural causes? If you have the right poison, you could make it look like a return of her cancer. It would be a long time before the public finds out that it was murder, if ever. Then you could get back to Moscow before anyone is the wiser. Of course, the CIA could still get your message, but it just wouldn't be made public. Either way, I can help set it up for you. It's what I'm trained to do."

"If I choose to go that way, do you have a specific plan?"

"I do. I could use the daughter to get close to Wolf . . . initial reconnaissance, information on her habits, access to her files and her house. I travel to the Washington, D.C. area at least once per year. I'm a marketing rep for a company in the D.C. area that sells security products internationally. While in D.C., I learn about their new products and how to market them. My next trip is planned for early September."

"Don't know if—"

"I'm about the same age as the daughter, and I don't like to boast, but I still pride myself on my ability to attract women. The daughter is in the security business as well. That gives us something in common to talk about and maybe develop friendship and trust. My research indicates that she works for the U.S. National Security Agency. By the way, that may be a connection that you may consider worth developing as well. Anyway, this year, I also plan to attend a security conference in D.C. in September. Perhaps I could encourage Miss Brandy to attend and hook up with her at that time."

"I appreciate the offer. I will think about it."

"That's all I ask. If you decide to use my help, perhaps we could meet when I'm in D.C. and nail down the specifics of our plan?"

"I will let you know. How do I get ahold of you?"

"You don't," Garcia responded. "You get ahold of Petrov and he will contact me. May I please leave now?" Garcia asked, looking at Markov and then Petrov.

They both nodded in the affirmative, and Joseph Garcia left, knowing exactly what he would need to do next.

Markov looked at Petrov and asked, "Can we trust him?"

"Absolutely," Petrov replied.

Back in his office, Joseph Garcia was pleased with what he just accomplished. He sent off a secure text message to another one of his clients. It was short and to the point.

Wheels set in motion. Will meet in D.C. – JGM

14

THE RUSSIAN PLAN

In early September, Joe Garcia flew to Dulles Airport and took a van to the hotel in downtown Washington, D.C. where he would stay. He normally came to the D.C. area around this time each year to meet with vendors of security hardware. There was also an expo that he would attend. It was an opportunity to become familiar with all the latest equipment and how to employ it. It was a legitimate business trip that his company would pay for. However, this year he would also meet with potential Russian clients to discuss his possible role in an operation that was clearly illegal.

He checked into his hotel, and then went to the hotel lounge for a late afternoon refreshment while he waited for his contact to show. He was nursing a ginger ale when a gentleman sat down beside him.

"My name is Aleksei Chaban," he said with a heavy Russian accent, "but just call me Aleksei or Alex. I work for Markov."

"Nice to meet you, Alex. Have a seat. I'll buy you a beer."

"Markov would like to see us in his room."

Joe looked at Alex quizzically.

"He wants to see us right now!"

Not to be intimidated, Garcia slowly finished his ginger ale, put a five-dollar bill on the bar top, and slid off his bar stool. He stood before Aleksei for a moment, looked him in the eye, and said, "Okay, let's go."

Then the two of them took the elevator up to Markov's room.

"Hello, Garcia. You have good trip?"

"It was fine but tiring. I thought our meeting was tomorrow."

"I'm eager to get started. I want you to tell me how you plan to accomplish my objectives."

"Uh . . . Please tell me specifically what you want to accomplish."

"First, I want access to Donna Wolf's classified emails and documents, and then I want you to take her out. How will you go about that?"

"Okay, my plan is to gain access to Donna Wolf's residence. I've already made an initial assessment of what is required. There will be door keys and a security code. Then, to access her computer, I'll need multiple passwords. I'll develop a relationship with her daughter because she'll help me get what I need. My plan is to essentially clone Wolf's laptop and give you the clone to use—"

Aleksei interrupted. "Why a clone? Why not just steal her laptop and bring it to us?"

"Because, as soon as her laptop goes missing, she will report it stolen, and as soon as it's reported stolen, the CIA will deauthorize its use. We're talking a matter of only a few hours. And it's not likely that the laptop has anything on it that's classified, so it would become useless to you. If I give you a clone, you can continue to access her accounts indefinitely. The network will think you are her."

Markov looked at his subordinate and smiled. "Our new comrade knows what he's doing. I think we should let him continue."

"Well, then you said you wanted to take her out. Are you leaving it up to me to decide how to do that, or do you have something in mind?"

"We have used many techniques in the past—radioactive isotopes, cyanide, heavy metals, antifreeze, nerve gas, various chemical injections, and so on. They all have limitations." His tone and demeanor were even and calm as he spoke. "I want it to be low-key. Make it look like a natural death—no publicity, no investigation. This time we try something new."

"Like—"

"Like cancer," he replied with an increased display of enthusiasm. Our labs back home developed a new chemical that can be ingested. They say it causes a form of blood cancer. That's what we use," he said with conviction.

"Okay, let me know how I can help with that, and I will do my part."

"Aleksei will let you know. He will work with you and keep me informed of your progress."

"This plan will take time to develop," Garcia said, addressing Aleksei. "I'll need to establish a residence near where the mom and daughter live, and establish my cover. I will also need some financial help to get started and cover my expenses," Garcia said as he turned toward Markov. "As my client, this would be expected. I'll open a bank account here in Maryland in the name of my company, *JR Seguridad, Srl*. My company wants eight-grand a week for my services."

"Make it four," Markov quickly replied.

"Two hundred dollars per hour for my time and expense is reasonable for this type of work. If I put in a forty-hour week, that's eight grand a week. We should make this look legit. Don't you agree?"

"Let's split the difference."

"Okay, then let's shake on six grand per week." They shook hands.

15

GETTING STARTED

Joe Garcia had already determined the addresses of Brandy Evans and her mother, Donna Wolf. The next step would be to find himself a place to live that would be convenient to both addresses. He found a three-bedroom townhouse on the south side of Columbia, Maryland, in the Kings Contrivance section. He agreed to a six-month lease. Donna's address was about three miles to the east of Joe's townhouse off Guilford Road. NSA was another five miles to the east, where both she and Brandy had offices. Brandy's address was in Ellicott City, north of Columbia, and about twelve miles to the north of Joe's place. Joe's next step was to put eyes on them and find out when and where they went each day.

He started with Brandy. Brandy lived in an older house on a half-acre of land. She left her house each day around seven fifteen and headed to her office at NSA. She returned between six and six thirty each day except on Tuesday and Thursday. On these days she returned home around eight thirty. Joe needed to find out what she did on the evenings she came home late. He made note of her car make, model, and plate number.

Then, Joe watched Donna leave her two-bedroom townhouse around seven thirty each morning and drive the short distance to NSA. He couldn't help but notice that she had her laptop with her. He hoped for a time when she would leave it at home. Otherwise cloning it would take longer than he first thought. Joe observed that Donna returned home between five thirty and six each evening, except on Thursday. On Thursday, she stopped at home and went right back out. Joe followed her to a Lifetime Fitness Center in Columbia, not far from her townhouse. When he got there, he also found Brandy's car in the parking lot. On that day, Joe kept his distance. He did not want to arouse suspicion, but he knew exactly what he would do next. He joined the fitness club. His membership would begin the Tuesday after Labor Day.

Joe was at the fitness center that Tuesday evening, and he reasoned that in addition to Thursdays, Brandy would be there on Tuesdays as well. He was right. She was there. She was using a stationary bike. He positioned himself on a treadmill just across the aisle from the stationary bikes. He watched her as she pedaled energetically, hardly breaking a sweat. She was trim and her body well proportioned. She had black hair tied in a short ponytail above her neck, and a pretty face with a clear complexion. He couldn't help but stare.

Brandy noticed and returned his stare with a few glances of her own. When she finished her required time on the bike, she dismounted and walked across the aisle to confront him.

"You were staring at me. Did you like what you saw?" she said mockingly.

Joe stepped off his treadmill and faced her directly. "I apologize if I creeped you out, but you are a very attractive lady . . . and I think you were also looking at me. Were you not?"

There was a pause, and Joe was not sure which way this conversation would go.

Brandy had noticed his well-chiseled body and six-foot frame, his lightly tanned skin, and his full head of short black hair. He was eye candy, and she had noticed. However, she decided to ignore his question, and finally said, "I haven't seen you here before. Are you new?"

"I'm afraid so. This is my first visit. My name is Joe. Pleased to meet you," he said and extended his hand.

She was impressed by his slight accent and formality.

"My name is Brandy," she said as they shook hands.

Joe was impressed by her assertiveness, but knew that winning her over would not be easy.

Over the next two weeks, Joe frequented the fitness center at the times that he expected Brandy and her mom to be there. He told her that he was on temporary assignment as a security system consultant and designer. Brandy told him that she managed an IT organization, and worked at the NSA. On Thursday the following week, he met Brandy's mother,

Donna, for the first time. Joe was entering the locker room area and he encountered Brandy and her mom on their way out. Joe said hello and engaged them in conversation for a few moments before they left. But while Joe's relationship with Brandy was friendly, it was still superficial, and it wasn't getting him any closer to Donna Wolf's classified files. The relationship needed to move to the next level. So far, Joe's attempts to do this were politely rebuffed. Brandy seemed reluctant to become involved.

****

Sometime during the last week of September, Joe got a call from Aleksei. "We must meet," he said. "Meet me tomorrow at nine at the sports bar in the plaza near the Metro stop for Glenmont, Maryland." Glenmont was the last stop on the Red Line from the District of Columbia. The trip was easy for Aleksei. All he had to do was hop on the Metro from wherever he was staying in the city. On the other hand, Joe had to drive down from his townhouse in Columbia. When he arrived, Aleksei was already seated in a small booth that offered some privacy to the conversation that ensued. Aleksei was already nursing a vodka. Joe ordered a ginger ale.

"What's wrong?" You don't drink?"

"No, I don't. Don't take it personally," Joe replied.

"But it reflects your hesitation to take risks."

"What are you saying?"

"Markov thinks things are moving too slowly. In Russia, we know how to get our women in bed."

"The objective is to compromise Donna Wolf's computers, not to have sex with her daughter. Tell Markov to be patient."

"He wants me to help you."

"How would you do that?"

"If an opportunity were to happen, I hope you would be smart enough to take advantage of it."

"What are you suggesting?"

"I'm told you have high IQ. No? When opportunity happens, you will know."

"I don't want Brandy to get hurt."

"She won't."

"Okay."

"I go now. Must catch Metro back to city before they stop running," he said as he put a ten spot on the table.

As Aleksei got up and left, Joe's ginger ale arrived. *Nice talking with you too*, Joe thought.

****

On Tuesday of the first week in October, Joe had changed into his workout clothes and was heading out of the locker room toward the exercise equipment when Brandy entered the building. They greeted each other and continued along their respective ways. Two hours later, Brandy was on her way back out. Joe had already changed back into his street-clothes, but had waited around, hoping to catch Brandy as she left. He really did need to move things along. He waited near the entrance and was talking with someone as she passed by. He waved, and she acknowledged, but obviously he missed another opportunity. After a few minutes, he headed out to the parking lot. When he got to his car, he saw Brandy a few cars further down the row. She was standing in front of her car, and she was on the phone. She seemed distraught. As he approached, it became evident what the problem was. Both front tires on Brandy's car were flat.

As he looked at her, she held up a finger to indicate she would soon be off the phone. While he waited, he stooped down and looked at one of the tires. It was totally flat, but did not appear slashed or punctured. Sure enough, when he removed the cap on the tire stem, it was evident that someone had loosened the valve stems and let out all the air. He stood up just as Brandy was finishing her call.

"Brandy, who would do this?"

"Good question. Whoever it is, is sending me a message. None of the other cars are affected. Maybe my ex-husband. We just had a legal dispute over money set aside for my son's college education, and he lost. He can be a real asshole at times."

"You were just on the phone. Were you calling a road service?"

"Yes, but they said they don't do tire repair, and they don't have air compressors on their trucks, so the car must be towed."

"How long?"

"Not till tomorrow."

"Oh, that's not good. Can I give you a ride somewhere?"

"Thanks for the offer, but I don't know. I tried to call my mother, but I got a message that says her home phone is unavailable, and she's not picking up on her cell. I left a message but don't know if she will get it."

"Okay, so let me drive you home. You can continue to try and reach your mother, and hopefully she'll be able to help you in the morning."

"I don't know . . . I don't want you to—"

"Brandy, it will be okay. I don't mind helping you."

Brandy locked up her car and followed Joe back to his. Joe could tell she was nervous as they pulled out of the parking lot. She was wringing her hands, and he could see the stress in her face.

"Who would do this to me?"

"Brandy, you need to relax. Everything will be okay. . . Which way?"

"Take Snowden River to Broken Land, then head west to Route 29 and go north to Route 100. It's about eleven miles."

"Okay."

"I don't understand why I can't reach Mom."

"Does she live nearby?"

"She lives in a townhouse off of Guilford Road."

"That's interesting. I live off Guilford Road also," he responded to get her talking.

"Where on Guilford Road?

"Eden Brook."

"Oh, okay. Mom lives further to the east, closer to Route 1."

"Isn't that kind of out of her way to come here to help you in the morning?"

"Yes, but she owes me a few favors. She was very sick a year and a half ago and I spent a lot of time with her, and when she goes somewhere, I water her plants and tend to her cat. I was thinking she could come stay with me tonight and come back here with me in the morning, and then if my car isn't available, we would continue onto work together. We both work at the NSA—different buildings—but I can walk from one to the other."

"Are you and your mom close?"

"We weren't for many years, but three years ago, after I got divorced, Mom helped me to deal with it, and then later when she got sick, it was clear that she needed me, so we've grown much closer now."

"You're lucky to have your mom around. My dad and my stepmom were killed in a car crash about five years ago. That's when I started my consulting business."

"I'm sorry to hear that your parents passed away," she said with sincerity. "Here. Get off at this exit. My house is on the opposite side of the highway, but there is no exit, so we need to loop around and cross over to the other side."

"Okay."

By the time they pulled into her driveway it had become dark, but there was some light from her porch lamp and a street lamp. "So here you are—safe and sound. Nice-looking house. Well landscaped too."

"It looks better in the daylight," she quipped. "Thank you for your help," she said and reached for the door handle.

"Brandy, before you go, I'd like to ask you something."

She sat back in the seat and looked at him. "Yes?"

"I would like to ask you to have dinner with me."

After a moment of silence, she replied. "Joe, I like you enough, but I'm not sure I'm ready to date anyone."

"Why? You've been divorced for three years. You need to have a life, don't you?"

"That's just it. I have a life and I'm happy with it. I don't need to get involved in a romantic relationship. You're a very attractive man. If you're looking for sex, you can do better than me."

"Brandy, that's not what I'm looking for, and if I were, I don't think I could do better than you."

"When we first met, it seemed that way. You were looking at me that way. So, what are you looking for?"

"I'm looking for a friend that will enjoy my companionship and vice versa. I don't expect sex. Just go to dinner with me. We don't have to call it a date. Think of me as you would a girlfriend if you want."

The way he said it made her smile.

"Joe, if I say yes, I need to know something first, I need to know if you're married."

"No! I'm not married, never have been, and I have no children. And if you say yes, I promise to respect you."

"Okay."

"Okay, yes?"

"Yes."

"Here. Take this." He gave her one of his business cards. "My local mobile number is on the back."

"I don't have a business card to give you," she said.

"Not a problem, just tell me. I'll remember it." She told him the number, and he repeated it back.

That Friday evening, they had a very enjoyable dinner together, and afterwards, they took a leisurely walk around the nearby lake. They learned a lot about each other—everything except Joe's actual mission in the States. By all accounts it was the start of a romantic relationship—but without sex. Joe was keeping his word out of respect—or was it out of necessity?

16

A CLONE JOB

Joe's relationship with Brandy developed, but it was not until late October that Joe had the first opportunity to accompany Brandy to Donna's townhouse.

The two had a date for Saturday evening. Brandy called to request a change in plans.

Joe, would it be okay if I pick you up rather than you driving all the way up here?"

"Sure, why?"

"Well," she said. "Yesterday, Mom decided to spend the weekend in D.C. with an old friend, and she asked me if I could go over to her house to feed her cat and water her plants. If I pick you up, we could go to Mom's place before we go out. Do you mind?"

"Not a problem." He said, as he recognized this was the opportunity that he had been waiting for.

Brandy drove them to Mom's townhouse and parked out front. As they walked to the front door, Brandy asked Joe to wait on the porch. Joe watched as she went to the edge of the townhouse and retrieved a key from the downspout. *How convenient*, Joe thought to himself. She unlocked the door and they entered the foyer. As Joe followed her in, he could hear the beep-beep-beep of the security alarm. Brandy went to the alarm box mounted on a nearby wall, opened the door and began to punch the buttons. Joe watched intently as she punched in the code '0-0-2-9-6'.

Then they walked down a hallway and into the kitchen. Joe looked around and spied the empty food dish for the cat. "Where's the cat?"

"Tabby's a little shy with strangers. But if we put some food into his dish, he may come," she said. Would you mind getting his food bag from inside the utility closet over there?" She pointed to a door along the side of the kitchen wall near the back entrance-way. "I'll be watering plants in the living room."

Joe went inside the closet and saw the bag in a corner. He also saw the panel for the security system, and noticed the key in the key slot. He couldn't resist. He opened the panel and looked inside. He noticed the AC power connection that came from a transformer plugged into the wall socket below. He also noticed the black brick that served as a backup power supply, and he also noticed the phone line circuit that communicated with the security company's monitoring service. All of this could be useful information in the future. He picked up the bag of food, walked out of the closet and over to Tabby's dish and poured a small amount of the dried food into the dish, but Tabby didn't come.

"He's probably upstairs in the bonus room," Brandy said. "Come up with me. I need to clean his litter box."

On the second level was a small extra room called the bonus room. It was at the rear of the house, just past the laundry room. In addition to Tabby's litter box, there was a bed for him to sleep in, and another food and water dish. Cleaning supplies, extra cat food, and miscellaneous who knows what, were on a shelf on a side wall.

"Wow! You mean Tabby has his own room? One lucky cat!" Joe exclaimed. Brandy laughed. "But I still don't see him."

After they took care of the litter box, they came back to the kitchen. Sure enough, Tabby was at his bowl eating. Joe slowly approached. Tabby looked up, but decided he was no threat and dipped his head back into his bowl. "Where do you suppose he was?"

"Probably upstairs in Mom's office. He likes to sit on the window sill on a sunny day."

"This is a nice place. How long has your mom lived here?"

"About three years now."

"She's lucky to have you nearby to take care of things when she's not here . . . Where did she go this weekend?"

"She has a long-time friend. His name is Ed Perez. He lives in Costa Rica, but every now and then, he comes to the States on business. Maybe you know him."

He smiled. "It's a big country. Lots of people."

"Well, anyway, they see each other once or twice a year. And when they do, they make the most of it."

"You don't mind?"

"No, my dad has been gone for about ten years now, and Mom needs a life outside of her work. I'm happy for her."

"She coming back tomorrow?" Joe asked.

"No, not till Monday, and that reminds me, Mom said she forgot to water her plant and wanted me to check on it. It's upstairs in her office. Come on up with me."

While Brandy put water onto a palm in a large pot to the left, Joe looked around. Straight ahead was a double size window overlooking the parking lot. The Venetian blinds had been pulled up and the sun beamed in. Under the window was a shelving unit, the top of which was covered with a cloth upon which Tabby liked to sit in the sun. The lower shelves contained books, manuals, CD ROMS, and a locked box. A file cabinet was in one corner to the left of the door, and a wooden desk with a swivel-chair was up against the wall to the right. Sitting atop the desk was Donna's laptop. He observed that it was a powerful Lenovo, not an Apple.

As they left, Joe watched Brandy reset the alarm. This time it was '1-0-2-9-6.' Brandy returned the key to the downspout, and then they went back to the car and drove to a nearby pub, where they met two of Brandy's friends for drinks, supper, and conversation. Brandy introduced Joe as a friend from the fitness club. Afterwards, she drove Joe back to his place and dropped him off. They both said how much they enjoyed the evening. Joe was tempted to ask her in but held back.

****

The next morning, Joe was up early. He had a job to do. After a quick breakfast, he gathered up his laptop and his gear, and drove over to Donna's townhouse. He let himself in but did not return the door key to the downspout. Instead, he slipped it into his pocket. Then he entered '0-0-2-9-6' into the key pad on the wall and headed upstairs to the office. He powered up Donna's laptop and verified that it required a password just to be able to use it. He tried a couple of obvious possibilities like *'password'* and like *'Tabby'* but as expected, they didn't work. He reasoned that multiple passwords would be required to access the CIA network, her email, and the various files and programs that she used. There would be too many to remember. She probably used a password manager program. In any case, he reasoned that she probably had all her passwords and user IDs documented somewhere. He began to search the office. He remembered the locked box on the shelf under the window. He pulled it out and set it atop the desk. It had a simple key lock. No key. No problem. He picked the lock and opened the box. Inside, he found several USB memory-sticks. A label on one of them said, *'pw mgr'*—just what he was looking for. It would have all the passwords and a backed-up version of the password manager program. He inserted the memory stick into his laptop and copied the contents bit by bit onto his laptop. He now had the password needed to log onto Donna's computer and the master password and user ID required by the password manager program. He returned to Donna's computer and entered the password to log onto the computer itself. It was *'TabbyCat1.'* Once on her computer, he was able to use the master password and access everything. However, that would not meet the Russian's requirements. They wanted to access the CIA network from their own computer.

He copied her MAC address and all her cookies onto his laptop. He copied the registry information, and he copied the network access protocol. Then he plugged a cable directly into her cable modem and attempted to access the CIA network from his laptop. It didn't work. Access to the CIA network required a unique access protocol program and a unique identifier for Donna's computer. Perhaps the MAC address or a special cookie was required during the connection process. Or, there may have been other reasons why it didn't work. He would need more time to analyze it and come up with a solution.

There was nothing more he could do for now. Time to leave. He made sure everything was back in its original place, and before he left, he took time to say goodbye to Tabby. Tabby was becoming his friend.

It took another two weeks and another trip back to the townhouse before he had successfully cloned Donna's laptop onto another laptop.

17

FALLING IN LOVE

It was mid-November and the three of them had driven to Philadelphia to attend a three-day computer security conference. After the second day of sessions, Joe, Brandy, and Brandy's friend Jill joined several colleagues and went downstairs to the Travelers Lounge for drinks and conversation. The sessions had ended late that evening, and dinner consisted of bar food. Joe, Brandy, Jill, and a guy named John sat at a table for four. Jill had met John at one of the sessions, and they seemed to hit it off. An entertainer sang and played dance music in one corner of the lounge while one or two couples danced.

Joe took the opportunity to dance with Brandy. He was an excellent dancer, especially to Latin music, and Brandy loved it. Meanwhile, John seemed to be sweet-talking Jill. At some point, John went to the bar to get himself another beer and Jill another Pina Colada. Joe just happened to glance over to the bar from the dance floor and couldn't believe what he saw. He watched as John took something from his pocket and slipped it into Jill's drink. He whispered something into Brandy's ear and they walked back to the table.

"Would you care to dance?" he politely asked Jill.

She hesitated, looked at Brandy and then John, as if to seek approval.

"Go ahead," Brandy said as John remained silent.

She got up from her seat, and took a quick gulp of her drink before walking off with Joe.

Once on the dance floor, Joe momentarily put a hand on each shoulder, pulled her close, put his mouth down to the side of her cheek, and spoke.

"Jill, I saw John put a roofie into your drink."

"Hah, hah, funny," she replied.

"Jill, I'm not joking. Don't drink that drink."

"I don't believe you. Let's dance," she said in a matter-of-fact manner.

When they returned to the table and sat down, Brandy and John were talking. John was still unaware that his secret was out.

Jill reached for her drink, and was about to take another sip. Brandy interjected just in time. "Jill, would you mind coming to the ladies' room with me?"

After they left, Joe looked hard at John and spoke sternly but calmly. "John, I saw you put a roofie into Jill's drink. But why? She already likes you. If you asked her to have sex with you, she probably would have said yes anyway."

"I wanted to help things along."

"Look, Jill and Brandy are friends of mine. I can't let you do it."

"Did you already tell her?"

"I did."

"Did she believe you?"

"Do you want to be here when they return? We'll find out."

Before John could respond, the ladies returned.

"Jill says she's not feeling well. We're going to go up to the room."

John waited for them to leave and then stood up and addressed Joe with hostility. "Thanks for messing up my evening. I'll get you back for this."

"Don't waste your time, John."

Joe watched John go to the bar. After being sure that John was not going to follow the ladies, he got up and headed toward the elevators.

****

Joe took the elevator up to the fourth floor. He was relieved that John did not follow. Brandy and Jill were sharing a room. He knocked on the door.

"Who's there?" It was Brandy's voice.

"It's Joe. May I come in?"

"Of course," she said. "C'mon in."

"Is Jill okay? Where is she?"

"She's in the bathroom. I think she's okay. She didn't have very much of the drink. I think she's mostly embarrassed. Joe, she didn't believe you.

She thought they were really hitting it off. Are you absolutely sure that John did what you said?"

"Yes. He admitted it to me after you guys went to the ladies' room. I asked him why he did it, and he said he wanted to help things along. I'd like to tell Jill I'm sorry this happened, but she shouldn't be embarrassed. Will she speak to me?"

"Have a seat. I'll see how she's doing."

A few minutes later, she entered the room.

"Joe, I should have believed you. I'm embarrassed that I allowed him to deceive me, but the fact is you saved me from being raped. I owe you."

"You have nothing to be embarrassed about. You had no way of knowing. Things happen. I'm glad you're okay."

"Look, Brandy, you don't need to stay with me. I mean, if you two want to be together, it's fine. Perhaps you have things you need to talk about in private?"

Brandy looked at Jill. "Are you sure?"

"I'll be fine . . . Go."

Brandy and Joe walked down the hall and around the corner to room 480. Once inside, Joe took a seat on the edge of the bed. She remained standing. "What is it that Jill thinks we need to talk about in private?" he asked.

"Joe, I think it's important that we talk about our relationship. I—"

He started to interrupt, but she cut him off before he could say anything.

"No, hear me out. We have known each other for two months now. We've had several dates. We've had dinners; we've gone hiking; we've been to concerts; we've gone out for ice cream; we've gone swimming. We even dressed up and went to a Halloween party. We've enjoyed each other's company. Last week we went dancing and tonight we danced. You've been to my house. You've been to my mom's house and you've met her. My mom likes you. She's happy that I have a male friend. We've been able to discuss topics that range from trivial to matters of national interests. We've shared personal information. You've shown me that you're a caring and considerate person, and I really like you—"

"Okay, I like you as well. I like you a lot. Aren't we good friends? What's the problem?"

She shook her head. "Joe, that's the problem right there. We're good friends and I know that's my own doing. I told you I was afraid of getting involved sexually, and you promised to respect that . . . and you have, but I know it's been hard on you to do that; it's been hard on me as well—"

"Are you about to tell me you don't want to be friends anymore?"

"No, I'm telling you that I don't want it to end, and I want to be more than just friends, but I need to know how you really feel about me. How is it possible for you to show so much restraint?"

"You said you didn't want to have sex, and I kept my promise not to pressure you."

"I know, and that was unfair of me, but you don't need to keep your promise anymore."

Joe sat there looking bewildered. She went over to him, pulled his head toward hers, and kissed him hard on the mouth. He hesitated.

"Joe, what's holding you back? You told me you don't have a wife or a girlfriend back home. Please tell me if you do. And you said you weren't gay. Is there something wrong with me? Don't you desire me?"

"Oh, God, no! There's nothing wrong with you. I think you're a wonderful person and I care deeply for you."

Emotionally, Joe briefly wished he could tell her everything, but he knew he couldn't do that. He had to complete the mission. Until a few days ago, he thought that Brandy's part in his mission could be completed soon. He had access to Wolf's house, and he had provided Markov access to Wolf's on-line accounts, and he was ready for whenever Markov gave the word to deliver the poison. After that, he could just disappear. It would be so much easier if he and Brandy were not sexually involved— at least that was his thinking. But then when he met with Aleksei, just a few days ago, he realized that the mission would require more time, and that meant more time with Brandy. Apparently, there was an issue with the email access process, and Aleksei said that there were other items on the network that he wanted to access. Perhaps Wolf had reset passwords. Perhaps something else. He would need to go back to Wolf's townhouse and find out. And then, when was the next part of the mission supposed to take place? He would need to know when Wolf would not be there, and he would need to assure himself that she had not changed the key-code for the townhouse security system. The poisoning would probably require multiple visits. Joe was conflicted. He thought he might be falling in love with Brandy, while at the same time he knew he was taking advantage of her to complete his mission, and he didn't like that. So, he told her what he could.

"Brandy, when I first saw you, I thought that you were attractive and my desire was to have a fling, a sexual one to be sure. But I quickly got to know you and realized how wonderful a person you are. I've never met a woman like you before, and I've never felt this way about a woman before, but that's the reason for my hesitation. My assignment here is short-term. I have no idea where I'll be four months from now. It's possible we won't see each other after my assignment is complete, and I don't want to hurt you."

She turned toward him and reached for his hand. "Joe, if you leave in four months without having made love to me, it will hurt me even more."

"Are you sure?"

"Yes."

He pulled her to him and they hugged tightly. Then they slowly undressed each other, exploring each other's bodies for the first time. He told her how much he cared about her.

18

THANKSGIVING

Brandy invited Joe to come to Thanksgiving dinner at her mother's house, and naturally he had to accept. Brandy said her son Brian would be there as well, and he wondered if anyone else would be there.

"No. Just us. Mom saw Ed less than two weeks ago, and so he can't make it, but he might come around Christmas."

Joe felt relieved that Ed Perez would not be there, but still felt uneasy about what he was getting himself deeper and deeper into. He had previously met both Brandy's mom, Donna, and her son, Brian, but only briefly. Now he would be having a long visit. They would ask questions. He didn't want is mission known, and if Donna knew, she would be very upset that he was romancing her daughter. And that was becoming more and more of a dilemma for him. He was beginning to have strong feelings for Brandy. He didn't know how much longer he could carry out the charade, and Markov was not yet ready for part two of his plan.

"Brandy, how much do we tell them about our relationship? Does your mom already know we have slept together? How does she feel about that?"

"Joe, relax. She's very happy for me and I'm sure she expects that we've slept together. And besides, this is the year 2003, and we're both in our mid-thirties. She's not going to judge us. I'm sure she's been sleeping with her friend Ed, and I don't judge *her*. So, like I said, relax. Just be yourself."

****

On Thanksgiving, Joe drove the short distance from his place to Donna's house. He was told that dinner would be at three o'clock but to come early, around two. He arrived on schedule and brought two bottles with him. He

"

had a bottle of Sauvignon blanc for Donna and Brandy, and he had a bottle of cider for Brian and himself. Brandy and Brian were already there when he arrived. Brandy was in the kitchen helping with the food, and Brian was in the living room playing a game on the TV screen. As he came in, he could smell the pleasant aroma of the turkey and what he thought to be baked bread. He greeted everyone and offered to help. They immediately put him in charge of setting the table. It had been many years since Joe had celebrated holidays with family. His head filled with pleasant memories of when he was young, and he, his dad, and stepmom had holidays together. He snapped out of it when he felt a tug on his arm. Brandy gave him a kiss on the cheek and asked if he would please say hello to Brian and tell him his mom would like him to wash up for dinner and come to the table.

They sat down to dinner, and Joe poured the wine and the cider. Donna said a short grace, a thank you to God. Then Joe raised his glass:

"I want to thank all of you for inviting me to join you."

After they each took a sip, Brian asked, "Joe, how come you aren't drinking wine?"

Brandy started to say something, but Joe held up his hand. "It's okay. It's a personal choice I made. My mother's brother was an alcoholic, and I found his behavior to be obnoxious, and at a young age, my mother was run down and killed by a drunk driver. I tried drinking in college but it made me sick. I decided I didn't want to be like my uncle, and I didn't want to harm anyone. I haven't had a drink since."

Donna then asked, "Joe, would you be willing to carve the turkey for us?"

"It would be my honor."

"I'm sorry about your mom," Donna said. "Brandy says you're from Costa Rica. Where about?"

"The San José area. Have you ever been to San José?"

Joe poured more wine into Donna's glass.

"Yes, I have. I have a friend that lives there."

"And where does he live?"

"Escazu."

"That's a rather upscale place to live. What does he do?"

"He has a high-level government job. And where do *you* work?"

"I work to the northeast of Sabana Park on Route 2, and I live several kilometers south of there. Brandy has my business card."

"Do you like living there?"

"I do, but I also liked living in the States. Don't know if Brandy told you, but I was born in Texas, and I lived there until my dad got a good job in Costa Rica and we moved. I was about six. I also went to graduate school in the U.S."

"So, wait a minute, aren't you a citizen of Costa Rica?"

"Yes, my dad was, so I have dual citizenship."

"How did your dad and mom meet?"

"He was in graduate school at the University of Texas and she worked at the school."

"You mentioned that your mom passed away. What about your dad? Is he still alive?"

"No, unfortunately, he and my stepmom died several years ago—So, Donna, tell me," Joe said changing the subject, "What did you think of Costa Rica when *you* were there?"

"Well, my friend would like me to retire there—with him of course. I think it's a beautiful country, but I'm not sure I would want to live or work in the city. The traffic in the morning and evening seemed almost intolerable. I remember hardly moving in traffic while motorcycles whizzed in and out between the vehicles."

"I'm afraid to tell you this, but on most days I'm one of those motorcyclists. And you're right, the traffic is terrible, but the bike allows me to cut significant time off my commute, and the gas mileage is a lot better than the car I share with my business partner."

"What model bike do you have?" Donna asked.

"It's a Yamaha 2000 XV-635. five-speed manual. Do you know bikes?"

"I had a bike once," she responded. "It was a small Suzuki, a souped-up moped really. I had it for the same reasons, traffic, gas mileage . . . and parking," she added.

Now, Brandy started to show an interest and looked at her mom with a degree of disbelief. "Really Mom?"

"I loved that bike," she said excitedly. "I nicknamed it little Susie. Your father and I, we . . ." Her voice tapered off as she realized the impact of what she was about to say.

"My father? Tell me about him."

"Brandy, we've been through this. I can't do that yet. Please be patient with me."

"Sorry Mom."

"Anyway, it was a long time ago—before you were born."

"I can't imagine you riding a motorbike, Grandma," Brian added.

"And I never saw you on a bike," Brandy added. "Why did you stop?"

"I had a very scary accident. I was lucky that I wasn't killed. And soon after that, I got pregnant with you, so I decided it just wasn't worth the risk. I haven't been on a bike since."

Joe, who was paying close attention to this exchange, decided to change the subject.

"Donna, did you say you were thinking of retiring?"

"Yes, I had originally planned to retire by the end of this year, but now it has slipped to the end of January. I'm counting the days," she responded.

"Grandma, how come you delayed it?"

"My boss wants me to help finish a project I've been involved with."

Joe thought about the significance of that. *Did the delay have anything to do with his mission? Markov only has another two months to get what he wants using her access codes, and if part two of his plan is for a slow death by poisoning, it would need to start very soon.*

"Well, here's to your future retirement," he said and held up his cider glass.

After the dinner, they agreed to take a break and come back later for pumpkin pie and coffee. Joe helped to clear the table. When he walked into the kitchen, he was surprised to see Tabby at his bowl off in the corner. He walked over and noticed the bowl was empty. Tabby looked up and meowed. Joe crouched down to pet him. Donna, who had just entered the kitchen, watched as Tabby rubbed up against Joe's leg and started purring.

"Wow!" she exclaimed. "Tabby usually doesn't warm up to strangers that fast."

Then Joe went to use the rest room near the kitchen, but apparently Brian was in there. He heard Donna telling him he could use the one upstairs if he wished. He thanked her and headed off upstairs. On the way back, he encountered Brandy. She was in Tabby's room looking out the window. He walked up behind her and put his arm around her shoulder.

"What are you looking at?"

"I was just thinking about Mom. You probably noticed how she reacted when she started to say something about my birth father."

"Yes, I did, and I was wondering what that was about."

"All my life I've wanted her to talk about him, and she just won't do it. Until tonight, I had the impression he was still alive, and it was always my hope to meet him someday. I thought maybe Mom needed to protect his identity for some reason, like maybe he was a secret operative or something. But what she said tonight implied that maybe he was killed in her motorbike accident, and I remember when I was a child, my grandma told me he was killed in the war in Vietnam, so maybe that's true. Anyway, that's what I was thinking about."

"I see. I always wanted to know more about my birth mother, so I understand. I hope she tells you about him."

After everyone had used the restroom, they returned to the dining room. The table was cleared and reset, and after the coffee was ready, they were ready for dessert. Donna brought out a home-baked pie, and Joe poured the coffee. More talk ensued. Joe made a point of complimenting Donna on how good the pie was. At some point Brian excused himself but after a few minutes he returned. A flash of light seemed to come out of nowhere.

"Brian, what are you doing?" Joe exclaimed in horror.

"I wanted a picture of you and my mom. Aren't you and Mom like boyfriend and girlfriend?"

"We're good friends Brian," Joe responded showing some annoyance.

"Do you really like her and care about her?"

"I do."

"You have been seeing each other quite a bit over the past two months. Are you sleeping together?"

Donna spoke up. "Brian, you don't ask something like that."

"I just want Mom to know that if they like each other, I'm okay with it. Dad says he doesn't want her back, and I want her to be with someone who cares about her."

"Well, we do care about each other, but we're taking things slowly," Brandy replied. Joe is only here on a temporary assignment and we don't know yet how it will play out. Okay?"

"Okay."

It was about ten in the evening when Joe excused himself. He thanked Donna again and gave her a good-bye hug. Then he kissed Brandy and gave Brian a man-hug. On his drive home, he concluded that the evening had gone quite well.

19

THE POISONED WELL

In early December, Markov gave the order to initiate part two of his plan. Aleksei met Joe at their meeting place in Glenmont. The day was chilly, and it was natural that they both wore gloves. This time, their meeting was brief. Aleksei reached into his coat pocket and pulled out a small package which he handed to Joe. The package contained a small liquid-filled bottle with an eye dropper top.

"Here is your weapon," he said. "Do a dropper full, five times over next two months and she is dead. If not, *you* are dead."

Joe gave him a look.

"I joke. Markov wishes you good luck."

Joe put the bottle in his pocket. The two shook hands, and they parted.

The next day, Joe parked in front of Donna's townhouse, walked up to the front door, and entered with the key he had copied from the one in the downspout. As he entered, he heard the low beeping sound from the home security system. He went to the wall-mounted box and entered '*0-0-2-9-6*'. He was pleased that Donna hadn't changed the code. The beeping stopped. As he went into the kitchen, he saw Tabby cowering under a chair. He offered a treat and was pleased that Tabby acknowledged him by coming out, sniffing the treat he held in his hand, and rubbing up against the leg of his pants. He placed the treat in Tabby's dish and proceeded to the refrigerator. Inside the refrigerator, he found a pitcher of iced tea sitting on the top shelf next to the milk and orange juice. As he pulled the small bottle of clear liquid from his pocket, he knew exactly what he had to do.

Two weeks later he went back to Donna's place to apply dose number two. He kept Aleksei informed. As before, he knew exactly what he needed to do. And once again, before leaving, he took the time to play with his new friend Tabby.

****

It was a short week. New Year's Eve was on a Wednesday, and Brandy had decided to have a small gathering of friends and neighbors at her house that evening to celebrate. Joe learned that neither Brandy nor her mom would go to work that day, and the two of them would spend most of the day at Brandy's house helping with preparations. Joe saw Donna's expected absence from her townhouse as an opportunity. He informed Aleksei of his intention on Tuesday evening.

"Markov wants to know if Officer Wolf has shown any sign of becoming sick."

"No, I was wondering about that. How long is this supposed to take?"

"Markov is getting impatient. He wants me to go with you for the remaining three doses."

"Sounds like you don't trust me."

"Just following orders."

Early the next morning, Joe met Aleksei at the Metro's Greenbelt station and they drove from there to Donna's townhouse.

Joe unlocked the door. They walked in and were greeted by the expected beep, beep, beep.

"What is the key code?" Aleksei asked as he went directly to the key-pad on the wall.

"Press '0-0-2-9-6'," Joe said, as he set the small bottle of poison on the counter top.

"It don't work!" Aleksei responded.

"What? What do you mean? Do it again."

"I did!"

"Oh crap! Keep trying," Joe yelled as he ran down the hallway to the utility closet. He opened the door on the panel and quickly disconnected the land line with only five seconds to spare. He was about to go back to the kitchen when he heard the alarm go off upstairs, as well as on the panel itself. *Oh damn*, he said to himself. He pulled off the wire for the back-up battery, and then, using the small screwdriver he kept in his pocket, he removed the AC connection. The alarms stopped. He hoped that no one outside the house had heard it. He closed the panel door and headed back to the kitchen, where he noticed that a red flashing light on the key-pad unit had replaced the beeping.

"I think I got it in time," he said to Aleksei, who already had the container of orange juice on the counter and was adding a dropper full of the poison, "but as soon as you're done, I suggest we hightail it out of here, just in case."

They locked the front door as they left, got back in Joe's car, and drove off.

"What happened? Why code don't work?"

"Could be Donna changed it. When she gets back, she will know someone was here."

"We come back two more times, no?"

"Yeah, I'll figure it out." Joe drove Aleksei back to the Metro station and dropped him off.

Later that evening, Joe joined Brandy, Donna, and their friends at Brandy's house and celebrated the new year.

****

Two and a half weeks later, it was Martin Luther King's Day, Monday the 19th of January, 2004. Donna and Brandy had the day off and decided to have mother-and-daughter time by spending the day shopping. This afforded Joe another opportunity. There was still no indication that Donna was getting sick. As Joe and Aleksei entered the townhouse, they saw Tabby scurry away and hide. This time, Joe went directly to the utility room and disarmed the system all within twenty seconds. When he exited the utility room, he encountered Tabby peeking at him from under a shelf. Joe couldn't resist saying hello. When he returned to the kitchen, Aleksei had already opened the refrigerator and was looking at the orange juice. The orange juice container was low. It appeared that Donna had been drinking it. Joe watched as Aleksei returned the orange juice container to its position and pulled out the iced tea container. He watched as Aleksei squirted what seemed to be less than a full dropper of the liquid poison into the tea. "That should do it. Let's go," he said.

"I need ten minutes," Joe told him. Joe had researched the alarm system and was able to reset it back to the way it was before they entered without knowing the keycode. It took ten minutes, but when he powered it back up, there were no alarms going off. After walking out the front door, he paused, no beeping, and no alarm. Then they left.

****

The poison was applied again two weeks later, on February first, Super Bowl Sunday. In the morning, Donna was with Brandy. They may have gone to church, and then afterward, Donna helped Brandy with preparation for a Super Bowl party that would take place at Brandy's house that evening. Many of the same friends that had attended the New Year's Eve party would be there, including Joe. Up to this point, Donna had not displayed any noticeable effects of having been poisoned, and once again Markov assigned Aleksei to accompany Joe to Donna's townhouse.

"It appears Donna has been drinking orange juice—there's a brand-new container on the shelf. Looks like it could use some of this," Aleksei said as he inserted the dropper into the bottle of liquid poison. Meanwhile, Joe went into the other room and befriended Tabby.

"Did you put it into the orange juice?" Joe asked when he returned.

"I put a dropper full in the juice but some poison left in the bottle, so I add it to tea."

Donna came home later in the afternoon to clean up and change for the party that evening. Joe did not know if she drank any tea or orange juice before she left for the party. However, after the party that night, Donna said she was feeling sick. So, rather than return home, she stayed over at Brandy's house. Brian was at his father's house that night, and Joe had planned to stay over, but realized that under the circumstances, the right thing to do would be to return to his place after the party and sleep alone.

20

MISDIRECTION

During the months of December through January, Ivan Markov had reaped a great deal of intelligence by tapping into Donna Wolf's CIA email account. As a result, he had uncovered the identities of several Russian officials, some within the FSB and the SVR, who had passed information off to the CIA. Arrests had been made. Of course, they all pleaded their innocence, but the emails spoke for themselves, and Markov was quite pleased with the cyber access that Joe Garcia had set up for him.

In early February 2004, Ivan Markov sat in an easy chair in his make-shift office with a laptop computer spanning his thighs. He had come across a Top-Secret email from the CIA in St. Petersburg, Russia. The email was addressed to Brian Matheson with Donna Wolf on copy.

> *Agents uncovered evidence that Putin worked with KGB and SVR to suppress and eliminate opposition leaders, especially in the Liberal Russia Party, and took further action to prevent or hinder opposition voting in the Parliamentary elections in December. Evidence includes photos and recording of Putin and associates. They identified one of the SVR participants as Ivan Markov, who is a person of interest to Officer Wolf.*
>
> *The full dossier is in the referenced file. The code word is "United."*
>
> *This information could have an impact on April's presidential election in Russia. Please advise if further action required. Reply to Chief of Station.*

Markov accessed the dossier and read with astonishment the extent to which he, Putin, and others were incriminated. He couldn't help but ask himself questions. Who was spying on them? Who was leaking secrets? How did this stuff get revealed?

A week later, Markov intercepted the following response from Matheson:

I will leak this dossier to the Washington Post. My agent will deliver thumb drive to WP rep at the coffee shop on 15th and K on Saturday mid-morn. President Bush gave go-ahead. Your sources will be protected.

****

Twenty-five-year-old Daisy Clark was called into her manager's office at the Washington Post. Daisy was a recent hire at the paper and was still learning the ropes. She was also eager to take on any assignment that might help her get ahead.

"Daisy, I have a field assignment for you."

"Yes, sir . . . A field assignment. That sounds interesting."

"Well, this assignment is very important because I want you to receive a digital file from one of our secret sources. Secrecy is very important. The information will result in a big exclusive story for the Post."

"Okay. Exactly what do you want me to do?"

"I want you to go to the coffee house on the corner of 15th and K around ten in the morning. Buy yourself a latte or whatever, take a seat, and wait for a man to arrive and introduce himself as Mr. Jay Smith. Allow him to initiate the conversation. You will respond with your name, and say, 'Pleased to meet you.' He will ask if you have been waiting long, and you will answer, 'Yes, actually I have.' Then he will apologize, shake your hand, and say he appreciates you waiting. The hand shake will deliver a USB thumb drive from his hand to yours. Don't fumble it. Put it directly into your purse. Stay seated for about five minutes and talk about the weather or whatever. Then excuse yourself and leave the restaurant. Come directly back here and give me the thumb drive. Got it?"

"Yes, sir."

Daisy performed her assignment as planned. She arrived at 9:50, enjoyed a double mocha latte, and met Jay Smith at 10:05. At 10:15, with the thumb drive secured in her shoulder purse, she left the coffee house and walked down the sidewalk toward her car. Before she got to her car, a man came up behind her, put his arm around her, told her he had a gun, and if she wanted to stay alive, she had better cooperate. She was scared out of her wits.

"Please don't hurt me," she whimpered. "I'll do whatever you want."

"Good. You get idea," he said in broken English with his mouth up against her ear. Then he grabbed hold of her arm and forcefully led her to the rear door of a waiting limo. "Now get in," he said gruffly.

"Please, you're hurting my arm. What do you want?" She was in tears as he forced her into the rear seat of the limo. The man slid in behind her. Once inside the limo, she found herself sitting between two beefy men, the one on her right who had accosted her and another on her left. The limo began to move forward.

"Where are you taking me? What do you want?" she pleaded.

"We want the thumb drive," the man on her left said as he grabbed her purse and began to rummage through it. "Ah, here it is," he finally said and held it up in the air as if to declare victory. She sensed a slight accent. "Now, tell me young lady, what were you planning to do with this? Did you think you would write a masterpiece article and become famous?"

"I don't even know what's on there," she pleaded.

The two men turned and looked at each other. "Really?" one of them said. "Can we really believe that?"

"Please, I'm telling you the truth. This is my first assignment. I was just told to deliver the thumb drive to my boss. I have no idea what's on it."

"What you think we do with her boss?" the man on the right asked.

"I think—"

Just then, two vehicles cut them off and forced them to come to a complete stop. Within seconds, FBI agents surrounded them with guns drawn. The FBI opened the car doors and ordered everyone out.

The man on Daisy's left objected. "We have diplomatic immunity," he calmly protested.

"Doesn't matter," the agent said. "The lady next to you needs to exit. You need to let her out."

"Okay, fine," he said reluctantly and stepped into the street allowing Daisy to slide out of the limo.

As soon as Daisy was out of the car, a female FBI agent escorted her away. At the same time, another agent forced the man who preceded Daisy out of the limo up against the roof of the limo and handcuffed him. The agent gave him a pat-down and recovered the thumb drive.

"You can't do this. I've done nothing wrong, and I have diplomatic immunity," he calmly proclaimed.

"Ivan Markov, I am charging you with stealing classified documents, kidnaping, and conspiracy to commit murder." Then, he was read his Miranda Rights.

"So, you know who I am? Then you know you cannot arrest me."

"You need to brush up on the law. We caught you in the act of putting someone's life in imminent danger. We can arrest you, charge you, and hold you regardless of your possible immunity from prosecution. And as far as your diplomatic immunity is concerned, I don't think you have any. I think you're in this country illegally, and I think your passport is phony, but we will deal with that later."

The Feds took Markov, his bodyguard, and the limo driver into custody, and impounded the car. They entered the thumb drive into evidence. It never made it to The Washington Post.

21

ESCAPE PLAN

Aleksei Chaban was not with Markov when Markov was arrested, but Aleksei soon got word, and now he was on the lam. On February 20, Joe received a message on his smart-phone.

Urgent. Markov arrested. We are at risk. Need your help. Call me on 999-555-4321. Identify yourself using your initials.

Joe did not recognize the number—probably a burner phone and not likely being tapped into, he decided. So, he made the call using **his** burner phone.

"Hello, who is this?" the voice answered

"JG. Who is this?"

"This is Aleksei. I need your help."

"Where are you?"

"Can't tell you. I'm safe now but think Feds may be on to me."

"Why would they be on to you? Would Markov give you up?"

"No, but his bodyguard might."

"What do you need help with?"

"I want to leave country and return to Moscow before they find me."

"Why me?"

"You're a friend. I trust you."

"Tell me what I can do."

"I want you to make plane reservation for me to Moscow."

Joe wondered why he couldn't do that for himself unless he thought his phone was tapped, but he played along. "Okay, he responded, but you need to give me some details."

"Tell me what you need."

"What airport do you want to leave from? Does BWI work for you?"

"Fine."

"You know there are no direct flights and this is last minute. "I'll do my best to get you to Moscow."

"Do best, but do it soon."

"Okay, now I need to know what name you want on the reservation. I assume it won't be Chaban."

"No, not Chaban. Make the name Alexander P. Sarnoff."

"What does the P stand for?"

"Doesn't matter. Just initial is fine."

"Okay. Now I'm sure you realize they may want a passport number with that name on it."

"Of course. The number is 45 02 987654."

"Issue date and expiration date?"

"16 June 2001 and 15 June 2006."

"And the nationality?"

"Russian."

"How soon?"

"As soon as possible."

"Anything else?"

"Yes. I need ride to airport. You pick me up at our pizza place in Glenmont. Bring tickets and small suitcase with three days of clothes and toiletries."

"Alex, you know you're asking for an awful lot from me."

"Look at it this way, Joe. It's in your best interest to get me out of country. If I get captured, I don't know what the Feds might force me to say." It sounded a little bit like a veiled threat, but Joe let it pass.

"Okay. I'll call you back and let you know the day and time that I'll pick you up in Glenmont."

"It must be soon. *Spasibo.*"

Joe made the reservations for Alex as requested. As he did so, he had a fleeting thought. *Wasn't Inga Sarnoff the real name for Maria Martin? Could Aleksei be related?*

Then Joe gave some thought to his own safety. His plan had been that at the end of his assignment he would disappear and return to Costa Rica.

No one would know of his true mission, but could he trust Aleksei to not see him as a loose end that had to be dealt with? He also needed to consider the possibility that the Feds might arrest both he and Aleksei. And there were other complications, like his involvement with Brandy. Could he ever see her again after this?

He decided on a course of action. After making the reservations for Alex, he made reservations for himself to fly to Toronto. His flight would leave after Alex's flight, also from BWI. He explained to Brandy that he had to leave on business, and made up a story as to where he would be and why. She came to his townhouse the evening before he was to leave, and they spent the night together. She was still at his house when he left to pick up Alex in Glenmont the next day, Monday, February 23.

Alex looked in the back seat before he hopped into the car. He noticed that Joe had brought more than one bag with him.

"Joe, I only need small bag. Why you have two bags?"

"Because I'm leaving the country as well."

"What about Brandy?" he asked.

"I'll have to live with that. I can't take the chance that Markov or his muscle man will rat us out."

The two drove directly to the car rental facility, turned in the car, and took the shuttle to the terminal building. Then they went to their respective airline counters to show their passports and check in. Alex waited for Joe, who seemed to take longer than expected. Then they followed each other through security to Concourse D. They stopped at the junction of two corridors. The flight to Toronto was down one; the flight to JFK and Moscow was down the other. This is where they said good-bye. Alex surprised Joe with a bear hug. "You good friend. I wish you well," he said. Then, Alex continued down the corridor to his gate. He would board shortly.

Joe looked around. He saw no sign of the Feds. Before heading down the corridor to his gate, he went to the men's room, made one final call on his burner phone, and dumped it into the trash. When he came out of the men's room, he saw them, two well-built gentlemen wearing suits and wing-tipped shoes. The Feds had arrived. He watched them head toward the gate for JFK. It was about to board, but the flight to Toronto would not board for another hour. The Feds could nab Alex and then come back for him. However, he had already considered this. He had spent extra time at the check-in counter changing his flight to go to Quebec. It would board in ten minutes, and he planned to be on it. He went to a neutral place until he heard the boarding call for his flight to Quebec. After boarding, he half expected to be dragged off the plane, but it never happened. His deception had worked. He breathed a sigh of relief. He had escaped. He doubted that Alex would have had the same luck.

22

HER FINAL YEAR

Donna lay on her back, staring at the ceiling, waiting for the next interruption from the hospital staff. She had had one medical test after another and they still couldn't tell her if she had been poisoned, or if she had some rare form of lymphatic cancer. Her condition was getting worse, and she knew it. At least the medication had dimmed the pain, and she still had clarity of mind. As she lay there with nothing else to do, she began to reflect upon all that had happened since returning from Costa Rica ten months ago in April 2003.

During the time following her return, Donna had worked hard to bring closure to all her projects. Her plan was to retire early in the spring of 2004, and with that in mind, she began training someone to take over her job. Together, they even exposed two more Russian operatives before September. She considered the possibility of retiring with Ed Perez in Costa Rica, but her priority was to have more time to spend with Brandy and grandson Brian. Perhaps she could make up for all the time she had not been there for them. Perhaps she could begin to give back to Brandy. *Would Ed be willing to retire in Maryland?* she wondered. She received a letter from Ed telling her it was safe to come back to Costa Rica. No charges would be filed. However, she politely declined. Before any of this could happen, there were things she had to complete.

Inga Sarnoff, the Russian spy she knew as Mary Lou, was dead. That was not the original plan. The original plan was to interrogate her and gain valuable information about her colleagues, other agents she worked with, her superiors, and the actions they were planning. Now that she was dead, they only had her computer hard-drive. However, the hard-drive was enough to get started. The DIS in Costa Rica had a copy, as did the CIA. The DIS and the OIJ in Costa Rica would begin an investigation into the corrupted Costa Rican authorities who were helping the socialist causes.

Meanwhile, the CIA would focus on the higher-ups that Mary Lou reported to in the Russian Federation's SVR. Matheson said he had a plan and Donna had agreed to it. She knew it was a sting operation, and she had helped to create phony documents and files that would serve as bait. Other than that, she knew very few details.

In the early fall of 2003, Donna had a follow-up medical exam. Her doctor had told her that while there was no visible cancer now, her blood test indicated the possibility that the cancer could return. He had recommended another round of chemo to be sure. After giving this much thought, she made the decision not to go through that again. The chemo sessions were too painful and she would have no quality of life during that time. She decided to enjoy the quality of life she had now, use it to accomplish something important for her country, and let nature take its course. She did not mind being a target of the Russians. If they managed to kill her, she would die for her country. If they didn't kill her, she would likely die anyway. Over the next several months, she traveled very little. She was home for holidays like the Fourth of July, Thanksgiving, Christmas, New Year's, and Super Bowl Sunday the following year. She was happy to spend a great deal of her free time with her grandson Brian, her daughter Brandy, and with Brandy's new boyfriend, Joe.

By the end of the year 2003, however, Donna began to get suspicious of Joe. Brandy seemed to be getting serious with this guy and he had come to Thanksgiving dinner. She had met him briefly before, but this was the first time they had a chance to really talk. He said he was from Costa Rica which seemed too coincidental to her. He said he was working for a large client here in this country but wouldn't say who. He seemed to travel a lot. His Costa Rican driver's license said Joseph Garcia but he told Brandy his name was Joe Martinez. When they saw him for dinner the week before Christmas, she noticed he had what looked like cat fur on his pant leg. And one day when she was talking with a neighbor, the neighbor mentioned that she saw a young man enter her townhouse during the day on more than one occasion. These observations could possibly be explained individually, but taken as a whole, they aroused her suspicions. This was especially true, considering that she had already been informed that she was a possible target. As she became more concerned about her daughter's boyfriend, she began to wonder if he was working for the Russians.

She had gone to Matheson and discussed her concerns, but got no help from him. "You promised me protection," she said, "and I want to know what it is."

"I can't tell you. Just trust me," he replied.

For a moment, she wondered if Joe was the protection. If so, she did not like the idea of Brandy's involvement with him. On the other hand, if he was the one stealing information or the one sent to kill her, that was even worse. Either way, if Brandy found out, she would be upset. Her instinct was to protect her daughter.

She recalled that at the Thanksgiving dinner, her grandson had taken a photo of them at the dinner table, which Joe was not happy about. Sometime in December, she had pulled out the picture that her grandson had taken, and thought hard. Had she seen Joe before? Was it in Costa Rica? Was Joe the man standing at the coffee bar in La Copa Máxima?

So, she had contacted Ed Perez for help and had sent him a copy of her grandson's photo. Perhaps Ed knew who he was. She also told Ed that she was concerned for Brandy's safety. She seemed to be falling for this guy, and she was quite certain that they were sleeping with each other. She had told Ed she was not sure that Joe was who he claimed to be, and she wanted to know who he really was. He had replied to her that he would investigate the matter and get back to her. Only he hadn't gotten back to her.

Why hasn't he responded? she asked herself.

****

During the month of January 2004, Donna's anxiety had increased. Someone had broken into her house on New Year's Eve and had disarmed the security system. The next day she had seen a text message on her phone from an unknown source that said:

DO NOT DRINK THE ORANGE JUICE. IT IS POISONED!

Naturally, she reported this to Matheson, and he claimed credit for the warning message. They agreed that it must be the Russians trying to poison her, but she wanted to know who specifically was doing it. She wondered if Joe was an assassin. Ed had not yet replied to her request, and she had become more anxious. It was right after this that she started having days when she was not feeling so well. She wondered if it was stress and anxiety, or if it was poison. And then on Martin Luther King's birthday, she received another text message from an unknown source.

DO NOT DRINK THE TEA!

Two weeks later, on Super Bowl Sunday, she helped Brandy prepare for a Super Bowl party. Brandy had invited her, Joe, and several friends to her house to watch the game on her large plasma TV. Everyone enjoyed the food, the drinks, and the hospitality. The fourth quarter was exciting. The Patriots edged out the Panthers by a score of 32 to 19. After the game, Donna did not feel well at all. Brandy convinced her to stay the night, much to the apparent chagrin of Joe, who told them it would be best if he went home.

Then on Monday, the day after the Super Bowl, she received another text message.

DO NOT DRINK THE ORANGE JUICE OR THE TEA. THEY ARE POISONED!

A few days after the Super Bowl, she became sick enough that she sought medical attention. Again, she wondered if she had been poisoned. She thought she had heeded the warning messages and had been careful. Yet she couldn't be sure. Her condition deteriorated rapidly. Two weeks later, she was hospitalized full-time.

Now, as she lay there, she realized that there was so much she wanted to understand, and she looked forward to Ed's visit later in the day. Perhaps he would explain why she had not heard from him until now, and perhaps he could give her answers about Brandy's boyfriend.

Her face lit up immediately when Ed entered her room. No sooner had he kissed her than she asked, "Ed, where have you been?"

He apologized profusely. "Donna, I wanted you to know everything, but Matheson never read me in to the operation and I didn't know that you weren't fully aware of Matheson's plan."

"Ed, I may be dying. Please tell me what is happening," she pleaded.

"Okay, but I'm not authorized to tell you everything, and you can tell no one what I'm about to say. It's highly classified."

"I understand," she said.

Matheson told her that the Russian spies were in custody, but Ed also told her everything he knew about Joe and reassured her that Brandy would be safe. Donna was dying. It was the right thing to do, he thought.

"Thank you," she said to Ed. "I'm pleased to hear that my final project with the agency has been successful, but even more important to me is setting things right with Brandy. Her welfare and happiness are my number one priority. Perhaps you could help her get past her relationship with Joe."

"I will . . . You also said she wants to know about her birth father. Were you going to tell her?"

"Yes, I left a letter for her. It will be up to her if she wants to pursue it."

"I think you've done the right thing."

A week later, with Brandy and her grandson at her side, Donna passed away. She died peacefully in the hospital, knowing that she had left matters in the best of hands.

23

DONNA'S FUNERAL

Donna was interred in March 2004. The day was dreary— cloudy and breezy with temperatures in the forties. The cemetery was just north of Bethesda, Maryland, the same one where Donna's parents and her husband John were buried. The ceremony was short but respectful. Donna's casket arrived in a hearse escorted by armed plainclothesmen— probably FBI. Several of Donna's local friends and colleagues attended. Her boss, Brian Matheson, and several colleagues, drove up from Virginia. Matheson said a few prepared words. Brandy, her son Brian, and her half-brother, Daniel, rode together from Ellicott City. Brandy said a few heart-felt words and became overwhelmed with tears. Matheson had never met Brandy, but he took the time to offer his condolences and support.

Ed Perez had flown up from Costa Rica. He came alone. After the ceremony, Ed walked over to Brandy.

"I'm Ed Perez. Don't know if you remember me. We met briefly a couple of years ago when your mom was sick. I was a colleague and a close friend of your mom, and I feel your sorrow," he said sincerely.

"Yes, I remember you. Mom has talked highly of you, but I wondered why we didn't see you more often."

"I live and work in Costa Rica. It's a long way, and your mom and I didn't see each other very often, but she always talked proudly of you."

"Were you and Mom close?" Brandy asked, even though she knew the answer.

"We worked together for many years, became close friends after your dad passed away, and I think you already know that we've been intimate more recently."

"Yes. She told me she spent time with you a few months ago."

"I'm going to miss her. We talked of retiring together. She also told me about your boyfriend, Joe. She was concerned about him. Wondered if he was taking advantage of you in some way."

"I assume she was just being my mom—always looking out for me."

"Where is he? Is he here?" he asked as he looked around.

"No, he is not! He left three weeks ago and I have not heard from him since."

"Sorry . . . any idea where he is?"

"He said he was on a business trip to Toronto, but I followed up on that. The company has never heard of him. Perhaps he went back to Costa Rica, but now, I don't even know if Joe Garcia is his real name. I'm angry! Mom was right. He took advantage of me!" She paused and looked Ed in the eyes. "Joe said he had a business in San José. That's where you're from, right? Did you know him?"

Ed felt for her, but all he could say was, "Brandy, I'll look into it when I get back and I'll let you know what I find out."

"I would really appreciate that. Thanks."

"Brandy, there's something I want to ask you . . ."

"Yes?"

"Did your mom say anything to you about your birth father?"

"Why do you ask?"

"I encouraged her to tell you. She said she would leave you a letter telling you about him, and leave it up to you as to whether you wanted to contact him."

"Yes, she left me items in her safety deposit box, but with the funeral and all, I haven't had time to look at them . . . Wait! You mean he's still alive?" she said excitedly.

"Yes. You didn't know that?"

"No. All my life, Mom and Grandma led to believe that he died in Vietnam. Ed, do you know who he is? Is it you?"

"Huh, no. I've never met him, but I would like to. Your mom had good things to say about him."

"I never understood why she would never tell me about him."

"She had very good reasons. You need to read the letter she left for you. It will explain a lot. Look, I would like to talk more, but my ride is calling for me to leave," he said, motioning to a large gentleman standing by a black limousine on the road nearby.

"Ed, I hope I will see you again."

"Likewise," he responded. "Please take this. It has my contact information on it. Feel free to contact me any time."

****

That evening, Brandy thought about the conversation she had with Mom's friend Ed at the cemetery. He told her that her birth father was still alive and did not know she was his daughter. A letter would be in Mom's safe-deposit box, he had said. Brandy had gone to the bank last week and now everything was in a shoe box on the top shelf of her bedroom closet. She pulled it down and thumbed through the contents until she found two sealed envelopes, one with her name, the other with the words "For Brandy's birth father."

Brandy opened the envelope addressed to her. In the enclosed letter, Mom provided the contact information for her birth father. His name was Peter Troutman, and he lived nearby. Mom said she had met him in Saigon where they had an affair. She said he worked with the agency over the years, but she never told him she was pregnant and that he had a daughter. Mom's explanation was that she married John who provided them with a happy home, and that Peter had a family as well. "No need to destroy families and careers, but now things were different," she said in the letter. The letter said that contacting Peter was her choice, but hoped that she would. If she did contact him, she should give him the other envelope addressed to him.

Brandy pondered whether to contact Peter. What would the impact on him be? Should she just leave things as they were? Mom had said that things were different now. Were they? She had many unanswered questions about the relationship that he and Mom had. She wondered how she would react to the answers. However, her curiosity was overwhelming, and she had an unexplained, innate desire to know him. It was not an easy decision to make. Three weeks went by before she decided.

24

AN UNEXPECTED PHONE CALL

It was a Saturday morning in April 2004. Peter Troutman was alone in his townhouse. He and his wife Carol already had breakfast, and she had just left for her community garden. Peter was sitting at the kitchen table, sipping his second cup of coffee, and working on the morning's crossword puzzle. It was his quiet time, and he was not yet ready to start work on a long list of Saturday chores. He was thinking of an eight-letter crossword, meaning peace and quiet, when RING . . . RING . . . RING ended his thoughts of serenity. It was still very early in the morning, and he wondered who would be calling. Was it Carol? Did she have car trouble? Hoping for the best, he answered with a simple "Hello."

"Hello, my name is Brandy Evans, and I would like to speak to Peter Troutman, please."

He was relieved that the call was not from Carol, but now expected it might be an annoying marketing call. "This is he. How may I help you?" he said. He always tried to be polite, but perhaps there was a hint of annoyance in his voice.

"Mr. Troutman, I hope I haven't caught you at a bad time. I believe you may have known my mother, Donna Wolf."

"I'm sorry but I don't think I knew her," he lied. The name was familiar, but he was wary and suspicious of the caller's intent.

Ms. Evans responded right away. "Mr. Troutman, you may have known her in 1967 as Donna Cinelli."

The mention of the date and the name was enough to provide some credence to the caller.

"Yes . . . I did know her. Why are you calling?"

"My mother recently passed away from cancer. Before she died, she specifically requested that I contact you. I'm honoring her wish."

"Thank you for notifying me. I'm so sorry to hear that your mother passed away, but more than thirty-six years have passed by since I was last with her. I'm not sure I fully understand."

Peter had tried to reconnect with Donna several times over the years, but had given up fifteen years ago when it became apparent that she did not want to see him. And now she had passed away, and someone claiming to be her daughter wanted to notify him. He was suspicious, but he was also curious.

Ms. Evans then explained, "Before my mother died, she had determined your whereabouts, and she gave me something she wanted you to have. Mom was very insistent that I deliver it to you in person. I would like to set a time to meet with you and talk about my mother. Would that be okay?"

Peter's curiosity really piqued at this point.

"Yes, that would be fine. I live in Columbia. Do you live or work in the area? Where can we meet?"

"I live nearby in Ellicott City. We could meet near you in Columbia."

"Okay, there's a coffee shop called Lakeside down by Lake Kittamaqundi. Do you know where it is? Would that work for you?"

"Yes, that's perfect. Could we meet next Saturday morning at ten?"

"Yes," he agreed. "Please let me have your phone number in case something changes."

Ms. Evans gave him her number. The number had not shown up on his caller ID and he wanted to check it out.

For most of his career, Peter had worked as an analyst and was quite good at what he did. Peter and his wife Carol were now in their early sixties. After Peter retired from the IBM Corporation, and after Carol retired from the FBI, they started a small consulting business. Their expertise helped business and government agencies make smart business decisions about telecommunications technology. They also did what they called audits or investigations. Carol had an office upstairs on the top level, and Peter had an office downstairs on the basement level.

Immediately after he got off the phone with Ms. Evans, Peter headed downstairs to his home office and logged onto his computer He wanted to know more about the caller. He entered the phone number into one of his computer applications. Within minutes, he knew the phone number was registered to James Evans. He also knew Mr. Evan's address in Ellicott City, Maryland. There was more information if he wanted it, but that was enough. He was satisfied that the call was legitimate and probably not a scam. He put a note on his calendar and began attending to his Saturday chores.

****

As he ran the vacuum cleaner, a mindless job, Peter began to recall the intense experience that he and Donna had in Saigon in 1967. Peter was in his mid-twenties then, technically very smart and creative, but socially naïve. In 1967, he had gone to Saigon as a private contractor to implement an intelligence analysis program called the PEN that he had developed in graduate school. In 1967, the war was getting closer to Saigon, and many enemy bombings and killings were taking place in and around Saigon. The PEN Project was intended to predict attacks so that preventative actions could be taken. Saigon is where Peter had first met Donna.

Donna Rice, as he knew her then, was an operative or agent with the CIA. Donna was about the same age as Peter. She had had military training and had only recently become a field operative for the CIA. The CIA had assigned her to work with him. Perhaps a more apt description of her role would have been to baby-sit. He was an asset and she was his handler. Saigon was also where Peter had first met Jon Wilson, Donna's CIA boss. Both Jon and Donna had legitimate cover jobs, but in fact, they were covert CIA operatives.

Initially, Donna's job was to escort Peter, to introduce him to the military people he worked with, and to keep him out of trouble. However, before they left Saigon in 1967, her assignment, and his involvement, had evolved into much more. Peter and Donna had an affair during that assignment. But then, after four assassinations, Peter and Donna were sent out of country for their protection. Before parting, they had promised each other to remember this experience and to stay in touch. Although Peter tried to keep the promise, Donna had not been responsive to his attempts, and they had not spoken since they said good-bye at an airport in South- east Asia more than thirty-six years ago. If Donna had continued in the same line of work, locating him would have been a cinch, but this was the first time she had initiated contact, and she was dead. Peter did not know why Donna would want her daughter, Brandy, to contact him after all this time, especially when she had avoided his efforts to reconnect with her. He could only speculate.

Later that afternoon, Peter's foot was on the frame of his upside-down lawnmower and both hands grasped the end of a socket wrench. He pushed downward on the handle of the wrench with all the force he could muster. He was trying to replace the blade on the lawnmower, but the damn nut was frozen tight. He set the wrench down and stood up to contemplate a new tactic. At that moment, it dawned on him that he would need to explain to Carol why he was meeting with Brandy Evans next Saturday.

This was the second marriage for both Peter and Carol. They often referred to events in their first marriages as occurring in their "prior lives." Their prior lives belonged to their private space and they had learned from their first marriages to respect each other's private space. Carol knew almost nothing about Peter's experience in Saigon and absolutely nothing about his affair with Donna Wolf. She did, however, know of his contacts with the CIA. After all, that was how they met seventeen years ago, and then after they were married, they jointly participated in another CIA project as part of their consulting business. But in the sixteen years they had been together, Peter had never mentioned Donna Wolf, and he hoped to keep it that way. Now, however, Peter realized that things would change. He would need to have a long discussion with Carol and he wasn't sure how it would go.

****

For the remainder of Saturday and for most of Sunday, Peter and Carol were busy with chores and social activities. Perhaps he was just using their activities as an excuse, but it was late Sunday evening before he broached the subject of his planned meeting with Brandy Evans. He told Carol about the phone call and why he needed to meet Ms. Evans. He told Carol that he had known Ms. Evan's mother, Donna, in Vietnam and that Donna had passed away. Carol and Peter communicated openly on most things, and he hoped she would understand. Of course, she was initially suspicious and asked many questions.

"Peter, how did you know Brandy's mother? Why did you never mention her before? Did you say her name was Donna? Had you been in touch over the years? Why would her daughter Brandy need to see you?

Did you say she wants to give you something? Have you ever met Brandy before?" and so on.

Carol and Peter talked about Saigon and Donna Wolf for an hour Sunday night, but there was only enough time to scratch the surface. Carol wanted to know the whole story—everything. Clearly, the whole story would take a while. As they both worked in their business during the day, they agreed to talk each night prior to Peter's meeting with Brandy the following Saturday.

By Friday evening, he had described his entire Vietnam experience to Carol, including the affair. Well, of course, he omitted a few intimate details out of consideration. Peter was relieved when Carol said she was okay with what he was telling her, "as long as it was not on her watch." He reaffirmed that he had been, and always would be, faithful to her.

Yet, he still did not have answers to two questions. Why, after all these years, was he notified of Donna's death? And, what did her daughter Brandy need to give him? Peter would meet with her the next morning.

25

MEETING PETER

On Saturday morning, Brandy walked into the Lakeside Coffee Shop in Columbia. It was five minutes after ten. She was only five minutes late.

The Lakeside was located on the bottom floor of an office building, and shared a parking lot with the Rouse Headquarters next door. Large windows afforded a view of a small park and a partial view of Lake Kittamaqundi. The lake was only about fifty yards down the stairs and across a grassy area where they held concerts in the summer. Inside the shop were tables with comfortable chairs and in one corner a sofa and three large cushioned chairs. Just outside the main door was a patio with tables. When the weather was warm, you could eat outside and enjoy the view, or the music.

Although she knew of the place, she had never been there before. She had pondered what she would say to Peter. A part of her was angry at him and her mom for keeping the secret for so long. She needed to keep those feelings in check. She was also unsure how her revelation would affect him. She wondered how he would react. She was nervous. Nevertheless, it was a week ago when she had arranged to meet him. There was no turning back now. She was committed.

As soon as she entered the shop, she looked around for someone who looked like he could be Peter. She spied an older man who rose from a small table on the far side of the room. It looked like it would be him, and he seemed to recognize her as well. She came over to the table and they greeted each other.

"Hello, are you Peter Troutman?"

"Yes, are you Brandy Evans?"

"I am," she said and smiled.

"Please have a seat," he said, motioning to the empty chair. "Brandy, you look remarkably like I remember your mother." Although she looked to be in her mid-thirties, her body was tall, trim, and shapely, like her mother's. But, unlike her mother, her hair was dark, like his. Somehow, he knew it was her right away. It was uncanny. "As you came in, you seemed to know who I was," he added. "How is that?"

She chuckled. "Mom had a picture of you from 1967."

"Surely, I no longer look like that, do I?"

She chuckled. "You also have a business website with your picture."

"Oh, I forgot about that. Would you like a coffee, and perhaps something to go with it?"

"Just a regular coffee," she answered. "No cream or sugar. Thanks."

"I'll be right back."

Peter went to the counter, ordered two house coffees, and to save time, brought them back to the table himself.

"Brandy, did you have any problem finding this place?"

"No, not at all."

"Have you been here before?"

"Not to the coffee shop, but I often stop here in Columbia on my way home from work. I work over at the NSA."

"Oh, may I ask what you do over there?"

"Nothing like what my mother did. I'm just an administrator."

"Nothing wrong with that," he responded. Then he changed the subject. "I was sorry to hear that your mother passed away. Did you say she had cancer?"

"Yes, ovarian, but it was in remission, and then more recently, the cancer came back quickly in a different form. She only had a few months to get her affairs in order."

"Where did your mother live?"

"After my dad died, they reassigned her to an office at NSA, and she moved from Potomac to a townhouse complex nearby."

"When was that?"

"Dad died in 1992, and she started at NSA in 1994 after selling the house I grew up in."

Her tone and the expression on her face as she answered his questions made it clear that she was eager to get to the point of their meeting. Peter sensed this and said, "I'm sorry if I'm asking too many questions. It surprises me that I am notified of your mother's passing. Many years have passed since I knew her. Why did your mother want us to meet?"

"Well, Mom left a letter for me. In the letter, Mom said she knew you a long time ago in Saigon. I had always thought she was in the military, but she told me more recently that she worked for the CIA and that she knew you then. When I was younger, I tried to get her to tell me who my father was, but she would not say much. She and my grandmother said that my biological father died in the war."

Brandy sounded angry as she continued. "However, when I was little, I overheard them arguing about something in which I thought they said my biological father was still alive. After Mom married, her husband adopted me, and I always thought of him as my father. Mom was not home very much, but Dad and Grandma spent a lot of time with me. When I asked where Mom was, I did not get answers, although sometimes I would receive postcards from strange places. However, several years ago, I came across some memorabilia and proof that she was lying to me about my biological father. It made me angry and we fought over this. Then after Dad died, she told me she was a CIA operative and that she worked with you in Vietnam. To hear that she was a CIA operative made me angrier. Another secret she kept from me, but it explained why she was never home. I want to know if you're my biological father, and I want to know if you and my mother were seeing each other behind my father's back."

Peter had to let this sink in before he could respond. "Well, if I'm your biological father, I never knew it. Your mother and I have not seen each other since 1967. I tried to contact her in sixty-eight and again in eighty-seven, but we never connected. Tell me your birth date."

"It's May the tenth, 1968," she responded.

Peter did the quick math in his head, and it hit him that she really could be his biological daughter. "Wow! I could be—" was about all he could get out before she interjected.

"Really? You never knew?"

"No. I did not!"

"Why would Mom not tell you?"

He shrugged and held up my hands. "I do not know."

In the back of his mind, Peter thought that this news was possible. Yet he found it to be shocking, nonetheless. He was feeling strong emotions but tried not to show it in front of Brandy. He was feeling a mix of emotions that he needed to understand and come to terms with. He was sad that Donna had passed away. It disappointed him that he was unable to see her again, yet he was pleased and happy that she remembered him. He wondered if Donna and Brandy had a happy life together. Brandy sounded angry with her mother and with him. He felt guilty that he was not there for her, and at the same time, he felt slighted that no one told him he had a daughter. He was anxious, perhaps fearful, as to what was going to happen next. Who needed to know about this? How would they react? Was Brandy here to serve her mother's interests, or her own? Did she want something from him? Peter tried to collect himself and appear in control, but inside, he was shaken.

"Brandy, when you called last week, you said your mother had something she wanted me to have. What is it?"

26

DONNA'S LETTER

Brandy handed Peter a sealed envelope with his full name neatly printed on the front. She then answered the question he was about to ask. "Mom's letter to me said you should open it now in my presence."

"Okay, I will," he said and began to unseal the envelope. They were both nervous with anticipation. He removed the letter and began to read in silence. Brandy watched his facial expressions as he did so.

Dear Peter,

I asked Brandy to be sure you received this letter. I told her that I hoped she would deliver it in person so she could also meet you and talk with you, but it was her choice. Although I have addressed this letter to you, I wanted her to see it as well.

If Brandy is there with you now, you already know that I have passed away. I have been fighting cancer for more than two years now. However, there is no longer any hope and the end is near.

I am writing this to you because I owe you an explanation about why I was not responsive to your attempts to see me over the years. After I returned home, I learned that I was pregnant. When I exchanged Christmas cards with you that December, I knew, but had not accepted the reality of it until I saw a doctor after the holidays. Your card and note told me you were happy, your wife had given birth, and you were going to finish your MBA and start a wonderful career. I also learned that you turned down an offer a year later that the CIA made to you, and went with IBM instead. In retrospect, I think you did the correct thing for yourself and your family.

Let me get right to the point. Brandy is your daughter. I made a conscious decision not to tell you and to keep that from you. I wanted to protect you and your family. You seemed so happy and that was all I wished for you; I did not want to destroy what you had.

My mom helped me take care of Brandy until she was five, so that I could do what I did. She knew about my USAID job but not about what I did for the CIA. During those five years, I thought of you often. I remembered how you comforted me after what I had done on that Friday. I have had to re-live that experience a few times, and I want you to know that I never stopped feeling something afterwards. Unfortunately, the only people I had to talk with afterwards were jaded CIA operatives. I could not confide or get emotional support from my mother. However, I was able to take comfort when I thought of you and what you said to me that night, and later that weekend.

Brandy was five when I married John Wolf. She probably remembers being the flower girl at the wedding. Just so you know, your name was never on the original birth certificate, and when I married John, we legally adopted Brandy and changed her name to Wolf. John's wife had died and he had a son, Daniel. Daniel was a couple of years older than Brandy. He left home to go to college and then he moved to California. John was tolerant of my travels and understood I could not tell him too much about my work. He was a good father to Brandy, and I relied on that. He suffered his first heart attack in 1987 and passed away four years later. Brandy and I both missed him. Without John to help out, I put in for a more normal job at Langley, and then transferred to NSA, where Brandy now works. You should also know that after John died, I looked you up (The Internet made it easy). I saw that you had remarried, so I let it go. Our timing was always off.

Now back to Brandy. I wanted Brandy to know you, the real you. Of course, Brandy knew that John was not her biological father, and she often asked who her father really was. My mom would say it did not matter because her father had died in the Vietnam War. My mother's attitude was that any married man who would get her daughter pregnant was no good. Nor did my mom approve of my traveling as much as I did instead of being home to take care of

Brandy. I fear that some of this attitude was projected onto Brandy when they talked.

When Brandy was about seven years old, we were at my mom's house, and I had an argument with my mom about whether Brandy should be forced to attend Sunday school. I wanted Brandy to have a say. Mom did not. The argument got loud. Mom reminded me that I had an affair with a married man and that I had left her in charge of Brandy for five years because I was never home. She did not want me and John to undo all the good she thought she had done for Brandy. Then she suggested that maybe the reason I had not been home was because I was still seeing you on the side. I did not know that Brandy had overheard the argument until years later, but it must have made an impression.

As she grew older, Brandy continued to ask about her 'real' father, about what I did in the war, and why I traveled so much. I could not tell her the truth. I repeated the lies about you having died and about what I did for a living, until when she was home after John had his heart attack. She was rummaging through my things, found your letters, and caught me in the lie. She was very upset with me. She blamed me for having an affair and for lying to her. I tried to explain, but then I think it upset her even more to think that I loved someone other than John. Then she said that her grandma was right and told me what she had heard. Brandy was pregnant, and she told me she was not going to do to her child what I did to her. (Yes, I was a grandma at 46.) All of this was happening in 1987 around the time when I received your letter. It was not a good time. I apologize for being so brief in my delayed response to your letter, but I hope you will understand after reading this.

My falling out with Brandy lasted until recently. She now knows I worked as a CIA operative, and why I was not home as much as we would have liked. I have apologized for not telling her the truth about you. I asked her to forgive me, but I think she deserves more. I want her to know what really happened, and that despite the circumstance she was conceived out of love, not lust. I want her to know that you did not take advantage of me as my mother believed. I know you never felt this way, but I always felt that if anything, I had taken advantage of you, not the other way around. I want Brandy to know the real you, the person I loved.

As you remember, before we left Saigon together, we had already understood that we were probably not meant to be together, and may not even see each other again, but we made a promise that we would always remember each other. You knew that Dona Rice was not my real name and you told me that you wanted to stay in touch and know that I was happy. You asked if you could send a Christmas card. When we parted at the airport in Hong Kong, I remember we both had tears in our eyes and we repeated our promises to remember each other, and I slipped my address and real name into your pocket, (A breach in protocol). Peter, I kept my promise. I always remembered you. Every day when I looked at Brandy, I remembered. She even has some of your features. You told me that you had no regrets about what we did, and you did not want me to have any either. You gave me Brandy. She's the best gift I ever received. I have no regrets.

Please help Brandy to understand and fill in the details of what happened in Saigon as you see fit. I always trusted your judgement.

Good-bye. I loved you both.
Donna

P.S. I know that you were trained to be skeptical, and Brandy often felt I had deceived her, so I am adding the following to what I wrote yesterday. Peter, I think you know that you were the only man I was with back then; but, if either of you have any doubts about your biological relationship, consider a DNA paternity test. Whether you let others know of your relationship, I must leave that entirely up to the two of you to work out.

P.S.S. I made an extra copy of this letter so you could both have it.

After he finished reading the letter, Brandy could not help but notice that Peter was rattled and could no longer hide his emotions.

"Are you okay?" she asked sincerely.

"Brandy, please excuse me for a few minutes. I need to use the restroom."

As he got up from the table, he pushed her copy over to her and said, "I think you should read the letter. We can talk when I return."

Peter washed his face with cold water, and took a few relaxing breaths before returning. When he returned, Brandy looked up at him and asked again, "Peter, are you all right?"

"Yes, please excuse me. This is sudden, and the memories are bringing forth many emotions. However, I want to tell you everything you need to know."

"I want to know if you loved each other, and why you stopped seeing each other. I think I know the answer to that." Her tone sounded almost like she was hoping for a different result. "I think she loved you, but I don't see how you could have loved her."

Before he could respond, she continued. "Peter, I read through the letter quickly. I don't understand what Mom meant when she said, '*I remembered how you comforted me after what I had done on that Friday. I have had to re-live that experience a few times, and I always felt something afterwards.*' Was Mom referring to having had sex with you and then other men later?"

"What? No . . . of course not!"

"What then?"

He could see the consternation on her face. He looked straight at her and calmly told her, "Brandy, your mom had just taken a life. It was the first time, and she was upset."

"Peter, I knew that Mom was a CIA operative. Is she telling us that she became a trained assassin and killed multiple times?"

Peter sensed some agitation.

"Brandy, it was self-defense. She had no choice. Your mother was concerned about having to kill someone again in the future. I told her that if she did and she did not feel anything, she may as well be dead herself. She would never have become a trained assassin."

"So, then what?" she said excitedly. "Are you telling me that you took advantage of her when she was upset, and comforted her by having sex with her?"

"No. I'm telling you that I didn't take advantage of her," he replied calmly. "It was not like that. Your mother and I already had strong feelings for each other."

"Peter, I know I should calm down, but I'm having a hard time with this."

"I guess that makes two of us. Brandy, we have been here for two hours. Your kids and husband are probably wondering where you are. You probably need to get going, but I think that you and I should talk more. I would like us to meet again if you're willing."

"I don't need to be anywhere. I'm in no rush. I only have a teenage son and I'm divorced. . . I have something else I want you to see. I brought a large envelope with Mom's memorabilia. Do you have time to have a look?"

"Sure, what have you got?"

She reached into the envelope, pulled out a picture, and handed it to him. "Is this my mother with the motorbike? The print says April, 1967 on the back."

Peter smiled and said, "Your mother loved that bike. She gave me many rides on the back. I took the picture. I mailed it to her in May after returning to New York, before I knew I would be going back to Saigon later in the year. Of course, she had to part with the bike when she left in August. What else is in here?"

She had a picture of Peter, the Christmas cards he sent in 1967 and 1968, and the note he sent in 1987 when he tried to reestablish contact. She even had the menu from *La Paix*, a French restaurant on the eastern side of Saigon. Peter smiled when he saw it. Donna also had kept a picture of herself when she was pregnant and one of Brandy when she was a baby. Peter smiled again and said, "Brandy, you were a beautiful baby."

Brandy then asked, "Do you want to keep all of these memorabilia?"

Peter looked directly at her and replied, "I think you should keep it. I think your mother would have wanted you to have it."

It was Peter's view that continuity from generation to generation was very important, and seemed to be lacking in today's NOW culture. He felt like giving her a father-to-daughter lecture on the subject but restrained himself.

He continued, "Perhaps you came here to hear what I had to say and close the book on your mother and move on. However, your mother said she wanted you to know the real me, and I think she wanted you to know her better as well. She apologized to you and asked for your forgiveness.

I think it's important that you forgive her and remember her in a good way. She tried to protect you, not just me. Her work was difficult both technically and emotionally. I want you to know that I am willing to spend as much time as you need to understand what happened in 1967 and why we were together. I would like us to meet again. I think your mother would want that."

"By the way," he continued. "I told my wife, Carol, about my affair with your mother. She says she's okay with it because it didn't happen on her watch. We've been married for almost fourteen years now, and I've always been faithful. Of course, she doesn't know you're my daughter, but I feel like I'll need to tell her. I hope you're okay with that."

"That's fine."

"Before we part, I need to ask a favor of you. It's very important to me. Would you mind if I visited your mother's grave? I would like to say good-bye to her. Is she buried anywhere nearby?"

"Well, I suppose you are entitled to that," she responded. "The cemetery is nearby."

Then Brandy provided the details on where her mother was buried, and how to get there.

"I'll plan to be there tomorrow afternoon at one o'clock, unless that conflicts with others that may visit." "Not a problem. That would be fine."

****

After meeting with Brandy, Peter brought Carol up to speed. He told her that Brandy was his biological daughter and let her read the letter from Donna. Peter shared his mixed emotions. He felt sadness that she died, regrets that they never reconnected, happiness knowing she remembered him, comfort about the birth of a daughter who gave meaning to her life, and angst not knowing where any of this was heading in the future. Carol said she understood and seemed to be supportive.

He told Carol he needed to visit Donna's grave site. She asked if Brandy was going to be there and he said he didn't know. He said he hoped she would come, but that would be up to her. He just wanted to say good-bye and have some closure.

27

PAYING THEIR RESPECTS

The next day on Sunday, Brandy brought her son Brian to visit his grandma's grave. The cemetery was a forty-five-minute drive from their home in Ellicott City. It was off Route 355 just north of Bethesda. They arrived a few minutes after one o'clock that afternoon. The sun was out and the temperature was in the low seventies. In Maryland, spring brings out blossoms on many different trees, including Cherry, Crab Apple, Bradford Pear, and Red Buds. Sometimes, they are all in bloom at once. This seemed to be one of those times. It was a beautiful spring day.

Donna's grave was a distance from the roadway that wound its way within the park. As Brandy and Brian exited the car and began to walk toward the grave site, Brian noticed that someone was already there.

"Mom, who is that man kneeling in front of Grandma's grave?" he asked.

Brandy took a close look. Then she took Brian's arm and stopped their forward progress. She remembered how Peter reacted when they met at the coffee shop, and now he was at her mom's grave. A warm smile came across her face. It was clear to her that he must have really cared about Mom. She was feeling very sympathetic and wondering if she could have been more sensitive when she had met with him.

"That's Peter Troutman," she said

"Who?"

"Brian, do you remember last Thanksgiving when Grandma started to talk about my biological father? Well, that's him. Grandma left letters for me and Peter and said she wanted us to know him. I met with Peter yesterday. I think he's alright. I want you to meet him."

Meanwhile, Peter had managed to find Donna's grave on his own. It was a family plot. Her mother and father were buried there, as was her brother Brian. Peter looked around but could not find a marker for her husband, John Wolf. Donna's headstone said,

Donna Wolf nee Cinelli

1942 – 2004

She served her Country

As Peter paid his respects, a good feeling came over him. He became lost in his thoughts, remembering all the good things he could about Donna. He was thinking about the life she must have had, so different from his, when he heard voices behind him. He stood up and turned to face Brandy. She had someone with her.

They both were finely dressed. Perhaps they had been to church, he thought. He assumed this could be her son with her. He was tall, thin, and good-looking. He looked to be about sixteen or seventeen years old, consistent with when Donna's letter had said Brandy was pregnant.

"Peter, I would like you to meet my son, Brian. Brian, this is Mister Troutman. He knew your grandmother."

"Hello, sir," Brian politely responded.

"Hello, Brian, I'm pleased to meet you."

Then he asked, "How did you know Grandma?"

"I worked with your grandma many years ago in Saigon."

"Where?" he asked.

"Vietnam. Haven't you learned about the Vietnam War in school?"

"Oh, yes, a little. Were you and my grandma in the war?"

"Perhaps sometime I could tell you about it."

"Okay."

After quickly paying his respects by placing some flowers on his grandmother's grave, he told his mom he would come back in about a half hour.

As they watched him take off, Brandy said, "Brian recently got a driver's license and I let him drive me here. He volunteered to pick something up for me at a nearby store."

"Brian is a fine-looking young man. Your mother had a brother named Brian," Peter said as he gestured toward the grave marker.

"Yes, it pleased Mom that I named him after her brother."

"You must have been rather young when you had Brian. How were you able to manage?"

"After I graduated from high school, I went to the University of Maryland for a year before I got pregnant with Brian. My husband and my grandma gave me enough support that I could work and eventually get an associate degree at the community college. I guess, to be fair, Mom helped as well. Getting pregnant before I got my associate degree was not the wisest thing I ever did. However, I decided that I was going to be at home for Brian as much as possible. But before he was five, I needed to get out and Mom helped me to get the job at the NSA. The NSA paid for me to finish my education and get a bachelor's degree and a master's degree."

Then she changed the subject. "Peter, tell me something about you. According to Mom's letter, you and your wife had a child in 1967. Do you have other children? What about grandchildren? According to Mom, you're about her age, but you don't look that old."

"Well, thanks for the compliment about my age, but I was born in 1942, so what your mother told you is true. Yes, I have two daughters within a year of your age, and my current wife Carol has three children. We have seven grandchildren between us and there may be more to come. My oldest grandchild is twelve." Peter was pleased that she was beginning to show some interest in him, but he saved a lot for future conversations.

Then he changed the subject. "You're dressed up. Did you come here from church?"

"Yes, we did."

"Your mother and I went to a Catholic Church in Saigon. We talked about religion. Are you Catholic?"

"No, we're Protestant. My grandmother was a devout Catholic, and I remember my grandmother being very upset with Mom because she did not force me to go to a Catholic church. When we moved in with Dad, we began to go to a Methodist church. When I was about ten, Mom explained how important it was to have God in my life. But she wanted me to learn about different religions, so that when I got older, I could decide on what church I wanted to attend for myself."

Peter looked straight at Brandy and said, "I'm pleased to hear this. Your mom had issues with the feelings of guilt and unworthiness bestowed on her by the Catholic Church. I told her that I was going to expose my kids to multiple religions and give them a say. She told me she thought that was a good idea and wished that she had been given that opportunity when she was growing up."

Peter found himself looking at the gravestones again. "Your mom talked to me about your grandparents when I was with her. She said your grandpa had a construction business. According to the gravestone, he died in 1976. You must have been about eight. You lived with them for the first five years of your life. Were you close? Do you remember it?"

"Grandpa was nice to me but he wasn't home a lot. I was much closer to Grandma. Grandma allowed me to see the coffin at the service, but it was closed. I remember coming here to the cemetery with Mom and watching the coffin lowered into the ground. I asked Grandma how he died, but she wouldn't tell me. Later, Mom said he was murdered, but they never found the person who did it."

"Wow, that must have been tough!" Then after a pause, "Did you know that I twice spoke to your grandma briefly on the telephone? The first time would have been the Christmas after you were born. Your mom was not home; I don't think she ever got the message. The second time was back in eighty-seven when I was trying to locate your mom. All your grandma would give me was a post office box number where I could mail a letter to your mother, which I did. You have that letter in your memorabilia box. I was hoping to see your mother again, but it did not work out. I see that your grandma passed away in 1996. She was not that old, only seventy-six. May I ask how she died?"

"Grandma died of cancer, after a long battle, just like Mom. I guess it's what I have to look forward to."

"No! Brandy, you can't think that way."

Brandy sat with Peter for a few moments in silence, and then said, "I've given more thought to our meeting and to Mom's letter. I know I need to be able to forgive you and Mom. It's hard to reverse feelings that have built up over many years. I don't know if I can, but I need to try. I do want to understand you and Mom better." She looked at Peter and said, "You're different than what I originally expected. Would you help me to better understand?"

He looked at her and nodded yes. "Brandy, I don't want to intrude on your lives, but I would like to know you and Brian better as well."

Meanwhile, Peter noticed that Brian had returned. "Brian is back, but I could come here again next Sunday," he said.

"Yes, I'd appreciate that."

It could never become a normal father-daughter relationship, but they both made an effort. Over the next month, they became friends, and learned more about each other. Peter and Carol even had Brandy and Brian over for dinner one evening. Peter enjoyed giving him a short history lesson on Vietnam, followed by a friendly discussion of the morality of it all. He was a nice kid—said he wanted to go to college and become a lawyer.

28

HELP

Early on a Friday evening, two months after Donna's death, Peter received a phone call at his townhouse. Peter and Carol were preparing dinner. Peter had his hands full, at that moment, so Carol answered. It was Brandy.

"Brandy, we're preparing dinner. Please don't keep him on the phone too long," she said to Brandy. Then, "Peter, your new daughter wants to talk with you," she said as she handed Peter the phone. Her tone suggested some annoyance.

Peter talked to her for several minutes and then hung up. Having overheard part of the conversation, Carol was interested to know more.

"What did she want?"

"She wants to see me," he replied.

"Why?"

"I'm not sure. Although it has been two months since her mom died, she said that she was just now going through her mom's things and she came upon some files that disturbed her. She thought that I could help her understand what she was looking at."

"What was she looking at?"

"She said that she came upon a scrapbook that had disturbing news articles and a picture of a dead person."

"How did she think you could help with *that*?"

"I asked her that same question. She said that she saw my name mentioned in this book more than once. She thinks that although I had said otherwise, I may have been associating with her mom prior to her death."

"Were you?"

"No, of course not. I've been truthful to both of you. I know Donna was a covert operative for the CIA, but I have no idea what she did after 1967. I did try to contact her a few times before 1989 to have closure. I just wanted to be sure she was doing okay and let her know that I was doing okay. Nothing more after that. I was in love with *you*. The last time I even had a glimpse of her was at Jon Wilson's memorial service way back in 1988. We both attended, and I saw her on the other side of the chapel, but as I went toward her, she ducked out on me. Of course, I learned later the likely reason. She didn't want to lie to me about Brandy being my daughter. Anyway, after that I married you and put thoughts of Donna aside until she passed away and I met with Brandy and learned the truth, and I've told you all that."

"Peter, please understand my uneasiness. This has all happened suddenly, and Brandy works for the National Security Agency—not clear exactly what she does. I'm unsure of her motives . . . I'm still trying to adjust. I hope you aren't getting into something more than you can handle."

Peter had shared the entire story with Carol and Carol had accepted his affair with Donna. "It happened thirty-six years ago, not on my watch," she had said. However, in the letter that Donna had left for Peter, Donna had suggested a DNA paternity test if there were any doubts. The paternity test had not yet been done, and the delay caused some tension between Peter and Carol. Meanwhile, over the past two months, Peter and Brandy had gotten to know each other and seemed to be bonding. Carol wondered if it all happened too fast. Carol was trusting, but she was also cautious.

"When did she want to see you?" Carol asked.

"Tomorrow morning. Is that okay?"

"Well, you should probably meet with her, and see if you can help her, but don't forget, the lawn needs mowing." Her remark reminded Peter that his prime responsibilities were Carol and their home.

"Yes. Why don't we plan to go out to dinner tomorrow night after I mow the lawn, and I'll tell you everything that I learn."

"Okay . . . fine. Tonight's dinner is ready now. Please help me serve." She had a tone of annoyance in her voice.

29

VISIT WITH BRANDY

On Saturday morning, Peter Troutman drove the seven miles from his house in Columbia to Brandy's house in Ellicott City. This was his first visit to her home. He arrived at nine. Summer weather had come early this year. It was going to be a warm and humid day and he hoped to be able to get back home and do the yard work later in the morning before it got too hot. He rang the doorbell. Brandy came to the door dressed in shorts and a T-shirt. At thirty-six years old she was still very attractive. She had a slim and shapely figure. Peter had to remind himself who she was. Nevertheless, he couldn't resist complimenting her.

"Brandy you are quite attractive. Good thing I'm your father," he quipped.

"You don't look old enough to be my father," she quipped back. At sixty-two Peter was also slim and had most of his hair with its original color.

"Peter, come in. I have coffee for us in the kitchen."

"Okay, thanks."

"How do you like it?" she said as he followed her into the kitchen.

"Black . . . Nice house . . . How long have you been here?"

"I moved here shortly after I got married. After the divorce, I got the house."

"By the way, where is my new grandson Brian today?" he asked.

"He's supposed to be with his father this weekend, but probably with friends right now."

"You said you were disturbed by some things you were finding in your mom's belongings. Did you want to discuss it?"

"I do, but before we talk about that I would like to talk about our relationship."

"What do you mean?"

"I'm getting a sense that Carol is uneasy about all this."

"You're right. She *is* uneasy about our situation."

"Tell me what she's uneasy about. I'm trying to be sensitive to this."

"Well, we've been married for fourteen years and until you came along, I never told her anything about my experience in Vietnam, or about my affair with your mom. She probably wonders what else I haven't told her. She also knows that I was married when I was with your mom, and so now she probably wonders if I may have cheated on *her*. Her first husband cheated on her and he covered it up with lies. The information caught off guard. I think she also has some doubts that you're really my daughter."

"I see. I can't do anything about the trust issues she has with you. My husband cheated on me, so I understand her uneasiness."

"Hey c'mon. I hope you're not still uneasy about me and your mom."

"I'm sorry. I know you said it wasn't like that with my mother. I'm just saying I understand her uneasiness. I wish that paternity test I had us take will come back soon. That would resolve at least one doubt," she said in a matter-of-fact tone.

"Yes, I agree."

"I'll let you know right away when it does. How about more coffee?" she asked as she held the pot ready to pour. "We can take it into the den. That's where I have Mom's stuff that I want to ask you about."

"Okay, just half a cup."

Peter followed Brandy to the den being careful not to spill coffee on the carpet along the way. She had given him more than half a cup. He took a sip and set the cup on a small desk as Brandy began talking.

"Peter, I'll get right to the point. I'm finding things that make me wonder if Mom was legit."

"What do you mean? Like what?"

"Like documents that indicate that she had an overseas account with HSBC. Her friend Ed contacted me and asked me about it. I found a trust agreement, and an address in London where we need to send a death certificate—something I only recently received. If she was legit, why would she need an offshore account? And how is Ed involved?"

"Good question, but offshore accounts are legal. If she was a covert operative, it may be something that the CIA set up. I wouldn't read too much into it. You should probably ask Ed those questions."

"Okay, but there's more."

"Yes, on the phone you mentioned something about a picture of a dead person."

"This is what I wanted you to see," Brandy said, pointing to a loose-leaf binder in the center of the card table.

Peter took another sip of his coffee and then walked over to the table to have a look.

"Please look through it and tell me what it means."

He pulled a folding chair up to the table and proceeded to review the book page by page as Brandy peered over his shoulder.

The book displayed a sequence of events that began in the year 1987 and ended in April 2003. Most of the events were described by newspaper articles and photographs with a few comments that Donna had scribbled onto the margin of the pages.

Peter turned to the first page. It was a newspaper article from April 1987. Jim Hoffman, a resident of Colorado Springs, had died suddenly after having lunch with a real estate agent. The death was suspicious and being investigated as a possible suicide or even murder. The next page in the scrapbook had a news article about a body found in Boulder Creek. The body was identified as a student at the University of Colorado in Boulder who was also a suspect in an attempted break-in at a nearby missile defense system compound. Peter remembered reviewing these articles in 1988 when he was in Boulder, and he remembered how his wife, Carol, had investigated the money flow to Hoffman's bank account. But why would this be of any significance to Donna and why would Brandy be concerned about it? Then he proceeded to the third page in the book.

When Peter saw the third page, he gasped. There was a newspaper article about an attempted car bombing in May 1988 that took place in the parking lot of a Residence Inn in Boulder, Colorado. The article said that a bomb had been planted in a car rented to an unnamed IBM employee there on business. There was a photograph of the bomb-squad next to the car. Peter recognized it immediately. It was his rental car and he was the unnamed IBM employee. He and three auditors were about to go to the IBM site that morning. If he had not noticed the bomb before they got into the car, they would have all been dead. He wondered why this would be in Donna's book. What was her involvement? Then he noticed the handwritten note at the bottom of the page.

Peter, what had Jon gotten you into?

The past tense of the comment implied that she did not know about this at the time but learned about it later. Meanwhile, Brandy could not help but notice Peter's reaction to what was on the page.

"Peter, you know something about this, don't you? Please explain," she said in a somewhat demanding voice.

Peter had to think for a moment. So far, nothing in Donna's book was marked as classified, not even the comments she had written in the margins. Yet, at that time, Peter was working undercover on the Boulder Creek Project for Jon Wilson, a CIA officer. The project was highly classified. The bomb was an attempt to prevent him and his audit team from discovering that someone had planted a virus in software that IBM was scheduled to deliver to the Air Force that week. Peter was quite sure that Donna was not involved in that project.

"Okay, I'm quite certain that your mom was not involved in the bombing. I was working on a highly classified project for the CIA. The bomber intended to kill me and the people on my team. I don't believe your mom had anything to do with the project."

"Why is all this in her book then?"

"Don't know yet. Let's keep going through the pages."

The next page was a news item about the death of an IBM computer room manager name Georgy Belinsky. According to the article, he died of an apparent suicide in his apartment over the Labor Day weekend in 1988. The article included a photo of Georgy. Peter remembered Georgy.

"What can you tell me about this one?"

"I knew Georgy. He was a likable guy who got involved with the wrong people. He did not commit suicide. It was murder."

"Did Mom have anything to do with this?"

"No."

"How do you know?"

"The person that murdered him tried to murder me later that same night."

"My God," she gasped. "Why is all this in her book?"

"I think your mom found out about this after the fact. The person at the CIA that I answered to was Jon Wilson, and I think your mom was in communication with him."

"I saw Jon Wilson's name later in the book. He died right? Who was he?"

"Your mom and I both worked for Jon in Saigon, and I continued to do occasional contract work for him afterwards. Jon and your mom may have continued a working relationship at the CIA, but I don't think she was part of any project I was involved with."

The next page had an obituary for Jon Wilson, followed by a memorial service program and a copy of the attendee list. Peter wondered how Donna obtained it. On the page with the program, Donna had circled the name Mary Lou McGuinness who was one of the speakers. Donna had handwritten in the margin:

I felt badly he had to die. She will pay.

"Why did he have to die?" Brandy asked. "Who killed him?"

"Mary Lou killed him."

"The attendee list shows that both you and Mom were present. You told me you had no contact with Mom after Saigon."

Peter knew he was being interrogated, but he understood.

"Brandy, everything I told you was true. If you remember, I told you that I had tried to make a connection with your mom but she always managed to put it off. Yes, we were both at Jon's memorial service, but we never spoke. I noticed her on the other side of the chapel but before I could walk over to her, she ducked out the rear door. I did not understand why she was avoiding me until after she died and we read the letter that she left for us."

The next page had a picture of an attractive woman. Donna's note under the picture said:

Mary Lou aka Inga Sarnoff—Soviet Spy

The next two pages in Donna's book had newspaper articles about people who were murdered or died mysteriously over the next twelve years.

"Do you know anything about these people?" Brandy asked.

"Nothing."

"Do you think Mom killed any of these people?"

"No."

"Do you know who did?"

"Let's see what's next," he said as he turned the page.

The next three pages had articles about the elections in Costa Rica in 2002. One article included a photo taken at a political rally. Donna had encircled the face of a female participant. It resembled Mary Lou.

The final page had a news article dated March 2003. It was about the murder of a woman named Maria Martin. The article suggested that she was a socialist with a Russian passport, and that the U.S. Central Intelligence Agency killed her. There was a photo of the dead woman propped up in a semi-prone position with a bullet hole in her chest. On the bottom of the page, Donna had written:

Justice at last

The woman was the same one encircled on the previous page. She looked like Mary Lou.

"Peter, who is she?"

"It's Mary Lou. She was a Soviet spy"

"Did Mom kill her?"

"It's possible, but I don't want to believe it any more than you do. I also question if the CIA took her out. Do you know if your mother was in Costa Rica when this happened?"

"I checked the calendar and she was not home then. She had asked me to feed Tabby while she was gone."

"What about her passport?"

"I had checked that. She probably traveled on her government passport. Her personal passport did not show anything."

"Well, I think that if she went rogue, she would have used her personal passport. I don't know what else I can tell you except that Inga Sarnoff, or Mary Lou as I knew her, was a sociopathic Soviet spy who killed several people without any feeling of remorse. In my opinion she deserved to die. If your mother did it, I can't fault her."

"Peter, I have this need to know. I can't seem to shake it. Do you have any idea as to what my mother actually did for the CIA?"

"Not really. I suspect that much of what she did was covert. In addition to not wanting me to know about you, and not wanting to rekindle the flame, being covert may have been another reason why she avoided talking with me. Do you have anything else from your mother that may give us more answers?"

"I'll be right back,"

She returned with a medium sized safe box with a built-in combination lock. It was obviously heavy. Peter took it from her and set in on top of the table.

"If you still have time, I would like you to go through the contents of this box with me."

Peter looked at his watch. It was only 11:00 a.m.

"Yes, Carol doesn't expect me home until around one. And later, I need to mow the lawn and do some other chores around the house, so I have time."

"Where did you find this?" he continued.

"I found it hidden on the top shelf of the closet in Mom's office."

"Let's see what you have."

****

Brandy opened the lock box as she explained. "Mom left a letter for me with the letter she left for you in the safety deposit box at her bank. Her letter to me gave instructions for everything, including the combination for this box. It was in the letter that she said who you were and she said I should connect with you and that I should trust you to help me answer questions. She made all these preparations in 2002 after she got cancer and thought she might die. I'm glad she did—not cancer—the preparations."

Peter smiled. "How would we have opened this lock box otherwise."

Peter looked inside the box. Among other items, he saw passports, a digital camera, memory cards, a burner phone, and a wad of cash.

"Wow, a regular spy kit," was about all he could say.

"I haven't removed anything. Everything is there the way I found it."

He thumbed through the cash, mostly fifty-dollar bills, perhaps $10,000 in total. Then he looked at the passports, all personal ones but in different names. One of them was in the name of Donna Rice, a name he recognized, but it had recently expired. Then he removed a memory card from the box. The label said, 'CR-01-02'. He inserted it into the camera, and began to scan through the large thumbnails. Almost all were photos. Most were pictures that included Mary Lou as Peter called her. They had dates imprinted on them, early 2002 for the most part. There was Mary Lou attending a political rally, Mary Lou having lunch at a café with another woman and some gentleman, Mary Lou walking into the Russian Embassy, Mary Lou walking into her house, and so on. These seemed to be surveillance photos. There was also a picture of the head of the PAC shaking hands with a local socialist candidate in the 2002 elections. They were giving speeches surrounded by their entourage. Mary Lou was not in the background, but the gentleman she had lunch with was. As Peter scanned the thumbnails of the photos, Brandy stood behind him peering over his shoulder. "Wait!" she said suddenly. "Go back."

"This one?"

"Yes, that's the one. Enlarge it please."

"Okay. What do you see?" he asked.

"It's Joe," she said, looking at the picture of the three people at lunch. The gentleman appeared to be a handsome Latino. He had a cup of java in his left hand.

"Joe?"

"Yes, Joe Martinez. I know him."

"Really?" Peter said with surprise. "How would you know him. These pictures were taken in 2002 in Costa Rica."

"Oh my God! Peter, I dated him this past year—here in the United States."

Peter pushed the chair back away from the computer, turned toward Brandy, and gave her a hard look. "Brandy, you need to tell me about him. How did you meet?"

"It seemed that we met by chance. It was at my fitness center. I was on a bike and he was on a treadmill just across the aisle. I caught him eyeing me and I returned the look. Obviously, we started talking. Things just seemed to mushroom from there. A year prior to that, I had been taking care of Mom. She was in the hospital, had surgery and was recovering. I helped with her meds, cleaned her house, took her to appointments. It kept me very busy, but by the spring of 2003 Mom was better. She was working and traveling again. I think it left a void in my life that I needed to fill."

"You're sure this is Joe in the picture? It's not the most resolute picture."

"Yes, it's his tan skin, his hair, and his expression. It's definitely him."

"What did he say he did for a living?"

"He told me he was the co-owner of a company in Costa Rica that designed and marketed security systems. He said he was responsible for setting up new markets and that they had a contract with an international company in the United States. He said he traveled a lot."

"Are you still dating him?"

"No. I stopped seeing him in February after Mom got sick again. He told me that he completed his project here, and he had a new assignment that required him to travel to Toronto. It didn't seem like our relationship could go anywhere. We had discussed this, and we parted amicably."

"Have you heard from him since then?"

"No. I hoped I would—I missed him terribly—but I never did after that."

"Brandy, did you sleep with him?"

"I don't like you asking me that. Mom asked that. Are you asking as my father? I don't think it's your business."

"Okay, I'm sorry. I'm just trying to get a feel for how close the two of you were. Did you introduce him to your mom? What did she think of him?"

"He celebrated Thanksgiving, Christmas, and the New Year here with us and he was also here for the Super Bowl party I held. Mom never said anything bad about him, but I think she had some reservations."

"Did Joe ever talk about his life in Costa Rica?

"Yes, he told me he grew up there and went to school there."

Peter decided that this line of inquiry was leading nowhere, so he changed course.

"Let's see what else is in the lock box," Peter suggested as he reached in and pulled out the burner phone. "Interesting," he said. He turned it on and found two phone numbers in memory. The first was a U.S. phone number when called from another country. The phone number was 00-1-703-555-9516 ext. 111. The second was a number with the foreign country code '506'. The number was '506-2519-2099'. Peter did not know the country but thought it might be Costa Rica.

"What are you doing?" she asked as he was about to dial a number.

"You're right. No dial-tone. No service."

"Here. Use my phone," she said and handed it to him.

First, Peter dialed the 506 number. This time it rang and rang. No answer.

Then, Peter put the phone on speaker and dialed the number in Virginia. A recorded message asked for the extension and he entered '111'.

They heard "I'm not available. Please leave a message."

The message did not identify who they had reached, so he just hung up.

"Oh well. Let's continue looking through your mom's stuff."

"Peter, would it be okay if we continue this tomorrow? I need time to process some of this information. Besides, Carol is probably wondering what has happened to you."

Peter looked at his watch. It was already after one. He was late.

"Sure, what time tomorrow?"

"Around two, okay?"

"Okay. See you then," he replied and hurried out the door.

****

Peter arrived back home around 1:30 p.m. Carol was not too happy. They usually ate lunch at one, and he did not call to say he was going to be late.

"You're late. I just started eating my lunch, but I made a sandwich for you and put it into the fridge."

"Yeah, I'm sorry. Time got away from us."

"Did she show you the picture of a dead person?" Carol asked almost mockingly. "Who was the dead person?"

Peter looked hard at Carol. "It was Mary Lou!"

Carol's jaw dropped. "The Mary Lou we knew?"

"Yup. One and the same."

Peter could see the puzzlement on Carol's face so he continued. "Apparently Donna had put together a binder with news clippings about Mary Lou's activities starting in 1987."

"I still don't understand. What did Donna have to do with our Boulder Creek project or with Mary Lou? Was she part of it in some way?"

"I'm not sure. I can only speculate."

"What did you tell Brandy about it?"

"Well, I had to tell her something. She had a picture and news clipping of the attempted bombing of my rental car in 1988 and she had knowledge of my association with Jon Wilson."

"I hope you didn't tell her too much. I don't want to lose my pension from the FBI," she quipped.

"Not to worry, nothing in Donna's binder was marked classified, and I don't think anything I said was classified. There was nothing in the binder about you, and I didn't mention anything about your involvement."

"So, is everything okay with her now?"

"No. I agreed to go back tomorrow and help her make sense of what she found in her mom's safe. . . Look, I know this is hard on you, but I figure the more we learn the better off we are. I'm also convinced that she's my daughter, and I don't get the feeling we're being played."

"Hope you're right."

30
RETURN TO BRANDY'S HOUSE

The next day, Brandy began the discussion. "Peter, I've been thinking about what we discovered yesterday and I'm even more troubled than I was when we started yesterday. I didn't sleep very well last night thinking about it. Do you think that Joe could have had something to do with Mom's death?"

"I thought your mother died of cancer. Is there something you aren't telling me?"

"Mom had a checkup and blood test just before Thanksgiving. She was cancer-free. Then in January Mom suddenly became sick again. When Mom was in the hospital, I tried to get the doctors to tell me what they were finding. I got the feeling that I was getting a run around. They would say things like 'her organs are failing and we don't know what more we can do' but they would not provide me with specifics and they never said specifically that the cancer had returned. I also noticed that her boss had come to the hospital to visit her more than once with another CIA employee and they had several conversations that I was not privy to. A couple of days before mom died, I ask her what was going on. All she would say was that it was better for me the less I knew."

"I see," Peter responded. He was thinking that it would not be unusual for her boss to come visit and discuss things they needed to know about her job. Nor did Peter think that a sudden and unexpected return of cancer was so unusual, but he did not say anything.

Sensing Peter's skepticism she said, "Wait here. I'll be back in a moment."

When she returned, she had several sheets of paper which she handed to Peter.

"What are these?" he asked as he began to look at them.

"Those are the results of medical tests that Mom had. The first one was done just before Thanksgiving. They were perfect—no sign of cancer. The next two pages were tests that were done in late January when Mom started feeling sick. I'm not a doctor, but the reports seem to indicate something other than cancer. In any case, I just found these when I was going through Mom's records."

"I see," Peter said somewhat unsure of where this was headed. "Could we take the report to a doctor now and find out what it means?"

"I already did," she responded.

"And?"

"And, he said that more tests were probably conducted after these, but he said that this report did not indicated the presence of cancer cells, and he expected poisoning. However, there were no traces of a specific poison."

"Was there a death certificate?"

"Yes, it took three weeks after she died before I was able to get a copy. It says that the *cause of death* was lymphatic cancer resulting in organ failure. It also mentions prior ovarian cancer. It says that the *manner of death* was indeterminate and pending investigation. The doctors asked if they could do an autopsy and I agreed. It has been more than two months now since Mom was buried, but I still haven't received an autopsy result. I asked as recently as last week and they told me they were still waiting for lab and toxicology results."

"So, are they investigating the possibility of murder? Have the authorities talked to you?'

"No, and I wonder why not?"

"You said there were conversations between your mom and the CIA just before she died. Perhaps they are involved. If it was murder, I could understand why they would want to cover it up, especially if it was murder by a foreign agent. But if it was murder, why do you think your boyfriend had anything to do with it?"

"I had trouble sleeping last night because I began to remember little things that did not seem important at the time, but may be important now that I have seen her scrap book and these pictures. I'm trying to connect the dots."

"I see. What are some of those dots?"

"Well . . . the morning after Mom went into the hospital, I went to her townhouse to check on her cat. I made sure that Tabby was fed and did a few other things while I was there. Mom liked iced tea and she made batches of it each week and stored it in the refrigerator in a large pitcher. I recall that at some point I opened her refrigerator and everything seemed to be in order. Well, four days later, that pitcher was not there. At the time I thought it odd, but maybe I just hadn't noticed it missing four days earlier. I gave Tabby a splash of milk and brought him back here with me along with the milk. The milk was fine, as is Tabby. But I wondered about the iced tea."

"Any other dots that you recall?"

"Yes, I'm angry that I never heard from Joe after he left. He left three days after Mom went into the hospital. I would have thought he cared enough to ask about her after that. Two weeks after he left, I tried to call him. I called his cell and it was no longer in service. I called the Maryland office of International Security Systems, the company he said he had a contract with. They had no record of a Joseph Martinez. Then I called the number on his business card in Costa Rica. They would not give me any information except that he was out of the country on a special assignment. I realized he played me."

Brandy's voice began to show some agitation as she continued. "Then I remembered the day he left. I had spent the night with him—yes, and I apologize for my reaction yesterday when you asked. Anyway, he was in the shower and I was in his living room where he had his laptop and his shoulder bag. He had printed out a few pages on a printer that he had connected to his laptop and the papers were sitting on top of his laptop. The top page was an airline itinerary with the name Joseph Garcia and a flight to Toronto. Joe had told me his name was Joseph Martinez, so that was confusing. However, I also noticed that a sheet of paper had slid off onto the floor underneath the table, so I retrieved it and was about to put it with the other papers when I noticed that it was also an airline itinerary for that day. The only thing is the name was not Joseph Martinez and the destination was not Toronto. It was for Alexander Sarnoff and the destination was Moscow via O'Hare."

"Did you ask Joe about this?"

"I did. He told me that his full name was Joseph Ricardo Garcia Martinez and that it was customary not to refer to a person's last name in Costa Rica. He also told me that the itinerary was for Alex, a colleague that he needed to meet with before they both left, and that Alex had sent him a copy of his itinerary so that they could fit it in. Joe said he had agreed to drive him to the airport."

"What was Joe's demeanor when he said all this? Did he seem upset with you for noticing this or anything like that?"

"No. He smiled and thanked me for retrieving the page and he spoke calmly. What he said seemed very plausible to me at the time and I didn't think any more about it until about a week later. I thought I would have heard from Joe. I thought he might want to know how Mom was doing, but I never heard from him again. That made me so curious that I used my position at NSA to follow up. Peter, neither he nor Alex ever boarded a flight to Toronto or to Moscow!"

"Anything else?"

"Yes. Joe had said I could have anything he left in his townhouse. Specifically, he told me I could have his printer, but he also said he had some clothes in the closet that I could give to Goodwill. I took them home, but before I gave them away, I checked the pockets and found a slip of paper with a phone number. It had the initials '*BM*' followed by a phone number. I can't remember the number precisely, but I do remember the area code was 703 and I think the extension number was 111, but I'm not sure. The number we found on Mom's burner phone yesterday was similar. Now I'm trying to put two and two together—may not mean anything."

"Do you still have the scrap of paper?"

"I may. I think I put it back into the pocket, and I have the jacket. It's hanging up in the closet. Let me go look."

When she came back, she had the slip of paper. "Here it is. The 703 number is *identical* to the one on the burner phone. I guess all we need to do now is determine who these numbers belong to."

"The 703 number is in Northern Virginia. My suggestion is to call it tomorrow, a work day. My guess is that it's someone at Langley, perhaps her boss. But that begs the question, why would Joe and your mom need to call the same number in Langley?"

"Okay. What about the other number on the burner phone?"

"You could try and call it tomorrow as well. Perhaps someone will answer. I checked out the 506 country-code last night on the Internet. Just as we thought, it is Costa Rica. Could the number be Joe's number in Costa Rica?"

"I have Joe's business card and when I called it, two months ago I'm pretty sure I dialed a 506 country-code, but I don't think it's the same number. Let me go get it just to be sure."

She returned waving Joe's card in her hand.

"Does the business card agree?"

"Nope, same country code, different number," she said and showed him the card. "Perhaps the number is for Mom's friend Ed? He lived and worked in Costa Rica."

"Again, call the numbers tomorrow and see where it leads you. Do you remember anything else that would help us connect the dots?"

"I don't know. I just have so many unanswered questions. Peter, do you think we should go to the police and start an investigation?"

"Hmmm . . . I don't think it would be wise."

"Why not?"

'Well, think about it. If they found evidence of foul play—and we have none now—I think you would be their prime suspect. You had the means, and they could also argue motive."

"**Motive? How so**?" she said loudly."

"They could argue that you wanted the life insurance money. They could also investigate your many years of estranged relationship with your mom."

"Ugh!" she moaned as she got up and began to pace.

"Hang on. I believe you said your mom had conversations with her boss before she died. It's possible that the CIA is already investigating this. Did you talk to them at all?"

"Only after she passed. Her boss expressed his condolences. He seemed sincere and he left me with a business card—said I could contact him if I needed to talk."

"I think you should take him up on his offer. Don't know if you will learn too much more, but I think it would be a safe avenue to pursue. What's his name?"

"Brian Matheson . . . '*BM*' were the initials on the slip of paper in the jacket pocket. You don't know him, do you?" she asked inquisitively.

"Actually, I do know who he is. I met with him once in 1988 and again in 2000," Peter said and then paused. "Brian was Jon Wilson's second in command and took over for him when Jon was killed. We crossed paths again when I was doing telecommunication consulting work for a large corporation. The CIA was interested in phone calls between someone who worked for my client and a certain party in Central America. He said he did not have enough for a warrant or to bring NSA into it, so he came to me. I thought it had to do with exchanging drugs for classified technology information. I gave him what he needed. I would be happy to go with you to see him."

She didn't respond. Her mind seemed to be elsewhere.

"Peter . . . I'm thinking about Mom's friend Ed. He came to visit her both times when she was sick, and he came to the funeral. I talked to him briefly. He gave me his contact information, but no phone number with the Costa Rican country-code. He said he was a long-time friend—told me how Mom had good things to say about me, and so on. I think he may be more than a close friend, and I'd like to know more about how he fits into all of this."

She paused and then continued.

"Last night, I searched through her personal email accounts. She had two personal accounts, a regular one, and another that she reserved for 'junk'—you know, one she used for vendors and people that might put her on a mailing list. She and Ed must have had some way of staying in touch, but I didn't see any emails from him in either account and if he sent letters, I didn't find them which is strange unless he was CIA and Mom tossed them to protect his identity. Anyway, I did come across an email in the 'junk' account. It was addressed to Sally Mae from the proprietor of a coffee plantation in Costa Rica. Mom once told me she would use phony names like that to hide her real name. Anyway, the proprietor was responding to a survey she answered indicating how much she enjoyed the tour of his coffee plantation. The survey was dated the Saturday before the newspaper said they found Maria Martin's body. So, now I'm certain that she was there. I'm also guessing that she was with Ed. I really hope Mom was not the assassin. I should talk with Ed about that."

"Did you say he gave you his mailing address?"

"I'll find the contact information he gave me at the funeral. Maybe I could send him a letter in the mail—"

Peter looked at his watch. "Brandy, I'm sorry but I need to get home. Just give me a call and let me know how I can help. I'm willing to go with you to see Matheson."

"Okay I'll call you as soon as I set something up."

****

Two days later, Peter received a call from Brandy. She had set up a meeting with Matheson at CIA headquarters. Unfortunately, it was not right away as Matheson would be traveling, but they scheduled the meeting for Friday afternoon in the first week of June. She told Peter that Matheson remembered him, and invited him. She would pick Peter up at his house and they would drive to Langley together. Brandy also mentioned that she obtained a home address for Ed Perez in Costa Rica and had written him a personal letter expressing her concerns and asking him a whole bunch of questions.

31

DRIVE TO LANGLEY

Brandy had arranged the meeting with CIA Officer Brian Matheson for a Friday afternoon early in the month of June. She took off work and drove from her office at Fort Meade. She picked up Peter at his home in Columbia and they drove to CIA headquarters in Langley. The day was sunny with temperatures in the mid-seventies, and the traffic was not bad. The drive was relatively pleasant, and took less than an hour.

"Peter, I received a response from Ed Perez," she said gleefully. "It came in today's mail. I thought you may want to read it while we're driving. It's in the glove compartment."

The envelope contained a two-page letter and a thumb drive. Peter pulled out the letter and began to read.

Dear Brandy:

It was such a pleasure to hear from you. I hope I can help with some of your concerns, but please understand that I can only speak to personal matters relating to you and your mom. I have known your mom for about fifteen years as a friend. Due to the nature of our work, I think we had a special and unique relationship, one which became intimate more recently. We were both close to retirement and we discussed retiring together. Your mom was a wonderful person, and I miss her terribly.

You should know that your mom loved you and that you were the world to her. She told me how over the years she struggled with balancing her job and her role as a mother. She also told me how proud she was of your accomplishments and how much she loved you for standing by her when she was sick, both in 2002 and recently. I believe she died with a clear conscience about the decisions she made during her life and was at peace with herself and her maker.

I am very pleased to know that your mom told you who your birth father is and that you have connected with him. I urged your mom to tell you because my own mother disappeared when I was three, and I understand the need to know about birth parents. In my case, she was my mother, and although we never really hit it off, I had a sense of closure after I met her. Although I never met Peter, your mom and Matheson had many good things to say about him and the work he and Carol did for us. I would very much like to meet him. I don't get back to the States that often, but I will contact you when I do.

You asked why your mom was here in early April last year. You wondered if the news reports of the murder of Maria Martin, believed to be a Russian spy, may have been more than coincidental to her presence here. Let me say three things. First, the CIA has denied any role in her death. Secondly, I can't imagine your mom killing someone except in self-defense. Finally, I was with your mom most of that weekend. I had dinner with her Friday night, and I was with her one hundred percent of the time from Saturday morning to early Sunday evening. As you discovered, we went touring on Saturday. In addition to the coffee fincá, we also toured Poás and a hummingbird park, and we had dinner and went dancing later. We had a very enjoyable and romantic weekend. Yes, the news did suggest that Maria may have been murdered earlier on Friday. However, your mom gave me a very plausible and verifiable account of where she was. Unfortunately, the Costa Rican OIJ has not yet arrested anyone for the crime, and the news media has suggested that your mom was the assassin.

Regarding your boyfriend, Joe. In December, your mom had expressed a suspicion to me about his intentions. She expressed a concern for your welfare as well as her own. Unfortunately, I was not able to tell her much at that time. Then in early January, she sent me a photo and asked me to investigate. I recognized Joe as the operator of a security firm in Costa Rica and I contacted him. He told me he was involved with a highly classified operation. Details could not be revealed. I asked about his involvement with you. He told me he cared about you and you were not in danger. I could not reveal Joe's involvement at that time. However, your mom's concern increased after there had been attempts on her life and she became ill. She thought he may be a Russian agent who was poisoning her and was concerned about his relationship with you. I did not want her to pass away without knowing the truth. I told your mom everything I knew, and reassured her that you would not be in danger.

I know it must be disconcerting to have Joe vanish on you the way he did, but Joe is in custody. The OIJ arrested him when he returned to Costa Rica, but has not charged him with a crime. I met with him on several occasions and he admits to no wrong doing. While in Costa Rica there were attempts on his life. To protect him, he is now in U.S. Federal protective custody and held at an unknown location in the States. During my visits, he reiterated his frustration that he can't see you again to apologize and explain. I told him I would see what I could do.

You told me that you had a meeting scheduled with Matheson. I hope that will be productive. I talked with him and requested that he read you in on certain matters that will resolve some of your remaining concerns. Whether or not he can be trusted to do that remains to be seen. Don't expect him to admit to anything that is illegal or that would expose an asset.

The enclosed thumb drive will explain a lot. You will need a password: CIOP410BM.

Fondly, Ed Perez

After reading the letter, Peter folded it back up, put it back into the envelope with the thumb drive, and set it in the tray between the seats.

"Very nice letter. I'm curious though. He didn't say anything about the overseas account. Had you asked him about it?"

"I did. Perhaps he chose to ignore it."

"Have you seen the contents of the thumb drive?"

"No. Let's do that as soon as we get back home," she responded.

****

As soon as they crossed the American Legion Memorial Bridge into Virginia, they took the George Washington Parkway. They passed an exit to the CIA for employees only. Brandy mused that she wished they allowed employees of NSA to use it because it would save a few miles if they did. However, they continued, exited onto Route 123, and drove to the main entrance.

Matheson had put their names onto an authorized visitor list and given them an access code that they could present to the guards protecting the entrance roadway. A guard came out of the booth and asked for ID. Brandy gave him her NSA ID and then he turned to Peter.

"And you, sir?"

"I'm with her," Peter replied

"Could I have your ID, please?"

Peter passed him his driver's license.

"Were you given a code?"

"Yes." Peter fumbled through his pockets for the code that Brandy had just given him no more than forty minutes ago, as Brandy rolled her eyes. "Here it is."

The guard took the license and the code to his booth, checked something on his computer, and returned with their IDs.

"You guys are free to go. Have a nice day," he said with a deadpan expression.

As they passed through the gate, Peter noticed the black uniformed guard. He had an automatic rifle pointed toward the gate.

32

MEETING IN LANGLEY

They parked the car and walked into the main lobby. After they were screened and signed in at the lobby, an administrative assistant named Jeannette escorted them to Matheson's office. On the way, they passed by the Memorial Wall with stars that represented the agents and operatives that died in the line of duty. Brandy wondered if her mom would qualify for a star and to have her name in the Book of Honor that sat on a pedestal in front of the wall. When they arrived upstairs, they found Matheson standing at his office door.

Matheson had been with the agency for at least twenty years. Titles and positions were not generally made known, but Peter knew that Matheson had replaced Jon Wilson in 1988 and now he was probably a Deputy Director of something related to counter intelligence. He was probably around fifty years of age. He looked very average and ordinary, but when he spoke, he captured your attention. His tone was sincere and compassionate, but direct and commanding at the same time. He was well liked. Donna had reported to him.

"Hello, Brandy. And Peter, haven't seen you in a while," he said as he looked at Peter. "How is Carol?" he asked referring to Peter's wife.

"She's fine . . . said to tell you hello."

"Brandy told me on the phone that she's your daughter. I must admit I was very surprised to hear that. Although, it does explain why you and Donna often asked about each other . . . I didn't see you at Donna's funeral—"

Brandy interrupted. "Mom kept our relationship a secret from both of us until after she passed. It's a long story, but she had her reasons."

613

"Well anyway, please, let's sit down. What is it that I can do for the two of you today?"

"Mr. Matheson, you said I could call—"

"Brandy, please just call me Brian," he interrupted.

"Yes, Brian. I have concerns about what my mother was involved with. I need to know how to remember her, and we have lots of questions."

"I see. What sort of questions?"

"Like, who killed Mary Lou?" Peter replied and handed Matheson the news clippings he had of Maria Martin from the Costa Rican newspapers.

Matheson took a quick look at the news clipping and then looked at Peter. "I'll tell you what. We have a sensitive compartmented information facility, a SCIF. Let's go there."

They followed Matheson into a small conference room. "Our conversation will be totally secure and private in here. Please sit."

Peter spoke. "The news implies that the CIA took her out, and we know that Donna was there at the time. Did she do this?"

Matheson looked directly at Brandy. "Brandy, your mom was a good woman and a patriot. That's how you should remember her. To answer your question—No! The CIA does not assassinate people," he said, quoting the official line.

"Did she have an alibi?" Brandy wanted to know.

"I don't know how you feel about this sort of thing, but your mother spent the weekend in question with a gentleman friend."

"Was his name Ed?"

"Yes, how did you know?"

"He sent flowers when she was in the hospital. I traced the order back to an Ed Perez in San José. He also came to the funeral," Brandy responded.

"He must have cared a great deal about your mother for him to risk revealing his identity." Then after a pause, "Did you have any other questions?"

"We do," Peter responded. "We need to know the truth about Donna's death."

"What do you mean?"

Brandy began to explain. "In January, Mom said she wasn't feeling well. I asked her if the cancer could be coming back. She told me she hoped not, but if it was, she didn't want to fight it again. We agreed to go to the doctor and find out, which we did. She got worse and we spent several days doing appointments and getting tested. She told me that the doctors thought she had been poisoned. She thought so as well."

Brandy continued her explanation. "I went back to her townhouse with the intent of finding the source of poisoning. She always kept a pitcher of iced tea in the fridge and Mom thought that could be the source. Well, there was no iced tea in the fridge. Was I losing my mind? I could swear it was there before she got sick. Then I noticed that the pitcher had been emptied and washed. It was sitting in the clean dish drainer. My thought was someone else had been there. Maybe the person who tried to kill her had come back and destroyed the evidence. Meanwhile, just prior to this time, her townhouse was broken into. They disarmed her security system, but it was not clear if anything was taken. Perhaps they added poison to her food. I'm sure she reported it to you."

"Who did you think poisoned her?" Brian asked.

"My boyfriend!" Brandy replied emphatically.

"Your boyfriend? How—"

Peter interrupted and tried to lure Matheson into saying more. "We have evidence that her boyfriend, Joe Martinez, was a spy and that he poisoned Donna. We have enough evidence that we're considering going to the FBI and requesting an investigation. However, we wanted to alert you beforehand in case the CIA had an objection."

Matheson stared at Peter as he gathered his thoughts about how to respond.

"I can tell you with one hundred percent certainty that Donna died of cancer, not poison. The death certificate and the medical reports are now released, and that's what they say. We delayed these being made public until we finished our own investigation."

"Investigation or cover-up?" Brandy snapped back.

"Brandy, you must realize that national security may be at stake here and there are certain things I can't reveal. Peter, you understand that."

"We have information that we're willing to share with you," Peter responded. "If you also share with us. It would be better than sharing it with the FBI, don't you think?"

"I don't want you going to the FBI."

"Then read us in." Peter suggested.

"Give me something first."

"Okay, we have a picture that Brandy's son took of Joe and Brandy on Thanksgiving. Then, Donna's friend took another picture of Joe on New Year's Eve," Peter said, and handed the pictures to Brian.

Realizing where Peter was going with this, Brandy interjected. "At Thanksgiving, Joe didn't seem to appreciate having his picture taken, but we didn't think much of it at the time. Then on New Year's Eve, he told Mom he didn't want her to take a picture and pulled away, but I think by then Mom was starting to get suspicious of Joe, and Mom had a friend take the picture of him with everyone else later in the evening when he was off guard. But I wondered why he wouldn't want his picture taken."

"Okay, not so unusual, is it?" Matheson said.

"After Mom died, we found this newspaper picture taken in 2002 at a socialist political rally in Costa Rica. Apparently, Mom was suspicious and she circled the head you see in the crowd. Who do you suppose that is?" Brandy asked sarcastically.

Matheson kind of nodded his head but didn't comment on the picture. It was obviously Joe in the picture. "Anything else?"

"Here's another picture," Peter said. "It's a picture of Joe and Mary Lou together with a third person in Costa Rica. We know Mary Lou was a Russian spy. Who is the third person? The implication is that Joe worked with them."

Brian seemed alarmed. "Where did you get this?" he demanded.

"Donna left it for us. It's not marked classified . . . just three people having lunch. I was hoping you could verify the identity of the third person."

"So, you think Joe came here to poison your mom?"

"Yes, I do! I had invited Mom, a few friends and Joe to watch the Super Bowl at my house. On the day of the Superbowl, Mom was at my house helping to get ready. I think Joe went to Mom's townhouse earlier in the day and poisoned the pitcher of iced tea that she kept in her fridge, and maybe also the orange juice. The next day, Mom was very sick!"

"Do you have evidence that he was actually in your mom's house?"

"He was in Mom's townhouse several times in December and January with me, but on that particular day, when he arrived at the party, I noticed cat hair on his pant legs where Mom's cat Tabby would have rubbed."

"Did he have a key? And what about your mom's security system?"

"He knew Mom had a key hidden in the downspout. He could have gone back after his first visit with me and copied it. At some point Mom removed the key from the downspout, but I still had a key in my purse, and Joe may have taken it, copied it, and returned it without my knowledge. Even without the key he probably could have picked the lock. Peter showed me how easy it is to do that. As far as the security system, he could have watched me enter the code when we went there together. But just before the break-in, Mom changed the code. If Joe went there after that and didn't know the code, it may have been the reason why Mom knew there was a break-in. An alert was never sent to her or the alarm company, but she said that when she arrived home that day, she found that the alarm system was totally disconnected. After that, Joe either learned the new code or learned how to disconnect it and reconnect it without the code. He was a security expert, wasn't he?"

"Brian," Peter interjected. "We have been forthcoming with you. Now it's your turn. Please tell us who is Alexander Sarnoff."

"I need to know how you heard of that name?" he responded.

Brandy replied. "On the morning that I said good-bye to Joe, I found a travel itinerary for Alexander Sarnoff. Joe said he was a colleague. Was that Joe's real name?"

"Okay, but before we go any further with this, I need to know that neither of you will reveal to anyone what I'm about to tell you."

"Of course, you have our word."

"Please understand, not only is this a matter of national security, but your lives could be endangered if you leak anything."

"Okay." Both Peter and Brandy responded simultaneously.

"Sarnoff, also known as Aleksei Chaban reports to Ivan Markov, an intelligence officer in the Russia's SVR-RF, the Russian equivalent to our CIA. Markov is a member of an elite group called *Dignity with Honor*. He's the third person in your picture. He oversaw the operation Maria Martin—Mary Lou to you Peter—was working on in Costa Rica to influence the 2002 elections and increase the socialist influence in the country. They were somewhat successful. He also oversaw an operation intended to take out your mom."

Matheson continued. "Early in 2003 your mom went down to Costa Rica to arrest and interrogate Inga Sarnoff, aka Mary Lou, who used the name Maria Martin at this point. Finally, after all these years," he said as he looked at Peter, "she surfaced, and her identity was revealed. Donna met with high-ranking officials at the OIJ to discuss the plan. We believe that either one of those officials leaked information to the Russians, or that the meeting room was bugged. We think that it was from what Donna said about herself at that meeting that the Russians learned of her responsibilities at the CIA. Your mom was a tracker," he said as he looked at Brandy. "She tracked down Russian spies, been doing it for fifteen years. Unfortunately, Inga Sarnoff was murdered before we could arrest her."

Matheson continued to look at Brandy. "Your mom became a target. Our intelligence sources told us that the Russians wanted to find out who your mom's contacts were, who her intelligence sources were, and what Russian agents she was still tracking. The Russians believed your mom killed Maria Martin. Once they got the information they wanted, they planned to kill your mom in retaliation. Markov was responsible for the operation. We believe that Maria Martin reported to him, so it may have been personal for him as well."

"Did they succeed?"

"No. They did hack into your mom's CIA accounts and they did steal your Mom's Blackberry. However, we were able to plant fake information and fake files on the CIA server, so what they got was not what they thought they were getting."

"What about the poison?" Peter asked.

"We thought we intercepted the poison before your mom imbibed it. However, when she had symptoms of cancer we went to Donna's townhouse and searched for it. We took samples of the iced tea, the juice, and the milk, and then we dumped what was left. We washed out the pitcher and left it in the drainer. Brandy, your mind was not playing tricks on you when you discovered that. It was us. We knew the samples contained a lethal chemical. However, our lab found nothing out of the ordinary—no poison, just iced tea and orange juice."

"If that's the case," Brandy interjected, "then why did it take so long do produce a valid death certificate?"

"Well, your mom did die of cancer. Our intelligence said that Markov's plan was to have your mom ingest a chemical containing cancer cells. I know that sounds preposterous, but the Russians may have developed a way to trick the immune system into not rejecting cancer cells from another person. A chemical containing these cells would be difficult to trace unless the medical examiner and the lab knew what to look for. We needed time. Eventually we did isolate the chemical in the iced tea, but we couldn't prove that Donna drank any of it. And, we wanted the Russians to believe that their plan succeeded. It would give us more leverage when we interrogated Markov and threatened a charge of murder."

Brandy looked puzzled. "Were you able to arrest him?"

"Of course. We set up a sting operation and arrested him. He may have had diplomatic immunity in Costa Rica, but he did not have it here in the United States. He was here illegally. We charged him with several counts of espionage and one count of conspiracy to commit murder."

"Doesn't sound as if you can prove murder," Peter suggested.

"Actually, we have a recorded conversation in which Markov orders the kill and provides the lethal chemical to do it."

"What about Chaban? I saw his itinerary. Didn't he escape?" Brandy wanted to know.

"We arrested him at the airport. We charged him as an accomplice."

"And what about Joe? Where did Joe Martinez fit into this," Peter wanted to know.

"We arrested him as well. He was Markov's inside man. He used Brandy to gain access to her mom."

"He used me alright," she muttered.

"It seems as if you had someone on the inside yourself. You had a great deal of intelligence that you were able to act on, and I think I know who *your* inside man was," Peter surmised.

Matheson and Brandy both looked at Peter. "It was Joe. Wasn't it?"

"Sorry, I can't comment on that," Matheson responded.

"Yes. It's all starting to make sense now," Brandy said excitedly. "Joe asked me to take some clothes he had left to the Goodwill. In one of the pockets, I found a scrap of paper with a phone number on it. I didn't think anything of it at the time and put it back into the pocket where I found it. But this past week Peter called the number and heard 'Hello, I'm not available, please leave a message.' The number was 703-555-9516 ext. 111. Sound familiar?" she said excitedly. Matheson could tell by her tone that she was also angry.

"Okay, look," Matheson responded. "I have no idea about that and I never received a phone call from Joe Martinez."

"Did Mom know that my boyfriend was working with the Russians?"

"We couldn't let her know. If we did, it would have jeopardized our ability to catch the Russians in the act of espionage and attempted murder . . . but we—"

No sooner had he said this than he realized the impact his revelations must be having on Brandy.

Brandy was livid. "How could you do this to me and to Mom? You allowed an agent to take advantage of me and you allowed my mother to be used as bait?"

"I'm sorry. I can only imagine how you must feel," he said, but it was too late.

"I feel like I was raped! Can you imagine that?" She immediately got up and stormed out of the room.

"Brian, I'm with Brandy on this," Peter said and followed Brandy out.

When he caught up with her, she was crying. He put his arm around her and tried to comfort her. She resisted at first but then they hugged. "I told him I was with you on this. I think what the CIA did was deplorable. Are you going to be okay?"

"I'm sorry. I guess I let my emotions get the better of me," she said as she looked up at Peter and forced a grin. "Peter, I want to go home."

"Yes, of course, I understand."

As they turned to go, Matheson stood in front of them blocking their way. "Brandy, I had no intention of hurting you. I didn't know that you and Joe were intimate. If he forced himself on you, I need you to tell me so that I can take appropriate action."

"He did not force himself, but if I had known who he was, it would not have happened. I was taken advantage of. I need to leave now."

Matheson didn't know what else to say. "Please wait here and I'll have Jeannette usher you out."

33

VISIT WITH MOM

Brandy and Peter didn't say much as Brandy drove north on the Beltway toward the Maryland state line. But when she approached Route 355 in Maryland, she slowed down and turned onto the exit ramp—several miles before they would normally turn off to head back home.

"Where are we going?" Peter asked.

"I want us to visit Mom's grave. I hope you're okay with that." He thought he detected a bit of residual anger in her voice but took note that she had said, **us**.

"Yes, of course."

They entered the cemetery grounds, parked as close to the site as they could, and walked up a slight hill to Donna's marker. Brandy was about to set herself on the ground a few feet in front of the grave stone, but the ground was damp, and newly grown grass was beginning to take hold. So, she remained standing. Peter remained a few feet behind her.

They remained silent for what seemed like ages, staring at Donna's tombstone. Then Brandy looked back at Peter and motioned for him to come next to her. She had tears in her eyes.

"Peter, I apologize for letting my emotions get the better of me."

"It's understandable."

"I'm still trying to figure things out . . . Do you think that Matheson was telling us the truth?"

"Well—"

"I mean, isn't it possible that Joe really did poison Mom. How do we know that Matheson himself wasn't working for the Russians?"

"Well, I think—"

"Or, on the other hand, maybe Joe was really working for the United States . . . like a double agent or something?"

Then she took a breath and turned her head toward Peter.

"Brandy, nothing is absolute, but in my opinion, it's most likely that everything Matheson told us is true, but I don't think he told us the whole story, and he was very vague about what Joe's involvement was. Ed's letter seemed to imply that Joe was not out to kill your mom, but if that was true—"

"Either way, I was used, and I'm having a hard time getting over it." She turned her head back toward the grave stone. "Mom, how were you able to tolerate this duplicity all those years?" she said in an agitated tone as she stared at the tombstone.

Peter put his hand on her shoulder to calm her down.

"Peter, you've worked with the CIA in the past. Did you have to deal with this sort of thing?"

"Yes, I did. After Mary Lou, aka Maria Martin, killed Jon Wilson, I swore I would never do another assignment with the CIA. But, unlike your mom, I had a choice, or so I thought. Ten years later, Carol and I won a telecommunications consulting contract with a large company. It was a big win for us. Then two weeks into it, our client's Vice President called me into his office to give him a status update. As I entered his office he motioned to his left, and lo and behold, who is standing before me? None other than Brian Matheson. Turns out that our contract was a guise by Matheson to get us to secretly do some intelligence work for him."

"Is that the assignment you mentioned when you were at my house?"

"Yes, it is."

"Did you do it?"

"Didn't have much of a choice at that point. I had a contract. It wasn't illegal, and the additional twenty-grand for the intelligence work didn't hurt. Yes, we did it. I didn't like how they had manipulated me, but after I began to see the bigger picture the way Matheson did, I got over it."

"What was the bigger picture?"

Matheson explained that his job was to accomplish certain objectives for God and Country, while minimizing collateral damage, and while keeping his actions legal. I didn't necessarily like it, but I understood it, and I accepted it. I think your mother got it as well."

"Are you saying that I was collateral damage?" she mumbled.

Peter didn't answer. He put his arm around her and pulled her close.

"I think," she continued, "what I'm most upset about is falling for Joe only to find out he was lying to me. I had real feelings for him. I wonder if he had any for me."

"It's quite possible he did, Brandy. Things are not always cut and dry. Either way, you're not doing yourself any good by dwelling on it."

"You're probably right," she said as she went directly up to her mom's tombstone. Peter watched as she crouched in front of the gravestone and put the palm of her hand over the engraving on its face.

"I love you Mom," she said softly. Then she turned back to Peter. "I'm ready to go now."

34
MORE TRUTH

They returned to Peter's house around three thirty in the afternoon. Before getting out of the car, Brandy motioned to the envelope. "I thought you would want to see it too."

"I do. Why don't you come in with me? We can view it on my desktop."

"What about Carol?"

"Not to worry."

Carol came down the stairs from her office and greeted them at the door. Peter detected that look of *where have you been.*

"I'm home. A little later than I thought . . . I know. We stopped at her mom's gravesite on the way home."

"Oh, hi Brandy. How did the meeting go?" Carol asked them.

"Okay, I guess," Peter replied halfheartedly. "Oh, Matheson said to say hello for him," Peter added in a cheerful tone and then said, "I hope you don't mind, but Brandy and I need to review something on my computer before she goes home. We won't be long."

And before Carol could respond, Peter headed down the stairs to his office with Brandy in pursuit.

Peter removed the thumb drive from the envelope and plugged it into the USB port, while Brandy pulled up a nearby chair. They were eager with anticipation, like two kids about to go on a carnival ride. "Here goes," Peter said as he clicked on the drive and entered the password required to open it. They both read the contents together. The thumb drive contained two folders: Folder A and Folder B. Peter clicked on Folder A.

Folder A

Brandy:

Here is my understanding of Joe's involvement.

Your mother was aware that the Russians had targeted her and she had agreed to Matheson's plan to entrap them. However, Brian Matheson is a strict believer in the "need to know" philosophy. Up until she passed, your mother was unaware of your boyfriend's role in the operation. Prior to January, I was totally out of the loop and unaware of the operation that your mother was involved with. Interestingly, Joe was not aware that neither I nor your mother knew of his role.

Joe's role was to work with the Russians to gather intel and set them up. It was also his job to protect your mom, but when your mom got sick, it was not clear if he had succeeded. This all came out after I had met with Matheson (BM) and Joe (JGM) in late January. Bottom line, Joe is one of us. I informed your mom of Joe's role just before she passed. However, she was sworn to secrecy.

Folder B contains transcripts of Joe's report to us of events that occurred on Friday evening, April 4, 2003. I trust that you understand the sensitivity of the contents. You may want to destroy the thumb drive after you read it.

Ed (EP)

"So! Joe was a double agent under deep cover? Matheson never indicated **that** when we talked to him," Brandy pronounced. Peter could see the agitation in Brandy's face.

"Take a breath," he advised. "We'll get through this. Are you ready to see the contents of folder B?"

"I'm ready. Let's do it"

The first thing Peter noticed after he opened folder B was that any security classification markings had been removed.

Folder B

Text message 5 a.m. April 5, 2003
TO: BM and EP:

I have included a transcript of what I observed on Friday evening April 4. I am not sure I can make sense of it. As you approved, I did report to Petrov the death of Maria Martin and that the possible assailant was Officer Wolf. He has requested a full report within the week. As of now, the authorities have not been notified. Please advise as to what else I should report to Petrov. (See Enclosure.)
JGM

████████████

Text Message April 6, 2003
TO: EP and JGM:
I am returning your original transcript with redactions. Langley wants Joe to report to his Socialist client the portions of his report that are <u>not</u> redacted (see attached). This will be the official report outside of the agency.

We want Joe to convince his client that CIA officer Donna Wolf was Inga's assassin, and that they will need his help to retaliate. Our objective is to identify Inga's puppet masters and expose their plans to retaliate—whether it be espionage or attempted murder—against Wolf and the CIA on U.S. soil. If on U.S. soil they will be subject to arrest and/or death. Please consider the following redacted report to be your official report.
BM

████████████

REPORT OF OBSERVATIONS ON FRIDAY APRIL 4 2003
I am tracking Donna Wolf, aka Donna Rice, a known employee of the American CIA. I follow her from the InterContinental Hotel in Escazu to La Copa Máxima, a coffee shop and eatery in the city of Heredia. She is driving a rented late model white Toyota Camry, plate number 8537161.Wolf is wearing casual business attire consisting of a white blouse, a silky neck scarf, black slacks with a black belt, and black slip-on shoes. She has dangling earrings, shoulder length brown hair and is not wearing glasses.

We arrive at La Copa Máxima at 5:15 p.m. Wolf enters the café and I follow her in. I go to the counter and order a coffee. While standing there I see Wolf walk over to a table in the back corner.

~~Two men are there. I don't know the one. Let's call him Mystery Man.~~ She says hello to the ~~other~~ man and there is an exchange of words. I recognize him as a Deputy Director of the DIS, Jafeth Balladares. He reports directly to DIS Director Geraldo Alverez. Wolf seats herself at a table on the other side of the room. I return to my car.

~~At 5:30 p.m. Mystery Man leaves the coffee shop. I think I have seen him before but I can't quite place him. He looks to be in his mid-thirties. He is about 5 feet 9 inches tall, slender, but with an athletic build. He is dressed more casually than the Deputy Director. He is wearing a white short-sleeved shirt, a tie but no jacket, black slacks, and black shoes. I notice he has a tattoo on his left forearm. I believe it to be symbolic of a faction of the Nicaraguan Resistance movement. He turns to his right and goes to the parking area around the side of the building out of my line of sight.~~

At 6:00 p.m., Wolf exits the café and heads for her car. She has a small cardboard carton in her right hand. She sits in her car a few minutes before leaving. I'm too far away to see what she is doing. Perhaps she is primping, I think. While I'm waiting, Balladares leaves the café and goes to the back of the building and out of sight. At 6:10 p.m. I follow Wolf out of the parking lot onto Route 3.

I follow Wolf to the Rohrmoser area of San José. Wolf makes a left turn from Via 104 and enters the neighborhood, but a black Ford sedan with tinted windows cuts in front of me and prevents me from following closely. I miss the light and must wait a few more minutes before I can continue. As I finally enter the neighborhood, Wolf is no longer in sight. However, I know the neighborhood and I know where Maria Martin lives, having once been to her house when I worked with her. I assume that may be where Wolf is headed. I drive to Maria's address at 23 Thirteenth Avenue. At 6:45 p.m. I pass by the residence and don't notice any activity at the house. The sun has already set and the only light is an outdoor driveway lamp. Then I notice a parked car, a white late model Toyota Camry. After a quick glance at the license plate, I determine it to be Wolf's car. The car is empty. After I pass by, I circle back and park where I have a view of both the residence and Wolf's car.

I sit in my car and wait for Wolf to come back to the Camry. Wolf returns to her car carrying a large shoulder bag. In the dim light I can't see her face, but I notice she is now wearing a black top and glasses. I follow Wolf out of the neighborhood, back to Via 104, and to the Grano de Oro Hotel.

We arrive around 7:25 p.m. Wolf parks on the street near the entrance to the lobby and I do the same. She has her shoulder bag with her as she exits the car. I exit my car and follow her into the lobby. She stops at the front desk, removes a small carton from her bag, and hands it to the desk clerk. They exchange a few words and then she proceeds down a hallway, toward the bar and dining area, presumably to use the ladies' room. Judi had mentioned that Wolf was planning to meet a friend there. I reason that Wolf could have altered her appearance and was now heading to the ladies' room to change back before meeting her friend.

~~If she's meeting a friend or staying for dinner, I expect her to return to the lobby. But, the light in the lobby area is revealing, and after no more than fifteen seconds, I sense that the woman that went down the hallway does not look like the Donna Wolf that I remember seeing at the cafe in Heredia. Of course, the black top and glasses are different, but other details like her hair and her gait seem different as well. I also wonder why she would park on the street if she were planning to stay for dinner. I become suspicious.~~

I slowly make my way down the hallway. When, I come to the end of the hallway, a new hallway goes off to the left. I see no ladies' room, and I don't see Wolf, but I do notice a side door far down the hallway that leads back outside the building. She must have gone out the side door and walked around to the front of the hotel where she left her car. I immediately run back through the lobby and out the front door of the hotel. I arrive just in time to see the woman drive off in the same white Camry that I had followed here. Damn, I've been played. The time is now 7:30 p.m.

I jump back in my car, a bit angry, and not knowing what else to do, I give chase. She had a good jump on me and with the traffic and the darkness I temporarily lose her. However, two blocks later, there's a break in the traffic and I spot her white Camry up the road ahead. I follow the car to a nearby fast-food restaurant on Via 104. The car sits for a few minutes in the rear parking lot before the woman exits the car. I watch her make her way to a nearby dumpster at the rear of the restaurant carrying her shoulder bag. She is in the shadows and has her back to me, but she is now wearing a white top like she wore when she left La Copa Máxima. I watch her drop the shoulder bag into the dumpster. ~~*Then she turns as if to come back to the car, but heads for a side door of the restaurant instead. Other cars and people partially obstruct my view. I wait in my car until she exits the restaurant two minutes later. She is facing me as she passes through a lit area near the door and heads back to the car. My view is unobstructed. I see clearly that she is no longer a woman! She is now Mystery Man!*~~

I now have a choice. Do I follow the Camry, or do I find out what was put into the dumpster? After the Camry drives off, I go to the dumpster where I discover the contents of the shoulder bag and the case. The bag contains items of disguise, latex gloves and black ladies' shoes. I look for blood spatter, but it's too dark. I open the case and find a small hand gun, an ammo clip, and a silencer. The time is now 7:45 p.m.

Judi said that Donna was planning to have dinner at the Gran de Oro with a friend who worked at the Embassy, so perhaps I would find her there. I'm also curious to know who will pick up the carton left at the lobby desk. As soon as I find a place to turn around, I head back to the Grano de Oro. I drive to the rear of the hotel and park in the guest parking area. As I start to walk to the nearest entrance, I notice a Toyota Camry that looks exactly like the one that Wolf drove—same color, same model. I place my hand on the hood and in front of the grill. The engine is still hot. I peek into the car window and see nothing on the seats. Of course, I don't know what might be in the trunk. Then, I check the license plate and it's identical to the one I had followed.

~~*How can this be? I ask myself. How could the car that Mystery Man is driving have the same plate number as the one that Wolf is driving? Did I misread the plate on Mystery Man's car? Perhaps I mistook a 6 for a 9 or reversed the order of the numbers in my head,*~~

but I didn't think my eyes or my dyslexia were that bad. I thought it more likely that the plates on Mystery Man's car were altered or forged. Wolf's plate number became public when she rented the car Wednesday night. The number 3581767 could easily have been altered to be 8537161. Black ink and white-out would probably do the job. If the DIS were behind this, I think they could even have manufactured new plates for Mystery Man in the two days they had before tonight.

I go inside the hotel and I see Wolf. She's wearing the same outfit she wore when she left La Copa Máxima. She is seated at the bar next to a man who I identify as a U.S. embassy courier. Another man, who I identify as Ed Perez, a U.S. government employee, appears and walks away with the courier. Perez heads up the main staircase while I follow the courier to the front desk. I watch him take possession of the carton, and I follow him up the staircase to room 299. I keep my distance so as not to be seen. Perez is waiting at the door and they both enter the room. Then at about 8:15, Perez rejoins Wolf at the bar and the hostess seats the two of them in the dining area. Later, I verify that Donna Wolf is back at her hotel, the InterContinental, before 11:00 p.m.

"Wow!" Peter exclaimed. "Read the unredacted version and then read the redacted version. It's amazing how the meaning of something can be totally different after it's redacted. This whole thing was a counterintelligence operation devised by Matheson. I wonder if he even had approval from higher up. It makes clear that Joe was not here to kill you or your mom. And if you believe Joe's unredacted report, it also exonerates your mom. Looks like she was set up—she's no killer."

"I wish I could be sure. The DIS and the CIA could have been in it together. One of them pulled the trigger and the other disposed of the evidence."

"Don't be so cynical. She's your mother!"

"Peter, I've had it with all this secrecy and subterfuge," she said angrily. "I'd like to leak this report to the media, or maybe to the OIJ in Costa Rica?"

"I think you know what would happen if we did. This report implicates the DIS and the CIA in illegal activity, including murder. The source of this information would be known. Both you and Joe would become targets, and you might end up dead . . . and what about the security classifications on these documents? They were removed, but my guess is that the security classifications are far above what we should be looking at. You never saw this. Ed could be in trouble for sending it to us—could lose his job and go to jail."

"I think he and Mom were very close. . ." She started to cry again. "I'm sorry. They took advantage of Mom and me. Mom was anxious about being targeted and about my welfare, and I was dumb enough to fall in love with a hardened covert operative. I just can't seem to get over it."

"Did you really fall in love? In his letter, Ed said he met with Joe and that Joe wished he could see you one last time to make amends. Would you be willing to do that?"

She paused . . . "I'm not sure. I'm so angry at him right now. Yet another side of me says maybe it would bring closure."

"Brandy, it's all going to be okay," he said. As he put his arm around her to comfort her, they became aware of Carol having come down the stairs to go to the food storage area in the other room. She probably overheard much of what they had said.

"Listen, we had best wrap it up." He unplugged the thumb drive, put it back in the envelope with letter, and handed it to her. "Keep this in a secure place."

They walked up the stairs to the front door. "You're going to be okay," he said as he pecked her on the cheek and held the door for her.

Carol had followed them up the stairs and watched them say good-bye.

"Did Brandy get all of her questions answered?" She asked.

"Some, but not all. She's upset."

"About what? Not with you, I hope."

"Well, I can't tell you much. Our meeting took place in a SCIF and the discussion was highly classified. However, I will tell you this. She's upset that she hasn't heard from her boyfriend since her mom got sick, and she's upset with Matheson for not telling her everything about the circumstances of her mom's death."

"I see, and I assume you're the one who consoled her," Carol said somewhat sarcastically. If I didn't know you better, I would think the two of you were having an affair," she mocked.

"Sounds like you're jealous. We had our appointment for a paternity test and we're hoping that the results will be back soon, but there's no question in my mind that she's my daughter. In any case, you know I love you," he said and gave her a hug.

"I just thought of something I need to do. I'll be downstairs in my office."

It was only four forty-five. Although it was Friday, Matheson would not normally leave his office before five. As soon as Peter got to his desk, he dialed Matheson's number.

35

GENETIC PROOF

On Tuesday the following week, Brandy received the results of the DNA paternity test. She was excited. She immediately called Peter. Carol answered the phone.

"Carol this is Brandy. Good news. The paternity test results are back. It's definite! I'm Peter's daughter! Is he there?"

"No, he's not, but that *is* good news."

"Well, I would like to bring you the paperwork. I know you have been a little uneasy about our relationship. I hope this will help."

"Well, yes. Peter and I were a bit wary at first, thinking that you may be conning him in some way. As Peter probably told you, I had a bad experience in my first marriage. My husband lied to me and covered up an affair. I know I shouldn't have felt suspicious of the two of you, but I did."

"Carol, I fully understand your feelings because the same thing happened to me in my marriage, and recently I was upset because my boyfriend turned out to be someone other than who I thought."

"You're welcome to come over whenever it's convenient."

"Is Thursday evening good?"

"Would you like to join us for supper?"

"Yes. I'd love that. What time?"

"Six thirty, okay?"

"Yes, I'll come directly from work."

****

Brandy's jubilation changed dramatically Thursday morning when she received the following message from Brian Matheson:

Joe wishes to see you. He has suggested the boutique hotel near Dupont Circle. I can arrange it. Please respond yes or no by 2 p.m. Friday. Details will follow.

Brandy became emotional as she read this. She remembered that weekend. It was just before Christmas. The air was crisp and cold that day. She and Joe had toured the city and many of its sights like the monuments, museums, embassies, etc. They had used the Metro system whenever possible but had also done a lot of walking. By the end of the day, they were cold, and they were hungry. They came across a small hotel with a restaurant not far from the Dupont Circle Metro stop. The hostess seated them at a small table, where they ordered food, and continued to enjoy each other's company. While waiting for the meal to arrive, Joe excused himself—men's room? When he returned, he said the hotel had a cancelation and persuaded her to stay in the city overnight. It hadn't taken much persuasion. At this point she was head over heels for him, but they had limited opportunities to spend nights together, as they were not ready to publicize to Mom or Brian that they were sleeping with each other. Later, Joe admitted to planning this overnight ahead of time. She didn't mind. It turned out to be a very romantic evening.

Now she had a decision to make. Was the message for real or could it be a trap set by the Russians trying to find out where Joe was? Could she trust Matheson? She wondered if she should let Peter know about this development. Could she trust herself? *I need closure, not sex,* she told herself.

****

Thursday evening, she arrived at Peter's house with a bottle of wine. Peter greeted her at the door and took possession of the wine.

"Come in. Dinner is almost ready. How are you feeling?"

"I'm feeling great," she said and gave him what he interpreted as a forced smile.

"Carol said you seemed very happy about the results of the DNA test when you called on Tuesday. I sense that something else is going on. Did something happen between Tuesday and now?"

Once again, she smiled. "Yes, but I'm dealing with it."

Peter gave her a curious look. "You heard from Joe, didn't you?"

She wondered how he knew, but nodded in the affirmative and put her finger across her lips.

"I received this message this morning," she said and handed him a copy. "I'm not sure what to do. It could be a trap."

Peter took a quick look at it and handed it back.

"I'm *glad* you heard from him. It's not a trap. I think you should go. You both need closure."

"You seem very sure of this," she said almost taken aback by the quickness of his response and the certainty in his voice.

"I am, but you don't need to decide tonight. Tonight, we celebrate."

Peter put his hand on her shoulder and escorted her into the kitchen where Carol welcomed her.

"Brandy brought us a bottle of wine," Peter said and showed her.

"Oh, thank you . . . very nice of you."

"Can we open it?" Peter asked, looking at Brandy.

"Absolutely, if it's okay with Carol. Will this go with supper?"

"Pinot noir goes fine with pork tenderloin," Carol replied. "Peter can get the wine glasses. Dinner's just about ready."

After they were seated and the food served, Peter poured the wine and offered a toast. "To new beginnings" he said and raised his glass.

Dinner conversation was cheerful and friendly between the three of them, but at some point, Carol asked Brandy about her mother. She asked Brandy how she was doing after dealing with so much.

"Well, looking back on it, I wonder how I got through it," Brandy replied. "First Mom got sick, then my boyfriend disappeared, then Mom died unexpectedly, and then a letter from Mom tells me I have a new father—all within a two-month period. However, I'm coming to grips with it now. I want to thank Peter for helping me. Everything Mom wrote about him is true." She raised her glass. "Here's to Peter and to Mom."

"And here's to Carol for her patience and understanding," Peter added.

"Yes, to Carol," Brandy repeated.

Then they clinked glasses and each took a swallow of the Pinot Noir.

"You know, Mom had a very interesting life. Doing what she did for the CIA while raising me must have been very challenging for her. I only began to fully understand her in recent years when she got sick the first time. I began to understand her and we became close. I was thinking that her story would make for a very interesting biography, a way to celebrate her life from the eyes of others."

"How much wine have you had?" Peter asked.

She giggled. "No really, what better way to honor someone than to write their life story?"

"Okay, have you ever written a book?" Peter asked.

"Nope. That's why I want you to help me write it."

Peter played along. "You mean like co-authors?"

"Yeah. It could be her story seen through the eyes of those who were close to her. Besides us, we could talk with my stepbrother, my son Brian, and maybe even Matheson could add something not classified . . ."

"And what would the title of this book be?"

"I don't know. How about '*Mom's Final Project*' . . . what do you think?"

Carol, who had remained silently amused by all this, now decided to say something. "I think you've both had too much wine."

36

FORGIVENESS

After much deliberation, Brandy replied "yes" to Matheson's offer to arrange a meeting with Joe, and received further instructions.

Come to the hotel on Sunday. Take the Metro. Arrive at 2:00 p.m.
Ask the front desk for a message in your name.

On Sunday, she drove to the Greenbelt Metro station and took the Metro to Dupont Circle. She walked from the station and arrived at the boutique hotel at 1:50 p.m., ten minutes early. As instructed, she went to the lobby desk and asked if there was a message for Brandy Evans. The lady behind the desk looked down and pulled out an envelope and handed it to her. Brandy opened it. The message was short.

Come to Room 354 and knock four times.

Strange, she thought, but she took the elevator up to the third floor, found room 354 and knocked four times as instructed.

The door opened a crack and a woman's husky voice said, "Come in, Joe is expecting you."

Brandy could feel her heart beat faster as she cautiously stepped into the room. A man that had been sitting on the other side of the room got up and approached her. Was that Joe? The man had a full beard and long dark hair tied in a ponytail. He wore jeans, tennis shoes, and a short-sleeved golf shirt. A pair of dark glasses dangled on a strap from his neck.

"Hello Brandy. Thank you for coming," he said.

Brandy stood in front of him. Her jaw dropped as she stared at him. Even his eyes were a different color.

"Joe, is this you?"

Before he could answer, Brandy was startled by the sound of the door slamming behind her. She turned quickly to see a stocky woman next to her. To Brandy, the woman looked like a German female prison guard in an old war movie.

"Who are *you*? Brandy asked excitedly.

"Brandy, meet Greta. Greta, meet Brandy," Joe said as Greta was in the process of displaying her ID. "Greta is with the U.S. Marshals Service."

"Turn around and put your hands up against the door," Greta ordered.

"What? No!" Brandy protested

"Greta, stop! Joe shouted. "There's no need for that."

"Whatever you say, sir. It's your life. You two behave yourselves. When you're done, bang on the door. I'll be right outside in the hallway." Greta left.

"Sorry for that. She was just assigned to me for the day. She can be over the top. Please sit."

Now almost speechless, she took a seat on the chair, while Joe sat on the edge of the bed.

"Brandy," he began. "Please forgive me. I know I have hurt you, but I really care about you and needed to see you. Please allow me to explain the situation." He sounded sincere.

"I've been in hiding. It's the CIA's version of witness protection. By now you probably know that I was working as an agent of the CIA. I want you to know I haven't been charged with a crime. I'm being held as a material witness to crimes committed by Russian agents. Until now, I've not been allowed any communications to the outside world. On Friday evening, Matheson told me you had met with him and he gave me a stern lecture about becoming involved with you. He said you told him that you felt like I raped you. That was not—"

"No," Brandy replied. "I was angry and I said I felt like you took advantage of me. You lied to me about who you were."

"Okay, you were right to feel that way, but it was not my intent to take advantage of you. I never wanted to hurt you. I was under deep cover. If I told you who I really was, it would have put you and others at risk. My feelings for you are real. I'm in my late thirties and my work doesn't allow me to live a normal life. This was the first time in my life that I felt like a normal person who could have a normal relationship with a woman. You made me feel that way, but I was wrong to think that was possible. I care deeply for you, but I realize now that I misled you and hurt you. For several weeks, I have been telling Matheson that I wanted to talk with you and ask for your forgiveness. He advised me against it, but said that after he met with you, and after he talked with Ed Perez and with Peter Troutman, your father, he decided he would not stop me. He said that both Ed Perez and your father had been very persuasive. By the way, when did your mom tell you that Peter Troutman was your father?"

"After she died, in a letter she had left for me."

"But you're glad to know, right?"

"Yes, he's been a big help to me."

"I also told Matheson that when this trial is over, I want out. Don't know if that's possible though. I don't know where I'll be, what my job will be, or what my name will be three months from now. I don't know if the Russians will figure out that I betrayed them and track me down—in fact they probably already have. There was an attempt on my life a month ago but it may have been the Costa Rican DIS. Anyway, after the courts are done with me, I may go into WITSEC for the rest of my life."

"That's the Federal witness protection program, isn't it?"

"Yes, it is, and that means you can't know where I am. I needed to see you now while it was still possible."

Brandy was stone silent.

"I'm sorry. Please forgive me."

Brandy stared at him and remained silent.

"Maybe this was not a good idea. You should go now," he said as he rose from the edge of the bed and motioned toward the door.

"Wait!" she said. "I need to know something."

"What?"

"Did my mother know who you really were?"

Joe sat back down.

"No, not until after she was in the hospital. Apparently, Matheson never told her what my role was. I did not know this when I started my assignment, but it became obvious to me after a while. Do you remember we visited her in the hospital just before I fled? And do you remember she asked to speak to me alone for a few minutes? She accused me of killing her. I told her who I was and what my role was. I was not authorized to do that, but I thought she should know. I don't know if she believed me at that moment, but Ed Perez also told her about me when he saw her a few days later."

He paused, but Brandy remained silent so he continued.

"Matheson had kept Perez in the dark also. Perez did not know the whole truth either until sometime in January. Your mother became suspicious of me—thought I was a Russian spy and suspected I was trying to compromise you in some way. Apparently, your mother expressed her concerns to Perez about me, so he met with me to find out more. You recall I had gone back to Costa Rica for a few days in January. I didn't realize until he spoke to me that neither he nor your mother knew what was going on. Officially, I couldn't tell him, but he appealed to my conscience and convinced me that he cared about you and your mom. He had the ability to expose my cover, but I didn't think he would have done it, I already knew who he was and I felt I could trust him. So, I gave him a document that spelled out the total plan that Langley had contrived."

Again, Brandy said nothing.

"According to Perez, your mother also went to Matheson and expressed her concerns about me. When she started to feel ill, she thought perhaps I was there to poison her. She went to Matheson again and told him what she thought she knew. She threatened to act if he didn't. Matheson never told her the whole truth though. Perhaps he was trying to maintain my cover in case the Russians showed up at the hospital—don't know. Matheson promised her I would be arrested and you would be safe. Apparently, he later lied to her and told her they had arrested me at the airport before I could flee. In fact, I was arrested in Costa Rica three weeks later. I felt badly that I couldn't be there for you at your mom's funeral, but I was in custody. So, no, I don't think she knew the whole truth until after Ed talked to her in the hospital."

Brandy finally responded. She rose from her chair and over to him.

"Joe, thank you for helping me to understand. I fell in love with you and you hurt me. I don't know if I'll be able to forgive you. If in the future your situation changes, perhaps we could start over—I don't know."

"Brandy, I'm so sorry."

They both had tears in their eyes as they parted.

37

SAFE HOUSE

After the meeting with Brandy, Greta took Joe back to his safe house. He had been kept there since they brought him back from Costa Rica near the end of May. The safe house was a large brick two-story home with an attached garage and it was in an upscale neighborhood. It stood on a half-acre of land. From the outside no one would know that a prisoner was kept there—and yes, although he had not been charged with a crime, he was a prisoner. Each morning that they needed to take him somewhere, he would enter the garage and get into the car. The garage door would remain shut until he was inside the car. A push of a button on a key-fob would open the garage door and they would be off to court, the FBI, the lawyers, CIA, or wherever that day's agenda dictated. No one would see who he was as he came and went.

Joe was also impressed with the state-of-the-art security system. Cameras monitored activity on the grounds outside, while sensors monitored all the doors and windows on the inside. If something bad occurred, alarms would go off, and the U.S. Marshals would be immediately notified.

On the inside, it was heaven—especially if you compared it to the alternative, a prison cell. Joe had everything a prisoner could want and a lot more. He slept in one of the three bedrooms upstairs, while his guard slept in the bedroom on the main level. In case there was a house invasion, there were two safe rooms, one on the second level and one on the basement level. These rooms were bombproof and impenetrable. Each room could also serve as a SCIF. They were soundproof and impervious to electromagnetic waves.

Right now, Joe was on the main level watching the news on TV with his guard, Bill. Bill had been his guard since they moved in a month ago. Joe was beginning to view Bill as a friend. They often engaged in friendly chit-chat. Who else could he talk to? However, Bill was a professional. Joe knew he could rely upon him in case of an emergency. Bill had told him how he once saved a whole family from a planned hit by the Mafia. Bill was ex-special forces, was in perfect physical condition, had an IQ above 140, packed a 9 mm semi-automatic, and kept a fully automatic military assault rifle in the hall closet just in case. He was the best!

Not much on the news—same old, same old. Then, Bill asked how his day went.

"Did you close things out with your girlfriend? You still seem down."

"It went as well as I could expect, but I still can't get over her,"

"Want to talk about it?" I'm a good listener," Bill offered.

As much as he emotionally wanted to, Joe had been advised not to talk about his assignment or about those involved.

"No. Thanks, but I'll be okay," he replied.

Shortly after that, Joe decided to retire and went upstairs to his room. He couldn't sleep and began to think about the conversation he had with Brandy that afternoon. He wished he could have told her everything he had endured over the past two months. Perhaps she could better understand and she could forgive him. As he lay there on his bed, he began to recollect his experience after he left BWI Airport in mid-February.

Joe had planned to go to Toronto, cool off, and decide what to do next, but he made a last-minute change and flew to Quebec instead. Then, after three days he decided to fly to Costa Rica. Perhaps he could resume his normal life. Not being able to sleep, Joe thought about the two and one-half months he had endured in Costa Rica before ending up at the safe house.

38

TESTIMONY IN COSTA RICA

Joe closed his eyes and recalled his escape from BWI. The original plan was to return to Costa Rica after he completed his work in the USA. Never, was the plan to fall in love with Brandy, or to be responsible for the death of her mother. This weighed heavily on his mind. However, after he arrived in Costa Rica, things got even worse. The OIJ was investigating the Socialist and Russian influence on government officials, and his name had surfaced as a supporter of those activities. He was only there three weeks before the OIJ wanted to bring him in for questioning.

He recalled how he was afraid of what would happen to him if he allowed the OIJ to question him, and what would happen if they arrested him. The Russians would know he betrayed them, and certain elements in Costa Rica would not want his knowledge of corruption in the government made known. Joe remembered how he feared that testifying in Costa Rica could easily result in his death. The United States had procedures in place to protect witnesses like Joe—Costa Rica not so much.

He had gone to Ed Perez at the U.S. Embassy for advice. After all, he was really working for the CIA and he was not sure what he could say or could not say regarding his undercover assignment. It was from Ed that he learned that the other shoe was about to drop. The FBI had hoped to turn Chaban and have him testify against Markov. However, this was not about to happen. He learned that the case against Chaban and Markov for conspiracy to commit murder would be weak without his testimony. The CIA and the FBI wanted him back in the States. He was a material witness.

The FBI arrested him in Costa Rica. While waiting to be transferred back to the United States, he was kept in a room in the basement of the

U.S. Embassy. This was for his own protection they told him. Ed advised him to seek witness protection and apply for admittance into WITSEC, the federal witness protection program. Ed provided him with legal counsel and helped him through the process.

Joe's lawyer explained that WITSEC is administered and operated by the United States Marshals Service, (USMS). The USMS is an organization within the Department of Justice, (DOJ) that has been around since the days of George Washington. The USMS is responsible for protecting witnesses that are in the program and not incarcerated in a federal prison. Applications to the WITSEC program go to the Office of Enforcement Operations (OEO), a department within the DOJ, that is responsible for authorizing or denying admittance into WITSEC.

Joe agreed to proceed. He found that the WITSEC application process was quite rigorous. There were interviews, forms, and paperwork, as well as psychological tests. Even, his possible testimony to a grand jury was considered. He had to prove that he was in danger and needed protection. Finally, after two weeks of effort, Joe was admitted to the program.

Meanwhile, the OIJ was pressuring the DOJ to release Joe to them. A negotiation ensued and finally, after another two weeks, and with the help of Ed, an agreement was reached. Joe would testify to everything for both the Costa Rican OIJ and the U.S. DOJ in exchange for full immunity from prosecution by both, but he would be given protection by the USMS. It was also understood that he would not answer any questions from the OIJ that would implicate the CIA or Donna Wolf. The deal had been made by early April.

Joe remembered the room he stayed in at the embassy. It was his home for about two months. Nothing like the quarters he had now. The room was down a set of stairs and at the end of a hallway lined with concrete walls. The room was sparse with a bed, a small closet to hang clothes, a chest of drawers, a table and chair, and a private bathroom with shower. There was adequate lighting but no windows.

The procedure had been the same each day. He would be up at 6:00 a.m., shower, dress in business attire, have breakfast delivered to him in his room, and then be escorted to a black van waiting in the driveway. The van belonged to the OIJ, but one bodyguard from the USMS would also be in the van. The van would make its way to the OIJ complex on the other side of San José. The guard would escort him to a secure conference room in a building adjourning the courthouse where he would wait until the first of a stream of Counselors came to question him. All the interrogations were recorded, often with video. His testimony would later be used in court. Violence was never threatened, and he cooperated. It was in his best interest to do so.

They brought lunch to him around noon each day. Lunch typically consisted of a burrito and a fruit drink in a carton with a straw. It wasn't much, but he didn't complain. However, on the sixth or seventh day, he had just opened his burrito and was about to take his first bite, when the guard burst into the room.

"Stop! Don't eat that," the guard had said excitedly.

"Why? What's going on?"

"We just found the regular food delivery boy. He's dead! Your food might be poisoned."

"Well thanks," he had responded. "Don't think I'm hungry now. Take it away."

Sure enough, the next day his lawyer told him that his burrito had been laced with cyanide. "You're lucky," his lawyer had said.

I'll be lucky if I ever get out of here, Joe had thought.

That night, like most nights, Ed Perez had come to visit him in his room at the embassy. The two of them had worked together as business colleagues—as spies, but now they were getting to know each other on a personal basis. They were almost friends. Ed had just sat down when a guard brought Joe his dinner. The embassy had no cook, and meals were prepackaged like those you would have on an airplane. Ed had watched him remove the tinfoil cover from the tray and the utensils from the napkin, and he had watched him pick up his fork with his left hand, scoop up several peas, and lift them to his mouth. After he sat his fork back down, he turned his head and looked at Ed.

"Ed, I need to know something."

"What's that?"

"I need to know if I'm responsible for Donna's death."

"No. She died of cancer but your poison did not cause it. If it had, you would not be sitting here and I would not be helping you."

"Why are you helping me? Did the CIA instruct you to be sure I didn't say anything that would damage their reputation?"

"No, that's not it."

"What then?"

"I was very close to Brandy's mom, Donna. Neither she nor I had been read in to your role. In December, Donna had become suspicious of you and she sent me a picture of you. She wanted me to determine who you really were. I went to Matheson. It took a while, but he finally agreed to read me in. Donna wanted Brandy to be safe and happy, and before she died, I told her what I knew and assured her that I would help. But Matheson didn't tell me everything, and now Brandy needs to know more. She thinks her mother could have assassinated Inga Sarnoff, and that you may have assassinated her mother. She has enlisted the help of her biological father. They've set up a meeting with Matheson. She needs to know the truth, but I don't think she will get it from Matheson. And . . . I also understand your situation. You and I have some things in common. I see myself in you when I was about your age."

"Yeah, how so?"

"Both of us are well-educated and highly intelligent; We both lost our birth mothers at a young age; We're in similar lines of work; We're both caught up in the quagmire of government bureaucracy; We're both Catholic, and we both have ethical and moral conflicts between our work requirements and our personal relationships. I had a wife once, but couldn't handle it. You sacrificed a lot and deserve another chance."

"And how did you resolve those conflicts, Ed?"

"I changed my expectations. Between moral and immoral, black and white, there are infinite positions you can be in. You will need to decide for yourself where in the gray area you are most comfortable."

"We're not normal people, are we?"

"No, we're not. Look, I understand your frustration with Brandy. We have kept in touch. Anyway, she's trying to understand what happened, why her mom died, and what you had to do with it. She has asked me for help. She also told me she has a meeting set up with Matheson. Perhaps there is some way that the two of you can meet to clear the air. You both need closure. Can't promise anything, but I'll see what I can do. You do want to see her again, don't you?"

"Yes, I do, and I appreciate your help." He then wrote something down on a sheet of paper and handed it to Ed.

"What's this?"

"It's the decryption code for a document that will help you and Brandy with the truth. I will ask my lawyer to retrieve it from my office and send it electronically to your office here at the embassy."

Then, Ed changed the subject. He asked Joe what he thought would happen to him when he returned to the States.

"Well, as much as I wish I could live in my home country, Costa Rica, I have too many enemies here, and Costa Rica has no witness protection program like the U.S. does. So, I'll be glad to return to the States. I'll testify and put the Russian spies in jail where they belong. After all, that was the whole point of the operation, wasn't it?

"Joe, I detect anger in your tone."

"Yes, I'm angry! I gave up my career, my heritage, and the only woman I ever loved more than my mother. Then, if I'm lucky enough to still be alive after I testify, I'll get a whole new identification and be relocated to a strange place so that I can start my life all over again, and today, someone tried to kill me for my efforts," he said, slamming his left fist on the table. Then he stood up and walked slowly around the room. After he calmed down, he said, "I'm sorry. I'm letting my emotions get the best of me."

"Joe, if you are relocated, where do you think you will be?"

"Don't know. I've heard that if they ask and you tell them where you would like to be, that's the last place they will send you." He was being cynical but it was probably true. "But if I had a choice, I would like to live in Albuquerque, New Mexico."

"Really. Why?"

"I've never been there, but I've read about it—medium-sized city surrounded by beautiful country—good job opportunities—large Spanish-speaking population—and the weather there is suitable for me as well. I can't stand the cold damp winters in the D.C. area."

"Well, maybe you will get your wish. Look, as far as your career is concerned, you can still do what you know. They will create documents and references for you and help you get employment. You're smart. You will do alright. I know you will."

"Thanks for the encouragement, Ed. You're turning out to be a good friend. Maybe after this is over, I can start over and have a normal life."

After four more weeks had elapsed, Joe had told the OIJ everything they wanted to know. He told them how he provided surveillance—often illegally—to catch important government officials in compromising situations. He described situations that included everything from sex to drugs to bribery. He told them how the Russian spy Inga Sarnoff, aka Maria Martin, would then use the information to extract political donations. These donations would then sponsor socialist causes, and help elect socialist candidates into office. The information that Joe provided was very useful to the OIJ, and helped them to clean up the political corruption.

After his testimony in Costa Rica was complete, Joe was flown back to the States. It was in the middle of the night when two armed guards from the USMS escorted him from his room out the delivery entrance and into a black van. They took him to the *Tobías Bolaños* airport in Pavas, only about one and a half miles away from the embassy. The Pavas airport was not very well known, but in 2004, it was the second busiest airport in Costa Rica. The airport was served by only one public airline that connected several cities in Costa Rica. However, the airport was primarily used to transport executives, freight, government employees, and foreign officials on privately owned aircraft. Four hours after boarding, they landed at Andrews Air Force Base near the District of Columbia and were quickly whisked away in another black van.

Now he was in the safe house and in the process of providing testimony to the DOJ that would be used in court to prosecute Markov and Chaban. Tomorrow would begin his third week here. He finally gave in and fell asleep.

39
TESTIMONY IN THE UNITED STATES

Joe had been back in the States for two weeks now. Each day, guards had escorted him from the safe house to an interrogation room at the FBI headquarters. Joe willingly cooperated. The CIA had provided a lawyer; the USMS had provided him with temporary witness protection; and they had given him full immunity.

Joe was pleased that he had full immunity. In the U.S., he could have been charged with a range of criminal offenses, including breaking and entering, theft of classified information, and conspiracy to commit murder. These were also the offenses that Aleksei Chaban and Ivan Markov were charged with. The DOJ also intended to charge Markov and Chaban with murder. They needed Joe to testify against them in court.

Starting today, however, the preparation for Joe's testimony would take place in his safe house. He had asked his guard, Bill, about the change in venue, and was told that the Marshals had uncovered a plot to intercept his transport, and they were concerned about his security.

Counselors would come to the safe-house and record the details about how he worked undercover to reveal the Russian plan for the theft of classified information and the murder of Donna Wolf. Each day, an FBI agent and two counselors were brought to the safe house and went to the SCIF in the basement. Joe was brought in while Bill guarded the door. The FBI agent and their counselor sat on one side of a conference table; Joe and his assigned lawyer faced them on the other side.

Joe told the FBI all the details of the events leading up to his involvement in the sting operation. He discussed the death of Inga Sarnoff and the Russian's motivation for revenge. Then he described his role in the Russian plan to clone Donna Wolf's computer, breach the CIA data base, and finally to assassinate Donna Wolf by using a poison that would make her death look like she died of cancer. He described how he got the Russians to believe he was working for them while at the same time keeping the CIA and the FBI totally aware of their activity. He explained how he had recorded his meeting with the Russians in D.C. and turned it over to Matheson at the CIA. He explained how he sent warning messages on his burner phone to both Matheson and Donna Wolf not to drink the tea or the orange juice. He also explained how he sent samples of the poison to the FBI lab for analysis.

Joe's testimony, or interrogation as he called it, lasted a full week. Joe's entire testimony was recorded. In the recordings, and in the transcripts, he was always referred to as Joe, never his full name. Only portions of his recorded testimony were presented to the Federal Grand Jury. The prosecution only needed to present those parts of testimony that made their case. The prosecution wanted a murder indictment, so they did not present the portion of Joe's testimony about him warning Donna not to drink the juice and tea. In a grand jury there is no defense or cross-examination like in a trial, and all proceedings are secret. In addition to Joe, others testified, including a medical examiner, an FBI agent, a young newspaper reporter, and a CIA employee who was working with Donna. By the end of the year 2004, Ivan Markov and Aleksei Chaban were indicted. The indictments included murder, theft of classified information, and several other lesser charges.

However, the prosecution took the death penalty off the table in exchange for a guilty plea to various counts of espionage and attempted murder. The prosecution wanted the Russians to believe that they had murdered Donna, but knew they could not prove murder. The CIA and the FBI knew it, but the grand jury and Markov did not. Everyone knew that Donna had died of cancer, but the manner of death was never known with certainty. During the grand jury proceedings, a medical examiner testified that the FBI lab had identified the poison used by Markov and that it could cause the type of cancer that killed Donna. This was true. What the medical examiner didn't say was that they had not detected it in Donna's body. An indictment of murder allowed the prosecutor to bargain with Markov. Markov and Chaban were eager to avoid death and the bad publicity that a public trial would bring to their country. They pleaded guilty to attempted murder and to the other charges. A trial was avoided.

Joe was also pleased that a trial was not needed. For him, it meant less public exposure and less chance of an attempt on his life before he took the stand. It also meant no cross-examination, something that he was not comfortable with. Although Joe had technically broken a few laws himself, he was given immunity and not charged.

****

Now that the testimony was over, and the Russians were locked up, Joe had a decision to make. He could drop out of WITSEC and go back to being the old Joe Martinez, or he could accept a totally new identity and be relocated to a place where he could start over. Joe faced the reality that he would be a marked man unless he was given a new identification. Surely, the Russians would know he betrayed them, and he had already been subjected to attempts on his life in Costa Rica. Even if he continued to be an agent of the CIA, he would need a new identity.

He had been told that as a condition for being in the program, he would have to say good-bye to all his friends and family and never have contact with them again. He had no family left, so that was not a problem. Did he have any friends? Was Bill a friend? Was his business partner a friend? They certainly got along. Although he was working counter-intelligence, he had thought of Maria Martin as a friend—until he discovered she was also a serial assassin wanted by the U.S. DOJ. Perhaps Ed was the closest one he still had to being a friend. He would miss him. Ed had shown compassion, had helped him get through the ordeal in Costa Rica, and had convinced Matheson to allow him to say good-bye to Brandy. Then there was Brandy. She had been a friend—it still hurt to think about her. Perhaps not having anyone close would be a blessing in disguise, he thought. Fewer complications.

Joe was friendly. People seemed to like him and enjoy his company, but his job had run counter to long-term close relationships. Now, however, he was no longer working covertly as a triple agent, and he felt confident that he would make friends wherever he ended up.

So, he decided to stay in WITSEC permanently. By the time Chaban and Markov were sentenced, Joseph Ricardo Garcia Martinez had become someone else. It was a popular name and would not stand out or arouse unusual interest. Joe was given a new birth certificate, new college records, new work history, and a new bank account. He was instructed to memorize who he was and be ready to act the part.

A prerequisite to joining the WITSEC program had been that he would attend two orientation meetings. These meetings were intended to help the transition. The first occurred when he entered the program. The second of these meetings occurred after he had his new identification, but before he knew where he would be relocated. The meeting took place at a secret location in D.C. and was attended by several others who also had new identifications.

One exercise was for each initiate to introduce themselves to another person—using their new identification of course. This might be someone you meet at a cocktail party, or at a meeting, or while interviewing for a new job. It was important that they felt comfortable doing this. A U.S. Marshals employee would supervise and give suggestions afterwards. Typical questions that they asked included:

"I'm so and so, and you are?

"Tell me about yourself. What do you do?"

"Where did you live before you moved here?"

"Why did you leave?"

Etc.

Joe had studied his new history the night before. He felt very comfortable with this. Afterall, he had been living semi-covertly for several years. This was just another cover, he reasoned. He passed the test without any help.

A Marshal ended the meeting by emphasizing the importance of staying with the program. "No one in the program has been exposed and killed," he said, and then added, "as long as they followed the rules and stayed in the program."

The USMS provided Joe with $75,000 in a checking account in his new name. This was a customary amount to allow him to have money to live on while he looked for new employment consistent with his prior income. Lawyers with powers of attorney closed out the accounts he had in the name of Joseph Garcia Martinez. They legally transferred the money through a third party and deposited it into his new account. This accounted for another $100,000. The CIA also gave him another $75,000 as compensation for the work he had done for them. So, he had about $250,000. It was more than enough to tide him over while he found employment at his new location.

Within the week, the USMS relocated Joe to an unknown location. They would monitor him periodically and provide a local USMS contact in case he had an issue. Other than that, he was free to begin his new life.

40

LIFE GOES ON

Brandy continued to stay in touch with Ed Perez. Two years after Donna's death, Ed retired from the CIA. Although not the life he envisioned having with Donna, he opted to become a permanent resident in Costa Rica. After he retired, he moved to a house in a gated community nearby, and began to attend the local Catholic church more frequently. The idea of a country setting within reach of the city and the airport appealed to him. He already knew more people in Costa Rica than back in the States. Although none were close or intimate friends, he did have a few buddies that he could go to the gun range with, go golfing with, or go fishing with off the coast and have intellectual conversations with. These included prior colleagues from the DIS and the OIJ. His connections afforded him opportunities for consulting work with agencies of the Costa Rican government. He registered as a foreign agent with the U.S. government. He kept busy, but not too busy to pursue his photographic hobby.

Ed was happy in retirement. He took pictures of nearby scenes using an expensive high-resolution digital camera. He improved his skills at mounting and framing his photos and managed to get a part-time job in an art photo gallery and store. He learned about the best backing materials, the best matting materials, and the best wooden frames to use. Working in the store afforded him discounts on the materials and equipment he needed to make the job easier and faster. After only two years of retirement, he already had the first showing of his work. The theme was Costa Rican volcanos. It was a success and a touring company offered to buy some of his pictures. But there was one photo he would never sell, one that had the view of Poás that he shared with Donna two years earlier.

When Brandy mentioned that she was thinking of a vacation in late June of 2006, Ed convinced her to bring her son Brian, her father Peter, and Carol to Costa Rica. Brandy's son Brian would graduate from high school and would enter Stanford in the fall. Ed had suggested this trip as a graduation gift. He would pay for Brian and Brandy. Brandy asked how he would have the money to do this, but was told not to worry about it. He would explain later. Peter and Carol agreed to join them but would pay their own way. Ed would arrange for a one-week stay at a resort in Sarapiqui. The resort was in the mountains north of San José, where temperatures would remain desirable.

Ed met everyone at the San José international airport in a small van. They spent the first night at Ed's new house in Escazu, not very far from the airport. The house had four bedrooms. Ed used the master bedroom for himself. Two others he planned to rent out for tourists. Peter and Carol would have one of those bedrooms, and Brandy would have the other. He used the fourth bedroom as a studio and workshop for his photography. For this night, he would set up a cot in the studio for Brian. The first thing that Brandy and the others noticed when they entered were the framed photographs that lined the walls. Ed was eager to show them off. Brandy found one of her mom, and another of the Poás volcano that she especially liked. "We will visit Poás tomorrow," Ed commented.

Early the next morning, they set out for the resort with Ed acting as their tour guide. On the way, they stopped at the Poás Volcano. Ed told them it was one of his favorite places and that he had been here with Brandy's mom three years earlier. Brian was impressed with the view. "Awesome," he said.

The resort consisted of multiple circular units; each unit had eight private rooms. Peter and Carol shared a room, and the other three each had a room of their own. There was no TV or other amenities, but the shower was nice, and each room had access to a balcony with lounge chairs that circled the unit. The resort also had a pool and a bar. It was there that he pulled Brandy aside and kept his promise to explain the overseas account that provided the funds for their vacation.

****

Ed and Brandy found a quiet table near the bar where they could talk. A roof over the bar area protected them from the sun. There were no walls. The pool was visible on one side, and the rain forest on the other. It was a sunny afternoon. People were in the pool, very few at the bar. Ed went to the bar and returned with two bottles of cold water—too early for liquor.

"Brandy, I want to talk to you about how I am paying for this trip. You deserve to know the full story. The money is from the overseas HSBC account that you asked me about. Your mom and I set the account up twelve years ago." Ed watched Brandy's eyes widen as he talked.

Brandy had discovered the existence of the overseas account two years ago. She had asked Ed about it but never got a complete answer. She looked at Ed with anticipation as he continued.

"We were on a temporary two-year assignment in Europe. We barely knew each other before that, but the assignment drew us together. Each of us was given extra pay to cover our living expenses. Your mother was the one who came up with the idea that we could save a lot of money if we pooled our resources and shared our living quarters. The idea fit well with our cover stories and we decided to do it. We rented a two-bedroom flat on the outskirts of London and that became the base of our operation. Please understand, we maintained our privacy, and there were many days that only one of us was there. We also got by with only one rental car while in the London area. The bottom line is that after two years we had each saved about fifty thousand British pounds. The money was gained legally, and we paid income taxes on it."

Not knowing what to say or ask, Brandy remained silent.

"However, during those two years, we had also become good friends, and even more the week before we parted. We had learned to trust each other. I was the one who suggested that we pool our money and invest it. We did. We were already doing business with HSBC under our cover names, so that is where we went. We put all our savings into a joint deferred annuity account and named each other as beneficiaries."

Ed could see the question mark on her face. "The account is legally under our real names, but our pseudo names appear on correspondence. HSBC is good at maintaining privacy."

He continued. "When your mom passed, I became the sole owner of the account. However, the law required me to begin taking minimum payouts each year. I've taken about $6,000 so far, and some of that I used for this vacation. But now we have a decision to make."

"What do you mean?"

"Well, half of the account was your mom's and is rightful yours. I've also added your name as the sole beneficiary for when I die, but in the meantime, if you or Brian needs money, like for college, I could help with that now. No need to wait until I die."

"Ed, how much money are we talking about?"

"There's about $500,000 in the account right now. Tell me what Brian needs for college."

"Ed, I really appreciate your generosity, but Brian and I are really doing okay. I have a good salary at NSA. I received money from Mom's life insurance, and Brian's father is supposed to pay half his college expenses— at least, that was the agreement we had. And, Brian had scholarship money as well. But Ed, you're retired now. Don't you need income?"

"I really don't. If I stay here in Costa Rica, I have more than I need, and I have no family or heirs. You and Brian are the closest thing I have to family. Your mom wanted you to benefit from this account and I want the same thing."

"I see. . . Suppose you continue taking as much as you are required to take each year—more if you need it. Then, when you die, it can come to me. That would be good with me if acceptable to you."

"Okay, that's what I'll do. What do you say we go for a swim before the others get back from the Pineapple plantation?"

"Sounds good."

****

It seemed like one week was not enough and went by too fast. During the week, they enjoyed hiking in a rainforest, spotting howler monkeys, a lecture on bats, swimming in the pool, enjoying the bar and the excellent food in the common dining area, and more. On one day they went white water rafting in the nearby Sarapiqui River and on another day, they toured a pineapple farm. When Ed asked Brian what he enjoyed the most, he didn't hesitate to say, "The whitewater rafting and the Poás volcano. They were awesome!"

41

A NEW LIFE

Brandy continued working for the NSA and attained the title of Associate Director of Information Technology. But despite her success, she was tired of her work. To make it more interesting, she began writing technical papers and gave presentations at a few conferences. Her lively personality made her an entertaining speaker.

In the fall of 2010, Brandy spoke at a major information technology conference in Las Vegas. It took much preparation, review, and security screening, and now she was in a large meeting room facing an audience of more than a hundred people. She breathed deeply, let out a long breath, and delivered one of the best talks of the conference. People applauded loudly, and afterwards, a group of 'fans' surrounded her to compliment her on a great talk, tap her for more information, ask more questions, impress her with their own knowledge, exchange contact information, and just plain schmooze.

As the size of the group surrounding her dwindled, a well-dressed middle-aged gentleman introduced himself.

"Hello, Ms. Evans? Allow me to introduce myself. I'm Joseph Ramirez," he said while using his left hand to point to the name-tag he wore below his right shoulder. "I found your idea about multi-dimensional surveillance to be of great interest. I'm the marketing manager for a security business and can relate to those concepts." He reached into the left pocket of his jacket and handed her one of his business cards. She looked at his card and then at him.

Joseph Francisco Ramirez had short, receding curly black hair, and a neatly trimmed goatee and mustache. He wore glasses that gave him an air of dignity. Brandy stood looking at him, her mouth agape. She was almost speechless. "Joe?" She finally uttered weakly.

"Call me Joey. If I were to ask you to join me for coffee, would that be too forward of me?" he asked.

"Uh . . . of course, I'd love to," she said.

They went to the break area and took their coffees to a table for two.

"Joe, I mean Joey, may I ask where you're from?" she asked, playing along.

"Albuquerque, New Mexico."

"You said you managed a security business?"

"Yup, the marketing manager for five years now. While I've been there, it's grown from a three-person operation to eight employees and six contractors. I'm doing quite well, and I really enjoy the work. . . And you? I saw on the conference brochure that you're an Associate Director at NSA. Impressive!"

"I'm the Associate Director of Information Technology. The title is more impressive than the job. Joey, could I ask you a personal question?"

"Sure."

"Are you alone? I mean, are you married or with someone?"

"No, I live by myself in a nice garden apartment with a pool. No girlfriend . . . and what about you?"

"No, just me, a cat, and my work. Joey, you're a very handsome man, eye candy to many women, I'm sure. I'm surprised you aren't spoken for."

"Well, I appreciate the compliment, but six years ago, I was in love with a wonderful lady, and it just wasn't going to work out at that time, but I remembered that when we parted, she said that maybe someday we could start over. I don't expect things to be the same, but I was hoping to take the first step . . . but only if she's willing."

"How could this work?"

"Could we talk about the possibilities over dinner tonight?"

Although hesitant, she agreed.

That night, they had dinner at a local restaurant, and they talked. He told her who the new Joey was. He told her that before moving to Albuquerque, he had worked with the General Services Administration headquartered in Washington, D.C. He told her his job was to work with building contractors on security, and he also helped to develop security related standards. He often traveled to the various regional offices of the GSA as part of his work.

"What kind of education did you need for that kind of work?" she asked. "Do you have a PhD?"

"No, I have an engineering degree and a master's in computer science. I considered a PhD, but I ran out of money and decided to work."

"Where did you get your degrees?" She was obviously testing him, and of course, he knew that.

"Cal Tech," he proudly stated.

"I'm detecting a slight accent. Is it Spanish?"

"You're very perceptive. I was born in Texas and grew up there, but both my parents were from Central America. For many years, I lived in the El Paso area. Most people in my neighborhood and the school system spoke Spanish, and I still speak it when I need to. I find that being able to speak more than one language can be very useful for work."

"Are your parents still alive?"

"No, sorry to say. They passed away, many years ago now."

After a pause, she smiled. "Joey, I'm impressed."

After dinner, they retired to her hotel room, where they could talk more privately. The chemistry was still there, but they both resisted the temptation. They needed to come to an understanding and an agreement on how they could move forward. He told her that he still loved her and how much he wanted to be with her. Their conversation extended into the next evening. He told her he was taking a big risk revealing that he was in WITSEC, the Federal witness protection program, but that he trusted her. He told her that to remain in the program and remain protected, he was not supposed to associate with anyone from his past or even be where someone from his past might recognize him. She said she understood and agreed to keep their conversation a secret. No one else would know they had met.

"What happened to the old Joe," she wanted to know. "Did he die?"

"No, he's still out there somewhere, but no one knows where. He disappeared," Joey stated facetiously. "Apparently, it's not like in the movies where the person fakes their death before going into WITSEC."

Joey told her how much he wanted them to have a long-term relationship together. He invited her to come see him in Albuquerque in a month. He said that he would understand if she decided not to pursue it, but really hoped she would. "In any case," he said, "regardless of your decision, please don't reveal our prior relationship to anyone." Once again, she promised.

By the close of the second evening together, they could no longer hold back. The fire between them reunited. He spent the night in her hotel room, and they made passionate love.

Over the next ten months, Brandy visited Joey three times in Albuquerque. Joey introduced her to his work colleagues and his friends. She was the girlfriend that he had met at a recent security conference in Las Vegas. It took time, but they got to know each other—again. More importantly, Joey was real, his business was real, and his participation in the community was real. People who knew him liked him, and Joey liked his new life. It was not long before Brandy fell in love with him all over again.

He asked if she would be willing to relocate to Albuquerque. They both wanted to be together and make it work, but there were some serious questions that needed to be resolved before she could agree. Mentioning a new boyfriend who she occasionally saw was one thing, but moving to be with someone in a close relationship was something else. She didn't want to lie to her son. Brian had already met Joe on several occasions in the year 2003 and early 2004. Eventually, he would need to know the whole truth. Same thing with her father, Peter, and what about Ed Perez? And then there was her ex-husband. He had met Joe once. What if he found out? Could he be trusted? And what about the life she would leave behind in Maryland?

Brandy decided that before she made such a monumental decision, she needed advice. She would talk to Peter. She could certainly trust him, and besides, Peter had been very instrumental in helping her learn the truth about her mother and about Joe. She called him and asked if he would come over to her house so they could talk. Of course, he agreed.

****

Over the years, Brandy's relationship with Peter remained about the same—occasional visits, emails, and phone calls.

It was now the summer of 2011. Although they had talked on the phone a few times, it had been more than a couple of months since she had seen Peter. They were both busy with their own lives—not unusual. He was glad to hear from her and be invited over, but he wondered why. It sounded important. She greeted him at the door with a hug, and she ushered him into the living room where they were seated.

"Peter, I'm so glad to see you. We don't see each other often enough, and it seems like when I do see you, it's because I need something."

"So, what's up? It sounded important."

"I need to make a very important life decision, and I want your advice."

"Okay."

"As you know, I met someone when I gave my presentation at the security conference in Vegas last year. We have kept in touch, and I have flown out to Albuquerque, where he lives, to visit him three times now in the past year. He wants me to move out there and be with him. I would need to sell my house, retire from NSA, get a new job, and move. I need your advice about that."

"Okay . . ."

"Do you think I should do that?"

"Could I ask you a few questions?"

"Sure."

"You must feel very strongly about each other to want to do this."

"We're in love and want to be with each other."

"It sounds like you have only been with him three or four times. How can you be sure that you will have a future with him?"

She seemed to be unsure as to how to answer. "We're sure," she finally said.

"Brandy, are you pregnant?"

"No! No! Nothing like that."

He looked at her and detected some deception. "What then? I sense that there is something you haven't told me."

"Peter, his name is Joey Ramirez. He's the same Joe that I was in love with in 2004. He just happened to be at the conference, and we talked, and we really care about each other."

"So . . . is he still a covert operative? Does he still work for the CIA?"

"No. He stayed in WITSEC, and they gave him a new life."

"If Joe is in WITSEC, and the Marshals Service gave him a new identity, the two of you are taking a big risk. You know that, don't you?"

"You don't approve, do you," she said despairingly.

"I'm not saying that. It's your decision, and I'll support you no matter what. It's just that I care about you and don't want to see you hurt."

"What about Carol?"

"What about her?"

"Will she know? Will she approve? She was FBI. Will she keep it under wraps?"

"I never told her the details of our investigation into the circumstances surrounding your mom's project or who Joe was, and she never tried to find out. But, if she did know, I'm sure we can trust her to keep the secret."

"I'm not sure what to do."

"If you do this, I suggest you take it one step at a time. Move out there and get your own apartment. Make it look to the outside like a slowly developing relationship. Don't reveal his prior identity to anyone. If it doesn't work out, no one will be the wiser, and you can continue with your life independently. If it does work out, and you end up living together, you will need to decide how you deal with people that are close to you, like your son."

Peter stood up, walked over to her, put his hands on her shoulders and kissed her on the forehead. "Bottom line . . . I think you should follow your heart."

She stood up and hugged him. "Thank you."

****

After talking with Peter, Brandy decided to retire from the NSA. She would have more than twenty years of service and would receive a decent pension. She would move to Albuquerque. Aside from Peter, a couple of girlfriends from work, and her mom's grave, there was nothing keeping her in Maryland. They would understand, she reasoned. Her son had just started a career as a lawyer in the Los Angeles, California area, and her stepbrother now lived in Kentucky and owned an auto body shop, and her cat—really her mom's cat—had passed away. She already knew she had support from Peter. So, she decided to sell her house and move to Albuquerque. She took Peter's advice to avoid suspicion, and rather than move in with Joey, she would rent an apartment for herself. She was only forty-three years old and an experienced manager with IT systems knowledge. It would be easy for her to find a job in her field, she reasoned. But even if it took a while, the money from the sale of the house would bridge the gap.

So, in August of 2011, she retired from the NSA and moved into her new apartment in a fashionable suburb of Albuquerque. For convenience, her apartment was in the same complex as Joey's. It only took her another month to land a job as the IT manager of a local company.

Brandy looked forward to her new life.

42

ED'S VISIT

Ed received an email from Brandy telling him that she left the NSA and had moved to Albuquerque. She enclosed the new address and telephone number and wished him well, but didn't say much else. After reading the email, Ed wondered what would motivate her to move, and why Albuquerque. In his reply email, he asked her that. She wrote back, telling him how great a place it was to retire, and listed some of the things that were great about the state. She also said she got herself a job, so apparently, she really wasn't retiring, and then she mentioned she had met a guy and was dating.

A couple of months later, Ed decided he needed to disrupt his routine. Throughout his career, he was not only busy but he dealt with the unexpected almost daily. He thrived on the uncertainty. Yet during those years with the military and the CIA, he often longed to have a "normal" life. Now, in retirement, life was slower and not so exciting. Of course, there was the photography, the golf game once a week, the gun club once a week, the church group, etc. But life had become routine. If this was normal, he needed to spiff it up. He needed to get away. He remembered how Brandy had praised New Mexico, so he got on the Internet and researched what it had to offer as a place to visit. Turned out, it had quite a bit. There was the famous annual International Balloon Fiesta in the fall. There were balloon rides over the Rio Grande Valley. There was Roswell, where aliens supposedly landed in 1947. An associated museum with artifacts made you think it was true. There was the White Sands Monument, where the first atomic bomb test took place. A nearby museum displayed missiles and other legacy weapons of mass destruction. There was the Silver City mining town, the Sandia Peak Ariel Tramway, and the reminders of the Spanish cultural heritage in the old towns of Albuquerque, Santa Fe, and Taos. To top it off, the scenery matched that of Costa Rica. How could he resist? He found a small group tour company and booked a trip for October 2011. There had been a cancellation, and he would get a great price if he could be ready to go in three weeks. His plan was to fly into Albuquerque, participate in the tour, and then rent a car and visit Brandy at the end of his trip before flying back home. He sent a text message to Brandy to let her know his plan and to be sure that it would work for her. It was short notice, but he could still modify his booking if necessary.

****

Three weeks later, on a Sunday morning, Ed drove into the parking lot of Brandy's apartment complex. Although she was expecting him on Sunday, they had never agreed upon an exact time. He didn't exit the car, but called her on the phone to let her know he was in the area.

"When can you be here," she asked.

"Any time now." He answered. "What would be convenient?"

"Can you give me an hour?"

"Not a problem. See you then."

Ed put his phone aside and set the satellite radio to a station playing country-western music. After a few minutes, he decided to take a short drive while he waited out the hour and kill time by exploring the area. After a while, he stopped at a local Mr. Donut and bought six jelly-filled to go. He returned to the parking lot and parked closer to Brandy's apartment this time.

Well, here goes, he thought as he walked up to her unit and pressed the doorbell.

"Hello, Ed. Come in."

They hugged politely with no kiss.

"What do you have in the bag," she asked.

"Oh, I brought a couple of doughnuts from Mr. Donut."

"Yummy. Let's go into the kitchen. I have fresh coffee in the pot. We can have coffee and donuts while we talk."

Ed took a seat at the kitchen table.

"Jelly donuts?" she said, peering into the bag. "Six of them?"

Brandy went back to the counter and was about to pour the coffee, when Ed spoke up.

"Brandy, before we dig into those donuts and coffee, would it be okay if I used your bathroom and washed up?"

"Oh sure, down that way and to the right."

While washing up, Ed could not help but notice the extra toothbrush and the small travel bag on the counter. He took a closer look and noticed the handwritten identification tag attached to the handle. It belonged to Brandy's boyfriend, he thought.

However, it was not the name, address, and phone number that was of interest. It was the fact that the writing was all slanted to the left like someone who was left-handed would do.

Back in the kitchen, Brandy had already positioned a full cup of coffee, a plate with a jelly doughnut, and a napkin and fork at his place.

"One reason I brought extra donuts is because I thought you were living with someone now. Will he be here?" Ed asked, sounding curious.

"Oh, no. We have separate apartments."

"Perhaps he could come over later. I'd like to meet him and take you both out to dinner."

"I'll call him and see if he can do that."

"How serious are you about this guy—what did you say his name was?

"Joey . . . Joseph Ramirez. We're serious, but we're taking things slowly, one step at a time."

"I see. What does Joey do?"

"Do?"

"You know, for work."

"Oh . . . He's in charge of marketing for a security systems company."

"How did you meet?"

"Ah . . . well—"

He was aware of her hesitation.

"Brandy, am I asking too many questions? You seem nervous."

"No, it's okay. We met at a security conference in Las Vegas about a year ago. I was giving a presentation, and after my talk, he approached me and we began talking."

"Interesting—"

"Ed, why are you looking at me like that?"

"I remember you had a boyfriend named Joe just before your mom passed away. He also had a Spanish last name. I find it interesting that you went with him to a security conference, and that he said he was also a marketing rep for a security company. I also think that the guy who shared your bathroom this morning is left-handed, just like that Joe. As I had told you, I knew Joe. I spent time with him when he was brought back to Costa Rica to testify. He knew he would be relocated and get a new identification. I asked him where he would like to live and he told me Albuquerque. He also told me how much he cared for you and how he needed to meet with you to clear the air before he disappeared into WITSEC. Peter and I influenced the powers that allowed that to happen. I want you to trust me. The coincidence is too much. Sounds to me like Joey and Joe may be the same person."

"Ed, I discussed this with Joey. We were still trying to decide if we would need to let you know, and how and when we would do it. Then when you said you were coming to visit, our time-table was moved up. We were not totally prepared. Joey has taken a big risk. You understand that, right?"

"More than you think. But it's a risk for both of you. You must love each other a lot to take this risk."

"Please promise you'll keep our secret."

He didn't respond to that right away but kept talking.

"I can't help but wonder what your mom would have said about this. Your mom knew how unhappy you were in your marriage. She never liked your husband—thought he was a jerk—said he cheated on you. She always wanted you to meet someone who you could be happy with. Then when Joe came along, she hoped he would be the one, that is, until she learned that Joe was a double agent and that you were being used. It upset her, and when she knew she was dying, I told her I would look out for you. If you or Joe had asked my advice, I probably would have advised against it. On the other hand, Joe's a good man, and I know he must love you to take such a risk. Look . . . bottom line . . . what's done is done. I'll support you, and you can trust me to keep your secret."

"Thank you. Mom always spoke highly of you. I can see why."

They spent several more hours talking, talking about Ed's life in Costa Rica, talking about Brandy's job, talking about Albuquerque, etc. Then, they went for a walk in the neighborhood and enjoyed the warmth of the sun. To Ed, the neighborhood seemed nice. At some point, Brandy called Joey, and he said he would come over later.

Joey rang the doorbell shortly after four. Ed stood on the other side of the room as Brandy let him through.

"Ed, please meet my friend, Joey Ramirez. Joey, this is Ed."

Joey and Ed looked at each other, and Joey was the first to speak.

"Hello Ed. You don't seem surprised to see me. Perhaps Brandy has already revealed our secret."

"I really didn't have to," Brandy piped in. "Ed pretty much figured it out himself."

"Welcome to our new inner family circle, Ed," Joey said and held out his arms.

The two of them walked towards each other and hugged each other in a manly manner. Then the three of them had a drink—a ginger ale for Joey—and they talked. Ed learned that, at present, the "new inner family circle" consisted of himself, the two of them, plus Peter. He wondered if they would expand that to include Brandy's son, Brian, and possibly Peter's wife, Carol. That evening, the three of them went out to one of Brandy's and Joey's favorite restaurants. Ed was happy to treat.

.

43
WEDDING PLANS

Brandy and Joey planned their wedding for June 6, 2012. It would be small, perhaps twenty people in total—very close family members, Joey's employees, and a few of Joey's local friends. There would be no big newspaper announcements or any other media publicity. For it to be otherwise would be too risky for Joey. Aside from herself, Ed, and Peter, her son Brian was the only other person invited to the wedding who knew what the old Joe looked like.

Brian had graduated from law school in 2011 and was in his first year working for a law firm in Los Angeles, California. The money from Donna's life insurance had helped to pay for his six years in college. Brandy had attended the graduation, as did her ex-husband, but that was the last time they had seen each other. Peter and Carol thought about going, but although they had friends in Los Angeles, it was a long way and Peter was involved with clients. They sent a card and a gift.

Brandy could not be married without her son being there. Three months before the wedding, she called him and convinced him to come visit her in Albuquerque. She said she needed to discuss some very important matters regarding her upcoming marriage and she wanted him to meet Joey. Brian wondered why they couldn't discuss it over the phone, but she insisted and he agreed.

Brandy met her son at the airport and they drove to her apartment.

"Mom, where's Joey?"

"You'll meet him later. Right now, he's still at work."

Brian looked around the apartment and commented, "I don't see any indication that Joey lives here."

"We both have leases that we can't break yet, but we have plans to buy a house together as soon as we marry."

"Mom, what was it that you needed me to come all this way to hear?"

"I'm going to reveal something to you that you must promise never to repeat."

"What's that?"

"I'm dead serious," she said with a raised voice. "You must promise that you won't repeat any of this to anyone, no one at the wedding, none of your friends, not your father, not your girlfriend—No one!"

"Okay, Mom. Relax. I promise."

"Do you remember my boyfriend Joe from years ago?"

"Yeah . . ."

"Joey is the Joe you met eight and a half years ago. Aside from you and Grandpa Peter, no one else at the wedding will know this."

Brian appeared stunned, and it seemed like ages before he could respond.

"Mom, I don't understand. Grandma thought Joe was trying to poison her. She had me take a picture of him. She told me she was sending the picture to a friend who could find out who Joe really was."

"Yes, and she did that. She sent the picture to Uncle Ed. You probably know that Grandma and Uncle Ed were more than just friends, and I'm sure you remember that vacation he arranged for us in Costa Rica. Uncle Ed found out what was going on, and informed your grandma."

"Didn't Joe poison her?"

"No, he didn't."

"How did she die then?"

"She really did die of cancer. I think you know that your grandma worked for the CIA. It seems that Uncle Ed did as well, and he knew who Joe was. Turned out that Joe was part of a covert CIA operation. Joe was put into witness protection and that's why he disappeared, but I didn't learn any of this until a couple of months after your grandma died."

"How did you find out?"

"Grandpa Peter helped me coordinate an investigation, and Uncle Ed was very helpful as well.

"So, did you say that Grandpa Peter and I will be the only ones at the wedding that can identify who Joe really is? What about Uncle Ed?"

"I heard from Ed. He doesn't think he should attend. He and Joe were both stationed in Costa Rica prior to 2004. Ed said his prior association could result in too much risk for Joe . . . and regarding Peter, there's something else you should know. I've asked Peter to walk me down the aisle . . . if that's okay with you."

"It's fine Mom. You deserve to be happy and I promise that you can trust me to keep the secret," he said, and gave his mom a big hug.

****

Brandy and Joey had received a wedding card and a note from Ed Perez indicating that he would not attend. He said that they should be on the lookout for a wedding gift that he would ship to them shortly. Ed's gift arrived on Friday two weeks before the wedding. It came in a rigid carton about three feet by two feet and four inches thick. Joe and Brandy open it together. They opened one end of the carton and carefully slid out two foam protection sheets. A note had been taped to one of the sheets:

Brandy and Joey:

I hope you enjoy your wedding gift. The picture is my favorite. Your mom was with me when I took it. All of us have shared this image of Poás, and I hope it brings you the same warm feelings that it brings me. Ed

Then they slid out the framed picture that was inside and propped it up against the coffee table.

"Wow. It's beautiful! Just like I remember it," Brandy exclaimed

"Brandy, the note says that we have all shared the image. When were you there?"

"Oh, I never told you. Yes, Ed invited me and Brian to come down for a vacation. Peter and Carol also came. That's when we went saw *Poás*."

"When?"

"June 2006. When we were at his house, he had a picture of Poás on his wall. Photography is his hobby. He does all the framing himself and he's displayed his photos in several exhibitions. When we went to the volcano site, Ed told me that he had brought my mom there in 2003, and that he asked her to retire with him. I think he really cared about Mom."

"Yes, when I was incarcerated in the U.S. Embassy, he told me how much he missed her . . ." Joey's voice trailed off and he began to gaze at the picture, almost in a trance.

"Joey? Are you alright?"

She got his attention. "Sorry, I was just remembering the times *I* was there. I grew up near there, and I often visited the Poás National Park with my father and stepmom. Those were enjoyable times. The volcano site is also where I first met Ed in 2001. That's when he recruited me as a CIA asset. I have good memories, but it's part of the life I'm supposed to bury."

"Joey, you don't have to bury all of it. If someone were to ask about the picture, you could truthfully tell them that you went there with your parents when you were young . . . like on vacation as a tourist."

Joey turned toward her and smiled. "Yes, you're right," he said emphatically and gave her a kiss. "I think the picture will look fine in our bedroom on the wall at the head of our bed in the new house."

"I agree," she said.

44

THE WEDDING

Brandy and Joey had chosen to have both the wedding and the reception at a local golf club and resort where Joey was a member. Playing golf was one way to make deals, especially when he could demonstrate his work at the same time. Joey's company had installed the resorts entire security system, video cameras, member ID cards, entry scanners, alarm systems, etc. The location was also ideal for a wedding, even a small one. The outdoors was picturesque, with mountains in the background. And afterwards, the hotel offered an overnight without having to drive anywhere.

The day was beautiful—sunny, warm, and dry. Twenty guests would sit in two sets of white folding chairs with an aisle in between. A small gazebo in front of the chairs would serve as an altar. Guests included work colleagues, local friends, Peter Troutman and his wife, Carol, Brian and his girlfriend, Eva, and a local friend of Brandy from work, Jennifer. Brandy had asked Jennifer to be her Maid of Honor, and Joey had asked Brian to be the Best Man.

When Peter joined Brandy at the head of the aisle, he told her how gorgeous she looked. She was wearing a baby blue blouse, dressy black slacks, and black high heels. A pair of blue sapphire earrings dangled from her ears. The stone was cut in the form of an elephant. Peter noticed this right away, but did not say anything. The wedding party outfits were coordinated. Joey was wearing a black suit, a baby blue shirt matching Brandy's blouse, and a black and blue striped tie. Peter and Brian wore charcoal gray suits, light gray shirts, and silver and gray striped ties. Jennifer wore charcoal slacks, a silver blouse, and heels.

Peter escorted Brandy down the aisle. Joey, Brian, and Jennifer were waiting for them at the altar. Recorded music played as they walked. When they arrived, Peter gave Brandy a kiss on the cheek and took a seat next to Carol. A non-denominational minister conducted the ceremony. Joey and Brandy recited their vows and became husband and wife. Some of the guests took pictures.

Joey and Brandy had discussed the possible risks of taking pictures, but people expected to be able to take photos at weddings. No way they could forbid it. It would look very suspicious if they did. However, they did request that the attendees not post pictures on social media. But who knows? People will probably do that anyway. They also decided to further minimize the risks by having Peter be the official photographer. Only family members would receive those photos. They also figured that over the past eight years, Joe had aged and changed his looks. Unless someone knew what they were looking for, the risks were small. So, pictures were allowed.

Before moving indoors for the reception, the guests had time to mingle on the grounds while Peter took pictures of the wedding party. Brandy and Joey had reserved a private room and had sprung for a full-course dinner with wine for their wedding guests. Peter and Brian gave toasts to the bride and groom. That was followed by Joey's boss, who told everyone that Joey was a hard worker who rarely took time off, but that if he didn't take the next week off, he would fire him.

"Where are you going on your honeymoon?" people asked.

"We have reservations for a lodge in the Taos area," Joey responded, and then added, "After we get back, we plan to close on a new house and finally move in together. I want to thank all of you for participating in our wedding and making it a joyous occasion for both of us."

Peter and Carol met Joey for the first time. Having had common experiences in the fields of security, communications, and detective work, they had much to talk about. Although Peter had seen an old picture of Joe, and knew what had transpired, he kept his knowledge to himself. The only person attending who had met Joe in his prior life was Brandy's son Brian. Brandy had been nervous about that, but Brandy had coached him ahead of time, and Brian kept his promise not to reveal anything. His girlfriend Eva seemed nice, and Brandy secretly hoped she might be the one for him.

After the dinner, the wedding guests were able to join the public in the Saguaro lounge, where they had live music and dancing. When Joey and Brandy entered the room, the band began to play "Here Comes the Bride," prearranged by the club owner. Peter danced with his daughter for the first time. As they danced, he commented on her earrings.

"The earrings look very attractive on you," he said.

"Thank you. They were Mom's. She showed them to me when I was only five. The stones are in the shape of elephants. I was impressed by that because I had just been to the zoo and had seen real elephants for the first time. I remember her telling me that in Asia the elephant is a symbol of good luck, happiness, and longevity. I remember asking her where she got them. She told me a special friend gave them to her before I was born and that they were very special to her. She told me that someday they would be mine."

Peter was smiling, and his eyes seemed to be tearing up. "What?" she said as she gave him a curious look. "Did you give them to her?"

"I did . . . the night before we said good-bye."

"She never told me," Brandy said and gave him a quick kiss on the cheek. "I think Mom would be very happy if she could be here now."

"I think so as well," Peter replied.

Everyone danced until midnight. The out-of-town guests stayed the night. Brandy and Joey stayed the night as well. Before she went to bed, Brandy removed the earrings and set them on the shelf inside the room safe. That night, Brandy dreamed about her mom.

In the dream, she saw her mom's gravestone. The earrings were resting on top. Brandy felt relaxed and warm inside. Joey was next to her, kissing her gently on the lips. Brandy told him she was happy, and he told her that he was happy to have her by his side.

She saw her mom's face, and then she heard her mom's voice. Her mom was speaking from above, from heaven. "Your happiness was always my final project," her mom told her. "I'm at peace now."

ACKNOWLEDGEMENTS

I want to give a special acknowledgement to the men and women who work behind the scenes to protect us from foreign intrusion. In addition to the threat of war, they protect us from acts of terrorism, financial manipulation, and interference with our political process. A small percentage of the time, their efforts fail. When this happens, the failures become headlines in the media. Sometimes, careers are ruined, and sometimes people die. On the other hand, when their efforts succeed, which is most of the time, these men and women remain anonymous and unheralded. All three stories in the trilogy are about such people.

DUPLICITY FOR LIFE is a re-edited version of **THE BOULDER CREEK PROJECT, FINAL PROJECT, and THE PEN PROJECT.** So, I want to re-thank those individuals who reviewed my original manuscripts. They pointed out the errors and inconsistencies, and they provided perspectives and suggestions for improvement. I list them here:

My wife Jean, a loving person, and my first reviewer.

My friend George Fleischman, an engineer in the defense industry;

My brother Bruce Eisenhut, an attorney;

My friend Bob Greiner, a retired analyst in the security business;

My friend Phil Gallagher, a retired analyst in the security business;

My friend Gary Battel, an expert on nature and weather;

My friend Col. Tom Genetti, Ret. A war veteran and pilot;

My friend Tim Sosinski, a retired architect and entrepreneur;

My friend, Robert Dale Headrick, a retired defense contractor;

Joe Hoolihan and members of the Savage Writer's Circle;

Dr. Thuy Nguyen. She grew up in Vietnam;

Dan E. Feltham, author of "When Big Blue Went to War."

Lt. Colonel Richard J Giddings, USAF Ret.;

Kenneth P. Moorefield, Deputy Inspector General DOD;

George Morales, Lily Green, and the staff at Bennett Media and Marketing, for their support and professionalism.

ABOUT THE AUTHOR

Peter S. Eisenhut is a graduate of Cornell University and the University of Rochester. He worked for two international organizations and as an independent consultant. After retiring, he has enjoyed doing volunteer work and writing. He is also an avid hiker. The inspiration for his novels comes from his career experiences and his travels. Peter lives in Columbia Maryland with his wife Jean.

Peter's stories are about people who work behind the scenes to protect their country. Duplicity is an underlying theme in each of his first four novels, The Pen Project, The Boulder Creek Project, Final Project, and Fateful Affairs.

You can preview or purchase his books at: https://amazon.com/author/petereisenhut-usa